THE MOVIE SET

THE MOVIE SET

A Novel by
June
Flaum
Singer

M. EVANS AND COMPANY, INC.
NEW YORK

This is a work of fiction. Any resemblance between characters and persons living or dead is purely coincidental.

M. Evans and Company, Inc.
216 East 49 Street
New York, New York 10017

Manufactured in the United States of America

For Sharon Bathsheba, eldest daughter

Acknowledgments

My thanks to Herb Katz for many things, but
most especially for his super enthusiasm,
great cheer, and good friendship.

The poem "Ever After" and the lyrics to "Love Grown Cool"
are copyright by Sharon Bathsheba Singer.

Ever After

When the man comes,
The orphan or the simple son,
The youngest daughter knows him.
With his rags, bravado, doubts,
A thing or two to prove,
She foresees him robed and crowned with vines.

They lay down in whispers,
Prescriptions and old women's wisdom
Flung off with scattered sheets,
They drink up visions from a single cup.

But a test always waits while heroes tarry—
The formless put on treacherous flesh
The deformed take up gaudy trappings
The glorious lie piteously in the way—
How should they know who must be struck
Or who embraced,
What gift refused
What provision shared
What scrap proves indispensable
What treasure fatal?

The wrong door has a thousand handles.
All may be lost
In one flawed moment. "Lost," he cries
Fading into distance. Bitter,
She warms her hands over betrayal
As over sputtering twigs.
Then the wandering
Or long habitation in twisted halls.

Most likely
A dim content must seem sweet enough
When harm done cannot be undone
And teacups before the fire must console
For even those who would cannot regain
The singing day.

Sharon Bathsheba Singer

PROLOGUE

1984

As I dressed for the wrap party for *White Lily* on Sound Stage Four at the King Studio I could not help but think of the dream I had the night before. I had dreamed of a college campus in an Ohio town, of a shabby little apartment with only a few unlovely sticks of furniture, occupied by a sweet-funny boy not yet twenty. And I had dreamed of a beautiful red-haired girl juxtaposed against the cobalt blue Midwestern sky.

I sighed and drew on a cream-colored satin jumpsuit; fastened cream-colored, ankle-strapped sandals; threw down my head and brushed my hair furiously so that when I righted myself, my hair would fall into place in glamorous profusion. Then I carefully placed the diamond clasp set in a perfectly matched string of pearls directly in the center of my throat and was ready to go. The party today signified that *White Lily*—the picture that was months over schedule and millions over budget, that Hollywood cynics had been laying bets would never be finished—was finally in the can.

It was going to be a very fancy party. Round tables draped with silvery white lacy cloths, a plethora of fresh white flowers, lilies naturally, fashioned into centerpieces composed of porcelain ducks and metal leaves and ivy vines, and for candlesticks—more lilies, these made of porcelain. The tables would be set with precious Lalique plates and copies of Napoleon III crystal glasses; the flatware reproductions of the silver used by Marie Antoinette, another foolish lady who did not know how to keep her own head. The menu was to be very posh—oysters in champagne sauce, eggs en cocotte, squab stuffed with golden raisins, and for dessert there would be white chocolate mousse, champagne sorbet, and individual white cream-frosted cakes in the shape of—what else—the lily.

The usual wrap party was almost never this fancy, but *White Lily* *needed* a big send-off and while studio parties are supposedly for the cast and for the endlessly long line of studio workers, this particular bash was really for the media—to impress them with the opulence of the production, to seduce them with food and champagne and elegance, to beguile them into loving our star-crossed, by now notorious, opus. Perhaps the notoriety would work *for* the picture rather than against. These days you never knew. The movie business was even more precarious than the lives of its players, the movie set.

Yes, we would all pose for the public and there would be photographers to catch the big false smiles . . . so many capped teeth flashing, so many glasses held high. There would be lots of spiritous hijinks and if there was a steady line into the restrooms for a quick snort, no one would take notice. And certainly the same laissez-faire would apply to a sexual encounter or two performed under a skirted table or in a hastily locked dressing room not far away. A Hollywood Movie Set party. Or was it a wake?

"Last night I dreamed I went to OSU again," I said aloud to the mirror, and the slim, green-eyed lady there smiled back at me with only a slight trace of bitterness. A scene flashed through my mind, still vivid in Technicolor memory despite the passage of time. . . .

The four of us walked back to the dorm: Suellen, my fair-haired sister who would graduate the following week and wed the week after that; Cleo Pulitzer from New Jersey, who, like me, had just completed her sophomore year and who thought that maybe she was in love with the campus fashionable neo-radical; Suzannah, my beautiful roommate who dreamed of being a Hollywood star but who was scheduled to leave the very next morning for New York with someone with whom she was decidedly not in love. And there was I . . . Bonita Ann Lewis, known to my intimates as Buffy, and in a day when practically everyone was high on *something,* I was high only on Todd King.

Suellen, Cleo, and I had just toasted Suzannah at Andy's Tavern with 3.2 beer, and she had toasted herself with ginger ale, believing alcohol was bad for the complexion and believing very much in her own unblemished pale-skinned perfection. We walked four abreast, laughing in the twilight of that lovely spring day, and I thought of how much I would miss Star Suzannah, as Todd had labeled her. She had been my friend since the very first day I arrived as a freshman at OSU.

We passed one of the campus parking lots now, and a fifties' aqua-and-cream Pontiac pulled in and a boy got out. The sound of his car radio filled the soft spring air. It was Elvis's voice, but an Elvis already past his prime. Suddenly, inexplicably, Suzannah darted over to the car and before our incredulous eyes, climbed to the roof and began to strip to the music. Under her mini she wore a white bikini bathing suit although it was only the end of May, and May days are still fairly cool in Columbus. Had Suzannah been sunbathing that day? I wondered. Or had she already packed all her underwear?

Suzannah—eyes closed, as if transported to some far-off, exotic place —was herself an exotic, breathtaking, red-haired goddess in two scraps of white silk jersey. Oblivious to us, to the boy who owned the Pontiac, and to the few other people who stood gawking in the half-light, Suzannah danced, head thrown back, white, graceful arms making ghostly motions against the oncoming night. She accompanied Elvis in his plea for love, crooning softly to herself, and even when the others began to clap and sing along, Suzannah took no notice.

It was such an incredible thing to do, I thought—incredible and unbelievably narcissistic, completely uninhibited. But I knew that it was not for us or for the others in the parking lot that Suzannah performed. I knew that Suzannah danced and sang only for herself. And I knew that it was a scene I would never forget.

That was a long time ago and Elvis was dead now—horribly dead of bloat and drugs, of self-inflicted degradation. And my friend Suzannah? Suzannah had the leading role in *White Lily*. And we could never go back, not any of us. . . .

I went downstairs and paused in the entry hall with its black and white marble floor, for a moment disoriented. I had dreamt of the Ohio State campus but I *lived* in a Beverly Hills mansion, with an enormous courtyard and emerald green lawns, with all the Hollywood status symbols—a black-bottomed pool, a complicated security system, and a tennis court—a north/south to be sure. And as I so often did these days, I asked myself: what was a small-town girl from Ohio doing here, anyway?

I called out for Leah whom I had brought with me from Ohio and who had been with me through almost all the years of my marriage, who still managed to intimidate me. Because of Leah's taciturn personality we kept no other live-in help and had to manage the running of the house with lots of in-for-the-day personnel. Receiving no answer now I went to the kitchen and found Leah at the long wooden table polishing silver.

"Didn't Bess do that just last week, Leah?"

Leah was old, no one knew exactly how old, and I wanted to spare her, if she would let me, but she never would. She grunted now and I took that for an affirmative answer. "So why are you doing it again? Don't you have enough to do?"

She didn't answer. So much for Bess's silver cleaning.

"I'm leaving now, Leah. You can answer the phone if you like or you can turn on the machine if you prefer." I knew that Leah did not enjoy the phone.

"Machine's broken."

"Again? Well, if you like, I'll call the answering service and tell them to take the calls."

"Them!"

So much for the answering service.

"Bobbie Jenson's mother will drop Mikey off around five," I told Leah apologetically. She didn't approve when I allowed Mikey out of the house in somebody else's care. "And Megan has dance class today so she won't be home until six. Mitch, I suppose, will be along right after school. . . ." My voice trailed away. I was grateful that Matty, who only went to morning kindergarten, was playing outside in the back garden with the little boy from across the street. He was in full view of the kitchen window, so I wouldn't have to discuss *his* schedule with Leah in the face of her scornful disapproval of my maternal behavior.

Not receiving any response again, I said, "Have a good day," like any good cashier in a Southern California supermarket.

I got into my white Seville that was parked in the corner of the bricked-over courtyard, eschewing as usual the Silver Cloud inside the garage. There were two Rollses there, my Silver Cloud and Todd's Corniche. Mine had been an anniversary present from Todd and I got more pleasure leaving it there unused and ignored, thus driving Todd crazy, than I would have driving it. (Much as I bought large amounts of fantastically expensive jewelry and left most of it locked up in the safe.) Now, he too hardly ever took his Corniche out, as if all the fun had gone out of owning such a special car.

Actually driving the old Caddie was easier on the nerves. One didn't worry as much about scratches or even dents or about the parking lot jocks going wild with the genteel, cultured Rolls. Such are the problems of the Beverly Hills privileged: vital issues such as the proper care and feeding of a luxury car, the availability or nonavailability of parking space, the latter being the reason I had had the whole courtyard paved over with brick, stylish used-brick, of course. Now, there was room for thirty cars when we entertained and the parking was scientifically choreographed by hired-for-the-evening valets. Oh yes, I had learned all the rules for proper living in the years I'd been in California. I had learned to be the perfect hostess; how to live perfectly in a Mediterranean villa that was close to the Pacific, where to get my hair done in the most trendy fashion, where to lunch, and where to shop. In Lotus Land, even certain supermarkets were trendy. When was it then that I had forgotten how to be the perfect wife to the perfect husband? I asked myself. Which was foolish of me, for I knew that exact date to the minute. It was etched into my brain. No. Not brain. More accurately, on my heart . . . probably, in blood.

The fancifully-worked black iron gates opened magically for me, then closed behind me and I drove to Benedict Canyon to make the descent to Sunset Boulevard. At Sunset, I took a left toward Hollywood. At the first red light, a woman in a brown Mercedes in the left lane stared. I smiled. People were forever staring, thinking they recognized me as a star of yesterday, not stopping to think that I was too young to be the movie star they had in mind. Vivien Leigh. Vivien with a face-lift? Before they remembered that I couldn't be . . . that Vivien was dead.

Everyone had always remarked on the resemblance. Todd had, when I first met him. And Suzannah. And Paulie, the boy Suzannah had gone off to New York with. Poor Paulie. He had been a movie buff. He had always tried to match up people with film look-alikes, old-time look-alikes, preferably. The old-timers had more glamor for Paulie. "You look like a *young* Vivien Leigh," Paulie always told me. He had tried to come up with a look-alike for Suzannah, but he had never really succeeded. Rita Hayworth, he would say, but hesitantly. *Or maybe Hedy Lamarr, a young Hedy with gold-red hair.* But Paulie had been reaching. Suzannah always was—would always be—an original.

The light changed and I charged ahead waving to the lady in the brown Mercedes as I left her behind, switching to the left lane, not meaning to, but still cutting her off. Buffy King in the fast lane. Not meaning to be, but just a tiny bit out of control . . . just like everyone else I knew. You were supposed to be laid back in L.A. but the actual truth was that if you were, you got *left* back, trampled on, maybe even maimed. Oh, I believed it! I had learned to believe it.

Only recently, just a few months back, my sister, Suellen, had asked: "Oh, Buffy, why oh why did we ever leave Ohio?" And I had answered her, not at all convinced: "For the good life, Suellen," and was glad when she didn't ask the next question: *And did we find it, you and I?*

I drove down Sunset Boulevard from where it was still prosperous and pretty to where it wasn't so nice anymore and where the presence of the burn-outs, drop-outs, and prostitutes made you wonder if you were on a movie set where they were shooting a remake of Sodom and Gomorrah in modern dress. Oh, where was the happy-go-lucky "Kookie, lend me your comb," of my TV youth who used to strut so cool and proud on the Sunset Strip?

Now, everyone said: "You should have been here thirty years ago . . . forty years ago. . . . That's when Hollywood was *really* Hollywood." But forty years ago I hadn't even been born. And thirty years ago, I was a little girl in Ohio dreaming of heroes, but not ever dreaming that I would grow up and marry a hero who would take me to Hollywood, a hero whom I would have followed into hell itself if he had but asked me.

I drove through the studio gate and the officer on duty hailed me, wished me a good day even though the day was almost over. In an hour or so the sun would be setting to the west of King Studios, illuminating it with an unearthly yellow glow. I parked in front of Sound Stage Four and walked inside. The tables were set, the waiters were already passing tulip-shaped glasses of champagne, and the band played the theme song of *White Lily.*

My eyes searched the crowd to see who was or who wasn't there. Talking to a prop man was Howard, Suellen's husband. My eyes moved away from him to look for some other familiar faces. It was hard to tell the players without a scorecard.

Then Todd rushed over and kissed me on the mouth and like the song went, my heart stood still. And cameras flashed. But it was only a kiss, a public one, and like a movie kiss, not quite real. And I thought of how it had been for me almost twenty years ago. . . .

PART ONE

*Spring
1964–1967*

1.

I was newly arrived at Ohio State University that morning and as I unpacked two unmatched suitcases, I kept a wary eye on the white steamer trunk with bright brass trim that sat in the middle of the dormitory room, dwarfing everything else in this less-than-large enclosure. The trunk awaited its owner, I assumed, my yet-to-arrive roommate. It reeked of affluence, of glamorous cross-Atlantic trips on luxury liners, of Paris . . . London . . . Rome, of wherever glamorous people traveled.

Did it contain glorious gowns of satin and silk and sequins? And to what end? What would the owner of such a trunk be doing at a state university in the year 1964? I was sure that there wasn't another trunk like it in all of Columbus, not even at the sorority houses. It was my bad luck to get its owner as my roommate! She was bound to be a petulant, spoiled princess with her nose stuck up in the air, and I knew from my sister Suellen who lived at the Theta house that the girl who shared your room was not someone to be taken lightly. I found myself wishing for perhaps the hundredth time that Suellen had never joined a sorority so that the two of us could have shared a dormitory room. (I, myself, had no intention of becoming a Greek sister.)

Then, a girl with red hair—brilliant sun-touched red—stuck her head into the room, a very tall girl in a too-big man's blue work shirt and the inevitable jeans, who despite her attire exuded a certain confident, glamorous presence that transcended even her startling beauty. She certainly looked like she belonged to the white steamer trunk despite the casual way she was dressed at the moment.

"I do declare," she announced. "If you're not the spitting image of Scarlett O'Hara."

I laughed. It was not the first time that I had been told this. Actually it was Vivien Leigh who I resembled.

She continued to study me carefully. "You're much too short to be a beauty queen, of course. But just the same, you're *almost* as beautiful as I am."

I *had* to laugh at that.

"Are you my roommate?" I asked, hoping she would say yes. She seemed to have a sense of humor, a top priority for a desirable roommate. And she certainly appeared to be interesting.

"I wish I could say that I was, but I can't. I'm in 303 and I already have a roommate." She rolled her eyes expressively.

"Well, come on in anyway."

She sauntered in, threw herself down on one of the two beds and proclaimed, "Scarlett O'Hara is my most favorite heroine. I saw the movie at least ten times and I even read the book twice, even though I try *not* to read all that much."

I had never heard anyone say that they tried *not* to read. "Why?" I asked.

"Why what? Why do I try not to read? To save my eyes, *por favor!* Don't you know that if you strain your eyes they lose their sparkle?"

"I never thought about it. I read a lot myself. Why is Scarlett O'Hara your favorite heroine?"

"Because she was one little gal who didn't give a damn about anything except herself. She was strong, she went after what she wanted, she was smart as a whip, and she had oodles of character. And all the men were mad about her. I always thought *I* should have looked like Scarlett . . . had her green eyes like you do. But I really don't *mind* my yellow ones. They're rather unusual, don't you think?"

I was forced to laugh again. This girl was fantastic, incredible. "You have beautiful eyes," I said with sincerity. Her eyes were the color of cloudy amber.

"Thank you," she said, still studying me gravely. "No, you can't be a beauty queen and you can't be a model either. Still too short."

I smiled. "It's lucky then that I never had any idea about being either a beauty queen or a model. I want to teach. English literature probably. But is that what you want to be? A model? Or just a Miss America?"

"I figure I'll see what comes down the pike. Play it cool. I'll probably be some kind of beauty queen, I guess. Maybe Miss America. Then, I'll model. In *Nueva* York, of course. *If* I don't get to Hollywood first. I do have a model's figure as you can see—no hips or boobs to speak of. When I was in high school, I stuffed my bra with socks. But you, sugar, while you can't model, you certainly do have the titties. My goodness, just look at you all!"

In an unconscious reflex action, I looked down. With my jeans I was wearing an old, shrunken T-shirt, and it certainly revealed my generous breasts.

"Now, if I were a little old boy," the redhead said, "I'd probably go out of my cotton-picking mind and just up and take a bite out of 'em right here and now—"

We both giggled like crazy and I was really sorry now that I wasn't going to room with her. "I'm Bonita Ann Lewis from Cincinnati," I said, "but everyone calls me Buffy. My older sister, Suellen, who's a junior here, gave me the nickname when I was little. She named me after the dog next door."

"My name's Suzannah and I'm a non-res. I'm from Kentucky and a soph. I spent my freshman year at the U. of K.Y. and no one would dare give *me* a nickname. No one's even allowed to call me Sue or Suzie or anything but Suzannah with one Z and two N's." She reached into her shirt pocket and pulled out a crumpled pack of Marlboros. "You want a cig? I don't *ever* smoke pot. I used to—in the back of the library when I was a senior in H.S. But then I found out it ruins the hair. It kills the follicles, you know."

(It would be the last time in many years that I would see Suzannah smoke a cigarette—she gave them up the very next day after reading a skin specialist's testimony in *Cosmopolitan* that smoking was bad for the complexion.)

"I'm waiting for you to unpack that gorgeous trunk," Suzannah said, blowing the smoke toward the ceiling through pursed lips. "Very, very luxe. I could die that your clothes will never fit me. . . ."

"It's not my trunk. It belongs to my roommate who has yet to make her appearance. I seriously doubt that I own *anything* you'd die to wear."

"Well, I surely wish you could room with me instead of that simp from *Nueva* Jersey that fortune has seen fit to bestow upon me. *Cleo Pulitzer, por favor!* Now, I ask you! What kind of an idiotic name is that?"

"I haven't any idea. But why do you say *Nueva* York and *Nueva* Jersey?" I asked, slightly irritated by this affectation even though I didn't know why."

Suzannah opened her amber eyes wide. "Because I'm studying Spanish. *Nueva*'s the word for new." She narrowed her eyes. "Why? Is there something wrong with doing that?"

I hesitated. I hardly knew her, but still, I decided to take the plunge. "It's kind of silly . . . tacky . . ." I smiled apologetically to take the sting out.

She considered this for a moment and then decided to laugh. "I declare. I think you're right. It really is too bad we can't be roomies. I think you must really be smart. It must be all those books you read. And if we were roomies, I could pick your brains."

"Oh?" I continued with my unpacking, placing cotton bikini underpants in the small top drawers of the chest. "I have the distinct feeling that *you* don't have to pick anyone's brains."

"Me? I'm just a little old hillbilly from K.Y. and I've just enough brains to make the most of my natural assets."

I thought about advising my new friend to stop saying K.Y. for Kentucky, which was in the same category as saying *Nueva* York, when there was a tap on the partially open door and I looked up to see yet another very tall girl standing there—this one with very long blond hair.

"I'm Cassie Hammond," she said, "and I believe this is my room." It was more question than declaration.

"Come on in," I said cheerfully. "If this is your trunk, this is your room."

The blonde smiled apologetically. "It's my trunk . . . I'm Cassie Hammond," she said again, walking in, holding herself very straight, offering her hand first to me and then to Suzannah. I could see Suzannah assessing her, taking in the beige cashmere sweater and the matching pleated skirt which came to a modest two inches above the knee. (Most of the girls I had seen around campus were wearing their minis inches higher.) I saw Suzannah's eyelids flutter, and reflected that my new friend probably was wondering exactly how much competition Cassie would be in a beauty pageant since Cassie *was* tall enough and certainly very pretty. But somehow I already got the impression that she was not the type to be interested in beauty contests. There was something diffident about her and while she had a certain well-bred, chin-up good cheer, there *was* a wistful quality too.

"Are you res or non-res?" Suzannah asked.

"I beg your pardon?"

"This *is* a state university." Suzannah was a bit impatient. "Are you from Ohio or out-of-state?"

"California."

"You certainly have come a long way—" I said, wanting to ask the reason she had chosen Ohio State but thinking better of it.

"Where in California?" Suzannah demanded.

"Los Angeles."

Suzannah opened her eyes wide. "Are you out of your cotton-picking mind? Why would anyone in their right mind leave Los Angeles—Hollywood—for Ohio?"

Cassie blushed. "I wanted to be on my own more . . . you know, not live at home. This is the first time I've ever been away . . . and when I told my mother that I wanted to go away to school she said that I should go to school in Ohio. You see, my grandfather came from Ohio originally and my mother admired him greatly. . . ."

"Is your family rich?" Suzannah asked bluntly and I writhed in the agony of embarrassment.

Cassie too was obviously embarrassed. Her cheeks reddened. "I suppose . . . there's only my mother, really."

"What did your family make their money in?" Suzannah asked.

I thought it was high time I interceded. "Come on, Suzannah, I want to go meet your roommate . . . that girl from *Nueva* New Jersey."

"Okay. In a minute. I'm just curious. My goodness, how am I ever to learn anything about anything if I don't ask questions?" She turned back to Cassie. "What *did* your father make his money in?"

Cassie's violet eyes clouded. "Oil. Only it wasn't my father. It was my mother's father."

"The one that came from Ohio?"

"Yes."

"When? I mean when was it that he got rich?"

"I'm not sure. Early in the 1900s I think."

"Really!" Suzannah pondered. "That's not so long ago. Not like the Rockefellers."

"It's long ago for California," Cassie said. "For Southern California . . ."

"Well, if your family's such a big name in California how is it you came here—to a state university in Ohio? How come you didn't go to a private college in California or one of those fancy schools in the East like Vassar or Smith?" Suzannah demanded.

"Oh, Mother despises what she calls the Eastern Establishment. I guess it's because she thinks they look down their noses at California. She said that if I was so determined to go away to school then I should come here because this is where our roots are." She paused a second and then gave a little laugh. "I guess what she really thinks is, that if I have a good, hard Ohio winter I'll be glad to get back to sunny California. And she believes in state universities. She has to—she's a regent of the University of California, you see. It's one of her civic responsibilities. At first I wanted to go to UC at Berkeley but she almost had a fit. She thinks the whole Berkeley campus should be closed down." Cassie blushed. "The radicals, you know. Mother's currently devoting herself to a campaign to eradicate radicalism from their campus since she can't accomplish closing them down." She smiled ruefully. "Mother's a very determined kind of person."

I thought all this about Cassie's mother was very interesting but Suzannah turned her attention to the white trunk.

"Did you pick that out?"

"No. Mother ordered the trunk from London. I suppose that's how she went away to school in her day—with that kind of a trunk."

"Well, come on, start unpacking," Suzannah urged. "I must admit I'm dying to see what you've got inside it."

"You'll be disappointed. I don't have anything spectacular. Just the usual sweaters, blouses, and skirts. Mother doesn't believe in college girls wearing anything ostentatious. . . ."

Suzannah was crestfallen. She could easily have worn Cassie's clothes —they were of a height and slimness. "Your mother sounds like a royal pain in the—"

Cassie turned bright pink and I quickly cried out, "Suzannah!" My red-headed friend might be funny but she was also completely outrageous as well. "Come on, it really *is* time for me to meet your roomie," I urged.

Heaven help you, Cleo Pulitzer. You're certainly going to have your hands full with Miss K.Y.

As I was going out the door with Suzannah firmly in tow, I saw Cassie looking after us wistfully. Didn't she know that I was just trying to cut her a break by getting Suzannah out of her hair? I guess she didn't. So I asked her, "Do you want to unpack later and come down the hall with us now?"

"Oh yes!" Cassie breathed in grateful appreciation.

I had a feeling that Cassie Hammond had always been a lonely girl, and that she was definitely hung up with a thing about her mother.

2.

Despite Suzannah's dire observations regarding Cleo Pulitzer I found her vastly entertaining—clever, bubbly, high-spirited and enthusiastic, and we seemed to have the same frame of reference—we had read many of the same books, had liked the same movies, loved the same songs, thought the same things were funny. We always understood where the other was coming from. She wasn't what one would call a real beauty, but she *was* trim, neat, and stylish. I decided that the antipathy Suzannah felt toward her was due to Cleo's self-confident Eastern preppie manner and her big-city sophistication. Cleo claimed not only to have seen the Beatles in concert at Shea Stadium but swore that she had been pressed up tightly against Mick Jagger in a crowded elevator in Bloomingdale's in New York City, and had actually felt Mick's *thing* pushing into her: There was nothing, absolutely nothing, that Suzannah could possibly come up with to match such an experience.

Still, in spite of this half-joking, half-serious adversary relationship that developed between them right from the start, we four—Suzannah, Cleo, Cassie and I—hung around together during that first week, Orientation Week, and we went to all the meetings and assemblies together and all the sorority parties and teas, even though I was rushing simply for the fun of it. But when I announced my intention of remaining an Independent to my new friends they were all surprised. Especially Suzannah.

"If you really want to be somebody on campus, you simply *must* belong to the best sorority. And I don't mean the one with the biggest collection of boring, intellectual types either. I mean the one with the cutest girls . . . the most popular ones. So the best boys know which house to come to right off the bat."

I considered this a pretty dated idea—a leftover from the forties and the fifties, and I was surprised that Cleo, whom I expected to be more advanced in her thinking—she *was* from the East, this time agreed with Suzannah.

"My mother," Cleo said, "would probably like me to get into that kind of house. She would call the sorority house with the prettiest, most popular girls the one best attuned to success. That's my mother's most favorite phrase—'attuned to success.' "

"But wouldn't she give any good marks for brains?" I asked.

"I suppose. *If* the brains went along with the beauty and popularity."

"And where are you going to find those three things in one package?" Suzannah demanded, almost as if she were baiting Cleo, implying that she herself was the one package and Cleo was not.

"Maybe in a package from *Nueva* Jersey," Cleo teased, winking at me. "We Eastern girls are on our toes, you know."

"I would hardly think *you'd* be that package, Cleo. Wise-asses are never popular with *anybody,*" Suzannah answered quickly. "As for myself, I've *always* been popular. And I belonged to the best sorority at the U. of K.Y. And *it* had the prettiest and most popular girls."

"One would wonder why you ever left there for here—" Cleo murmured.

"I was Homecoming Queen and it was only my freshman year," Suzannah said, pointedly ignoring Cleo. "And I was practically engaged to the most important boy on campus. But then I said to myself, 'Suzannah, honey, do you want to spend your whole life being a big fish in a little old pond, or do you want to jump in the ocean and swim with the other big fish?' "

I laughed. "And what did little old you answer little old you?"

"I have opted for the ocean, as you can see. The U. of K.Y. was all right as far as it went, but if I stayed there, I figured all I'd get to be would be Miss Junior Commerce of Louisville or maybe Miss Hardware or something like that. Now, OSU might be full of pushy Yankees," she smiled at Cleo, "but it *is* more cosmopolitan than the U. of K.Y. and I figured it probably would be a lot better to be a beauty queen here than there. I *could* end up Miss America. With a big modeling contract. Or maybe even end up in Hollywood. Why, look at Jean Peters! She won the Miss Ohio State contest back in forty-six and wound up marrying Howard Hughes. And if I stayed in K.Y. maybe *I'd* end up marrying Harvey from the grocery store and spending the rest of my life hanging out the wash and drinking straight vodka at eleven o'clock in the morning. Now if you had your druthers, which would *you* choose?"

I, for one, could see Suzannah's point. Who in her right mind would want to end up nipping straight vodka at eleven o'clock in the morning, for God's sake?

"Did you know," Suzannah continued, "that statistics say that if a girl goes to college, she usually marries a boy she meets there?"

"But you just said you wanted to be a model or a Miss America, then go to Hollywood and be a star. I didn't know catching a husband was also part of your plan for the future," Cleo teased.

Suzannah chose to take the remark seriously. "True. That is not my main goal. But who knows? If the right man came along—a rich, important, powerful man. I wouldn't turn down, say, John Kennedy. If he weren't dead. I mean, both rich *and* president! Or I wouldn't mind marrying Howard Hughes, for that matter, if he weren't already married to Jean." She thought a moment. "Of course if I met him and he fell madly in love with me, he could divorce Jean, couldn't he? That's what Scarlett O'Hara would have done if she wanted him. She would have made him divorce his wife."

"But Ashley never did divorce Melanie for Scarlett, did he?" Cleo stated with relish, sure she had Suzannah.

But Suzannah fixed her with a furious eye, then stated witheringly, "But people didn't divorce in those days. Maybe once in a blue moon. . . ."

"But even in the end *after* Melanie died—he still didn't really want her, did he?" Cleo persisted.

"That's true," I said. "She never got Ashley and in the end she lost Rhett Butler too, and he was the *real* hero. He was the real loss," I mourned, loving heroes, loving fairy-tale endings.

Suzannah thought about it. "Well, Ashley *was* a mistake. The trouble was she should never have wanted him in the first place. He was a weakling and a wimp. As for Rhett, I got the definite impression she would get him back. Very definitely so. Assuming she still wanted him."

"Oh, I think she'd still want him," I said, sure. There was a fitness to things, and if Scarlett was the heroine then she would still want the man she finally saw as hero. I smiled at Suzannah, feeling touched by her real devotion to a make-believe heroine. She really believed in Scarlett O'Hara. "Well, who knows? Maybe someday you'll really go to Hollywood and you'll be a big star and they will make a sequel to 'Gone with the Wind' and they'll choose you to play Scarlett."

Suzannah dimpled, as if my saying so made it really possible.

"And maybe if pigs had wings, they would fly," Cleo offered, buffing her nails ostentatiously. Cleo had very long, perfectly manicured nails and had told us that she and her mother, along with the other well-groomed mothers and daughters of Tenafly, N.J., went to the neighboring town of Fort Lee, N.J. to a salon where they *only* did nails—no hair.

Suzannah had resented Cleo's nails from the minute Cleo had told us about the elitist Fort Lee salon. "And maybe if pigs had manicured nails, they would look just like you," she trilled now triumphantly.

Cleo had really walked into that one. Still, to try to save the situation I turned quickly to Cassie. "How about you, Cass? Will you pledge a sorority?"

"I think so," she answered thoughtfully. "As far as Mother is concerned, my first year here is kind of an experiment, and if I pledged a sorority that she considered the right kind, that might count for a lot toward whether she allows me to stay on when the year is up."

"Which sorority would your mother consider the right kind?" Cleo asked, and we were all interested in hearing the answer. From what Cassie had so far revealed about her mother, we all found her fascinating.

"I guess it would be the one with the girls from the best families . . . the *nice* girls . . . which would probably mean *not* the prettiest nor the most popular. . . ." she groped for words. "Mother would never associate those kinds of girls with being nice—"

"Really?" Cleo asked. "What would be your mother's definition of *nice?*"

Cassie looked at all of us in turn in a helpless sort of fashion, as if she could not possibly find the words to explain. Finally she laughed and said, "I guess the first term of definition would be first family Californian. And I guess you'd have to meet my mother to really understand."

I got the distinct impression that Cassie herself had been trying to figure her mother out all eighteen years of her life.

Earl Blackstone, Cassandra Hammond's father, had not always been the aristocrat she depicted him as. Actually he had been a ne'er-do-well from Ohio who had wenched, drank and brawled his way west to a city named for *Nuestra Señora de Los Angeles* where he decided to stick around—the sun shone every goddamn day and it was easier on a man who often as not had to sleep in the open. And it was sheer dumb luck when one day he stumbled onto the *brea,* the tar pits, the black stuff the Indians used for everything from salves to fuel, and he had his one great idea of a lifetime. He married Tessie McCarthy, a barmaid with a nest egg (she had planned on opening her own saloon), and they bought the leases on the land from which the tar bubbled, and the two of them started digging for oil, at first with merely a pick and shovel. They prospered but when *everybody* started to buy up land leases and drill, there was a glut of oil and prices fell. Then the land leases were going for almost nothing. It was Tess who urged Earl to buy up the leases—she foresaw the day when there would be a demand and a market all over the world for the black gold. The rest was California history.

Ten years into the twentieth century found the Blackstones in control of most of the oil production in the state, as well as holders of extensive parcels of land, and established as Southern California aristocracy. It was of no matter to the Blackstones that they were looked down on by the robber barons from the North—those who had made their money in gold, railroads and land, frequently stolen from the Spaniards who held the original land grants, and who formed the nucleus of San Franciscan society, and who, in turn, were looked down on by the aristocrats of the Eastern coast. Earl and Tessie decided to build a baronial domain and start a lineage of well-born Blackstones.

Accordingly they built Blackstone Manor on twenty-four acres of beautiful hillside in a village (later to be incorporated as Beverly Hills) where bear and deer and mountain lion still roamed. There were forty-four rooms in all with seventeen Spanish-tiled bathrooms. There was a tap room, a music room, a paneled library with five thousand books ordered in one fell swoop, a garden room with a handpainted ceiling of leaves, flowers, birds, and angels; fifteen fireplaces, gold-plated door handles, and acres and acres of garden frankly copied from the Villa de Medici. There was even a gallery for the portraits of twenty-three former Blackstones for whose features the artists' imaginations were given carte blanche.

Tessie McCarthy Hammond died giving birth to her daughter, Cassandra, in the year 1918, and Earl then gave up half his estate to development, leaving himself with only twelve acres—he no longer was keen on running such a large place without his wife. He was already saddled with the difficult enough task of raising his daughter alone and Cassandra was never easy. At the age of sixteen she was determined that she had a mission in life. She was sick of hearing that her place of birth was an artistic wasteland. She decided then that she would be the cultural saint of the City of Angels. She would establish museums, an opera house, launch a world of theater and ballet, possibly develop a philharmonic orchestra. In order to attain all these goals, she would have to forge a proper alliance with a man who was a match for her, one who might weld his strengths with hers.

By the time she was eighteen, her father was anxious that Cassandra find her proper mate so that he himself might be relieved of her judgmental eye and critical tongue. Accordingly he eagerly presented her with eligible, illustrious names but none were deemed suitable by the discerning Cassandra. Earl Blackstone wondered if the man whom his daughter would find suitable even existed.

Sometimes Cassandra accompanied Earl when he visited with his friend Willy Hearst at San Simeon, although she professed that for her this was hardly a pleasure. A snob herself, Cassandra claimed to detest the San Franciscan snobs and abhorred Hearst's San Franciscan connections, although by this time Mr. Hearst himself was pretty much out of it and even in his prime had not bothered much with San Franciscan society himself. Furthermore, she decried the Hearst castle as vulgar. Nor was she impressed, as most young women would have been, to be dining with the likes of Gable or Cooper. She did not, like most Americans, idolize film stars. As for Willy's friend, movie star Marion Davies, who retired to the powder room with alarming frequency, only to return each time more flushed and high-spirited, Cassandra had two words: alcoholic tart. Earl Hammond could only envy his friend's good fortune in having his bed warmed by the glamorous, good-natured blonde while he had Cassandra, who watched how much he drank and corrected his speech, manners, and dress.

However, no matter how much Cassandra eschewed the pretentious San Simeon, it was there she first laid eyes on Howard Hughes when she was twenty and he thirty-three. She weighed his gifts and accomplishments, and decided that she had found a man worthy of her or at least as worthy a man as could be found. She would forgive him his first marriage, though as a rule she did not approve of divorce. Hughes, known to be somewhat appalled by women with matrimonial designs, might have fled had he known what Cassandra had in mind for him, but as it was, he found her attractive, young and physically appealing.

Still, eight years later, Cassandra had to admit that she had pursued the elusive Hughes in vain and married Walter Hammond on her twenty-eighth birthday in the year 1946, shortly after her father had passed away. The war was over and she felt free to arrange a splendid affair. Spread under pink and white striped canopies, the buffets were adorned with great swans of carved ice filled with the pinkish-red caviar selected to adhere to the color scheme, and sparkling silver fountains spraying California pink champagne, also selected for its hue rather than its drinking qualities. The champagne actually consumed by the five hundred guests was fifty cases of Dom Perignon offered up by one hundred waiters, a ratio of one waiter to every five guests, and a case of the Perignon for every ten. The guests danced to three orchestras as they speculated as to what had happened with Hughes, and wondered about this Hammond character. Who was he?

Only Cassandra herself knew that Walter Hammond was a second choice. He was not the achiever Howard was, but he was intellectual and well-mannered, and unlike Howard he was easily manipulated and managed. As an art history professor, he would be of invaluable help to her in the development of the Blackstone Museum.

Yes, after almost eight years of trying to catch and tame the beast, she had decided she could not go on in a continued effort to try to wed Howard. One, there was the question of his character. Two, it was demeaning to someone of her stature to go on with the chase, and three, there was the question of an heir. She was nearing thirty—her childbearing years were rapidly diminishing.

She could not deny that she had been taken in at first by Howard. He was tall, rich, dashing, and a great achiever, but in the end she decided he was dour rather than charming, ill-dressed and ill-groomed, and those sneakers he affected had grown rather noxious. Besides, no one would deny that he was a persistent, obsessive nag, eccentric to a fault, and she could no longer ignore those stories about all his women . . . how he kept them in apartments in Santa Monica and Hollywood, in bungalows at the Beverly Hills Hotel and in leased houses in the hills above Sunset. At first, the chase had been a challenge, and she had taken her own satisfaction in the fact that only she, of all the women he had known, had remained inviolate; that she was the only pure, unattainable woman Howard had ever known. It had even been amusing—their cat-and-mouse game. *He* was the mouse *her* cat never quite cornered into submission and marriage; *she* was the mouse *his* cat never quite managed to bed. But even that amusement had worn thin after eight years. So it had been with great relish that she summoned Howard to tell him that their relationship was over and that she was marrying Walter Hammond.

She made an appointment for Howard to present himself at Blackstone Manor at two in the morning.

"Come alone, Howard, and in an unmarked car," she said with a certain amount of malice. "One of your old beat-up Chevrolets will do just fine."

Howard sputtered and she laughed to herself. Howard thought she knew nothing of his habit of meeting people in strange parking lots in the middle of the night, or how he liked to travel incognito in battered Chevrolets when on an assignation.

She answered the door herself, regal in an evening gown of pale blue chiffon that matched her eyes. She could hardly keep servants up till two in the morning merely to embarrass Howard who enjoyed his secrecy and loved intrigue. "Come into the drawing room," she said, feeling very much the spider. "I have something to tell you that will be of interest to you." Ill at ease, he sat nervously with one long leg crossed over the other while he massaged his soiled white sneaker waiting for her to speak. Finally, after deliberately prolonged minutes, she said, "Our friendship is at an end. I'm going to marry Walter Hammond, a professor of art history," and waited for his reaction.

He scratched his head and said, "Who the hell is Walter Hammond and when have you been meeting him? It's impossible that you've been seeing him and I didn't know anything about it: For God's sake, Cassandra, how did you pull it off?"

She laughed. Surely she was entitled to glean some crumbs of pleasure from the long, wasted affair. "You'd better fire those detectives of yours, Howard. For years you've had me under surveillance and I've outsmarted your men at every turn."

He was stunned. It was true. He had had Cassandra under surveillance and had assumed that not only had she been unaware of it, but that he had been informed about every man she had seen. Now, a specter of all the men with whom she might have betrayed him tainted the whole relationship and he was furious. At the same time, the rather vague urge to claim her virginity (or assumed virginity, at this point), the desire that had waxed and waned over the years, intensified sharply. He crossed to the pale blue satin sofa where Cassandra sat, a thin smug cat. "I'll sack every goddamn one of those detectives!" he snarled and sat down hard by her side, draping one arm around her bare shoulder. "And you, Cassandra! How could you deceive me like this?"

"*I* deceive *you*, Howard? Now, really!" she purred.

"You allowed me to think that you didn't know you were being observed. That's the height of deception." His hand trailed down her bare arm. "You allowed me to think that you were faithful." His hand trailed up her bare arm and rested on her slim neck.

"Perhaps I was faithful, Howard, but perhaps I wasn't. . . . Now you'll never know, will you?" she said with an uncharacteristic coyness.

She plucked his hand off her neck and threw it aside. "But *you*, Howard, have been flagrantly promiscuous."

"Don't be silly, Cassandra." He moved his hand back and let his fingers play with the soft white flesh of her nape.

"Oh yes you have, Howard," she said with a certainty calculated to alarm him, and he removed his hand from her neck abruptly.

"How can you be so sure?" he demanded.

"Because I have had *you* under surveillance too, Howard."

"You what?" he rasped harshly.

"Yes." She smiled, knowing how the revelation would sting in light of his elaborate efforts to safeguard his privacy.

Furious yet at the same time sexually aroused, he ripped at her bodice, exposing a small but otherwise perfect breast. He lunged for it with his mouth, biting the nipple sharply while one hand reached under the long gown and up her thigh. She had not anticipated such a tactic; still she maintained a cool control. Why not? she thought. She was past twenty-five and about to wed Walter Hammond. Should she not have some experience? Shouldn't one at least test the waters before commencing to swim? Besides, she had waited for Howard Hughes for years and surely she was entitled to know what it was like with a lover of his reputation, especially since she could do so without compromising her morality or allowing Howard to think that she had succumbed.

She fell back on the sofa as if it were only the weight of his body that had caused her to do so. She voiced no sound but permitted her face to record abject terror and then submission, but only under duress. Then she groaned in such a manner that Howard, in the midst of pulling up her gown, could not tell whether it was in passion or horror. But he could not stop to find out, and as he struggled into her soft inner space, he was gratified to know that at least the symbol of her virginity offered resistance. He slipped into place, and, exercising all his restraint not to discharge prematurely, he was uncertain how his attentions were being received. Then he felt her long uncolored nails claw his back and he moaned both in pain and pleasure, not bothering to determine if the raking was an attack or an unbridled response. His mouth found hers and he felt the sting of her teeth digging into his lip, and then her shudder and then her sigh, and then he released himself, convinced that, after all, she *had* wanted him.

But then as he lingered within her a few moments more, enjoying his exhausted repose, he was stunned by the force of a table lamp striking his skull. Dazed, he demanded, "Why the hell did you do that, Cassandra? Are you out of your fucking mind?"

"How dare you use such vile language in my presence! And after you have taken advantage of our friendship in this unspeakable manner!" She wept.

It was the first time Howard had seen her cry. *Cassandra Blackstone didn't cry!* Her tears confused him. Had it been rape or seduction? Or, in the final analysis, had it been simply an act of compliance? He would never know for sure and it was damn annoying. To be on the safe side, he attempted an apology although it did not come easily.

My God! An apology for making love to her? The most unstylish thing she had ever heard of—It was unbelievable. . . . And worst of all, the lovemaking itself had been like the years she had spent in search of the finer Howard Hughes, unrewarding. Well, she had no one to blame but herself. She had been foolish. After all, Howard was a Texan and not a Californian.

Two weeks after her wedding Cassandra had indication that she was with child. It was something of a dilemma. Should she give birth to a child whose paternity was in doubt, which meant, of course, that she would be guilty of behavior that smacked of duplicity, a practice she frowned upon. Still, what were her options? Abortion? On religious grounds, she was opposed to what she considered a basically ungodly act. And she despised the idea of putting herself into the hands of anyone so shabby and shady as to perform such a deed. However, if she decided on such a course she would not hesitate to take it. One did what was necessary, no matter what, and only the fool dallied or hesitated.

On the other hand, if she gave birth to the child, what of the two possible fathers? Would Walter suspect that the child might not be his? No. Never. Walter was not the hardest person in the world to deceive and he stood in absolute awe of her. He would never allow himself to doubt her. Howard was another story. He was an enigma—his mind a tortuous labyrinth of odd thoughts and notions, his thinking process entirely unpredictable. Would it occur to him that the child might be his? He was maniacally, compulsively possessive about anything he presumed to be his. He could possibly cause trouble, attach scandal to her name, but in the end could he really harm her? She could always respond by labeling him an insanely jealous madman and as many people would believe her as not. Besides, she really didn't believe Howard would risk public ridicule.

In the end she decided to continue with the pregnancy. She wanted an heir. Who could ascertain if she would conceive again?

Cassandra gave daily inspection to the daughter she brought forth, but she could come to no definitive conclusion. The baby was pretty enough with her own coloring of blue eyes, fair skin, and pale hair, but she thought she detected a certain commonness of feature. The nose, for one, was broader than her own and shorter, nearly, but not quite, snub. Now *that* was Walter's nose. But the eyes, a deeper blue than her own, almost a cornflower blue, were shaped like Howard's. The mouth was small but the lips full, almost what was called "bee-stung," a feature that she *had* to lay to her mother's influence. Her mother's pictures betrayed that same defect. And the hair seemed to have more gold than her own, but almost exactly the shade her own father's had been. So be it. It would be necessary to observe the child's development to determine whose bent she followed—Walter's or Howard's. Would she be ambitious like Howard—an achiever, but willful and self-obsessed? Or artistic and bookish like Walter, soft and easily controlled? Would she lend herself willingly to the training required to mold the proper Blackstone heiress?

Nice . . . No, she could not actually define the word for her friends as her mother would use it, but she had started learning early in life the different facets of the word. For one, a nice girl did not do anything naughty . . . ever. She did not disobey her mother, and was not, if it could be helped, beautiful. People were always saying that she was a little beauty but she learned not to let that give her any pleasure. Beautiful definitely was not nice.

When Walter Hammond died at an early age, six-year-old Cassie sat next to her mother on the Queen Anne sofa in the yellow drawing room dressed in a black velvet mourning dress while Cassandra received the condolence callers.

"At least you have Cassie," they comforted the widow. "Such a sweet, darling, beautiful little girl."

"Some of the most beautiful things in life are the most useless. Take the rose, for instance. Lovely, certainly. To look at and to smell. But useful? I would hope Cassie will grow up to be more than a vain little snip of a flower."

Walter had been handsome to be sure, Cassandra thought. But of what use had he been to her outside of his duties as curator of the Blackstone Museum? She had tried to make a man of him but instead of rising to her provocation, he had wilted like a lily in the field. For the thousandth time she studied her daughter. Was she Walter's? Decorative but spineless? Or was she Howard's? Would she evolve as stubborn and strong-willed? Only time would tell. In the meantime, she seemed to be a thoughtful little thing . . . quiet and introspective.

Cassie sat and tried to make heads and tails of the different conversations her mother had with the callers while at the same time she worried whether her daddy had gone to heaven where the good people went. She knew that often he had displeased her mother and displeasing Mother was *bad*. She already knew that to be beautiful was bad. And beautiful was also useless. And useless was worthless. And worthless was bad. To be beautiful was also vain and vain meant spoiled and spoiled was bad. Good meant pleasing your mother no matter what. A good girl was a nice girl.

Finally Cassie smiled at us in a conciliatory fashion and said, "I'm sure Mother would say all three of you were really nice girls."

Somehow I had the feeling that this wasn't entirely the truth, that Cassie, in her own nice way, was being more tactful than honest.

"Well, when I do get to Cal I'll surely look up your mama," Suzannah said. "Maybe she'll introduce me around to all her influential friends."

"Certainly," Cassie murmured and Cleo said, "I bet if Mrs. Hammond knew what was in store for her she'd just jump for joy." Suzannah wheeled around angrily to counter this verbal attack with a remark of her own, and I knew we were off and running once again.

3.

Suzannah and I made a vow at the end of that first week. We promised each other that we wouldn't go steady. We would play the field our first year and just have fun. We even shook hands on it and went over to Andy's Tavern on High Street to seal the bargain with a beer. Rather, I had the beer while Suzannah took only a sip. "Beer," she said, "while nutritious—it has lots of B vitamins—is extremely bloating. And *that* is definitely not good. Neither is falling in love. Only fools fall in love, you know. If you're clever, you only allow men to fall in love with *you*. Actually, boys *and* men have been falling in love with me ever since I can remember. Even my stepfather was forever making passes at me. On the sly, of course, but I think Mother knew and she was forever trying to get rid of me. She always sent me to different relatives to live with for as long a time as she could get away with it. Yop, old Hubie had roaming hands, all right."

I was shocked. "Your stepfather?"

"You better believe it." She smiled at me crookedly. "And I was only ten when she married him. At ten when a man you call Daddy puts his hands on you you think he wants to be a father to you."

"But you said your mother knew. Why didn't she do something about that instead of sending you away?"

Suzannah laughed bitterly. "I guess she wanted him more than she wanted me. He was the insurance agent the railroad sent around to settle the claim. Daddy, you see, worked for the railroad and died by the railroad. Somehow, he fell under the wheels and got so chewed up they couldn't even open the coffin at the funeral. I never did get to say goodbye to Daddy. And he was pretty sweet, my daddy." Her eyes filled and she wiped at them with her long, aristocratic fingers. Then she took a gulp of my beer. "Any-hee-how, Hubie Dopson was the agent and when he saw all the money Mama was getting—and Mama is pretty even if her hair is losing its bright red color—he married her. And Mama was thrilled to get him. The second big thrill of her life was when I finally went off to college. Hubie has more hands than an octopus and Mama wanted them all for herself. Well, she's welcome to them. For all I care, she can fuck herself to death with Hubie. What really bugged me was that Mama thought I *wanted* Hubie. Can you beat that? Me, of all people! Why, I don't believe in giving away anything for free that others will pay for. You got to save the old temple for better things. And I don't mean a ten dollar bill either. There are thousands of rich, important men out there that are just dying to be of some help to a desirable woman and I intend to meet up with them."

"All of them?" I giggled. I wanted to make Suzannah smile.

Suzannah batted her eyelashes at me. "Well, if I must—" And we both laughed, and Suzannah took another sip of my beer.

That night Suellen came to dinner at the dormitory. I had hardly seen her all week. For one she was engaged to Howard Rosen, a senior with all the qualities Suellen admired in a man—sincerity, gentility, honesty, and kindness—so she had to spend a lot of time with him. And secondly, she had been busy with her sorority duties—helping out with the rushing and what not. She felt guilty about neglecting me my very first week at school but I relieved her mind quickly, introduced her to my new friends so that she could see I had had plenty of company. And then we all ate together. I was eager for Suellen to like Suzannah, Cassie, and Cleo. I wanted all five of us to be friends, for no matter what else happened, or whomever else I was friends with, Suellen would always be first in my heart. Suellen was like a mother to me, if truth be told. We had always been close, and especially so since we had been orphaned five years before when our parents had been killed in an automobile accident on an Ohio highway. And we had stayed close even after Suellen went off to Columbus and I stayed with Aunt Emily in Cincinnati finishing high school.

Everything went well at dinner. We all talked and laughed and I was pleased that everybody was getting along so well. But afterwards, Suellen took me aside and cautioned me: "It's a mistake to make friends too quickly. Take your time. Go slowly. Look around. The friends you make in college can turn out to be the friends you have for the rest of your life!"

I gathered instantly that she wasn't referring to Cleo and Cassie with this warning—both of them were nice and well-mannered and in no way offensive. Suellen was definitely talking about Suzannah. I really couldn't expect my sister Suellen to appreciate someone like Suzannah. Suellen, who I always thought looked exactly like Doris Day, *acted* like Doris Day. I mean she was the embodiment of the American girl next door. She was friendly, polite, and earnest. She was full of ideals and high principles. She was concerned with the world, the peace movement, and civil rights. She was actually sick in bed for a week when the president was assassinated, and was already concerned about the country's growing involvement in the affairs of another country. She was even thinking about joining the Peace Corps. And Suzannah? I had to admit she was high-handed, totally self-absorbed, deeply in love with herself. No, Suellen could never really understand a girl like Suzannah.

"Oh, she's fun! And I'm *not* making a lifelong commitment to her.

Honest, I didn't promise her a thing," I joked. How could I possibly explain to Suellen that Suzannah somehow fascinated me like some strange, exotic bird of gorgeous plumage?

4.

On the very next day after Suzannah and I had exchanged our vows not to go steady, I walked into Speech 101 and spotted a boy with dark red hair sitting toward the rear of the room and I felt something stir within me. I quickly took a front seat, the first empty seat I saw and I pondered the turn of events. My glimpse of the boy had been but cursory. What was unusual enough about him to cause my stomach to do butterflies? He didn't appear much older than I, and he wasn't even startlingly handsome. Lean and kind of muscular looking in a slim way and . . . cute? Yes, cute, I decided, for want of a better word, although I found the word embarrassing. And he had looked back at me with a kind of steadfast gaze. Cute and steadfast? I laughed at myself. I, who believed in heroes out of books, out of fairy tales, being struck dead in my tracks by one quick glimpse of a slim, cute boy with a steadfast gaze and an upturned nose?

I longed for another look but I did not dare turn around. I would take a second look when the class let out, I decided. The instructor came in, collected the registration cards, then explained what we would be doing in class and told us what texts to buy. The course, though titled Speech, was actually Public Speaking, as we all knew, and our first assignment would be a humorous speech on any subject we chose. Everyone would be prepared, and he, Mr. Schlamm, would call on as many students as time allowed. The class would then discuss the speeches and, hopefully, offer constructive criticism. He then wished us a good day.

I took several minutes to pull myself together, gathering up papers, books, and purse, and then I looked up. He was passing my seat and he grinned down at me. It wasn't a smile, and for the first time in my life I really gathered the difference between a smile and a grin. The mouth sort of went up in one corner and down at the other and the eyes crinkled. Bright brown eyes, flecked with yellow, crinkling. And a plethora of dark red curls. Why, he was straight out of one of those stories in the *Ladies Home Journal* that my mother used to enjoy so.

I didn't smile back. First of all, I was too shaken up. And then, I was affronted. Affronted by my own reaction to those crinkling eyes and crooked grin.

That was a Tuesday. Unfortunately, Speech 101 was a two-credit elective, which meant it met only twice weekly and would not meet again until the end of the week, Friday to be precise. Between Tuesday and Friday I met a few other interesting boys to whom I gave my telephone number, but I was really simply holding my breath until Friday, eager to see if I would have the same reaction to the red-haired boy. It would be really interesting to find out, I told myself and Suzannah, who only shook her head in disapproval.

I walked into class and looked immediately to the rear. Our eyes met and yes, there was that same reaction again—something inside me turning over. Mr. Schlamm asked for a volunteer to give the very first speech and only a few hands went up. *His* hand was one of them and he was chosen and I wondered if that meant anything. Did this boy possess a magnetic quality that drew people to him instantly?

"Hi," he began. "I'm Todd King," and he grinned at the class bringing his gaze to rest upon me. The textbook instructed, "Pick out one person in your audience and address yourself to that person." Apparently I was to be Todd King's *person*. Instinctively I wanted to smile back but I resisted the urge. I had to be prudent, see what developed.

His speech centered on how he was determined to try always to be of help to his fellow man. One of the things he did toward this end, although he himself didn't smoke, was to always carry matches on his person. In his experience, the people who most needed matches were always those lacking them, especially those who smoked things *other* than your usual cigarette. This, naturally, got a big laugh from the class. Even Mr. Schlamm's lips twitched. I, too, only permitted myself a small twitch of the lips.

Then he described his first opportunity to be of service to mankind. A very pretty young woman needed a light for her cigarette, but owing to his nervousness and inexperience in dealing with matches—since he didn't smoke—each match went out before it had served its function. Titters from the class. "Then along comes this very debonair guy and he

produces a *lighter*. . . . lights the lady up and walks off with her.
. . ." Big laugh. I smiled faintly.

"But I was not daunted . . ." he went on. Another opportunity soon
presented itself, he told the class. He and a group of friends were on a
picnic when it began to pour. The group ran to a deserted cottage which
was cold, dark, and dank, but with a fireplace and a handy pile of
firewood. A fire was laid and the cry went up, "Who has a match?" "I
have," he called out and pulled out his book of matches. . . .

I anticipated the next line.

"And in my hand I held this soggy mess of cardboard and running
pink sulphur. . . ."

A really big hand from the class.

Todd King concluded by drawing a book of matches from his pocket.
"But I despair not, friends. Here I stand, ready to be of service. If you
are ever in need of a match, call on me."

And he winked at me!

This time I suspected that it was not my stomach at all that was
turning over but my heart.

Lots of applause from the class and even Mr. Schlamm appeared
pleased. I found myself clapping along, even though I felt that the
speech had been juvenile, cutesy, and coy. But it was also charming. *He*
was a charmer. And I wondered what else he was.

Mr. Schlamm asked for criticism and I was drawn to my feet by a
compulsion.

"Mr. King's material was a bit sophomoric . . ." I found myself
saying to my horror. I suppose I only wanted to be provocative but I
was immediately ready to cut my tongue out. He would think I was a
bitch and he would be right. *My God, honey caught flies, not hydrochloric acid.* "But his delivery was excellent!" I added triumphantly.

*Say something else, quick. Say something that will make you look
good,* I told myself.

"All in all, I would have to say, 'His speech flowed from his tongue
sweeter than honey.' Homer—*The Iliad.*"

"Nicely put, Miss—" Mr. Schlamm smiled at me as if he found me
cute.

"Lewis. Bonita Ann Lewis. But I'm known as Buffy. My sister Suellen named me after the dog next door."

And I got a laugh from the class, which was of course my intention.

Mr. Schlamm asked for further criticism. Everyone pitched in and
the general consensus was that the speaker had done a bang-up job.

When the class was over I gathered my possessions together slowly, waiting for Todd King to come forward. When he didn't, I rose in a pique and started to leave. Then from behind me I heard: "I want to thank you for your criticism. 'I disapprove of what you say, but I will defend to the death your right to say it.' Attributed to Voltaire."

I was stunned by his words; I was thrilled. I spun around to look into those smiling eyes.

"Where are you headed?" he asked.

"Back to my dormitory for lunch. I have another class at two."

"I break now too. Why don't you invite me to have lunch with you?"

This was a surprise and for a moment I was at a loss for words. Then I said, rather querulously, "I can't just take people to lunch. I'd have to have your lunch charged to me on a guest pass."

"That would be all right," he said, taking my arm. "Bonita Ann," he added.

"Everyone calls me just Buffy."

"But *you* can't be 'just' anything. At the very least, you have to be Buffy Ann."

We filled our plates from the buffet tables and sat down. Egg salad. Tuna salad. Carrots jelled into the orange Jell-O. Rice salad. Lettuce and celery submerged in green Jell-O. And for desert there was red Jell-O crowned with a dab of whipped topping. I shrugged half-apologetically. "Dormitory food."

"Oh, it's great," he said. "It's one Jell-of-a-meal."

Wonderful! I thought, looking at him from under my lashes. "You can have seconds. Except at dinner you can't have seconds on the meat."

He raised his eyebrows. "Are you inviting me back for dinner?"

Nervy, I thought. Or just trying to be piquant? Probably. "I wasn't thinking of it," I said. "I thought maybe you'd invite me out to dinner."

"That would be very nice, but no."

"Oh." Well!

"But how would you like to go to the movies tonight?"

I was almost afraid to say yes—he might come back at me with a "that's nice, have a good time." Warily I said, "What's playing?"

"I'm not sure. But I'd like you to come to the movies with me just the same."

I decided to take a chance. "All right."

"Good. Do you know where the Cinema is? On the corner of High and Walnut?"

I nodded.

"Goodo. Meet me there at seven thirty. Not in front. On the Walnut side."

"I'll be there."

"I'll be looking for you."

"Goodo," I said.

He nodded. "You know . . . you look like Vivien Leigh. A *young* Vivien Leigh."

I nodded. I knew.

After he left I realized that I had a million questions to ask him that I hadn't managed to over lunch. Why I didn't even know his major!

I showed up at the Cinema's side entrance at exactly seven thirty as I had been instructed. I guessed that he was playing some kind of game of intrigue with me. I only prayed that he would not stand me up. I didn't think that I would get over that in a month.

But the theater's side door opened and he materialized, dressed in a short red jacket. He beckoned me inside. "Quick!"

"Oh my God!" I gasped. "I didn't realize—"

"Sh!" He held a finger to his lips and pushed me down into an aisle seat. "I'll be back in a few minutes," he whispered.

Up on the screen Victor McLaglen was being gross and sweaty. Apparently the Cinema was a revival theater. After twenty or so minutes had passed and Todd hadn't returned, I started to wonder if I had been abandoned after all. I chewed a fingernail just as he popped up out of nowhere and sat down beside me with a furtive air. He pushed a bag of popcorn at me. "You can have it all," he said. "I'm not crazy about popcorn."

"No one could ever say you don't treat a girl right," I whispered. He smiled, nodded, and patted my thigh, and an electric current ran through me. Then he got up and left again. I nibbled at the popcorn and watched Victor up on the screen drink himself into a stupor, and didn't blame him a bit.

After another fifteen minutes or so, Todd returned again. This time he handed me a box of Good & Plenty, said, "Enjoy," and vanished once more. Victor snuffled and sniffled, and I popped one sugar-coated piece of Good & Plenty after another into my mouth until the box was empty and I wondered whether I was in love or merely infatuated.

He was back. "Got a free few minutes now," he said and plopped himself down in my lap. When I laughed, he commanded, "Shh! Do you want to get me fired?"

Then he kissed me. At first his lips were dry and sweet and closed, and then they were open and his tongue was sweetly wet. Just as I was recovering from the surprise and starting to savor what was happening, he jumped up and started back up the aisle. "Listen girlie," he whispered loudly, "you've really got to keep your hands to yourself!"

Toward the end of the picture, after Victor had informed and was falling apart, Todd was back with a Milky Way. Apparently he was stealing the candy stand blind. The bar of candy felt mushy and soft in my hand, and I spoke up loud and clear: "Hey, Buster, I hate 'em soft . . . I like them *hard!*"

I sat through the second showing. By the time the theater closed I was nauseated from the overdose of sugar, and it was past eleven thirty. We barely had time to get me back to the dormitory before the midnight curfew.

"Meet me for breakfast at Smitty's tomorrow morning," he said as the lobby door was closing after me. "Smitty's. High and Oak. Ten o'clock."

"I know. Don't tell me," I said. "You're the busboy."

I met him the next morning as directed. I was in a state of intense anticipation. I felt as if anything could happen. We had a big breakfast —juice, pancakes, eggs, and sausage. And then we sat over coffee until nearly lunchtime. I found out he was a sophomore and an accounting major.

"Really!" I marveled. "You don't seem an accountant type. What are you doing in a Freshman Speech class?"

"I don't intend to be an accountant for life. And you never know when you might have to give a speech."

"What do you intend to be?"

"A rich man," he said.

For some reason I didn't laugh, although it *was* kind of funny.

"What's your major?"

"English Lit."

"You don't seem like an English Lit type to me."

"Oh? What type do I seem?"

"The type that marries a rich man."

"Oh."

"Look," he said. "This has been a really nice breakfast but now I have to split. I'm hawking refreshments at the game today. Thank you very much for the lovely meal."

I was incredulous. "You mean I'm buying?"

"Well, it *is* your turn. Didn't I treat you to the movies last night?" He picked up the check, looked at it, then handed it over to me. "If I were you, I wouldn't pay it."

"Groucho Marx," I said.

"Groucho Marx," he agreed. And he kissed me right there at the table in front of Smitty's window.

I had only one other date with another boy. In a last spurt of independence and also to mollify Suzannah, who was furious that I was so quickly breaking our vow not to go steady, I made a Saturday night date with a boy named Roy, a perfectly nice pre-med student. We went to the Monkey Bar downtown and although Roy was sweet and attentive, I found it difficult to concentrate on him. My thoughts were elsewhere.

Then I looked up and there, at a table across the aisle from us, was Todd, and a curious feeling of contentment engulfed me. He smiled and waved, made faces while I tried not to look at him. I made an effort to concentrate hard on Roy, who, after all, deserved that much. But it wasn't long before Todd came over, actually sat down at our table. "Hi," he said. "You don't mind, do you? I just got sort of lonely over there by myself."

I felt a surge of exhilaration. It was such an *exciting* thing to do. I didn't know of another boy who would do such a thing. It was straight out of a book. But at the same time I wanted to laugh. It was so funny, altogether outrageous. Still, I felt sorry for Roy. He was at a loss. Finally he asked Todd, "What is it you want?"

"Oh, I just want to sit here and talk. I'm in love with Buffy Ann, you see." He shook his head up and down in affirmation.

Roy stared and I didn't know what to say, although my heart was singing. "Don't pay any attention to him," I told Roy, and proceeded to ignore Todd myself. The whole scene was right out of a forties' movie, and I pitied the girls who were bogged down with boys who were into the sixties. *This* was romance and what did they have? Sex? Drugs? Sitins? Mere dismal distractions.

Todd refused to be ignored. He continued to insert his observations into Roy's and my considerably stilted conversation. Roy stood up and asked Todd to leave. Todd shook his head. "No. It's all right. Really.

I'll just sit here. Don't pay any attention to me, just like Buffy Ann said. I'll just sit here quietly and look at her. I just love looking at her. Don't you? Look at those green eyes. They're the same color as this old cat I used to have—"

Roy sat down again. I could see that he was in an uncomfortable situation. He couldn't even *hit* Todd, if he was of a mind to do so— Todd was just too damn amiable for that. "Go away," I told Todd. "I mean it. This is not nice."

But he paid me no attention. "What are you studying?" he asked Roy with a large show of interest.

"Pre-med," Roy mumbled, and then he looked at me and I suppose I was watching Todd with an all too obvious fascination. He stood up again, threw a bill down on the table. "See you around," he said.

Todd got to his feet, grabbed Roy's hand and shook it. "Nice guy," he said, looking at Roy's retreating back. "Bright guy. Leaving was the intelligent thing to do." He took my hand in his. "So," he said.

"So," I agreed.

"I guess that's it."

"I guess so," I said.

Then he kissed me, leaning over the table, right there in the Monkey Bar with everyone looking. The Monkey Bar, after all, was a pretty small place, and it would have been difficult to miss the red-haired boy and the girl who looked like Vivien Leigh holding a kiss for what seemed to the girl like an eternity. Right out of a book. Right out of a forties' movie.

5.

Time was our enemy. We were forever fighting the clock to find the time to be together. There were classes, studying, and all of Todd's many jobs to contend with. And when we were together, there seemed to be no place where we could be alone. There were no mixed dorms. Men weren't even permitted upstairs in mine. There certainly was no way a girl could entertain a gentleman caller in her own bed while her roommate slept in the next bed, as I had heard was the style at some more sophisticated private colleges.

And none but the barest intimacy was allowed on the comfortable, poisonously bright green couches in the lobby of my dorm. There, we were permitted to talk to male friends, or study with them, or even to play cards at one of the bridge tables set up all around. But there was no touching allowed other than shaking hands, though I guess nobody would really bother you if you only *held* hands. But there was no kissing, and certainly nothing heavier. There was a sign posted on the bulletin boards promising disciplinary action if the rules were violated. (I was on probation several times after being discovered with Todd's lips on mine, with his tongue in my mouth, with his hand suspiciously positioned on my sweater, on one occasion with his hand *under.)*

Todd's room was off limits to us too. He lived in a boarding house off-campus where no girls were allowed upstairs. (His landlady accepted only male students since girls were too much trouble. They used too much hot water, their long hair clogged the drains, and the University demanded that the landladies monitor the hours the coeds kept.) There weren't even living room privileges in that boarding house and Todd had no car. The only place we could reasonably be alone was the movie theater where we managed to get to first base and occasionally even to second, but rarely to third and never, never to home plate.

When I, excruciatingly frustrated, complained to Suzannah, she drawled, "Poor baby. He brings her popcorn when what she's dying for is *nuts!"*

I told her she was vulgar. Actually, Suzannah did not sympathize with me at all. She was all for virginity but not for the usual moral reasons. As she had stated the first week we met, she simply did not believe a girl should give it away, but rather save it all up for a rainy day when she could barter it for a magnificent prize . . . like maybe just the sun, the moon, the stars, or even the whole galaxy.

Of course, we did have the great outdoors—the campus, the grass or bushes to hide behind, assuming the season was right. Frantic for consummation, I urged. "We could, at night, you know, in the bushes. Everybody else does!"

"No, Buffy Ann, not the first time, certainly. The first time has to be right, beautiful."

"It would be, Todd. We'd make it beautiful."

"No, Buffy Ann, I demand only the best for you."

Of course a motel was the obvious answer but I had a hard time convincing Todd. "Sleazy," he resisted. Unburdened by Todd's high standards, I persisted until he finally caved in. "If it's sleaze you want, it's sleaze you get."

"Sleaze can be very sexy," I assured him.

Todd managed to borrow a car for Saturday morning. (Todd worked Saturday afternoons and the owner of the car on Saturday evenings.) When I got into the car I saw a blue canvas gym bag on the seat. I knew one needed a piece of luggage to check into any half-respectable motel. "What did you put into it?" I asked. "Silk pajamas?"

"Sneakers. It *is* a gym bag."

But after we'd checked into the rather drab motel room, Todd started unpacking. First, he withdrew a green glass vase and then a red rose. He filled the vase with water, stuck the red rose in, placed it on the bedside table. He then thrust his hand inside the bag and came up with two wine glasses and a bottle of New York State champagne.

"Champagne!" I marveled. "You really didn't have to get champagne. Any plain wine would have done."

His eyes crinkled. "Haven't you heard? Todd and Buffy Ann drink *only* champagne. They're famous for it."

"Oh yes. Famous," I agreed. "Pour!"

"Not quite yet, if you please." He went back into the bag and pulled out a little dish and a can of salted peanuts. "I've heard tell that you were getting a little sick of popcorn and were yearning for some nuts."

"Oh, Todd, *you're* a nut! Oh, Todd, I do love you!"

"Please! Not yet. You are being premature in your declamations. First we must undress the lady—"

"Oh . . ."

He had felt of my flesh before and I of his, but we had never seen each other nude. I held my breath as he removed my clothes, piece by piece, kissing each part as it was revealed. Then, as he removed his own clothing, I watched him very closely and I saw tears rolling down his cheeks.

I was terrified. Was he disappointed? "What's wrong? Why are you crying?"

He smiled at me then, despite the tears. "It's just that you're so beautiful and I love you so much—"

He poured the wine and we drank solemnly. Then, suddenly, he jumped onto the bed with a display of wild abandon and said, "I am now prepared to give you the break of a lifetime. I'm going to let you make love to me. All you want!"

Playing at being outraged, I beat him over the head with the bed pillow until I was out of breath, and then I said, "Oh, I want."

And suddenly he was serious again. "Me too," he said. "I want!"

We drove back to my dorm. Todd had to return the car and report to work. As I got out of the car, I asked: "Are we engaged now? Or are we still going steady? Or perhaps now that you've finally seduced me, are you going to demote me to a one-night stand?"

I did not catch Todd off-guard. Earnestly he dug into his pocket and pulled out a ring. Strangely enough, it was not a ring from the dime store but a real gold ring with a real pearl. Small but real.

Thinking of how hard Todd worked and usually for so little recompense, a lump formed in my throat, and tears gathered in my eyes. "You shouldn't have," I murmured as I thrust my left hand forward.

"Wrong, Buffy Ann. I should've. Of all the things I've ever done this is the most should've."

He put the ring on my finger and kissed my hand.

I ran through the lobby of the dorm. My only thought now was whom I should show my ring to first. . . . to whom would I reveal my state of engagement. Suellen of course! But she would probably be upset that I had moved so quickly, had not been nearly as cautious as she had with Howard. It had taken Suellen almost two years before she had agreed to marry him. Suzannah? Suzannah would throw her hands in the air, call me a fool for tying myself down to a virtual nobody. But what could Suzannah know of a boy who could make you laugh one minute and who himself could cry the next because he thought you were beautiful and he loved you? What would Cleo say? Sympathetic and understanding as she was, what could she really know of a boy like Todd? She judged boys by the standards of her mother. "Is he attuned to success?" were the words that would pop into her mind. Now Cassie might not *know* about a boy like Todd, but possibly, very possibly, she had dreamt about one just like him.

Yes, I would tell Cassie first so that I could enjoy her look of happiness for me. Yes, Cassie was a girl who knew about heroes.

I went to my room to look for her. When I saw that she wasn't there, I decided to call Suellen next. And when Suellen wasn't in either, I went down the hall to Suzannah and Cleo's room. I had to tell somebody!

I found Cleo out in the hall, hysterical. She was surrounded by tennis racquet, skis, books, piles of clothes, everything strewn helter-skelter.

"She's locked me out of my room, my own room! That bitch! My mother would have a fit if she knew what kind of a girl I live with . . . a disgusting, nauseating, filthy cracker, that's what she is! And look what she's done to my things, all my beautiful things! Look! She's a pig, that's what she is. She keeps the room looking like a filthy pigsty and now look what she's done!"

I tried to calm Cleo down, to find out the reason Suzannah had locked her out and thrown her things after her, but she just kept screaming. "Pig! Dirty coffee cups all over the place with yukky mold growing in them. Dirty panties under the bed, not to mention dirty, filthy socks. And she hasn't made her bed *once* since she came! She hasn't even changed her sheets even once. They're not white—they're black! And she never, ever hangs anything up! Her clothes lying all over the floor, on the chairs, on the dresser tops! On my dresser top too! Piled to the ceiling practically! First she grabs the bigger closet because she's a selfish sow and then she doesn't even use it except for its floor! I—"

"Come to my room, Cleo, and let's talk it over."

"What about my things?" she screamed. "They're all over the hall."

"After we talk about it, we'll come back and I'll help you pick everything up. Okay?"

"All I asked her to do was remove the moldy coffee cups from the room, keep her dirty clothes off my desk, dresser, and chair, and return my grandmother's pearl necklace that she borrowed three days ago. And do you know what she said? She said she didn't have an idea in hell where the lousy pearls were and she told me, *told me* to look for them myself under the pile of clothes and books and papers on my dresser. And when I did look for them and couldn't find them, do you know what she did then? She *threw* five dollars in my face and said, 'There! For your crummy pearls!' My grandmother's pearls that are an heirloom and that she left me *in her will* and my mother will absolutely die when she hears that they are gone. So that's when I called her a filthy pig! Do you blame me?"

I shook my head from side to side in a kind of ambiguous answer. Truthfully, I didn't blame Cleo at all.

"Well, then she shoved me out the door. She's bigger than I am, the Amazon! And meaner! And then she threw my things after me. What am I going to do?" She ran her hands over her hair, whipping her curls into a wild froth. "You do understand that when I first asked for my pearls back and requested she remove the coffee cups and things from my dresser, I asked *politely. I* was brought up a lady. And you do understand that I can't put up with her and her slovenly ways anymore, not to mention her essential nastiness. Frankly, I don't know what I'll do if I have to go on this way."

I couldn't think of anything to do but offer to trade roommates with her. I would have to give Cleo sweet Cassie and take Suzannah myself in exchange. I could handle Suzannah, make her toe the line. Better than Cleo could, anyway. Besides, I wouldn't get so upset when Suzannah didn't behave.

"It's all right, Cleo." I put my arm around her to soothe her. She really did look like a deranged person with her hair so disheveled that it stuck out in points all over her head. Even her clothes were wrinkled and askew and she usually was so meticulously groomed—not your quintessential, pointedly sloppy college girl. You never saw Cleo walking around barefoot, carrying sneakers or sandals in hand. Why, she even wore matched sweater sets with her jeans. "I'll change roommates with you. Suzannah can room with me and you can have Cassie who is not only a love but as neat as you are—"

Cleo's dark eyes opened incredulously. "But why? Why would you take Suzannah when you absolutely don't have to?"

"She *is* my friend and I can cope with her. It'll be all right." And then to change the subject, to distract her, I extended my left hand. "Look what I got today, Cleo. It's an engagement ring."

"Todd King?" Her voice rose as if the ring had upset her further.

"Yes, silly. Of course Todd King!" Good God! Was there anybody else in the whole world?

"But it's only been a few weeks—Do you know what my mother would say?—"

I really didn't give a damn what Mrs. Pulitzer would say but I had a good notion, and I sighed heavily. "Would she want to know if Todd was attuned to success?"

Cleo broke out in a fresh torrent of tears.

"Cleo! What is it?" I wondered now if she had really gone berserk.

"It's my parents . . . they're getting a divorce!" Cleo sobbed in a state of absolute hysteria. "Mother just called. She's on the verge of collapse."

"Oh . . . I'm so sorry." So it was more than Suzannah that had driven Cleo over the line. "These things do happen, Cleo," I tried to console her. "At least you're grown. It's not as if you were a little girl. Why, you probably would never have lived at home again anyway."

"You don't understand. My parents were *perfectly* attuned. We were the perfect family in the perfect home . . . on East Clinton Avenue in Tenafly. You just don't understand. East Clinton is a lovely street, full of beautiful homes and successful people. Tenafly is a beautiful town and we were a model family. My father's a successful labor lawyer. My mother kept a perfect house. She was a lawyer too but she never really practiced. She gave it all up to make a home for my father and me, to be supportive of my father's career. When my father came home from New York at exactly six thirty every day, my mother would be waiting in a tea gown. Nobody else's mother wore tea gowns. My friends would absolutely *die.* Do you know anybody who wears tea gowns for dinner with the family?"

I shook my head. My Aunt Emily who wore tailored blouses and skirts to work would come home and change to pants and an old sweater.

"Well, my mother did. And she would have cocktails waiting with ice in a silver bucket just for the two of them. Sometimes I would sit with them too and maybe have a sip of wine. Mother said this was the gracious, civilized way to live. And Hilda would have dinner ready to serve on the dot at seven thirty. We ate in the dining room every single evening and the table was always set perfectly, almost as nicely as when there was company. With candles. And Hilda would always wear a uniform. Pink for every day, and black for company. Mother always says if a person is dressed properly for a job, she'll do a better job. I can hear her now. 'Cleo, dress for success no matter what it is you're do-ing. . . .' " Cleo's voice ran down and I thought she was through, but then suddenly she spoke again. "She always wanted me to have my nose fixed. Did I tell you that? She wanted me to have the Standhope nose—"

"My goodness, what's the Standhope nose?" I broke in. It sounded as if Cleo was talking about the Hope diamond or the Curse of the Bas-kervilles or something like that.

"It's the nose all the girls at my school had. They were all done by Dr. Standhope in Englewood and they all looked the same. Small, like maybe a half inch, and narrow with a little tilt at the end. You can recognize a Standhope nose all over the world. Why the other day I saw a girl at the Union drinking coffee and I *thought* I recognized the nose. I couldn't very well walk up to her and ask her if she had had a nose job, but I did ask her where she was from. Sure enough, she was from New Jersey. Teaneck. That's a town right next door to Tenafly. Bergen County. Englewood is a bordering town too. I guess *all* the girls from Bergen County have the Standhope nose."

"So why didn't you have your nose done too? If that's what your mother wanted—"

"I'm not sure. I guess I didn't want to have the same nose as all the girls in my school. I guess I should have done it. It upset my parents very much when I refused—" And she started to heave violently.

"Come on, Cleo. Don't start blaming your parents' divorce on your refusal to get a nose job—"

"I don't know. They used to get very upset when I was afraid to put on a pair of skis, until finally I did. We always went on skiing vacations, you see. Mother says skiing and tennis are *the* two sports for really successful people. Tennis much more so than golf. Actually, it was Mother who got angry at me for not having my nose done. My father was more upset about my *chin*. He said . . . he said . . . it was weak!" she sobbed.

I put my arm around poor Cleo's narrow shoulders and smoothed back her hair. I searched for words to comfort her. "Hey, come on. Your parents didn't break up because your mother didn't like your nose and your father didn't like your chin."

"No, actually they didn't," Cleo said, calming down, only sniffling now. "Mother said that Dad left her for an associate of his. A twenty-eight-year-old lady lawyer in his office. And after Mother gave up her career in law just to be supportive of him. It is rather ironic, isn't it? And Mother did keep herself up all these years. She kept herself perfect. Hair. Nails. She always read all the latest books. She always said that successful men, men who go straight to the top, wanted really attractive women who were up on things at their side. And now she's lost Dad to this snip who doesn't even dress up for work. She wears jeans to the office . . . jeans and T-shirts with writing on them. . . ." She resumed sobbing.

"Cleo, Cleo . . . people are getting divorced all the time these days. Maybe your mother'll find herself another husband. Or a lover! Divorce is not the end of the world—"

"It's the end of *our* world. Our world on East Clinton in Tenafly, New Jersey. And now I'll have a stepmother."

"Maybe they won't get married. Maybe they'll just live together."

"Oh my God, I hope not!" Cleo screamed. "My mother would really have a heart attack if Dad disgraced us both like that."

I had to laugh. It *was* funny.

"Come on, Cleo, I'll walk you back to your room. We'll tell Suzannah about the switch. At least you'll have that. Cassie instead of Suzannah."

"I'll bet *she'll* be glad. She's getting the best of the bargain. Just like she always does."

"But she *is* right," I told Suzannah. "You *are* a terrible slob. I hope you mend your ways before I'm forced to lock *you* out. The miraculous thing is how you manage to look the way you do, emerging from that incredible pigsty of your possessions."

Characteristically, Suzannah chose to take the remark as a compliment. "I do look pretty good at that, don't I?" She ate strawberry ice cream from a cafeteria take-out container as she spoke, and I contemplated the container, wondering what Suzannah was going to do with it once it was empty.

"I was not complimenting you, Suzannah," I said kindly but firmly. "I was merely trying to point something out to you in a nice fashion. That I have taken you in whereas nobody else would, but I would appreciate your neatening up your act." Then I watched the ice cream carton slither its way from Suzannah's fingers to the floor. I picked it up and threw it into the wastebasket. "This thing here," I kicked the basket, "is known as a wastebasket and it is a receptacle for trash. Use it!"

She sucked her fingers clean. "I told you I was an ignorant hillbilly, didn't I? That is not to say I am unintelligent. I am intelligent enough to know that I'm ignorant. I am also intelligent enough *not* to get myself engaged so early in the year to a boy who has no money, no background, no credentials and probably, no potential. Why, he's a nobody, honey. A very *charming* nobody, to be sure . . . why that boy could charm monkeys out of the trees, and he's cute as the dickens, but still a nobody!"

I was getting madder and madder but I determined to wait until she was finished before I lit into her.

She went on, "Why you're throwing yourself away, sugar. Just like my friend, Poppy. Poppy and I were in high school together. She was cute as the dickens. *Short,* but really pretty. Like a doll. And clever. And she started going with this no-account hillbilly—Herman Beaufort whose family was really trash. And Herman himself was just about this short—" she held her fingers an inch apart, "this short of being a real, genuine, homegrown retard, but he sang and played the guitar and she decided she was going to manage old Herm into the big-time. So Poppy up and quit school and that's what she's doing, nursing this ape. And Poppy's no fool. It's just a clear case of misdirection. She's just throwing herself away on a no-account no-quality moron."

I thought I was going to kill her. I really did. I was going to put my fingers around that white neck of hers and squeeze as hard as I could. I said in a dead, icy tone, "And you, you ignorant stupid no-account cretin, are implying that that's what I'm doing? I mean, are you comparing my Todd, my beautiful, brilliant darling Todd with this hillbilly moron? How dare you, you . . . asshole!" I finished up, using *her* word.

She completely ignored the insults I hurled at her. "No, of course not, honey," she said, smooth as cream. "I'm just talking about Poppy. This really cute, bright girl who's clearly misdirected. As I said . . . I think Todd is charming, a darling, and terribly clever, but still, he is a nobody. And I think you should look for someone with a little more *potential.*"

My anger was already spent. "Oh, Suzannah!" I said wearily. *"You're a stupid little fool. Who* do you think is a somebody? Your dumb football players? Your silly fraternity boys? Why, you know, you wouldn't recognize quality if it hit you in the face."

Suellen, who *liked* Todd, was not much more enthusiastic, although of course, not insulting or defamatory. Suellen was conservative by nature. She *had* dated Howard for two years before deciding to marry him, was planning on marrying him two years hence when she graduated. Conservative.

"How can you put your faith and trust in a man you hardly know, Buffy?"

"I *know.*"

"Unless you do not take this engagement as seriously as I take my commitment to Howard. I suppose you could be one of those who might be engaged several times before you're through—"

"I am quite serious, Suellen."

"But how can you be, so soon?"

"Because all the parts of me tell me that I am—my eyes, my nose, my mouth, my ears, my heart, my brain, my soul. I am the sum total of these parts and they all tell me the same thing—Todd loves Buffy, Buffy loves Todd."

"I can see that Todd King is lovable and sweet. But if you're planning on really marrying him, you must think about other things. Stability . . . practicality . . ."

"Todd is all things, Suellen," I said with a finality in my voice.

He *was.* He was all things, and they would all find out.

6.

Most people had a dream and Todd had told me his. He dreamed of being a rich man. But unlike most dreamers, Todd already had a Plan. A Plan and a set of Rules.

One of the essentials of the Plan, he said, was for me to drop English Lit in favor of Accounting. And I must say I never hesitated, not for a moment. I would be an accountant.

"Are we going to be in business together?" I asked him. "King and King, Accountants to the trade?"

"Maybe. But that doesn't matter. Accounting will only be a first step. When you're an accountant, you learn everything about all the accounts you service. You discover which businesses are doing well and why. You find out which businesses aren't doing well and why not. Then maybe, if you're smart enough, you can step in and take over a failing business and make it a success because you've already learned why certain businesses fail and others succeed. Pretty clever, eh?"

"I hope I'll be able to do it. I'm not sure that I'm smart enough—"

"You're smart enough. Would I pick out some dope to go bananas over?"

"Really? You're bananas over me?"

"It ain't grapefruit, Tomato."

"No, really . . . Todd. I don't think I'm smart enough to do it."

"You're smarter than I am. You got me, didn't you? And look what I got!" He shook his head in disgust.

I hit him with a book. "Yes! What did you get?"

He became serious then. "I got a girl so exquisitely perfect, a girl I

hadn't even dared dream about . . . not even in my wildest fantasies."
And there were those tears in his eyes again.

Who needed English Lit? Could Shakespeare have put it better?

Part of Todd's Plan was the Bank Account, the reason for all his jobs.
He had already had the account when he came to Ohio State—money
saved up from various jobs all through his high school years and summer vacations. He had been raised in an orphanage (a real Victorian
novel) and had no one to help him. His idea was to have a bankroll
ready when it came time to make that first business investment. Unfortunately, one of his easier jobs, that of usher in the movie theater, came
to a premature end soon after we became engaged.

I sat in my usual place on the aisle to the far left of the theater that
Friday night and Todd made one of his frequent visits to my seat armed
with a box of Goober chocolate-covered peanuts freshly purloined from
the candy stand. Bela Lugosi was playing Count Dracula on the screen
that night, and as Todd sat down, he made a dive for my throat with his
mouth. As I giggled and Todd nibbled, I glanced up over Todd's head
and spotted Mr. Schwartz, the theater manager. I tapped Todd's shoulder just as he was bestowing a loud and succulent hickey. "Mr.
Schwartz," I hissed.

Todd turned, simultaneously dropping the box of Goobers. "Hi, Mr.
Schwartz," he said. "Glad you could stop by. I've been wanting you to
meet my fiancée, Miss Buffy Ann Lewis, for the longest time. Miss L.,
I'd like you to meet my good friend and employer, Mr. Arnold
Schwartz."

"King, you're fired! And give me back that box of Goobers. Then
take your fiancée and get the hell out!"

Todd looked at me. "All right, Buffy Ann, I will!" He turned back to
the manager. "My fiancée, Miss Buffy Ann Lewis, says 'Go fuck yourself, Schwartz.' "

I rose with dignity, put my coat on with a great flourish. "Come
along, Todd dear. This place is a dump, d-u-m-p, dump!"

Todd presented his arm, I took it, and we marched out the side door,
almost as if to trumpets. When we were outside, we ran up the block in
triumphant exultation. "Great exit line, Buffy Ann!"

But then I stopped short.

"That *was* a great exit line, Todd. But I'm afraid we'll have to go
back."

"Why?"

"You will take note of what you're wearing, Mr. King." It was the short red usher's jacket. "Mr. Schwartz is still in possession of your own somewhat shabby, but reassuringly warm forty percent goose-down jacket."

Todd immediately got a new evening job at a diner dishing up hamburgers, and I grew very tired of eating burgers every night, especially since my dormitory meals were already prepaid. "All this grease is going to ruin my complexion," I complained one night, sitting at the counter.

"That does it!" Todd exclaimed, untying his slightly soiled white apron and throwing it up in the air. "Mike," he addressed the puzzled owner of the diner, "I quit! You're giving my girl zits."

We did well selling Fuller brushes. Todd did the selling and I made the deliveries. The housewives were unable to resist Todd's contagious grin, his twinkling eyes, and superb line of gab. He was really doing terrifically until he was offered the job of district manager, a job he could hold even as he was finishing school. That was when he quit and taught me his first rule for success.

"One must be careful not to be *too* successful at something one really doesn't want to be doing. It's seductive. Soon, one gets sidetracked from one's real goals. The important thing is to keep your eye on the main goal. Always remember that, Buffy Ann."

"I'll remember, Todd. I'll always remember."

By the following day Todd had a new job—telephone solicitation. "Definitely not seductive," he assured me.

In order to fortify our Bank Account further, we worked out a scheme to save on Todd's food expenditure by means of my dormitory cafeteria. I would pile my plate as high as possible—take as many rolls as feasible and surreptitiously make sandwiches, slipping them into handy waxed sandwich bags, then stuffing them into the very large handbag I carried around specifically for this purpose. Then I would go around to the other tables, grabbing a stray apple or orange—anything that wasn't being consumed. It became a game all my friends joyously entered into, and at the end of a meal I would be virtually deluged with leftovers, once in a while even snagging such a highly desirable item as a pork chop. (Only Suzannah was not entirely cooperative. She was going through a vegetarian stage, convinced that meat in any form formed toxic bodies in the bloodstream of her body, her temple. So when I requested that she accept the animal portion of the meal from the server in order to pass it along to me for my collection, she refused. She said she could not taint her plate with the blood of sacrificial animals.)

Occasionally I would take Todd into the dining room on an official guest pass, but then we would try to avoid handing in the pass as we completed the cafeteria line, so that we could alter the date and reuse the pass. One night, Mrs. Henchey, who collected the passes, apparently thought she detected an altered date and came over to our table and waved the pass in my face.

"I would like to consult with you, Miss Lewis. The date on this pass —" she began as Todd grabbed at his abdomen and groaned.

"Jeez, I think I've been poisoned. Don't eat the chicken salad, Buffy Ann! Help! Nobody eat the chicken salad!" He fell off his chair onto the floor.

Mrs. Henchey sniffed. "We're not even serving chicken salad tonight."

"Really?" I commented. "Is that so?"

Mrs. Henchey and I studied Todd rather impassively as he rolled about on the floor. Finally I said, "Don't you think we'd better call an ambulance, Mrs. Henchey?"

"No, I don't think that will be necessary. We'll just overlook the matter of the pass for tonight. However, you will not employ this tactic again. Now, will you tell your crazy boyfriend to get up from the floor before somebody trips over him?"

As she walked away I proclaimed loudly, "Boyfriend? I don't even know him. What's your name, kid?"

Todd picked himself up and resumed eating. "I hope you've learned something today, Buffy Ann. When faced with an enemy attack, divert and distract. Distract and divert. Always remember that, will you?"

I watched him attack the apple brown Betty. "I'll remember, Todd. I'll always remember," I said, believing every word he uttered was gospel.

Bank Account or not, once a month we dined out in style. We would go to the Deschler or another one of the hotels downtown and order Brandy Alexanders, shrimp cocktails, chateaubriand and strawberries Romanoff, accompanied by a six-dollar bottle of wine. The first time we went, however, I was so consumed with anxiety over the expense that I could hardly enjoy the dancing.

But Todd only smiled. "Rule, Buffy Ann. A learning experience is always a justifiable expense. We have to learn to be accustomed to the good life so that we will always demand it, accept nothing less. Also, we have to be reminded that saving money is not an end in itself."

He *was* smart. "I'll remember that too," I said as I pressed my body closer to his.

We visited a local motel as often as feasible, a schedule we found completely inadequate for our needs, not to mention the damage to our Bank Account. So Todd taught me another Rule. "In any venture, one must search for the holes where the money is leaking out. Once having located said holes, the astute businessman plugs them up." And he moved out of the boarding house where girls were not permitted and located a room with a tiny kitchenette on the third floor of a dilapidated apartment house not too far away from campus.

"A fleabag," Todd admitted, taking advantage of the situation to teach me another Rule. "One has to be occasionally prodded into remembering where one is going. It's not too good to be too comfortable before one reaches one's ultimate destination."

We furnished the apartment with a card table, a couple of folding chairs, a beat-up dresser and a double bed, all gleaned from the local Salvation Army resale shop.

" 'Nothing is more simple than greatness; indeed, to be simple is to be great.' Emerson," he said. "Do you agree, Buffy Ann?"

I agreed. I thought he was only wonderful. I threw my arms around him. " 'The fewer our wants, the nearer we resemble the gods.' Socrates."

"You know, you're extremely cultured for a lady who is going to be an accountant."

I lay down on the bed. "Come. Do things to a cultured lady."

He patted the mattress. "We *do* have all the necessary equipment. Rule, Buffy Ann. 'A good worker always picks the right equipment for the job.' "

When he was tightly inside me, I rejoiced. "I must be a good worker. I picked the right equipment for the job."

"And I must be a good businessman. I have plugged up all the right holes." He sighed with satisfaction.

7.

It was June, and only Todd and I, it seemed, were staying in Columbus where we both had jobs for the summer and where I could move into the apartment with him for three months of bliss. Everyone else was leaving and going off in different directions. Howard and Suellen were going back to Cincinnati where Suellen had a job at a Y camp as a swimming instructor, and Howard, who had graduated in Business Administration, was beginning a new job at an insurance company. Cleo was going home to Tenafly, New Jersey, to stand by her mother through the official, painful dissolution of the perfect marriage. And Suzannah, who had asserted so often that she was *never* going home again, was going to work as a hostess at the South Carolina resort of Hilton Head, where she not only would have a fun summer of dancing, men, and water sports, but also would get to meet people who might be of use to her in the future when she was out in the real world.

Only Cassie was leaving Ohio State for good, and tearfully. Even though she had joined the right sorority with the right sort of girls and even dated a few boys—a *very* few boys, that her mother would have judged the right sort—in the end her mother had decided that a year in Ohio, the ancestral home state of the Blackstones, was quite sufficient for one whose true destiny lay in California. Cassie would spend her next college year at the University of California in Los Angeles and live at home.

I was saddened by Cassie's departure. I had grown very fond of the California girl and would miss her. As for Suzannah, she could not understand Cassie's reluctance to return to the land of movie stars, sunshine, and promise, a place where her family name was so prominent. "You must really have a few screws loose," she summed it up, as I shook my head at her insensitivity.

Cassie didn't try to explain to her friends that Los Angeles meant only two things to her: the place where her mother ruled, a mother who still frightened her, and a city populated by terrifying strangers.

One Friday, when Cassie was in second grade at the Dacey Day School, she was permitted to take her Mickey Mouse Club pocketbook to school as a special treat for getting all "excellents" on her report card. Very proud of the purse, she had brought it outside with her during recess. When the girls were herded back inside after the playtime was over, Cassie suddenly realized that she had left the red pocketbook outside. Unobserved by her teacher, Miss MacDonald, she ran back to the playground to look for it. It would be terrible if she came home without it. Her mother would be furious over her carelessness.

She recalled that she had put it down under one of the palm trees in the far corner of the schoolyard while she skipped rope. As she approached that section of the yard, she saw an odd-looking old man in dirty clothes.

"Hi, there, Sis," he called out.

"Hello, Sir. I'm looking for my red Mickey Mouse Club pocketbook. Have you seen it?"

The man looked around. He pointed behind a tree. "Isn't that it over there? Yessiree, that's it!"

"Oh, yes, it is!" Cassie cried with relief. "Thank you very much." She ran to retrieve it. As she did, the man took a funny-looking red thing out of his pants. "Do you want a nickel, Sis?"

"Oh no, Sir." She had been taught not to take money from strangers.

"Do you want to be a good girl?" he asked.

"Oh yes, Sir. I *am* a good girl." She stared at the funny-looking red thing sticking out of the man's pants.

"Then you have to kiss my pecker." He wiggled the red thing.

Cassie laughed. "Pecker" was a funny word.

"It hurts and if you kiss it, it will be all better. Go on!" he urged in a louder voice. "You just put it in your mouth. Go on!"

She hesitated. Her mother didn't like people who dressed in old, dirty clothes. She wondered if her mother would want her to talk to this man at all.

"Hurry up!" the man said. "Hurry up or I'll tell your teachers you've been a bad girl . . . not obeying your elders. . . ."

Finally, in fear and indecision, Cassie inched forward and tried to put the red thing in her mouth, but it wasn't easy. It seemed to be bigger than her mouth and it tasted awful . . . salty . . . icky. . . . The old man was trying to force it in with his two hands when she heard Miss MacDonald's scream behind her.

"Cassie! My God! What are you doing?"

She felt her arm being wrenched and then Miss MacDonald dragged her back toward the school building at a run. Inside the principal's outer office, Miss MacDonald shouted at Miss Mulcahy, the school secretary, "Call the police! There's a pervert out there with his . . . you-know-what . . . hanging out!" She brought her voice down to a loud whisper, "Cassie was sucking on his—"

Cassie sobbed.

Then Miss Dacey appeared from the inner office. "Be quiet, you fool!" she snapped at the teacher.

Cassie sobbed louder. She knew that she must have done something terribly, terribly bad since everybody was upset and yelling.

"You two come into my office," Miss Dacey told the teacher and the secretary. "And you, Cassie, stop crying! Sit there and don't move!"

Cassie sat there petrified with fear as she heard the women screaming at one another through the closed door.

"How could you have done such a thing as to allow Cassie Hammond to remain out in the playground alone?" Miss Dacey raged. "You imbecile!"

"But I didn't—"

"Quiet! If we call the police we have to tell them *and* Cassandra Blackstone Hammond exactly what happened. And when that happens, I might as well lock the doors on this school. She'd have me out of business in a day. Do you understand that? And you, MacDonald, and you, Mulcahy, would be out of jobs . . . with no references either. Once word got around what happened at our school, no one would hire anybody from here! Can you get that through your thick skulls?"

"But Cassie—"

"You leave Cassie to me. Tomorrow we'll have a security guard on the grounds. Actually, this has been a fortuitous incident. No harm has really been done but we have been alerted to the possibilities. Even of a kidnapping. But once I have hired a guard nothing so unfortunate will ever again occur at the Dacey School. Now back to your duties and send Cassie in here. Not a word to anyone!"

"You were a very naughty girl, Cassie, to do what you did to that awful man."

Cassie rubbed at her red eyes with clenched fists. "I only wanted to help him. He told me his pecker hurt—"

" 'Pecker' is a nasty word, Cassie! Do not ever use it again!"

"Yes, Ma'am. But that's what he said that thing was—"

"Nice girls do not use that word! They do not ever talk about it and they certainly do not do such a terrible thing as to put the nasty thing in their mouths!"

Cassie screamed and broke into mournful wailing.

Miss Dacey hurried to conclude the distasteful business. "So you can see, Cassie, that you did a disgusting thing. A naughty, disgusting, dirty thing and your mother will be very displeased with you . . . very angry!"

"Oh, yes, she will be!" Her heart hammered.

"I feel sorry for you, Cassie. I don't think you meant to be naughty. So I am *not* going to tell your mother what happened!"

As the woman's words sank in, Cassie couldn't believe her good fortune. "Oh, thank you, Miss Dacey, thank you," she said fervently and grabbed the schoolmistress's hand to kiss it.

Miss Dacey pulled her hand back in horror. "Don't *do* that!"

Then more kindly. "It will be our secret, Cassie. Ours and Miss MacDonald's and Miss Mulcahy's. And no one will ever mention it again. I will not tell your mother and you will not either. Only, don't *ever, ever* go near strange men again!"

"Oh no, Miss Dacey, I won't! I promise! If I ever see a man with his thing out, I'll run away. I'll never be bad again!"

The headmistress sighed. The poor thing was going to develop a complex for sure, but there was nothing to be done. "Cassie, you did do a bad thing, but you didn't *know* it was bad. It wasn't your fault. That man was bad and he *made* you do the bad thing. It wasn't your fault but his."

"But why was he so bad? Why did he make me do that bad thing?"

"Some people are just that way, Cassie . . . evil. We live in a city, Los Angeles, that's a very big place with lots of people. Any place with lots of people is bound to have many bad people, evil people. We have to stay away from them. Now try and forget all about it. Never say a word to anyone. I'm going to take you to the nurse's office. She'll wash out your mouth with some nice antiseptic so that it will be very clean again and you can lie down until it's time to go home."

Lying on the cot in the nurse's office, Cassie screwed her eyes closed tightly. She was grateful that her mother was not going to learn of what she had done but she was also full of terror. *Evil,* Miss Dacey had said. Los Angeles was a bad place with lots of evil strangers.

"God, wouldn't I just love to go to UCLA? Why I bet if a good-looking girl was enrolled in Dramatic Arts there—the right girl, that is —why she could be discovered for the movies in a jiff," Suzannah said enviously.

I couldn't exactly see Cassie enrolled in Dramatic Arts—she was far too withdrawn for that. But Cassie *must* have thought about it herself at one time because she said, "I doubt very much Mother would allow me to enroll in UCLA's Drama School. I think that would be the last thing she'd let me do."

"Well, for God's sake, why don't you stand up to her?" Suzannah demanded. "Granted, my mother never wanted me around much; still every time I showed her a flash of temper, it scared her half to death. You'd be surprised how people back off when you show a little back-bone. You have to learn how to control people. That's what life is all about. Control!"

Around the beginning of July I received a letter from Cassie. She was working as a nurse's aide at the hospital at UCLA. (Her mother was on the board.) In the fall she would be attending UCLA and living at home since it was only a ten-minute drive. She was majoring in Art History as her mother wanted her to work eventually at the Blackstone Museum. She hoped to take a couple of courses in Dramatic Arts if she could manage it. "I think it would be fun," she wrote.

8.

It was our anniversary . . . a year from the day we had first met. I really didn't expect Todd to take much notice. I was back in the dormitory again, after having spent the summer with him in the apartment, and we were rushing around again, trying to make do with scant time and funds.

That particular afternoon, I was on the corner of High and Elm, waiting for Todd so that we could take the bus to work together. We were currently employed by a caterer—I as waitress and Todd as bus-boy. An old white Cadillac, big as a boat, pulled up in front of me but I scarcely took notice—I was anxiously looking up and down the street for the sight of Todd, who was almost ten minutes late.

"Hey, can I give you a ride, Beautiful?"

Without even looking at the car or its driver I was about to tell the joker to get lost when I realized that I recognized the voice. "Todd!" I screamed. "What are you doing in that car?"

He was wearing a motoring cap, driving goggles, a long white silk scarf tied rakishly about his throat. He looked like somebody out of *The Great Gatsby*, or the way I imagined such a character would look.

"Don't you mean, what am I doing in *your* car?"

"Mine?"

"Happy anniversary, Buffy Ann. You've known Todd King for one year, you lucky girl!"

I was speechless. I got into the car. On the seat lay a cap, goggles, and white scarf that were the match of Todd's. "These are mine too, I take it?"

"You take it correctly," he said. "As you have taken *me.*"

"You know? I think I love you," I said, tying the silk scarf about my throat.

"Of course you do. How could you not?"

Suzannah, needless to say, was not impressed with my car. "A broken-down, beat-up wreck. A convertible with a top that won't or can't go down! How tacky can you get?"

Usually I could ignore Suzannah when she was annoying, but this time I was hurt. I felt as protective of my old Cadillac as one did of a sick child. Suzannah, of course, drove around in fancy, sleek cars in the company of fancy, sleek boys. Corvettes were more her style. In fact, she traded her boys in for their cars according to her need of the moment. She had been Homecoming Queen the November before, and while campaigning for that crown, she had swished around campus in a bright green Continental convertible that belonged to a boy named Harris whom she had allowed to become her best friend just in time for the event. A contestant for Homecoming Queen *had* to make appearances sitting on the top of an open car. It was traditional. And then when she campaigned for May Queen the following spring, she befriended a boy named Taylor who owned a bright red convertible. After all, one wouldn't make appearances in the same dress, would one?

"You're blind," I told her. "Your problem is that you don't know the difference between men and cars." Sightless Suzannah.

All things considered, it wasn't the easiest thing in the world to be Suzannah's friend and I often wondered why I bothered.

There was the time Suzannah accused Gladys, the proud, middle-aged black woman who cleaned the halls and public rooms on our floor, of stealing her new pink wool suit. With a dignity accented by an obvious contempt for "white trash," Gladys took one look around the mess that was Suzannah's half of the room, then from under her bed flushed out the pink suit, along with dust balls, cut-off jeans, a collection of odd and soiled socks, one black sandal, one brown sandal, two cafeteria coffee cups, and several soiled tissues, and then disdainfully left the room. But Suzannah merely shrugged her shoulders at me. Shameless Suzannah.

However, the next day Suzannah did offer Gladys a large bottle of Tabu by way of an apology, and was genuinely upset when Gladys refused it.

The other girls on our floor considered Suzannah selfish, egotistical, in every way a bitch, which, of course, even I who was fond of her had to admit was true. She never hesitated to take a boyfriend away from another girl if he interested her in some slight way . . . not even if the other girl was crazy about the male in question and Suzannah knew beforehand that she would discard him after one evening. Suzannah the Spoiler.

No, I could not deny any of the charges levied against her. But denial and defense were two different things. And I did defend her. In some weird way, I had become responsible for her. People came to complain to me, much as they did to a mother of the bad kid on the block. And maybe it was only I who saw her good qualities—amusing, even touching in a certain way, fascinating, interesting, and fun. She could light up a room. Scintillating Suzannah.

I wouldn't admit it to Cleo, or to Cassie, and certainly not to Suellen, but the truth was that next to Todd, I found Suzannah the best company. Sometimes we would lie in our twin beds, one next to the other, and laugh the whole night through. That had to count for something. Suzannah was a friend for the good days, I decided, and I only hoped that I would never have to count on her for stormy weather. Still, I had the feeling—slight as it was—that even then, she might, just possibly might, come through for me.

Yes, we were a foursome—Suzannah, Cleo, Suellen and I—even though I frequently had to remind Suzannah that Cleo *was* her friend (they bickered constantly) and remind both Cleo and Suellen that Suzannah was theirs. The Unlikely Four, Todd called us—Star Suzannah, as he liked to refer to her; Carbonated Cleo, because she was so zippy and full of energy; Saint Suellen for obvious reasons; and me, Buffy Ann.

"But don't I get an adjective?" I asked him. "Am I just plain old Buffy?"

"In this particular case, I would have to dub you Binding Buffy for *you're* the glue that holds them all together. I'm afraid that without you, oh most Beauteous Buffy, they wouldn't give each other the time of day."

It was true, I laughed ruefully. Still, Suellen and Cleo had recently gone to jail, bound together in a common cause. During a demonstration in behalf of civil rights, Suellen and Cleo had prostrated themselves in the street in front of the state capitol, holding up traffic for hours before being carted off to jail. And I reminded Todd of this.

"Yes, but you will have to admit they did not go off to jail in the same spirit exactly. Suellen is your true idealist who acted out of principle. And Cleo, as you well know, did it only because she's enamored of Leo."

I knew he was right. Cleo had recently taken up with Leonard Mason, who wore his hair like Paul McCartney and was president of Students for Peace, Equality, and the Rights of Man, known on campus as SPERM. In fact, Leo looked a bit like Paul and affected a Carnaby style to his dress. At first, I thought that was the reason Cleo was so attracted to him—she simply adored the Beatles—that and the fact that he was called Leo. *Cleo and Leo.* Everybody remarked how adorable that was—surely a couple who belonged together. But I realized that it went beyond this. Her parents had just broken up and she wanted somebody and something to take the place of her family unit. With Leo, she got a strong-minded man *and* an organization. An organization with an admirable cause and a man who was a handsome smoothie, highly articulate, and energetic . . . a man definitely attuned to success. So when Leo told Cleo to march and to lie down in the street, that was what she did.

I often wondered if Cleo was convinced that Leo really believed in what he so loudly espoused. None of the rest of us could quite swallow that. (Especially Suellen, who detested him and considered him an opportunist.) And Leo himself, egocentric to the nth degree and a communications major, often boasted that his political activity would one day help him write the definitive drama of the sixties, which he would then turn into *the* screenplay of the seventies which he would also direct, or even produce. Yes, Leo had his future laid out in very definitive terms.

I thought I knew the secret of assuring a future. You could only count on people—*some* people. Like Todd. Leo, who had arranged the demonstration, had not been there on the firing line but back in the office directing things. And it was Todd who had not demonstrated at all because he did not believe in the ultimate worth of demonstrations, and who had gone downtown to the city jail to take Cleo and Suellen home; who had been ready, if required, to invest our Bank Account to secure their release. "Rule, Buffy Ann," he said. "It's always prudent to invest in people, for in people alone lies our eventual security."

Whenever Todd spoke like this, the words always sounded like those of a prophet. "Who was it who said that, Todd?" I wondered.

"Who? Why, Todd King, of course."

But of course! Who else?

It was the weekend and I had a three-day pass from the dormitory. It was also Valentine's Day and I wanted to make a special meal for Todd, so I immediately drove over to the apartment to prepare our dinner in time to surprise him when he came back that afternoon. I planned on pot roast and little browned potatoes and a cake that said in pink sugar, "I love you, Valentine."

After I frosted the cake, I laid out as pretty a table as I could from our meager assortment of accessories. We did have some white dishes decorated with violets. Todd had bought the dishes but insisted on calling the flowers forget-me-nots. And then I went to make up the bed with fresh sheets, thinking how wonderful it would be to have sheets too that were covered with violets called forget-me-nots. I pulled off the cotton bedspread and found there was already a fresh sheet on the bed —a sheet covered with red hearts! One hundred of them! I counted them. And they were all painted by hand, every last one!

I could hear Todd bounding up the stairs and he burst into the apartment, his arms full of neither violet violets nor blue forget-me-nots nor even red roses, but orange and yellow marigolds, bunches of them.

"They didn't have violets and they laughed at me when I asked for forget-me-nots. They thought I was screwy. They said nobody ever asked for forget-me-nots. It seems they're a lost flower. This is what they did have—" And he dropped his arms, pouring the marigolds all about me in a yellow and orange shower as I sat kneeling in the middle of the bed.

Their pungent odor filled the room. "I love marigolds!" I said, inhaling their fragrance as he climbed in beside me.

"They don't smell very sweet, do they? More spicy than sweet," he said regretfully.

"Don't you recognize that fragrance?" I asked, breathing in, breathing hard. "That's the fragrance of love . . . like my red hearts. Smell them and tell me they don't smell of love."

Instead he buried his face in my breasts and then lifted his head to kiss me. "It's *your* heart that carries the scent of love," he whispered in wonder.

I should have known better, I suppose, but I told Suzannah about my sheet with the hundred red hearts.

"Honey," she drawled, "why, I think that's the sweetest thing I ever heard of. But isn't it kind of impractical? What are you going to have to show for your present a couple of months from now? Why, if he hand-painted them, it'll probably run and smear all over the place the first time you wash it. All you're going to have is one soppy, red, smeary sheet. Wouldn't you have been better off with a piece of jewelry?"

I didn't even try to explain to Suzannah that it didn't matter what happened to the sheet, it only mattered that the sheet had existed for that one moment in time, that it had been a magic moment, making our love on that sheet, that he had done it for me and we had made love on love.

Of course, I had to tell Suellen about my sheet when she showed me all the many Valentine presents Howard had sent her from Cincinnati—lovely things such as a heart-shaped pendant, a lacy handkerchief, a crystal vase with a silken rose. Howard, at least, had the soul of a poet and believed in romance, and I was glad for my sister. And Suellen pleased me with her response to my gift: "What a perfectly lovely thing to do. Todd is really a very sensitive person."

But then she immediately launched into the solution to the laundering problem. "We'll spray it with fixative then wash it quickly in cold water using a diluted dishwashing solution and hang it up to dry *out* of the sun."

Now, I knew that Suellen was the personification of goodness—she worried about all the right things. Still, I wondered about *her*. For all her infinite saintliness, would she always manage to take the romance out of life?

Cleo cried when I told her about my present. "Oh, that's so romantic!" But then I suspected that maybe Cleo was crying because it was something Leo would never think to do, or having thought of it, would never take the time out from his many activities to carry it out.

Then it was springtime and romance had to be in the air, I thought, as I watched Suzannah do an about-face. Suddenly, it seemed, she dropped all her former boyfriends—the rich boys, the fraternity men, the athletes, and became involved in a serious, *meaningful* (a new word for Suzannah), platonic (she claimed) relationship with an extremely nice guy, Paulie White, although she had known him really almost from the moment she had arrived on campus. He was extremely tall and lanky, had curly brown hair and freckles, and was always smiling, good-natured to the nth degree, and completely without guile. As soon as I realized that Suzannah was seeing Paulie to the exclusion of anyone else, the first thought that crossed my mind was: *Oh dear, I hope she doesn't break his heart!* And then I was ashamed. Suzannah was my friend; it had been only last week that I had had one of those viruses that had attacked suddenly, and it had been Suzannah who had held my head while I threw up all through the night, and who had then cleaned me up so gently.

She had first met him when she was running for something or other. Paulie wrote a "what's doing" sort of column for the campus paper, and he also did a show for the campus broadcasting station along the same lines. It naturally followed that he would write about her and interview her on the radio show—Suzannah *was* a campus personality—Homecoming Queen, May Queen, and so on. Besides, he had fallen in love with her right from the start—a love that bordered on idolatry, for Paul White was enamored with movies and their stars, especially with the old timers like Garbo and Davis and Dietrich, and to him Suzannah was the glamorous personification of his mania. There *was* something about Suzannah that reminded him of Hayworth, he would say. But no. While Rita had the glamour, she didn't have the classic beauty of . . . say Garbo . . . or the elegant sensuality of Dietrich, while Suzannah had it all—the glamour, the beauty, and the haunting sensuality.

Being so adored was naturally gratifying to Suzannah and certainly useful. Paulie was like having her own personal public relations representative. Still, she said she could never take him seriously—romantically, that is. He just did not possess those qualifications she considered essential in a boyfriend. He was neither rich nor socially eligible. Nor was he especially physically prepossessing. She *did* like his eyes—they were puppy dog eyes—bright brown, wise, and filled with worship for her. Also, he said sweet and funny things.

I guessed that Suzannah began to take Paulie more seriously when it became clear that he was laying the foundations for a real-life career. In addition to his column for the campus paper, he started writing movie reviews of old movies for the Columbus paper. Then he became something of a local celebrity when he secured the job of host for the Columbus television station that showed old movies. He became a stringer for *The New York Times,* one thing led to another, and he also became stringer for several New York-based magazines. And then, finally, he published an anthology of old movies with *all* the credits (he named even the most innocuous bit players) along with pungent, witty reviews, and there was actual talk of syndicating his local TV show.

I guessed that's when Suzannah must have reevaluated her own priorities, along with Paulie's assets.

I questioned Suzannah about her intentions toward him. Someone else might have gotten angry but Suzannah laughed. "You *are* the most cynical person, Buffy Ann. Did it ever occur to you that I might just have grown fonder and fonder of Paulie, considering that we've been friends for almost two years? Isn't it just possible that my feelings of fondness, which I've maintained for Paulie all this time, have matured into something that's more than friendly affection?"

"Possible but not probable," I responded. "I think it's your values that have matured and this matured sense of value tells you that Paulie has a great deal of potential that can do you a great deal of good."

She gave me that professional smile she had developed, the practiced one that showed her bottom teeth and forced dimples.

"What are you so worked up about? You always thought I should go with a more worthwhile person and now I am. Now you don't have to worry about me anymore."

I didn't tell her that it wasn't she I was worried about.

By the end of the school year it was clear that Paulie's local TV show wasn't going to be syndicated after all. But his book of movie reviews had done sensationally well and he was offered a column reviewing old movies for a major New York City daily. So he was graduating and going off to New York. And he wasn't going alone—Suzannah was going with him. She would become a name model. Paulie would do his column, write another book, and help publicize her. Hollywood would naturally follow . . . for both of them.

I had mixed feelings. For one, I would miss her. I knew all her faults and I was frequently upset with her but I loved her, as I knew she loved me, selfish as she might appear at times. Secondly, I was glad for her too because I felt she was going to be the rage of New York—there was no stopping Suzannah. And third, I was concerned for Paulie.

"Do you really love him?"

"Oh, for God's sake, Buffy! Love! Paulie and I have a *relationship* . . . for the time being. . . . The world is in a state of chaos . . . there're dramatic changes going on and there's a what do they call it? A cultural revolution going on. You're an anachronism. You're living in another decade like Paulie's old movie stars. I agreed only to go to New York with him. I didn't swear an all-time allegiance. He *wants* to manage my career."

"Yes," I said softly. "But he is also terribly, terribly in love with you."

"So he says." She tossed her head. "But who knows? People are devious. Maybe he just wants to use me to further his own career."

"I don't believe that and neither do you. He's crazy about you."

"Like Todd is about you?"

"Like Todd and I are about each other."

"But you *sleep* with Todd. I've never allowed Paulie to touch me . . . not in any extensive way."

"You mean you're going to New York with Paul and you're going to live but not sleep with him?"

"Well, you know how I feel about a girl's virginity. But I'll see. You know I'm not rigid. Maybe I will and maybe I won't," Suzannah laughed, and flipped her golden-red mane with long white fingers. "You can be sure I'll do whatever I have to do. But I really don't foresee any problems. Paulie *is* a sweetie."

So, Suzannah planned on going away with Paulie, and Howard and Suellen made plans to get married. She was graduating and Howard was doing well in Cincinnati. He was assistant manager of the insurance company he worked for. (Suellen's conservative side believed in insurance.) Suellen would be the swimming counselor at the same Y Camp where she had worked previous summers (she believed in swimming as the best form of exercise), and in the fall she would be practice teaching at an elementary school. She hoped to secure a regular teaching position in her field the following year, at which time she and Howard would be able to put a down payment on a house in the suburbs (preferably of Colonial architecture). Then after a few years, perhaps four, she would have her first baby, quit teaching, and devote herself to raising her family. She would certainly raise her children by Dr. Spock's manual, as she and the doctor believed in a lot of the same things.

So she was off to Howard, Cincinnati, and marriage, peace of mind and security, and of course I wished her only the very, very best. And Suzannah was off for New York and fame and fortune, and I wished her, too, only the very, very best. As for myself, I wouldn't trade Todd for anything . . . not for Suellen's security, nor for Suzannah's razzle-dazzle quest for the end of the rainbow, be it in New York or even Hollywood.

9.

Both a minister and a rabbi of the Reform denomination officiated at Suellen and Howard's June wedding in Aunt Emily's garden. Some of the more mature guests had never seen or even heard of such a thing—a ceremony combining elements of both faiths. And then, as if that weren't enough to shock them, Suellen and Howard recited their own version of vows. Naturally, these guests immediately attributed all this to the radicalism of the sixties, which was funny, for essentially, outside of Suellen's causes, she and Howard were as traditional, as Establishment as you could get in the things that really mattered.

"Flower children," a few of the guests sneered. That was all right. I rather liked thinking of Suellen as a flower child. "Hippies," someone said, which was really ridiculous. Suellen had never gone barefoot outside, except for the one time she had developed a blister on her heel; neither had Howard. And both of them were extremely neat and clean and Howard's hair was only a little long.

As for Suellen's hair, I dug up a picture of Grace Kelly's wedding picture and we fixed her hair like Grace's, in a great chignon with pearls threaded through. (Nobody could deny that Grace was both beautiful *and* conservative in nature.) But, Grace's hairdo to the contrary, Suellen still looked like Doris Day—Doris wearing a chignon with pearls threaded through, and as sturdy and pleasantly firm as ever, with all the old-fashioned virtues showing glowingly through.

I was maid of honor and Todd was best man, and I had worked out the vows with Suellen. "I know what I want to say," Suellen told me, "and I know what I want Howard to say, but I think you can probably phrase it better than we can."

"How about starting out with you taking Howard's hand and simply saying, 'I love you, Howard'? And then Howard will take your other hand and respond, 'I love you, Suellen.' "

"I love it," Suellen said. "I really do."

Suellen was not at all nervous, just confident as always that she was doing something *right*. She stared steadfastly into Howard's eyes the whole time and Howard positively beamed back at her. I brushed away a few tears but it was Todd who cried through the whole ceremony. My sentimental hero.

Then Suellen and Howard went on their honeymoon—a camping trip in Yellowstone Park (something they had always wanted to do), and Todd and I went back to Columbus to work through the summer. And I thought about how in the fall, there would only be Cleo and me left from our original quintet. We had been five little Indians, then Cassie had gone back to California and we were four. This year we had lost two more Indians, and now we were two.

That summer I received a letter from Cassie who said that she was "going with" someone, a man named Douglas Fenwick. He was a lawyer.

"Mother is pleased," Cassie wrote. "Douglas, who is very good-looking, has all the qualifications she approves of—he's Episcopalian, of excellent stock, and he works for a top Los Angeles firm. He belongs to the California Club and he plays superb tennis. (Tennis is one of the things we have in common.) Actually, he and Mother believe in all the same things—heritage, position, involvement in the right philanthropies. . . ."

To me it sounded like Cassie was not at all thrilled with this Doug Fenwick, and that as usual, she was doing what pleased her mother instead of herself.

I sighed and read on.

"In the meantime, I'm going to classes through the summer. Art History, etc., all courses which are not terrible but not fascinating either. In the fall I'm going to register for a drama course and just keep it a secret from Mother, I know it sounds really sneaky, but it will be much easier . . ."

In answering her letter I decided to throw caution to the winds and tell her exactly what I thought.

Dear Cassie,

While your friend, Doug, sounds like perfection—looks, employment, etc., etc., I do hope you don't stop looking for somebody so exciting, so romantic, so thrilling and so thrilled with you that the sight of him makes your heart stop!

I looked at the words I had written. Sappy words to be sure. But words from the heart. That's what the sight of Todd did to me . . . made my heart stop. I could wish no more than that for Cassie.

10.

Todd cried when he told me we would have to abort the baby I was carrying.

"Oh no! I can't! You know I don't believe in abortion, Todd!"

My feelings weren't religious or political. I didn't care what others felt or did—I just knew it was wrong for me. For me it was like killing love.

"Can't we have this baby?" I pleaded. "Why can't we just get married now instead of next June when you graduate? What difference can a year make?"

"Buffy, don't!" he cried in obvious agony. "I want the baby too. I love that baby inside you just as much as you do. It wouldn't make any real difference if we got married now instead of next June, but it would make a difference if we had a baby now . . . instead of when we were really ready. It would jeopardize all our plans for the future. It would jeopardize the future of all the babies we're going to have. I'd have to leave school now and get a real job . . . a full-time job. It would be the end of the Plan."

"But you wouldn't have to quit school. We have a lot of money in the bank. Why couldn't we just use some of that money and get married and have the baby and then—"

"We don't have *a lot* of money, for one. And if we use up that money, our bankroll, we use up the Plan. The bankroll is the basis of the Plan. I'd have to work for other people instead of getting started in my own business, *our* business. We'd never get ahead. Before we saved up enough money for another bankroll, you'd probably be pregnant again. We'd be stuck in a cycle. That's why there aren't more big successes in the world: People get bogged down in the no-money, more-babies cycle. Believe me, Buffy, I do want this baby, but the timing is all wrong. I want more for you and for the children we're going to have. That's why we have to sacrifice today for tomorrow. Timing is everything."

He was wrong. I knew it. How could timing, a lifeless intangible thing, be everything? For once, my hero's thinking was flawed.

He cried and I cried. Finally, when it seemed as if I couldn't stop crying, he said, "All right, Buffy Ann. We'll get married now and have the baby. I can't bear for you to have this pain, for you to cry. I want you only to laugh."

But I had already acknowledged to myself the fact that the baby was lost. My tears were not a plea but a lament. A baby was, after all, expendable, and I would sacrifice it for Todd's dream. Loving him as I did, I could not do less.

I called Suellen. I wanted to go to Cincinnati for my abortion so that I could have her at my side . . . helping me . . . sustaining me. With her odd blend of conservative and liberal thinking, Suellen was definitely pro-abortion. (Overpopulation was one of the things Suellen was definitely against.)

Aware of my despair, she tried to comfort me: "There's a time and place for everything, Buffy. Obviously, this isn't the right time for Todd's and your baby to come into the world. And who would gain? Not the baby. The baby would *sense* that it had been the wrong time . . . it would be insecure."

I didn't believe that. That sounded like nonsense to me. But I did believe in Todd.

Suellen thought I would be better off in New York than Cincinnati. "They have clinics there, I understand, where they make things easy for you. You just go in and no questions asked. Routine. And it's over before you know it. It will be better for you there. Kind of impersonal. And you could stay with Suzannah. *She has to be good for something*, doesn't she?"

That was Suellen trying to make me laugh, I guessed.

I thought about it. New York and Suzannah might be just the answer. I had heard from her a few times since she had gone to New York. Hastily scribbled notes. She and Paulie had taken a very small apartment on the Upper East Side—not much in the way of space but a very good address. That was very important in New York, she had written. People judged you by your address, and the Upper East Side was the very poshest. They had a living room, a bedroom, and a kitchen that wasn't much more than a closet, which really didn't matter since all they kept in the refrigerator was orange juice, a jar of Nescafé, and a bottle of olives. Paulie slept on a sofa bed in the living room while she had the bedroom, so they managed quite well. And she had started modeling, *just.* But she was also getting her name in the columns and that was really good, especially since she hadn't been in New York all *that* long. Earl Wilson had devoted two paragraphs in one column to her while bigger names got only a sentence or two. In fact, Paulie was so good at getting her name in print that sometimes she wasn't even at the gatherings or clubs where they had placed her.

That was pretty funny. Suzannah was pretty funny. I would call her, I decided, and tell her I wanted to come.

At first, I couldn't get a word in.

"I'm free-lancing," she told me excitedly. "And I'm only using the one name. Paulie says that just using the one name—Suzannah—implies a certain greatness from Square One. Paulie does have the most wonderful ideas. He's a genius at publicity. And he doesn't want me to sign with any agency in particular until my name is known . . . really known. So I'm not doing all that much modeling. But I'm taking all kinds of lessons—acting, singing, dancing. It's what everybody in show business does and that's what modeling is—show business. And the publicity stunts Paulie dreams up for me . . . that's show business too."

"How's Paulie's own career going? How's his column doing?"

"Oh, he's given it up. It was too time-consuming, he said. I guess maybe he wants to go into Public Relations instead." Her voice trailed off. "What about you, Buffy? What are you and Todd up to?"

I told her what was on my mind.

She gave an angry little squeal. "Oh, Buffy, how *could* you let yourself get caught? I know loads of girls who let themselves get preggie and then they have to have an abortie, but *they're* real dodos. I thought you were smarter than that. But I see you're just another little fool when it comes to these things."

I said nothing, but an anger rose inside me. I was not in the mood for a lecture from Suzannah of all people.

"Only a fool doesn't protect her temple against defilement."

I wasn't sure now which was supposed to be the defilement—the pregnancy or the abortion. I said nothing.

"But of course I'll help you. Even if you are a little fool you're my darling, sweet fool. Buffy, are you there?"

"Yes, I'm still here, Suzannah."

"When will you arrive?"

She *had said* that she would help me, even if her other words had annoyed me, I thought . . . and that was the bottom line, the important thing, I told myself.

"I'm not sure. I'll see if Todd will go with me—"

"Todd! And where was he while you were getting yourself preggie? I guess it's true what I've always said. If a girl doesn't take care of herself, no man's going to take care of her—"

I hung up. She *was* a bitch, and a stupid one. And I would not listen to any more of her talk about the defilement of temples and about men and women and who took care of whom. Inexplicably I started to cry. And I had assumed that all my tears had dried up.

Later, I was sorry that I had hung up on her. She really wasn't that bad. She had said she would help me. She had wanted me to come to New York. Poor Suzannah. She couldn't help it if she had a perverted view of life. It was probably because she had been rejected by her own mother in favor of a husband who had more hands than an octopus.

Still, I had lost my taste for going to New York. I would stay in Columbus with Todd and we would help each other through our bad time.

In the end, the abortion took place in Todd's apartment and it was Leo who found the intern willing to do the job for a hundred dollars. Leo did get around, after all. "Don't forget, Todd, old pimple." (Leo thought that was funny—calling people "pimple.") "You owe me one—"

That was Leo, for you. Good old Leo.

Cleo offered to stay with me but Todd told her no. "We're going to stay with each other."

"It's perfectly safe," Todd reassured me and himself. "He *is* a doctor."

"I know. I'm not worried. Not the least little bit."

"Leo got me a few pills. They're not exactly pain-killers but they'll help float you through."

"I don't need Leo's pills," I said scornfully. "It doesn't take long. I'll be all right."

Todd insisted on staying in the room while the deed was done. He held my hand, tried to get me to take one of the pills, tried to make me laugh. And I tried to, for his sake.

After Bob the intern left, cheerfully taking with him two of our pills, Todd and I both took one and lay in each other's arms, closer, maybe, than we had ever been before. Still, I wasn't floating. Suzannah had worried about the defilement of my temple but I worried only about my heart. I imagined it as a big chocolate Valentine but with a little bit of the edge nibbled away.

When Todd whispered, "We'll make up for this, Buffy Ann. I promise. We'll have a half-a-dozen kids."

I laughed weakly. "That's too many."

"All right then, we'll have five."

"All right," I said. "Five it is."

We sealed the bargain with salty kisses.

11.

Todd, graduating, was full of plans. He wanted us to be married two weeks after graduation—a June wedding. Previously the Plan had been that we would marry after I graduated the following year, but according to the new Plan, my graduation was to be eliminated altogether.

"But I have only one year to go to get my degree," I protested. "I've put in three years. I don't want them to go down the drain. What a waste!"

Todd only laughed at me. "We've been together and you call that a waste? It would be wasteful for you to stick around here in Columbus when I need you in Akron."

I had wanted us to start our careers and married life in Cincinnati where Suellen and Howard were, but that too seemed not in the cards. Todd was from Akron and it was there he wanted us to live. He said he *knew* Akron, and that would give him something of a headstart.

"But wouldn't I be of more help to you with a degree? What kind of accountant am I going to be without one? Who will hire me?"

"Anybody. Everybody. You're smarter now than any C.P.A. Nobody's going to actually ask you for a diploma, you know. Besides, Buffy Ann, do you really want to be in Columbus when I'm in Akron?"

"You could work in Columbus, you know, until I finished school."

"No, I can't. I'd only be marking time instead of really getting my career started. I have to be in Akron and we do have to be together."

"Yes."

Of course. How could it be any other way? If Todd needed accounting, who needed English Lit? And if Todd needed a wife in Akron, who needed a diploma?

I made plans for the wedding quickly. Aunt Emily's garden with Suellen as matron of honor. And Cleo, Cassie, and Suzannah would be bridesmaids.

But Suzannah called and said that while her little old heart was broken up about it, she couldn't *possibly* come to Ohio at this time. "You simply have no idea. . . . busy, busy, busy."

Paulie had taken a job again (they needed the money), but he wasn't doing his own column. It was on the *Post,* on the rewrite desk, the graveyard shift, so that he could handle Suzannah's career during the daytime. And of course, being on the *Post* did enable him to get her name in the papers. But since he was working evenings, he wasn't able to escort her places that she just had to be seen in order to enhance her "image." But that wasn't a problem—not having Paulie as escort. There were escorts aplenty begging for her time. And there were always the "sweet boys" to take a girl out—they played an important part in the New York scene. Lots of socially prominent women in New York went about only with these boys—they weren't threatening, they were fun and full of the best gossip, and, God knows, she didn't need any sexual entanglements. That could only be a headache, especially when one was on the brink of stardom, which she definitely was. I *had* seen her picture on several magazine covers, hadn't I? Some people were already calling her the model of the decade. And it was a secret—so would I please keep it under wraps—but she was on the verge of signing an exclusive contract to be the official spokeswoman for the biggest cosmetics firm in the world. The president of the company was slightly crazy over her.

When I finally hung up, my head buzzed. Suzannah had gone on and on. And I *was* miffed. Not only was my wedding so unimportant to her that she wouldn't make the sacrifice of one or two days to attend, but she had been so tuned in on herself she hadn't even remembered to congratulate me or send her best wishes to Todd. But then I realized that Suzannah wasn't the only party guilty of self-absorption. *I* had been so centered on Todd and myself the last few months that I hadn't even been aware that Suzannah *was* on the covers of some of the biggest magazines. (Who had the time for magazines?) She *was* something of a sensation and we had taken no notice and that wasn't nice either. So much for Suzannah and self-preoccupation.

Cleo was delighted to be a bridesmaid. She even asked if we wanted Leo to be part of the wedding ceremony. But we had to decline her offer regretfully. Todd's best man was to be Howard, and Aunt Emily's garden wasn't large enough for ushers. Cleo wasn't returning to Ohio State for her senior year either, since Leo, like Todd, had graduated and already had a job lined up in New York writing and directing at a local TV station. And they were getting married too and moving in with her mother into the big house in Tenafly. (Her mother had gotten the house in the settlement.) Their wedding wouldn't be until August since it was going to be a huge affair and they needed more time for the arrangements. It seemed Cleo's mother was simply crazy about Leo! She thought Leo was probably the most handsome man she had seen in a long time and that certainly he seemed destined for success.

Unlike me, Cleo was going to finish her fourth year at New York University, after which she planned on getting a job in publishing. Then she and Leo would get an apartment in New York and be a bright New York couple (both with great careers) with a stunning apartment. They would go to all the right places, which meant stylish restaurants, first-nights, and vernissages. And they wouldn't have children until they were married at least ten years so that they wouldn't be burdened down, would be free to travel, and Cleo could concentrate on her career.

"Is that what you really want, Cleo? To put off having children for ten years?"

"I want what Leo wants," she said with absolute certainty. "I want a successful marriage like the one my mother *had* but I want mine to last. So I have to give Leo whatever he needs from a marriage."

I thought about that and I couldn't argue with her thinking. Was I any different? Wasn't that exactly what I intended to do—give my whole life to Todd? But it was out of the enormity . . . out of the completeness of my love. And Cleo? I couldn't imagine her loving Leo the way I loved Todd. But that was my smugness. I was so sure that *nobody* loved anybody the way Todd and I loved each other.

Cassie arrived the day before the wedding and although it was two years since I had actually seen her, it was only minutes before I remembered how fond I really was of her. She was as sweet and nice as she had ever been and perhaps even lovelier.

"You're prettier than ever," I told her, "and you look happy. How are things going? Really?"

"Oh good. Really. Remember when I wrote you that I was thinking of taking a course or two in theater arts? Well, I did it. Of course I didn't tell Mother. She wouldn't have liked that very much. . . ."

Wouldn't have liked it? She would have been furious. She would have said that acting was for young men who didn't want to work and for girls who wanted to sleep with Jewish producers.

"Well, I just love it. I'm not really thinking about a career—I couldn't possibly do that, but the classes are such fun. And I think that I've really come out of myself more. I've made a lot of friends that are really exciting and interesting."

"It sounds to me like you've met a special man."

"Well, I have, kind of—" Cassie laughed almost apologetically. "I mean, I've been going out with somebody from my acting class . . . not a lot but some . . . because Mother doesn't know about him yet. Mostly, I'm still going out with Doug. I wrote you about him. He's the one Mother likes—"

"Then you're going out with both of them?"

"Yes. I think Douglas wants to marry me when I graduate next year, but we don't have an official understanding yet. So in the meantime I'm going out with him and Guy."

"Guy's the actor?"

"Yes. Guy Savarese. He's from La Jolla. That's down the coast from L.A. It's a resort area. Guy's actually the star of the class. All the girls in the class are mad about him. He's incredibly good looking. Beautiful white teeth and wavy hair. I know it sounds terrible but the girls in the class actually call him *Beefcake*."

"He sounds devastating. Are you in love with him, Cassie?" I asked softly.

"Oh, I don't know, Buffy. I'm not sure. I'm afraid that perhaps it's his looks, his extraordinary sex appeal. Oh, Buff, I don't know how to explain it. He has . . . a . . . raw, animal sexuality. . . ." She flushed and her voice trailed off.

"Are you and he making it? Are you lovers?" I knew Cassie wouldn't resent the question.

Cassie was almost ashamed to answer. "No."

"Why not?"

She shrugged. "Because he hasn't made that kind of move. *Nobody's* ever tried to have sex with me. Not Douglas either. And I've been going with him for almost two years. All he's ever done is kiss me." She was embarrassed and she laughed ruefully. "Doug *is* an expert kisser . . . I think he must have learned his technique from a manual. But I think with him the technique is more important than I am. I guess I just don't have sex appeal."

"Of course you do! It's just that you're such a lady that everyone respects you—" I said, but I wasn't sure that the two—respect and premarital sex—were necessarily exclusive. Then, as if she were reading my very thoughts, Cassie said: "But you and Todd have been lovers almost from the day you met and he respects you. He adores you!"

Ah yes! But that's Todd.

I found myself wishing that there was a Todd for Cassie too. "Maybe your Guy will turn out to be like Todd, Cassie." I said this although I knew that this was impossible. There could only be one Todd.

Cassie laughed wistfully. "What would I do with him then? What would I say to my mother? 'He's an actor and a social nobody and Italian and his looks are so overwhelmingly gorgeous that they're almost vulgar, but he's really a Todd King and he'll love me forever. Can I have him, Mother?' "

"If he *is* a Todd King, Cassie, take him and love him and *don't* ask your mother," I told her passionately.

We hugged and tears rolled down her cheeks.

It was prom night for Guy Savarese's graduating class, and his intimate friends Greg, Bull, and Paco wanted to put in an appearance, but he himself wasn't interested.

"I know it's strictly batshit, man, but what the hell—it's our high school graduation too, man," Bull urged. "Let's get tanked, then go to the dance and move in on the jocks' chicks. What the hell—we'll have a few laughs."

They didn't have dates for the prom, but then, they seldom had "dates." They had no need. They always got more girls than several jocks could handle, for free, without the necessity of putting up with some La Jolla princess's crap. They didn't call themselves the Fuck Bucks for nothing. All four of them were muscled and well-endowed and word got around, especially in a beach community. And Guy, tanned and sinewy, was kingpin with his extra-size Saturday Night Special, as he himself had named the organ he was so proud of, and with his ability to stay "firmo intacto" indefinitely. Paco, who idolized him, called him *El Guapo,* the handsome one.

They were different from the rest of their graduating class. With the exception of Greg, they were not from La Jolla's affluent. And instead of doping (which consisted mainly of smoking "kief," the cheaper variety of *mota),* they drank. And for fun, instead of surfing or sailing, they started fights and broke into the houses of La Jolla's rich, which they vandalized rather than burglarized. And twice they had torched a house, once for fun and once for pay. They had been arrested only once, when they were caught red-handed systematically smashing windows in a beachfront villa, but the case had been dismissed as a mischievous prank rather than the vicious act it was, thanks to the intervention of W. P. Harrington, Greg's father, who pulled some strings. And while the rest of their schoolmates were content to copulate with each other, Greg, Bull, and Paco preferred older women, ones with big breasts, while Guy had a penchant for girls from the junior high, usually selecting small, childish, underdeveloped virgins. Maybe it was because these girl-children had difficulty accommodating him and that pleased him. Certainly he didn't think about it much.

"All right, we'll go to the fucking prom," Guy finally acquiesced. "But we better get a load-on first. I can't stomach those turkeys without a gutful."

Greg, who had his phony I.D. handy and looked older than the others, went in and got four pints so that they could each have his own bottle, along with three six-packs. After an hour or so of aimless driving around and verbally abusing other drivers, the boys had finished their pints and fourteen cans of beer.

"How about we boogie for the prom now?" Paco asked. He was eager to indulge in his specialty—provoking free-for-alls.

"Hold your piss," Guy said. He had spied a girl walking up the road from the beach, and he elbowed Bull, who was driving. "Pull up."

Bull peered into the darkness. "What for? She don't look like she's out of kindergarten yet."

"Shit, man! I said, pull up!" Guy barked.

Bull did as he was told.

"Hey!" Guy called out to the girl. "What you doing?"

"Going home."

"You shouldn't be walking by yourself at night. Don't you know it's dangerous to be out by yourself in the dark?" he laughed. "Hop in! We'll give you a ride home."

The girl was nervous; she could hear the tension in his voice. "No, thanks. I don't live far."

"Hop in, I said!" His tone became more insistent.

The girl started walking faster.

In an instant, he was out of the car grabbing the girl's arm.

"Let me alone! I have to get home!"

"I said we'll drive you home."

"No. My mom doesn't like me to take rides with strangers."

"We ain't strangers. We're real friendly guys."

She pulled away from him and started to run. In a moment he'd caught her and thrown her to the ground. She began to sob.

Greg came up.

"Jeez, what are you doing? She looks to be about ten."

"Shut up!" Guy said, unzipping his pants. When the girl opened her mouth to scream, he threw himself upon her and slapped her face viciously from side to side several times. Still she fought, trying to scratch his face, flailing out with her thin arms. He laughed and pounded her head against the dirt.

"Take off her shorts!" he ordered Greg who stood behind him watching.

Greg did as he was told, the excitement getting to him as he tore off the girl's shorts and panties. In the meantime, Bull had driven the car into the bushes at the side of the road where it was almost obscured by the dark night. Then he and Paco got out.

"Pull her into the bushes more, man!" Paco offered, his own weapon exposed now. "And pull off her shirt!"

Guy and Greg each took a leg and dragged her a few feet farther. Still she screamed and resisted.

"Shut her up!" Bull growled. "Coldcock her!"

"No, I like to see their eyes when I go into them," Guy said and worked to push himself inside her. He could tell that it was going to take a little extra effort. She was small, and he narrowed his eyes, concentrating.

She screamed still, until Paco said, "I'll shut her up," and sat down on her face, forcing her mouth open until it enveloped him. Then there were no more screams.

When Guy finally withdrew, there was blood dripping from him and blood smeared all over the girl's thighs. It was too dark to see it, but he could feel it, and the smell of it roused the two boys who were waiting like hyenas for their share.

When Paco got up, there were no more outcries, and Bull and Greg took the two positions vacated. When they were finished, Guy contemplated turning the now rag-doll body over and assaulting her from behind, but the others whispered to him fiercely and their eagerness to flee the scene became suddenly contagious.

"Park a couple of blocks from the school so no one will be able to spot us pulling into the parking lot and then no one will know exactly what time we got there," Greg told Bull.

They combed their hair, straightened their clothing, and entered the gymnasium quietly. Then after they mingled a bit Guy told Paco, "Do your thing, man, so *everybody* will know the Fuck Bucks were here!"

When early the next morning Adrienne Fisher's limp body was found, all four boys were safe in their beds, having left the dance only after the brawl they started had been brought to a satisfactory conclusion by the local police. When Adrienne Fisher became conscious, she was able to give almost no information to the detectives who questioned her—it had been almost pitch-black on the road leading up from the beach and all she could absolutely say was that there had been four boys, all tall, one on the heavy side. There was a routine investigation and the police decided that the attack had probably been perpetrated by some out-of-town kids. After all, La Jolla *was* a tourist town. Adrienne Fisher cried a lot, almost uncontrollably, and her parents decided to call in a psychiatrist and did not press for a more thorough investigation, hoping to keep Adrienne's name out of the newspapers.

After a few days, the boys relaxed. Obviously they were not even going to be questioned. Still, Guy decided that it would be better to get out of town. Suppose the girl was in a taco joint one day and recognized not a face, but a voice. Besides, now that school was out, his father had been on his back to get himself a job, and what did the future hold for him in La Jolla? He didn't want to go to college and he didn't want any nine-to-fiver. He had always thought about the possibilities of being a movie star, what with his looks and all. An easy buck. And in Hollywood, from what he heard, his epic joint would be like money in the bank. Besides, where else but in Hollywood could a man find such a variety of tail? Yeah, that was the place for him. Hollywood, home of the big bucks, a natural for those with outsized talents.

Guy Savarese did not find Hollywood the warm and receptive place he'd anticipated. He found out you were supposed to get an agent. The agents told him to get some experience. Casting directors told him to get an agent. A big-name actress he banged one night advised him to get some theatrical schooling. She herself had studied at the Yale School of Drama. Big blond studs without talent or training were like sand on the L.A. beaches—everywhere. Very quickly he ran out of money. Then there was nothing left for him but to hustle women. That was easy. There were a thousand places to pick up broads who wanted to be screwed and there were thousands of them willing to pay for his kind of sex. But he didn't find it an easy buck. Their aging, flabby bodies repelled him; the sweet talk they demanded made him ill.

Voicing his complaints one night to a fellow-hustler in a joint on the Strip, he got some trenchant advice. "You're working the wrong side of the street, sweets. The boys pay a lot better, and after it's all over, they're usually in a hurry for you to leave. And no sweet-talking shit either."

Guy was offended. "No one fucks *me* up the ass!"

The other man merely raised his eyebrows. "Just pick the catchers, not the pitchers. If your wad is as big as you say, they'll be standing in line to get pronged. Sometimes, all they want is for you to beat the shit out of them. Now, that ain't so hard to take, is it? Wise up, sweets. That's where the real bread is."

One of his clients, a man calling himself Patrick Henry, a devoted "catcher," grew truly impressed with Guy's sexual equipment after a long night of athletic encounter. Exhausted and sated in the small hours of the morning, he revealed himself as a producer of films and made Guy a proposition, a business one. "Johnny Stick," he said to Guy, who had adopted that alias for the night, "I'm going to make you a star!"

In a year's time he had made six porno features. Even his sexually jaded co-stars were eager to work with him. No one in the business wedded size and staying power like Johnny Stick. But Guy wasn't happy. He wanted to be a real movie star, or at least a TV one. He was every bit as good-looking as Brando or Newman and years younger. He told that to Patrick Henry one day when they were dickering over money, thinking that Henry would grow alarmed that he would quit the business and thus give him the raise he demanded.

But Henry only laughed. "God, you're a fucking-stupid kid! Listen, you schmuck, once you've made pornos, nobody's going to use you for movies. Not TV either. This is *it* for you! This is all you're ever going to get! You better make up your mind to enjoy it." Then he said with a touch of contemptuous pity, "Who'd you think you were going to end up like? Redford? Reynolds? Jesus, man, they've got class! They have respectability!"

For a minute or so he saw red, he wanted to smash Henry's face in, he wanted to smash everything in the room. But the minute passed and then his arrogant enthusiasm overcame his rage-filled depression. He didn't give a shit what Henry said! He wasn't even twenty yet. It couldn't be too late! He *wouldn't* let it be too late! Johnny Stick *would* be instantly terminated and Gaetano Savarese would be reborn! He would dye his hair black. Italians were *supposed* to be dark-haired anyway. He would grow a mustache. And this time, he would do everything by the book.

Johnny Stick has provided him with enough money to support him for a while. He would enroll at UCLA and get the training and experience everybody told him was necessary. School. Little theater. He would acquire some polish. And he would find himself a girl with enough respectability for two. Oh sure, even with his hair dyed black, the new mustache, and his old name, word *might* leak out. The stories would go around about him being a porno star. Patrick Henry, furious that he had lost his star cock, would probably be one of the first to spread them. But after he had made it, the stories wouldn't matter. For one thing the times were different. People weren't so uptight. Nobody really gave a shit. After all, they said Joan Crawford had been in those kind of movies before *she* made it. Everybody knew that Marilyn Monroe had made the rounds of the studio offices on her knees. So what? After he was a star, he would deny everything. After you made it big in Hollywood, nobody could touch you. You had it all—the money, the respectability, all the little chicks chasing you up and down the block, panting to make it with a star.

"I guess I'll just have to wait and see what happens," Cassie said. "Guy hasn't said anything to me at all about being serious. I really haven't the slightest idea how he feels about me. To be honest, Buffy, I am attracted to him but I can't say that we're really close."

12.

Suellen, dressed in mauve, stood up for me, holding her newborn baby in her arms. Her schedule, which had called for her working for four or five years before starting a family, had gone awry. "A baby is security too," Howard had told her, and Suellen, for once, had been pliable.

Cassie and Cleo both wore pink and Leo, who was *not* a member of the wedding party, nonetheless wore chalk-striped gray flannel, his new style of dressing that went with his new lifestyle in New York. He had definitely and for all time put aside his campus radicalism.

"I love thee, I take thee, I will light up thy life with the glow of my love, I promise you, Todd."

"I love thee, I take thee, I will cherish every breath of life you take, I promise you, Buffy Ann."

Howard beamed and handed his new brother-in-law the plain gold ring.

The minister pronounced us man and wife and the groom passionately kissed the bride. Howard and Suellen's baby gurgled. I laughed with delight and Todd cried with emotion.

And there was a telegram of congratulations from Suzannah and Paulie. Gladdened, I turned to the others: "See! She remembered!"

Todd had said we could afford a *little* time out for a honeymoon. All things considered, it wouldn't be *too* wasteful. But he had kept his plans a secret. And I hadn't even tried to worm them out of him. Location . . . whether it was the locale of our honeymoon or our entire life's adventure . . . meant nothing to me as long as we were there together.

We flew to New York and checked into the Plaza. It was my first time in New York, but I was positive that there was no hotel lovelier than the Plaza. We drank champagne and made love, looked down on Central Park and the lights of the city like people did in the movies, and we made love. In the morning, we made love, breakfasted in bed and made love, and I thought: Nobody has ever made more beautiful love than we have here at this moment.

Then Todd said, almost as if he knew exactly what I was thinking, "Making love is not an act of love."

"What is an act of love then?" I asked, just wanting him to say the words.

"The things we'll say to each other and the things we'll *do* for each other every day for all our days . . . for the rest of our lives."

"That's lovely. Still, this will probably be the loveliest love I'll ever make . . . the loveliest honeymoon I'll ever have."

"Huh!" he said, inelegantly. "You think *this* is lovely? In that case I'm sorry to inform you that you'd better get dressed. We've got a plane to catch."

I dressed, fighting back tears of disappointment. Talk about waste! We had flown to New York to spend one night at the Plaza! Why, we hadn't even seen the Statue of Liberty or Suzannah, for that matter.

We were almost ready to board before I figured out that we weren't going back to Akron at all! We were taking the flight to Paris! *Paris!* Todd and I were going to Paris: That was my first ecstatic thought. My second was one of anxiety—the money! How could we justify spending so much of our precious bank account on such a glorious, extravagant fling?

"The money!" I anguished to Todd.

But he only smiled. "We've worked hard for the past three years. And there may be hard times ahead. But in between must come the solstice . . . a time to refresh our souls."

Oh, the man was a poet. And besides, he had the answer for everything. How could I ever doubt him?

"Now for the fountain," Todd said after we had watched the sun come up from behind Notre Dame and breakfasted on croissants and *café au lait.*

"What fountain?"

"You *dare* ask that? *You,* who were going to major in Literature? My God! It's really fortunate that you switched to Accounting."

I didn't know what he was clowning about but I trusted that I would soon find out. He led me to the Place St. Michel—to the fountain with the stone dolphins, and quick as a bunny, he was *in* the fountain, the silvery spray of water leaving drops of silver on his face. He held out his arms to me. "Zelda Buffy Ann, come be my love—"

I jumped in. I could do no less. The water-wet kisses tasted sweeter than wine. "I love you, Scotty King. You're cornier than Ohio cornfields but I love you more than life itself."

This, then, must be an act of love.

We sipped calvados on a terrasse on the Champs Élysées in the shadow of the Arc de Triomphe de l'Étoile.

"But why are we drinking apple brandy?" I asked Todd. "How come we're not drinking champagne?"

"Tsk, tsk, where is the romance in your soul? It was the second time you came to the High Street Cinema. You ate one jumbo bucket of popcorn, one Milky Way, one Baby Ruth, and two Mary Janes. They were showing the *Arch of Triumph* with Ingrid Bergman and Charles Boyer, and I beg you to recall. What did *they* drink on the Champs Élysées?"

Calvados! But of course.

"But of course," I said.

An act of love.

PART TWO

Summer
1967–1977

13.

When we returned to Akron the first thing we did was make a small down payment (a *very* small down payment, since Todd believed in making the smallest down payment possible in order to keep working capital free) on a small Cape Cod on a street called Honey Lane. (Todd also said that it was ridiculous to pay rent when we could be building equity.) I loved the name of our street, and we both quickly secured employment in two separate accounting firms, I as a junior accountant and Todd, without that qualifying title of junior. We proceeded to furnish our new home, went to work every day, and kept our eyes open for opportunities.

The first opportunity came when our old Caddy broke down for the twentieth time. Someone told Todd about a kid, one Prentis Hobson, who was still in high school but fixed cars in his spare time. Hobson, reputedly, was a mechanical genius. Todd admired the finished work and the price was right. Soon, Todd was buying a couple of old cars a week and Prentis was fixing them up, and Todd resold them for a profit. Within a couple of months, there were too many cars for Prentis to work on in his spare time and not enough space to store and work on the cars. Todd took another piece of our bank account and put a down payment on an empty lot. He said to Prentis, "Do you like school?"

"Not much."

"How well are you doing in school?"

"Not too good. I'm not so hot with the books."

"What do you plan on doing when you graduate?"

"Be a car mechanic. What else would I do? It's the only thing I'm good at."

"So why don't you quit school now and come work for me full-time?"

Prentis scratched his head. "Not finish school?"

"You'll first graduate in two years, right? And then you intend to become a mechanic? But if you come to work for me now, in two years you'll have four other guys working under you and you'll be head mechanic. You'll have a two-year jump on the guys you're going to school with."

"You mean that, Mr. King? You'd make a guy without a high school diploma a head mechanic?"

"I would and I will. And I'll promise you something else, Prentis. You really do a job for me and when the lot gets going, I'll give you a percentage of the whole deal."

Prentis went to work full-time and the used-car lot prospered.

I was two months pregnant when I discovered the Westervelt Lumber Company. I was working on their account in my capacity as junior accountant for Ryan and Feldman, and found that the lumberyard was losing money . . . a little every day. Todd went to Charles Westervelt and offered to buy him out, but Mr. Westervelt said he wouldn't dream of giving up his forty-year-old business.

"But you're losing money every year," Todd pointed out. "You've been drawing more money out of the business than you've been making, which means you're depleting your capital assets. At this rate, you'll be in bankruptcy sooner than you realize. If I buy you out now, you'll have money to retire on—you can go down to Florida or out to California and enjoy life."

"But my son Charlie's in business with me. If I sell out, what will become of him?"

"I'll make Charlie manager of the yard. I'll be glad to have him. He knows the business, right? He's a valuable man. And if he works hard for me and we prosper, as I strongly suspect we will, I'll give a percentage of the business back to him, and that's a promise."

That was the bait Charles Westervelt, Sr., went for, but I was a little concerned about those percentages Todd was giving out. "Why are you giving away pieces of our businesses?"

"Elementary, my dear Buffy Ann. If a man has a piece of the business he'll work that much harder. He'll work his heart out for you."

I could understand that. *I* worked for Todd and I did so with all my heart. So much so that sometimes I wondered if there was any of it left for anyone else.

By the time I was five months pregnant and still working for Mr. Ryan and Mr. Feldman, I discovered a liquor store that was slowly expiring from old-fashioned merchandising concepts. The last chunk of our bankroll went to buy it and I left my job to supervise the renovation and expansion of the store into a supermarket operation, which I managed and kept open even during the renovation. And I worked until the moment Todd bore me off to the hospital in our very old Cadillac. Eight days later I bundled up our new baby daughter, Megan, in her pink bunting and went back to the supermarket, but this time in a brand-new white Cadillac, my giving-birth present. I was driving the symbol of our new prosperity.

Just as I was sending out the announcements of Megan's birth, we received an announcement of Cassie Hammond's marriage to Gaetano Savarese. It was quite a surprise. I hadn't heard from Cassie for some time and I wondered why, considering Cassandra Blackstone Hammond's social standing, there hadn't been a big wedding.

When Cassie's mother discovered that she was seeing Guy Savarese, even as she was dating Doug Fenwick, she never did say absolutely, "I forbid you to see him." Instead, she insisted on meeting him, inviting him to dinner, and then immediately launched a campaign to belittle him, demean him in various subtle ways. Even at that first dinner, as Guy sat uncomfortably on the rose-colored cut-velvet chair at the vast enameled bronze table in the tapestry-hung Blackstone Manor dining room, Cassandra stared at his fingernails, making both Cassie and Guy suspect that his nails were dirty, even though he had strenuously scrubbed them before coming to the house.

The funny thing about it all was that at this point, Cassie was not half as infatuated with Guy as she had been at the start of their relationship. Even before Cassandra launched her campaign of disparagement, Cassie had had her doubts. There were things about Guy . . . a certain dispassion when he kissed her . . . the way he never, ever had a good word to say about anything or anybody . . . how he always described people as either *filthy rich* or *piss poor*. And then, having met her mother, how he went on and on about her . . . what a great lady she was, how rich she must be, and what a goddamn palace Blackstone Manor was. It did leave a certain taste in Cassie's mouth.

But Cassandra never said: "Desist!" So Cassie went on seeing Guy, much in the manner of the small child who dares to go further and further, testing to see how far she can go before she's ordered to stop. And maybe she waited for the moment when Guy Savarese would forget she was Cassandra's precious princess and take her—one way or another—so that she would know he felt some sensual passion for her, and would know too what it was like to share a passionate, sexual experience with this man the girls at school referred to as "a hunk."

Probably if fate hadn't interceded, she would have gone on like that for months . . . even years (if Cassandra didn't intercede either) . . . dating both Doug and Guy, not in love with either, waiting for Doug to propose formally, waiting for her mother to say something, waiting for someone else to come along and claim her . . . that warm, loving man of her dreams.

But fate, in the form of Darren Prouty, a film director teaching a course at the University, did intercede. He asked Cassie, who was enrolled in his class, to come back to his office so that he could help her with a scene. The office was tiny and cramped with a leather couch squeezed in, and as she sat there on the black couch next to the overweight director with his fleshy thigh squeezing hers, she suspected that it might have been a mistake to be there at all. So almost immediately she tried to excuse herself but he would have none of that. Then, without the grace to at least seduce her nicely, he was all over her, all two-hundred-and-twenty pounds of him. When she resisted, he turned ugly. He called her a bitch, a cockteaser. He told her she was like all the other girls who wanted to make it in films.

He pushed her down, choking her with his weight. He slapped her hard across her cheek until she literally saw stars and couldn't believe it. He hit her again, this time on the side of her head, and she grew deathly afraid. *Why, he doesn't care if he kills me! He just doesn't give a damn!*

He thrust a finger, a single thick finger, into the indentation at the base of her neck. She wondered whether the finger would pierce her flesh and the blood would pour out, or would she choke to death. She stopped struggling to lessen the pain. She lay breathless as the hairy hand pulled at her skirt, plucked at her panties. She felt, rather than heard, the thin material tear. He lifted himself up slightly, unzipped his fly. She closed her eyes as he thrust into her, one hand keeping her thighs spread apart, the heavy finger pressing into the hollow of her neck. He felt so enormous jamming into her and the pain was intense. She felt as if she were being torn apart. Surely she must be bleeding down there. Would she bleed to death?

Suddenly, he let go of her throat, screamed, calling her a whore, and she felt his hot liquid start to shoot into her. Then he pulled out and directed his stream of ejaculation over her face and hair. Its foul taste splashed her lips.

She didn't move, didn't open her tightly clamped eyes. She heard him adjusting his clothes preparing to leave. "You better clean yourself up," he said. "And turn off the lights before you go. And if you have any idea about telling anybody about this scene, I'd think twice. I'll say *you* wrote the scenario. Everybody knows what little whores you bitches are —throwing yourselves at anybody with a little influence. All of you, you'll do anything to get your little cunts in the door."

He was gone and she was alone. She had to summon up all her strength to get up. She finally managed to get to her feet and slowly, stiffly, made it to the ladies room down the hall. She prayed no one would see her. Oh, God, she hurt so much! She scrubbed her face even though it was bruised and painful. And her hair! How would she ever get it clean? She dabbed at the hair with wet paper towels, combed it, wiped at it some more. Then she sprayed it with cologne from a small bottle she carried in her purse. But it didn't really mask the odor. She washed her face again. The red mark from his hand was still there. She put on makeup but it didn't cover.

She went back to the office, found the ripped panties on the floor. She took the manicure scissors from her bag, went back to the ladies room and laboriously cut the material up into little pieces, then flushed the shreds down the commode. As she did it, she asked herself what she was doing. She was destroying evidence that she should be saving for the police. She knew that you weren't even supposed to clean yourself up, that you were supposed to go to a hospital for examination first.

But she had already made her decision, she realized. She would not be going to the hospital or to the police. She would not be filing charges. Cassandra Hammond would never countenance the public washing of such disgusting linen. And at that moment, Cassie realized that she had no intention of advising her mother of her debasement either. Worse, even, than being raped would be the look on her mother's face. She would despise her daughter as something soiled, corrupted.

She looked into the mirror, the red bruise still vivid, her hair a mess. She despised herself!

Not only would her mother despise her, but Doug would too . . . *if* she told him. She had heard his ideas on rape—his personal and legal thoughts. No girl was raped. There were only girls who in some way provoked attack. Except for those cases in which the rape was performed by a legally certified maniac. In his eyes, as in her mother's, she would be soiled. Soiled and not above suspicion.

Guy would probably believe her . . . if she told him. He knew Darren Prouty, the kind of man he was, and he knew how such men behaved. Still, he wouldn't feel the same way about her either. In his eyes she would no longer be a princess. She would just be another chick who had fallen off a few barstools.

She would be a fool to tell anybody. Anybody! It would only mean more pain and humiliation.

Four weeks later, she was responsible for the death of a rabbit and was almost out of her mind with anguish. Her mother! She didn't know what to do. She didn't even have a close girlfriend with whom she could discuss the possibilities. And she didn't possess the mental stamina to obtain an abortion, not all alone. She could run away. But to where? Could she tell her mother *now* that she had been raped a month ago? Or Doug or Guy? And she wasn't enough of a fool to think that she could be one of those unwed mothers who raised their illegitimate babies alone with style and élan. Not she!

Doug. She knew he intended to ask for her hand any day now, and would probably expect to wed an appropriate three months after that. That would be funny. Proper Doug Fenwick with a bride five or six months gone. He would never elope with her on a moment's notice if she asked him to, playing it as a whimsical inspiration. No. He would insist on the proper engagement, the proper wedding. She could not very well afford the time.

But Guy was another story. Guy would probably marry her in a minute, considering that she was Cassandra's daughter, so impressed was he with the Blackstone Hammond credentials. And if she told Guy that her mother was pressuring her to become officially engaged to Doug, he would be hot not to take a chance on losing her, heiress as she was to that castle just above Sunset Boulevard.

She and Guy were married in one of those wedding storefronts on the Las Vegas Strip where even the 10K gold-filled wedding band was included in the flat price. After the ceremony her new husband took her to a second-class motel and made violent, almost brutal, but curiously impersonal love to her bewildered body. In fact, the second coupling of her life was not that different from the first. There were only two differences. One was the size of the weapons they used, Darren Prouty's being almost insignificant in comparison. The second was that while Prouty had called her dirty names, Guy called her nothing . . . nothing at all. Still, she had married a man to whom sex was not an act of love but an act of rage.

When Guy was finished, completely oblivious to what she was feeling, he dismounted and asked, "Once your mother gets used to the idea that we're married, what are the chances, you think, of us living with her in that castle?"

Distantly she heard his question. She was lying flat on her back, staring at the ceiling. What would her mother say about a girl who married one unfeeling stranger after another stranger had violated her? Who was married in a storefront wedding mill with dirty windows by a man in a spotted suit, while outside, neon lights flashed in the mid-day sun? Cassandra would undoubtedly say that such a foolish, worthless girl deserved anything that came her way.

She turned over on her side, away from her husband. "Maybe," she murmured.

She wouldn't tell him that moving in with her mother was the very last thing she intended, even if Cassandra were to extend that invitation. For one, she hated that gloomy house. And not least, there was no way she was going to allow her mother to know for sure what kind of a stranger her daughter had married. Her mother was going to think that she, Cassie, had made a wonderful choice if this was the last thing she pulled off.

14.

Suzannah called to congratulate us on the birth of Megan. "How does it feel to be a mother?" she asked me and without waiting for an answer, launched into a discussion of her career. "You *have* seen me all over in the mags and on TV, haven't you? *Women's Wear* has called me not the model of the year but of the decade. And my decade has just started—"

"That's super! And what does Paulie say? He must be thrilled."

"Oh, Paulie! What a pain in the ass he is! Frankly, Buffy, I don't know what to do about him. He doesn't do any work of his own, and he wants to oversee every little detail of my life—my photography sessions, my wardrobe, my makeup. When I go on location, he insists on packing my clothes. Would you believe that?"

"But you *wanted* that, Suzannah. You wanted Paulie to manage your career."

"Well, it was convenient before . . . it simply isn't anymore. Paulie's a real drag, if you must know. He's always drinking too much and then he makes scenes . . . terrible scenes. Between you and me, Buffy, I would very much like to lose Paulie. He's driving me out of my cotton-pickin' mind."

"Did you tell him that, Suzannah? That you wanted to end your relationship with him?"

"Well, for God's sake, I haven't exactly been keeping it a secret from him. But he's such a son-of-a-bitch. You see, there's another little problem . . ."

It seemed Suzannah was seeing a certain prominent, very social, rich politician who was being really helpful to her in many ways, but who, unfortunately, was married. They—she and the politician—had discussed a divorce on his part, and a marriage on their part, but of course the whole thing could possibly damage his career and she was not at all sure whether the publicity would damage her career, or help it. So the whole thing was on the back burner for now. But Paulie said that if she broke off with him, he was prepared to expose them. He would give the whole story to one of the scandal sheets, not to mention the legitimate columnists. Of course, she *was* concerned about said politician's career, but it was *her own* that was uppermost in her mind naturally. Her career centered now on her image for Durell Cosmetics. She was their official model, their official spokeswoman; they were naming a whole line after her. It was going to be Suzannah lipsticks, Suzannah bath oil, etcetera, and best of all there was the Suzannah perfume. . . . She couldn't afford a breath of scandal. "If only he hadn't become so goddamn dependent on me. After all, he *is* supposed to have a career of his own and not feed off mine like a goddamned leech."

Remembering that the last time I had spoken with Suzannah about Paulie, she had still claimed she wasn't sleeping with him, I asked now, "Don't tell me you're still not sleeping with him?"

"Only when he rapes me," she replied.

"Oh, really, Suzannah! I find that hard to believe—"

"You just don't know. He really does. The first time it happened I had been out with Wes—he's the politician—and his wife, and Wes's administrative assistant, Bob Ging. Bob was my date . . . our beard, you know, so that Wes's wife wouldn't catch on that we're seeing each other. Well, I came home and Paulie was in his bathrobe . . . unshaven and drunk as usual. And he said to me, 'You're fucking that son-of-a-bitch and now you're going to fuck me,' and he grabbed for my tittie. Well, I was afraid he was going to tear my dress, which was a Tovito original and borrowed, so I said, 'Stop, you stupid, filthy drunk! I have to give this dress back!' But he didn't give a damn, he just pushed me down on the sofa and started mauling me. Well, I was afraid for the dress, and when he started sucking on my nipple I was deathly afraid he might just *bite it* right off! My friend Poppy from back home had once told me a story about this girl, Eunice, who had had her nipple bitten completely off when a man had forced himself on her and she had fought back, so I decided to just submit and save the dress *and* my poor little nipple. . . ."

I had heard enough. I didn't want to hear another word. "I have to go now, Suzannah," I said. "It's time to feed Megan."

"Well, for God's sake, let the nurse do it."

"I don't have a nurse and I'm breastfeeding."

"I don't believe you. You're still working, with the baby and all, and you don't have a nurse? And breastfeeding? My God, Buffy, you're only twenty-two. By the time you're twenty-three, your boobies will be down to your knees. Don't you care *how* you violate your body, the only body you'll ever have?"

Oh, for God's sake, Suzannah, can the bullshit!

"I mean, Buffy," she went on, "it was bad enough that you went and had a baby when you were only twenty-two . . . in the prime of your life you went and tied yourself down, not to mention the stretch marks your boobies and belly must endure! Not to mention how Todd must resent those stretch marks."

"Don't you worry about Todd," I snapped. "He's very happy with the baby and with me, stretch marks and all."

"Well, you don't have to snap my head off. You know I was only thinking of your good. . . . Really, Buffy, I'm so happy for you. I think of you all the time. You and Todd and baby makes three. . . ." she said sweetly.

Cleo and Leo sent a package from Bloomingdale's for the baby—a comforter quilted and appliquéd with pink and green elephants, plus an assortment of tiny T-shirts, each one adorned with the picture of a different animal. There was a note inside.

Dear Buffy,

We're thrilled to hear about the baby. Hope we can take a trip real soon to see you and Todd and little Megan. Your announcement made me almost sorry that Leo and I decided to wait for at least ten years to have *our* little one. But that's still our plan. Leo is still with the TV station and he's working terribly hard, but he says they don't really appreciate him there. It's local, you know, and he's trying to make a connection with one of the networks. As for me, I've landed the most wonderful job in publishing. I'm an associate editor and it's so exciting —reading manuscripts and meeting with writers (lots of lovely lunches on an expense account). Between you and me and the notepaper, I think Leo's nose is a little bit out of joint because my job is more glamorous than his. And would you believe that I'm making almost as much money as he?

Keep me posted on Baby Megan's progress and what's doing with the Kings.

Love ya,

Cleo

The next day another package arrived from Bloomingdale's in New York—Suzannah's present for Megan. It was a pair of "rubber pants," plastic-lined blue denim with a tiny red-checked bandana peeping out from a back pocket. Accompanying it was a tiny T-shirt with the legend: "Tough Guy."

15.

I received a lovely baby present from California from the Savareses—a tiny white dress with a smocked yoke, hand embroidered in pink, blue, and yellow. And I sent them a wedding present—a Dresden porcelain figurine of a shepherdess that reminded me of Cassie herself. Not knowing where else to send it, I addressed it to Cassie's mother's house, where I had always corresponded with her. A few weeks later, Cassie called me to tell me she had received the present, that she loved it, and that she was pregnant.

I was thrilled for her. "How is your mother taking all this? The marriage to Guy and a baby on the way?"

"I'm not sure," Cassie said. "It's hard to figure Mother out."

When she had been informed of the elopement, Cassandra's response had been surprising. She neither raged nor berated, which was what Cassie expected and which she had anticipated with something akin to terror. Instead, Cassandra had smiled a sour little smile and folded her arms across her chest as if to say, "Well, now you *have* made your bed, Cassie, you little fool, and you will certainly have a time lying in it, won't you?"

At first, there had been no wedding present from Cassandra, and Cassie thought maybe her mother assumed that if there weren't a large gift of money, her new husband would be sorely disappointed and would walk out on the marriage. But when, only a few weeks later, Cassie had announced that she was pregnant, her mother surprised her again. She presented the newlyweds with a house . . . a big, handsome house in Bel Air. It appeared almost as if Cassandra was giving her blessing to the new marriage. She *did* make Guy sign mortgage papers stipulating a sizable payment each month, with a variable interest clause—the interest for the year would be calculated at the going rate. But it was understood that these payments would not be made. It was a formality, the lawyers said—a legal technicality necessitated by estate and community property laws, especially since the divorce rate was so high in California.

Then, once they moved in, it seemed to Cassie that it was almost as if her mother had settled back in her chair to watch the proceedings, as if Cassie's marriage was a play and her mother an audience of one. Cassie had a vague notion that something was off-key. She couldn't quite figure it out. But when they tried to furnish the house, maintain it, keep up the grounds and the pool, all on the strength of Cassie's small job at the Museum, she better understood her mother's strategy. Besides the financial requirements of the house, they had extraordinary daily living expenses. Two cars were an absolute necessity given their Bel Air location. There were Guy's wardrobe requirements as an aspiring movie idol, not to mention his weekly haircut, his gym expenses, etc. And his occasional few days' work of modeling or TV bit parts did not add a lot to their income. Her mother was *forcing* money problems into their marriage. But Cassie thought the solution was simple. "If we can't maintain the house and we can't pay our bills, we'll just have to move out—give the house back to Mother and move into an apartment we *can* afford."

But Guy flew into a rage. "What makes you think we can afford an apartment? We can't even afford a fucking garage until I get my big break." He told Cassie that no way was he moving out of the big, beautiful house. Oh no! He had come too far for that. He wasn't making a move . . . not until he was ready to move into the grandest house of all—Blackstone Manor itself! Even the fucking witch of Sunset Boulevard couldn't live forever!

"We have to find other ways of making it in this house. You think about it," he told her, offering his solution: She, Cassie, had to squeeze money—an allowance—out of the old lady. "Goddamn it, your mother's the richest old bitch in the Southland, isn't she? Are you, her only fucking heir, and the kid you're having, supposed to starve while she lives it up in that castle?"

Cassie shut herself off mentally from her husband's words and his rage, much as she did from their sex. No matter what he said or did, there was no way she was going to beg her mother for money. Was that the reason her mother had given them the house then? Simply to put her in the position of begging her mother for money. The very thought was enough to make her sick.

"But she *is* happy about the baby, isn't she?" I persisted.

"I suppose," Cassie said. "I guess she would like to see a grandchild . . . somebody to carry on the Blackstone name. Though I think she would really have preferred an immaculate conception. A baby but no Guy." She laughed but it was the saddest laugh I had ever heard.

As the months passed Cassie reconsidered her mother's motives. Building Guy's character? Forcing her to beg for money? Too simple. Her mother must be playing a different game, a power game much more contrived. Perhaps what her mother wanted was for Guy to walk away from the marriage, to fold under the responsibilities of house, wife, baby. Then what would she, Cassie, *have* to do with a baby and no husband? Go crawling back to Cassandra . . . on her knees. . . .

Sometimes, especially when Guy was inside her, jamming in and out, and—she could swear—trying to hurt her more than trying to make love, she wished it could be that simple for her—that he would walk out on her so she would be left only with a baby and no husband. She wished that he in this way would make the choice for her. But then there would be her mother. It seemed no matter what happened she was going to end up the loser.

When her baby was stillborn, Cassie would not talk for two days, despite the efforts of the hospital staff. All she would do was lie facing the pale green wall of her room.

All for nothing, she thought over and over again. Her marriage to Guy, pointless. All her misery, pointless.

Guy came to see her on the third day. "I never get a break," he told her bitterly. There were real tears in his angry eyes.

She was surprised and touched at this sign of his grieving. She held out her hand to him, searched for words to console him. "The doctor said it was an accident of birth. He said there wasn't any reason we couldn't have a healthy child in the very near future."

Yes, she owed him that much. She had deceived him, after all, married him without telling him that she was impregnated with Darren Prouty's child. She owed him another child, a healthy one.

"Yeah?" he sneered. "When are we going to have this kid? It's *now* that we needed it. *Now* that we need your fucking mother's help. She's not going to give us a fucking dime without that baby."

She recoiled as if he had struck her. She had thought he was actually mourning the loss of the baby. She closed her eyes in pain, turned her face to the wall again, and he left.

She would leave him, she resolved. Yes, she would! To hell with her mother and what she said or thought. There was no baby so she wouldn't have to go live with Cassandra. No. She would get herself a job. And not one at the Blackstone Museum either. She would get her own place. She would live in one room if she had to. She wouldn't live with either of them. Not ever again.

Cassandra came to visit, arriving amidst a great flurry of doctors and nurses dancing attendance. She was on the board, after all. But her cold, haughty, imperious manner would probably have demanded the same respect even if she hadn't been.

"I *am* sorry about the baby, Cassie, but perhaps things have worked out for the best. Perhaps now you can admit that, as usual, you messed things up badly. You don't have to go on with this pretense. You married a worthless, vulgar man. A man who can't even support himself. One without any redeeming qualities. Are you going to be stubborn about this or will you admit that the man you married is only after our money and position?"

Is it really so impossible that a man might love me for myself, Mother?

But Cassie said nothing. The fact was her mother was one hundred percent correct.

Cassandra took her silence for acquiescence. She smiled triumphantly. "It really was provident about the baby—"

Provident? Her baby not living was provident? And that smile! That Cassandra-smile that stated that she was right, that only Cassie was wrong. Time after time after time. *How dare she use that word? She isn't God! Not yet she isn't!*

"No, Mother, you're not right! Not right, not right, not right! You're wrong about my baby! It's not provident! It's . . . it's the worst thing that has ever happened to me! You're wrong about my baby and you're wrong about my husband! He's a wonderful, fine man and he's going to be a big success! You'll see! And we're going to have another baby. A wonderful, live baby!"

Cassandra smiled a tight, cool, controlled smile this time. "You always had a tendency to be willful, Cassie. So much like your father—"

"My father? I don't remember him as being willful at all. He was a dear, sweet man and you always—"

"You don't know anything about your father," Cassandra said coldly. "Someday I will tell you all about him."

She left and Cassie stared at the ceiling. No, now she couldn't leave Guy. She had to win out first! She *was* going to win this one time! Once she would triumph over Cassandra! She could only leave Guy *after* she had a beautiful, live child to parade before Cassandra and *after* Guy was successful. Then she would be able to tell them both to go to hell, Guy and Cassandra! But first, she was going to win out over Cassandra. . . .

Cassandra sent her chauffeur and car to take Cassie home from the hospital, without even inquiring whether or not Guy would be performing the task. As the car wended its way up the hills of Bel Air, it occurred to Cassie that she hadn't really needed to accept the ride home from her mother. She could have done without either one of them—

Guy or her mother. She could have simply called a cab. Why hadn't she? And then she wondered whether Guy would be at home when she arrived. She desperately hoped he wouldn't be . . . she could no longer bear the sight of him.

Guy Savarese cruised the Strip, his eyes alert. At first he thought he would go to one of the bars he frequented, but he had changed his mind. He knew what he needed more than a drink. And then he spotted the very thing to fill the ticket. She was little and thin . . . almost spindly, wearing a pair of red shorts with sneakers to match, and she was looking into the window of a record shop. As he pulled in to the curb, he put his free hand down and felt under the seat until he found the little plastic container of pills secreted there.

"Get in!" he yelled out in invitation. When the girl spun around, he winked at her and held up the pills for her to see.

16.

By the time we celebrated Megan's first birthday, we had two used-car lots, two King supermarkets, and Lerner and Wiston, the accounting firm Todd still worked for, offered to make him a junior partner. Instead, Todd tendered his resignation, ready at last to go completely out on his own.

"I've found the big one, Buffy Ann. They've already filed for bankruptcy. It's a construction company with equipment and land options, and a half-finished development of one hundred and twenty houses. It's a very big, fancy operation and it'll go for ten cents on the dollar."

"Why did they go bankrupt?"

"Overexpansion, undercapitalization, sloppy workmanship, and slipshod management."

"And you think you can correct their mistakes?"

"I'm sure we can. You and I."

"Then what are you waiting for?"

"Your approval. We'll have to sell the markets and the car lots. Prentis will keep his percentage of course. And we'll keep the lumberyard

. . . make it part of the operation. The thing is, you're going to have to be completely involved, which means that you're going to have to leave Megan at home with a full-time housekeeper."

Actually I had been thinking of retiring, of starting a new baby, not becoming even more involved in a new business. But I didn't hesitate. "Okay. We'll hire a full-time housekeeper. As usual, you have my complete approval." I put my arms around his neck.

"There's one more thing. You understand that we could lose everything we already have—even the house. We're going to be mortgaged up to our chins."

"I understand that. What I *don't* understand is why you didn't simply marry a rich girl in the first place. Look at all the time and work you would have saved—"

"Ah! But look at all the fun I would have missed!"

I found Leah—a small, wiry, black woman with a crusty disposition, to take care of the house and Megan. At first her noncommunicative ways and baleful looks turned me off, worried me. But Todd was reassuring, "Consider her dedication. It's her work that counts, not her attitude."

Gradually we became accustomed to one another, Leah and I, and I saw that it was only adults with whom she was uncommunicative. She and Megan related to each other really well, which was indeed fortunate because the completion of the half-finished housing development, the prime asset of our construction company, assumed an overwhelming priority in our lives.

"We have to get a cash flow going," Todd said. "And we can't get a cash flow until we start selling the houses. And we can't begin to sell houses until we have at least a few completed. Therefore it follows that not only do we have to finish construction, we have to do it yesterday. Time, Buffy, is our enemy," he told me and proceeded to assault it.

The loan officers at the banks crumbled before his business acumen and his persuasive charm. When he told them that he intended to employ three shifts of working men around the clock, seven days a week, a 168-hour week instead of a forty, thereby completing the entire job in less than one-fourth the normal time, they were appalled. The labor costs would be prohibitive, if not suicidal, what with time-and-a-half, double, and triple time. But Todd pointed out that by completing the project in five or six months instead of two years, he would actually be saving money on labor and materials, due to rising costs. He planned to complete the last house by late spring—the costs of building in '70 as opposed to the accelerating costs of '72. And he didn't fail to mention that everybody involved would start recouping his money a year-and-a-half earlier. And they gave him the money we needed without further delay. I always said Todd was irresistible.

I showed Cleo around my new house, which was the sixth completed house in the development and still very sparsely furnished.

"I love the minimal look," Cleo said. "That's how we've done our apartment too. Minimal, spare, functional . . . almost no color except for accents."

"Stark's more the word. Only ours is not intentional. I intend to have more furniture when I get the time to shop for it but I don't know when that's going to be. Certainly not before we've sold the last house in the development. I really didn't need a new house. We were only in our other house about three years. But Todd said we'd show everyone our own faith in the houses if we lived here ourselves, and we did make money on the sale of our old house and that's what it's all about. Todd says you buy and you sell, as long as you make a profit, and every time you move, you move *up*. You know Todd. He always makes everything sound easy. The funny thing is, it always turns out that way."

"Todd's smart," Cleo said, narrowing her eyes. "Leo always said Todd's smart."

"And lucky—" I added, wanting to sound modest on Todd's behalf in order not to tempt the jealous gods. "We've been very lucky."

"Leo always says that people make their own luck."

Even if it was Leo who said that, I silently agreed. Todd did seem to make his own luck.

"How long will you be in Akron, Cleo? I want you to stay with us."

"Oh, I'm just staying overnight. I have this author to see and it's back to New York tomorrow. We have a dinner party at one of the station's bigwig's. And you know Leo. If I'm not back in time he'll have a hemorrhage."

"Yes. How is he doing?"

"I'm afraid he's still only an assistant director but he's just written something . . . a play that the station is going to put on, so that's progress. Of course Leo won't be happy until he at least makes the networks. And *my* being promoted . . . losing that little word 'associate' before my title of editor . . . didn't make him any happier," she giggled, "not to mention that I'm making more money than he is."

"What do you hear from Cassie?" Cleo asked, as we had tea.

"I think she's still depressed about the baby. But she said her husband was doing better, getting more parts. He had a pretty good part in one of those TV cop shows recently, and Cassie called to tell us to watch and we did. It was kind of funny—Cassie asked that we call up after the show and tell Guy how much we enjoyed the show and his performance—"

"So did you?"

"Sure. Actually, Todd called. He spoke with Guy and told him how much we liked him in the show."

"What does he look like?"

"Gorgeous. Cassie had told me that he was extremely good looking but I really didn't expect him to be *that* handsome."

"I wished I'd watched the show . . . had seen him."

"You probably will get a chance. I'm sure the teenagers are going to love him and make a star out of him."

"That will be nice for Cassie. And how about Suellen? What's she up to?"

"Oh, she's busy with her son Petey and Howard and cooking these days. She *was* into politics . . . she actively campaigned for Bobby Kennedy. But when he was assassinated she went into a funk and quit everything. She was very depressed . . . especially since that assassination came so soon after Martin Luther King's. I know it sounds a little strange but she really never got over Bobby's death. I imagine Leo must have taken his death hard too."

Cleo looked at me curiously. "Of course he was shocked when it happened. We all were. But it *was* some time ago. And Leo's no longer interested in politics. He doesn't even rage against Nixon these days."

I nodded. I wasn't a bit surprised. But I was concerned that I had made Suellen sound "peculiar." "Suellen's a wonderful mother," I said. "She's completely devoted. In fact she thinks I'm terrible to go to work and leave Megan with Leah so much of the time."

"I bet you're a wonderful mom and Leah . . . well, she seems very able. . . ."

"Yeah," I laughed. "Able *and* terrifying . . ."

Cleo rolled her eyes. "To tell you the truth I would just love to take her back to New York with me and sic her on Leo. . . ."

We both went off into gales of laughter and it was almost like we were back in school again.

Then she sat up straight. "Oh, I forgot to tell you. I ran into Suzannah the other day at Tavern on the Green. She looked gorgeous and was as full of herself as usual. Paulie was with her and *he* looked god-awful! He must be on something! They were with this other couple. Real country-cousins, if you know what I mean. Accents thick as corn syrup. The fellow's a singer who plays the guitar and the girl was his manager. She was *something!* She was wearing a mini so short you could see her tonsils. Her name was Poppy and it seems she's from the same hometown as Suzannah. A former schoolmate. Would you believe they're staying with Suzannah and that Suzannah's trying to help them make a connection? Our girl's actually trying to help somebody?"

"Come on, Cleo. Suzannah's not all that bad. Why wouldn't she help somebody if she could? Especially an old friend."

Cleo sucked in her cheeks. "For sure . . ."

We talked and laughed late into the night, long after Todd went to bed, and when Cleo left the next morning, I found myself wishing that we got to see each other more. She must have been thinking the same thing.

"I wish you and Todd would come to New York for a visit. We may only have an apartment—not like this great big house of yours—but we do have a guestroom. Well, actually a den-guestroom with a sleeper. It *was* comfortable living with Mother in her house in Tenafly but of course we were dying to have our own place in town. And besides it was difficult to entertain in New Jersey. Nobody who's anybody wanted to cross the river. Promise me you'll come for a visit and stay with us. . . ."

As her cab pulled away I found myself thinking of all the questions that had been left unasked.

Are you happy, Cleo? Are you deep-down in love with Leo? Still? Are you satisfied with your life? Is it all turning out for you the way we planned it back in Columbus not so long ago?

17.

Leonard Mason awoke with both a terrific idea and an erection. He poked at Cleo with his elbow until she came fully awake, thinking that if he poked her one more time maybe she would gather the courage to kick him in the balls.

He climbed on top of her.

"What time is it?" she asked.

"Time for you know what," he smirked and thrust himself into her, even though she was dry and unprepared for his entrance. She closed her eyes and tried to will herself into the mood to make love, but Leo, even as he pushed himself in and out of her, told her the great idea he had had while half-asleep.

"For the part of Greta," he said, referring to the name of the female lead in his TV play that was ready now for casting. "Suzannah!"

Cleo opened her eyes. "What about Suzannah?" she asked, as Leo said, "Shit!" and ejaculated.

"I want Suzannah to play the part of Greta!" He pulled out and lay flat on his back.

"But she's no actress. She's only a model!"

"She's more than a model. She's the Durell Woman."

Obviously, Leo was going to overlook the fact that she had not achieved gratification and she was just as willing to forget it herself. She got out of bed and went into the bathroom.

"I don't *need* an actress," he yelled after her. "I need a *name*. And Suzannah's probably dying to try her hand at acting. Every model wants to be an actress if she gains enough celebrity."

Toothbrush in hand, Cleo came back into the bedroom. "You must be crazy to think that Suzannah would consider making an acting debut on a local TV station. If she would consider TV at all. Knowing Suzannah, I don't think she'd go for anything less than a real movie. And if you think about it, with the exposure she has from those cosmetic commercials, she'd be nuts to do it. Those commercials promote her as much as she promotes the Durell products. That Suzannah perfume one makes her appear as the most desirable woman in the world. She probably could get a theatrical movie. If she could act, that is."

She went back into the bathroom to brush her hair vigorously. Since she had followed her mother's suggestion and had had her hair streaked, it had lost much of its gloss. Still, her mother had been right—people did notice her more now that her hair was no longer mousy brown.

Leo came into the bathroom.

"You're always so goddamn negative. That is, when it comes to *my* career."

"That's not true, Leo. I always try to help—"

"Then help me now."

"I don't know what I can do. How can I possibly help?"

"Help me talk Suzannah into doing it."

She looked at him, speechless.

"Well?" he said, removing the hairbrush forcibly from her hand and putting his face an inch away from hers.

"How can I do that?"

"We'll have a party. We'll invite Suzannah, some of my people from the station, and the big shots from the Durell company. Geoffrey Durell himself. I heard he and Suzannah were fooling around. Maybe we can even get Durell to sponsor the show."

Cleo stepped out of her nightgown and into the shower. "What makes you think Suzannah would even come to any party we invited her to? She probably only goes to name parties." She turned on the water, and closed the stall door, hoping against hope for an end to the conversation. But she knew it wouldn't happen.

Leo jerked the door open in a fury and turned off the water so hard that the plumbing reverberated. "You don't want me to succeed, do you? All you're fucking interested in is your own fucking job. You just get Suzannah to come to the party and *I'll* talk her into it!"

"Leo," she said with desperation in her voice, "Suzannah and I never got along. She never liked me. We were never really friends. It was only Buffy that drew all of us together."

"Then you get Buffy here. Say the party's for Buffy and Todd! Say anything!" And he turned the water on again, stormed out, and slammed the door shut.

As the tears rolled down her cheeks, Cleo quickly turned off the torrent of scalding water. Thoughtlessly Leo had turned the tap to the extreme left. What could she possibly tell Buffy and Todd to make them leave their daughter and their business and come to New York just for a party?

The development was mostly behind us when Cleo called, urging us to visit in New York and attend her party, and I had been thinking that Todd and I deserved a breather while we were still between projects. At the moment Todd was studying his land options, trying to decide where to strike next. And I wouldn't feel guilty leaving Megan for a few days. She had been with us much of the time, practicing her toddling, as we sold each and every house. We had salesmen of course, but in the end no one could sell better than Todd.

"Cleo said it was sort of a reunion," I told Todd. "Only it isn't. Not really. Suellen said she and Howard couldn't possibly go and leave Petey behind, and I hardly think Cassie would come all the way from California. So actually, it would only be us, Cleo and Leo, and Suzannah and Paulie, as far as a reunion goes. And Cleo said Suzannah would only come if we did."

"Otherwise the party wouldn't be worth her time?" Todd laughed.

"Exactly. Though there will be a lot of other people there . . . non-Reunionites, you might say."

"And you want to go?"

"Well, we do owe ourselves a break. And it will be fun to see Suzannah. And Cleo did ask me to come as a favor. Frankly, she sounded kind of desperate. Don't you think it will be fun?"

"Sure. We'll go. But on one condition. We're nobody's houseguests. Not Leo's and not Suzannah's. We stay at the Plaza."

"It's a deal."

18.

We checked into the Plaza and I wasn't a bit surprised that we had the very same room where we had so beautifully celebrated our wedding night. It was the sort of thing that I had come to expect from Todd.

He went off that morning to inspect a shopping center, of all things, in Paramus, New Jersey, and I went to meet Suzannah for lunch at the

Russian Tea Room. I was really excited. I hadn't seen Suzannah since that day when she had first left for New York four years before, if you didn't count her pictures on magazine covers or the TV commercials starring the Durell Woman.

Suzannah had told me on the phone that she was making a reservation for us at the Russian Tea Room because it was called the Polo Lounge of the East, and that the Polo Lounge was *the* meeting place of the stars in Hollywood. In other words, I surmised, the Tea Room was where the West Coast people lunched when they were in New York. I really didn't understand what this had to do with Suzannah since she was a New York model and not a Hollywood person. Nevertheless, I was led to what seemed to me a "good" table to await Suzannah's arrival—she was late. When she arrived she was something of a sensation. Everybody looked at her, and she threw kisses in the general direction of several tables. She was rather spectacularly and over-warmly dressed (it *was* the end of May) in a long green suede coat with a voluminous skirt, boots to match, and her flamboyant hair was wild in artful disarray. There seemed enough of it for two.

"Buffy! Buffy! Buffy!" she screamed and wrapped her arms around me. "I've missed you so! You'll never know! Why, I don't think a day has passed that I haven't thought of you with love."

I kissed her back with feeling, touched, forgetting already that I heard from her only intermittently.

"You look sensational!" she cried. "Not one day older than the first day I set eyes on you. You little devil, you still look like Vivien Leigh."

I mumbled something about it not being *that* long but she turned to the maitre d' and said, "Isn't she the picture of Vivien?" He murmured his agreement. "Madame is lovely."

I knew it was silly but I did feel a glow, and I was exhilarated at being in Suzannah's company. So much so I ordered a martini with an olive even though I would be drinking that night at Cleo's party. Suzannah ordered club soda. "Still protecting the old temple?" I joked, recalling that Suzannah didn't drink hard liquor in deference to the holiness of her body.

"I still don't ingest alcohol into my system," she said primly. But then she leaned forward and whispered, "But I *did* have an abortion last year."

"Oh Suzannah, I'm sorry," I burst out, remembering the desolation I felt when I had my abortion, that feeling of total emptiness.

"For goodness sake, don't be sorry. *I* wasn't. God! Think of what *not* having the abortion would have done to my career."

"But you could have gotten married. And then, after the baby, you could have picked up your career again—Paulie would have married you even if it weren't his baby."

"But what makes you think I wanted to keep the baby? And whose baby do you think it was if not Paulie's? When I *know* I'm going to do it with somebody, I'm always protected. It was Paulie's alright. It was one of those times when Paulie raped me," she said with ingenuous indignation.

I struggled to keep my face straight. *One of those times when Paulie raped me,* as if she were being automatically raped on an on-going basis. That was pretty funny. "You could use the Pill," I said. "Then you would be protected even in times of rape."

"Oh no, Buffy! You don't know what the Pill is doing to your hormones! You have to *protect* your hormones. If you don't, who will?"

I had no idea. We ordered and I threw caution to the winds. I ordered lobster Newburg, calorie-laden as it was. Suzannah ordered a lettuce-and-tomato salad and removed a bottle of her own dressing from her bag—a special blend of apple cider, vinegar, and herbs, she informed me.

"I'll give you the recipe. You mustn't persist in eating things with sauces, Buffy darling, or you won't look like a *young* version of anybody anymore." And we both laughed.

"Oh those days . . . our college days . . . those were wonderful days, weren't they?" she asked as if those wonderful days had occurred light years ago.

"Yes they were, but the days aren't so bad now either. Are they?"

She looked into my eyes with a kind of sadness. "Oh, *you* . . . you're still a romantic, aren't you? That's one of the things I've always loved about you best. But Buffy, don't you know? Nobody can afford to be romantic anymore. . . ." Her voice trailed off.

I wanted to tell her that *I* could but instead I asked, "Are you still seeing that married politician? And if so, why?"

She blinked a few times as if she were dragging her thoughts back to the present reluctantly. Then she spoke briskly, "Because he's rich, prominent, top drawer, and definitely presidential material."

"I'm surprised at you, Suzannah. A lot of good any of those things are going to do you if he's married to another woman."

"They're going to get divorced—"

I sighed, looked at the orange Newburg sauce without appetite now, and said, "Talk about being unrealistically romantic. They're *always* going to get a divorce, from what I hear. Does it make sense that he would divorce his wife for you when he's dreaming about the White House? If he did divorce, he wouldn't have a chance."

Suzannah smiled that sly smile I remembered so well, the one that showed her bottom teeth. "He would *if* she's the one who has strayed, if she's the one who's fooling around. Then people will feel only sorry for him. And then, my public exposure, my glamor, will be an asset. Assuming that *my* name is free of any scandal. So you see I have to keep Paulie in line so that he doesn't make any trouble for me."

"So the two of you, your senator and you, are waiting for his wife to stray?"

"Wes says he thinks she's fooling around right now." She leaned across the table the better to whisper confidentially. "He's having her followed."

"And what about Paulie? What's the current understanding between you two?"

For a moment . . . only a moment . . . Suzannah's eyes clouded over with pain. Then they darkened with anger. "I'd like to strangle Paulie, that's what. He's completely washed up. He doesn't do *anything* now. Anything at all. He's completely of no use to me. Not in any way. He's an albatross around my neck. All he does is drink and threaten me physically. To tell you the truth, I'm afraid of him. And I can't even get rid of him. He keeps threatening to blow the whole story of Weston and me to the press." She ran a hand across her forehead. "I just wish I knew how to get rid of him . . . without a fuss. Wes says I should just let it all rest. That Paulie makes the perfect cover for us. But Geoffrey Durell is not at all pleased about Paulie being in the picture. He sees me as the personification of both glamor and class . . . that's the image he wants me to project for his company . . . for the Suzannah perfume. And he says there's nothing classy about me living with an unshaven, unpredictable, unemployed drunken lout!"

"Oh, Suzannah, don't!" I gasped. I couldn't bear to have Paulie described in this manner. Not the boy I remembered—so sweet, smiling, jaunty. Oh yes, that's what Paulie had been then. And self-confident, with self-esteem and self-pride. And laughing.

"What about Geoffrey Durell? Where does he fit into the picture? Besides being your employer?"

This time, Suzannah showed her dimples *and* her bottom teeth.

"Geoffrey's *old*. He requires my attentions only once in a while. And besides," she leaned over the table, "he's just a teensy bit queer."

Before I could ask what she meant by that precisely, she fished in her big shoulder bag and withdrew a gold flacon. "This is for you, Buffy darling. It's the Suzannah perfume and the flask is eighteen karat gold and it's refillable. There were only a very few of the real gold ones made up. They gave me three and I want you to have one."

She pushed it on me. I took it and ran my fingers over the name Suzannah etched into the gold. "I don't think I should take it, Suzannah. It's too valuable—" I protested.

"But I *want* you to have it, Buffy. You're my dearest friend. The only true friend I can trust. Besides, my little old friend from Kentucky, that guttersnipe Poppy, has one, so you might as well have one too. Do you remember me telling you about her? I used to talk about her when we were in school."

"Yes. Cleo told me that she met her with you, that she and her boyfriend were staying with you. That you were trying to help them get started professionally. He's a singer? I thought that was awfully nice of you, trying to help them . . . letting them stay with you."

Suzannah grimaced. "That's not exactly the way it happened. Believe me, I didn't *want* to help them. It was more like I was forced into that situation."

Sometimes, I reflected, waiting for Suzannah to continue, she could be surprisingly candid.

"The truth is, one morning, they, Poppy and Herm, appeared at my door—barefoot out of Kentucky, in a manner of speaking—and they just moved in on me, with barely one suitcase between them. I hadn't had the littlest inkling that they were going to show up."

Poppy had been thinking about leaving Kentucky for some time. And then that evening she made up her mind definitely. It began when they left the Big Drink that night.

"They really went wild over me tonight, didn't they, Poppy? They sure as hell went crazy over me tonight," Herm glowed.

"Just go on and get your fucking truck, Herm. I'm freezing my ass off." She wrapped her arms around her shoulders, hugging herself. She wore a strapless knit tube that barely covered her breasts and bared her midriff. When Herm came back with the pickup she yelled at him without any particular rancor, "Get your butt down here and help me up, you dumb bastard."

He followed instructions. "I forgot I was supposed to do that," he mumbled, pushing back the brown hair that persistently hung in his eyes.

"You'd forget your ass if it wasn't nailed on."

He grinned in pleasure at her words and said, "You didn't tell me how good I was tonight."

"Maybe it was because you wasn't, asshole. You didn't do like I told you, you fucking stupid hillbilly bastard. I told you a thousand times—country singers are a dime a dozen. You gotta be a little different. I told you to get more of a wail in your voice."

He was wounded. "It ain't easy to sing one way when you're used to singing another."

"If you weren't so fucking lazy, you'd practice more and then maybe you'd get it right."

"I'll try, Poppy." He put his hand on her thigh where her skirt was hiked up.

She gave his groin a squeeze.

His hand on the wheel faltered. "You better stop that before I drive us off the road."

She pinched him there.

"Jesus, Poppy, ain'tcha better wait until I pull up someplace?"

"Just shut the hell up, keep driving, and stick your finger in."

"I cain't while I'm driving."

"Goddamn it, Herman. Stick your finger in! I want to be frigged and I want to be frigged right now!" She pinched him again, this time more viciously.

"Jesus, Poppy, you better cut that out! I almost ran us off the road!" He was sweating profusely. "I can't stand that while I'm driving."

"Take your fucking finger and put it where I tell you."

"How can I? Ain'tcha wearing no panties?"

She wriggled her skirt up to her waist. His eyes left the road for a second. "Je-sus!"

"Now I know you're not very bright, Herm, so I'll spell it out for you. You need one hand to hold the wheel, that leaves you one hand with nothing to do. You take the middle finger of that hand that ain't doing nothing and stick it in the hole."

Finally she said, "There you are . . . you can do anything if you make up your mind to do it."

"I'm burning hot, Poppy. Unzip me!"

"Okay, clowny. How's that?"

"Jesus! I'm gonna pull over!"

"No. Don't you know it's better when you're moving?"

"Are we going back to the Big Drink tomorrow night?" All of a sudden she was filled with dissatisfaction. "That stinking hole. You ain't gonna get nowhere in those stinking toilets. For five years now we've been doing that and we still don't have any bucks and nobody knows you're alive."

He was bewildered. "But you said I had to start somewhere."

"You've *been* starting for years. Don't it ever occur to you that you're not getting anywhere? You ain't cut but that one stinking record and we never could get anybody to play it except for the few asshole disc jockeys around here. It's fucking time to move on."

"Where to?"

"Someplace where it's happening."

His eyes bugged. "You don't mean Nashville?"

"No, I don't mean Nashville, dummy. Country singers are a dime a dozen there and everybody's hustling. And you ain't smart enough to hustle. Besides, who wants to go to fucking Nashville?"

He was impressed with her lofty attitude toward the mecca. "Where do you want to go?"

"Shit! To Hollywood. To Vegas. Or right now, I think New York."

"New York? Quit your fooling. How will we make out in New York?"

"God, you're a dimbulb! I don't know why I even waste my time with you."

"Cause you love me?" he entreated. "Cause I sing good? Cause I fuck good?"

"You don't sing that good and your balling is only passable," she said sourly. "And who ever said I loved you?"

"Where will we stay in New York, Poppy? And where will we get money?"

Telling him about Suzannah would serve no purpose. He wouldn't begin to understand the hold she had on Suzannah, the hold being the information that Suzannah had volunteered herself when she had written her a scribbled note. She must have been stoned when she had written it . . . complaining about her troubles with her boyfriend and that politician guy, the one with the wife with the big social connections. Yeah, she could blow the whistle on Suzannah, embarrassing the hell out of her, and not only her but her big politician friend too. And there was that big cosmetics deal Suzannah had mentioned. If she spilled the beans on Suzannah, it surely would blow the cosmetics deal. No, she didn't think Suzannah would wail about putting them up in her fancy duplex on Fifth Avenue for a while, helping Herm get a start. Suzannah had connections, Poppy was sure, and she would really try to help them considering that she would get rid of them that much faster if she did.

"When are we gonna go, Poppy?"

Now impatience was eating at her. "Tomorrow."

"Tomorrow?"

"Yes, you got it. Tomorrow. And we're not saying a fucking word to anybody. We're just up and leaving."

"How about my mom?"

"Send her a Christmas card."

"I can't believe it," he enthused. "New York!"

"Yeah. And if you can stop acting like a big turd and not end up in some jail for the criminally stupid, who knows what our next stop will be? Vegas. Maybe Hollywood." She would like that. Hollywood!

Herm giggled. "I'm lucky to have you, Poppy."

"Bet your ass."

She laughed. She was thinking about the look on Suzannah's face when she and Herm and the guitar showed up on the doorstep of her fancy New York apartment.

"They just moved in on me, simple as that. He's sweet but moronic, but she's sharp enough for two. That little bitch blackmailed me. What I had told her in confidence, fool that I was, she held over my head. She threatened to spill the news about me and Wes to one of those scandal sheets unless I supported the two of them while I tried to get people to listen to that idiot sing. I can tell you I was beside myself. I didn't know what to do to get rid of those garbageheads, to get them out of my hair. And the one day I discovered one of the perfume flasks was missing, I knew immediately that Poppy had filched it. She was always light-fingered. She used to steal the drugstore back home blind. But it gave me an idea. I announced that a diamond bracelet was missing and I told Poppy that I was going to the police and swearing out a complaint against her unless she and Herm got the hell out of my life. And even if she blew the whistle on me she would still go to jail because I'm a person of importance and the police would believe me and after all, who was she? As a matter of fact, I suspected that that little bitch had made some kind of connection and was doing some kind of trafficking in drugs and probably using my apartment to *store* her merchandise!"

"But you didn't know that for sure?"

"I didn't have to. I suspected it! And she *was* blackmailing me, holding me up! And believe me, it wasn't bad enough with Paulie a walking embarrassment, you can imagine what it was like with those two hanging on me too."

"So you threw them out?"

She looked surprised. "Of course. What would you have done?"

"I don't know. Where did they go?"

"I haven't the slightest and I couldn't care less. But I don't doubt for a minute they'll make out. That Poppy is as smart as they come, as sneaky as a snake, and as wily as a she-fox." She was pensive for a moment. "Believe me, I only wish I could get rid of Paulie the way I did Poppy."

I had a mental image of Poppy and Herm walking the streets, homeless and hungry. I knew she was speaking only figuratively . . . still I was upset that she could put Paulie into the same category with them.

"Oh Suzannah! Does it have to end this way with you and Paulie? You've already made it big. Why can't it be you and Paulie? You can still save him. My God, Suzannah, Paulie isn't even twenty-five. You can't discard him like a soiled tissue. Why do you have to chase after this Wes or that Durell? These men will only try to use you, even as you're using them. Paulie loves you. Why can't you choose love? Choosing love is the only salvation, Suzannah! Believe me!"

My urgency was for Paulie, but for a moment it frightened Suzannah. I could see it in her eyes. But only for a moment. Then she laughed and said, "But I don't love Paulie. I never did."

"Can you love anybody?" I demanded.

"Yes, of course. Me! I adore me!" And she laughed some more, laughing at herself. And finally, I laughed too. It was hard not to go along with somebody that laughed at herself. But for the rest of the lunch, even as I tucked the perfume flacon away in my purse carefully so that the fanciful swirls of the engraved Suzannah wouldn't scratch, I felt there were ghosts at our table: Poppy and Herm and dear Paulie.

19.

So this is a glamorous New York party, I thought. They even had a terrace crowded with tubbed trees and white tubular chaises. What matter that it looked down on Third Avenue and the view was less than charming? It *was* New York and the tubbed trees did have little sparkling lights artfully concealed among their leaves. The living room contained, as Cleo had told me, very little furniture—white canvas-covered sofas, black glass-topped tables, huge, exotic plants, and vermeil accessories. Chic: Cleo always did have a flair. The guests, inadvertently, complemented the color scheme. The men wore black and the women, for the most part, were dressed in white or black, with only an occasional flash of color. Cleo wore understated black and I myself was in white silk jersey draped in the Grecian manner. Todd liked me in white. He said that beautiful women with shiny black hair and porcelainlike skin should always wear white.

But it was Suzannah, making a late entrance with Paulie in tow, breaking her own rule of not allowing her attire to vie for attention with her face, who positively glittered like a true star in a gold lamé mini party dress, her red hair a jarring but exactly right note of discord. Who there could avoid looking at her alone, dazzled by her brilliance?

I turned to Todd to share my observation with him. He was staring as if mesmerized, but it was not Suzannah he was staring at but Paulie . . . emaciated, ashen-faced, his eyes hollow, his clothes hanging on his frame. His eyes lit up when he spotted us and he rushed over, hugging us, kissing me then Todd. I loved Suzannah, but my heart broke over Paulie. He whispered in my ear, "You're *still* a young Vivien and those green eyes still make my heart beat fast." I reached up and kissed him again.

We talked and laughed, and I was fervently hoping that he wouldn't take a drink and for a while he didn't. He did light many cigarettes with shaking hands and I knew that once again I was being the naive, romantic dreamer.

A waiter passed tall thin glasses of champagne and a waitress in black silk served canapés of Scotch salmon on rounds of toast and tiny potatoes stuffed with red caviar. I made a mental note to tell Suellen about the stuffed potatoes. A very expensive party, I thought, and Cleo, as if she read my thoughts, murmured, "At times like these, Leo's glad to have my salary to add to the family income and doesn't worry about who has the better job or who is more important."

Still, two salaries notwithstanding, I wondered how they managed so well. I guessed that Cleo's parents, independent of each other in their divorced state, were both contributing. Cleo's mother, in particular. She was so eager for Cleo's marriage to be a success.

I glanced over at Leila Pulitzer, in for the evening from Tenafly. She was fashionably dressed in silver and white and talking to one of the people from Cleo's office. Like Paulie, she smoked one cigarette after the other in compulsive fashion. Nervous, I thought, and probably drinking too much too. Still in despair over her failed marriage? Well, no laughing matter, that. And if it were I in her place, it wouldn't be liquor I'd be drinking, but more likely hemlock from a silver cup.

I spotted Leo and Suzannah out on the terrace, deep in conversation, and I wondered what those two, who had never held each other in any affection, were talking about with so much concentration.

"But I don't need you, Leo." Suzannah smiled with a tinge of contempt. "I probably could go to any network and get a production. Especially with Durell as a sponsor. Why should I hand you both me and Durell for your itty-bitty station?"

"Because *I'm* the one who can handle your problem discreetly."

"What problem?" Suzannah asked warily.

"Paulie. Your nemesis, Suzannah. If you're not careful, he's going to drag you down so far, you'll be choking for breath. I'd give Paulie a job on the show. A small job but something to keep him busy. Something to straighten him out."

Suzannah breathed an inner relief. She was worried that Leo knew about Weston and was about to threaten her with that mess. Relieved, she sneered, "If I deliver Durell as a sponsor I could demand a job for Paulie anywhere. I don't need you for that. Besides, it wouldn't keep Paulie off my back for long. At this point, he's too far gone even to keep up the pretense of a job. One alcoholic binge and bingo! He blows up in everybody's face."

"Not if I take him to this doctor I know of—"

She looked at him with a renewed interest but with suspicion. "What's your doctor going to do for him? Give him a lobotomy so he'll forget he ever knew me."

"No," Leo laughed. "He'll give him shots to get him off the booze and at the same time mellow him out."

"Mellow him out?" she repeated.

"Yes. No more rages. No more jealous scenes. Just a mellow, tranquil Paulie that you'll be able to manage . . . help him up out of his decline so that you can ease him out of your life gently and gradually."

Oh God, that would be wonderful! If only she could help Paulie get on his feet . . . his old self again . . . and still get him out of her life.

She narrowed her eyes. "What, exactly, are these shots?"

By the time we sat down to dinner, Paulie was glassy-eyed and held his body in that stiff, carefully upright manner of drunks who are trying to behave in a correct, normal way. He was quiet. I had kept an eye on him; had not seen him take anything to drink. When had he drunk? And where? Out of a pint bottle in the bathroom? And where was the drunken rage Suzannah had spoken of? I saw that he was only morose. Stiffly and gravely morose. What a pity he couldn't have gotten more pleasure from his drinking. He could, at least, have been a happy drunk.

We rode back to the Plaza in a cab holding hands. We were both thinking about Paulie. "That bitch Suzannah . . ." Todd breathed, which was out of character for him. He always viewed everyone with tolerance . . . had always regarded Suzannah with a kind of amused affection.

"But it's not all her fault," I justified her once again. "Paulie must have an inherent weakness. There are lots of cases of unrequited love. Lots of people love someone who doesn't love them back. But they don't go to pieces for the most part, do they? They pull themselves together and go on. . . ."

Todd's mouth was a thin line. He shook his head. "It's not just a case of unrequited love. That's an oversimplification. Suzannah's used him . . . badly . . . unpardonably. She's delivered him a mortal wound."

I shivered. Strong words . . . *mortal wound* . . .

We sat silent until I said, "Leo hasn't changed at all, has he?"

Todd gave a little chuckle. "Nope. Old Leo's still the same. And Cleo hasn't changed much either except that her hair is frosted."

"I think she's changed some. I think that she's storing up resentment against Leo now, while before she thought every word he said was gospel."

"And do you think all this stored-up resentment will erupt?"

"I just don't know. Not yet. She's got this thing about a successful marriage that her mother's drummed into her head. And it's worse now that her mother's divorced. Now Cleo has to do it for both of them."

I sighed heavily. Everything seemed so depressing. Then Todd was lifting my chin with two fingers. "Don't be sad, Buffy Ann. I love you with every breath. . . ."

Thank you, God. He kissed me and the cab pulled up in front of the hotel.

Alighting, Todd spied the hansoms that carried romantic lovers through the park across the street. "Come on," he said, pulling me along. "You've never been properly mauled in a horse-and-carriage, have you?"

As the horse trotted sedately through Central Park, I murmured into Todd's throat, "Thank you."

"Why thank me? It's the horse and driver who are doing all the work."

"Thank you for not changing. Thank you for still being the same Todd I fell in love with . . . *my* Todd."

We stood at the Plaza's fountain that sparkled in the star-filled night. "She's called the Fountain of Abundance," Todd told me, referring to the bronze statue of the nude woman that graced the fountain. "The Abundance is that basket of fruit she's holding. Representative, I suppose."

"Yes."

"I like her. I think she looks just like you," which of course was nonsense.

"Oh, I'm not so abundant. I've only produced Megan so far." I was thinking of the five children Todd and I had promised each other not so many years ago. But Todd said, "I was thinking of the other fruits you bear so beautifully . . . friendship, understanding, compassion, and grace. Not to mention love."

Oh, Todd, you always mention love.

Then I saw excitement grow in his eyes. "Do you know what I'm going to do? I'm going to commission a statue just like this one but exactly in your likeness and I'm going to center it in a fountain and put it right in the middle of our shopping mall!"

He knew full well that he was dropping a bombshell. Still, I played along. "What shopping mall?"

He grinned at me. "I haven't decided on a name yet. What do you think of the Buffy Ann King Mall of Abundance? Like it?"

I ignored that. "How long have you been thinking about this?"

"Oh . . . two, three months. We had an option on the land and I thought *why not?*"

"Why not? Because I thought you were stewing about another development of houses. I thought that was the business we were in—"

"So did I. But then I thought, 'Hell, we've just done that. Why don't we try something else?' "

"Something else? You call a mammoth project like a shopping center 'something else'? You're talking about millions and millions of dollars—" Then I added, "Aren't you?"

He smiled smugly. "I already have commitments from the banks for the money. And a list of department stores positively begging to be part of the mall."

I shook my head, scared. "It sounds like too big a project."

"Don't be frightened by the thought of success, Buffy Ann. I've got it all on paper. We're going to finish the shopping mall in less than a year. We're going to build it like we did the houses. With crews around the clock. You know my motto—"

He had a lot of mottoes. "Nothing ventured, nothing gained?" I guessed.

"Uh-uh. With love, we can do anything—"

"Oh, *you!*" I pretended to be angry. "Why didn't you say anything to me about this before?"

"Because it was to be a surprise. I wanted it to be a birthday present to you—"

"It's not my birthday. What made you change your mind and tell me about it now?"

"I thought about it and I decided it would be kind of hard to have a shopping mall jump out of a birthday cake."

I pretended to be disgusted. "That's a pretty lame joke—" I shook my head. "A shopping mall jumping out of a cake . . . Really!"

We smiled at each other and held hands, still looking at the lady in the fountain, the mist dampening our faces. Then I giggled and Todd turned to me with delight. "Did you decide my joke was funny after all?"

"No. Not at all. As a matter of fact I was thinking how you've changed. How, in spite of your dumb jokes, you're getting old—"

His eyebrows shot up. "And what makes you say that, if I may ask?" he asked with extreme politeness.

"I was thinking of our honeymoon . . . of Paris . . . of the fountain at the Place St. Michel . . . with those stone dolphins—yes, you've grown old and stodgy."

He hesitated but a second and then he said, "The hell you say—" and he was *in* the fountain, splashing me with water. "Come," he held out his arms. "Come and be my love."

"My dress," I protested, laughing.

"Ah, Buffy Ann, it's *you* who have grown old."

"That time in Paris . . . I wasn't wearing a three hundred dollar dress." Still, I wavered and finally I, too, was in the fountain, my tears and the magical spray intermingling as Todd's arms wrapped tightly about me . . . as if he were holding on for dear life.

20.

I unpacked, relieved to be back home. We had been gone only three days but it had been sufficient time for me to count my blessings. I took the perfume flask Suzannah had given me and placed it on my dressing table, and I thought about Suzannah's friend, Poppy, who had Suzannah's other gold flacon. I couldn't help but wonder what had happened to the girl from Kentucky after she had left Suzannah's.

Poppy returned to the High Roller Motel and found Herman lying on the bed sweating and fondling himself.

"What the hell do you think you're doing, Birdbrain?"

He grinned at her sheepishly.

"Do you think I carried you on my back to Las Vegas so you could lie there like a stale jug of piss and play with yourself?"

"Didn't have nothing else to do. You said I shouldn't leave the room."

"I told you a hundred fucking times—when I'm not here you rehearse, you practice. Over and over and over again, so you'll be ready."

"I been rehearsing, Poppy. Like you said. Over and over for weeks."

"Yeah? Well, Friday night you're singing. Your first fucking date in the big town and you sure as hell better be good 'cause I'm sick to death of hustling for a no-account hillbilly who don't know his prick from his asshole and got nothing better to do than to lie there playing with his ding-dong."

"I'm really gonna sing? I got an engagement? A real-honest-to-God engagement?"

"Yes, you clown. In the Silver Lode Lounge."

"Holy shit! How did you do it, Poppy?"

"Oh, Jesus, you make me want to puke. By working my ass off, you asshole. Now listen to me carefully. Tomorrow morning early, you're leaving for El Paso."

"Why am I going there?"

"To do somebody a favor. You do somebody a favor, they do you one. You're picking up a package and bringing it back here."

"Ain't you going with me?"

"No, I can't. I gotta take care of business. You want to sing Friday night, don'tcha?"

He nodded.

"Then just do as I say and don't fuck up the delivery. If you do, just don't show your fucking face around me ever again. And oh yeah, from now on your name's Beau Beaufort."

His eyes popped. "How come?"

" 'Cause it's prettier than Herman Beaufort, stupid!"

"Yeah, I guess so," he said, pleased. "Beau Beaufort . . . I like it, Poppy!"

"Jesus, ain't that super?"

"You really stunk tonight."

"I was up all night driving the pickup back from El Paso. For months now I been driving back and forth to El Paso. Back and forth. Back and forth. I'm wore out, Poppy."

"Listen. A week from Saturday you're singing at the Showboat. The Showboat is a real high-class place. If you're really hot that night, maybe you won't have to go to El Paso no more. I got some people coming to see you there so you better be hot. We're gonna bleach your hair yellow and before you sing your regular songs, I want you to do a couple of Elvis's early numbers, the ones he did when he was just starting out. And like Elvis, I want you to whirl your cock around up there, throwing your hips around like a crazy man."

"That ain't my style, Poppy. I'm strictly country."

"Oh, shit, you fucking moron, I'm so sick to death of you whining all the time. You'll do what I tell you. By a week from Saturday you be ready with these. . . ."

She pushed the musical arrangements literally into his face.

Beau strutted around the tiny dressing room in his new, tightly fitted sequined cowboy suit, tossing his newly yellowed hair back and forth. "Ain't this something now?" he admired his image in the mirror. "These here pants make my nuts look like watermelons."

"That's the idea, joker."

Poppy had a new outfit too. A black satin short skirt styled exactly like the jeans skirt she usually wore. And a black satin tube top. Under the skirt, she wore a pair of red lace panties, an item of clothing she seldom bothered with.

"Listen to me carefully, Beau. After you finish with the Elvis songs, I'm gonna take off my panties and throw them at you."

His eyes goggled. "What for?"

"You catch them, nuzzle them, lick them, rub them up against your cock, then you throw them back to me."

"What for?"

"Just do it! Then, if somebody else throws their panties at you, do the same thing. Kiss them, rub them, hump them, wipe your sweat with them! Then toss them back."

"But why do I want to do that with their shitty panties?"

"Just shut up and do it! We're going to be a sex symbol, dummy. Like Tom Jones. Like Elvis. You gotta knock yourself out up there, really tear that stage apart! Throw your Elvis-pelvis around like it was a rubber ball. Here," she rummaged in her purse. "Take these." She handed him a couple of red pills. Before he could ask her what they were, she said, "They'll give you a little extra pep up there so no one takes you for a corpse."

The panty-throwing bit worked as Poppy knew it would. Once she did it, she knew that the sex-starved old bitches sitting in the audience with their bald, fat hubbies, would do the same thing. And the pills had worked. Beau had been real frenzied up there. And the big boys in the black suits she had brought into the house saw it all come together, had seen a star born tonight. And she had done it! The Christmas season, 1970, and she, all by herself, had given the world a new star!

"Was I good tonight, Poppy? Those women liked me, didn't they? Didn't I do just like you said?"

"You weren't great," she said. "But you weren't bad either," she relented.

"Am I going to get a contract like you said?"

"I think so. If you don't fuck up. And if I work real hard. You better get in some sacktime now. Tomorrow night you're doing three shows."

"But I can't sleep now, Poppy. I'm so wound up I think I'm going to explode."

"Here," she handed him a capsule. "To help you unwind."

He grinned at her. "It's gonna take more than that."

"Take off your suit and hang it up. Then take that pill and lie down."

He did everything she told him. He always did.

"Now just close your eyes, you dumb fuck, and Poppy will put you to sleep."

As she worked him over with her tongue, he asked, "How long do you think it'll be before we get to Hollywood?"

21.

Todd had started work on our shopping center in June of 1970, and now, only eleven months later, we were officially opening the mall. True to his word, he really did commission a statue for a huge fountain positioned in the main plaza of the King Galleria, and it did look almost like me in a bronzy kind of fashion. The fountain itself was tiled in shades of almost every color of the rainbow, and surrounding the fountain were manicured English boxwood hedges bordering flowers of every possible hue.

"It's gorgeous," Suellen admitted. She and Howard had arrived in Akron that morning to be present for the opening ceremonies the following day.

"We didn't think the sculpture was going to be ready. It took the artist almost as long to complete it as it took to build the whole galleria."

"She's lovely, Buffy," Suellen said, gazing at the bronze figure. "And what a testament to Todd's feelings for you. He's even made an idol in your likeness."

"An idol? Really, Suellen! That's nonsense!" I protested but I was pleased just the same.

Proudly I walked Suellen around. "Todd's idea, as you can see, was to incorporate the old with the new. You know that arcade in Cleveland that was built around 1890? Todd's always loved it. So he told the architect to start with some of the arcade's old-fashioned charm and go on from there. So," I said pointing, "there we have Victorian balconies combined with all that expanse of glass. And we have those brass railings and white bleached wood in contrast with those beautiful old-fashioned overhead trusses. And the Doric columns in combination with the giant skylights. . . ."

"And trees and flowers everywhere—" Suellen helped me out.

"And the whole thing is temperature-controlled. Right now there are only a few shopping malls in the country that are totally enclosed like this one. They'll all do it eventually, but in the meantime we're a forerunner. Todd is an absolute prophet. And we're probably the only mall in the country that has a car dealership right in the midst of it all."

"It's breathtaking, really! And you have every right to be proud. You and Todd—"

"It's Todd alone that's responsible. He's a . . . visionary!"

Suellen smiled at my obvious pride. "Howard says that more than anything, Todd's a financial wizard . . . the wizard of Akron."

"I don't know. He makes it all seem so easy. As if almost anybody could have done it if he had put his mind to it."

"I don't believe that. And you really don't either. To pull off something like this—" she shook her head. "Todd's not even thirty yet and he started off with practically nothing."

I thought of the precious bankroll we had worked for during the years we were in school, and now it did seem like it was almost no money at all.

"I must say it was almost like the banks were dying to lend Todd money. And it seemed like everyone in the world wanted to be part of this—Why, Todd was selling leases even before the foundations were laid. And all the department stores wanted to have a branch here. Todd had to fight them off. Of course we owe enormous amounts of money—" and I giggled. "Really, one has to be very rich to owe as much as we do—"

"In the meantime, Todd is planning the mall in Columbus?"

"Yes. Did I tell you? It's going to be fashioned in the style of the Galleria Vittorio Emanuelle in Milan. Combined with American modern—"

"You two are certainly expanding your horizons."

I made a face. "I wish it were *I* who was expanding."

Suellen looked at me blankly for a moment. "Oh, you mean a baby . . ."

"Well, Megan is two-and-a-half and if I started a baby now, there'd be over three years difference in ages. But Todd wants to wait a while longer. He says he needs me. He doesn't have anyone else to rely on. Not someone he can absolutely depend on."

"Well, you have time, Buff. You're young. You *are* two years younger than I am, after all, and Petey will be four-and-a-half by the time *I* give birth."

"Oh, Suellen! You're pregnant and you didn't tell me?"

Suellen laughed. "I'm telling you now! And I hope it's a girl."

We joined Howard and Todd for lunch at the *Fleur de Lis* on the Boulevard St. Germain on the second level of the mall. "I have news for you, Suellen," Howard said, smiling nervously.

"Oh?" Suellen looked at him, and then at Todd, and then at me with a question in her eyes. She smiled tentatively. "Why do I have the feeling there's a conspiracy going on?"

She must be a witch, I thought. Wasn't it witches that always divined everything?

"Todd wants me to join him . . . in his business," Howard blurted out as if he couldn't hold the words in any longer. "He wants us to move here, to Akron."

Now Suellen looked from me to Todd as if we had in some way betrayed her.

"Meet the new Vice President of King Enterprises," Todd said, smiling broadly, as if he detected no adverse vibes at all from Suellen.

"I don't believe the three of you! To decide all this without even consulting me." She turned to me. "You! What did you say before? 'Poor me. I can't have another baby because Todd doesn't have anyone else he can rely on. . . .'"

"Oh Suellen, come on! It will be wonderful for all four of us. You'd think we were asking you and Howard to go to Siberia instead of—"

"The land of success and prosperity?" Suellen finished for me. "We aren't doing so badly in Cincinnati, you know. Howard is the assistant general manager at Ohio Security. We have a very nice house. It's not as grand as your new house but it's ours, and we've been very, very happy there."

"Todd has very generously offered to double the salary I've been making at Security," Howard said in a soft tone, apparently embarrassed at Suellen's reaction, although, obviously, he had anticipated it. "In addition, he's offered us a share in the company."

"Is this what you want, Howard? No. You don't have to answer that. Apparently it is." Suellen seemed more sad now than angry.

Todd took her hand. "You'll have a home here as lovely and as happy as you ever had. I promise you."

"Yes, Suellen," I piped in. "You will have a lovely home here. What's the problem? Don't you want to live close to us? After all, you're the only close family I have. You're like a mother to me—"

But I knew what the problem was. It was Suellen just resisting change. She always had.

"Where's your spirit of adventure, Suellen?" I brought up next. "You who were going to join the Peace Corps? Remember?"

She looked at me as if I had said something outrageous. "I was going to join the Peace Corps to try and help the disadvantaged of the world, *not* out of a spirit of adventure. We have our roots in Cincinnati. Our security."

I looked at Todd. Somehow, he had to say something that would convince her.

"*Real* security is only people, Suellen," Todd said, taking her hand again. "People you can count on."

"And you *know* you can count on us, Suellen," I added. "Your family and our family will be each other's security."

Suellen looked at Howard who looked back at her entreatingly. And I saw her face go soft. I knew what she was thinking. *I can deny Todd. I can even deny Buffy. But I cannot deny Howard.*

I knew then that it was over, and I could have cried with relief. Suellen living near me was the only important thing my good life had lacked. And now Todd had given her and her family to me too.

I jumped up, kissed Suellen, then Howard, and last but not least,

Todd. He beamed at me and called for the best wine in the house for we were truly celebrating. But hours later, Suellen was still not smiling.

"Oh, Suellen, what is it with you?" I asked, losing patience.

"It's *you*, Buffy! You and Todd. You two want *everything!* And nobody can have everything."

"You're wrong, Suellen. I don't want everything. I just want the people I love around me with all of us happy. Is that everything? Can that be wrong?"

"Oh Buffy, you still believe in only happy endings."

She was right. I did. As long as there was Todd, how could I not?

22.

That summer Leo's TV play starring Suzannah finally aired, a year after its inception. I was chagrined that we didn't get to see it. It wasn't a network production and although many local stations around the country were showing it, it wasn't being shown in our area. But Cleo called the following week to inform me that it had been a huge, unqualified success.

"And believe it or not, your friend Suzannah actually got good reviews."

"Great!" I was delighted for Suzannah.

"What Leo did was use her visually rather than giving her too many lines. He wrote the play around her central character and allowed her to move through the scenes as a presence, without letting her carry too much of the dialogue. Leo was writer, director *and* producer, you know, so everything was left entirely to him," Cleo told me with loyal pride. "And as a direct result of the play's success, Leo's received an offer to go to Hollywood."

As far as Leo was concerned, everyone had benefited from the success of his TV show. Everyone but him. Durell, who had sponsored the show, enjoyed a large spurt in the sale of Suzannah perfume; the station had received tremendous new interest from new sponsors, while Suzannah, unbelievably, had been offered a role in a legitimate theater presentation of an important play; but he himself had only received an offer to work for Goldman-Lessor Productions, a company that developed properties for prime time TV. Although it meant Hollywood, it was still TV. And it was the legitimate theater he lusted after!

He approached Suzannah, asked her to speak up for him, to *demand* him as director of her play. He told her that it was because of him and him alone that she was in a position to do this. It was he who had put her into this enviable position.

Suzannah practically laughed in his face. "The playwright would probably throw me off the stage if I asked for you—a TV director and not even network," she sneered. "And really, Leo, why do I need you?"

"Because it was my direction that kept the critics from tearing you apart."

"Oh really? I know what it is you want, Leo. You want everyone to think that I can't act without you. First on TV and then on the stage. You want to be credited with Suzannah's success, like Steiner and Garbo. Well, I'm not going to let you ride my coattails. And besides, what could you do for me in return?"

Leo fought to suppress his rage. "I'm going to sign a contract with Hollywood, which I would do *after* the play. And I would stipulate that you are to star in so many projects . . . two . . . three. Features. That's what you really want, isn't it? Movies?"

Suzannah laughed nastily. "Do you think I'm a fool? The whole town knows it's a TV contract you've been offered, not features. Big damn deal!" she said contemptuously.

He thought about strangling her. His hands itched with it. But he controlled himself. He said reasonably, "You need me, Suzannah. It was I who made you look good on TV. I'll know how to make you look good on the stage."

"You know shit, Mason! I don't need anybody to make me look good. And besides, all your promises stink! You promised to help with Paulie and what happened? He's still on my back and he's still vomiting all over my living room rug. That job you promised to get him . . . it lasted all of one week—"

"I tried. Was it my fault he showed up dead drunk the first day?"

"And how about those shots from that damn quack? You almost killed him! I wanted him off my back, not dead!"

"He wasn't supposed to drink with those shots. Everybody except that moron knows you're not supposed to mix tranquilizers with alcohol."

"Nobody told him it was injections of *drugs* that he was getting. He thought it was vitamins—*you* implied it was vitamins."

"What are you trying to pull, Suzannah? *You* knew it wasn't vitamins. *Everybody* knew it wasn't vitamins."

"No, I didn't." But she didn't sound positive. "To get back to my original premise, Leo, why do I need you? Actually," she laughed, "I think it was *I* who made *you* look good."

He wanted to take her by the scruff of the neck and slam her head against the wall. "You're going to fall flat on your face, you'll see! You'll come begging me to put you in something in Hollywood! And you know what? I'll piss on you!"

"But I don't want to move to L.A., Leo. I don't want to leave my mother, my friends, my job. . . . My job!" she wailed. "I'm getting another promotion, Leo. They promised me that—It's not fair, Leo," she pleaded.

"It's not fair either that I write a play, direct it, produce it, make that bitch Suzannah look like a star, and she gets to do legitimate theater and I don't. Either I go to Hollywood and work for Goldman-Lessor or I stay here and keep on with this cockamamie station, and there's no way that I'm going to do *that*. If I can't have the stage I'm going to have Hollywood. And not you or your stupid little job are going to keep me from it. If your job means so much to you, why don't *you* stay?"

He slammed into the bedroom and she ran after him. "You don't mean that, Leo!"

"The hell I don't. The more I think about it, the more I realize that going to L.A. is exactly what I want. They can stuff the *theatuh* up their asses. Milty Sears went to L.A. last year and he's living the life. Sun. Tennis. Parties with heads of studios. Lunches at Chasen's. That's where it's happening. There, not here. Here, there's only decay. Look out the window. What do you see? Dirty streets. Gray faces. Derelicts. Not palm trees and orange blossoms. I won't stay in TV for long once I get out there. I'll meet the right people and before you know it, I'll be doing features. And if it means more to you to stay here in your lousy job, well, what can I say except good luck!"

To emphasize his words he started pulling suitcases out of the closet. Cleo panicked. "When do you intend to leave?" *Her marriage! Her apartment! Her beautiful furniture!*

He smiled at her maliciously. "Changing your mind? Coming along for the ride?"

It took her a few seconds to answer. "I'm coming along because our marriage means something to me," she said as quietly as she could and with as much dignity as she could muster.

"Then you better give your bosses notice. I'm leaving next week."

"But why so fast?"

"If I'm going, I'm going. Why kill more time here? But if you're more worried about your employers than about me—" His words hung in the air.

"No, Leo, of course I'm not," she said quickly. "You know—I bet Judson knows somebody at one of the studios. I bet I can get a job in the story department at one of them. There's no reason I shouldn't be able to—It's a related field. I—"

So, you think you're going to out-perform me in Hollywood, do you? That you're going to go to work at one of the big studios while I try to fight my way out of TV? No way! he told himself.

"I don't think you'd better bother, Cleo. I don't think you're going to have the time."

"Why not? What do you mean?"

"I think it's time we had a family. A man with a family, a real family, that is . . . gets more respect on the Coast. They think he's solid, not a flake. And California is a great place to raise a kid. Kids grow big and beautiful there. It must be the sunshine and the o.j. And we'll need a house there. Anybody who's anybody there lives in a house, not an apartment. A house with palm trees outside. And a house means you have to decorate. But you're good at that, Cleo. It's one of the things you're so good at. . . ."

One of the things you're so good at? Now, what did that mean? Cleo wondered.

"And after we have the house, we're going to have to entertain," Leo went on. "A lot more than we do here. That's how business is done in Hollywood. At parties and around the swimming pool. So you can see you're going to be pret-ty bus-y. Pret-ty bus-y. And I want you to go to work for some of those charity organizations. All the big parties there are charity things. So you see," he smiled happily, "you're going to be much too busy to work."

"What about the money, Leo? All that is going to take a lot of money. A lot of *mon-ey,*" she aped him. "We'll *need* my salary."

"*Your* salary? Peanuts. Pea-nuts. Goldman-Lessor is offering me *two thou* a week. This is no shitty local TV station. This is the big time. And that's only the beginning. Five thou a week is the kind of salaries they

pay out there. With options. With percentages. With a piece of the gross
. . ." he was warming up.

"But you want to buy a house, Leo. We don't have anything saved
up."

He thought a moment. "In California, you buy a house for a couple
of hundred thousand but you put down a thousand. Don't you know
anything?" Then, "I have an idea, Cleo. I know how hard it is for you
to give up everything here. Why don't you ask your mother if she wants
to come along? She could live with us for a while until she gets her own
place. She probably could sell that house in Tenafly for big bucks and
find herself a nice condo. And she could help you with the baby."

Help me with the baby? I'm not even pregnant yet. But yes, her
mother would probably like to go to California; she would probably
enjoy a change. And her mother was so crazy about Leo. Cleo
shrugged. What was she complaining about? Life in Hollywood the way
Leo described it didn't sound all that bad. As a matter of fact, it
sounded like fun. And after she had the baby and had the house all
done and had everything under control with a good housekeeper, why
then she could always go back to doing something. Anyhow, it did
sound like the good life.

23.

By the time Christmas rolled around, Suellen had forgiven me for having dragged her to Akron. She had settled in, joined the local chapter of
the women's movement, became active in the PTA at Petey's prekinder-
garten, and gave a cottage party for an aspirant to the school board only
three days before she gave birth to Rebecca.

Cleo, who had moved to the West Coast, had better luck at getting
pregnant than I had. Her Christmas card gave me that news. Also, she
was really up about life on the Coast. And she was *so* looking forward
to the baby, as were Leo and her mother.

And before I could count the months, it seemed it was almost summer again and time to send a present to Joshua Mason, born in the land
of the setting sun. I bought the gift at the HeavenSent shop in our newly

completed Galleria Via Veneto in Columbus, and a couple of weeks later I received a thank-you letter from Cleo.

The Masons
570 N. Palm Drive
Beverly Hills, California
June 10, 1972

Dear Buffy,

We just adore the darling carriage cover and pillow set you sent baby Joshua. It will go beautifully with the pram Leo ordered from England. Needless to say, in Beverly Hills, English prams are as *de rigueur* as German cars (except for the Rolls, of course). To tell you the truth it beats the hell out of me why all the Jews here want to drive German cars but to each his own, I guess.

We have moved into our new house— a really lovely hacienda. Two-story. As you can see from our new address (please note), we are on Palm Drive in the north flats. That's the *right* side of town. However, we are not north enough to please Leo. We're in the 500 block but the higher you go the more prestigious the address. Leo won't be completely satisfied until we go to at least 800. But Leo says the (N.) 500 block is better than being in the Valley. I tell him that Bob Hope lives in the Valley and everyone knows he's richer than God. Leo says that's okay for Bob because everyone says he owns *half* the Valley. (It's the San Fernando Valley that I'm talking about.)

Needless to say, we have a swimming pool. (Leo doesn't even know how to swim but he wanted a pool for looks if nothing else.) (Also a spa.) A pool is nice for entertaining. And we are already doing that. We moved into the house when Josh was only three weeks old but Leo said he *needed* a housewarming immediately because he had to entertain a particular executive producer. (He wanted a particular assignment.) And there we were with the house only partially furnished, and certainly not decorated. Luckily Mother is still with us or I never would have managed what with the baby and all.

Leo, as you can remember, is *such* a perfectionist. He wanted the house to be just so, and there we were with only a week to prepare! And five nights before the party he walked through the house and yelled, "More lamps! This place is like a morgue! We need more lamps!" I tried to explain that accessories such as lamps really take more searching-out time than regular furniture takes. But would you believe it? The very

next day I went out and *found* eight lamps! And then just two days
before the party, Leo decided that the color of the sofa in the den was
wrong, that it would have to be recovered in time for the party. There
was no arguing with him. I knew there was no way that I was going to
find anyone insane enough to slipcover that sofa in two days so I just
stayed up the whole night through and cut out and *pinned* a new cover
into place and just crossed my fingers that nobody'd sit down and get a
pin up his ass.

I *did* have the house ready in time. And Leo said: "See! See what you
can do once you put your mind to it. All you have to do is put yourself
behind it, like I do!" I wanted to kill him just a little, but to tell the
truth, I thought he would kill *me* when the caterers *didn't show up* the
day of the party! Kill me or have a heart attack himself. Those idiots
(the caterers) got their dates mixed up. I couldn't really blame Leo for
being so upset. There we were with a hundred and fifty people coming
and no food! I did the only thing I could think of—I ran right over to
Nate and Al's (that's *the* delicatessen here—real New York-style corned
beef) and bought out the store. Then I went to Ah Fong's (the Chinese
restaurant next door) and bought every egg roll and barbecued rib
they'd give me, and we had those for hors d'oeuvres. Luckily, the caterer did send some people over to serve. (I had to threaten them that if
they didn't I would badmouth them all over town.)

Anyhow, it turned out to be a beautiful affair. The party was around
the pool and the weather was divine and Joshua didn't cry once and
Leo did get the show he was after.

As I mentioned Mother is still with us but she has bought a condo on
Wilshire (two bedroom) and will move when the complex is finished.
She's been a big help. She gave us the down payment for the house. She
has generally been very supportive. She's always loved Leo and *she's*
one of the few people Leo likes. And it's so cute—Leo is encouraging
Mother to have a face-lift. And what's really funny is that Leo has
gotten Mother a couple of dates! It's really tough on over-forty women
here. There are so many gorgeous young things floating around who
only go out with older, *substantial* men who can do something for them.
(I guess that's nothing new.) Practically every one of the older men Leo
works with has dumped the little woman he started out with for something young and tender. And there's just no place for these older
women to go. No one wants to date them and all they can do is cling to
what they have, which is usually the old homestead and the charge
accounts. No one even invites them to parties. Of course Mother has

always kept herself up. Who knows? Maybe with a face-job she *will* be able to latch on to somebody. But they say a lift only takes about ten years off. And if Mother looks in her early forties, I don't know if that's good enough to do the job. Not in Hollywood!

I invited Cassie to our housewarming. And she and the hunk came. She was kind of quiet and pale. She just had another miscarriage, you know. Poor Cassie. She's my idea of the poor little rich girl. She always seems so down, although most women would give their eyeteeth to have Guy Savarese in bed with them every night. And believe me, you have to know L.A. to realize how her mother is regarded out here. Like the Queen Mother herself. Her name's on every charity in town and if it isn't, you know that it's a charity not worth cultivating. Of course, Madame Hammond's society world is *not* the entertainment world. When you see Guy Savarese you wonder why he hasn't made it. He seems like such a natural. (Leo is convinced he *will* make it.) There *is* a certain truculent air to him, although truculent's not exactly the word I'm searching for—You just get the feeling when you talk to him that he doesn't much like you . . . or the whole world for that matter. When you write to Cassie, don't mention that I said that, please. I want us to be friends. In Hollywood, one learns to value real friendship for there's so little of it. But don't get me wrong . . . I love Hollywood!

It *is* fun out here and I hope you and Todd will come out to visit. Maybe you'll like it so much you'll want to build a King's Galleria out here. All my love to Todd and Megan and Suellen and Howard and their two kids. It must be wonderful for you to have Suellen living near you. I envy you having a sister to share things with. But of course, I do have Mother.

Love as always and forever,

Cleo

All in all, it seemed like Cleo was doing well in Hollywood and was happy. As I was. I was finally pregnant and the new mall seemed bound for success and I had Todd and Megan (not to mention Leah) to look at every day, to remind me to count my blessings. And not far away were Suellen and Howard and their children. As far as Suellen was concerned she had the perfect family for the seventies—two children, one of each kind. I thought about Cassie. I would have to write her right away to tell her how sorry I was about her miscarriage . . . to let her know I was thinking about her. And I would have to write to Suzannah too. Her play had just opened in New York and closed a day later.

Poor Suzannah! Her stage debut had been a horrendous personal disaster—the critics had really chewed her up. "Stinkbomb laid by the lady of perfume." "After a whiff of Suzannah what the stage needs next is a breath of fresh air." "As an actress, Ms Suzannah makes a breathtaking mannequin. She should be emoting in a department store window." One critic bothered to elucidate: "Leonard Mason, who has departed New York for what one assumes are greener fields in Hollywood, has been proven an intelligent director-playwright by his absence. Directing Suzannah for the TV screen, in the vehicle he himself wrote, Mason wisely chose to let the action and dialogue center about the beauteous model-actress rather than to rely on her oh-so-meager talents to carry the play. Would that Ron Hershey, the author, and Bob Kurtz, the director of *Exits* had had the sense to emulate him. But in the absence of *their* wisdom, one wishes that someone would have advised Suzannah to stick to her perfumes and creams, or perhaps, like Mr. Mason, depart for Hollywood where they would appreciate her cinematic beauty far more than her thespian qualities."

Still I was sure that Suzannah would pick herself up and go back to her commercials and the pages of *Vogue* and *Harper's Bazaar* while she worked out her next move. Nothing could be a total disaster for Suzannah . . . especially when she still had her Durell contract.

24.

I was three months pregnant when Suzannah's terrible call came. Paulie was *dead!*

Oh no, not dear, sweet Paulie!

An accident, Suzannah said. A fatal accident. A fatal combination of drugs and alcohol. . . .

At first it was I who felt the need to comfort Suzannah. "She wants us to come to New York immediately," I told Todd. "She said that she needs us to help her get through the next few days."

And at first it was Todd who resisted. "Needs us? She doesn't need anybody. Not Suzannah! She's got herself. That's all she needs. It's Paulie, God damn it, who needed somebody, and now it's too late for him." And he sat down, buried his face in his hands and cried.

"Oh Todd, she sounded so crushed. Not like Suzannah at all. I think she really does need us."

"And what about you? I don't want you upset when you're pregnant—"

"I'm fine. Really. I'll be fine."

We flew out that night. And I didn't suspect that in the next couple of days it would be Todd who would be urging me to be supportive, instead of the other way around.

"The police are investigating," Suzannah said furiously. "They're determined to call it a suicide. What does it matter to them anyway whether it was an accidental combination of drugs and alcohol, or suicide? As long as it wasn't murder. It couldn't be suicide anyway. Everyone says that in suicide, there's always a note. And there *wasn't* any note. No note!"

Suzannah looked marvelous in black. Black with a superb string of pearls. She was a bit thinner than when I had seen her last, if that were possible, and her face was especially pale and drawn so that the yellow cat-eyes appeared overly large. Yes, she looked marvelous, which I found myself resenting. How dare she look so exquisite with Paulie lying in the cold, cold morgue?

"He was completely out of control," Suzannah cried, trying to enlist our sympathy for *her*. "Completely unmanageable. And I warned him. You know I warned him," she started to sob. "Every single day I told him that drugs and alcohol were a lethal combination. I told him he was fooling around with dynamite, defiling his body. And it was true. If he hadn't defiled his body, he would still be here, wouldn't he?" she asked piteously. Her mascara began to run and somehow, this small display of imperfection gratified me. She shouldn't be so perfect with Paulie lying dead. . . .

"I just thank God that he didn't commit suicide, that there *wasn't* any note. It was an accidental overdose . . . a combination of—" She broke off in the middle of the sentence. "Still, there *is* a cloud hanging over my reputation now. Everyone will think we were lovers and—"

That was the remark that did it for me.

"What do you mean—*think* you were lovers? That's the most ridiculous statement I've ever heard. What would you expect people to think, for God's sake? You and Paulie were living together for years. Do you think they thought you were holding hands? He sacrificed his career for yours right from the start. For God's sake, he sacrificed his *life* for yours and don't you ever forget it!"

She fell back on the couch from the velocity of my attack. "Buffy, how can you? You of all people. You know how fond I really was of Paulie . . . you *must* know how I feel."

Todd put a calming hand on my shoulder, his eyes clouded over with anxiety from the intensity of my reaction. And he looked at Suzannah now with concern too, convinced of her true grief.

She spoke to him. "I know Buffy doesn't believe it but it's the truth. We weren't *exactly* lovers. The only times I went to bed with Paulie were under duress. When he was drunk and forced me to—When I couldn't refuse him because I was afraid of what he might do. I never once did it with him willingly. . . ." she told Todd almost with a hint of pride in her voice.

I became enraged all over again. *What the hell is she so proud of?* That Paulie was dead and never once when he was alive had she—his goddess—given herself to him, if not with love, at least with respect and affection?

I felt sick. Todd had been right. We never should have come. She deserved no consideration. I got to my feet. I waited for Todd to get up too. He did, but hesitantly. He looked from me back to Suzannah, his expression clearly saying that we had to be sure that we were doing the right thing in leaving.

I saw panic on Suzannah's face once she realized we were thinking of leaving. She rose quickly, came toward me, her face entreating and her arms extended. She stumbled and fell. "Buffy!" she screamed, on her knees now, her fingers clutching at my dress. "You can't leave me now. I don't have anybody else. Even Wes has deserted me. Especially Wes, that bastard! He's so afraid of his goddamn name being connected with me! Nobody here really knew Paulie, like he was . . . how it was for all of us together . . . the good times before Paulie—That's why I need you two here. You two remember—"

I wasn't sure of anything now. I looked at Todd. He nodded at me encouragingly, put his arm around me, and then helped Suzannah to her feet.

"What hurt me most is that Paulie never realized his dream," she smiled at me now, begging me with her eyes to join her in her lament. "He never did get to Hollywood. . . ."

She tore at her hair. "He loved the movies so much." She looked entreatingly at Todd. "You remember, don't you? How he always talked about the movies and the old-time stars. He wanted so much to be part of it. He wanted to go there and write about it all . . . to tell the whole world about the fantasy of it all."

We all sat down again.

"Oh, how I wish we had gone there instead of New York," she went on in a hushed voice now. "Maybe it would all have turned out differently."

How could it? Would you have loved him more? Would you have used him less? Would it have served Paulie more to die in Hollywood of drugs and alcohol and broken dreams instead of New York?

Todd consoled her, sent her into the bedroom to get herself a fresh handkerchief. When she left the room he said softly, "We came to see Suzannah through this thing and we will, no matter what. Even if she failed Paulie, we won't fail her. It's not a question anymore of Suzannah, is it? It's more who *we* are."

I never could fault Todd's reasoning. He seemed always able to cut through everything and get to the bottom line. *What kind of people were we? One didn't judge, one only tried to help.* I thanked God silently for letting me be the one to find Todd.

When Suzannah came back into the room Todd said, "If there had been a note, it would have been foolish of you to keep it. And really unnecessary. But there was no note . . ."

"I told you," Suzannah said, her eyes big. "There was no note."

"Yes you did. That's what I meant. *If* there had been one—"

Once the coroner's office gave their verdict of death by accidental overdose, the services were held. It seemed there was no family. There was only Suzannah as closest of kin. And I thought the worst of it was over for all of us. But Suzannah, receiving callers, was beset with a new terror.

"Geoffrey Durell didn't come to the funeral," she wailed, all the color drained from her face. "He hasn't been here at all."

So Suzannah was no longer mourning the betrayal of her married politician-lover. Now it was Geoffrey Durell she was concerned with.

"Maybe he's sick. Maybe he's been out of town on business," I offered by way of consolation.

"No. It's the scandal. Suicide or not, it's still a scandal, a black mark on my name. And he was about to renew my contract. And it was going to be an even better one than before. They were getting ready with a big promotion for a new shampoo . . . *my* shampoo. They were going to call it Redhead!" she cried. "Geoffrey's absence means he's not going to do it. He doesn't want his company to be associated with me anymore! Oh, damn Paulie!" Then she looked at me aghast at her words, and then at Todd whose face was tight. "I didn't mean that like it sounded. I just meant that I need him so! I miss him so! If only he were here. He was so sweet, especially when I fell on my face in that goddamn play. So sweet . . ."

She turned to Todd. "Todd, you're so smart. Tell me what to do. I *need* the new contract. That Broadway play hurt me. You know how people are. When you fail at just one little thing they don't want to know you. They're afraid the failure will rub off on them."

Todd thought only a moment before he offered to have the King Gallerias declare Suzannah week, where every appropriate shop in each Galleria would carry and push the Suzannah line, with a special push for the new shampoo. And they would have additional related promotions, with Suzannah herself making appearances, with entertainment—maybe a whole line of dancing redheads. That would mean something to the Durell people. The Gallerias were constantly being besieged by various companies for that kind of promotion, many more than they could possibly accommodate.

Suzannah hugged him. "Oh, that's wonderful of you, Todd. And it should count for a lot. But I don't know if it will be enough to counter—"

Todd licked his lips as if they were very dry. "There is something else you can do. I'm surprised you haven't thought of it yourself. It's the oldest one in the books."

"What? What?" Suzannah asked eagerly.

"Have you ever slept with Durell?"

Suzannah flushed. "I . . ." She looked at me. She had told me the last time we were in New York that she had. She couldn't very well deny it now. "On occasion . . . on *rare* occasion."

"Then do it again quickly," Todd said flatly. "Then tell him you're pregnant. It's an offer most men can't refuse. And pray that you can bring it off."

I couldn't believe my ears. Was Todd kidding? No, I guessed that he wasn't.

Suzannah's eyes lit up as she smiled delicately, lowered her lashes. "He'll have to divorce his wife."

We were going back to Akron the first thing in the morning. We stared into the Plaza fountain morosely. Neither one of us was about to jump into it tonight, especially since I had had those vague pains in the area of my uterus all day.

"If she succeeds in weaning Durell away from his wife, there'll be blood on our hands," I said mournfully to Todd.

"I know," he moaned. "I can't forgive myself. But I didn't think—I had no idea he was married, did you?"

"No . . . I don't recall that she ever—" I felt a sharp pain and then there was another. And I recognized the pain this time. It was a labor pain!

God help us, Todd! The blood isn't on our hands at all! It's between my thighs.

I turned to my husband. "I think I'm having a miscarriage," I started to cry. "And it's not my fault," I said, bewildered. "I didn't do anything I shouldn't have—"

Suzannah came to visit me in the hospital room.

"Oh, Buffy," she wailed. "I feel so guilty. If you hadn't come to New York—"

"Yes, Suzannah, but nobody's responsible," I said tiredly, not even wanting to bother reassuring *her*. "They say that almost all miscarriages are nature's way of aborting its mistakes. That's the way I'll have to look at it. It just wasn't meant to be."

I wasn't sure that I believed what I was saying. *Had* I traded my baby for the one that Suzannah was going to trick Geoffrey Durell into siring? Was this nature's revenge for Todd's part in the conspiracy to save Suzannah's contract? If it was, it was one hell of a trade.

"How long do you have to stay here?"

"I'm going home tomorrow."

"Oh, how I wish you lived here in New York so we could see each other all the time."

I did not reply.

"I'm really so lonely, Buffy. I don't have anybody now. I miss Paulie so. I had no idea how much I would miss him. Do you know how much I miss him?"

I didn't answer again and she sat down on the bed. I saw that she was not as well groomed as usual. "You really miss someone who loved you *that* much." She lay back on the bed next to me and I moved a few inches so that her head could share the pillow. "Nobody will ever love me that much again."

She was right. Nobody would ever love her again the way Paulie had and now that she realized it—too late for the knowledge to help either her or Paulie—her loss was all the more terrible. And did it matter all that much who loved whom more? Love given or love received? It still was love lost.

I had Todd and Megan, and next year I would have another baby. And Suzannah's loss was forever. My hand crept out from under the covers and found hers.

Still that date, August 20, 1972, would always be engraved in my mind. My sister Suellen always referred to 1963 as the year Jack Kennedy died, and the year 1968 as the year Bobby died. For me 1972 would always be the year I lost my baby and Paulie died.

25.

When Suzannah married Geoffrey Durell, after his wife divorced him in Santo Domingo, even the Ohio newspapers carried the story.

"Now she has everything, doesn't she?" Suellen asked, not expecting an answer. "Big career, all that Durell money and her own shampoo, not to mention that Suzannah perfume being piped into *our* shopping malls. I was shopping at the Galleria yesterday and the whole place reeked of it. I could scarcely breathe."

I laughed at Suellen's exaggeration. "Todd promised her a big promotion. And she doesn't have *all* the Durell money, only half of it. Mrs. Durell, the first one that is, got a very large settlement, I understand."

"I don't care. It just doesn't seem right," Suellen persisted. "She practically killed Paulie single-handedly, she made you lose your baby, she broke up a marriage that had lasted forty years, and she still ends up with everything."

"For one, I think I would've lost the baby even if I didn't go to New York. Second, Paulie, in the final analysis, was responsible for his own life. And you know what they say—no one can break up a healthy marriage."

I really believed this to be true, but it still didn't keep me from feeling guilty about the first Mrs. Durell. And there was no way I was going to tell Suellen of Todd's part in the matter.

"And furthermore, I *am* pregnant again, so I don't even want to think about that baby. That would be to deny the baby I'm carrying now. After all, if I had had *that* child I wouldn't be having this one."

If Suzannah had really made good on the lie she'd told Geoffrey Durell, she and I would be giving birth about the same time, give or take a month. Of course Suzannah had to hope for a premature baby or convince Mr. Durell that really late babies ran in her family . . . late, late babies. I had to smile—the idea of Suzannah with a protruding belly was enough to give one pause.

But a few weeks later, Suzannah called to say that she had suffered a miscarriage and was off to Acapulco where Geoffrey was taking her to recuperate.

"She *was* pregnant then?" Todd asked me when I told him about the call. "She *did* become pregnant?" It was as if he were seeking some kind of justification for the heartless advice he had given her.

"I don't know for sure. She told me she had the mis and I didn't question it." Poor Todd. He would never forgive himself for his part in the whole sorry business. Suzannah had managed to draw him into her duplicity and left him forever in some tiny way marred . . . in some tiny way a damaged hero. But all of us were living life, after all, and not some fairy tale.

The King Galleria in Cleveland and the firstborn King male heir made their debut the same week. I named my son Mitchell, instead of Todd as I had planned, after Howard mentioned that in the Jewish religion, a child was named after a deceased person, and although we weren't Jewish, I was taking no chances with Todd's life.

And I didn't want to tempt fate by going to Venice either, which was where Todd wanted us to go immediately for a brief fling. He had an idea about doing a new galleria in a Venetian motif. He said that there was no reason we shouldn't go—we had a nurse to see to baby Mitchell and Leah to look after Megan and the new house—a Georgian colonial this time—and Howard to look after the business.

"What do you mean it's tempting fate if we go to Venice?" he demanded.

"People say: 'See Venice and die.' "

He laughed. "The expression goes 'See Naples and die,' and 'See Venice and fall in love.' In our case it would be: 'Fall in love all over again.' "

"Are you sure?"

"Absolutely. Venice is a city for lovers."

"All right. I'll take your word for it." Hadn't I always?

When we returned Todd was full of ideas for the new galleria to be situated in Cincinnati. It would feature canals laid out between gardens of extra-spectacular beauty and gondola rides.

"Fantastic. Will you charge admission?"

"I'm not sure," Todd said in dead earnest. "I'd like not to—but if we don't, the same people would probably hog the gondolas and the others would never get to ride at all. The greedy ones spoil it for everybody."

Yes, I could see that. Greedy people did tend to spoil things for everybody else.

"I have an idea of my own. If I start now, I could have another baby ready for the Cincinnati opening!"

He had to smile at my enthusiasm. "You just *had* a baby."

"Yes, that's true."

"So what's the big rush?"

"We *are* planning on five, aren't we? You already have three shopping malls and I have only two children. I have to hurry to catch up before you run out of cities."

"I didn't know this was a race. Besides, there are other states after we've used up Ohio. What are you going to do when we have ten shopping malls? Or twelve? And what about poor Leah? How many kids can she handle?"

"That's her problem. Whenever I mention hiring more help around here she tells me to go to work and let her worry about the house and children. She says, 'Mister King might needs you to help tend his business but I'm managing fine with mine.' Maybe it's time you argued with her. She respects *you*—"

"Are you crazy? I wouldn't do battle with Leah even if you promised to make love to me tonight."

"How about if I sweeten the deal? Tonight *and* tomorrow night *and* the night after that *and*—" I whispered in his ear.

He laughed heartily. "I'm weakening . . ."

Nonetheless, Leah was not persuaded into allowing more help into the house. Rather it was I who was persuaded—into waiting a while before becoming with child again.

26.

The New Year, 1974, came in with a bang.

"Suzannah called," I told Todd. "She's coming for a visit."

He looked at me with raised eyebrows. "Did she say why?"

"No. She's coming tomorrow."

"Oh? How long is she staying?"

"She didn't say."

"Well, I'm leaving for Cincinnati first thing in the morning, but I'll be back the next day in case you need me."

Now I looked at him with raised eyebrows. "Do you anticipate some kind of problem that I might not be able to handle alone?"

"Of course not. Why? Do *you?*"

The advent of a visit from Suzannah seemed to be making us both anxious.

She was all in black—mink, silk blouse, wool suit, even the "Garbo" slouched fedora. It was more than a year-and-a-half since Paulie's death, so it was all right for me to say in jest, "You look like you're in mourning."

"Maybe I am," Suzannah offered cryptically, looking around the entrance hall, peeking into the French blue and ecru formal drawing room. With silvered fingertips she touched the Sèvres vase that reposed on a Regency table decorated with bronze gilt. "An antique?"

"Yes."

"You're really rich, aren't you?" she asked in astonishment.

I smiled. In some ways, Suzannah hadn't changed at all. "Hasn't anyone told you it's bad form to ask somebody how much money they have?"

She threw back her head and laughed heartily. "Oh, Buffy, you know me. I never did have any manners. I told you, honey child. I'm just a redneck from old K.Y." She hadn't given me that line in a long time.

"Sure you are. That neck of yours looks like pure alabaster to me."

She looked at me hard. "That's sweet of you, Buff. But then, you always were sweeter to me than I deserved."

"Come on, Suzannah, what is this? Humility week? It doesn't become you. Let's go into the den and relax. You can take off your hat or even your shoes. Then you can tell me why this sudden visit. Or first, you can see Megan and Mitchell, if you like."

We went into the den. "Of course I want to see your children." She threw herself down on the leather sofa. "But first, I'd like a glass of white wine, please. A very dry wine with a twist of lemon—"

"Wine? You? How about that temple you wouldn't defile with alcohol?"

"I've read that white wine is good for the digestion," she said primly. "And my goodness, fiddle-dee-dee . . . what's the big fuss over one little glass of wine?"

"No fuss. What's with the fiddle-dee-dee? Why, honey chile, that expression will not do for New York's top model. That expression is gone with the wind."

"Oh, Buffy," she burst into tears. "It's *all* gone with the wind. . . ."

I installed the almost hysterical Suzannah in our green and white guestroom, put her to bed, pulled the green satin comforter around her thin shoulders.

"I didn't see the children yet," she protested as she sobbed.

"That's okay, you'll see them later. I'll get you your glass of wine and then we'll have a nice long talk."

She grabbed at my hand. "Don't go. Don't leave me. Sit down here next to me . . ." she said piteously, the sobs distilling sniffles. Then, abruptly the sobs stilled. "My goodness, don't you even have a maid to fetch and carry?"

I laughed. "Fetch and carry? Sherman marched through Atlanta a hundred years ago, remember? No more fetching and carrying. I *do* have a part-time cleaning lady plus a housekeeper named Leah, but she's not exactly into bowing and scraping. Sometimes, if I ask very carefully, she may agree to do as I ask."

"You never were assertive enough," Suzannah sniffed. "And if I had your money I'd have a dozen lackeys."

"*If?* I would bet that Geoffrey Durell has a thousand times more money than we do."

"But that's gone with the wind too," and she burst into a fresh torrent of tears.

"All right, Suzannah, tell me all about it."

"I did what Todd told me to. I went to bed with Geoffrey at the first opportunity and believe me, it wasn't easy. I had never done it with Geoffrey before in a manner that would enable me to say I'd gotten pregnant, if you know what I mean. I mean for him to get an erection stiff enough to stick it in, well never mind. I *did* it and a couple of weeks later I told him I was with child. And Geoffrey was thrilled out of his cotton-pickin' mind. His wife had been as barren as an abandoned sparrow's nest. It was enough for him to come in his undies just thinkin' about all this virility he never knew he had before—enough virility to makc a baby. It blew his mind! But at first he refused to divorce his wife. It seems she was . . . is . . . an invalid. What he had in mind was to provide for me and the unborn heir with trusts and stuff, and maybe after his wife died—if she died—Well, a hell of a lot of good that would have done me considering I *wasn't* pregnant. Not to mention canceling my contract once he found out the truth. So naturally I told him that either he marry me right away or I'd have to have an abortion. Well, he wasn't willing to kiss off his proof of virility that easy. He was desperate enough to talk his wife somehow into going to Santo Domingo for the quickie and we were married immediately. And three weeks after that, I told him I'd miscarried—"

"But I thought you were going to try and *get* pregnant right away and tell him that late babies ran in your family. You were only going to use the miscarriage story *if* you weren't able to get pregnant—"

Suzannah smiled in a strange way and her eyes rolled upward in a peculiar fashion as if she were going into a convulsion. It was chilling.

"That was assuming one *could* get pregnant in a certain period of time." She still had that funny smile on her lips.

I didn't understand what it was she was getting at but I stayed quiet, waiting for her to go on.

"After I told him I miscarried he wanted me to get pregnant again. I kept telling him that the doctor said no . . . that my health wouldn't permit it. Finally, after months of that, he spoke to my gynecologist without my knowledge and found out. . . ."

"He found out that you were never pregnant?"

"No. He found out that I never *could have been* pregnant—"

I stared at her, not speaking.

"He found out that I was empty inside."

"Empty?"

"He found out that I had had a hysterectomy—"

"Oh my God, Suzannah!" My heart went out to her. "I never knew. When?"

"I had an abortion a while back. I told you about it. Remember? It was soon after that."

"But what was wrong? Was it?—" I was terrified for her, terrified even to say the word.

"No. It wasn't a . . . tumor or anything." Her eyes rolled upward again, making me sick to my stomach. "Nothing was wrong. It was just the surest way I knew never to get pregnant again."

My mouth fell open as I stared at her bewildered. "You mean you *chose* to have a hysterectomy? It was your choice?" Surely I had misunderstood her.

She nodded, smiling foolishly. She put her hand to her mouth as she spoke, as if she were saying something a little funny. "The latest in birth control."

"But that's crazy! It's criminal. My God! Why didn't you take the Pill?"

She opened her eyes wide. "But the Pill is hormones, Buffy. I would never fool around with hormones. Don't you know you can get cancer fooling around with hormones? I hope *you* don't take the Pill, Buffy darling," she said, her eyes entreating.

"You could have had your tubes tied," I said harshly.

"I heard of a girl who had her tubes tied and got pregnant anyway. Besides, it sounded so awful . . . so messy."

Messy? I felt as if she and I were two inmates having a discussion in an asylum.

"I thought . . ." she paused for a breath. "I thought this way seemed so *clean.*"

I turned away. I found it difficult to look at her and not want to slap her face.

"Where are you going?" she asked in a panic.

"Downstairs. To get you your wine and me a double vodka."

Maybe the wine *was* good for her digestion, and how badly could it damage her damn temple now anyway?

For the next few days Suzannah lolled about in dressing gowns, each more lavish than the last.

"What's going on?" Todd asked. "Isn't she ever going to get dressed again?"

"I don't know. She's recuperating."

"But she's not sick, is she? What exactly is she recuperating from?"

"Being thrown out on her backside. It's a terrible malaise."

The first morning Suzannah was with us Leah had brought her breakfast on a tray while the bedridden guest languished against the pillows. The next morning she waited in vain while Leah muttered into her kitchen sink, "I'm sicker than that one is."

After the second day, she refused to make up Suzannah's bed or even straighten up the messy bathroom.

"I do declare," Suzannah complained. "What kind of a hired girl is she?"

"Are you sure you want to use the word *girl?*" I asked. "She's at least thirty years older than you are. Besides, I told you—she's the housekeeper."

"Then why don't you get a real hired girl? You can afford it."

"I told you, Suzannah," I said, losing patience. "Leah doesn't like the idea and I must respect her wishes. She's important to me. I rely on her, and there aren't too many people you can say that about. We've worked out our arrangements, she and I. On the days when I go off to work, she makes my bed but when I stay home, I make it myself. And if you're going to be staying on any length of time, I suggest you work out some kind of arrangement with her yourself."

"You mean if I stay, Leah will make me scrub floors for my room and board?" Suzannah pouted.

"Oh no," I said cheerfully. "We do have the part-time cleaning lady for that."

"Don't you want me here, Buffy?" she asked pathetically.

I hugged her. "Of course we do. For as long as you want to stay." And I meant it. My feelings about Suzannah were truly ambivalent—I did get so mad at her when she was insensitive or downright callous but in the end she was still and always ours.

"But you do understand, Suzannah, that I can't stay home with you all the time. I still go into the office—"

"But why do you have to? It seems to me that—"

"Because Todd depends on me. Even with Howard. We're still a family business. And we're all over the state now. I don't have to keep nine-to-five hours, but I do have my duties and responsibilities."

"One would think you'd want to stay home with Megan and Mitchell," she said reprovingly. "I mean . . . *if* one does have children one should—"

"Honestly, Suzannah! You're too much!" She really was. "I just finished telling you Todd needs me. Howard and I are actually the only two people he absolutely can rely on—"

"You see," she said plaintively, "you rely on Leah, and Todd relies on you and Howard. Who do I have to rely on?" She started to whimper. "Nobody."

I sighed. Poor Suzannah. She hadn't learned yet that if you wanted to rely on somebody, you first had to be a reliable person yourself. But I said, "Yes, you do. You can always rely on Todd and me. We'll always be there for you."

And I was sincere, even though there was a little voice in my head that said, "I hope you never live to regret that statement."

She dimpled. "Oh, Buffy, I knew you'd say that. I never doubted it for a moment. You and Todd have always been so good to me. And you're a sweetie. You always were. And so pretty too—" and she laughed. "Even if you don't have red hair and are pretty damn short for a beauty. Why, you know, I think you're *almost* as beautiful as I am."

Then we both laughed, remembering that first day at Ohio State. And then the laugh turned into one which had the taste of something bittersweet on the tongue.

Suellen and Howard came for dinner, Suellen reluctantly.

"You know that I was never crazy about that one, and why you're putting up with her now is beyond me. Don't you have enough to do without that self-centered neurotic taking over your lives?"

"It's not like you to be uncharitable, Suellen. Suzannah's going through a difficult time and what are old friends for?"

"I'm sorry but I think she's despicable. And I'm not even talking about what she did to Paulie." She shook her head as if trying to shake free the memory of him. "I'm talking about what she did to her body. Anyone who does that is beneath contempt."

"I think she's more to be pitied. And if you get right down to it, it was her choice, wasn't it? Her body? You go around campaigning to have dogs fixed, don't you? Well, some women should be fixed too. It's better for them and the world and their unborn. Maybe, just maybe, Suzannah was wiser about herself than others would be wise for her."

"Her method was rather drastic, wouldn't you say?"

"Suzannah is a drastic person. I *was* shocked myself when she first told me. Shocked and sickened. But I've come around in my thinking. Since it was her body, and she hurt no one else, she had the right to go any way she pleased."

"Well, I still think that that doctor should be shot!"

"Maybe that doctor, whoever he was, didn't have a chance standing up to Suzannah once her mind was made up."

The evening was a challenge to Suellen's innate good manners and she was correct, if distant. But Howard, at least, was his usual pleasant self. After dinner we sat in the library before the fire and Suzannah, in a flowing satin robe the color of emeralds, curled up on the apricot velvet sofa, basking in the orangy-red glow of the flames leaping on the hearth. She sipped from a goblet of golden-colored brandy and bowed her head to delicately sniff at the peach-blush blossoms that reposed in a crystal bowl. It was a picture as rich as any of Suzannah's glossy advertisements. "She's wearing Suzannah," the legend would read.

"I'm washed up in New York," Suzannah sighed. "I'm washed up as a model altogether."

Howard looked at her with commiseration as Suellen stared at the dish of smoked almonds on the coffee table, offering no comment. But Todd rose to the occasion. "That's ridiculous," he protested. "You were a top model before Durell and there's no reason you can't still be one."

"You don't understand," Suzannah said softly, sadly. "I was the face and name for the *top of the line.* The other top cosmetic firms wouldn't use me now—not once Durell is through with me. Why would Estée or Revlon want me after Durell has used me up, overexposed me? In the public mind, my face, my image, would still be associated with Durell, with the Suzannah line." Suddenly, she started to cry. "My Suzannah line," she moaned as if her baby had just died.

I could understand how she felt and automatically I put my arm around her to offer some comfort.

"I can't step down to a less prestigious company . . . not after that. You can see that, can't you?" She took a large gulp of the brandy. "I'm almost thirty already, Todd," she said looking directly at him as if she and he were alone in the room. "They're using seventeen-year-old girls for the magazines, for God's sake. In the modeling business, you're a hag at thirty. You *can* go on, but you're a freak. What's the percentage in it? What's the point if you can't be the top of the line?"

I waited for Todd to answer her, reassure her that she wasn't through as a model, but instead I heard him agree with her now. "I guess modeling *is* out. And if modeling is out, you have to consider your other options. Movies. TV. The stage. You've already flopped on the stage though, so I would think that's out for the present."

Oh my God! I thought. Now *his* knife was getting sharp, sharp as the surgeon's who had—I wouldn't think about that. What Todd was doing now was chopping away the dead wood quickly, getting to the heart of the matter.

"So that leaves TV and movies. And you were already a hit on that one TV show you did with Leo. And most of TV has moved to the West Coast—" Todd said, thinking hard.

"So you think I should go to Hollywood? That's what you're saying, isn't it? Yes, I could go to the Coast. All I would need would be an agent. A top agent. And that won't be a problem," she said, warming up. "I do have a name. I *am* famous."

"You are," Todd said and I nodded my head.

"But I hardly have any money. I spent everything I ever made. When it's coming in you feel like it's going to last forever. And Geoffrey swears I won't get a red cent from him. So how can I go to the Coast without any money an still put up a big front so that they won't know I'm flat on my ass? Without a big front, you have to go down on your knees on the West Coast, one way or another. You know that, don't you?"

I assumed now that Suzannah wanted money. And it was no problem. Todd would give her whatever she needed, I was sure. But I heard him say, "You're not thinking clearly, Suzannah. Of course you'll get money from Durell. The Geoffrey Durells of the world don't go into court and say, 'She made an ass out of me, she deceived me, she made me divorce my wife who's old and sick by trickery.' Even if he didn't care what an old fool that made him look personally, he would consider the company's image. All you'd have to do is *hint* at what you might say in court. For people *not* to have certain images in their head when they look at future ads of the Durell product should be worth a half million. The company must spend twice that much on a campaign to put positive thoughts in their heads. And when it's *you,* their former image, who's the one who made an ass out of *the* Durell—why, it's probably worth more than a half mil. You probably could get the whole million."

Suellen appeared disgusted. Howard seemed upset, and Suzannah dimpled with delight. "Oh, Todd! You're right! You're a genius!"

Todd looked at me and I wondered, for what? My approval? The truth was I was filled with dismay. To have advised Suzannah to trick Durell into marrying her and not cancel her contract was one thing—he hadn't known about the existence of the first Mrs. Durell, and Durell *had been* having an affair with Suzannah. And to advise her to go to Hollywood was just plain good sense and hurt no one at all. But to advise her to hold Durell up for ransom—a man she had already wounded? That was entirely another matter and I was not only dismayed, I felt ill.

I tried to avoid Todd's eyes but he would not let me do so. Watching me, waiting for me to glance in his direction, he did catch my eye and he shrugged and shook his head at me, and I knew him so well I knew exactly what he was telling me: The disposed first Mrs. Durell and the imaginary baby were already *fait accompli,* out of the picture, and now we were only talking about money. Only money, and Geoffrey Durell was a very rich man. Right?

But he was wrong. We weren't talking about money at all, but about morality. Suzannah *had* affected lives with her self-centeredness. Her deceit and selfishness *had* caused pain. Should she emerge now victorious, untouched, her pockets lined with gold? She was my friend, for better or worse. Still, was it right?

She was like an excited child now. "And Wes, that self-righteous bastard! He deserted me when I needed him after he had used me. He's going to pay too!"

She turned to Suellen and Howard, explained who Wes Hamilton was and her relationship with him. "Why should *he* get off scot-free after everything I went through for him? After I protected his name. Not to mention the pain he caused my poor Paulie! Well, I don't have to protect him any longer, do I?" She smiled at them, asking for their approval. "Where was he when I needed him? Did he rush to my side when Paulie died, when *my* reputation was at stake?" She looked at me and laughed, *"He* was gone with the wind, wasn't he?"

But I was in no mood to laugh at the use of that expression. I averted my face. She then turned to Todd and like a professional victim who sensed certain people's sympathies, she demanded of him: "What do you think, Todd? Don't you think my *not* telling my all to one of those scandal sheets about Wes and me should be worth a half million too?"

But Todd frowned now, not answering. Again he turned to me. I guessed that he wanted to separate himself from Suzannah's financial demands and ambitions at this point, and wanted to put himself on my side. He smiled winningly at me. The smile said, "Wow! I guess I've done it again . . . stuck my foot in it—She *is* a bit much, isn't she?"

But I wouldn't smile back.

He came up behind me as I sat in front of the dressing table mirror brushing my hair, and his arms encircled me.

"It's only money, Buffy Ann."

"Yes, but it doesn't seem right after what she did. And we helped her, we advised her in New York that day, and tonight—"

"But she's Suzannah. She would have thought of it herself as soon as her head cleared. And what if Durell and Hamilton are going to part with some money? The point is she couldn't fuck Durell or Hamilton now if they hadn't fucked her first, right?"

"Yes. Hamilton, I suppose, fucked her over. But Durell? How did he?—"

Todd smiled at me. "But he *did,* didn't he? In the very literal sense of the word. He fucked her and what happens when you fuck somebody? They fuck back or it's no deal. When you fuck, you have to be prepared to be fucked back."

I thought about it and finally I had to laugh. His logic was irrefutable. "And if I fuck you now, what will you do?"

"I'll fuck you back as hard as I can. I promise."

Suzannah left the next day, her head full of plans. After she'd gone Leah cleaned the guestroom as if it had been inhabited by lepers, or at least by tuberculars. Smiling to herself, humming a hymn, she was a Lysol-bearing wraith.

I handed her the envelope Suzannah had left for her. She tore it open, pulled out a note and a twenty dollar bill. Wordlessly, she handed me the scarlet notepaper. "Dear Leah," it read in bright green felt-tip ink, "Thank you for all your kindnesses." Her signature was sprawled half across the page.

Leah marched into the bathroom, and I saw her flush the bill down the toilet. I knew Todd would have told her: "It's only money, Leah.

No name. No face." But I said nothing. I never questioned Leah, not in words, or by deed. Leah was always Leah, and her instincts were uncanny.

27.

We heard from Suzannah quite often once she was in Hollywood. "It's almost as if she's reporting in," I remarked to Todd, after a weekly call.

"Like we were her parents?"

"Yes. Or at the very least, her sponsors."

She had not gotten her first role yet, either in films or in TV. But she wasn't worried, she told me. She had her money from Geoffrey and from Wes, so she wasn't hurting for funds. And she was represented by the biggest talent agency in town.

"That's the most important thing . . . who's representing you," she informed me during one call. "That, and keeping your name alive while they put together a deal for you."

The job of keeping her name had been relegated to the "top public relations firm in L.A." "But this isn't difficult for them—the name Suzannah still *means* something—everyone knows who I am. Wherever I go, I get the red-carpet treatment. And CTA . . . those are my agents . . . are working on a deal for me to play opposite Burt . . ." and then she added ". . . Reynolds, you know."

"In the meantime, you can't imagine how busy I am. Why, honey, I'm as busy as a bee in June." Voice lessons, having her hair done, her skin pampered, her body massaged, her toes pedicured, her muscles exercised. "I have the best work-out person in all L.A. It's the same one who does Jane Fonda. She's really into the body."

Another call and she divulged that she was trying to meet Burt Reynolds. "It would do wonders for my career if I could have an affair with him . . . Dinah Shore is a Southern girl, you know."

In the meantime, incredibly, she was seeing lots of Cleo and Leo. Leo was doing very nicely for himself. At first, he had been as mean as anything to her, still holding it against her that she had not insisted upon him as director for her ill-fated stage debut. But once it appeared that she was going to play opposite Reynolds, if not Newman, he had come around. Leo and Cleo gave wonderful parties . . . Cleo did have a certain flair for entertaining and she was looking much better these days. "It's a wonder what a little nipping and tucking can accomplish."

I had already learned about Cleo's plastic surgery. Cleo was nothing if not an efficient correspondent—she wrote wonderful letters in perfect textbook penmanship on French gray stationery embossed with her latest address—the ten hundred block of North Beverly Drive. This time her house had a "name."

Beverly Mews
July 22, 1974

Dear Buffy,

As you can see, a new baby is not the only thing new with the Masons. Our new house is just up from Sunset and just behind the Beverly Hills Hotel. It was remarkable how quickly we made this move. We were living quite comfortably in the house on Palm Drive and we were there only two years. The problem there was we had a swimming pool but no tennis court and one day Leo came home and said we needed a championship quality north/south *immediately!* When I told him it would take weeks or even months to have a tennis court installed, even if we had room for it which we didn't, he told me to go out and find a house that already had one. Well, you know Leo. When he wants something it's like being chased by a mad dog. You run faster than you think it's humanly possible. Luckily, Mother helped. She's in real estate now. You know Mother. She's a lot like Leo. Maybe that's why she likes him so much. Whatever either of them decides to do, they make a success of it.

Well, Mother knew the story behind *this* house, whose owner (Craig Burroughs the actor) was in trouble financially (was in a hot series which was suddenly canceled) and he needed a fast sale. Luckily, you don't need a large down payment out here and Mother got it through escrow almost immediately. From start to finish, we were in the new house in a little over two weeks. (Our old house is still unsold but Mother's working on it.) And we had the party Leo wanted in just another week. You see, although Leo is tremendously successful doing TV movies, he's desperate to get into theatrical features, and when he heard that Hack Jagger—he's a very important producer (you must have heard of him)—had a script about tennis players caught in terrible psychological competition (you know the sort of thing I mean)—Leo was desperate to direct the picture. So the tennis court and the big party were to *catch* Jagger, who's a big tennis addict himself. (He's always in the local charity matches.) Leo figured if we had a really great north/south—you get the idea.

The party was outside with the tennis court as the focal point, so Hack couldn't miss it. As if anyone could. The damn thing is a mile long and lit up like a prison yard. To make a long story a little bit shorter, Jagger didn't show up! As it turned out, it wouldn't have much mattered if he had. Hack didn't need *our* tennis court. Hack, we found out later, plays tennis with *Chuck Heston!* Besides, it turned out, he had already signed another director.

But that night we didn't know any of that and Leo became temporarily irrational when Hack didn't show up. He said it was all my fault—I must have sent the invitations out too late. I thought he was going to choke me to death. I mean *literally!* He had his fingers around my throat and—Luckily, Mother was still there helping me clean up the mess the caterers left. She calmed Leo down. And then *me,* after Leo had gone to bed. I was really furious! To be found fault with after all I had accomplished in such a short while! Mother kept telling me that Leo is a great talent and *all* great artists have a temperament.

Mother said that no one gets *everything* and that I was a lucky girl to have everything that I do have, and I shouldn't mind putting up with a few unpleasant facets of Leo's personality. Especially since I was not *really* a raving beauty in a town full of raving beauties. And so I had better get on the ball and keep pleasing Leo—dress better than anyone else, entertain better, have the most spectacularly decorated house in town, serve the best food, and have the best guest lists. And take tennis lessons. Mother said there were hundreds of cute and willing chicks who wouldn't mind taking Leo, even with his little quirks. And if I didn't get on the ball and stop complaining, I'd live to regret it all my life. I'd be part of the walking dead out there on the streets, all those abandoned wives who hadn't kept up. And it really was time I had my nose bobbed.

So, as they say in the commercials—*ta ra*—Cleo Pulitzer Mason has a brand new nose. And Leo loves it. The funny thing is, it looks just like a New Jersey *Standhope* nose, the one I was supposed to have when I was a teenager back in Tenafly. If I didn't know for sure that I had had Dr. Stanley Price (the latest "hot" plastic surgeon in Beverly Hills), I would have thought that Dr. Standhope had moved his practice out here. Anyhow, now Leo *and* Mother want me to have my chin done. And I guess, sooner or later, I must. *If* I can fit the operation in between my cooking classes and the tennis lessons.

Desperately wish you two would come for a visit. It would be so super to see you and Toddy. We could have a reunion of sorts. You, me, Suzannah, and Cassie. I do see Cassie every once in a while at parties. Guy is getting hotter and hotter. Leo says that every time Guy does a bit on TV, they get bagfuls of fan mail from the teenybopper crowd. So there's lot's of talk going around about his getting his own series. (Leo has an idea for a series for Guy. Leo says that if he's going to be stuck in TV—for a while, anyway—he wouldn't mind having a hot series. You can't imagine the big money involved in a hit series—the reruns.) There is also a lot of talk going around about Guy having been in pornos. But who knows if it's true and who cares? Nobody in this town except for Cassie, I daresay, or her mother the grand dame.

About Cassie. I hope we get to see more of each other. I get the feeling she could use a friend. Everybody needs a great friend. I'm lucky. At least I have Mother.

28.

Cassie arrived home from the museum at six. As she came up the driveway, she noted with relief that Guy's new car was not in the courtyard. He was not at home. She parked her Valiant at the extreme left to leave plenty of room for the bright red Ferrari, the beloved acquisition. Guy had celebrated the signing of his contract for the series by buying himself the car. As for herself, she thought she was the only person on the West Side of L.A. who still drove a vehicle of American vintage . . . *ancient* American vintage.

Getting out of the car, she automatically checked the neighboring house high up the hillside as she did each night when she returned home. Still there and still dark. She checked her watch. It was exactly ten past six. The lights would go on in five minutes. Every night, they went on at exactly fifteen minutes past six.

The mailman had told her something of the house's history. Its owner was Jenny Elmann—an actress who had come from Germany in 1939. She had not found cinematic success in Hollywood but had found a husband, a California aristocrat, heir to a railroad fortune. But one black night, several years after she married, Jenny had emptied a rifle into her handsome husband's heart, having mistaken him for a prowler. Then, soon after, she had gone back to Germany, leaving her house to be closed up tight, attended only by a gardener who came every week, and then every month or so.

Cassie thought it was the *prettiest* house from what she could see of it from the windows and terrace of her own house. (From the road it was not visible at all.) It was California pink with a red tile roof, with turrets and terraces and giant palms standing guard all around. Cassie wondered why it had been allowed to stand empty all these years without a family or barking dog to fill its silent barren rooms. Why hadn't it been sold?

She watched the lights come on then walked to her own door, taking a customary note of her own overgrown grounds. Ivy out of control. Evergreens shaggy and shapeless. Hedges and vines reaching unevenly toward the darkening blue sky. Here and there, a cluster of the exotic birds of paradise. To her, they were grotesque rather than beautiful, more bird of prey than of song and twitter. She sighed. Eventually, she would be forced to pay a landscaping crew at least three weeks of her museum salary to give the grounds some semblance of order. But she didn't even know why. When she came home at night she welcomed the overgrown abundance—it was a shield from the world. Who could peek over its vast disorder to detect the disordered turmoil of her life?

And there was no one, after all, to reprove her for her unkempt grounds. Not Guy certainly. He was too immersed in himself, especially so now. It was all his new show, his new car, his newly refurbished wardrobe, his weekly hair treatments, his voice coach, his gymnasium, and his private pursuits of the night, which interested her not at all.

And her mother could not reprove her either. She did not even visit Cassie's house. She, Cassie, went *there*—once a week, to the big gray stone castle, and forced herself to walk up its exquisitely maintained walkway to the huge cast bronze doors, to enter the immaculate interior, to sit in the elegant drawing room, to drink tea or very occasionally a glass of sherry, to watch her mother warily, to parry carefully worded questions with guarded, noncommunicative replies. And all the while that she sat there, she could think only of the childhood bedroom up on the second floor. She was sure it was exactly the same as she had left it the night she eloped with Guy Savarese; kept so, awaiting her return . . . her surrender.

It was her seventh birthday and she was having a party, as she did every year. She had been allowed six guests of her choice from among her classmates at school. The seventh guest (seven guests for a seventh birthday) was Audrey Booth, the daughter of her mother's good friend. Cassie hated Audrey who came, nevertheless, to her birthday party year after year. Audrey was two years older than Cassie and her other guests, and easily took over the games that followed the refreshments.

The year before, Audrey had managed to turn the other guests against the birthday girl so that she was taunted and laughed at. While the mothers had *their* refreshments downstairs, Audrey had the girls playing house upstairs, each girl enacting a member of a family group— mother, father, granny, sister, brother, and Cassie was not even granted the role of cook, but of the family dog, down on all fours and barking.

It did Cassie no good to tell her mother she didn't want Audrey at her party again. Cassandra informed her that she was not being gracious. How hurt Audrey would be to be left out, not to speak of Audrey's mother, Cassandra's own friend. Cassie must learn to be not only gracious, but also kind, more charitable.

Cassandra gave Cassie her present the morning of her birthday—a large baby doll with big blue eyes that opened and closed, with a tag tied to her arm that proclaimed her name to be Barbara Jean. And that afternoon, as the mothers sat downstairs drinking cocktails and sipping tea and taking dainty bites of birthday cake, Audrey Booth poked at the baby doll's china blue eyes with a yellow pencil until the eyes fell back into the recesses of the doll's head, lost forever, leaving two black holes in Barbara Jean's baby doll face.

Cassie screamed when she saw the black holes, screamed and kicked and attacked the smiling Audrey, until all the mothers rushed up the grand stairway and along the hall to the playroom to find Audrey hysterical. She, Audrey, felt terrible enough over the accident that had befallen Cassie's dolly without the insult of having Cassie try to poke *her* eyes out with the pencil. She got all this out while screaming and crying.

The assembled mothers were shocked. Cassie's behavior was not that of a little girl only seven; she was behaving like a wild, uncontrolled animal. One might even say, a *vicious* animal. The mothers and their daughters departed save for Audrey and Lorna Booth, who sat with Cassandra Hammond waiting for an unrepentant Cassie to apologize.

The two mothers conversed as they waited, as Audrey gazed at Cassie with a sweetly malicious smile. "I had no idea she could be so willful," Cassandra said to Lorna Booth. "Willful and obstinate . . . just like her father."

"Willful? Walter?" Lorna Booth remarked and mused. "Really?"

Finally Cassie gave in. First she apologized for thinking that which was an accident had been purposefully done. Then she had to apologize for attacking Audrey physically. "I'm sorry that I acted like a vicious, uncontrolled animal," she dutifully repeated and only then was allowed to go to her room.

That night, Cassandra placed the sightless baby doll on the shelf along with Cassie's other dolls, and there Barbara Jean stared down at Cassie in her bed, the doll's painted red mouth smiling, her empty eye sockets reproachful. "We will keep Barbara Jean right there," her mother said. "She will be a reminder to you that you were not only naughty, but extremely obstinate."

Cassie lay in terror all that night, sleepless, seeing the black holes in the doll's face even in the dark. The next night she fell asleep but had a nightmare. And then every night after that, she carefully turned away from the collection of dolls as she went to bed, averted her eyes whenever she came into the room, and gave up playing with *any* of the dolls on the shelf.

On her eighth birthday, there was no party at all, for which Cassie was grateful. Audrey Booth would not be able to attend. But her mother did remove Barbara Jean from the shelf. "I trust you have learned a lesson. Your father was a very obstinate, willful man. Those are unpleasant traits and we must guard against those traits in you."

Cassie was only grateful for Barbara Jean's departure. She did not pay too much attention to her mother's words. She had only a faint recollection of her father, that he was sweet and nice and had kissed her and loved her. She was pretty sure that she remembered *that.* As for Barbara Jean, she would always remember her, very, very, clearly.

As soon as Cassie walked into her own house she called Guy's answering service. Rarely, very rarely, he would have them relay a message to her—that he would not be home until late, or perhaps, that he wanted her to join him at a certain place, maybe a party. She knew from experience that these were occasions when he had somebody or a group of somebodies to impress, to show everyone that his wife was not the usual flashy Hollywood tootsie but a classy beauty—an heiress of an old, rich, socially impeccable California first family. And she was, by token of their marriage, one measure of *his* worth. *And that was her worth to him.*

Gratefully, Cassie heard the voice on the other end inform her that there were no messages for Mrs. Guy Savarese. She went into the kitchen. In the sink she found a couple of dishes and a cup that Guy had left there. She rinsed them and put them in the dishwasher. She considered making dinner but decided against it. A waste of time—Guy was practically never there for dinner. She decided that she would give the floor a quick once-over. First she swept and then she mopped, even though the floors at Blackstone Manor were never mopped but scrubbed. But her standards could not possibly match those of the Manor. She did all her own cleaning piecework style after she came home from the Museum. One day vacuuming, the next—dusting and polishing; one day downstairs, one day upstairs. The house was far too big for her to maintain herself without that kind of scheduling.

As she put away the mop and broom, Cassie thought how many eyebrows in town would go up if they knew that Cassandra Hammond's daughter and Guy Savarese's wife—he who had just signed a contract guaranteeing a weekly salary of five figures—could not afford weekly, or even monthly help. It was hard even for her to digest.

Standing at the tiled counter in the kitchen, Cassie ate yogurt straight from the waxed container. Yogurt was nutritious and filling enough for a person without appetite. Her dinner eaten, Cassie went into the den to savor the time she had been awaiting all day long. She flicked on one low light, poured herself a half glass of vodka and sat down in the chair she had placed by the windows so that she could look up at the house on the hill.

Would the house ever fill with the sound of human voices and laughter? Would its lights ever come on by human hand? Or was it to remain, like she herself, in a kind of stalemate?

She sipped at her vodka. She *knew* that what she was doing was wrong, even sick—sharing her life in a nearly empty house with a stranger with an empty heart, just to try to win a battle with a woman who *never* lost. Everyone knew that about Cassandra Hammond.

But now that Guy was getting his own series she was getting nearer to her own freedom. Soon she would be able to say, *See, Mother, he's not just a low-class climber. He is a success. I did choose well. But now, having chosen well, I can discard him. Having chosen well, it is my option to do that.*

Still, she wanted to have the baby too. If she could take something good out of this marriage, *that* would be a form of victory, a triumphant exhibit. *See, Mother. I have done something right after all. I am not entirely worthless. My marriage has produced this worthy little bundle of joy, your posterity, and someone for me to love.*

Then, it could and would be: *Bye bye, Guy. Bye bye, Mother. Neither of you have any love to give anybody.*

In the beginning, Cassie had often wondered why Guy had stayed with *her*, since he obviously had married her for the Blackstone fortune and her mother was clearly not forthcoming with support. Certainly he had not stayed with her for her sexual attractions. That too was obvious. And she surmised that since he was away from the house almost every night, he was fulfilling his sexual needs—whatever they were— somewhere else. She supposed that part of the reason he did stay with her was that she did fulfill his outward needs, his façade. But there had to be more reason than that. It had to be that he too wanted an heir, all the better to force Cassandra into submission. Failing that, he was waiting for Cassandra to die. Then there would only be Cassie and possibly their heir, to inherit. And Cassandra had to die—not even she was immortal.

So they stayed together and once or twice each month, they copulated, she in cold terror and he in his brutal rage, joined together in their mutual desire to produce Cassandra's grandchild.

As the vodka started to go to her head, she wondered if it had ever occurred to Guy to wonder why she stayed with *him?* Endured their relationship as strangers, the sexual encounters that were as passionless as they were brutal? Did he think, in his colossal conceit and narcissistic pride in his colossal organ, that she was in love with his body, if not he himself?

Was it possible that he didn't know that his embrace did not provide her pleasure but only pain and terror? No. Not possible. Then, with the help of the vodka, the answer came to her. *He knew everything.* He had figured out that for her their marriage, their sex, had very little to do with him at all. That it was all just between her and her mother. For both of them, for her and for Guy, coitus was not only not an act of love, it wasn't even an act of sex. Only an act of rage.

29.

Another one of Cleo's newsy letters arrived while Todd was in Marietta, attending to the finishing touches of the latest King supermall—this one with a Swiss motif, with the stores modeled after the cute little shops in the Alpine villages and the restaurants resembling chalets. (Next year, in '76, we planned on opening in Toledo and we were already discussing a theme for that location.) I hoped that he would return soon because I loved sharing Cleo's letters with him. She was the best letter writer I knew.

". . . I don't know which to tell you about first," Cleo wrote, "the series Leo is doing with Guy Savarese, or Suzannah's engagement. . . ."

Suzannah's engagement?

I definitely wanted to read about that first and when I saw that Cleo began with Leo, Guy, and the series, I skipped to the second half of the letter. Yes, that was more like it.

. . . Suzannah is going to marry Heinz Muller. You must have heard of him, or at least Todd has. He's the airlines biggie and God-knows-what-else from Dallas. (A conglomerate person.) Millions. I'm referring to dollars. ($$$$$$$$$$) He's most recently of Dallas, that is. He is originally of German origins. (He does have a rather heavy accent.) Well, anyhow, he is mad for our darling Suzannah and intends to go into the movie producing business, producing pictures starring our girl only. He says he's going to make Suzannah the biggest star the world has ever known. He says it's all a matter of promotion and putting enough capital into the venture. (Rumor has it that he wants to buy Fox! But it's only a rumor.) But Fox is where Suzannah plans on getting married. On the Twentieth Century lot, with the "Hello Dolly" set in the background. I have to hand it to her, even though it hurts, I think it's a very chic idea, and it will probably start a trend. And what's more they'll have room for two thousand guests!

It seems she and Heinz met in Cannes at the Film Festival. She was giving out press interviews, I understand, like crazy, even though she has *yet* to make a film. But even I, who can't qualify as her biggest fan, will have to admit that Suzannah acts more like a star and looks more like one than anyone else in this here town. Well, upon meeting Heinz, she immediately captured his fancy and he hers, which is not hard to understand considering the money and power there. Heinz has taken offices in Century City (a whole floor) as the new center of his operations and has moved into one of the bungalows at the Beverly Hills Hotel, where he is living with our gal Suzannah. (I think she doesn't want to let him out of her sight.)

They are the funniest looking couple—Suzannah so tall and spectacular looking and Heinie (that's what she calls him and now so does everyone else), five feet five even in his cowboy boots and Stetson. (He *is* from Texas.) And he dotes on every word that comes out of her luscious little mouth as he's laying out the campaign for the promotion of Suzannah Superstar. And there was a mention in the *Hollywood Reporter* that he's going to have a song written especially for her. It's a contest and the title of the song is to be—guess—*Suzannah Superstar.* Heinie plans on using it in her first film. I'm not sure if it's going to be the theme song, or if Suzannah will sing it herself. I also read in *Variety* that she's taking voice lessons, and not with one of your everyday coaches but with the great Palucchi himself whom Heinz brought over from Italy just for S.S.

Surprisingly, Leo and I are mixing with them quite a lot. Heinie likes to throw parties at all the name spots and we're usually invited. (Lucky for me or Leo would be livid.) In fact, she's asked me to help with the wedding at Twentieth Century. You know—the food, the decorations, the theme, the invitations, all the things Leo told her I do so well. To quote, "You can rely on Cleo for everything—she does those things better than anyone else in the big H."

So, expect an invitation within the next couple of months. And you had better come. It's time you and your boy saw California anyway. And you certainly don't want to miss this circus. The most amusing thing of all is that Suzannah *really* seems crazy about Heinie. She's always hugging him and sitting on his lap. If anybody didn't know better they'd assume she was crazy for his body. But everybody *knows* Suzannah doesn't fuck men—she only fucks herself. She stands in front of her mirror and gives herself the cockeyed *aigele* (eye in Yiddish— read as sexy look) and she strokes her breasts and fingers herself a little and then she humps the mirror. What a hot love affair. Steam rises out of the mirror. . . .

I had to laugh. I was gratified that Cleo hadn't gone so Hollywood that she had forgotten how to be funny. For my money, she was cleverer than the self-styled genius Leo. Still, I was a bit miffed that Suzannah herself hadn't called to give me the news of the imminent wedding.

There was another page or so to the ending of the letter, but I went back to the beginning before proceeding.

. . . When Leo realized that it was only a matter of time before Guy Savarese was in a hit series, he took things into his own hands. First, he developed a concept for a series about a special squad of L.A. police that covered the Hollywood and Vine area, and then he took it to his people who took it to the network and said that Leo already had a commitment from Guy to do it. And then Leo went to Guy and told him that he had a commitment from the network to do the show and he, Leo, was going to "let" Guy star in it. Leo, without help from any agent, put the whole deal together himself. It was brilliant of him. So, not only is Leo going to direct but he's also the creator of the series, plus its chief writer—he'll write as many of the shows himself as he chooses and will supervise the rest. They're just starting production and the first show will air any month now.

My mother is going around crowing to anybody who'll listen that Leo is a genius. And I must say it all happened at the right moment. We were really over our heads keeping up this house and everything. Terrific expenses. Especially now that we have Tennis Sundays at the Masons. Sounds darling, doesn't it? Every Sunday we invite a group of people over for tennis. (People who are *somebody* in the Industry and who are also proficient at the game.) And we serve champagne and hot dogs during the afternoon (what do you think of that combination? inspirational?), and we finish up with a supper. At some Sunday courts, the crowd is not allowed to talk shop at all during play or while they sit around waiting to play but at our Sundays, you're *only* allowed to talk shop—no politics or anything else allowed. You see, it's *the rules* that you establish and having the *same* chic refreshments every week that makes it special, a ritual—And it's been terribly successful. Everyone is dying to get an invitation. I call everybody at the last minute on Sunday mornings—that's to keep everybody expectant. And don't think Leo doesn't stay up till three Saturday night working on the list of invitées. It's really been the making of us socially. We're getting lots of biggies. And it didn't hurt that the Vice President in charge of programming at the network that Goldman-Lessor took *Hollywood and Vine* to is one of our regulars. That's where Leo prepped him *before* they made their pitch—at our Tennis Sundays.

But frankly, we don't know what to do about Suzannah and Heinie. Suzannah refuses to learn the game. She says she doesn't care *who* plays —Farrah or R.J. or Clint—she's not developing tennis elbow or muscles in her legs. And Heinie is hardly the type. He's more comfortable sitting at a baccarat table in Vegas than wearing tennis whites, if you know what I mean. That's one of our very strict rules too—*whites only* on our court. Guy doesn't play but Cassie does, and very well too. It seems she had lessons when she was growing up. Only it's really weird. She *always* wears the exact same shirt and shorts.

I went back to the last part of Cleo's letter.

We were in Vegas just last week with Suzannah and Heinie. We flew in for Frank's opening at the MGM on Heinie's personal jet. Now, *that's* posh. And Heinie, of course, is a high roller. We saw him drop fifty thousand in one shot without a bat of his lashes. Or Suzannah's, for that matter. They just laughed as if it were really funny.

Guess who we ran into at Frank's show? None other than Suzannah's old friend, Poppy. (Remember Suzannah's little friend from Kentucky who moved in on her when she was modeling in New York?) Well, Poppy is married to the boyfriend now. And his name is now Beau Beaufort, he's newly blond, and he's headlining at the Desert Paradise. (In case you haven't heard—I know you're into shopping malls and probably not cognizant about singers but Beau is *big!*) He does mostly country and some rock and is constantly on the charts and does the usual concerts all over the country. Frankly, I'm not into rock stars or country singers myself and if it weren't for the fact that we *are* in the entertainment business ourselves, I wouldn't even bother keeping current. But as it is I do read all the trades and the gossips, so I usually know who's who—who's on the charts, and who's sucking whom.

As for Poppy Beaufort, I knew that she and Suzannah had not parted the best of friends in New York. And I understand that the whole thing became pretty dirty although I don't know the details. But you never would have guessed it from the way Poppy and Suzannah fell all over each other. And then Poppy invited us over to the Desert Paradise to hear Beau as her guests, and of course we went. Later I casually asked Suzannah about their past falling out and how come she and Poppy acted like long-lost relatives. She just dimpled at me and said, "Oh, Poppy and I go back a long way. We understand each other. God, yes!"

Yes, that sounded like Suzannah to me. One thing you had to say for Suzannah was that she was not one to hold a grudge. And it was always the immediate that held her attention. And probably, she and Poppy *did* understand one another. They were birds of a feather. Poppy had tried to blackmail Suzannah and Suzannah had retaliated in kind, and they were even, and neither one, being the kind of people they were, blamed the other for what each was capable of herself.

But let me tell you—she's something: Very pretty but—: She was wearing a red tube top with sparkles and a red satin jeans skirt that covered about two inches of thigh and not much else. Her hair which is inky black is cut really short with a point on the nape of her neck and with points in front plastered to her cheeks. Sort of an extreme *Vidal*. And she was wearing *red* eyeshadow! And he—Beau—well, he didn't have much to say, he just kept on sort of bopping. Either he is a case of arrested development (as Suzannah says) or he's so doped up he's out of it! But Suzannah says that Poppy is as smart as the devil!

I had to agree with Suzannah's estimate of Poppy. A few years ago she had been out on the street without any money, and now, her husband was at the top of the charts and the toast of Vegas. How had she pushed him so far in so short a time?

30.

When Beau came off the stage—his sequined cowboy suit wet with sweat and his face glistening in the semi-darkness of the wings, Poppy threw him a towel and decided to take him home without even waiting for him to shower and change.

"Was I good tonight?" Beau asked, running in place like a prizefighter. It was the question he asked every night.

"Fair," she answered crisply and told Virgil to bring the limousine around to the service entrance. "Here, put this on—" She helped him with the terry cloth robe. "Careful, you ape," she barked as he tried to put his arms around her. "You're stinking wet and the dress is new—"

She was wearing a black silk dress with long sleeves and no glitter. Just last week she had decided to change her image. If you were in the big time, you had to change, for if you didn't change, you stagnated and stunk like a mosquito-logged swamp. Her only adornments were a pear-shaped diamond on a chain that she wore around her neck and another pear-shaped diamond, bigger than the first, on her third finger left hand.

"Do we have to go home? I don't feel like going home, Poppy. I wanna have a drink—You said last night I could have a drink in the lounge after the show tonight. You said, Poppy—"

"Yeah, but you're tired tonight. Maybe tomorrow night."

"I'm not tired," he said defiantly.

"Yes, you are!" Then she added, "Who knows better than Poppy when you're tired, you stupid son-of-a-bitch?" She had determined to clean up her language, too. She was going to be a lady now that they had made it, but she had to talk to Beau that way. He expected it, and if he didn't get what he expected it would throw him off.

She and Smokey hustled him out the back door and into the limousine.

"I'm hungry," Beau whined.

"You ate two hours before the first show."

"It was a long time ago."

"Listen, stupid, you're gaining weight. And the chicks ain't gonna . . . aren't going," she corrected herself, "to like you fat like a pig."

He grinned. "You'll like me still, won't you, Poppy?" He tried to slide his hand under her dress oblivious to Smokey and Virgil in the front seat. She slapped at his hand and he laughed, "Okay, Poppy, I'll wait till we get home. Can we play strangers on a bus tonight?"

"Sure," she said, thinking of how much it would take to bring him down tonight, so that he could sleep. She liked him to get ten hours of sleep—that doctor in Birmingham had told her that sleep was the great healer, that it made up for a lot of the other abuses.

"I'm starving, Poppy," he grouched, his mood changing again. "Can't we stop for some chicken? Or burgers and fries?"

"That shit ain't . . . that stuff isn't good for you. I have a turkey at home. You can have some turkey."

"Rather have burgers and fries," he muttered, slipping his hand under her dress again.

She frowned. They said the crap killed the appetite for food and sex, but they were sons-of-bitching liars in both cases.

They'd be home in another five minutes. She'd put him in the spa first, turn the temperature up to hotter than hell, turn on all the jets, relax him. It was the best thing she had done, getting that house. It meant they didn't have to hang out at the hotels. She didn't need a million prying eyes keeping tabs on Beau Beaufort. And she didn't have the problem, like she did on the road, of all those fucking dumb groupies lurking in the corridors, outside their door, *behind* the fucking doors sometimes. Every once in a while, she fed him a groupie, but she didn't like to do it if she could help it—it was a fucking dangerous business, she knew. Especially if he roughed one up . . . like that time in Wichita. And the stupid asshole girl didn't even know the reason he turned ugly on her was because she didn't rough *him* up. That time was one time she was glad she had Ben Gardenia and his bunch to help out, to earn their fucking fifty percent for once, the mothers.

She stripped Beau of the costume, helped him into another terry cloth robe, while Virgil got out the remains of a cold turkey from the refrigerator. Then he and Smokey turned on the TV in the dining room and sat with Beau as he gorged on the turkey, ripping the meat off the carcass with eager fingers.

She went into the combination bathroom-dressing room that was almost as big as her satin and velvet blue bedroom. There was a bike in there and a rowing machine, but in order to keep Beau using them she herself had to sit there screaming invectives at him until she was hoarse. She turned on the jets and watched the water foam out. She'd have to think of something to deal with Beau's ever-growing weight problem. You'd think he would lose weight with all the water he lost during a performance.

She went back into the bedroom and picked up the perspiration-stained costume, fingered the sequins at the collar. She guessed that it could stand one more cleaning. You'd think with forty costumes almost exactly like this one hanging in the closet, and with all the money they had made, she wouldn't have to concern herself with penny-ante stuff like getting a couple more wearings out of a suit. But all the fucking expenses came out of *her* fifty percent, not theirs. They got the cream and she got the leftover shit.

He was still way up when he got out of the spa. She wrapped the bath sheet around him, as he danced around, sang a phrase or two, tried to paw under her negligee. At least he wasn't all jittery and jangly and ugly, she thought as she rubbed him dry. She had seen other performers when they were high, too high. No, Beau was almost always good-natured: up and down, on stage, almost always. Always sweet. Maybe just a touch less sweet than he used to be. A bit more demanding, a bit more insistent on getting his way.

"Now you ask me what I'm doing in your house," he prompted.

"I thought you said you wanted to play strangers on the bus."

"Naw, I want to play rape."

"We did that last night."

"It's my favorite," he grinned.

She would have preferred the bedroom, the king-sized bed, or the thick blue carpet but Beau preferred the bathroom, with its hard tiled floor.

She took her position before the dressing table, brushed at her hair while he came up behind her. Seeing him in the mirror, she screamed.

"What are you doing in my house?"

He grinned. "What do you think I'm doing?"

"What do you want?"

"I want to fuck you, lady."

"No!" she screamed. "Get out of my house!"

He grabbed at her, pulling her negligee from her shoulders.

"Watch it!" she said. "Don't tear my robe, you turkey!"

They wrestled. She hit at him with her fists, taking care not to rake his face with her nails.

"More! Harder!" he breathed. "You have to fight back harder!"

She closed her eyes and kneed him in the groin. He grunted and she kneed him again. He moaned and she pushed him down to the white tiled floor, and he collapsed, his head striking the tiles more viciously than she had intended. Jesus! One day he was going to split his head wide open and then what? As he lay on the floor, his eyes narrow slits, he begged, "Don't hit me!"

She knew the scenario. She bit her lips and took out a thin leather strap, and yanked the bath sheet that still covered him away. Seeing her standing over him with the strap raised, he shuddered and moaned, shuddered and moaned.

She put him into a warm shower, called Smokey to give him a massage, finally gave him two white pills from a silver box, and tucked him into bed.

"Ain'tcha gonna kiss me goodnight?" Beau asked as she was ready to leave the room. She hesitated a moment then said, "Sure, you stupid son of a bitch."

She promised herself then she was going to see Ben Gardenia, pitch him to let them ease up on the goddamn road trips, let them live somewhere else than Vegas. A lot of the big stars lived in California, in Hollywood, had mansions in Beverly Hills, and only came to Vegas when they were performing. If she and Beau lived a regular life like *they* did she would wager that Beau wouldn't—There was no reason they couldn't be like everybody else in show business . . . lead regular, normal lives. If only Ben would let them.

She had made an appointment to see Ben that morning. She was going to insist that he allow them to move out of Vegas, even if he wouldn't let them ease up much on the concerts. Or maybe it would have to be the other way around. She would see. She would trade, negotiate—get a little, give a little. She would be a touch arrogant, so that he wouldn't know that it still made her nervous to talk to him, in spite of the fact that theirs had been an association of some years. Ben was low-key enough, it wasn't even that he was hard to talk to, but there was that edge to him. Threatening. And he had told her when she had asked for an appointment that he had something he wanted to discuss with her too. Now, what was that all about? Something else to worry her as if she didn't already have enough problems.

But before she met Ben she had an appointment with the lawyer so she hurried. She did her face—no blush, no red eye-shadow, and not even false lashes. Just lipstick, mascara, and a dark gray smudge of color on the lids. Her new face. To go with her new manner. She should let her hair grow long, wear it back in a twist maybe . . . sophisticated. She put on a white silk dress, a designer dress that she had bought at one of the shops in the arcade at Caesar's. It was tailored with long sleeves. She would wear only her pearls with the dress. Let Ben see that she was ready to move on to another plateau.

"Bring the coupe around," she told Virgil.

"Don't you want for me to drive you?" he asked.

"No. Rick and the boys will be here in half an hour. Rick's got the new arrangements. And I want Beau to rehearse with them all morning. And I want you and Smokey to sit in the studio and watch out for things." Their own recording studio was one of the best things about having their own place. She would have one built on their new property once they moved to L.A.

She was at the lawyer's for only ten minutes. It was a mere formality —the signing of the contract with Lee Jameson. He understood the rules quite well. For a fair remuneration, he was relinquishing to Beau Beaufort all rights and titles for all time to the words and music of "Really Down Low." Understood was that he was also selling his silence. As far as anyone was to know, Beaufort had written both the music and lyrics himself. And Jameson understood that there was not only the contract to enforce the legal position, but there were Poppy's friends and business associates to enforce the silence.

Way back, Ben had explained to her that a singer's reputation and credibility was enhanced when he performed the music he himself had written. Not to mention the take on the tapes and records. Poppy saw instantly that Ben was right. And how long could a singer last singing old Elvis Presley songs, after Presley himself had wrung the best out of them? And why should they make some nobody of a composer rich on the strength of Beau Beaufort's talent to put the song over?

And if anybody complained about the inequity of this arrangement, Poppy only shrugged. *If you don't like it, take your mother-fucking song and cut your own record!* There were thousands of them and there was only one Beau Beaufort and she knew what it took to make a Beau Beaufort and it wasn't easy.

As Poppy walked into the Regent Club to meet with Ben she thought of how she would be missing Suzannah's wedding in Hollywood because they would be touring again. Shit! And she had only worried that they wouldn't be invited. Suzannah was going to be on the inside again, while she was still out, looking in. And she had thought once Beau was a star, they too would be respected insiders. It hadn't happened yet, but it would . . . if it took her last breath. She was going to save Beau yet, with respectability.

Ben was dressed in his usual dark suit with his gardenia in his lapel, even though it was only ten in the morning and the usual sunny day in Vegas.

He greeted her at the door and led her to a table and offered her tea and blueberry muffins, the same morning meal he had every day.

"You're looking well, Poppy. I like your dress. Very tasteful."

She nodded her head at his compliment. He was almost always the gentleman. It was a game he played.

He got right to *his* point. "I wanted to talk to you about Beau's weight problem. He's gained again, Poppy, and you know that don't look so good when you go out on tour. Now you're going out in a few days and he's overweight. Those little girls out there aren't going to react so good to a *fat* boy, are they? I think you had better get him on a losing streak there . . . and right away."

"That's not so easy, Ben. He's always hungry."

"Nobody said it's easy. Of course it's not easy. But I know you'll do what you have to. We can't have Beau overweight for his fans. In Vegas it doesn't hurt him to have a few extra pounds, it's a different crowd. No giggly teenagers."

She took a deep breath. "I don't want us touring so much anymore. I—"

"What are you talking about, Poppy?" An edge in his voice appeared. "You have to tour." He laughed. "That's what the business is all about."

"I didn't say *no* tours. I want that we should only do like maybe three or four concerts a year."

He shook his head. "You surprise me, Poppy. You know how it works. The road sells the records and the records sell the road."

"The records will sell without us being out on the god—" She caught herself. She started over. "Every record's been a winner, Ben. They'll sell with only three or four big concerts a year. Does Jagger tour? He only picks his spots, doesn't he?"

He looked at her with a sad smile. "Of course Jagger tours. He's no fool. And Beau's no Jagger either. It'll be a long time before he's Jagger. If he ever is. If he lasts—"

Lasts. That was Ben's warning word to her. The voice was soft but the word wasn't.

Her own tone changed. "It's too hard out on the road, Ben. The whole situation is too hard, too dangerous. I can't control it like I can here or even better if—"

"If what, Poppy?"

"If we lived someplace else than here."

He shook his head at her. *"Here* we can help you, Poppy. It's better if you're here."

She wouldn't continue with that right now, she decided. She couldn't push for two objectives at the same time. That was a mistake. "It's hard on the road, Ben. We get too tired. Beau and me. Too many things to watch out for. The girls . . . the guys always slipping him stuff . . . the hard stuff." Her tone got angrier. "I didn't come this far to spend the rest of my life on a bus—"

He laughed out loud. "You won't, Poppy, I assure you. Beau won't last that long. I've seen plenty of Beaus. You have to milk them for what they're worth *now.* So at least, later, you'll have the money."

"I have money." *Even with what you bastards cream.*

"What is it you're after, Poppy?"

"The albums, yes. A couple of concerts a year. A couple of months in Vegas. *And movies."* Finally, she had spit it out.

His expression didn't change. He didn't laugh at her. Still he said, "Nobody's going to put Beau in a movie, Poppy."

"Why not?" she screamed. "Elvis made a string of movies. And they sold records—"

He shook his head. "Even for Elvis who's got the magic, that's ancient history. Catch up, for God's sake, Poppy. You're a sharp girl. You're living in the past and you hardly were there. *Elvis* couldn't make a movie today."

"Beau's better looking than Elvis—"

"For God's sake, today Elvis is fat, and he's just managing to perform, but he's a legend, Poppy. An idol. And he can't make a picture. You have to keep *au* current, Poppy." He always said it that way. It was one of his favorite expressions. "You have to *act* in movies today. And we're not even sure Beau could read the lines, much less remember them." His tone was becoming more impatient. "You'd better hold on to what you've got and not go chasing rainbows. It wasn't long ago you were a ten dollar hooker and your boy was just another witless wonder. You're goddamn lucky to have what you have and don't forget it. Hold on to it with both hands, trim your boy down to fighting weight, and keep winding him up for as long as you can."

He stood up, signaling that it was time for her to go. He put his arm around her, walking her to the door.

His tone was more kindly again. "You've come pretty far, Poppy, since that first day I saw you. And you were a pretty girl. Now you're a beautiful woman."

She had slept with Ben then, in those first days, but she didn't any longer. They were business associates now, and Ben didn't mix business with sex.

"And I always said you were smart. You were always smart enough to do as you were told. That's why you've done well."

Warnings. Still, she said, "Yes, I've done well but I intend to do even better!"

And she would! She'd be fucked if she'd let Ben and friends hold her back. She'd sold herself and Beau a thousand times; she'd whored and she'd pimped, stolen and merchandised, and it hadn't all been to ride a bus, no matter how fucking fancy it was, or to spend her nights in Holiday Inns. She knew what she wanted and it was the top of the shit pile, the biggest goddamn mansion in Beverly Hills, or maybe Bel Air, with closets of ladylike clothes. She would party with the best of them, and she wanted Beau to do what Sinatra did—a concert every now and then for some big charity benefit. And in between making movies and cutting a disc, he would maybe play golf, like Deano did, and Bob Hope. Sinatra, Martin, Crosby—they'd been only singers and look at them—big shots who played golf. She was willing to bet Beau could learn to hit a little old ball. How much learning could that take?

"Sinatra and Martin . . ." she blurted out.

"What about them?" he asked with some irritation.

"They play golf, don't they?"

"So?"

"They were singers. Then they made movies and they play golf."

He looked at her as if he found her very strange.

"Let Beau play golf it that's what you want. You live right on the course." He took her arm and led her outside to her car. This was a big concession for Ben, she knew. Walking someone to her car was a sign of respect. Was it respect now? Or just a show of friendliness? Or another warning? She didn't care. This was too important to her. She couldn't give up.

"Beau could do movies I tell you . . . just like Sinatra."

"Forget Sinatra!" he said now, his patience at an end. "Get it through your head! Beau's no Sinatra! He never will be! They're not in the same league!"

He opened up the car door for her but she hung back, not getting in. *So you won't give up,* Ben thought. *Maybe you need a lesson to get off my back.*

"Tell you what I'm going to do for you, Poppy. After you come back from the road this time out, I'm going to see if I can get you in to see the Old Man . . . the Old Man in the Tower. If anyone can get Beau into movies, it's the Old Man. He's got the power." He looked up at the pinnacle of the Golden Fountain, the gold-covered hotel with its liquid gold-spraying fountain from which it took its name. It stood right next to the smaller building housing the Regent Club on the Strip.

She looked up too and whispered incredulously. "The Old Man?"

She'd heard the stories about him . . . about how he had lived up there in the tower secreted away like a hermit . . . richer than God . . . controller of men, countries and presidents . . . ancient as Methuselah and some said, mad as a hatter. Anybody who lived in Vegas had heard all the stories. But he was *dead!* They had brought him back from Mexico dead, hadn't they? With long dead fingernails and a long white dead beard?

"But he's dead!" she said to Ben.

"Is he? Don't believe everything you hear. Believe me! If anyone can get Beau into the movies it's him!"

Now he put his hand firmly on her elbow and guided her into her car and closed the door after her.

"Drive very carefully, Poppy. I worry about you, you know."

She drove home, thinking about what Ben had said. The Old Man! What had Ben actually implied? That he was still *the* top man on the ladder, and not Ben himself? That he was still in control? But what did she have to do to get him to use that power for her? Maybe it was all a load of horseshit? Maybe Ben was just teasing her, or just stringing her along? Well, she was sure as hell going to find out! And she would do whatever she had to.

Then she thought about what Ben had said about Sinatra. That Beau wasn't in the same league with him. Maybe she could do something about that too! Sinatra didn't wear costumes, satin jumpsuits covered with sequins and silver and crap like that. And he sang ballads, not rock and roll and country. Shit! Beau could sing ballads too and he could wear a tux with the best of them. She had brought him along from rock and roll, turned him into a country singer, had taken him from the toilets to the lounges, and then into a headliner. And now he could do ballads too. Why not? As soon as they came back from the road this time she was going to throw away the freak suits. And if Beau sang ballads, she wouldn't have to pump him up with drugs so he could prance around doing bumps and grinds and throw himself around until he was covered with sweat like some hopped-up freak in a sideshow. She fucking well was going to turn Beau Beaufort into a class act!

The musicians were gone and Beau lay sprawled out on the pretty blue upholstered bed, his face wet with sweat. He was *out.*

"What happened?" she asked Smokey.

"He wanted to take a nap."

"Don't lie to me, you fucking liar. He's not sleeping—he's zonked."

"Somebody . . . I guess it was one of the guys in the band . . . slipped him a fifth," Smokey said sheepishly.

"Oh you dumb bastard! Is that what I'm paying you for? Is that what the two of you are hanging around for, always stuffing your faces? So I can't turn away for a minute? Are you trying to kill him? How many fuckers have you seen dead from booze and—? Oh, what's the use?" She burst into tears. She knew she shouldn't . . . not in front of Virgil and Smokey. But she was beyond caring. "Get out! Just get the hell out of here, you two fucking shits!" she sobbed, not forgetting that she wasn't going to talk that way any longer but too worn out to care.

They left and she threw herself down on the bed. Beau turned over and mumbled, "Poppy . . ."

"Oh, shut up, you dumb bastard and go back to sleep!" She had an hour or two before she'd have to get him back on his feet.

But then, with a weariness, she got up and went to get a towel. She came back and gently wiped the clammy wetness from the fair brow. "It's all right, Beau. You're going to be a class act. I promise."

31.

I had anticipated that Suellen wouldn't want to go along with us to Los Angeles to attend Suzannah's wedding but that didn't stop me from trying to talk her into it.

"You're such a stick in the mud, Suellen. Why won't you go?"

"I just don't want to."

Suellen was baking bread and blond wisps of hair escaped from the topknot she was wearing. It was amazing. I had just seen Doris Day on TV on the Carson show and she was wearing a topknot too. But Suellen had been wearing the topknot for a few months now so I knew she wasn't just copying Doris.

"I could not care less that Suzannah's getting married—I don't like her. I never did. And in college she wasn't *that* bad. Selfish but almost harmless, and I suppose, amusing. But once she went to New York? You might as well be friends with a rattlesnake. Take that article in *People News*. That awful interview. Just because she's marrying a Texas millionaire, did she have to let the cat out of the bag about her affair with Weston Hamilton, just as he was set to try for the Presidency? It was such a malicious thing to do."

"I guess she wanted to get even with him—"

Suellen kneaded the bread viciously. "I thought that's why she held him up for all that money before she went to California. She got the money. Did she have to ruin his career as well?"

"One story in a gossip magazine isn't going to ruin his career." I chewed on a roll that had just come out of the oven. "And why are you so concerned with Wes Hamilton? You hate his politics and he *did* cheat on his wife, didn't he?"

"That's *his* immorality. I'm talking about Suzannah's. And because I do not approve of Mr. Hamilton's political views does not mean I wish to see him destroyed. That's *my* morality. What Suzannah did was wrong and disgusting. And you're defending her? Where's *your* sense of what's right?"

I sighed deeply and put on my coat to leave. "I think it's right to get even with somebody who's hurt you and betrayed you. And Wes Hamilton did betray Suzannah. Betrayal is a terrible thing. An immoral thing of the highest order of immorality. The Bible says an eye for an eye, doesn't it?"

Suellen flipped the dough over. "I repeat—that's what the money Suzannah got from him was for. That was to even the score."

"Not enough," I shook my head. "That was only money. And money doesn't know about rejection and humiliation and betrayal. Only the heart knows about that. And the heart must have its revenge too."

"Oh phooey, Suzannah doesn't have a heart."

I made a face at her. "Don't come along for the wedding then. Just come along for a good time. We're going to be there a couple of weeks at least and the wedding is only one afternoon. Wouldn't you like to see Cassie and Cleo?"

"Cassie is a darling but I hardly know her anymore. Cleo is okay but I never liked Leo either. If you ask me they're two of a kind—Suzannah and Leo."

"Well, why can't you and Howard simply take a trip to someplace you've never been before?"

"When I'm ready to take a trip, when I don't have to worry about who's minding my children, there are other places I'd rather see than California. Greece, Italy, Israel . . ."

"Israel? Why would you want to go to Israel?"

"Howard would like to see Israel. Our marriage is a partnership, after all. I do care what Howard wants—"

"What point are you trying to make now, Suellen? That *my* marriage isn't a partnership."

"You and Todd have a wonderful marriage. I was just thinking about what kind of wife Suzannah was going to make—"

"Oh, for God's sake, Suellen. Drop it. Forget Suzannah! Forget that I ever came over here to try and persuade you to go along with us. I will see you when we get back. And don't forget—you'll look in on Leah and the children?"

"Of course I will, Buffy darling!" Suellen beamed at me now. "I'll have them over for a dinner a lot."

I laughed at that. Fat chance. "Good luck!" I could just see Leah bringing the children over to Suellen's for dinner. In a month of Sundays.

We checked into the Beverly Wilshire, having chosen it over the Beverly Hills Hotel where Suzannah and Heinie were living. A little Suzannah went a long way, Todd said. But the Wilshire seemed like a good choice. The doorman greeted us by name, the desk man did as well, as did the bell captain and the elevator man. Considerate and painstaking management.

"Thank you, Mr. King," the bellboy said, accepting his tip. "I hope your stay with us will be very pleasant."

Immediately I spotted a lavish arrangement of flowers. *Cleo? Suzannah?* I read the card. "They're from the management. Isn't that nice?"

"Good public relations," Todd agreed.

Only a few minutes later, Cleo called from the lobby. "I couldn't wait another minute. I'm coming right up, all right?"

"For heaven's sake, why aren't you on the elevator already?"

A few minutes later and Cleo stood in the doorway. "Ta ra! Here she is—Mrs. Beverly Hills."

Cleo was startlingly attractive with her new nose and chin, not to mention her hair which was a beigey blond. She only looked a trifle plastic, I decided, a tiny bit manufactured.

"You look stunning, Cleo! Doesn't she look stunning, Todd?"

"Most stunning," he agreed, kissing her hand. "And I love your outfit."

"You're teasing," Cleo laughed. She wore a black satin tunic with several bulky gold chains, skintight black leather jeans, and very high-heeled black leather boots.

"Back in Ohio, I know what we'd call that outfit and it rhymes with *gory,*" I said, delighted with my own wit. "What do you call it here?"

"Casual, sexual chic. The slightly S & M look is very *in* you know." Then she checked out the suite, peeking into the his and hers bathrooms. "Don't you adore the phones right next to the johns? It's really super to see you two." She picked up the card that came with the flowers. "Is that *all* they sent up? Just the flowers?"

Todd and I looked at each other. "Is something missing?" Todd asked.

"Well, they do have a routine in the good hotels. If you're strictly nobody, you get nothing. But if you're a cut above your usual tourist, you get the flowers. If you get a bowl of fruit or a bottle of champagne, it means you rate. But you know you've arrived when you get a white terry cloth monogrammed robe—" Then she swiftly looked at the bowl of flowers and back to us. Realizing she had been a bit tactless, she said,

"Oh, but you know, you'd have to be—" she spread her hands "—Albert Einstein, or the head of—Columbia Pictures, maybe . . . or Warren Beatty!"

"Not just your usual shopping mall operator from Akron, Ohio," Todd smiled, apparently teasing her. But it was not his usual *big* smile, I noticed.

Cleo was visibly embarrassed. "I was just trying to fill you in on the Hollywood way of doing things. I thought you'd think it was amusing —Anyway, let me tell you about Suzannah's wedding. It's going to be a real blast. Considering the length of the guest list, I told Suzannah it would be silly to have something terribly formal. That we should go into something really different. So, considering that it's going to take place on the Twentieth Century lot and have all those backdrops to work against, I recommended a real Western hoedown affair. Maybe even have stuntmen dropping from the roofs of the old saloon sets, and she could serve barbecue and chili on red-checkered tablecloths. . . ."

My goodness, I thought, just like a Texas-style fantasy mall.

"Suzannah loves the idea of honoring Heinie's Texas connection. So that's what it's going to be—a real Hollywood Western set wedding."

"Fabulous."

No sooner had Cleo left, promising to return to pick us up for cocktails and then dinner at the Bistro, than Suzannah showed up in a white angora sweater, white satin jeans, an armful of turquoise and silver bracelets, a western style belt, short silver kid boots, and *huge pointy breasts!*

"Suzannah!" I cried, startled. Both Todd and I could look nowhere but at her loaded bazooms.

"Do they have a life of their own?" Todd finally asked.

Suzannah dimpled. "Dazzling, aren't they? And they are hard! Hard as rocks! Touch one."

When neither Todd nor I made a move in their direction she urged us on: "Go on, it's all right. I don't feel a thing there," and she stroked her appendages herself. "Heinie thought I should have a sexier image. He said, who ever heard of an American movie star without tits?" Then she frowned, biting her lip with very white teeth. "You don't think he was wrong, do you? You don't think they were a mistake?"

"No, of course not," I hastened to say. "They're . . ." I spread my arms, "magnificent. . . . Aren't they, Todd?" But I was appalled. Contrary to Suzannah's credo about allowing nothing to compete with her natural assets, *they* competed for attention with all Suzannah's *true* glories—the flawless white skin, the crown of wild, red-gold hair, even with the elegance of her long-legged, lean, slim-hipped body.

Todd backed me up. "Truly magnificent," he said. Then he apologized for having to leave the moment Suzannah arrived. He explained that he had made an appointment with an industrial realtor before he left Ohio, which came as a surprise to me. "He's going to show me around some of the local shopping malls." He consulted his watch. "It's past lunchtime. Why don't you girls order up some lunch?"

"Oh, I don't want any lunch. I'll just have something to drink. Some champagne, I think—" Suzannah looked around. "Didn't they send up any champagne? They *always* send up champagne. . . ."

Todd scowled at the cocktail table that was empty save for the bowl of flowers.

Hastily I offered, "I'll call room service—"

"Imported . . . French . . . ," Suzannah said, sitting up erectly as her rigid breasts pointed straight ahead. "The French water's better—"

"Water?" I asked, terribly confused.

Suzannah had finished all the Dom Perignon almost by herself. "I have to go. Heinie really doesn't like me out of his sight for more than a few minutes. He adores me, he worships the ground I walk on. Did I tell you that?"

"Yes, you did. And I think that's lovely. But I don't know if you should drive now—"

"Oh heavens, honey, I don't drive. I've got a great big white Fleetwood stretch downstairs with a chauffeur. I'd like a Rolls personally, but Heinie—he's from Texas, you know—he *loves* big Cadillacs. I never did get my California driving license. Driving here *is* complicated. I have to hand it to Cleo. She's as good as a New York cabbie. She knows how to get *everywhere*. She even drives on the freeways. And she whips around, up and down the hills. Of course she's from New Jersey. Everybody drives in New Jersey, they say. Like in California. People in New York City don't drive that much, you know. I haven't driven since I left Kentucky. Do you think I've forgotten how? Leo says that Cleo drives like a man."

I couldn't believe what I was hearing. I knew Cleo said, "Leo says this," and "Leo says that," but now even Suzannah was quoting Leo.

But then Suzannah leaned forward and said contemptuously, "Leo's after us like crazy. He says he's written a screenplay *especially* for me and naturally he wants to direct it."

"And are you going to do it? Leo's screenplay, with him directing?"

"Heinie says we'll wait and see. We haven't seen the screenplay yet. To give the devil his due, Leo *is* good, you know. Even if Cleo *says* that Leo himself *says* so."

And we both laughed heartily, but in the middle of the laughter, Suzannah got up from her chair, threw herself down on the king-sized bed, and burst into tears.

"Oh, Buffy, they're so hard and stiff," she said, cupping her pointed appendages. "Stiff as a man's peenie. They don't even . . . jiggle!"

I sat down on the bed next to her, "It's okay, Suzannah. Where is it written that breasts have to jiggle?"

"Oh, Buffy, you're so lucky. You have such wonderful titties all your own. You haven't changed one bit. You still look like Vivien Leigh. An older Vivien Leigh, of course . . . slightly older, that is."

When Todd returned I asked him if he had enjoyed his tour. "Interesting," he said. "Very interesting. I'm going out again tomorrow. And what have you been up to?"

"After Suzannah left I went through my things . . . the things I brought with me—" I hesitated and he looked at me searchingly. "Frankly," I continued, "after I saw how Suzannah and Cleo were dressed, I was a little concerned that maybe I would look . . . too, you know, Akron, Ohio."

But Todd didn't laugh as I thought he might. Instead he said stiffly, "Your clothes come from the very best shops in all the King Gallerias. And I don't think I have to remind *you* that we have branches of some of the very best stores in the country."

"I *know* that, Todd. Still, our stores carry lines that fit *Ohio.* But not necessarily California. I just didn't want to look like . . . you know—a tourist."

He grew even more reserved. "I don't think you'd look like a tourist in that black import you got at Je Reviens just before we left—"

"I guess I used the wrong word. *Tourist.* I guess what I meant was that I wanted to look like, you know, California—" I smiled a little sheepishly and hoped he would let the whole thing drop. It wasn't like him at all to go on like this, when he knew I felt uncomfortable with my position.

But he did go on. "I see. You wanted to look *California.* But we're in

Southern California. And all California is not Southern California. And I daresay that *all* of Southern California is not Los Angeles, where we are this very minute," he went on pedantically. "And I would daresay that *all* of Los Angeles is not Beverly Hills . . . or if you prefer the term, Hollywood. So when you say you want to look California perhaps what you really mean is you want to look *Hollywood* . . . like Cleo and Suzannah. Personally, I thought the two of them looked like clowns, and I must say I am most heartily surprised that you would wish to emulate them. Surprised and disappointed. I have always thought of you as a person with good taste despite your insignificant *Ohio* background, and I would say that good taste is *not* a matter of geographic boundaries."

I was ready to cry. "What's gotten into you, Todd? You're not acting like yourself. You're testy, that's what you are." Maybe he was just tired, I thought. Jet lag. And then riding around all afternoon looking at shopping centers. "Would you like a drink? Maybe you'd like a little nap. You have some time before dinner."

"No, thank you. What I *would* like is to know what you decided to do, after having examined your Ohio wardrobe and found it wanting."

"I went shopping," I confessed. "I walked down Wilshire Boulevard to Saks—"

"*Saks?*" he demanded indignantly. "You came to California to go shopping in Saks when we have a Saks in—"

"I couldn't find what I was looking for in Saks," I hurriedly interjected. "So I went to this store on Rodeo right up the block from the hotel. It's called Giorgio's—it's supposed to be *the* 'in' store—"

"*In? In?* I don't think I know what you mean."

I snapped. "Oh yes you do, Todd King. You know *exactly* what I mean. You know what *in* means in Akron, Ohio, so don't tell me you don't know what it means in Beverly Hills."

"And did you buy a dress there?"

"Yes I did!"

"Well then, by all means put it on! I'm terrifically interested in seeing what an 'in' dress from an 'in' store looks like. It must be sensational."

"I don't think I care to try it on for you just now. The mood you're in, nothing would look sensational."

"Oh, I'll be fair. I promise I'll be fair."

Was I wrong? Did I see the beginning of a smile on his lips?

"All right. If you promise. No more sarcasm."

"Was I being sarcastic?"

"You *know* you were."

"All right. I promise to be both fair and nonsarcastic."

I disappeared into the "hers" bathroom and came out in a few minutes rustling, wearing the red taffeta dress, the wide skirt just clearing the knees, the stand-up ruffles encircling the neck proceeding in cascades to a deep V-cut. I watched his face as he stared at my prominently displayed breasts for a full minute. Finally he said, his lips twitching as they did when he tried to hold back a laugh, "So now I know why we came to California."

"Why?"

"So you could compete with Suzannah in the big boobs department."

I lowered my lashes with a great show of coyness. "I think that if you'd make the test, you would see that it's no contest. . . ."

He came over to where I was standing and buried his face in the swell of my protruding bosom, moved his lips slowly and deliberately over each breast. "The winner . . ." he murmured.

"Do I get a prize?"

"I think so," he whispered. "But you have to lie down over there to collect." And we moved in unison toward the bed. But then, his lips twitched again. "Tell me, how much did that 'in' dress set us back?"

"Six hundred dollars."

"In that case, you had better remove it first."

"It's a fabulous store, Todd. They have a bar where you can order anything you want, and there are couches and chairs where husbands can wait around for their wives, and a billiards table. And they have men's apparel too."

"How many floors?"

"There's only a mezzanine upstairs. Ladies' shoes."

"Do they have a branch operation?"

"Not that I know of."

"Then if I were in the shopping center business in California I'd put a Giorgio's in every center I opened."

"Maybe they wouldn't want to do it. Maybe they just want to be in Beverly Hills on Rodeo Drive—an elitist sort of thing."

He grinned at me. "Then I'd have to talk them into it, wouldn't I?"

So he *was* thinking about California shopping centers. Or maybe he was only thinking about installing California-style shopping centers in Ohio?

I put on my face in the "hers" bathroom and Todd yelled from the "his." "Did Cassie call?"

"No, she didn't. I tried to call her. I tried that museum where she works—the Blackstone Museum—but they said she was out for the day. So I tried her at home but I didn't get her in. I did get an answering service and I left a message, but I never did hear from her. But we'll see her tonight. She and her husband are joining us for dinner. Still, I wonder why she never got back to me."

He came into my bathroom. "She was too busy, I guess, shopping for an *in* dress for tonight."

"Oh God! If I promise never to use that word again, will *you* promise to drop it?"

Leo and Cleo arrived to take us over to the Beverly Hills Hotel where we would have drinks in Suzannah and Heinie's bungalow before we proceeded to the Bistro, where Guy and Cassie would meet us.

Todd made a point of taking grave note of Cleo's attire—a pink ruffled silk shirt, wine-colored velvet knee britches, white stockings, and black patent pumps. "That's a very fetching outfit," he said. "Is that the latest Hollywood fashion?"

"God! I hope not!" Cleo responded. "The idea is to be a trendsetter, not a Johnny-come-lately." And as I threw Todd a dirty look, she added, "As I'm sure Buffy's dress is—a trendsetter, that is—in Akron."

"It might not be now, but it surely will be in a couple of weeks. You see, she bought it in . . . what's the name of that fabulous store?— Giorgio?"

"Gorgeous," Cleo said.

As Cleo drove Leo demanded of her: "What time did you make the reservation for?"

"Eight thirty."

"It's almost seven thirty already! By the time we're through having drinks we'll be late and you know how they act when you're late for your reservation. They'll put us in Siberia. Why did you make it so fucking early?"

"Because last time you said we got there too late—And they gave all the good tables away. Remember . . . the Pecks were there, and the Carsons, and we got stuck where nobody could see you—"

We pulled up in the porte cochere and the parking attendants leaped forward to open the car doors.

"I'll call right now and tell them we'll be there at nine," Cleo told Leo in an appeasing voice, and we waited in the pink and green lobby while she made the call. Leo's handsome face was dark with emotion. When she returned we proceeded through the loggia to the bungalows.

"Don't worry," Cleo told Leo. "When they see that Heinz Muller and Suzannah are in our party, we'll probably get the best table they have."

"What are you trying to say, Cleo? That Heinie Muller can get a good table and *I* can't. We've been going to the Bistro for years."

"I didn't mean that at all—"

"Maybe *I* can get us a good table," Todd interjected with a straight face.

Leo glared at Todd suspiciously and Todd said, "Well, we *did* get the loveliest arrangement of flowers at the Wilshire."

Suzannah greeted us at the door of her bungalow in a white sweater dress sparked with silver that showed off her pneumatic breasts and several inches of thigh.

"That's what I call a devastating dress," Todd said. "Is that the latest in Hollywood? In Akron, they must really be behind the times. We just *gave up* the mini a couple of years ago, I think. Isn't that right, Buffy Ann?"

I ignored him, but Suzannah said, "Oh, I don't give a damn what anybody else wears or what the latest is—I dress to please myself. And Heinie, of course," she added sweetly.

Heinie, all smiles, came forward to greet us. In a heavy accent, he said, "It's a great pleasure to meet my baby's good friends." He wore a big Stetson, a white cowboy suit, and very high-heeled cowboy boots, which added at least three inches to his height, distinctive only in its lack.

"I didn't order anything to drink sent over. Or anything to nibble either. What's the use of sitting around here drinking when we can do it just as well at the restaurant," Suzannah declaimed. "Let's go."

"But I just changed our reservation to nine o'clock," Cleo said in exasperation.

"Who cares about reservations? Heinie will take care of everything, won't you, Heinie darling?"

Heinie nodded and smiled and Leo threw Cleo a black look.

"And if Heinie can't, I will," Todd assured us all ingenuously. "You should see how I rate at the Wilshire. They sent us up the biggest bowl of flowers," he slyly confided to Heinie who nodded and smiled broadly.

"We might as well all go together in our car," Leo said.
"What are you driving?" Suzannah asked.
"The Mercedes."
Suzannah turned to Heinie with a significant shrug of her shoulders.
"We'll never squeeze in six people."
"We'll take the stretch," Heinie said.
"And then we can have drinks on the way over," Suzannah declared with satisfaction.

"Nice car, Heinie," Todd said as the driver closed the door on us. "Glad to see you're driving a good old U.S. of A. Caddy. We always drive a Caddy. Buffy Ann loved them."
Heinie smiled his approval, leaned back, and stroked Suzannah's right breast while I wondered what would happen when we arrived at the restaurant almost an hour early. I looked at Leo, who appeared to be fuming, and I surmised that he was thinking about the same thing. And while Cleo efficiently handed out the drinks from the built-in bar, Todd told Heinie all about how we did things in Akron. He was playing the wide-eyed yokel for all it was worth, but I don't think he fooled Heinie Muller for a second.

Leo leaped forward at the sight of the maitre d'. "Good evening, Tullio. How are things going? I know we're a little early—" He had a bill tucked into his right hand which he extended for Tullio to shake.
But apparently Tullio didn't notice his hand for he turned to Suzannah and reached for her hand, which he kissed enthusiastically. "Suzannah . . ." he murmured. "Mr. Muller," he bowed. "Please, right over here."
As we all followed Tullio, I could hear Leo whisper to Cleo, "He didn't even call me by name. He acted like he never saw us before. I *told* you to make the reservation in my name—"
"But I did. Of course I did!" she fervently whispered back.
After we were seated at what I could only presume was the best table in the house, I recognized Angie Dickinson at the next table, and Danny Thomas at the table next to that one. And I heard Todd say, "Heinie, old boy, you should have let me give *my* name. I bet we would

have gotten a really good table." Then he turned to Leo. "Leo, old man, how come we're sitting on top of the kitchen?"

Both Leo and Cleo automatically turned around and *looked* for the kitchen, although they knew exactly where they were sitting and that the kitchen wasn't anywhere in sight.

As for me, I was having the time of my life. I hadn't seen Todd in such high form since we had first met.

Suzannah sent her martini back to the bar. "Look at that martini," she told the waiter. "I declare it's positively *yellow* with vermouth."

"Give her a martini that's not yellow," Heinie told the waiter. "It must be clear . . . clear."

Just then the most sexually attractive man I had ever seen appeared at our table. I recognized him at once. Guy Savarese. But where was Cassie?

Guy Savarese flashed white teeth at Suzannah and Heinie, nodded curtly to Leo and Cleo, and smoothed his hair as he was introduced to Todd and me. I figured out that he had flashed so large a smile at Heinie that he had used his smile up.

"Where is Cassie?" I blurted out, then explained, "I'm dying to see her."

"She wasn't feeling well," he said shortly, and looked over at the next table at Angie, then over at Danny Thomas, then all around the room to see who else was there, intermittently squaring his shoulders, smoothing his mustache, touching his hair.

"What's wrong with her?" Cleo asked. "Is it the virus? It's going around—"

Guy waved to somebody across the room. "Just feeling a bit off her feed," he said, giving a little laugh. "Cassie's delicate," he said, sounding a touch sarcastic, I thought. Then he added, addressing Heinie, "She's Cassandra Blackstone Hammond's daughter," as if that explained her delicacy.

Heinie smiled as the waiter brought Suzannah a crystal-clear martini. All conversation stopped as Suzannah brought the martini to her lips and she tasted.

"Good," she said and smiled and everyone breathed a sigh of relief and Heinie said, "Wonderful . . ."

"I love your jacket, Guy," Todd said, touching the fabric of Guy's cream cashmere sport coat. "You'll have to tell me where you got it. I'm not going home to Akron until I have one just like it—"

Guy measured Todd with narrowed eyes. "It's from Bijan's. You can't go there without an appointment."

"Bijan is a tailor then?"

"No," Guy sneered.

Leo helped out. "It's a shop but their doors are locked to the public. You can't get through the door without a reservation."

"Wow! Just like a high-class restaurant. Imagine! A store that's locked to the public. I don't know what they'd say about that in Ohio. What do you think of that, Buffy? I think I'll call them the first thing in the morning. Whose name do you think I should use so they'll break down and let me in. Yours, Guy? Yours, Leo?" And then without waiting for an answer, he said, "I know. Yours, Heinie."

And Heinie moved his head up and down. "Wonderful," he smiled.

Leo sent back his steak as overdone and Cleo her lamp chops as underdone.

"Have to keep them on their toes," Leo explained as Suzannah gave a little cry.

"I forgot to tell you, Buffy—you're the matron of honor and you have to get a special dress. It's only a few days to the wedding, so you can't have anything made up. We'll just have to shop for the right thing. Since the theme of the wedding is Western, I thought a long dress but with a prairie look—"

Leo was amazed. "I thought Cleo was going to be the matron of honor. She already has a dress—"

"Why did you assume that?" Suzannah asked haughtily. "Buffy's always been my best friend."

"But Cleo's doing all the work, the planning, the invitations, the caterers—she already has her dress. I think you owe it to her, Suzannah," Leo said firmly.

I found the situation very embarrassing. I didn't care if I were matron of honor or not, but I felt that Leo was way out of line. After all, who *demanded* a position of honor? I waited for Cleo to hush Leo, as a matter of pride, but Cleo said nothing, much to my amazement. She too waited for Suzannah's answer, apparently hoping Suzannah would change her mind.

"I don't owe anything to anybody," Suzannah finally said. Actually, *sneered.* Then she turned to Heinie and her face relaxed. "Except for Heinie, of course." She threw her arms around his small figure and hugged him to her huge breasts. "Isn't that so, Heinie?"

Still, Cleo and Leo looked from Heinie to Todd, even to the oblivious Guy, in indignation.

Finally, I said, "Why don't we share the honor? Cleo and I?"

But Suzannah lowered her lashes, set her mouth, and shook her head. No one save Heinie was going to tell her what to do. And Heinie, for the first time that evening, was unsmiling. He looked at Leo coldly, his mouth a straight line. And then he smiled at me, "You'll make a most charming matron of honor, darling. . . ."

"I'll drink to that," Todd raised his glass. "And to tell you the truth, I can't wait to see the dress Buffy gets. Why don't we all go to Giorgio's and see what they have in the way of matron of honor prairie dresses? I'll just bet they'll have exactly the right thing. Now tell me, Suzannah. Give me the straight dope. Is this prairie thing really what's being shown for matrons of honor this season? I know how you feel about wearing exactly what you like and to hell with what's in, and I respect you for that, but as far as Buffy's concerned, I feel it's incumbent on her as a fashion representative of all Ohio, to wear what's 'in,' you know?"

I had been holding off but now I kicked him under the table. Suzannah looked puzzled, as if she were wondering if Todd had lost his mind. Then she burst out laughing, "If that's the case, she can wear anything she goddamn pleases."

Suzannah and I repaired to the ladies room where Suzannah took out her old gold perfume flacon with her name on it and touched her fingers first to the flacon's opening, then to her throat. I wondered what scent filled the gold case now that Suzannah the perfume no longer existed. Perhaps Heinie would buy up a perfume or cosmetic company and reintroduce the line.

"Can you imagine the nerve of that little worm, Leo, trying to foist Cleo on me as matron of honor?" Suzannah spoke loudly, ignoring the presence of the washroom attendant. But I, very much aware, kept my voice to a whisper: "Frankly, I'm not surprised at Leo, but I was by Cleo. She seemed as determined as he. And while I'm really pleased to be your matron of honor, I really don't understand all the fuss, why it means so much to them."

"Honestly honey, can't you see? It's the publicity. The columns . . . the trades . . . they'll all cover my wedding and they, Leo and Cleo, want Cleo's picture in the paper . . . to be named in print for all the world to see . . . Mrs. Leo Mason . . . matron of honor at Suzannah's wedding. They want the whole town to think that Mr. and Mrs. Leonard Mason are *the* best friends of Suzannah and Heinie Muller! It would do wonders for them socially, not to mention professionally. Even with the new series with Guy going on the air in three weeks, Leo is *still* only TV," she said with contempt. "Why, the publicity alone would get them a hundred invitations to the parties where they're still not invited, even with Cleo knocking herself out."

"But you *are* thinking of doing Leo's screenplay? Letting him direct?" I fervently hoped so, for Cleo's sake.

"Of course. I told you. Leo might be obnoxious but he's *good.* I can detest Leo as a person, but that doesn't mean we can't use his talent."

We went into adjoining booths and Suzannah yelled over the divider, "So! What do you think of Guy Savarese?"

I knew already I didn't like him. As far as I could see, there *was* nothing to like. His sulky good looks? But I wasn't about to say anything derogatory about Cassie's husband, and certainly not in a public toilet.

"He's certainly sexy looking," I said, as Suzannah brushed her hair. "Probably the sexiest looking man I've ever seen. Don't you think so?"

"I suppose he's sexy." She wrinkled her nose.

"Doesn't turn you on, huh?"

Suzannah laughed. "You know how it is with me, Buffy. *Nobody* turns me on. Except me." And she stroked her new breasts tenderly for emphasis as the matron stared. *"I'm* my greatest lover."

And Heinie?

Suzannah looked at me, reading the question in my eyes, and she laughed again. "Oh, Buff, grow up! How much do you think dear Heinie would love me if I were just plain Suzannah?"

Then, two women came into the ladies room and we departed and luckily for me, I didn't have to answer.

"Guess what, Buffy Ann?" Todd said when we got back to the table. "Heinie here has asked me to be his best man. What do you think of that?"

I was nonplussed. What a strange place this Hollywood was. Where a man like Heinz Muller asked a perfect stranger to be his best man. "I think it's wonderful!" I enthused. Why had Heinie, a man so rich and powerful, picked Todd to be his best man when he must have a thousand friends here and in Dallas? Even this evening at least twenty people had come over to the table to greet him.

Heinie put his hand over mine and smiled into my eyes. *What is he telling me? That he too, like me, knew a best man when he saw one?* No fool he, Heinie Muller. And I hoped that Suzannah, for her own sake, realized what kind of a man *she* was getting.

"And guess what else?" Todd enthused. "Heinie and I are going to that place Guy likes . . . Bijan's? . . . to get our suits. Western suits. What color do you think I should get?" He turned to the others and said, "Buffy Ann knows all the 'in' colors. I respect her judgment completely."

For the others I smiled. As for Todd, I kicked him under the table again.

As we finished dessert, Leo, who had obviously decided to give up his pique, announced: "Tomorrow night everybody's coming to our house. We're giving a party in honor of the Kings . . . to officially welcome them to our little town. We're inviting a few close friends. About a hundred people, right, Cleo?"

Cleo practically dropped her demitasse spoon, but quickly answered, "Oh, yes. Right. About a hundred."

Fast on her feet, I thought. Aloud I said, "But you can't possibly do that. It's too much. How can you arrange a party like that in one day? And you have enough to do what with the wedding and all . . ." My voice trailed off.

I was exhausted from the one day we had been in this place. These people were exhausting, even Guy Savarese, who had spoken almost not a word all evening except to Heinie, and had spent the whole evening looking around the room to see who was there and if they were looking at him. His silent frenzy was exhausting.

"Oh, it's nothing for Cleo," Leo said. "By ten o'clock tomorrow morning, she'll have everything arranged. Cleo is the best little party-giver in all Hollywood." And Cleo beamed.

"Are you going to call Hank Grant at the *Reporter* tonight, Cleo, or will you wait until tomorrow morning?" Suzannah asked, seemingly guileless. "I do hope he doesn't have another party he's going to—You really should have waited until you knew if he were free or not—And how about Army at *Variety?*"

Cleo smiled firmly, refusing to be rattled. "Oh, I'm sure they both can cover more than one party a night."

"Be sure and tell them that Heinie and I will be there. Then they'll be sure to make it," Suzannah grinned.

Abruptly, Guy gave Cleo the benefit of his flashing teeth. "Be sure and tell them that Guy Savarese will be there."

"And Cassie?" I asked nervously. I was beginning to feel I was in one of those mystery movies where the heroine is mysteriously missing and nobody but me suspects anything is wrong.

"Natch," Cassie's weird husband said and looked at me coldly. I could feel myself flush. I wondered if I was turning into one of those women who resented any man who gave no sign of being attracted to them. Was that my problem? I didn't like Guy Savarese because I didn't feel any wave of sexual interest flowing from him to me?

"Well, I certainly *hope* we see Cassie tomorrow night," Todd laughed, but eyeing Guy. "We're beginning to think she doesn't want to see us."

"I'm sure she does," Guy mumbled.

I was relieved that Todd had helped me out but then he said, "We're really looking forward to seeing her, and seeing the first episode of your show too."

"You're going to see that first episode really soon," Leo interjected. "We're planning to screen it tomorrow night at the party. It's going to be the entertainment feature of our evening, but don't say anything to anybody. It's going to be a kind of sneak screening just for our friends."

Even though Leo seemed to be addressing Heinie alone, Todd said, "I won't tell a soul. Isn't this exciting, Buffy Ann? A real Hollywood sneak preview!"

Leo demanded the check, declaring, "My party," but Heinie waved a desultory hand. "When Heinie Muller is present, there is no check—"

Leo's face darkened and I saw Cleo sigh with a great show of patience. It seemed that Leo had lost another round. The ultimate here, it appeared, was *not* signing a restaurant tab, much less using a credit card —*it was not even having it appear at all.* Hollywood magic!

"Gee!" I heard Todd say. "I could have let you use my American Express card. Do you know, we've gone all over Europe on this card, even without my picture on it. Isn't that right, Buffy Ann?"

"I really feel sorry for Cleo," I said as we rode up in the elevator back at the Wilshire. "I bet she's going to be up all night making lists for that party tomorrow night. I'm sure it was the first she heard of it when Leo announced it."

"Never mind Cleo. The important question is: what is Buffy Ann King going to wear to this star-studded event?"

"Don't you dare start that with me again. You were impossible!"

"Really? And I thought I was being pleasant, agreeable, and lively, so that everyone would like me. Do you think everyone liked me? How about that Guy Savarese? I don't think he was all that crazy about me."

"Why would he be? You're only a hick tourist from Akron, Ohio. A nobody."

"Oh, is that so? Well to tell you the truth, *I* wasn't crazy about him, so there!"

"Me too."

But the question in my mind was not why Todd wasn't crazy about Guy but why Cassie *was.* Or was she? I felt a terrible urgency to see her. I had a terrible anxiety about her.

"They're all really something, aren't they? I think Heinie Muller might be the sanest person there tonight. There's something very nice about him—"

"A real fun bunch," Todd said, opening the door. "Do you see what I see?"

I looked where Todd was looking. A bowl of magnificent fruit, towering and overflowing, stood next to the vase of flowers on the coffee table. "How could I miss it?"

"Did you ever see such beautiful fruit? Look at those grapes." He plucked one and popped it into his mouth. "Delicious! Taste one."

I took one and placed it in my mouth. "I don't know . . . it tastes a little sour to me."

I thought Todd was asleep but suddenly he turned around and asked me if I thought the bowl of fruit had been destined all along to be there when we returned that evening, or did I think it had been Suzannah's presence in our suite that afternoon, elevating us to prominence, that had prompted the management to send it up?

"It was *you.* They discovered that you were really royalty incognito. That you really were a king. King of Ohio."

"Hah! You think you're kidding?" he responded.

Actually I didn't give a damn about why the management had sent up the fruit. I was thinking about Cassie.

Cassie sat by the window in the bedroom, staring out at the black night. When she saw Guy's Ferrari come roaring up the driveway, she would get into bed, pretend she was asleep. Although she was dying to know about the evening, about Buffy and Todd, she wouldn't ask him. Buffy must think she was terrible not to have shown up tonight. Maybe by tomorrow morning her appearance would be improved enough that she could—

She touched her cheek gingerly. It still hurt. She went into the bathroom, put on the light, looked into the mirror to further examine the damage. The mirror sent back a reflection—*the face of a fool.* She wanted to smash it! Either the mirror or her own face, but her own face was already smashed, wasn't it?

She had waited for him to come home that night, waited for their once-a-month copulation. The room had been in semi-darkness. He had come into the room, eyes fixed on her face, his own face tight, suffused with the rage that had become ordinary for him. The angry eyes had raced up and down her body as she held her breath, thinking that perhaps she would suffocate.

He came up to her slowly, halted an inch or so from her. Slowly he revolved the lower half of his body against her, not touching her with his hands. Then slowly, deliberately, he shucked his jacket, unbuttoned the monogrammed shirt, and tugged at his fly. Her mouth was dry as his hands went inside the negligee and then he shoved her against the bedroom wall and as her body slid down to the floor, his hand cracked against her cheekbone. . . .

She hadn't been able to go to work that morning, hadn't been able to see Buffy and Todd. She had nursed her angry, bruised cheek, its bright red welt turning to violet-brown in the area directly under the eye.

How many days out of her lifetime would she miss nursing wounds? How many months, how many years would it take before she fought back? Before she, the worm, turned? Before she left him? Was proving her mother wrong worth this? Was even a baby worth this? And what kind of a father did she propose to give her child? Some kind of a brute-monster? Was the compulsion to prove her mother wrong, the compulsion to have a baby stronger than her pride and reason? It was a compulsion that could destroy her. And yet, she felt powerless to fight it.

Once I started thinking about Cassie, I was unable to sleep. Todd still wasn't sleeping either. He turned to me: "The oranges in that fruit bowl are really beautiful. Big as a grapefruit. Do you think you'd like to have one now?"

I giggled in the dark. "I think I'll wait for morning."

Then he rolled over on top of me, allowing his body to drop its dead weight upon mind, crushing the breath out of me, until I begged for mercy, laughing so hard I could hardly speak. "All right, I'll eat the damned orange."

"That's better," he said, but he didn't get up to fetch the orange. Instead, he nuzzled my neck, then suddenly stopped. "I'm going out to look at some more shopping centers tomorrow. Why don't you go and see Cassie the very first thing in the morning?"

He had been thinking about Cassie too. And I knew for the second time that evening why Heinie Muller had chosen Todd to be best man. Heinie Muller, a truly clever man.

32.

Since she had decided not to go to work again that morning, Cassie pretended to be asleep until Guy left the house. Then, still in her robe, she dragged herself down to the kitchen where she found the note he had left her. There was a party at Cleo and Leo's that night in Buffy and Todd's honor. That was all it said. Not a word to indicate that he was aware of her damaged face or whether or not there was any question of her attending.

She could try to go. She *would* go. She would cover the bruise with a lot of foundation, wear big black glasses. It was not uncommon to be seen wearing dark glasses in the evening, after all. A lot of people did. This was Hollywood.

The question was, was she ready to see Buffy? Could she bear it? Buffy had that way of not only looking you straight in the eyes with those green eyes of hers, but straight into your head and heart as well. Buffy had a sixth sense, a clairvoyance.

She put up a pot of coffee. That was all the breakfast she could stomach. Then she went into the laundry room off the kitchen and separated whites from darks. She put the whites into the washer, waited for the machine to fill with water, measured out detergent. While the whites washed, she would have a cup of coffee and vacuum the nearly bare living room.

As she started to take the vacuum from the closet, the door chimes sounded, startling her. No one ever came to her door. It was probably someone collecting for a charity. Or maybe it was the mailman with a letter that had to be signed for. She waited to see if the caller would give up and go away.

The chimes rang again. She would have to answer, try to get rid of whoever it was quickly. Shielding her face with her hand, she opened the door but a crack. *Buffy!*

Forgetting her face, she dropped her hand, opened the door wide. "Buffy! Oh Buffy!"

For a moment, I thought Cassie wasn't going to let me in. But she did and I tried to smile at her, but I was appalled. It was eleven in the morning and here was Cassie still in her robe, painfully thin, her hair unbrushed and her face *bruised* . . . the area around the eye discolored. Involuntarily, my hand reached out to touch her poor face. But quickly, protectively, her hand flew to cover her cheek and she started to say, "I had an acci—"

I had this lump in my throat and I felt the tears, hot ones, come to my eyes. "Oh, Cassie! Oh Cassie, *why?*"

We sat in the kitchen at an old oak table.

"Oh Buffy, you don't know what a relief it is to tell somebody—"

"Yes. You've told me, Cassie, but I don't *really* understand. I can understand why you married him. You were pregnant and scared and you couldn't tell your mother. And you had never told her even about being raped. And I know how you felt about Guy. You knew you weren't in love with him but you were attracted to him just the same and you thought that possibly you might come to love him. But then your baby didn't live. And by this time you *knew* what he was really like . . . a brute who didn't love you even one tiny bit. Really! I don't think *anyone* would understand why you stay married to him!"

"But I've explained it all to you!" Her voice was filled with hysteria. "I *will not* admit to my mother that I've made another mistake. That she was so right again and I so wrong. Don't you see? That's been the pattern of my life. And it's what my mother's waiting for—for me to admit I was stupid again and wrong and go crawling back to her! I can't do it again! I just can't!"

"Cassie, oh Cassie, what kind of a reason is that, stacked up against the kind of life you've been leading with Guy? Even if he didn't do *that* —" I gestured to her face.

"I don't think he *means* to, you know," she entreated. "It's . . . it's . . . just the way he makes love. . . ."

"Love?"

"Performs the act, then. Sex is a violent act to Guy. It's not *always* like this." She touched her face again.

I became furious. "Well, that says a lot. Maybe the next time, he'll break your nose or your jaw or . . . kill you, for God's sake! I can't believe that you're a willing partner to this—because you are, you know —a partner."

"I have to have the baby—"

I was sick to my stomach. I shook with the need to persuade her that she was acting in an irrational way, that she was killing herself. "Oh God, and what about the rest of it? What about the loving marriage you might be having instead of this ugly, sterile life—marriage to a decent, loving person?"

"But it's not going to be forever! Don't you see? I just have to wait until Guy is a big star and until I have a baby to show Mother—Then I'll be able to walk away proudly . . . not crawl to her."

"But you don't have to crawl now. You're not a teenager. You can stand up straight and tell them both to go to hell! Guy and your mother! This is the twentieth century, Cassie, and these are the seventies, for God's sake!"

"It's easy for you to see things that way, Buffy. You're strong and— *This* is the only thing I have the strength for . . . now. I have to stay here and endure everything . . . even the sex . . . if it means I'll have a baby. I have to stand everything to show my mother!"

"I don't believe you," I said bluntly.

She drew back as if I had hit her, rejected her. "What don't you believe?"

"I don't believe that you stay here with Guy to prove to your mother you didn't make a mistake. Or that you have sex with Guy when you know how bad it's going to be because you want to have a baby before you leave him—"

Cassie's mouth twisted in a weird smile. "You always were an amateur psychiatrist—"

I was determined to tell her whatever it was that needed to be told. "Frankly, I don't think anyone has to be a psychiatrist to see what you're about . . . to see why you remain in this situation, why you allow yourself to be physically tortured by Guy and mentally tortured by your mother. I think it's pretty obvious to anyone with the slightest bit of insight. Cassie, you *want* to be punished!"

Her face contorted with anguish, her hands clawed at her unbrushed hair. My God! I thought. Maybe I had said the wrong words? Maybe I *was* playing amateur psychiatrist and would do more harm than good? "Why, Buffy? Why would I want to be punished?"

I didn't know whether to go on or not. What was the right thing to do? But having said so much already, did I have a choice?

"I think you must know yourself, Cassie. Down deep you know. You want to be punished because you think you're no good, that you're worthless."

Cassie was calm now, outwardly anyway, but I had the feeling that everything I had said to her hadn't made a dent at all. She turned on the light under the pot of coffee, set out cups and saucers. She took a carton of half-n'-half out of the refrigerator and reached for a small pitcher on a shelf.

"Oh, just put the carton on the table, Cassie. You don't need the creamer," I said, almost irritably. *I* wasn't calm.

Still she took down the pitcher and filled it from the carton. "I guess I'm a creature of habit. Or my training." She smiled at me apologetically. "My mother's daughter, you know," she said with mock derision.

"You don't have to apologize for doing things nicely, Cassie. Or for being a lady. That's my point," I said, not able to leave it alone. "You *are* a lady, you *are* a nice person, you *are* good—there's no reason for you to *need* to be punished. What did you ever do to merit this kind of abuse?"

"But I never said that I wanted to be punished. That's your idea." She put the coffee pot down on the table and sat down. "Besides, I haven't always been so nice. I did deceive Guy, didn't I? In one of the very worst ways a woman can deceive a man. I married him pregnant with another man's child, allowing him to believe he was the father. Besides marrying him when I didn't love him. That was pretty terrible, wasn't it?"

"Maybe it would have been if he loved you. But it's obvious he didn't and doesn't. He married you for your mother and her money. I would think that would make you even."

But she wasn't listening to me. She was thinking of something else. "My mother never loved me either. The only person that ever loved me was my father and he died. Maybe it was because of him, my father, that Mother doesn't love me. She always said things about him . . . weird things. One time she would say, he was stubborn and conceited and willful, and other times she would say he was weak, with no backbone, that he was a mouse. It doesn't sound like the same person. It's confusing. She *always* speaks of him with contempt. And I'm his daughter. So she treats me with contempt too."

"See? Your mother made you feel unworthy—unworthy of love and therefore deserving of punishment. Any psychiatrist would tell you that you're a classic case. But Cassie, you *are* loving and *worth* loving. You *deserve* love," I pleaded.

"Thank you, Buffy, for your concern. But really, you don't have to worry. This won't go on for much longer. Guy is getting closer to success and . . . Really! It won't be that long. But if I'm going to be able to live with myself I have to win this battle with Mother. And I *am* going to win it if it's the last thing I do!" She made a fist and struck the table so hard the coffee in her cup sloshed over the rim into the saucer and then over its edge onto the table, and both of us sat motionless watching the brown liquid creep across the table.

She showed me through the house. *"Ma Maison,"* she giggled foolishly and when I looked at her with a worried frown, she said, "That's the name of a fancy restaurant here. And my house—it's very fancy, isn't it?"

It would have been, I thought, except for the ceiling showing brown stains of leakage and where the paper gently peeled away from the walls. And maybe, if the rooms held more than a few pathetic pieces of furniture.

We went out onto the back terraces that circled the empty pool which time and perhaps a violent storm had left cracked and strangely at home with the wild and uncontrolled flora. There was an air of genteel disintegration. Again I felt compelled to speech although I had probably already said too much. "This is something else I don't understand. Why is your house so unfurnished and run-down, and your grounds so overgrown? Guy's been working in Leo's series for a couple of months at least, hasn't he? And I've heard enough to know that stars in series make very big money. And he was doing fairly well before the series? He was getting parts?"

"Yes, he *was* getting parts before the series, and making some money, but there were always expenses, big expenses. He always had to have a new expensive car for his image, an extensive wardrobe, his hair is trimmed and styled every week, and his nails manicured. Gymnasium and a masseur . . . lessons, and a voice coach and a publicist and the agent's percentage. It all went . . . quickly," she said tiredly. "When I asked for money for the house, he always told me to go to my mother. He always laughed when he said it, knowing I wouldn't . . . couldn't —And of course I couldn't.

"And then with the series, when he started getting that five-figure salary every week, as they say, I thought that at least that part of my struggle was over, the financial struggle. But it didn't work out that way. You see when my mother gave us this house it was supposed to be a gift, an outright gift. But the lawyers made us sign papers . . . a mortgage agreement that was only a formality they said, to protect us all. And while we didn't have to make monthly payments, it was still a terrible financial burden to run this house. But that's beside the point— We didn't have to make any monthly payments, but the moment the news was released that Guy had the series, my mother *sold the paper* . . . the mortgage agreement that we had signed . . . on the house, so now we do have to pay it . . . the monthly payments and they're huge . . . the interest rate is fantastic. And besides that, we have to pay for all the months in the past! Nothing was given to us. It was all deferred, all payable on demand. We have all that deferred accrued interest to pay!"

Her mother was indeed Machiavellian. If I thought that Cassie had exaggerated about her mother before, I was now convinced. "Why don't you just move out? If you didn't put any money into the house all this time you have nothing to lose. Only the appreciated value. But that would still be better than—"

Cassie shook her head, smiled wearily. "My mother's lawyers are better than that. We would still be responsible for all the past payments . . . all the accrued interest . . . that's the way they wrote it. And Guy won't turn his back on this house, he says, not with its appreciated value, not after the years he spent struggling to hold on to it. Empty and run down, it's *still* a Bel Air estate. He says he's going to wait until the market goes up, explodes. Everybody says it will, you know, with the Arabs coming in with all their oil money.

"But that's only what he says. It's not that that he's waiting for, not really."

"What is he waiting for?"

"He's waiting to have the last laugh. He's waiting to move into Blackstone Manor. He's waiting for Mother to die."

Her words fell on the golden air, the *bel* air. Strange, darkly Gothic words amid all the foliage and sunshine.

"And what about you, Cassie?" I asked softly, while somewhere a bird chirped. "What about you? Is that what you're waiting for too? For your mother to die so that you can leave Guy without having to admit to her that you were wrong?"

"No, of course not!" she cried. "Mother has to live so that she can see she was wrong about me . . . that I can win too! If Mother died before that, it would be winning by default, don't you see?"

No, I didn't see, and I didn't understand and I just wanted to go some place and be sick. All I saw was that Cassie was destroying herself.

And then Cassie was smiling at me. This time, it was a strangely sweet smile. "Look up there at the pink house. Isn't it beautiful? That's really *ma maison*. I love it! I look at it each night. At night it's all lit up because nobody lives there now. The lights are to keep burglars and vandals away. A German actress lived there once. Her name was Jenny. Jenny Elmann. Isn't that a beautiful name? She married a man from Northern California. A man who was a railroad heir . . . John Starr Winfield was his name. John Starr Winfield from San Francisco, and one night she mistook him for a prowler, an intruder, and picked up a rifle and shot him right through the heart. Isn't that a terrible story? So sad. She closed up the house and went back to Europe. And my lovely house stands there all alone bravely in the night. I think about her often . . . poor Jenny Elmann. Think how her heart must have ached. To have shot with her own hand the man she loved." She turned to me, her smile fading. "*If* she loved him . . ."

I looked up at the house transfixed. I could almost see the beautiful Jenny standing in a darkened room, taking aim at an intruder's heart, blowing it away. Only her husband had been the intruder. Had she wanted him dead? Did Cassie want Guy dead as Guy wanted her mother dead? I was frightened for Cassie, now more so than before.

I turned to Cassie who stood motionless, still looking up at the pink house. I wanted to take her hand, to take her away with me, away from her own empty house, away from the pink house on the hill, away from this crazy Lotus Land, back to Akron where the sun didn't always shine but where people like Suellen and Howard lived. But I knew that she was committed, that she wouldn't leave . . . not yet.

I said with a little laugh, "Well, don't go buying any rifles."

Her eyes widened. "Oh, but we have one. Guy just bought one. There've been a lot of burglaries in the neighborhood lately. We don't have much to steal but Guy . . . Guy thinks everyone wants to take away what he has."

It was time for me to leave. Todd was probably back in the hotel waiting for me.

"Cassie . . ." I said hesitantly. "I wish you would see someone . . . just so you had someone to talk to—"

"You mean a doctor? A psychiatrist? You think I'm sick? Crazy?"

"No. Of course not. But I do think you're having a bad time and that you might be acting in a self-destructive way. I told you that before. And just talking is good, just to get everything clear in your own mind —what you *think* you're doing as opposed to what you actually are doing. And since you don't have any money available to you . . . I . . . we . . . would gladly lend you the money—"

"It's good of you to be concerned but no, no thank you. It's not as complicated as you think. And it *is* clear in my mind. It's really very simple. Three easy steps. First the baby. Second, Guy's success, and then the third—Mother will have to say, 'Yes, you were right, Cassie, and I was wrong.' Then, you see, I'll be free. Simple."

But there's a catch to that, Cassie. Who is to say what constitutes success? Maybe your mother will never admit it. Maybe she will turn her nose up at your baby. Maybe she will say: "Why, your baby is no more worthy of love than you yourself are. Just look at who its father is . . ."

Oh, Cassie, what will you do then?

33.

For the evening's festivities I put on the dress I had bought at Je Reviens in our Akron Galleria. Todd said, "Even if that dress *is* Ohio, you're still going to be the most beautiful woman there."

"Suzannah is going to be there," I reminded him.

"She never could hold a candle to you."

Hold that thought, will you?

Sighting Cassie the moment I walked into Cleo's house, I thought what a miracle it was that she had pulled herself together to make it this evening. You couldn't suspect a thing from the way she looked. She *was* wearing dark glasses but so were a few other people. But then Hollywood was supposed to be the land of miracles where the projected image was bigger and probably better than life, and Cassie was a true child of Hollywood, born and bred only a half mile or so away. Her face appeared smooth and tanned—you were supposed to be tan in the country of sunshine, weren't you? Her hair, obviously freshly washed and waved, flowed down her back in gorgeous pale lemon-yellow technicolor. And her excessive slenderness? Well, who could possibly be too thin here in the land of rich narcissistic people hyped on diet, massage, and exercise? As for her dress, while it wasn't high couture or Rodeo Drive, it was of a violet blue that matched her eyes, which were every bit as violet as those of cinema star Liz Taylor. The only thing missing from the star image was the white teeth flashing. No flash. No smile. She didn't know how to turn that on, as her husband did. Maybe that was why he was destined to be a star, he knew how and when—when he was looking in the direction of a person with power. Industry power.

Like tonight. This party, given in my and Todd's honor, was an Industry happening, filled with people only from the Industry and Guy Savarese was on, smiling all over the place, much different from last night. Looking all around me at Cleo's splendidly partified living room and the dazzling crowd, I could not but admire how adroitly she had pulled everything together. And her guest list was truly sensational—I recognized several faces from the television screen.

When Suzannah came running up to hug me, resplendent in a silver jumpsuit with a neckline cut down to here, I commented on the terrific job Cleo had done. But the soon-to-be bride tossed her head: "TV people, for the most part. And most of this bunch would go to the opening of a funeral home if they got an invitation. They're desperate to get out, to see and be seen. Not to mention the free food and booze. Cleo does do well in that department," she said grudgingly. "Let's get ourselves a drinkie-poo, speaking of booze."

There was a bar set up in the sunken living room, in addition to the twenty foot built-in mahogany one with its wine-colored leather armchair stools that was the pièce de résistance of the paneled library. Waiters passed hot barbecued shrimp and miniature avocado quiches, and through the open dining room doors, I saw a table already laden with a buffet that would quicken the heart of even the holder of the most jaded appetite. Beyond the dining room, through the French doors that led to the terrace surrounding the pool, there were small tables set up, draped in mauve moiré tablecloths and surrounded by little gilt chairs.

Cleo, in mauve silk pajamas, rushed up, "You have drinks? Great! Have you met everybody or anybody? We're not doing place cards tonight. We're just being very informal and everybody will sit wherever he or she pleases. Leo thought this would be all right since we do have quite a crowd. So we'll all sit around almost as if we were all en famille. Suzannah, do introduce Buffy to everybody. I have to make sure the projectionist will show up on time. Leo is a little uptight tonight, what with the showing of the Hollywood and Vine pilot. Did I tell you we're expecting Zsa Zsa tonight?"

"Not Eva?" Suzannah asked, her eyebrows raised.

Cleo swept off and I turned to Suzannah: "Really! You're certainly on her case. Why?"

Suzannah waved a white, red-tipped hand. "They're such opportunists, the two of them, they make me want to puke."

"It's not her fault," I defended Cleo, much as I always did Suzannah herself.

"Isn't it? She married him, didn't she? And she puts up with his crap, doesn't she?"

I struggled for an answer. "Sometimes people just don't know how *not to* put up with something—they just get submerged . . . gradually."

"Let's not get into this. I don't want to fight with you, Buff, over Cleo —This is your party. There's Heinie over there—" and she pulled me over to where Heinie was holding court.

"My little girl," Heinie was saying, "wanted to retire. She wanted to give up her career to make a little nest for me. But I told her no . . . a star is a star . . . and she owed it to her public . . . to the world. I could not accept such a sacrifice."

I looked at Suzannah speculatively. I found it hard to believe that she had actually been prepared to give up her stardom for a "little nest," no matter how grand, with Heinie Muller. She shrugged now, modestly, smiled demurely, sat down plumb in Heinie's lap (an incongruous picture) and when Heinie started to boast of Suzannah's magnificent intelligence quotient, I took the moment to drift out of the enthralled circle and seek out Todd or Cassie.

As I wandered through the clusters of guests, Leila Pulitzer, the mother of the hostess, in gauzy yellow pajamas, grabbed me. "Buffy darling!" she exclaimed, introducing me to the couple she was with— Hilda and Tommy Stanton. "I was just telling Hildy and Tommy that they can't afford *not* to sell their ditzy little house south of Wilshire and buy up . . . up . . . up on the North Side. And I have just the house for them on Camden in the 600 block and they can nail it down with a mere $100,000. What with the deduction and the fact that this property is going to be worth easily a million dollars in the next couple of years, they can't afford *not* to buy it. You're an accountant, Buffy. Tell them how much they *need* the write-off."

At that moment I remembered that Leila was now in real estate. I shook my head. "I couldn't possibly, unless I had all the figures. And I don't know anything about Beverly Hills real estate." At the look on Leila's face, I added: "But real estate of course is always the best investment . . . tax shelter. . . ."

Hildy and Tommy took the opportunity to excuse themselves and they made a dash for the buffet.

"Stupid idiots!" Leila dismissed them. "You're looking good, Buffy sweetie. And how do you think Cleo looks? Isn't it a miracle? And when I think how she looked when she was born—the original ugly duckling. She's turned into a swan."

I tried to say that it was hard to believe that Cleo was ever an ugly duckling but Leila wasn't listening. "Leo's done wonders with that girl.

I mean, look at her tonight, the perfect hostess, gorgeously dressed, in this absolutely gorgeous house. Look at this ceiling with those wonderful beams. And she does *everything* herself. Most of the food *was* catered, but did you taste the pâté? Cleo made that herself. She stayed up half the night doing it."

I wondered why Cleo had found it necessary to do this. If she was having other things catered, why bother to make something herself when she was so short of time? Because in her way she was as compulsive as Cassie was in hers. Compulsive about excelling in *something*.

"She's come a long way." Leila was still talking. "But it's only what Leo deserves. That's what I told Cleo all along. I'm so proud of her I could bust!"

I thought of Cleo when we had first met, when she was bubbly, spunky, and independent, when she gave even Suzannah tit for tat. And I thought of her when she was still full of beans when she was working as an editor in New York. And now I couldn't help but wonder what it was Leila Pulitzer was so proud of—that her daughter had become a glorified Hollywood doormat for Leo Mason?

Unable to look Leila in the eye, I looked down . . . at her chest. Her neckline was unbuttoned nearly to the waist, as so many of the necklines present were, but her skin was dry, lax, finely wrinkled; it was an old skin in contrast with her taut, almost ageless face. If women Leila's age wished to wear décolletage, they should really have the skin of their chests tightened along with their jawlines, I thought dourly.

I saw Todd with Cassie in the garden, in earnest conversation and I thought of the two daughters and their two mothers. One mother observing some kind of a death vigil, waiting for her daughter's marriage to fail, and the other frantically scrambling to keep her daughter's marriage whole. Which one was doing the most damage, not to the marriage but to their child?

Unwilling to interrupt Todd and Cassie's conversation, I started to turn away but there was Cleo again: "You're not mingling, Buffy. And it is *your* party," she reproached me. "I bet you haven't eaten anything either."

She spotted Todd and Cassie and called out, "Come on, you two. No têtes-à-têtes allowed. And Leo has somebody who's dying to meet you, Cassie. Someone who claims he knew your mother when she used to visit at San Simeon. And everybody who hasn't eaten had better hurry."

We're almost ready to clear for dessert. We'll be desserting right after the screening. . . ."

Cleo led Cassie away and Todd said, "Shall we buffet?"

I smiled at him gratefully . . . for remaining himself in wacky, tacky crazyland.

"I *tried* with Cassie," he said as we walked toward the dining room, "but I don't think I made even a dent—After all, Cassandra Hammond's been at her for nearly thirty years. What can we do in one day?" But I could see that he was disappointed. Todd always believed that you could move mountains if your will was strong enough and your heart was pure. "But we won't give up." He squeezed my arm.

We moved along the table of formerly spectacular dishes, by now sorely depleted by the horde of greedy partygoers. But still remaining was curried beef, ham stuffed with artichokes, oysters en brochette, and warm duck with grape cognac sauce. (I knew what sauce it was because I asked the waiter.) I also helped myself to tiny portions of cold pasta salad, green rice, and mushroom farci only so that I could tell Suellen, who was interested in cooking, all about the latest dishes being served in Southern California.

We went out with our plates to the terrace and saw Suzannah sitting on Heinie's lap again and hugging him. "You'll never guess what my Heinie has done. He just told me—it's my wedding surprise. You know the old Worth Studio on Sunset in Hollywood? It's been closed down for years and years. Well, Heinie's bought the whole works—why, it's almost as big as Twentieth Century! And guess what he's going to call it? The Suzannah Studio! Our very own studio! Is that a sweetie?"

I looked at Todd, waiting for him to do the honors in the congratulations department, but he was gazing at the beaming Heinie with such admiration, he seemed incapable of speech. I myself said, "I think that that's sensational. And Heinie is certainly a sweetie!" I kissed Suzannah and then the sweetie.

"Nein . . . nein . . . I didn't do it to be sweet. I did it because it makes good business sense. If you're going to be in the movie business, you should have your own place to work in. And if you have the biggest star in the business, why not have her name on it? Free advertising, no? Besides, I am a businessman first and always and I got it all for a song!"

Now Todd looked at Heinie not only with admiration but with something that was almost (could it be?) envy.

"A song?" Todd said. "Well, I think we should all drink to Suzannah

the Studio, to Suzannah the bride, and to Heinie the astute businessman, movie person, and not least of all, the sweetie."

And we all laughed. It was a wonderful moment. And we hit our
glasses. Now Heinie was our friend too.

As for Suzannah, what next? A cosmetic line, a shampoo, a perfume,
and now her very own, major movie studio.

"You know what?" she said. "Tomorrow night, Heinie and I are
throwing a party to celebrate both our studio and our friends, my darling Buffy and Todd."

"Oh no!" I protested. "It's too much. Heavens, you're getting married in a few days. I'm sure there are still a million things to do—"

"Oh, Cleo's taking care of all the wedding details. And besides, we'll
throw the party at a restaurant so there will hardly be anything to do.
We'll have it at La Scala and there'll be just the people to be invited, the
menu to be decided on, and the color scheme of course. Oh, you know
what?" Suzannah dimpled. "We'll just let Cleo take care of it all. She's
so good at it. Much better than I. And when Leo hears about the new
studio and knows this is his really big opportunity, why he would just
break little old Cleo's arm if she didn't jump in with both feet to help—
Besides, she's such a dear friend."

I wanted to protest again, on Cleo's behalf, but before I could say
anything, Suzannah was waving Cleo over to our table.

"Heinie and I are throwing a party tomorrow night to celebrate . . .
well, to celebrate something about which we will make the announcement at the party. Right, Heinie? And in honor of Buffy and Todd, of
course. Maybe only a hundred people . . . or a hundred and fifty.
. . . And I thought it wouldn't do to have anybody but our own best
little partymaker, Cleo Mason, make the arrangements. Isn't that right,
Heinie?"

Cleo flushed and didn't answer.

"I'm sure Leo would agree—" Suzannah threw in.

"Wait a moment," I said, not able to stand it any longer. "I think it's
all too much for Cleo. She's doing the wedding and she did this party
and I think she needs a rest—"

"But I was planning on La Scala. I wasn't asking her to make the
party in her house."

"But it's for tomorrow night," Cleo said, seemingly losing patience.
"They're bound to be filled up with reservations. They always are, you
know. Weeks ahead for a party. They won't be able to accommodate so
many."

"I'm sure you can work your usual miracles, Cleo. Just tell them who's making the party. And I think for a party scheme it would be nice to have a movie set theme—cameras and floodlights worked in with the flowers and maybe little miniature rhinestone stars as favors. . . ."

Heinie chuckled in admiration. "Who would think of such a thing except my Suzannah?" He tapped his head with two fingers. "Beauty and brains!"

"We're going into the theater now," Cleo said stiffly. "Dessert will be served after the screening."

The theater was a room converted from some previous function. Now it was outfitted with a large pull-down screen and some thirty old moviehouse seats freshly upholstered in maroon velvet. In the rear was a projection room, converted from a large, walk-in closet. Waiters were setting up the gilt folding chairs from the terrace for the extra seating required.

I saw Guy nervously pacing in the rear, refusing to sit. He kept looking over at the network people who were sitting with Leo in the front row. His whole career could be riding on the reception of this first viewing of the first segment of *Hollywood and Vine*. At the very least, it was some kind of test to be passed.

Todd wanted to sit next to Heinie and Suzannah who were in the second row, nuzzling each other. But I nudged him over to Cassie who was sitting alone. Then Leo called out, "Lights!" and the projector started to whirr, but still the room remained brightly lit. Leo stood up and whirled around to face the rest of the room where Cleo stood next to the wall with the panel of switches, looking obviously flustered. "Cleo, the lights! Douse the lights!"

"Something's wrong!" she answered in a panic. "Something's stuck! I can't seem to throw the switch!"

"You stupid bitch! Can't I count on you for *anything?* Do I have to do everything myself?"

The room fell into a shocked, embarrassed silence. Then an anguished Leila Pulitzer ran over to Cleo to see what she could do to help. And then several of the male guests rushed over too while Leo, realizing that he had made a gaffe, smiled sheepishly and laughed heartily to show he was only kidding.

As *Hollywood and Vine* dimmed from view and Cleo, standing by her post, triumphantly threw the switch that lit up the room brightly once more, Leo got to his feet to accept the accolades and compliments for the show that were due him while Guy—still in back of the room—frowned and clenched his jaws, waiting. The crowd started to get to its collective feet to press forward toward the expectant Leo, when Suzannah climbed on top of her velvet theater chair and clapped her hands for attention.

Leo stared at her, amazed. I could tell he was overwhelmed. Suzannah was actually going to make a public tribute to his talent—

"Ladies and gentlemen, Heinie and I were going to make our official announcement tomorrow, but while you are all here, I . . . we . . . decided to let you all in on our little surprise. You're all familiar with the old Worth Studios in Hollywood, closed for too long. Well, Heinie and I decided it was time to bring real moviemaking back to where it belongs . . . the real Hollywood, and not out in Burbank or the Valley or whatever—So we've purchased the Worth Studios and we want you to know that we're going to do all we can to make the real Hollywood live again! The new name of the studio that is going to resurrect the Old Hollywood will be the Suzannah Studio—"

"She makes it sound as though they bought the studio as a public service—" I whispered to Todd and Cassie. But Cassie was watching her husband, whose eyes were riveted not on Suzannah but on Heinie. Todd wore a vague, bemused smile, and his eyes too were on Heinie.

Poor Leo, I thought, for once feeling sorry for him. He stood there with his mouth hanging open as Heinie helped Suzannah down from her chair and everyone crowded in on them, offering congratulations and best wishes, even the network TV people. It really wasn't nice to rob a man of his rightful applause and acclaim in his very own house.

Todd tore his eyes away from Heinie and said, "We've already congratulated the studio owners. Why don't we go over and tell Leo that we think he has a hit on his hands," and then looking at Cassie, "and Guy too. He's going to be the TV success of the season."

We went over to Leo who stood practically alone. How could he, a mere TV writer and director, vie for honors with real movie moguls?

As we took our leave with the studio owners who were giving us a ride back to the hotel, Suzannah tapped the hand of the exhausted Cleo. "Cleo, honey, I couldn't help but notice that neither Army nor Hank made it here. Please try and see to it that they make it to *my* party tomorrow. *And* Jody. I do think society coverage of a first-rate party is every bit as important as coverage by the trades, don't you, Leo dear?"

"To be sure. I'm sure Cleo will do her best," he said bravely and firmly. Apparently he had recovered from the initial shock of having his big moment stolen and was now looking to the future. *"Won't* you, Cleo?" he elbowed her.

I squeezed Cleo's hand in commiseration, and stared at Suzannah meaningfully. "Say something nice to her, for God's sake—" I whispered.

Suzannah stared back at me, perplexed, and after a few seconds said, "And as for the Gabors, it was a perfectly lovely party without them."

Sitting on Heinie's lap in the limousine, Suzannah suddenly giggled. "What's funny, my darling?" Heinie asked.

"My little old friend, Poppy. When she hears about the studio, she'll go out of her cotton-picking mind with jealousy. She's dying for Beau to do pictures."

"Cleo wrote me that you two renewed your friendship when you were in Vegas. How come? After what happened when she was in New York—"

"Oh you know me, Buffy honey. I'm not one to hold a grudge. Besides, I had already evened up the score. When we were in school, we were always playing jokes on one another. One time, I remember, I told her I had fixed her up with the richest boy in town who was home from college, or something. Poppy was always dying to date a really *tony* boy, you know, and she was to meet him in this little old broken down motel. Well, she went there and who do you think she found in the dark? This old, crummy, broken-down old coot. I thought she'd kill me. But then she fixed me. She stole this plant from our homeroom teacher's desk—she was forever stealing things—and the old bitch made the biggest fuss. You'd think it was government secrets that were missing. And they searched the whole school and where do you think they found it? In *my* locker!"

The three of us laughed, but not nearly as hard as Suzannah herself. "Yeah . . . we understand one another, Poppy and I."

"Is she coming to the wedding? I'd like to meet her," I said.

"No. She was absolutely dying to but they were going on tour, much as she says she despises it."

"I never heard him sing. We'll have to buy some of his records."

"Is he good?" Todd asked.

Suzannah considered. "Yes. You have to give him that. Poppy's pushed him and molded him and told him what to sing and how to sing it, but old Herman . . . that's his real name . . . he always could sing. Even back in the old days. He was a cretin as far as I was concerned, but he sang as sweet as a honeybird. . . ."

We walked through the doors of the Wilshire—the night doorman saluting; through the lobby—the bell captain asking if there was anything he could do; into the elevator—the elevator man bowing.

"God, am I tired," I yawned. "What an exhausting evening."

"Yeah, but it was kind of fun, wasn't it?"

Todd opened the door with the key and immediately saw the bottle of champagne reposing in a magnificent cooler, next to two fluted glasses on the long coffee table, next to the newly replenished fruit bowl. "Well!" he said "What do you think of that?" His eyes crinkled. "I guess they heard that we went to a party where the Gabor sisters were *supposed* to make an appearance. We'll have to open it."

He picked up the white napkin that lay beside the cooler but I placed a restraining hand on his arm. "Tomorrow. I've had more than enough to drink tonight."

"Are you sure? I thought maybe we should toast the fact that we got the champagne."

I lay in bed thinking how it seemed like ages that we had been in California already, and that I missed the children. "Maybe instead of staying another week *after* the wedding, we should go back—"

"But we planned on going up to San Francisco and the northern part of the state—I'd hate to miss seeing the shopping centers there."

"Oh, you know what they say about shopping centers. You've seen one, you've seen them all."

"I can't believe that you—the co-creator of the most innovative shopping centers in the country—made that statement." He fell on top of me. "Now, take it back!"

"No . . ." I giggled, wrestling with him.

"Take it back," he warned. "Or else!"

"Or else what?"

"You'll find out!"

I found out.

34.

Drinking my morning coffee from room service, I told Todd, "I'm supposed to go shopping with Suzannah today but I'm really not in the mood. I think I'll skip it. I really don't think I can bear to hear once more what a little old sweetie Heinie is—"

Todd laughed. "Maybe she really believes it. I think she really likes him. He's hard not to like. I like him. You like him, don't you?"

"You know I do. But that's not the same thing as Suzannah liking him . . . or loving him. It's hard to tell. I think she loves having him love her. Be that as it may, I think I'd like to go around with *you* today. You're going down to San Diego, aren't you? I'd love to see the centers down in San Diego."

"As a matter of fact, I'm not looking at centers today. Heinie asked me if I'd like to tour the new studio and I said yes—"

I ended up going shopping with Suzannah and we found a dress for me to wear for the wedding. Then we had lunch at one of her favorite places—Ma Maison. I found out why she had chosen that particular place for lunch. As soon as we walked into the patio everyone at lunch stood up and gave her an ovation. Hail to the new owner of a moving picture studio! News traveled fast in Hollywood and obviously, Suzannah knew it.

After lunch, I went back to the hotel to wait for Todd. He'd said that he would be back early in the afternoon and I was hoping we could sneak off to do a little sightseeing on our own. But he didn't come back until late. "I'm sorry," he said. "But there was so much to see and it was all so fascinating!"

"I'm sure it was," I said just a little coldly.

He missed the intonation completely. "You just have to see it for yourself!" he enthused.

"Yes, I really must but what about tonight? Are Heinie and Suzannah coming by for us?"

"No. I hired a limousine for the evening."

"You hired a limousine to take us to that restaurant? It's only a few blocks from here. Why couldn't we have just taken a cab and someone would have dropped us off later?"

"What's the big deal? We can afford it."

"That's not the point. It just seems ridiculous to have a car and driver waiting around all evening just to take us a few blocks. Wasteful and ostentatious. Whom do we have to impress?"

He was a trifle embarrassed. "Come on, Buffy, that's the way the system works. If the people who can afford it *don't* spend money, how is everybody else going to make a living? Take this party tonight. Not a necessary expenditure and surely ostentatious but think how many people are going to earn their daily bread from it. The chauffeurs and the waitresses, the restaurant and the people who grow the food and raise the beef and the stores where the dresses came from and the sales-women and—"

"Enough. I surrender, dear."

The color scheme was emerald green, Suzannah's favorite, and even the flowers—giant gladioli and calla lilies—had been dyed to match. Suzannah herself wore an emerald green satin slip dress slit to the thigh and a diamond and emerald necklace with earrings to match.

Well, look at all the dyers of flowers that have been put to work, not to mention the miners and setters of diamonds and emeralds, wherever they may be.

"You've done a magnificent job," I told a very much deflated Cleo, whose hair lay limply on her head instead of standing up in bouffant curls as it had the night before and whose eyelashes bunched together in black mascaraed clumps, suggesting a very hasty application.

"Oh, thank you," Cleo said gratefully, sighing deeply. "I never did get to the hairdresser's today, and God knows, I needed to—" Then she smiled as if she were going to say something funny. "Leo wanted to know if I had to look like I'd gone through a clothes wringer—"

"I know Suzannah leaned on you hard but you didn't *have* to accept this assignment. You could have said that it was sufficient that you were taking care of the wedding arrangements."

"Let's not kid ourselves. I'm not doing either the wedding or this party tonight because I love Suzannah. I'm doing it for Leo. For both Leo and myself. Heinie can be Leo's big chance to switch from TV to films."

"But what about *Hollywood and Vine?*"

"Leo's the creator of *Hollywood and Vine* so he'll get his, week in and week out, whether he personally continues with it or not. Besides, once he's into features, his future isn't going to be riding on the vagaries of one series. He won't have to worry so much about how it's doing in the ratings or whether it's going to be picked up each season. A TV series is the worst form of pressure. It's hell. The first show hasn't aired yet and look at Guy Savarese. He's the biggest bundle of nerves. Even Leo isn't *that* nervous. And Leo is really high-strung.

"I don't give a shit for Suzannah. And she knows it. And she knows that right now we're at her mercy. That's the way the game is played. Anyhow, I'm going to be able to really rest up tomorrow. I'll get to my work-out at eight and after that I'm going to collapse at Liz Arden's. Let them give me the works. You do know, don't you, that Sara and Willy Ross are giving a party for Suzannah and Heinie out at their place in Malibu? You and Todd can drive out with us. If I tell you a secret, will you swear not to tell?"

She lowered her voice to a whisper, *"We* weren't invited originally. We don't even know them. They're the real stuff out here. Old Hollywood. Willy is still a big star and he has his own production company. And he won the Oscar a few years ago. And their friends are all the big shots. You've heard of Maeve O'Connor Hartman, haven't you? The widow of Harry Hartman, one of the Hollywood greats? And Chrissy Marlowe, of course." I nodded. "They're Sara Ross's best friends. And Sara's real society. She was a big New York debutante and she's the heiress to Gold Enterprises. To tell you the truth, I was really shocked to hear that *they* were entertaining for Suzannah until I learned that Willy Ross and Heinie are old friends. I mean, I really couldn't envision Sara Ross having anything to do with somebody like Suzannah—"

"Hey," I laughed. "Hold on. When you put it like that you're putting *us* down too, not only Suzannah—"

Cleo frowned, not understanding what I was talking about. But she was tired, I knew. "Forget it," I said. "Tell me what happened. How is it that you and Leo are going if you weren't invited?"

"Manipulation," Cleo said matter-of-factly. "Yesterday morning I called to invite them to *our* party. I told Sara that since it was a party in your and Todd's honor, the two people who are going to stand up for Suzannah and Heinie, I was sure they would like to be there. Well, she declined. She said they had other plans. So this morning I called her again, in Suzannah and Heinie's name, inviting her and her husband to *this* party. Again she declined, saying they had a previous commitment. So then I said how sorry I was, that I had been looking forward to meeting her, but how nice that she and Willy would have the pleasure of meeting you and Todd tomorrow night at *her* party for Suzannah and Heinie. Well, she *is* a lady so she invited us to come along too."

"Whew!" I said. "That was a close one. Nobody would say you aren't artful."

"Oh Buffy, don't make fun of me. It isn't easy for me to do that kind of stuff."

"I'm sure it isn't, Cleo. Why do you do it?"

"I have to—You know I do. Can you imagine how Leo would feel if we were the only ones who weren't going to the Ross party?"

"Yes I can. And I'm glad you're going, Cleo, really I am."

She hugged me. "You're the best friend, Buffy, really the best—" And then she laughed . . . at herself. "It's hard to be a professional social climber, you know, and I'm so good at it. And sometimes, it can be *very important* work. Careers can live or die by it. I'm really a do-gooder."

I laughed too. "You are . . . you are."

"And you promise you won't breathe a word of this to a living soul?"

I promised, sure that Todd didn't count as a living soul.

"Buffy?" Suzannah rushed up. "You can't stay here all night gossiping with Cleo. This party's in your honor and I want to show you off to some people. And I'm sure Cleo has a lot to do," she said, dismissing her and dragging me off.

"I want to go over and say hello to Cassie first—"

"You can't. Later. First you have to help me rescue Heinie. Leila Pulitzer's chewing his ear off. Can you imagine the nerve of that Cleo? Bringing her mother tonight. This is *my* party, after all, and I never gave her permission to bring her mother. Pushy, that's what she is, Cleo, and that mother of hers, not to mention Leo. No wonder the old lady's so crazy about him. They're two of a kind . . . three of a kind. It's not natural for a mother-in-law to be so crazy about her daughter's husband. Especially Leo. I wouldn't be a bit surprised if they weren't sneaking in a little fuckey-fuckey on the side."

"Suzannah!"

"Well, *she's* not getting any, and Leo—why he'd sleep with an alligator if it would do him any good, or if it flattered his ego a little. The man *is* an egomaniac."

Leila did have a death grip on Heinie's arm. "What you need is a place worthy of your and Suzannah's position," she was saying. She included us in the conversation. "And I don't mean anything picayune either, Suzannah." She lowered her voice dramatically. "What do you think of the Harold Lloyd estate, Greenacres, or, at the very least, Pickfair?"

"Are they for sale?" Heinie asked.

"I always say, you never know what's for sale until you make them an offer. Make the offer and if the price is right, everything in Los Angeles is for sale."

As I talked to different people I kept an eye on Todd as he wandered from group to group, listening intently. Finally, I couldn't restrain myself any longer. I went over to him and asked: "Well? Have you heard anything worth repeating? Anything interesting?"

"It's amazing. Nobody out here talks about anything but *the* business. Unless it's something that's in some way related, or catering *to* the Industry. Even the talk about real estate is show business talk. So-and-so paid a zillion dollars for a house in which Rudolph Valentino made love to Judy Garland. And Jean Harlow lived there before Jack Benny moved in, not to mention Marilyn Monroe *and* Groucho Marx *and* the lion from Metro-Goldwyn-Mayer!"

"Really! Who lives in the house now?"

"I missed the name. But you know, not one person here has asked me a single question about shopping centers!"

"Really?"

"I'll show you what I mean. Do you see those two gentlemen standing next to us? To our right?"

I nodded.

"I'm going to engage them in conversation. I'll say something about shopping centers and you watch what happens. I'll bet you they will not respond. Just watch."

He took my elbow and steered me over to the men. We heard one say to the other, "I got a verbal commitment from her. An absolute commitment. She said she'd definitely do my picture next year."

"Christ!" the other man said. "Really! Christ!"

Todd stepped between them. "Me too! I've got a verbal commitment from her too!" He nodded his head up and down enthusiastically. "She said she'd absolutely come to my Cincinnati shopping center sometime next year to do our annual kiddie show promotion, which we do every August just before school starts. Isn't that so, Buffy Ann?"

"Oh yes," I confirmed as the two men stared at us in amazement. "She even gave us her verbal commitment to put it in writing next month. *Really!*"

Then they looked at each other and walked away.

"You see?" Todd said. "I told you. Absolutely no interest at all in shopping centers."

"I see what you mean. Come on, let's get Cassie and make her sit with us and have something to eat. Have you sampled the salmon mousse yet? The rumor is that the salmon were especially spawned for this occasion."

"Christ! Really! Oh Christ! Just for tonight?"

"Well, actually they made the verbal commitment last year. And guess what they're calling the mousse?"

"Hurry! Tell! I can't wait!"

"Salmon Suzannah?"

He snapped his fingers. "Of course! How not?"

As we were taking our leave, Cleo drew me aside. "About tomorrow night. Suzannah insists *they're* driving you out to Malibu in their car."

"Fine. Whatever."

"Would you do me a favor?"

"Of course, Cleo. What can I do?"

"Would you suggest . . . insist . . . to Suzannah that we . . . Leo and I . . . come along too? In the same car? It would . . . look good for us, under the circumstances."

"Of course, Cleo. Consider it done. I'll twist Suzannah's arm, if necessary." But then I couldn't resist. "How about your mother? Why don't I suggest to Suzannah that she come along with us too?"

"No . . ." Cleo said regretfully. "I don't see how—It's a pity though. Mother would love to see the Ross house. They're in the Colony you know, behind the gates."

As we entered our suite, Todd's eyes went to the coffee table. The bottle of champagne, still unopened from the night before, reposed in its cooler in freshly replenished ice, and the bowl of fruit was as magnificent as ever. I held my breath as Todd went to the "his" bathroom, and then to the "hers." He was going to check if the management had sent up the crowning jewel of recognition, the terry monogrammed robe, I knew. He came back empty-handed.

"Elusive little buggers, those robes."

"Oh well," he said, reaching for the bottle of champagne. "Shall we drink to a more rewarding tomorrow?"

"Neh . . . We don't have to," I said. "We've already had plenty of rewards."

It took some doing but I finally persuaded Suzannah to let Cleo and Leo ride with us in the limousine out to Malibu to the Rosses' party.

"I'd love a little house on the beach, Heinie," Suzannah said as we drove through the security gates after being checked by the sentries in the guardhouse.

"Why not?" Heinie agreed pleasantly. "A little hideaway . . . why not?"

"We're thinking of getting a beach house ourselves," Leo said, much in the manner of the small boy making sure he wasn't left out.

"Why not, Leo? Why not?" Heinie said kindly.

As we drove down Malibu Road, I was surprised to see that the houses were so close together. "They're really on top of one another."

"That's how it is in the Colony," Cleo said with her usual expertise. "They're built narrow from the beach to the road. Waterfront property is so tight, you know. Of course they're all grander than they look, once you get inside."

"Ah, but you've never been to Sara and Willy's, have you, Cleo?" Suzannah asked pointedly. "They're at the very end of the road and they have a much larger piece of property. They have a house that looks just like Tara. That's what I would like, Heinie. A house like Tara."

"Why not?" Heinie patted her hand.

And then the driver stopped in front of a big white house with columns and I fully expected to see Scarlett come through the door in an antebellum gown of white muslin sprigged with green flowers.

"Do you see what I mean, Cleo?" Suzannah said as she swept out of the car. "I bet Angela du Beaumond and her sister, Kiki Devlin, will be here tonight. They're good friends of Sara's. Perhaps they'll want to work for us, Heinie? They *were* big stars, even if they are over the hill now. We could always give them little cameos to do."

I gave Todd an elbow. Two of the biggest actresses around and Suzannah was going to give them bit parts in *her* movies.

"Why not?" Heinie agreed.

I found Todd outside on the veranda-like deck, staring out to sea in a dreamy trance. Then, realizing I was there, he said: "God, this place is magnificent! The white sand, the waves, and then when you turn around you see those mountains. Incredible!"

"Oh, I don't know," I said. "They're not really *mountains*, more like hills."

Back in our hotel suite I watched Todd come out of the bathrooms, again empty-handed, trying to grin, trying to laugh at himself, but obviously disappointed.

"There *is* another bottle of champagne tonight. Let's drink it and count our blessings."

He picked the bottle up from the silver urn and examined it. "California," he said with an ironic smile. "The first bottle was French."

The next morning I suggested to Todd that we hire a car (and not a chauffeured limousine) and drive down the coast to San Diego all by ourselves, stopping at every shopping mall on the way down.

"It will be fun. And then we'll—"

"I can't, Buffy. I promised Heinie I'd go out to the studio with him again, and make some suggestions for the remodeling."

I looked at him unbelievingly. "But what do you know about movie studios?"

He was hurt. "I do know something about construction, don't I? Some of the buildings have to go. Some can be saved. It needs a whole new electrical system and—"

"Oh Todd! I was so looking forward to our going off on our own!"

"Don't you have to get your dress for the wedding?"

"I bought it the day before yesterday. I told you—"

"Oh. Why don't you spend the day with Cassie? You said you wanted more time to spend with her, talk to her. And she'll be restful for you after Cleo and Suzannah."

"She's working. Besides, ever since that day when we really talked, she's closed me out. She's been avoiding me at the parties. But don't worry about me. I'll wander around by myself. Sightsee. I might even take one of those bus tours. You know—see the stars' homes."

"That sounds like fun. I tell you what—Why don't you wander around this morning and I'll pick you up for lunch? And then we'll take the tour together. We should have plenty of time before—"

"Before what?"

"Well, I understand there's nothing on for tonight so I thought that maybe it was time for us to entertain the gang—"

"We're from out-of-town. *We* don't have to entertain. And I think we've had enough of parties for—"

He broke in. "I don't mean a real party. I just thought a dinner party in honor of the bride and groom. Just the few couples."

"But we need a reservation someplace. Why didn't you say something?"

"I just thought of it this morning. What's the big fuss? A few couples going to dinner. Cassie and Guy. The studio owners. Cleo and Leo—"

"How about Cleo's mother?"

"I guess. And I thought maybe you'd call Sara and Willy Ross. He's an awfully nice guy."

"Uh-huh. And where did you want to have this party?"

"How do I know? Why don't you ask Cleo? She knows all the right places. No, wait a minute. Why not the restaurant right here at the Wilshire? What's the name of that room?"

"The El Padrino Room?"

"No. The other one. Isn't it the La Bella Fontana? Yes. I think that would be very nice." He seemed especially firm about his choice. "And make sure they know exactly who it is who's giving the party—"

I laughed. "You're beginning to sound like Leo."

"Well, Leo is a man who knows what he wants."

My God, I thought, he's not even thinking about restaurants. It's terry cloth robes that are on his mind. It was insane.

"What is it *you* want, Todd?"

He grinned at me. "I just want everyone to have a good time. At my expense. I want to be a Hollywood host."

Now he was making fun of Hollywood again. He was certainly ambivalent about how he felt about the place. Or was he?

"You really like it here, don't you?" I asked suddenly, not having intended to ask the question at all. I wasn't sure I really wanted to hear the answer.

"Hey, Buffy Ann. Lighten up. You make it sound like it's the question of the century. Look. Why don't you call Cleo and let her call the maitre d' and make all the arrangements?"

"No, I think I'll let Cleo be. And I don't think it's really necessary. *I* know how to talk to a maitre d', even one in Beverly Hills."

"But you could ask Cleo if there's someone special we should invite?"

"Like whom? Army Archerd or Hank Grant?"

"Why not? And Jody Jacobs, the society editor at the *Times.*"

"Oh my God! You take a perfectly nice Ohio boy to California and

look what happens? He turns into Leo Mason. Or maybe it's really
Suzannah you're turning into?"

"On that note I leave you," he said, heading for the door.

"Already? It's only eight o'clock."

"I'm meeting Heinie for breakfast at his hotel. At the Polo Lounge.
Did you know it's the 'in' place for breakfast?"

"Really? Who said so?"

"Leo said so."

It took me almost an hour on the phone to get Cassie to agree to
come to our dinner party.

"I haven't gone out as much in a year as I have this week."

"What of it? After we've gone back to Ohio, you can go back to
sitting by your window looking up at that pink house on the hill, if
that's how you want to spend your life."

"I told you. It won't be my whole life."

And she did come, meeting her husband at the restaurant. Our little
dinner party ended up a party of thirty-eight. Suzannah had given me a
list of several other people she wanted—certain "behind-the-scenes"
people (prominent all the same)—and I'd complied.

Afterwards, Cleo complimented me. "*You* could have called on me,
but I think you did a very nice job. The crêpes de la mer and the veal
grillades were excellent choices, and the mocha meringue was delicious.
But tell me," she lowered her voice. "How did you ever get Sara and
Willy Ross to come?"

"It was simple, really. I just called up and asked Sara if she would
like to come and she said, 'Sure.' That's how we do it back in Ohio, you
know. We just call folks up and invite them."

35.

Finally it was all over. Suzannah became Mrs. Heinie Muller, dressed in
a truly original creation—an Old West version of a wedding gown fashioned of pearl-seeded satin and old lace. The bridegroom was attired in
a cowboy-style tuxedo with a large white Stetson, and there were one

thousand four hundred and fifty guests, many of whom flew in from various capitals of the world, on Heinie's own airline. Stuntmen fell off the roofs of movie set saloons and the guests sat down to picnic tables and benches to eat chili from Chasen's and kumquat tarts from Ma Maison, a truly eclectic menu.

Now we could leave for San Francisco, I thought, relieved that it was all over. Or maybe we could skip San Francisco and just go home. I was eager to get back to my children and it seemed as if we had been in California for a year.

"When are we leaving for San Francisco?" I asked Todd, as the workers were already clearing away the wedding debris from the movie lot.

"Hasn't anyone told you? Didn't I? Since Heinie's bought the studio and he's anxious to get started on the renovation, he's canceled their Mediterranean honeymoon. Instead, he's flying us to Vegas in his jet for a couple of days."

"When?" I asked, horrified. I couldn't believe that Todd was so delighted.

"Tonight. We're just going back to the hotel to pack a few things."

I wondered if Todd had really forgotten to tell me all this, or if he had planned it this way and then I reproached myself for being such a skeptic.

After the sojourn in Las Vegas, Heinie Muller's plane took us to Palm Springs, where his socially, financially, and very politically prominent friends, the Wallburgers, who had missed the wedding for some reason or other, were giving a party for the happy couple. It was a very impressive guest list that attended the party, and I really couldn't blame Todd for being impressed. I supposed *anybody* would have been impressed by a gathering that included the Agnews, the Hopes, Frank Sinatra, *and* Betty and President Ford. It was never clear to me if the President was a friend of Heinie's or if he was just taking a golf holiday at his friends, the Wallburgers, and was therefore included in the party. But Suzannah chose to think that Gerald and Betty were there in her honor, and all those Secret Service men were there to safeguard *her* security.

At last we were really going home. I packed the last suitcase with presents. "I hope Leah likes the red robe I bought her at Giorgio's."

"When you tell her *where* you bought it, she will probably be overcome with emotion," Todd said.

"Yes. She might even be moved to a grunt. I still can't believe we never got as far as Carmel. I heard there's such a beautiful mall there—"

"You know what they say. 'See one mall and you've seen them all.' "

The bellboy accepted his tip, thanked Mr. King, and took our luggage down while Todd checked the suite out once more to make sure we hadn't left anything behind. Then we went down to the lobby where Todd took care of the bill.

"It's been a pleasure to have you with us, Mr. King. Come back again soon."

Then we were outside waiting for our limousine to pull up. "One minute," Todd told me. "I have to check on something," and he went through the doors back into the lobby.

When he came back chuckling I asked, "What is it?"

"I went to check at the service desk. To see if there was a package or something for us. I thought that maybe they'd heard we had partied with Gerald Ford and had decided to reward us with one of those robes . . . sort of posthumously."

"No luck, huh? So why are you laughing?"

"How long ago did we check out?"

"Five minutes maybe?"

"And were they Mr. Kinging me all over the place? Everybody? The bellhop? The deskman?"

"I'd certainly say so."

"Well, five minutes later they forgot who I was. Would you believe that not one single person in there recognized me? As a matter of fact, the man behind the desk looked at me like I was a vagrant. You know what he said? 'What's your name, *buddy?*' "

"Buddy! He did not! I don't believe you! Did he really?"

"Yes, Ma'am. He did!"

I climbed into the limousine and Todd started to get in after me. But just before he did, he turned to the doorman and raised a fist. The vanquished hero declaimed, "I *will* return!"

I sincerely hoped he was kidding.

One of the first things I did on my return home was to run over to Suellen's to fill her in on everything, all the news and the gossip; to describe the wedding and all the parties; to tell her about every delicious dish we had tasted.

I sat down at Suellen's kitchen table to nibble at her potato pancakes, *latkes* as Howard called them.

"Hmmmm . . . good! Tell me, did Leah ever bring the children over for dinner?"

"Didn't Leah tell you?"

"Of course not. Leah never tells me anything."

"Well, she did. In fact she and the children had dinner here three times."

"You're kidding? Three times? I can hardly believe it. How did you do it?"

"How? I called her up and said, 'Leah? This is Suellen Rosen. Why don't you bring the children over to dinner tonight? We're having lamb chops and blueberry pie and Mr. Rosen will pick you up!' It was as simple as that."

I was delighted. "Oh Suellen! You're wonderful!" I leaped up to kiss her with my mouth full of *latke*.

Suellen's cheeks pinked. "I am? Why am I wonderful?"

Because you're a sweet innocent. Or maybe because you're very wise. Or maybe because you really believe that having a joyous life can be a simple thing. Or just because you're you, you're mine and I'm happy to be home, and I cannot think of home being really home without you being somewhere close by.

"Oh, just because you're my sister," I said, "and the only one I have." I took another bite of pancake. "Lushy. What's the recipe?"

"Will you ever make them?" she asked doubtfully.

"Probably not," I confessed, "but maybe Leah will."

"Well, you have to grate your raw potatoes and press out all the water. That's very important—to get them really *dry*. And you mix in a little bit of flour, an egg for every cup of potatoes and some salad oil and pepper and salt. And some people grate in *raw* onion but—"

"Yes?"

"My very own secret is that I sauté the onions *first* and that's the difference!"

I was delighted.

"You see? *That's* why I love you. In Hollywood no one would ever tell you to fry the onions first."

"Why not?"

I thought about it for a second. "Because they want everything *you* have, but they don't want you to have anything that's better."

"What about Cassie? She would tell, wouldn't she?"

"Yes. She would. If she *knew,* but she doesn't."

"And Cleo? Cleo would tell, wouldn't she?"

"Yes, she would, *but* only if Leo would let her. And he never would."

"Oh."

I could see that Suellen was not even considering asking about Suzannah, having already made up her mind about what Suzannah would do. But she was wrong. Suzannah was just the person who might—*know* and *tell.* But she would probably try and raid your whole cookbook later.

36.

Suzannah took the joint Poppy handed her, drew the smoke deeply into her lungs, held her breath, leaned back against the overstuffed sofa pillows, then let her body go loose.

"What's going down here?" Suzannah giggled.

"What do you mean?" Poppy answered stiffly.

"I hear funny noises coming from there." Suzannah nodded her head toward the hall that led off to one side of the living room.

"That's our bedroom wing down there—" Poppy sat on the edge of the chair. *The bitch had to drop in without calling first, probably just hoping to catch her off guard.*

"But what are those noises?"

"Nothing. Probably just the maid. Forget it."

"Don't you want to take a look? Or send that person I saw hanging around outside to take a look?"

"That's Smokey. He's just a gofer." Then, quickly, as if to draw Suzannah's attention to something else, she said, "I don't smoke myself anymore. Not pot and not cigarettes."

"I don't like to overdo it myself. It gives me the munchies and one thing I can't afford to do is eat."

"Oh, I can give you something for that, to kill the appetite."

"No thanks! I can't afford to be jittery either. At least not until we're through shooting, which won't be for a couple of months at the very least. Leo, he's my director, you know, he says that the secret of sensuous acting is to be loose, very loose . . . in mind and body . . . to be so utterly relaxed one oozes sensuality. In fact, Leo *makes* me take a few hits between takes. That's the image Heinie wants me to project—sensuality. He wants me sexy like Dietrich was, not in the way Marilyn Monroe was. The voice . . . the glance . . . the eyes . . . languorous body language rather than . . . *obviousness.*"

"Then why did you have your tits—your breasts," she corrected herself, "made bigger?"

"Heinie thinks that might have been a mistake. We're thinking about a revision. Or I guess you might say, a reversal. But of course we can't do that before *Love and Betrayal* is in the can. And after I do Vegas early next year."

Now Poppy opened her eyes wide. *"You're* going to do Vegas?"

"That's the plan. That's why we're in town today. Heinie's seeing some people. I've been taking lessons in singing and dancing for years, you know. And we have some top people developing an act for me—with chorus boys and all that. I'm *singing* in *Love and Betrayal.* The theme song. And I'll cut a record too. Heinie's buying us a record company—"

"But what's the idea? You're making a major feature. With all the publicity and the promotion, all the movie has to be is passable, and you've got it made. What do you need with Vegas?"

"That's part of our campaign. Heinie wants me to be an international star. And a multi-medium star. Guest shots on TV. Everything. The Vegas gig is just a hype, really. Just to really show all my stuff. Even Dietrich did a one-woman show. And after Vegas, Heinie's taking me to Broadway. A musical. And then we'll translate the musical to the screen. Poppy, your little old gal friend from Kentucky is going to be the biggest star the world has ever seen."

Poppy looked at the dress Suzannah was wearing—an elaborately draped white clinging silk jersey with exaggerated shoulders and little rhinestone buttons running up the sleeves. "But why are you dressed like that in the middle of the day?" she asked abruptly. "Nobody dresses like that in the daytime here."

"Oh, Heinie wants me to dress like a star, to look like a star at all times. He says, whoever heard of a star in jeans and a sweatshirt?" She laughed gaily. "And look at you! My goodness! You look like a little gray mouse in that dress. What ever happened to those tops you were always addicted to, and your sequins?"

Poppy automatically straightened the pleats of the skirt of the gray shirtwaist. "I guess I outgrew them. I've a new look now. Ladylike, you know. Beau may not be a movie star but he's a big star all the same, and I don't think the wife of a big star should look like a . . . like she's on the make, or something."

Suzannah giggled. "I'll say you don't look like you're on the make. You look more like you *dropped out—*"

Poppy's stomach churned. *Bitch! Having everything handed to you while I've worked so bitching hard.*

"You want a drink?"

"Oh, all right. A wee bitty one. Scotch. Neat. I think it's the ice cubes that are detrimental to one's insides. I think they just give you a chill all over. But a little bit of Scotch just raises the energy level."

Poppy handed her a highball glass half-filled with the amber liquid. "How come you ended up with Leo Mason as your director? Isn't he strictly TV? I would have thought you'd have the biggest—"

Suzannah took a large swallow, turned her head again in the direction of the hall where still louder sounds emanated from Poppy's bedroom. She was certain she could hear a human voice crying. "Those sounds are getting worse, Poppy. Don't you think you should take a look? Maybe you've a burglar in there?"

"If you must know, there's a pro—a working girl in there with Beau," she blurted out and was instantly sorry. She knew Suzannah. She would never let it drop now. You couldn't let your guard down one fucking minute.

"Really?" Suzannah grinned. "What's happening, Poppy? Are you getting frigid or only squeamish?"

"What does that mean?"

"Oh, come off it, Poppy. Everybody in town knew that you beat up on Herm and he really liked it, *really liked it.*"

Poppy looked steely-eyed at her. "If I were you, Suzannah, I'd drop it. When it comes to talking about the past, there are certain things I remember too."

"Well, don't get offended, honey," Suzannah dimpled. "I'm the first one to say, whatever turns you on. Personally, I think a little kink is interesting. But what I don't understand is why you've hired outside help. Aren't you afraid of losing some of your control?"

"It will never happen. It doesn't mean noth— anything. It's just that I can't do everything myself. I don't have anybody to do any of the important things I have to do. I have nobody to rely on. Like you got Heinie. So I just have to let some things go. The unimportant things."

Suzannah giggled. "Since when is sex an unimportant thing?"

Poppy shrugged. She wasn't about to tell Suzannah that the girls-for-hire did the things that she no longer could bring herself to do, that made her sick to her stomach. She just wanted to change the subject.

"How come you picked that Leonard Mason as your director?"

"You asked me that already."

"But you didn't answer me. That one time I saw you with them, Leonard and his wife, I got the impression you thought so little of him."

"Heinie was thinking of Scorsese. He does admire his work. But Scorsese does DeNiro and Liza. I wanted somebody that would do *me*. Only Suzannah, that would be associated with Suzannah automatically. And then Heinie thought of John . . . Huston, you know. He's always liked *his* work too. But for God's sake, I told him, he did Bogie way back when. He's a man's director, I told Heinie, and besides I wanted somebody younger, *au courant*. That means with it, you know, *current*. Somebody who would be on the same wave length with me. We went over and over the names. And there was Leo . . . waiting and panting. Absolutely panting. And I had my first success, theatrically speaking, with Leo . . . in Leo's TV play. He's a brilliant writer and director, even if he's *merde*—that's the French way of saying shit—as a man. Well, Leo was pushing, and waiting in the wings, and sweating. That's what we like—Heinie and I—somebody who's really sweating to kill himself for you. And he had a script ready—a hand-tailored-for-Suzannah script. He had written it for me as soon as Heinie and I connected. And knowing it was his big chance, it was polished to a fine sheen. No actress could have asked for more." She looked around. "How about another little hit?"

Expertly, Poppy rolled another joint, lit it without really drawing it in, and handed it to Suzannah, who inhaled soundly. "It *is* relaxing," Suzannah said in a haze of contentment. "Anything that is relaxing is good for your body, you know. Well, I thought, does it really matter that Leo Mason is an asshole personally? He *feels* the movie and he *feels* me. It's really amazing. The actress-director vibrations between us are extraordinary. As it must have been for Dietrich and her director, that von Sternberg. One would never think Leo Mason possesses the sensitivity, but he does. I think it's that he sees me on the screen just as I see myself. . . ."

There was a piercing shriek from down the hall and Poppy stood up and said flatly, "You'll have to exuse me for a few minutes."

"Well," Suzannah grinned. "I certainly should think so!"

But then a woman, not young but strong-looking, appeared in the doorway to the living room, with a robe thrown over her shoulders, carrying a huge tote bag, and a black patent leather handbag, wearing black patent leather boots to the knee. Her naked body glistened with perspiration, her black hair slicked back with the sweat.

Suzannah stared at the woman's pubis, shaved clean. She smiled with delight. This was all very fascinating.

Poppy stalked over to the large, pendulous-breasted woman. "What are you doing? You're not to come in here," she said in a low but furious voice. "Didn't Smokey tell you what to do?" She would kill him for sure.

"Cool it! I just wanted to know if it's all right if I use the shower facilities in there," she pointed back in the direction of the bedroom. "I guess I shoulda just done it."

"No!" Poppy gestured to the kitchen off the hallway. "Through there. There's a maid's room in there with a bathroom. And when you're finished, Smokey's in back of the house, off the kitchen. He'll take care of you."

The woman shrugged and turned her back, sauntered through the kitchen.

"I'll be right back," Poppy told Suzannah without looking at her. God! No matter what she did, they had to paint her with shit.

Suzannah ran over to the doorway, watched Poppy disappear down the hall into the bedroom. Then she went through the kitchen, found the maid's room, crooked her head into the bathroom, where the woman was already stepping out of the shower, wrapping her head in a towel.

"Hi," Suzannah said. "I just wanted to see if there was anything you needed. If everything was all right?"

"Everything's just super-duper and what's it to you?"

"Just trying to be friendly," Suzannah smiled beguilingly. "What was going on in there? With Beau, I mean? It sure sounded like a good time."

"Go fuck yourself," the woman said indifferently and turned her back on Suzannah who smiled to herself and went back to the living room.

"You want for me to freshen up your drink?" Poppy asked when she returned.

Suzannah considered. "Just a teensy bit. Did you just give Beau an injection?" she asked casually.

Poppy thought maybe she would strangle the bitch. "What kind of an injection are you talking about? Beau's no diabetic."

Suzannah's mouth curled into an innocent, cupid-bow smile. "I didn't mean that kind of injection. You *know* what I mean."

Poppy laughed shortly. "What do you think I'm running here? A shooting gallery?"

"I thought maybe something for his weight problem. I've heard that when Beau's back from a road tour, he starts getting fat as a hog."

"He gains a little weight. Everybody's got to relax a little once in a while. But he trims down again."

"I heard that sort of thing is dangerous," Suzannah said primly. "It's not good for the body, the up-down syndrome . . ." but her voice trailed off, as if she were trying to remember something.

"Beau's fine. I make sure he takes his vitamins."

"Sure you do," Suzannah giggled, drinking from the freshened drink.

She wanted to hit the red-headed bitch. She wanted to really bad but instead she leaned forward and asked, "Do you play golf?"

"My goodness, Poppy. You've known me a long time. Do I look as if I would play golf?"

"How about tennis? Do you play tennis?"

"God, no! I hate to get all sweaty. But Heinie's taken it up. He runs around the court on those cute little legs of his in his cute little white shorts." She tossed off the rest of her drink.

Suddenly Poppy blurted out, "I want for Beau to be in the movies."

"Really? Why?" Suzannah shook her head, fighting the slight disorientation she felt.

"Why the hell not? Elvis made movies, and Johnny Cash. And Beau is better looking than they are. Isn't he?"

"Well, *they're* hardly what I'd call *au courant*. As for the looks, I suppose. Elvis lost his looks when he got fatter. But then again I hear Beau's fat and bloaty too."

"He isn't! And if I could get him a film, believe me he'd be as thin as a starving sparrow. I'd make sure of that. And you know how the girls go crazy over him. He'd be a natural for a movie. It's the kids who go to the movies. Everybody says so. You wouldn't believe the mail we get. And the concerts—they want to rip him to pieces, they're so fucking wild over him!"

"I'm willing, honey. Go for it!" Suzannah said, looking around for her bag at the same time. She rummaged in it and finally said, "Have you got a ciggie-boo?"

Poppy took a box off the glass table, flipped it open, shoved it at her, grabbed a silver lighter from the table, and flicked it with her thumb until a flame shot up an inch and a half high.

"Watch it!" Suzannah said irritably. "You almost singed my eyelashes. You always were so incredibly wild! You have to watch it."

"Suzannah, tell Heinie!"

"Tell him what?" She blew smoke in Poppy's face.

"That he should make a picture with Beau—"

Suzannah looked at her as if she were crazy.

"Do you think it's that simple? You need a script, you need a director, you need an actress, one with a box office history."

"But couldn't Heinie do that? That's what he does, doesn't he?"

"You don't understand the business, Poppy. Today, you just don't decide to make a movie because you have somebody with blond hair that can turn a teenybopper's cuntie a-twirling. Or just because he can yodel. A studio today has to be doing a lot of things to survive. Some TV . . . both films and series. And we have people that we work in conjunction with—we do the distributing for, you know. And we have some things in the development stage, but right now *Love and Betrayal* is actually *the* only feature film Suzannah Studio is producing by itself."

"But you just said you've got things in the development stage. Why couldn't Heinie develop a film for Beau? I bet he could. Right this minute, if he wanted to—if you asked him to, if you recommended that he do it. Please, Suzannah?"

"Oh, Poppy honey, I wish I could!"

"What do you mean 'wish'? Why can't you?"

"This is a business, Poppy. Not a friendship circle."

"Beau would be good business."

"Would he?" Her head was whirling but she knew one thing. Beau was a joke. Beau was bad news.

"Look, Poppy, I came here today because we're friends. But why would Heinie want to bother with Beau? Considering everything."

Poppy reared back, as if she had been stung. "Considering *what* everything?"

"My goodness, you know. The drugs, all the kinky stuff that goes on around here. You just don't know Heinie. He believes in good business and clean living. He deplores kink, prostitutes, drugs."

Oh, you bitch! You stinking, rotten bitch!

"The only drugs I saw going down today was the dope you smoked. What drugs did you see?"

"Oh, come on, Pop!" She took Poppy's hand and Poppy snatched it away. "I don't mean to be unkind, honey, but you've just got to know your limitations. Yours and Beau's. I think you've done a perfectly marvelous job with him. Really, Poppy, you have. Why without you he'd be digging ditches somewhere. I surely hope he appreciates you. But honey, you can only go so far pushing this thing. Why, if I suggested to Heinie or to anybody else that they put Beau in a movie, they'd laugh themselves sick. You have to forget this crazy idea. You used to be so much fun. You're so serious now. You really have to learn to relax. When I think of all the fun times we had together. Remember that time when we both were getting old Charlie Black hot, and then we turned a hose on him. We didn't stop laughing all night. I've got to go now. I'm meeting Heinie at the Grand. We've got our plane waiting to take us back to L.A. I'm shooting tomorrow. Would you go out and tell my driver I'm ready to leave while I take myself a little wee-wee," and she quickly started down the hall that led to Poppy's bedroom.

"Just a fucking minute!" Poppy ran after her, grabbing hold of her shoulders and forcibly turning her around like a rag doll. "The powder room is over there. Out in the entrance hall—" and she gave her a push in that direction. Suzannah, startled, offered no resistance. But then Poppy shrieked: "No!" and turned Suzannah around again and pushed her toward the kitchen. "You use the toilet in there unless you want to pee in your pants! And when you're through urinating, you can get the hell out and tell your fucking driver yourself that you're fucking leaving. And one more thing! You're not exactly fucking *au courant* yourself, baby! You're over thirty and you still haven't got one picture in the can. In your business, that's *old,* sweetheart, and you know what else? You don't look like a star in that dress, you don't even look like a whore. You just look like a fucking fool. *Au courant,* your ass!"

Poppy watched through the window as Suzannah's limo pulled away. *Garbagehead!* She wiped at her eyes with her hand. It would be time soon to get Beau up and into a shower. She glanced at her watch. She would have to give him a red after the shower to wake him up. Or maybe she would give him a little coke instead. Dr. Pettigrew said it was better for him than the amphetamines, that the coke didn't harm the body. And Pettigrew wasn't one of those walk-up-a-flight-of-wooden-stairs docs, either. He was a top man.

If she had been smart, she would have offered Suzannah a snort and laced it with uncut heroin. That would have given the great actress a jolt! Fixed her butt. She would even the score one day. She would pay Suzannah back in kind.

It was time to call Ben's bluff about meeting the Old Man. Ben had been saying for months that he would let her meet him and that maybe the old guy would do something for her, that he had the power to make Beau a movie star. An idol! Well, it was time for her to find out once and for all if Ben was just shitting her, or if she and he could make a deal. Time to pee or get off the pot for all of them—she, Beau, Ben, and the Old Man.

37.

The Toledo Galleria would be opening in a few weeks and plans for the Galleria in Canton had been in the works for a couple of months. We had been planning an Oriental theme. But, all of a sudden, Todd announced that he was scrapping these plans.

"But why? We had such wonderful things planned. The Shanghai teahouse and the pagodas and—"

"Well, think about it. Does the Orient really belong in Canton, Ohio? All of a sudden it just seems silly—irrelevant."

"What kind of theme are you talking about then?"

"What do you think of a Southern California influence? You know— open air with lots of lights and sunshine, potted palms and masses of tropical flowers . . . even orchids. And cacti too. We could have Desert Row and Ocean Promenade and Mountain Vista, with a different type of building for each level!"

There was an excitement in his voice which I hadn't heard, really, since we had returned from our California visit several months ago. Was it possible that he had been stewing about all this ever since?

"Hey, wait a moment. Did I hear you right?" I asked. "Did you say open air? For Canton, Ohio? After you were one of the first to totally enclose all the malls? I'd say that would be a step backward, to have people strolling through Desert Row with a blizzard raging."

He was hurt. "I didn't say it wouldn't be enclosed. I think I said it would have an open air *feeling*. That's what I meant anyway. I've been looking around—I think if we use fiberglass for the roof, we could have the same effect. We'd get that outdoor feeling and still have protection. We'd have plenty of daylight, and at the same time, we'd be conserving energy. There's a Teflon-coated fiberglass that would reflect almost 80 percent of the sun's rays."

"And how would it be supported?"

"With metal arches. That part's simple. It's getting the general tone that's difficult. You know what I'm looking for, Buffy? Main Street, USA. That's what I want. You know what's happened to this country? The downtown shopping areas in the big cities are in a state of decay and the old-time Main Streets in our smaller towns have disappeared. And the shopping malls that have replaced them, ours included, aren't giving the people the same sense of community. That's what I want to give back to the people that come to our mall. That sense of community."

He paced. "I want the kids growing up to *feel* it. A Main Street they've never known. I want this shopping center to be a place where the older people can do all their shopping *and* take a stroll, stop off at the corner drugstore to have a soda pop and say hello to their friends, where the little kids can play in the sunshine and the older kids can hang out. I want it to be a community center with all the old-fashioned attractions, with the old-time values, the place that everyone, young and old, is crying out for—"

It was as if he wasn't even talking about a shopping center anymore but about an unreal place—a movie set. What was all this about? Was he dreaming? Was he being a visionary? Or was it all just wishful thinking?

"We're going to do it, Buffy Ann! We're going to make it look like Southern California and we're going to call it Main Street, USA!"

He was so excited, so earnest, and so sincere that my eyes filled with tears.

"It sounds wonderful, Todd. It sounds like a Shangri-la," I said, but I knew that he had everything mixed up. Where and how did the Southern California theme . . . the Hollywood theme . . . get all mixed up with Main Street, USA?

He really should have known better. He should have known the difference. He should have known that the differences were irreconcilable.

38.

She had asked Ben for an appointment, determined that the time had come for her to meet the Old Man. Ben had stalled her long enough. She walked into the Regent Club, not immediately spotting Ben. When she did she realized why she had missed him at first. Gone was the black suit with the gardenia in its lapel. And gone was the inky black hair. It was salt-and-pepper now . . . more distinctive . . . less obvious. Ben had changed his style too.

He was dressed in tan, and there was no flower at all in his lapel. When she sat down at his table, she saw that his beige shirt was unbuttoned at the neck. And while the tan suit was inconspicuous, its fabric was a silk noil, a type of silk that looked like slubbed cotton. And the shirt that was so silky in appearance was really a fine cotton. *Nothing was as it appeared.*

"Black again," Ben commented on her dress, and shook his head, smiling. "You don't look like Vegas, Poppy."

Her fingers played with the discreet double strand of pearls, they had cost many thousands of dollars, but only those truly cognizant of such things would have known it.

"Is that why *you're* not wearing black anymore?" Poppy asked. "Because you don't want to look like a mortician?" It was a bold statement, and perhaps dangerous, but she was testing the waters.

He continued smiling, although the eyes turned to slits, and he said in a very low voice, so low that she had to incline her head to his mouth to hear: "Maybe I don't want to look like an executioner. They wear black too."

Her body snapped back. Had she gone too far? Ben's jokes were seldom exactly that.

"Have a drink, Poppy," he said, and she quickly said she would take a glass of dry white wine.

"Good. Perhaps you need a little cheer. Kind of out of sorts, are you?"

He ordered the wine and smiled at her. "I'm told that Beau's new release is going straight to the top. That's good. We're all pleased. I was right about him sticking to rock and country. Them ballads are for older people, people like me. And I don't buy records or tapes. Kids buy them. If you want him to sing some ballads here in Vegas, that's fine. For the road—no. Here, he's a saloon performer. A saloon performer can sing ballads. On the road—no ballads." As the waiter set down her glass of wine, Ben said, "Drink your wine, Poppy."

She touched the glass to her lips.

"You said you'd make an appointment for me with the Old Man. It's been some time. How about it?"

He studied her carefully. Finally he said, "All right, Poppy. I guess you waited long enough. It's almost Christmas. I'll set up a meeting and we'll call it a Christmas present. But one thing—when you go for the meet, *don't* wear black. The Old Man don't like black. He don't like to be reminded of funerals."

"You're sure he still has some ties left to the movie business?" she asked nervously.

"Ties? Yes. If anybody can do it for you—But he does have certain . . . peculiarities, let's say. You'll have to follow certain procedures—"

"Like what? What will I have to do?"

"You'll figure it out. You're a big girl and smart. You'll figure it out."

She walked through the lobby in a dress of pure white silk. She proceeded to the rear of the hotel where there was a special unmarked elevator that expressed up to the tower suite. In order to gain access, she pressed three numbers on the special phone next to the elevator, gave her name, and the elevator door opened and closed after her and started its ascent.

She broke out in a fine sweat as she thought again about what she would say to the Old Man. She had rehearsed and rehearsed, endlessly. And then she worried about the clamminess she felt in her armpits, under her breasts, and between her thighs despite all the toiletries she had administered to her body. Ben had stressed the fact that the Old Man had a thing about germs and dirt, that she was to be hospital clean and deodorized.

The elevator door opened and she stepped out into what seemed a combination of a living room and office. The first thing she noticed was the television set dialed to *General Hospital.* She recognized the show because Virgil and Smokey watched it every day. In fact, the two men who came forward to check her out resembled Virgil and Smokey, both in dress and physical appearance. The next thing she noted was the extreme coldness in the room. The air conditioning must have been turned to its highest possible setting. And all around the room were the remnants of half-eaten meals.

"Here, put this on. You can use that bathroom over there." One of the men handed her a hospital gown, white and starched, and a pair of paper slippers.

"Are you snowing me?" she asked, furious. She was wearing a brand new Mary McFadden purchased just for the occasion. The ink was hardly dry on its label.

Obviously the asshole wasn't kidding and disgustedly, she went into the bathroom and changed into the hospital gown, took off her shoes and stockings and put on the white slippers. When she came out, she was handed a pair of white paper mitts.

"Don't speak unless you gotta answer him."

"What? I came here to have a conversation!"

"Sure. If he speaks to you, you'll have a conversation. Otherwise, keep your mouth shut." Then he frisked her, his hands even darting between her thighs.

"Where do you think I'm holding something? Inside my cunt?"

"It's been known," he said dispassionately.

He opened the door that led to what looked like a tiny cubicle, a small square between the room she was in and another room, its door marked with a small square of glass. He peered through the glass and said, "Okay, send her in."

The other man pushed a button.

She walked through the cubicle into the room beyond and held her breath. The room was dark, airless, hotter than hell, and stinking. And on a hospital bed was a *really* old man, older than anyone she had ever seen. *He must be a hundred-and-twenty if he's a day!* He had a white beard that reached way down over the sheet that covered him. A hand more gray than white but almost transparent in its silkiness, lifted from the sheet and beckoned to her; the nails on the skinny fingers looked like talons. She approached the bed slowly, willing her legs to move, one in front of the other while her knees strained to buckle. As she came nearer and nearer, the stench grew more intensified and she wanted to retch. His eyes were sunken in his skull but the pupils were curiously bright and the lids completely blue. He gestured for her to remove the sheet and she did so, fighting back the urge to hold her nose. She couldn't believe what she saw; the almost fleshless, skeletal form was covered with bright red, pustular sores. Even his ridiculous, bone-thin, wrinkled erection.

She was nauseated. Now was the time to split, she told herself. But could she take the chance of missing out on her big opportunity? And Ben would be as sore as hell if she just lit out of here without making a stab at what she had come to do, after he had gone to the trouble of setting up an appointment for her. She *had* to do this—commit this fucking obscenity before she got to make her pitch. This was the worst, but she had committed obscenities before. At least if all went well, this would be the last one she'd ever have to live through. She wondered if Ben knew that she would be expected to fuck before she got to talk. But he had said "certain procedures," hadn't he?

The Old Man indicated she should mount him and gingerly she did so, fitting herself carefully about him. Then he closed his eyes and lay there still. She started to pump and as she did she looked around for the first time. She saw jars filling the shelves that lined a white wall. What the hell was in them? *My God! They're full of shit!* And as the heap of bones beneath erupted into her, she vomited—into and onto his face.

The Old Man gave a piercing shriek, the first sound to come out of him. "Get her out of here!" he screamed, and the two men came rushing in with guns drawn.

"Holy shit!" one of the men said, forgetting that he was never to curse in the Old Man's presence.

When she came out of the bathroom dressed in her immaculate white dress, still shaking, only one of the men was in the room. "You're a stupid bitch. What did you think you were doing? Ben oughten not to pay a stupid broad like you!"

Pay? Pay!

So Ben had known what was going to happen; she had been set up as the lowest kind of a whore, and there had never been a question of a conversation, of her pitching that senile horror. She started to scream but nothing came out. The scream was in her head. Yes, she had been set up, as a warning from Ben to her.

"Tell me one thing. What are those jars of shit doing in there?" She had to know or she was going to go completely out of her skull.

The man laughed. "That's *his* shit. We save it. He don't like for nothing that's part of him to go down no drain."

"Yeah? Well, maybe you *had* better tell Ben to pay me!" she snarled. "And I'll tell you what I'm going to do with the money. I'm going to hire a couple of doctors. A head doctor for you fucking punks, and a doctor for that old geezer in there. He looks like and smells like he's been dead for years . . . and no doctor's been close enough to tell him!"

He laughed heartily. "No doctor has. Don't you know? It's the doctors that are trying to kill him."

39.

I decided to take a couple of weeks off from business to get ready for the holiday season. It was becoming more and more complicated each year as the children got older. Last year Howard and Suellen had decided to celebrate Hanukah, the Jewish festival of lights, so that their children would be acquainted with that holiday as well as Christmas. And they didn't want to leave Megan and Mitchell out of their fun, so we had all trooped over to their house, eight nights in a row. Each night the Hanukah candles had been lit and each child got two gifts, one from the Rosens and one from the Kings, besides their Hanukah *gelt*, the gold foil-wrapped chocolate coins. Then, on Christmas eve, we went to the Louise Wyler Martin Home for children, the orphanage where Todd had been raised, to distribute gifts to all its little residents. (That was not only our pleasure but our obligation for there was a new building there—the King building, with a gymnasium, an art room, a library and a theater, with a photographer's darkroom and science room to follow.) Todd, the accountant, believed in balancing out the books.

On Christmas morning, the Rosens came to our house to spend the day. The festivities began with breakfast, followed by the opening of the presents. This took hours, since Todd insisted on having lots and lots of gifts for each of the children piled under the tree, each one intricately wrapped, and only one child was permitted to open one present at a time. By the time we were all through unwrapping, oohing and aahing, it was time for dinner.

Naturally, this year we were going to have to repeat it all so I had a list of presents to be bought about ten pages long. I took the list with me that morning as I set out for the Galleria, hoping to accomplish at least one page of shopping before lunch. Mr. Barkley, our mailman, intercepted me as I got into the car, handing me a bundle of mail.

"It seems like there's more and more Christmas cards each year," he said cheerfully and I made a mental note to increase his present this year. One had to keep up with inflation.

I flipped through the pile of mail as I waited for the car to warm up. When I saw Cleo's return address on a fuchsia-colored envelope, I immediately tore it open.

Inside was a specially designed, oversized season's greeting with a picture of the Masons—the two children, Leo and Cleo standing in front of their oversized fireplace with their dog, a Russian wolfhound named Spot. (The name was reverse chic, Cleo had previously informed me—a corny, banal name for an obviously pedigreed dog.) There were reproduction signatures of all five of them (Spot included). There was also a short note from Cleo enclosed.

I know I have been very lax in corresponding lately. Busy, busy, busy. I am going to let this note take the place of a proper letter as we're having a really big blow-out for the holidays—an open house that will start at ten in the morning with a champagne brunch and go on through the day with an early dinner, followed by a midnight supper laid out about ten and continuing through. We have an invitation list consisting of literally hundreds, which includes everybody we know and a few that we don't! I hope those who come for brunch will leave before dinner, and those who eat dinner will leave before supper is served. We've decided to do this every year and thus whenever the holiday season rolls around, everyone in town will, I hope, be waiting for their invitation to the Masons' annual do. Don't you love it? A holiday marathon.

Leo is still working on *Love and Betrayal*. It goes on and on and on. It's millions over budget, thanks to our friend, Suzie Superstar. Leo says she simply was not meant for the major leagues. Not to mention her prima donna antics. (In the middle of a scene she yells for the cameras to stop so that the hairdresser can rearrange her hair.) Plus, she insists that she's co-producer, and keeps sticking her nose into things she knows nothing about. So now they've decided they have to reshoot about half of what they've already shot. Poor Leo! He's positively exhausted. He's been working with Suzannah day and night. He says it's like trying to breathe life into a wooden mannequin. That is his new name for her. The Great Wooden One. Don't you love it? Have to run now. Love and kisses from Cleo and all the Masons.

It was hard to believe that it was already over a year since we had been in California, that Suzannah and Heinie were married that long, and that Suzannah's movie, *Love and Betrayal*, had been in production for almost as long.

And I was disappointed that Cleo hadn't given me any news of Cassie, since I hadn't heard from her myself in a few months.

Driving home from work each night, Cassie had gotten into the habit of going beyond her own driveway, farther up the hill some several hundred feet to pass the pink castle that was not viewable from the road; to pass black iron gates spotted with rust and erosion, guarding the driveway which circled out of sight; to pass its eight-foot-high stone wall beginning to crumble. Directly behind the wall, the trees and shrubbery formed a wall of their own.

She knew from many, many months of observation that, at first, a landscaper's truck had appeared almost monthly and two or three men would make a small onslaught against the rampages of nature. But with the passing of time, the truck came ever less often, once every two and then three months, and then not at all. The neglect of mercenaries or unpaid bills?

She would continue driving until she was past the pink house's tennis court, its state of decay only slightly in view. Once past the court, she would make a three-point turn and drive down again to her own house. Tonight, after the turn, on the way down, she saw something she had never noticed before—a small space between the padlocked iron gates and the crumbling stone wall on the side nearer to her own property—a space large enough for a child to slip through, or perhaps a very slim adult.

She parked in her courtyard, not seeing, and not expecting to see, Guy's car. Now that the series was into its second season, he was less visible than ever as far as she was concerned. And she knew now where he was much of the time when he was not at home and not at work. She had seen where with her own eyes.

Twice, and the second time only to confirm the first, mildly curious as to where he went in the evenings, she had followed him in her car when he had left the house. The first time his trail had taken her to Hollywood Boulevard and at first she thought that perhaps he was just checking out the ambiance for his role as the cop who patrolled the area. But it was not long before he opened the door of the Ferrari to allow into the car a girl of fourteen, maybe fifteen, dressed in a tank top and cut-offs.

The following week she trailed him again. This time to the beach at Venice and in a very short time he picked up another pubescent girl— this one with stringy blond hair and embroidered dingy white jeans. Both times Guy himself wore a blond wig and mirrored shades.

Except for the bad taste in her mouth she was almost completely disinterested, as if she were but a stranger observing him. Yes . . . disinterested.

Unlike the night she had accompanied him to the awards ceremony when he had been nominated for best actor in a continuing dramatic series. That was a public appearance and he had insisted that she go with him. Then, when they had announced his name as the winner, he had kissed her first and then went up to claim his trophy. That night, she had been excited . . . thrilled.

Now, Mother will have to admit that he's a success . . . she will have to surrender, congratulate, acclaim . . . oh yes! Now I can leave him! I will forget about the baby! An innocent baby really deserves better than Guy! And won't Mother be confused! She will declare Guy a real winner and then I'll turn my back on him! That will show her what I think of her opinion! In effect, I will be turning my back on her too! It will be my moment, as this moment—winning the prize—is Guy's!

But it had all turned to ashes, that dream, when, instead of applauding, Cassandra's lip curled in a sneer of a smile and said: "A vulgar prize for a vulgar man in a vulgar business." She had admitted to watching the show *once* . . . just to verify what she already knew, she said. Then Cassie knew for sure that it would have to be more than a TV series to make a dent in her mother's armor.

Tonight, she had brought home with her some Christmas decorations to cheer her own private world—a wreath to hang on her door, holly to drape at the French doors of the den, a string of colored lights to decorate the mantel. She hung the wreath, ran the colored lights up the wall, across the marble ledge and down the wall again, and plugged them in, pleased when the red, blue, and green lights twinkled at her.

She had saved the holly for last so that as she worked at the doors she would see the lights come on in the pink house. But when they did, her heart sank as she saw that another room of the house failed to be illuminated. For months, she had seen the lights fail, one after the other, window by window, as bulb after bulb gave up its ghost. When would some caretaker come to replace them? Would anybody come at all? What would she do when the house lay entirely in darkness? *Poor house.*

She thought again of the opening in the wall formed by the crumbling stone. She could not get into the house to replace its bulbs, but she *could* hang a wreath on its front door . . . *if* she could get through the opening in the wall. No one would see the wreath, not even she would be able to see it from her French doors, but she would *know* that it was there when she sat looking at the house. And she wouldn't have to take it down, not even when the holidays were over.

She put on a sweater coat, stuck some nails and a hammer in the pockets, and holding a flashlight, she removed the wreath from her own door. Her heart beating rapidly, she walked down the length of her driveway and up the road hugging the sweater close to her—it was cold tonight, but tonight she was going to see the house up close!

It had grown dark quickly but the flashlight found the opening in the wall. With a sinking heart she saw that she had misjudged the opening. Much as she tried to wiggle through sideways, the jagged edge of the wall ripped at her hose and through the hose, tearing at her flesh. She should have put on pants, she realized, crying, and sneakers. But even that would not have helped, she thought, as she dropped the flashlight and began clawing at the stone with her hands, trying to make more of it fall away. She reached into her pocket, withdrew the hammer, and struck at the stone, smashing at it until she was exhausted. Rivulets of perspiration ran down her face, into her eyes. Finally, her body aching, she gave up. She would come back tomorrow night and she would bring a chisel.

On the third night she squeezed through and she sat down on the damp ground and cried. Now that she was on the inside of the stone wall, she was afraid. Afraid that once she walked up that long driveway and around to the house she might never want to come down again.

She directed the yellow glow of the flashlight onto her wristwatch. It was nearly eleven. She had been here chipping away at the wall for almost four hours. She would go home now. She would come back in the morning, would not go to the museum at all. Early in the morning she would come back and in a wink she would be through the wall, before anyone could see her. And once in, behind the wall, she would be lost from view, lost in the overgrown jungle. She would run up the palm-lined driveway all the way around until she came to the pink, green-trimmed castle.

It was a flawed jewel—coral, set within emeralds, mounted on a high terrace, surrounded by a stone balustrade with obelisks and cracked statuary on lofty pedestals. She tried to take everything in at once—the rose-tinted carved stonework, two-story balconies, medallions and moldings of terra-cotta, arched French windows, the red tile roof, the bell tower composed of Spanish Renaissance campaniles. In front was a ruin of a lawn. She hung her Christmas wreath on the massive green front door, using its giant knocker as a hook, and then she wandered.

To the left was a tennis court that had succumbed to triumphant weeds. To the right was what was left of formal gardens . . . a curving promenade that led to a lattice-roofed teahouse, and beyond that, the drained and cracked Moroccan-tiled pool with the remains of a casino —a once very elegant pool house with a tiled floor, ancient cherubs, and marble columns. And all about were the palm trees, the giant oaks, the hibiscus and oleanders growing wild. To the rear were flat terraces against the towering hillside.

Back and forth she went, from the tennis court to the teahouse, where she sat for a while on a rusted-over white wrought iron chair, imagining herself drinking tea with Jenny Elmann. Then she proceeded to the casino where she ran her fingers over the pink marble fluted columns. And then in one corner of the pavilion she found a toy fire truck, its bright red paint corroded with orange-colored rust that came off on her hands. Jenny Elmann had a child. . . .

She sat in a wicker chair, its white paint almost completely peeled away, on the rear terrace, studying a two-story building that was connected to the main house, but still separate. These were obviously servants' quarters with an entrance of their own, a wooden door fitted with glass panes. If she broke one of the panes, already cracked, she could stick her hand inside and open the door just like that! She had seen people do that in the movies, hadn't she?

She walked slowly over to the door, tried to peer through the glass. Yes, it would work. But there was a padlock on the door—it too covered with red rust but a couple of blows with a rock or the hammer would probably take care of it.

Tomorrow, she promised herself. Today had already been complete. Tomorrow, she would bring some bulbs with her. She would go into the house and she would replace all the lights that had gone out.

40.

Mitch had been tucked into his bed and Todd and I were helping Megan practice her lines for her school play. Outside, the lawn was covered with only a fine dusting of snow, but the weather forecasters had said the first really large storm of the new year was in the works. I prayed that it would be delayed for a few days. Megan's play would go on Friday afternoon in the school auditorium, and a really heavy snowstorm would cut down on the attendance considerably. I so wanted everything to go right for Megan. She had thought of nothing but this play once Christmas was over.

Todd took the part of the Happy Giant, giving Megan her cues. I could see that he loved doing it, and he made all the appropriate gestures, lifting his eyebrows, spreading his arms, talking in a deep bass so that Megan kept giggling.

The telephone rang and I told Todd to take it in the library so that I could go on rehearsing with Megan. "I'll take the part of the Happy Giant," I told her and she said earnestly, "I don't think you'll be as good as Daddy."

I sighed. I was sure that she was right.

Then Todd came back. I could see that he was upset, so I told Megan to go upstairs and get ready for bed, that we would come up in a few minutes and finish going over the lines after she was under the covers. She protested, but when her father told her to run along, she did.

As soon as she left the room, Todd blurted out, "It was Heinie on the phone."

I registered surprise, while at the same time I felt a prickling sensation at the back of my neck. Suzannah called often but Heinie hardly ever at all. "Well?"

"Heinie said . . ." He paused. "Heinie said—It seems that he walked in on Suzannah and Leo. They were rehearsing. They were supposed to be rehearsing. But they were in bed."

"Oh! Oh my God! Where?"

"In the bungalow at the Beverly Hills Hotel."

"Poor Cleo! Does she know?"

"I don't know. Heinie didn't mention Cleo."

"Oh my God! That bitch! That bitch Suzannah! How could she?"

"She could! She did. The question is *why.*"

"They didn't even like each other. She detested Leo. She *said* she detested Leo. Is it possible that she lied? That all along she was attracted to him. But you can usually sense these things. I never saw the slightest bit of attraction there. Did you?"

"No." He shook his head. He seemed as dumbfounded as I.

"And how was Heinie? How was he taking it?"

"He sounded . . ." Todd lifted his shoulders helplessly. "I don't know. He sounded destroyed."

"Why, do you think, he called us?"

"I'm not sure. Because we're his friends and we're close to Suzannah? I'm not sure. Maybe because he thinks we *know* Suzannah. I think he wants me to come out there . . . right away."

"Why? What does he want you to do?" I asked with a sharpness that surprised even myself.

"I guess he thinks of me as his friend. And he needs a friend."

"Yes, I suppose he does. I imagine there are not many people out there that he feels that way about."

"He was just crying out for help, I guess."

And the telephone rang again and we looked at one another. We both knew who it was. "You get it," I told Todd. "I can't talk to her right now."

I heard Todd say, "If you keep crying, Suzannah, I can't understand you—"

Then he was quiet for a few minutes. Finally I heard him say, "All right, Suzannah, as soon as we can." He hung up. "I told her we'd come out as soon as we can. I'll call the airlines. I'll see what's leaving first thing in the morning."

I was angry now. I could feel it surging through me, threatening to erupt all over everything and everybody. "Why, for God's sake? Why did you tell her that?"

"She says she's locked up in the bungalow. That they had to take Heinie away from the door. He was creating a terrible commotion. She says she's afraid . . . she's afraid Heinie's going to kill her."

"Good! I hope he does!"

"You don't mean that, Buffy Ann!"

"The hell you say! I mean it!"

He refused to accept it.

"What about Cleo?" I demanded angrily. "Think what Suzannah has done to her, not to mention poor, sweet Heinie! And what about Leo? Doesn't Heinie want to kill him too? Doesn't Leo deserve killing?"

Didn't anybody blame the man? Didn't anyone want to kill Leo? I wanted justice. If Heinie was going to kill Suzannah, he had to kill Leo too.

"What about Leo?" I demanded again of Todd. "Doesn't Heinie want to kill him?"

Todd went to the phone. "Nobody mentioned Leo. Not Heinie and not Suzannah."

"Why not?"

"I don't know why not, Buffy Ann. Maybe nobody thinks he's important enough to talk about at a time like this."

There it was. Even Todd didn't think Leo was *really* a factor in this matter. Cleo's happiness, her very life, was destroyed and nobody, including Todd, thought it was important.

"Don't you make a reservation for me. *I'm* not going."

He put the phone down. "But you have to—They're our friends and they need us."

"Suzannah's no friend of mine. I'm through with her."

"But what about Cleo? And what about Heinie? He's our friend too."

I realized that Todd had already decided to go *before* Suzannah had called. He had made up his mind to hold Heinie's hand.

"You go. But I can't go," I said firmly. "Megan's play is in two days. I have to help her get ready and I have to make sure that one of us, at least, is there in the audience. There *are* priorities, Todd."

After Todd left for the airport that morning, I sat by the phone knowing that I *should* call Cleo, but fighting my reluctance. It was like having to say consoling words to a friend after a loved one has died— you just never knew what to say and you dreaded the moment. Maybe even *that* was easier than making this call. At least in the case of a death, there was no sense of acute embarrassment involved.

I dialed but the line was busy and I was grateful for the reprieve, but in a few minutes I had to dial again and Cleo answered.

"Cleo darling, this is Buffy."

"Buffy! Then you've heard—"

"Yes. Heinie called. Oh Cleo, I'm so sorry. . . ."

"Yes. I just don't know what we're going to do now that Heinie's closed down the set on *Love and Betrayal.*" She broke into sobs. "It looks like Leo's washed up in the movies."

I was stunned. I was speechless.

"And it's all her fault, that miserable bitch! She's ruined us."

While Cleo cried, I tried to sort things out in my mind. She was crying not because she had been betrayed but because the movie set was closed down; because Leo's big chance at features had been aborted; and she blamed Suzannah! And I was furious! If a woman was a real woman, she had to stand up for herself—she had *to* have strength and courage and dignity, and she had to demand that she be treated accordingly. And if she didn't, then she was not a real woman—she was shit!

Cleo was shit! She was satisfied to worry about a movie being completed; she was satisfied to blame Suzannah and spare Leo her recriminations. Cleo was not concerned with her own personal betrayal.

What could I possibly say to her? If I decried Leo's behavior—after all, what did Suzannah owe Cleo compared to what Leo owed her?—then I was only a meddlesome busybody who wanted to cause trouble. And I would not be that. Cleo was, I had always thought, an intelligent individual. Her interpretation therefore was a considered evaluation and I had no right to interject my own analysis. I could not add my words to her sobs.

"Everything will work out," I said. "It will all get straightened out. You'll see." And while I was completely disheartened, I *was* sincere. I hoped it would all work out for her.

But I no longer wished to be involved. I wanted to separate myself from these people and their strange, shoddy lives.

Todd called that evening, asked to speak to Megan first, to tell her how sorry he was to miss her play. She heard Megan say, "Yes, Daddy. I know you have to help your friends."

Tears welled up in my eyes. She was everything I could ask for in a daughter—to have so much understanding and compassion when she was so young. And she made me ashamed of the anger I felt for Todd for going off to California and leaving me to escort Leah to the school play by myself.

"It's all right, Daddy. Leah is going to the play, and so are Uncle Howard and Aunt Suellen," Megan reassured him, "and of course Mommy and Mitch." Then she handed me the phone. And I made up my mind to be no less compassionate and understanding than my young daughter.

"Well, I've talked Heinie out of killing Suzannah though of course it was never really going to happen. It was more Suzannah's dramatics than Heinie's threat."

"What about Leo?" I still had to ask. "Doesn't Heinie want to kill him?"

"No. Do you know what Heinie said? 'Leo's only garbage. You can sweep him out with the trash. But Suzannah? I loved her more than life itself.' "

"Oh, that poor man. He is such a sweet man."

"Yes, he is. I'm going over to see Cleo now."

"Yes, you'd better. She was hysterical when I spoke with her; she could hardly talk. It seems she and Leo are both terribly upset over Heinie closing down the set on the movie . . . upset that they're going to have to go back to being mere TV people instead of being part of the movie set—"

Todd chuckled at my ironical remarks. "I thought that maybe that was what was eating at Suzannah too, that the set was being closed down. But I don't really think it's so. She's really heartbroken about her marriage."

"Then what was she doing screwing Leo? That's what I haven't heard. *Why?*"

"She thought that she *had to*—that if Leo was really to help her be a great dramatic star, they both had to *feel* it. She said something about Dietrich having von Sternberg and Garbo her Stiller. She thought if she and Leo had a great romantic affair she could become Garbo. She thought that was Garbo's secret."

"And you believe *that?*" I asked, incredulous.

"Suzannah *does.* She really does."

No, I thought. She couldn't. Garbo was of the long ago . . . more fantasy than real. And Suzannah was living in the seventies . . . the "me" seventies. If there ever was a *me* person, it was my friend Suzannah.

41.

Friday afternoon I set out for the school with Leah and Mitch beside me. It was extremely cold and I knew that the big snow that had been threatening was almost upon us. Even after the heater filled the car with warmth Leah still huddled in her old cloth coat with the worn fur collar. I felt like a selfish bitch in my new golden Christmas mink, and I had an overwhelming urge to wrap Leah in fur befitting the proud queen she was, which, of course, she would never permit. Then seeing her sit so nervously on the edge of the seat holding on to the armrest for dear life, something she *always* did when I was in the driver's seat and never when Todd was, I had another urge—to really give her a jolt, to go around the corners on two wheels, to step on the gas until the Seville was doing ninety. But I didn't, of course.

Megan didn't make a single slip and it didn't make a mite of difference that she was so unprofessional as to wave to us all before making her exit. After the play Howard and Suellen took Leah and Mitchell in their car to their house, while I waited for Megan. We would all have dinner together at the Rosen house—a dinner in honor of our actress. And still the snow hadn't started.

Suellen was so special, I couldn't help thinking. She had one of her very special dinners, and even baked one of her special cakes—a big mocha fudge rectangle. Across it, in butter cream letters: *Hurray for Meggie!* There were even candles for Megan to blow out. I was mad! Here were all the smiling faces I loved—Megan and Mitchell, Suellen and Howard and their children, Petey and Becky, and Leah . . . and even she was smiling. And where was Todd? With that great bitch Suzannah, that rat Leo, and with infuriating Cleo who didn't even have enough backbone to be hurt and angry that she had been stepped out on . . . that she had been humiliated and cuckolded.

"Can I have a piece to take home for Daddy, Aunt Suellen?"

"Of course, honey. It's your cake. Whatever's left you'll take home for your father."

"I don't know how much is going to be left after I have three pieces," Peter teased her.

"If Petey's going to have three pieces, so am I," Becky said.

"Me too," piped up Mitchell.

Howard took one look at Megan's anxious face and reassured her, *"Nobody's* getting more than one piece, Meggie. Not even me. There'll be plenty of cake left for your daddy."

"If he ever gets here." I muttered under my breath so that Megan wouldn't hear me. Unfortunately, Suellen did, and she looked at me with a worried glint in her eye. And we both looked out the window and saw the first big flakes start to fall fast and heavy.

Suellen's mouth was a straight line. I knew that expression. It was always there when Suellen was angry or disapproving. And she had already told me what she thought about Todd taking off for California.

"Sometimes you have to put your foot down, Buffy. I know that you think everything Todd does is wonderful, and fortunately, usually it is . . . but do you have to go along with *every* single thing he does or wants to do? I'm not sure that that's the mark of a good wife, or a good friend, for that matter. Sometimes we show our love best by setting limits—"

"We're not talking about a child here, Suellen."

"No. We're talking about Todd. And *you* tell me why he had to go rushing off to California. To hold Suzannah's hand? Suzannah doesn't deserve that. And Leo? Well, we won't even discuss *him.* As for Cleo, you told me what Cleo was worried about and I must say, I find her values very, very weird. And for Todd to go galloping off on his white horse to defend those values and miss his daughter's school play, well, I think that's weird too."

"I think Todd wanted to console Heinie," I offered in rebuttal, defending Todd now, although I too was angry with him.

"I never met the man," Suellen said, "so I suppose I shouldn't judge him, but I would think that any man who marries Suzannah knows exactly what he's getting, and he shouldn't be surprised afterward."

"You're too hard on people, Suellen. And besides, Todd's only flown to the Coast for a couple of days. He hasn't run off and abandoned me and the kids. He'll probably be back tomorrow."

Still, her air of impending doom was contagious. Seeing the snowfall picking up steam so quickly, I felt a kind of panic. I wanted to be home, in front of my own fire, with my kids safely in bed. So, refusing Suellen's offer for us all to stay the night and Howard's offer to drive us home, I quickly piled the kids and Leah and the remains of Megan's cake into the Cadillac.

"I'll drive as carefully as you would yourself, Howie," I promised, trying hard to smile at him. "For God's sake, there's barely a half inch of snow on the ground. I've been driving these Ohio winters for years and God willing, I'll be doing it for the next fifty years."

"Call me the minute you get home," Suellen said into the car as I started the engine.

"What's *wrong* with you? It's only been snowing for about ten minutes and I'll be home in another ten. And you know, they don't call me Buffy King of the Road for nothing."

Leah took the kids off to bed and I called Suellen to let her know we were safe. "Thank God!" Suellen breathed, then in the next breath, asked: "Have you heard from Todd?"

"No, I haven't," I snapped. "I just walked in the door, and I'm tying up the line speaking to you—"

"Goodnight, Buffy. Sleep well." Suellen's voice was a soft reproach. "I'm sure you'll hear from Todd first thing in the morning."

I paced and looked out the window. The snowflakes were more goosedown than snow, and the wind blew in angry gusts, getting angrier by the minute. Drifts began to form and grow higher by leaps and bounds. I thought that if Todd called, I would tell him not to make a move out of California until the storm in Akron was over. I wouldn't have been a bit surprised if the airport was already closed down. I called to see if it were so but I couldn't get through.

I tossed and turned throughout the night. Megan was upset in the morning because it was a Saturday. She was old enough, and cynical enough, to have wanted it to be a weekday so that she could have gotten a day off from school because of the heavy fall.

Mitchell only wanted to go out and play. I told him that he could go out and make snowballs *after* the fall had ceased and the skies started to clear.

I listened to the weather forecasters on the radio, switching from station to station all morning, hoping to find a prediction that was palatable, but by noon I was forced to accept the fact that the storm would continue into the night. By one o'clock I figured out that since it was ten o'clock in Hollywood and that the sun was probably shining, Todd must have been up at least two hours already. By two o'clock our time, he *would certainly have* finished his breakfast, at which time he would most likely call.

But he didn't. At two o'clock our time, I decided to call him, realizing then that he had never told me at which hotel he was staying. But I had a feeling it would be the Wilshire so I called there only to find out that he wasn't registered. Then I called the Beverly Hills Hotel. It figured that if Todd went to see Heinie first and then Suzannah, since one or the other was probably still in the bungalow there, that's where he would have booked a room. But the Beverly Hills had no record of him. They did ring the bungalow that was still registered in the name of Muller, but there was no answer there.

I could call Cleo, I thought. Quite possibly she knew at which hotel my husband was staying. But thinking it over, I decided against it. Not that she wouldn't know, but it wasn't the best idea in the world to let her know that *I didn't know* where my husband was. I was getting paranoid.

At six o'clock our time, I heard the forecasters say that the brunt of the storm had passed and was moving east. It was only three o'clock in California and I presumed it was still all sunshine there. When Suellen called to find out if I had heard from Todd, my answer was less than pleasant.

"Oh, I wouldn't worry, Buff. It's probably the storm. Trouble with the telephone lines."

That was sweet of her. She could have said, *"I* had no trouble reaching you."

By nine o'clock the last faltering snowdrop had fallen and I imagined that I could see the sky clearing, although it was pretty pitch black up there. I picked up the phone to check with Suellen, to ask her if she thought the sky was brightening, and then I discovered, now that the storm had passed our area, my telephone line *was* out.

That was the last straw and I crawled into bed exhausted. Sometime later, I wasn't quite sure how much later because I had dozed off, I heard a car door slam outside. I ran to the window and looked out. By the glow of the outdoor lights that I had left on, I saw Todd, my Todd, paying off a cab.

I flew down the stairs, not even stopping to put on a robe. I wanted only to throw my arms around my husband, to rain kisses on his sweet face, grateful that he had come back to me and our children, after all. I opened the door wide and there he was, grinning at me like crazy, a self-satisfied conquering hero.

"Would you believe that I left California this morning, eight o'clock their time? Do you know how long they held us over in Chicago? They wouldn't clear us until they opened up the airport here. Do you know how long it took the cab to get here from the airport? I think we were in the cab longer than we were in the air. . . . But neither rain nor hail could keep—"

I wasn't even paying attention to his words for once. All I wanted to do, and all I did, was fling my arms around his neck and kiss him desperately. *Then* I saw the fur-draped figure behind him.

"Look who I brought home with me—"

"Oh, Buffy!" Suzannah wailed. "I had no other place to go. . . ."

Todd bounded up the stairs to catch a look at the faces of his sleeping children and to change, while I helped Suzannah off with her ankle-length white mink and big matching toque, led her into the library where I lit a fire, gave her a large drink of Scotch, all stiffly, with only the most obligatory words.

She wept and drank. "Todd saved my life by bringing me here," she told me between sobs. "Heinie was going to kill me as sure as I lived!"

"That's ridiculous," I said without any passion. "People always say things like that in the throes of their anguish. It doesn't mean anything. I've said the same thing to my kids when they've done something to make me mad. Needless to say, *I* didn't mean it."

"Oh, Heinie meant it. I know he did. Todd talked him out of it. Temporarily," she added darkly.

"I hardly believe he meant it. Heinie's a sweet, gentle man," I said very pointedly.

And as she broke into a stronger torrent of tears, I steeled my heart against her. "How could you do that to him, Suzannah? And with Leo of all people?"

"But I did it for Heinie," she sobbed. "For the sake of the movie. I thought that if Leo was enthralled with me, dying with love for me, he would be inspired to genius and would transmit that genius into my performance . . . that it would show up . . . on the screen. A great director said that. I read it somewhere. He said that a director has to fall in love with his leading lady. That working closely with a beautiful woman you get to know her well and she you, and that it's very intense for both of you when you're really communicating. Then when he looks at the actress through a camera she grows even more beautiful and something happens—he falls in love. Maybe not with the actress but at least with her portrayal—"

"But he didn't say the actress had to go to bed with her director, did he? *Did he?*"

She didn't answer my question. She only said, "Don't you understand? I had an affair with Leo in order that *Love and Betrayal* would be the most inspired love story ever filmed!"

I knew her reasoning was faulty but taking into account the kind of person Suzannah was, I could understand how it all made sense to her. Was it such a farfetched hypothesis, at that? She couldn't possibly have wanted to make love with Leo for love's sake, or for sex's sake, or even for Leo's sake. I knew that she had nothing but contempt for Leo when he was not wearing his director's hat. I knew that sex meant nothing to Suzannah except as a tool. As for love, what was love for Suzannah but an illusion? As illusory as the images on Hollywood's big screens.

"And now I've lost everything," she moaned. "My Heinie . . . my sweet Heinie . . . my life."

And although I resented it, and resisted it, I felt the stirrings of sympathy beginning to warm my stone-cold heart. She had indeed lost Heinie and he was, for her, a great loss indeed.

"He loved me so."

It's a pity you didn't think of that before you embraced Leo Mason's body. I didn't want to forgive her so quickly, to cave in so fast. "Yes, he did," I said, trying to speak sternly.

"I don't know how I'll go on without him."

You'll manage, as you always have.

"You'll find a way. You have before and you will again. You still have your career."

"Do I? *Love and Betrayal* will probably never be finished now. And after everything I've sacrificed for it—"

This was getting really heavy, I thought. *Now we're into sacrifice.*

"Going to bed with that egomaniac! He never thought of anything but his own pleasure, satisfying himself. And I told him I loved him! God!" she screamed. "Don't think *that* didn't nearly kill me!"

Even though I knew that Cleo herself was more disturbed about the picture being closed down than about her husband's perfidy, I still had to ask: "Granted you were making a sacrifice for the sake of the picture, didn't you ever think of what you were doing to Cleo? You are . . . were . . . her friend."

"Cleo!" she dismissed that person. "She's a dirty little schemer if ever I saw one. I wouldn't be a bit surprised if she *urged* Leo to screw me. There's nothing she wouldn't do for Leo . . . for his career."

Her words came as a shock to me. It was something that I hadn't even considered—Cleo, in cahoots with Leo, *urging* him to make love to Suzannah the Star. Of course it wasn't necessarily so just because Suzannah said so. Could it be? Had Cleo changed so much that she had become *that* kind of a person? I didn't really know, had no way of knowing, would probably never know.

"They used me . . . both of them! They're shits. But Heinie . . . Heinie's sweet and he loved me so. They're only shits, but Heinie . . . he *was somebody.*"

It struck me how terrible it was that she spoke of Heinie in the past tense, as if he were dead . . . dead to her, as much as Paulie White was.

I took her upstairs and put her to bed. "Things won't look so bad in the morning," I said, tucking her in.

"What will I do, Buffy?"

"You'll think of something . . . tomorrow."

She smiled at me in a sweet-sad way. "Damned if you don't sound just like Scarlett O'Hara . . ."

Todd was waiting for me in the library. He took me in his arms and kissed me like leading men kissed leading ladies on movie sets. After the kisses, I laid my head on his chest. Suellen was right about one thing. There was nothing I wouldn't do for Todd . . . nothing probably that I wouldn't go along with. As ever, I loved him far too much to doubt either his goodness or his wisdom. And then I thought of what Suzannah had just said about Cleo. *There's nothing she wouldn't do for Leo.*

What was it with women like us? Didn't all the propaganda floating around about women's rights and women's privileges and women's prerogatives mean anything to us? Were we, teenagers in the late fifties and early sixties, born too early for the proper independence of heart? Only five years too early?

And then I grew cold at the very thought that if I had been born five years later, I would have missed loving Todd King! The thought was enough to turn me to stone. Far better not to be a liberated woman than to have missed loving and being loved by Todd King! *Far better?* No, it was the difference between life and death.

But still there *was* a difference between Cleo and me, and it lay in the man. Todd as opposed to Leo. And there was one very significant difference between Cleo and me. *I* would never be able to tolerate even the slightest infidelity. The flame of my love for Todd burnt too hot, too high, too intensely for it not to be a greedy, jealous, all-consuming love.

"I'm sorry about bringing Suzannah home with me. I know you weren't feeling particularly generous toward her when I left. But she kept crying . . . begging me not to leave her alone. And I wanted to fly home desperately. I had to talk to you right away and frankly, I didn't know what else to do with her. I just knew I couldn't turn my back on her when she was in need."

"It's all right. Of course you couldn't turn your back on her."

Would any hero do that? Turn his back on an old friend? No hero of my acquaintance.

"But there *is* one thing," I said. "You'll have to be the one to break the news to Leah that Suzannah's here. That's only fair."

And we kissed again and then went rapidly up the stairs to bed. And after Todd fell asleep, leaving me to offer up my thanks to God for bringing my husband safely home to me, I remembered what Todd had said—"I wanted to fly home desperately. I had to talk to you right away—"

What had he wanted to talk to me about? It sounded so . . . urgent. I wanted to wake him up and ask him. But he looked so peaceful and innocent in his sleep that I didn't have the heart to do so. It would have to wait for morning.

42.

We were awakened by the children who were delighted that it had stopped snowing, that their father was home, and that it was Sunday, which meant that he could take them and their sleds outside to play. So all four of us went down to breakfast, while Suzannah slept late. Then Todd bundled up the kids and went outside with them, while I prepared a breakfast tray for my guest. Leah was coping with Suzannah's presence in the house by ignoring her.

I set the tray down in the guestroom and pulled the draperies open, letting in the cold bright light. I watched Todd and the kids playing for a minute or two. We still hadn't had the chance to discuss what was on Todd's mind, what he had been so eager to talk to me about. Then I heard Suzannah coming awake and I turned to her. "How are you feeling?" I asked.

"Buffy, I had a dream—"

Oh dear, I thought, she's going to tell me some wistfully sweet dream about a reconciliation with Heinie. And I didn't think Heinie was the type of man who could forgive this type of betrayal, no matter what the reasons. And I could feel for him. I believed in the strength of his love. If he loved so hard, it was that much harder not to hate after the disillusionment.

"Oh Suzannah! Don't get your hopes up over a dream."

"But it all worked out so beautifully. Let me tell you what happened—"

"Okay." I sat down on the edge of the bed. I guessed that it would be better to let her get it out of her system. She smiled at me, the calculating smile with the teeth and the dimples. And that should have told me something, should have warned me that her dream might be more fabrication than dream.

"In my dream, Todd went to Heinie and talked to him . . . convinced him to finish the picture. Heinie, because he admired Todd as a person so much, listened to him. And we finished the picture and it was a smash. Worth everything that had happened before. Wasn't that a lovely dream?"

"Lovely." Yes, I should have known that any dream Suzannah told me about was sure to be some kind of a scam.

"Buffy?" she said tentatively. This time I knew exactly what she was going to say.

"Buffy," she repeated, "I know it's really a difficult thing to ask. But do you think Todd *would?* Talk to Heinie about finishing the picture?"

I sighed. "I don't know if he can, Suzannah. It's all so personal. It's personal with Heinie, you understand? And I don't know that Todd could intrude in such an intimate matter."

"Oh, that would be all right," she pooh-poohed, shrugging her shoulders. "You see, Heinie sets a big store by Todd. He thinks the world of him. He admires him. Buffy, don't you think Todd *might?* He would, I bet, if you asked him to, Buffy. . . ." she cajoled like a child might.

Well, why not? I thought. Did it matter anymore? "All right, Suzannah. I'll speak to Todd. Maybe he could, would."

Who knew anymore? Maybe Heinie might just listen to Todd.

Suzannah started to cry again. "I've lost Heinie. I can't lose *everything*. You can understand that, can't you?"

"Yes."

I did. In one way, I understood everything. But for the life of me I would never be able to explain it to anybody.

By the time I came downstairs, the kids and Todd were sitting at the kitchen table consuming bowls of steaming, homemade vegetable soup, along with chicken salad sandwiches, while Leah brewed hot chocolate and mumbled under her breath about idiots and wet clothes and the dangers of killing chills.

I sat down with them and Todd whispered, "We're going to build a snowman after lunch. Do you think you can find some dry mittens and stuff without letting a certain person know?"

I nodded, watching Leah's back and whispered, "What was it you wanted to talk to me about? You said you were eager to fly home to—"

Todd rolled his eyes at the children and then rolled his eyes at Leah, then whispered, "I guess we'll have to discuss it later."

After lunch, fortified with dry mittens, scarves, fresh jackets and pants, they trooped outside again to work on the snowman. Then the men who did our landscaping in the spring, summer, and fall, came by to shovel the walks and I decided to go out too. With Suzannah still in bed and Leah slamming about, muttering, it would be more fun outside than in. So I bundled up, put on my heavy boots, and joined everybody.

"We're going to need a carrot for the nose and some buttons for the eyes, Mommy," Todd said. "And what do you think we should use for the mouth?"

"How about a strip of red pepper? I think Leah might have a red pepper."

"What do you think, kids?" Todd asked. "A strip of red pepper?"

The kids yelled their approval and turned back to their work, while I decided to broach Todd about Suzannah's request. "How angry is Heinie? I mean, really?"

"Very. Why?"

"Suzannah wants you to go to him and persuade him to finish the picture. What do you think?"

"It will never happen."

"Are you sure?"

"Positive," he said with a finality, looking straight into my eyes and then I knew what it was he had been waiting to say to me. Perhaps I had even sensed it before he had left for California in such a rush.

"How come you're so sure, Todd? You had a discussion with Heinie relating specifically to the future of the picture?"

"Yes, Buffy. Heinie is through with Hollywood. Heinie is going to sell the studio—"

"I see," I said. *"And you want to buy it?"* I remarked without missing a beat.

"Yes! . . . but how did you guess?" He took my hand. "That's what I wanted to talk to you about."

"Then let's talk about it!" I turned to go back into the house.

He leaped in front of me. "And you'll think about that strip of red pepper, won't you?" he implored. But he had to go back to the children.

Todd and the kids finally finished their six-foot snowman and we found the requisite hat, scarf, and pipe to outfit him in style, not to mention his grinning red-pepper mouth. Then I started dinner. Leah, it seemed, had developed a bad case of aching back and had taken to her bed. I was sure that Suzannah had given several people a pain in the neck in her lifetime but this was probably the first time she had triggered a bad *upper* back.

Todd came into the kitchen as I bustled about and suggested that he call Suellen and invite them all over to dinner. I shook my head. "Not a good idea. Suellen, like Leah, can't stand the sight of Suzannah."

"Our charitable Suellen?"

"Our highly moralistic Suellen," I replied firmly.

"You know, I never realized it before, but Leah and Suellen are very much alike. Leah's charitable too. She must give half her salary to her church. And she's about as stiff-necked about morality as you can get . . . as is sweet Sue." Then he added thoughtfully, "Unlike Howard."

"Howard? Howard is very charitable and one could hardly call him immoral."

"Yes," Todd said munching on celery with relish, "but he's not rigid —he's . . ." He groped for the right word. "He's much more *tolerant* and open-minded. You'll admit that Suellen's much more narrow . . . slightly rigid in her thinking?" he asked carefully, unwilling to offend me. "Howard's not *judgmental.* That's the word."

Todd was right. Howard wasn't judgmental as Suellen was. And I wondered why we were having this discussion but only for a few seconds. The answer was clear—Todd was launching a campaign. And that was the correct word too—*campaign*. And there was such a lump in my chest I could scarcely breathe. And that lump was pure resentment. Todd was trying to mount his forces—Howard, for one—and we hadn't even begun to talk about this whole movie studio thing.

"It won't work, you know," I said.

"What won't?" He had switched from the celery to a bowl of olives and now sucked on a pit.

"Trying to work it through Howard. Suellen has the last word in that family and she would never approve of Hollywood and movies and that kind of stuff. Besides, why do you need Suellen's and Howard's approval or blessing? It's only I who has to give the final word, isn't it? I mean, I do still have the right of refusal, don't I?"

"Buffy Ann!" his tone reproached me. "You know *we* never do anything that we both don't want—"

Oh, the words were right but still I wasn't sure that what he said was true. The complete, unvarnished truth was that I was incapable of denying him anything he wanted. And he knew it. And I knew by now, that for Todd, the studio and Hollywood were an irresistible siren.

We didn't get to our discussion until very late that night. Suzannah managed to rouse herself from bed in time to join us for dinner, then played Candyland with Todd and the kids while I cleaned up the kitchen. By the time I joined them in the family room, Suzannah had consumed about a third of a quart of Jack Daniel's. I knew this was so because the bottle had been an unopened one and Todd did not drink Jack Daniel's.

Todd and I went up to put the children to bed while Suzannah put on the radio after going through all our records and tapes and eschewing the entire collection. When we came downstairs again we found her moving about the room, dipping and swaying, eyes closed, in accompaniment to a melancholy wail from the radio proclaiming:

Hittin' the road again,
'Cause can't be stayin' then,
Countin' to ten again,
While ya makin' up your mind again,
No more, no more . . .

"That's Beau, you know," she cried out. "I'd recognize his voice anywhere . . . even from the old days."

She dabbed at her eyes. "Did you ask him, Buffy? Did you ask Todd to prevail upon Heinie to finish the picture?"

I opened up my mouth to speak, to break the truth to her but Todd spoke first, and gently: "I'm sorry, Suzannah, but Heinie's not only closed down the set, he's prepared to close down the whole studio. He's through with Hollywood. He's going back to Dallas. He said he's going to sell the studio as soon as he finds a buyer. He said whether he sells it or not he's never going to step foot in California again."

Suzannah collapsed on the sofa in a series of little cries that evolved into sobs. Suddenly she stopped wailing and snarled, "You see what happens when a woman doesn't make sure she has everything in writing? Heinie bought that studio *for me.* Or so he said! But he never put it in my name. Oh, what a fool I've been. Oh, that crummy bastard!"

Finally we helped her upstairs and put her to bed as if she were our third child. In many ways she *was* a child. Most children didn't understand the concept that life was a two-way street.

We went back downstairs. "I can't help myself," I told Todd. "Regardless of what she's done I can't stop feeling sorry for her. She seems so vulnerable."

Todd shook his head. "No. One thing Suzannah isn't is vulnerable. She just seems that way at certain stages. Yesterday she was decrying the loss of Heinie the sweetie. But tonight we saw phase two. Heinie's a bastard who ripped her off . . . took her studio away. I'd be surprised if we didn't get to phase three any moment now."

Todd and I seemed to veer back and forth with Suzannah—alternating between support and resentment. It had been that way too when Paulie had died. We sat in front of the fire in the library, drinking a plain red wine of uncertain vintage. Now we looked at one another, eyes meeting . . . warily. The time for our serious talk was at hand.

"Why, Todd, why?" I pleaded.

He didn't pretend not to know what I was asking.

He smiled a little, raised his eyebrows. "I'm not sure. I guess I'm kind of tired of malls. It's not a challenge anymore. The fun's gone out of it, Buffy Ann. The fun and the excitement. . . ."

I, foolish woman, plucked at straws. I was only grateful that he had said the excitement was gone from shopping malls and not from our marriage.

"I guess it's the striving, the goals that I miss. All my life, ever since that day in the Home—I guess I was about eight—when I realized that if I ever wanted to be anything more than a skinny orphan without change in my pocket, I'd have to start running . . . fast. I started concentrating hard on the ball games in the playground. At ten, I knew I wasn't going to be a baseball player. And I thought about being a boxer. At twelve, I realized where my talents lay and getting myself through college became my goal. And there was the string of goals all laid out for me, to be attained one after the other. Now I have you and the kids, a beautiful house, and a string of shopping malls and I'm worth several million dollars. But you know, Buffy, after the first shopping mall and the first million, the thrill was gone."

I was desolate. He could have fooled me. I had had no idea that he had been operating without excitement-charged electricity. He turned to the bar to get himself a drink that was stronger than wine. I immediately consoled myself—I thought, well, at least he hasn't said that the thrill was gone after the first wife and the first couple of kids.

Todd came around from the bar and handed me one of the two Black Russians he had mixed.

"Please, Buffy Ann! I want it! I need it!"

"I can see that. But there is one thing! What do you know about the movie business?"

"Nothing. Absolutely nothing. But I don't see why if one proceeds in a correct, businesslike fashion, making movies should be any different from building shopping malls. Instead of buying a piece of land—a property, and developing it—you buy a screen property and you develop *that*. Instead of architects, you use a director; instead of construction crews you use production crews, cameramen, prop men; instead of buildings you have actors. And then when you're ready, instead of leasing out your finished product to store owners, you lease out your movie to theater owners. And there may be far less chance of losing money. If you keep your production costs from getting out of hand, you can always get your money back, even on a turkey. You can always sell it to TV or cable or to the foreign markets. Besides, you divide your operation into movies and TV. One covers the other. It's an old concept," he smiled at me. "It's called not putting all your eggs into one basket."

"I see."

What I saw was that Todd had given this all a lot of thought. He didn't know anything about making movies per se, but he had been thinking about the business part of making movies.

"What about the money? A studio has to run into millions and millions. . . ." I spread my hands. I really had no idea at all what a studio cost. I thought I had read somewhere that the numbers on Twentieth Century Fox were something like $400,000,000, an incredible figure, and who knew if that figure was accurate. But I did know that the Suzannah Studio was nowhere in this class. I knew enough to realize that much of Fox's value was due to its location on the edge of land-rich-per-square-foot Beverly Hills. That was a matter of real estate. And the Suzannah Studio was located in Hollywood, where the value of land was much, much less.

Still, it had to cost much more than we had. We did have a string of malls all over Ohio but if you subtracted what we owed the banks from what the malls were worth—well, simple arithmetic—

"What is it going to cost, Todd?"

Todd crooned, "We can get it for a song."

That line gave me pause for thought. Or pause for anxiety. I remembered Heinie using the same phrase when he first announced that he was buying the studio. His song had turned out less than sweet.

"What's a song, Todd?"

He didn't start off with the bottom line, the actual figure. "Heinie paid twenty-five million for a nonworking studio. For the land and for the existing plant. He renovated, he rebuilt, he acquired the latest in technical equipment. He probably spent at least another twenty-five. Then, of course he acquired properties, he developed, was developing. He has contracts with producers in association with—"

Still no bottom line. But Todd had taught me well. I knew the questions to ask. "What's the studio worth? . . . just give me a ball park figure. Assets against liabilities?"

"I'd say maybe $100,000,000. There *are* a lot of intangibles involved in the movie business. What certain options are worth. The financial returns on any particular property that is listed as an asset. There are a lot of dark horses."

"I can well imagine. But give or take a few million, your guess *is* about $100,000,000."

"The movie business is not an exact science," he said a bit defensively. "That's what makes it so exciting—"

"The asking price, Todd?"

"He's willing to sell it to me . . . to us . . . for $50,000,000."

"And that's the song?"

"It's fifty cents on the dollar." Again, defensively.

"Why, Todd? I assume Heinie is one of the most astute businessmen in the country. I mean, he *is* a billionaire. And self-made. Why is he willing to sell it at a fifty percent loss? It's been losing money, hasn't it? He's been pouring it in, hasn't he?"

"Yes, it has and he has. But he was only getting started. You have to expect that in any business when it's getting off the ground. You know that, Buffy. But that's not why he's willing to let it go cheap. It's because he wants to be rid of it quickly. He wants to forget it ever happened. You can understand that? And he likes me. It's as simple as that. A billionaire can afford to indulge himself—"

My mouth was dry, and inside me I was quaking. But I was prepared to be fair and I could understand that Heinie wanted to leave Hollywood and the studio behind him, to go back to Dallas and try to forget Suzannah and the Suzannah Studio. And that he could afford to indulge himself, even if it meant losing a lot of money. Why bother being a billionaire at all if one couldn't afford to indulge oneself?

"But how about the studio losing money? Granted it was just getting off the ground? That fact is still there to deal with—"

"How did we get our start, Buffy Ann?"

We both knew the answer to that one but still, I gave it. "By buying ailing or failing businesses for far less money than we would have to pay for a business that was doing well."

"And then what did we do?"

"We plugged up the holes where the money was leaking out—"

"Exactly," he said, pleased with my responses.

"But are you sure the studio is really worth $100,000,000 in the first place? Did you look at a financial statement? Did you examine the books? You were gone only two days or so. How can you possibly know where the money is leaking out?"

"I didn't have to look very far or very hard. I knew the answer to that before I opened one ledger. And if you think about it for a few seconds, so will you."

I thought about it for about a half minute and then I said, "Heinie threw good money after bad into *Love and Betrayal.*" I made it a statement, not a question.

Todd was pleased with me again. "Now think. What else was Heinie doing wrong?"

This time, I had to think for a full minute. "He neglected all the other phases of the studio's business while he concentrated on Suzannah—her movie and her career." *A fool in love.*

I was rewarded with Todd's widest smile of approval. "You have it in a nutshell."

But somehow the figures still didn't seem to jell.

"*Did* you look at the books?"

"No, of course not. I hardly had time for that. I took a fast glance but for the most part, I'm taking Heinie's word for the figures." He smiled at me again. "If you don't know when to accept figures from whom, then you don't belong in a big game at all."

True, true. But still I felt my pulse accelerating. Had I found the flaw in Todd's figuring? Was it possible that my boy genius had missed what seemed to me as plain as the cute nose on his face?

"But *Love and Betrayal* has been in production for well over a year. I don't pretend to know anything about the movie business but I do know enough to realize that the costs must have been astronomical . . . forty to fifty million dollars, you think? From what I've read, that figure would not be too far out of line for a picture that's gone way over budget, would it?"

Todd shook his head.

"Would it be out of line to say that at this point, our hypothetical forty or fifty million is probably *all* liability?"

"Absolutely not out of line," Todd agreed.

My eyes opened wide. How could he not see what I saw so plainly? "But did you see on which side of the ledger the picture is listed? Is it listed as an asset, due to its potential earnings? Did you question it at all? Are there really enough assets at the Suzannah Studio to encompass the huge liabilities? If the movie is listed as an asset, and its costs are part of the property's worth, then it just inflates the value of the property—It's fancy bookkeeping—creative bookkeeping, they call it, I believe—where the liabilities are moved over to the other side of the ledger. Actually, until that movie is finished and sold, *it's really all liability,* isn't it? Actually, if the studio is worth $100,000,000 and *Love and Betrayal* bombs at the cost of $50,000,000 or $60,000,000, and the studio has to eat it, then what is your studio worth? Simple subtraction."

Todd laughed in delight. "Excellent, Buffy Ann. You get an A plus for financial analysis. But the thing is, *Love and Betrayal* doesn't enter into the figures at all. It's completely out of the picture and off the books. All the costs—every single penny—are being personally absorbed by Heinie Muller. *They're his personal loss.*"

I was dumbfounded. "How come? Why?"

"Because Heinie wants to make sure the picture is never finished. That it will never be shown anywhere, at any time. This way, he can simply light a match to every scrap of film already shot, and to the picture's production schedule, not to mention the script itself."

Of course. Why be a billionaire if one couldn't indulge one's fancies and one's desire for revenge! Poor Suzannah!

"Poor Suzannah!" I uttered.

Still, I was impressed by the extent of Heinie's feelings. A forty, fifty million dollar vengeance. *Oh Suzannah, how much he must love you!*

So in the end, it was the force of Heinie's love and Heinie's revenge that cut off my last avenue of escape from the inevitable.

"The money you have to pay . . . the fifty million?" I still squirmed on the hook. "How will you finance it?"

"You know Heinie. The minute I call him with my final answer, it's a deal and the studio is ours from that minute on. I don't have to sign anything and I don't have to give him any money until I'm ready . . . until I sell the Gallerias. Whenever they're sold, whenever I receive the money, I'll pay him. A gentleman's agreement."

Yes. They were both gentlemen. My Todd and Suzannah's Heinie.

"Oh, our beautiful shopping centers. We made them so special. . . ."

"They're only brick and stone and concrete, Buffy Ann."

He waited now for my final answer. I looked into his hazel eyes that held the final question. Didn't he know there had never been a question of a question? Hadn't I once said that I would follow him to hell and back? A long time ago when he was a boy and I was only a girl. For me, he was still the same boy, my hero. And my heart told me, even if my mirror didn't, that I was still the same girl, still bedazzled and bewitched.

I smiled at him with tears in my eyes. "I've never said no to you, have I?"

Realizing then that this was complete surrender, he squeezed me tight. "And you've never been sorry, have you?"

"No. Never!"

"Then why did you scare me to death by hesitating so long? What are you afraid of, Buffy Ann?"

"It's scary out there, Todd. It's an alien land. I guess maybe I'm afraid of the change—afraid that we'll change there—you and I."

"Don't be afraid, Buffy Ann. I'll never change. And neither will you. Not to each other, at any rate. I want you to be as excited and thrilled as I am! Remember—'I pledge myself to thee? Be not afraid as we venture out on life's adventure together . . .' Our wedding vows. . . ."

On my wedding day I had only laughed. Now tears welled up in my eyes, and I was touched by his remembering. Suddenly I recalled and I was sure: He had *never* said anything like that. He had just made that up!

He took my hand and we went up to bed.

"We'll have to tell Suzannah that we're buying the studio right away, Todd. It's only fair. It'll be quite a shock to her and the sooner she hears about it the sooner she'll get over it."

"We'll tell her together the first thing in the morning."

Todd fell asleep quickly. The sleep of the victorious. I tossed and turned, thinking about everything I would be leaving behind. The house didn't matter—a home was where your love was. Leah? She didn't have any family that she ever mentioned, but she did have her church to which she was very much attached. Life without Leah was unthinkable. Would we be able to talk her into coming with us?

And Suellen! Suellen and Howard and Becky and Peter! The only family we had, besides our own children, since Aunt Emily had passed away. How would I ever do without them? And our lovely, beautiful shopping centers? Todd was wrong about them. They *were* more than stone and concrete, brick, and glass . . . certainly more than the money they would bring. They were the realization of our springtime dream.

Suzannah gave an anguished whelp—a gasp—when Todd told her we were buying the studio. She appeared shaken to her core but then her face lit up. *"You'll* finish *Love and Betrayal!* Oh how wonderful! It will all work out after all." She looked at Todd with something very close to adoration.

"No, Suzannah, I'm sorry but I won't be able to. *Love and Betrayal* is not part of the deal. Heinie is taking the picture with him in a manner of speaking."

Now her face really registered shock and then something that closely resembled hate.

"Oh that bastard! I'll kill him. And you two call yourselves my friends?" And she turned away from us, ran up the stairs to her room. I was very much shaken. "Do you think she's packing?" I asked Todd. "I feel terrible. I feel like we've betrayed her. Is *this* Phase Three, do you think?"

"No. I don't think so. And I don't think she's packing . . . *yet."*

When Suzannah didn't show her face again for a couple of hours, I went upstairs and knocked on her door tentatively.

"Yes?" Her voice came through, hard and cold.

"Are you all right, Suzannah?"

"Get away from my door!"

Todd put on his coat, scarf, and gloves. "Are you going to the office?" I asked.

"Yes. I want to talk to Howard."

Yes, of course. He had to talk to Howard. Howard and Suellen had twenty percent of the King Gallerias. If Todd was putting all the Gallerias on the market, Howard had to be told right away.

Todd called me from the office. "Has Suzannah emerged from her room yet?"

"No. Have you told Howard?"

"Yes."

"Well, what did he say?"

"He was surprised."

Yes, indeed. I was sure he was.

"Are you coming home now?" I really wasn't eager to be alone when Suzannah came out of her room.

"Not yet."

"Oh?"

"I'm going over to see Suellen now."

"Oh!"

I knew how the conversation would begin. Todd would sit in the kitchen with Suellen. She would give him coffee and whatever it was that she had baked that day. Perhaps apple strudel. And slowly Todd would pitch her. The only thing I didn't know was how the conversation would turn out . . . whether or not Todd would be successful.

"I need Howard with me, Suellen."

"You'll have Buffy. She's always helped you."

"Buffy needs *you*, Suellen. She says she's not going without you." He smiled at her winningly.

Suellen made a scoffing noise. "Look, Todd. I love Buffy and I love you too. But just because you get this crazy idea in your head it doesn't necessarily follow that Howard and I have to go along with it. We're happy here and with all due thanks to you, we're financially set for life. You've been more than generous . . . you didn't have to give us twenty percent of your business but you did—"

Todd shook his head. "I was just being canny. I counted on Howard working twice as hard as anyone else because he was Howard."

"I don't believe that's why you did it. But it's beside the point. The fact is we *are* financially secure. Why should we risk what we have to go looking for more? We already have it all!"

He shook his head. "Nobody has it all!"

"Are you so sure then, that you're going to find it *all?* In Hollywood?"

"No, I'm not sure. But I sure as hell want to go for it. I want to give it my best shot."

"You can lose everything you have . . . everything you and Buffy have worked for—"

"No, Suellen. All I can lose is money."

"I'm not so sure about that," she said ominously. "I read the magazines and the papers. The divorce rate in California. The children going bad."

"That's bull. There's divorce and bad kids everywhere. I *could* lose the money but my family—That's one thing I'm one hundred percent sure of."

"All right. Let's just consider the money. You should rejoice knowing that your family will never have a financial worry for the rest of their lives. Why do you want to risk it all on something as shaky as the movie business?"

Poor Suellen, he thought. She didn't understand the joy of risk, of challenge, who had never experienced the rush that gambling on yourself brought. "I'm not risking anything on the movie business. I'm risking it all on myself. And I guess I need to do that. But I'm not going to press you, Suellen. If Howard wants to stay on in the Gallerias, that will be arranged. And if the two of you want to get out altogether, you'll have enough money to do whatever else *you* want."

She did not miss the emphasis on the word *you.* "What are you trying to say? Are you implying that Howard wants to go to California? That Howard wants the risk and the gamble too, and it's I who's keeping him from living his life to the fullest?"

"I'm implying nothing, Suellen. I spoke to Howard and he didn't give me an answer. He only said that I should speak to you."

"You're implying that Howard wants to go but he's afraid to tell me that this is what he wants."

"You two will have to talk it over between you."

"It's true then? Howard does want to go?"

"I have to be honest with you, Suellen. I think he does."

She gave an anguished moan. "I see. Howard wanted you to talk to me, didn't he? For him. You men! Does it always have to be your way? It's still the heady gamble and adventure of the new frontier, isn't it? It just has to be your way."

"It's glorious when the two people in a marriage think of it as *their* way."

"You're talking about Buffy," Suellen said bitterly. "But I'm not Buffy."

"No." He leaned down and kissed her. "You're Suellen and the second most beautiful woman I know."

"All right, Todd. You win. If it's what Howard really wants, I have no choice but to go along. But I can't say that I *want* to—All I can say is I'm *willing*—"

"Is there a difference?"

"Come now, Todd," she smiled with sad eyes. "You may be a ruthless bastard but you're not insensitive. You know the difference between wanting and willing."

"I'm sorry, Suellen. But you'll see. You'll love the Coast. The sun shines all day and you can pick the oranges off the trees."

She shook her head. "It *used* to be like that. Now I understand that unless the oranges are commercially grown and shot full of stuff and sprayed and dyed, they're puny, pale, misshapen, and sour."

Todd threw back his head and laughed hard. "As long as it's only the oranges that are that way."

"Oh, you're a magician!" I said, throwing my arms around his neck. "A veritable miracle worker!"

But Todd looked depressed.

"What is it?"

"Suellen called me a ruthless bastard. She practically accused me of ruining the rest of their lives. And she thought that I came, like John Alden, to speak for Howard."

"And you didn't?"

"No. Not really. I came to speak for *you*. You were my Miles Standish."

"Oh! I guess then that we're both ruthless bastards because I'm so happy you convinced her. What does Suellen know anyway? She didn't want to come here from Cincinnati at first, either, did she? And she's been very happy and content here, hasn't she?"

I almost forgot that only hours before I dreaded this move too. Todd *was* a magician.

"And Howard? He *really* wants to go, doesn't he?"

"Yeah, he does," Todd said, cheering up. "He's really excited."

"Great! But there's still Leah! I can't possibly go and leave Leah behind."

Todd waggled his eyebrows at me. "Where is she? Lead me to her—"

I knew that Leah didn't stand a chance.

A few minutes later I came off my high. Were we right in dragging Howard and Suellen along? I was far from sure that *I* wanted to go, and here I was, pulling Suellen along with me. What *was* I doing? Taking the All-American Girl, the girl next door, perky Doris Day to Crazy Lotus Land? But then it occurred to me. Doris Day, the real D.D., was alive and well and living in Hollywood, U.S.A., wasn't she?

A radiant Suzannah came down to dinner dressed in a magnificent robe of burnt-orange velvet much too grand for our family-style repast, but I was relieved to see that her mood of the morning had changed to one of sunny graciousness.

"I've decided it's silly to look back. Instead, I'm going to look forward to the next movie that I'll be making for the Suzannah Studio."

I looked at Todd. The possibility of our newly acquired studio making a new picture with Suzannah had not even crossed my mind, and I doubted that Todd had thought about it yet either.

"There's another thing you'll have to accept, Suzannah," he said. "I will rename the studio. I want to call it the Buffy Ann King Studios."

"*My* studio! You're changing the name . . . my name?" She rose from the chair so fast she tipped it, and fled upstairs.

"Phase Three?" I asked.

"No. Not yet."

"Were you serious about calling it the Buffy Ann King Studios?"

"Yes. Why not? If it was Suzannah, why can't it be Buffy Ann King?"

"Because it sounds like a memorial—to the dead. King Studios will do just fine."

In the morning Suzannah didn't wait to have her tray brought up. She appeared at the breakfast table along with Megan and Mitchell, as bright-eyed and bushy-tailed as they.

"Where's Todd?" she asked, and I told her that Todd had left the house more than an hour before.

"He has a lot to do. We're selling the shopping centers and that means tons of paper work."

She sat at the table drinking coffee and humming to herself while Leah and I got the children off to their respective schools. (Mitchell was newly enrolled in a nursery school.) When I sat down to join her for another cup, she said, "I'm sorry about last night, Buff darling. Of course you wouldn't keep my name for the studio. It was very foolish of me to get so upset. It's just that I'm losing *everything* at the same time. Heinie. My movie. And then my name on the studio. You can see that I'd be upset?"

"You'd be an ass if you weren't."

"I think it won't all seem so overwhelming once I get started on a new picture."

I said nothing. Sometimes it was much better to keep one's mouth shut.

"I've decided to stay with the studio, no matter what. When do you think you all will be moving out? And how soon will Todd be taking over? I can't wait to get started on my new film."

Here we go again.

"You *know* it's not going to happen overnight. It might be months before Todd actually takes over and then months before he gets the studio organized. It might take quite a while before Todd can even think about a film for you."

That sounded reasonable to me. And instinctively I was trying to shield Todd from her onslaughts. I didn't have any idea whether the studio would have a contractual obligation to Suzannah.

"What am I supposed to do in the meantime? Shrivel up?"

"Look, Suzannah, at this point none of us knows what's going to be. This whole thing has happened pretty fast. Right now Todd has to concentrate on getting all the financial statements and papers ready to put the Gallerias on the market. And he has to talk to all the banks involved. There's a dozen of them. The banks probably own a bigger share of the shopping centers than we do."

"If you don't mind, Buffy, I'd rather not hear about your problems. I have enough of my own. What *I'm* going to do . . ."

I considered for a few moments. "Why don't you start reading scripts? You know, look for a property that seems right for you," I said, much as I suggested things for the children to do on a rainy day. Busy work.

She thought about it. "You're right. That's what I will do. And I guess I have to find myself a new agent. To look out for me." She threw me a dark look implying that she would certainly need to have someone to guard her against friends like us.

I forgave her for that. Paranoia would certainly be part of her present condition.

"With Heinie taking care of everything, I didn't even have an agent. I'll have to go back to the Coast at once, get myself an agent, and then start reading properties and—But where will I go?" she asked, her eyes wide open.

"What do you mean?" I inquired carefully.

"Where will I go?" she demanded. "All I had was the bungalow at the Beverly Hills Hotel. And Heinie's there! If he hasn't already given it up. Do you realize that I don't even have a home to go back to?" she asked angrily, as if this were in some way my fault. "Oh my God! I've been a fool! Heinie was forever talking about buying me a house in Beverly Hills or Bel Air, not to mention the little hideaway in Malibu. But he never did anything about it. Talk, talk, talk. I've got nothing out of this marriage, not one fucking thing! Not even a house! And I've been sitting here in Akron, Ohio, of all places, like some idiot when I should be in California getting myself a good divorce lawyer. God knows what Heinie's been up to all this time—"

Again she gave me a dirty look as if I had been detaining her in my home, working with Heinie to keep her in constraints.

"I'll tell you what Heinie's been up to—making sure I'm not going to get one fucking cent, that's what!"

She pushed back the chair and got up in such a hurry that once again she almost knocked the chair over. She headed for the stairway. I ran after her.

"Suzannah! What are you doing?"

"I'm going to pack. Call the airport for me. I want the next flight to the Coast. And make sure it's first class. And after you're through calling the airport, get Cleo on the phone for me."

"Cleo!"

"Yes, Cleo."

"What for?"

"Because I need the name of the best bomber in L.A."

"Bomber?" I asked, confused. She had told me to call the airport for a plane reservation and now she wanted a bomber. The only connection I could make was a bomber plane. But that was *crazy!*

"Honestly, Buffy, don't you know *anything?* A bomber is a divorce lawyer! The kind that milks blood out of stones. Because that's what I need. I'm going to take Heinie to the cleaners!"

Ah! Phase Three.

But there was one more thing I didn't understand. How could Suzannah expect *anything* of Cleo? *What gall!* And besides, even if Cleo weren't directly involved in Suzannah's mess, why Cleo?

"Why Cleo?" I asked, looking up at her at the top of the stairs.

"Because Cleo knows about these things. If nothing else, Cleo's *au courant.* She knows all about *le dernier cri.* That's French for the latest thing."

I called all the airlines and got a reservation for Suzannah on the red eye that evening. Then, with great trepidation I dialed Cleo.

Suellen had called Cleo weird and she was right. Without any questions, without expressing any resentment toward Suzannah, she gave me the name of the latest bright star in the bomber firmament. And then, and only then, she said: "It's all over town that Todd is buying the Suzannah Studio. And Leo says that if Todd wants to keep the whole studio from falling apart, he'd better get out here in a hurry, but definitely."

I gave the name of the lawyer to Suzannah but I worried all day about transmitting Leo's message to Todd. I had been comforting myself with the fact that we would be staying on in Ohio for several months to come, but now it appeared that I couldn't count on that breathing space either.

We were, one way or another, on our way. And our tenth wedding anniversary celebration would take place in Hollywood.

PART THREE

Autumn
1977–1981

43

The moment Todd told Heinie that all systems were go, Heinie lit out back to Dallas. As a result, the new King Studio was just hanging fire, immobile. And according to the Todd King theory, anything immobile quickly decayed. Besides, I could see that Todd was like a racehorse, champing at the bit, and the shopping centers, and Akron, Ohio, for that matter, were yesterday's horse race.

In a couple of weeks, he said, "I've set everything in motion, Buffy. What I have in mind is to leave for the Coast myself immediately and let you do the mopping up and whatever other preparations for moving that are necessary."

I was panic-stricken at the notion of Todd going on ahead without me.

"Why can't we all go now—you, me, and the children, and leave the mopping up to Howard? Suellen won't take her children out of school before the end of the school year anyway."

"Howard's going to have his hands full, just administering the Gallerias, keeping everything running smoothly until we have a buyer, not to mention finishing up in Canton. You're going to have to help him and take care of everything else. Get our personal affairs in order—the house, everything. It shouldn't take more than a couple of months. Probably, once we do have a buyer, Howard will have to stay for a transition period. It's the price we have to pay for running a closed shop all these years."

He could see that I was still upset. "It will only be for a little while. And I'll be flying back and forth . . . I'll be here on weekends—"

"But where will you live?" I asked as if that were my major concern. "Will you find a house for us?"

"I'm not going to have time for house hunting. I'll leave that for you when you get out there. I'll just check into a hotel. Maybe one of those bungalows at the Beverly Hills."

Oh good, I thought spitefully. *Why don't you just do that? I hope you do and I hope Suzannah's staying there too, and she makes your life miserable, besieging you daily with her wailing. It will serve you right for leaving me behind.*

I thought about the magnitude Suzannah's onslaughts could assume, *and* the ramifications possible. During our visit to the film capital I had chanced into a store that specialized in Hollywood artifacts—little notions such as toilet paper with a faked Gucci logo and greeting cards with cute Hollywood salutations. One had been *Starfucker! Suzannah the Starfucker!*

Then I was overcome with shame. I felt petty and small and debased by my own anxieties. Suzannah might well be a starfucker, but I knew she felt something for me—an affection that passed for love between friends. And besides, even in the year 1977, it still took two to tango. And while I might not have total faith in Suzannah, I did have total faith in my great love, my Todd.

So Todd flew off promising to be back in a few days for the weekend. And I thought: Well, if it turns out to be hell that I'm following Todd into, then this period must be purgatory.

Todd called his first night away. He was at a hotel called L'Ermitage. He had gone to the Beverly Hills Hotel, he said, but when he found out that Suzannah was staying in one of the bungalows, he had left.

"I decided it would be in my best interests to be somewhere else. I could just picture her pounding on my door morning and night with her tales of woe, not to mention demanding a picture commencing immediately."

"I don't know how much protection staying at a different hotel will afford you. If Suzannah wants to reach you, she will."

"But at least she won't be able to bang away at my door at three in the morning."

"No?" I wasn't so sure about that. Suzannah would have her due, no matter what.

In a few days' time, though, Todd reported that he had been called by Suzannah only once. It seemed she wasn't overly concerned about being on a movie set just yet. She had engaged a very hot lawyer—one Lee

Philips—and they were working together full-time on preparing her divorce case.

"They're inseparable," Todd said.

"Are they living together? Is that what you mean?"

"No, not formally, anyhow. Even a dumb lawyer, and Philip's no dummy, would know better than that. The word is they're going after twenty million dollars."

"Really? That sounds crazy to me. She and Heinie were only married a year or so."

"Would that stop our girl? And not Philips either. I hear he *always* gets twenty million. That's his absolute bottom price."

We both laughed.

"I guess Heinie will get himself a twenty million dollar lawyer too," I said and Todd agreed.

"Look, when this divorce business gets settled, Suzannah will be camped on your doorstep again. Do you or do you not have a contractual obligation to her?"

"No. Heinie, it seems, had only a gentlemanly husband's agreement with her. But we do have a contract with Leo that has several years to run. And a contract to produce thirteen segments of Leo's *Hollywood and Vine* series. It seems the show's ratings were dropping and was about to be canceled, and Heinie bought it up. And now we have a contract with Guy Savarese too."

At the moment, I wasn't interested in those contracts. I still had Suzannah on my mind. "What will you do when Suzannah finally does demand a picture? She will, whether she has a contract or not. I'm afraid that any picture with her will have a lot of difficulties—And yet, how can you turn her down?"

Todd sighed. "Why don't we wait until that happens?"

I waited for Todd to come home for the weekend, as he had promised, because I was concerned with another promise—the one we had made to each other about having five children. The time to get busy was at hand. I was past thirty, I was going to start a new life in a new home, and I had already decided that I had no desire to be involved in the workings of the studio. I planned on being only mother and housewife . . . if Todd would let me.

I met his plane, and he looked different to me, and I couldn't figure out why at first. Then I realized it was his tan. In a week's time he had gotten a deep, bronzed tan. And he hadn't been sunning himself on any beach, I knew. Where had it come from?

"At the studio. There's a gym right off my office, and it's outfitted with three different kinds of sun lamps."

It was a movie-set tan.

"You know the funniest thing happened. The first day I was there I went to lunch with Leo. It was a restaurant called *Ma Maison* . . ."

I was about to interrupt him, to tell him I had been there with Suzannah just a few days before her wedding, just after Heinie announced he had bought the studio, and that when we walked into the dining patio everyone had stood up and applauded her.

". . . It was the most amazing thing. As soon as we walked in, everyone there stood up and gave me an ovation. I didn't even know these people and they applauded me! It was as if I really were a *king*. . . ."

You are, you are. I only hope that you can remain one.

Todd came home for another weekend three weeks later. He could talk of nothing but Hollywood, of the studio, of projects in development. In his usual steamroller fashion he was buying up certain kinds of property—slipping or defunct TV series that the networks had dumped or were dumping. "I'm going to shine them up so bright, they'll be dying to buy them back again."

I listened with only one ear. I still had my own project for development on my mind and I had to persuade Todd to forget the studio for a few hours, which did not prove all that difficult.

And I asked him for news of Cleo, Suzannah, and Cassie.

"I've been so busy, I haven't seen anybody but Leo and Guy. The *Hollywood and Vine* segments are starting to shape up. They only started to go down in the ratings once Leo had gone on to *Love and Betrayal*. With Leo back directing and supervising the scripts, it should be a winner again. Oh yeah, I did go over to Cleo's for dinner. She and Leo invited me so many times I couldn't keep refusing. And come to think of it, I did run into Suzannah and her lawyer friend in a restaurant. She was clinging to him and rubbing his hand against her face, just like a cat. But Cassie? No, I haven't seen her at all."

44.

That morning Cassie let herself in through the rear door that led from the servants' quarters to the main house as she had done nearly every day for weeks now. She hurried to the front hall with the little bag of necessities for gold leafing. She was repairing as best she could the huge, square gilded mirror that covered nearly one whole wall in the entry. She sat down on the black-and-white tiled floor and opened the bag, took out the tiny sable brush, the impossibly thin sheets of gold leaf, the oil, and the adhesive. She had about two hours to work before she had to get ready to go to the museum. She had been working in this manner ever since that first day she had gained entry to the house . . . the day she gained access to a fantasyland.

She had gone through the service quarters examining the rooms thoroughly, deliberately controlling herself, saving the best for last. Then she had gone through the kitchen, big and old-fashioned, with its white tiled floor, dark oaken cabinets; through the pantry with its cupboards crowded with all kinds of dishes and glass—blue-and-white flowered plates; white, gold-rimmed dishes; flowered Limoges; lead crystal goblets. And then she had gone into the dining room. She held her breath, sat herself down at the burnished wood table centered under a globe-style, twenty-branched, crystal-trimmed glass chandelier which hung from a yellow-tinted ceiling. She dared to touch the table—there was only a fine patina of dust.

She had walked across the hallway, stepped into the formal drawing room. She was grateful then for her years at the museum. She knew that the armchair she sat in oh-so-gingerly was Chinese Chippendale and that it was upholstered in a Genoese cut velvet; that the rug she tiptoed on was a Savonnerie worked in a "Lion of Leon" design—its colors of beige and red and blue and black faded only a bit.

That day, she had forced herself to leave then, but she had returned the next morning and treated herself to the first view of the library. She touched the magnificent paneling of Circassian walnut with trembling fingers, afraid to touch the Italian silk damask draperies, so delicate a fabric that she feared it would disintegrate in her hand like a powdery cobweb. She looked at the rows of leather bound and gold-stamped volumes, put a tentative toe on the gilded bronze spiral staircase that led to the gallery, and gazed with awe at the huge allegorical painting on canvas that stretched across its ceiling. She was almost certain she recognized the art of Giovanni Antonio Pellegrini, who had died over two hundred years before. She decided then that she would try to identify every stick of furniture in the house and every objet d'art. She could do it—she had the books to consult. She would make a list. Write everything down.

It didn't even cross her mind that the house she had been raised in, the legendary Blackstone Manor, was a much grander house than her pink castle. But even if she had thought of it, it would not have mattered. This house was her own.

Still, it was all too much to be taken in, even on this, her second visit.

She had returned the next day and gone upstairs this time, going through bedroom after bedroom until she came upon the nursery— clowns and teddy bears sat on shelves surveying the room, balls of all sizes lay in one corner. Lead soldiers stood at attention on a table. Yes, there had been a child in this house—a boy. There were no dolls. And she remembered the fire engine she had found outside in the pool pavilion.

Oh, if only she could have a child—one unsullied by Guy's bad blood —whom she could bring here to raise. She would cook in the kitchen, eat in the beautiful dining room, put the baby to bed in this old-fashioned four-poster crib topped with its white muslin canopy. She touched the canopy. The material was parched with age, covered with dust.

She certainly had her work cut out for her, she had thought that day. A thorough cleaning was first of all. If she came at six every morning, she would have at least two hours to work. After the cleaning, whatever restoration she could do herself with her limited ability and financial means. She doubted that Guy would ever notice her absence in the early hours of the day, and if he did, she could always say that she'd been jogging on the hill along with the other early dawn runners. Or she could counter with a question: Where was *he* in the late hours of the evening, the early hours of the morning?

Oh, if only she could have a baby by immaculate conception. She made sure to laugh at herself just so that she knew she hadn't lost all touch with reality.

She was touching a tiny piece of the gold leaf with her brush when she heard a noise behind her on the staircase of Caen stone and bronze. She whirled around. There on the staircase stood not Jenny Elmann, nor the ghost of John Starr Winfield, but a *real* man. He was sleepy-eyed, his dark blond hair touseled, and he wore a short terry cloth robe. He was not frightening and not a ghost.

"I hope I didn't startle you," he said with a half-smile. He approached her slowly and she saw high cheekbones and bright blue eyes. "I was wondering who my cleaning lady was. Somehow, I *did* know it was a lady." He stuck out his hand. "I'm John Winfield. May I ask who you are?"

Cassie thought many times in the weeks that followed her first meeting with John Winfield that he must think her mad to have gone to his house all those weeks—cleaning, scrubbing, dusting, mopping, polishing, working on picture and mirror frames, mending tiny rips in silken draperies, washing, bleaching, starching, ironing ruffled kitchen and pantry curtains. But he had not been judgmental in any way, had seemed to accept what would be puzzling and disturbing to the ordinary person.

He had told her about himself. He was a historian at Stanford University; he hadn't been in the pink castle in twenty-three years—since he was nine. He had gone back to Europe with his mother then, had come back to the United States when he was eighteen to attend Stanford. His mother had recently died in Switzerland and now that he was on a sabbatical from his position at the University, he intended to spend the time restoring his house, doing much of the work himself. A labor of love, or maybe—he said with a wry smile—a labor of working things out. Then, eventually, he planned on selling it.

Sell the house—her house? Cassie was appalled, even frightened. What would she do when the house was gone? Then, she thought, perhaps he *wouldn't*. Perhaps he would change his mind when the house was perfectly restored, perfectly beautiful. Perhaps she could help change his mind. "Maybe you'll change your mind and keep the house?"

She couldn't read his eyes: the high cheekbones transformed them into long, narrow slits.

"Being a historian has taught me one thing," he told her. "There are times when one has to close the books on the past so that one can enter the future with a clear perspective. Actually, it's not easy for me to be here. So much has happened here—things that were pretty hard for me to accept. Things I didn't understand."

She yearned to ask him the question that wouldn't leave her head. Had his mother intended to shoot his father? But it wasn't a question one asked a stranger and that's what they were so far—little more than strangers.

"My father was a historian," she said. "He was a sweet, gentle man and he taught at UCLA . . . before he became curator of the Blackstone Museum."

She continued going to the castle in the early mornings. He adjusted his schedule accordingly so that he would be in the kitchen fixing breakfast for the two of them when she arrived. After they ate, they would work on a project together, talking all the while. It was as if she were making up for all the years she hadn't really conversed with anyone at all.

She would come home from the museum in the evenings and find that her own grounds had been worked on: gradually all her hedges were trimmed back in symmetrical fashion, her ivy clipped to perfection, her lawn manicured, the ficus shaped into great round balls, and there wasn't a weed to be found anywhere. Then one day she came home and found a whole new bed of old-fashioned roses laid out in the manner of an English garden in an array of colors that dazzled the eye—pink, blush and crimson, yellow, white and lavender. The trimming, the weeding—the gifts of a good neighbor repaying favors received. But the roses—oh, they were a gift of love.

She had become convinced that her stillborn child, her subsequent miscarriages, and more recently, her inability to conceive at all, were all part of a greater plan, the workings of Nature or a merciful God protecting her from bringing forth an imperfect child with imperfect genes. But now she knew what she would do. She was going to conceive and be delivered of a beautiful child, lovely of gene, lovely of spirit, worthy of love, capable of giving love, as loving as its father. And she wasn't going to do it for her mother but for herself.

The weekend that Guy went away on location, she packed a small bag for herself and went up the driveway to the pink house. Win wasn't at home—his little red MG was gone, but she knew he would be back soon. The few times that he had been gone overnight, he had told her so in advance.

She knew Win admired her . . . desired her, even though he had not proclaimed this by word or gesture. He was not the kind of man who would make that kind of move on a woman who lived with another man. They had barely discussed Guy, and never her marriage, but she guessed that he knew how it was with her and Guy. She and Win were friends now, and friends sensed this sort of thing. She thought that Win even understood about her mother.

She waited in the master bedroom for him to appear. Then she heard him coming up the stairs, two steps at a time. Did he guess that she was here? It was growing dark but she had put on no light. Breathlessly, she waited. He opened the door. She came forward to greet him, wordless, unclothed, her long pale hair and white breasts glimmering in the twilight, a smile on her lips, her arms outstretched. She saw no surprise in his eyes, but joy. He took her in his arms for a few moments, just holding her close. Then he picked her up effortlessly, carried her to the bed, and made love to her slowly and gently, as if they were both innocents, as if this was the first time at lovemaking for both of them, and as if they had the rest of their lives to be together. And she kept her eyes wide open, not afraid to look into his, for in his eyes she saw love.

45.

It all happened quickly then. We had a buyer for the Gallerias, and the new owners, a conglomerate, moved swiftly. They didn't even want Howard to stay for the transitional period: they had their own people. Three days later, all that remained of our shopping center dynasty was the name King Galleria on each center, and that would be gone in time —as soon as the new owners gained a gradual acceptance by the shoppers of their own name.

So we all flew out to the Coast together. Leah and I and my kids, Todd who had flown in to sign papers, Howard and Suellen and their children.

Suellen and I went house hunting together. With Cleo along as adviser and her mother, Leila, as real estate agent. I chose a Mediterranean villa off Benedict, with a pool and tennis court, because that's what Todd said a studio head needed: a grand Beverly Hills house with all the accoutrements—a front. And Suellen chose Encino in the Valley because she wanted to raise her children in what was more a suburb and less a sophisticated metropolis—closer to the real world as she put it. And while I wished she lived next door to me rather than twenty or thirty minutes away, I couldn't dispute her logic. Cleo did sniff a bit. There was no cachet to the Valley, and Leila Pulitzer put her nose in the air as if she were smelling something distasteful. But all Suellen had to say to her was, "If you can't handle a place in Encino, perhaps I should get another broker," whereupon Leila put on her best behavior like a fur coat.

I giggled at that. I was early into my pregnancy and I thought everything was amusing. And I was so thrilled for Cassie who had told me she was pregnant too.

I made every effort to separate myself from the daily mechanics of the studio, intent on being only wife, mother and, at present, pregnant lady. Still, Todd insisted on consulting me on most decisions.

"That's the way it's always been and that's the way it's going to be," he said. "I wouldn't know how to make a decision without you. I'm stuck with a dependency."

Statements like that still caused my heart to beat fast and my stomach to flutter, but I countered with, "You make me sound like a drug habit."

And he answered with a Humphrey Bogart imitation. "But you are a drug, baby. You're in my bloodstream and I'll never get you out." And my pulse raced.

I decorated the house, shopped for furniture, settled the children into their schools, tried to gather a part-time staff to keep the huge house going (still bowing to Leah's refusal to accept full-time domestic assistance). And I had to admit it was all fun. As the owners of a studio, we had a full social schedule. In addition to the usual parties, there were screenings, award dinners, charity black-tie functions. And Todd would never let me beg off, even when my pregnant belly preceded me by a full second into a room. "We've always done everything together, and nothing's going to change just because we're in Hollywood," he said again and again.

But I vowed that no matter how busy I was, I would always make time for my old friends. Accordingly, since I was enjoying an easy pregnancy, and Cassie had been ordered to a strict stay-at-home regime (because of her past history of miscarriages), I often went to see her.

But I could see no pale delicacy about her. She had fashioned a bedroom for herself downstairs so that she would not have to mount the stairs, and she pattered happily around the lower level of her house in *bare* feet and long, flowered dresses, her blond hair flowing loose and long. Suddenly, she was the proverbial rose in bloom, a smiling flower child in the truest sense of the world, although flower children had gone out of style. And surprisingly, there seemed no doubt in her mind that she would carry and deliver a strong healthy baby this time, although I would have thought she'd be a jangle of nerves and anxiety.

I paid a visit to Cassie that morning, arriving around eleven, ascertaining before I parked my car that Guy's car was gone from the premises. And just before noon, as we sat in the kitchen drinking tea, a blondish man in jeans and T-shirt, tall, tan, and Viking-like appeared, without benefit of bell or knocker (that immediately should have told me something, had I been paying attention). But I was struck dumb by his startling resemblance to Jon Voight. Did everybody here look like some movie actor? Or did I just think in those terms?

I noticed then that he carried a bunch of peonies in one hand, and a quart jar of what looked like chicken soup in the other. And I had to smile, bemused. It was the kind of gifts Todd would have brought me before he started bringing home golden bangles and bejeweled baubles.

Cassie introduced us. "My friend, my very good friend, Buffy King," she told him as if she were giving him a message, telling him I was on her side. And then, turning to me, "And this is my good neighbor, John Winfield. Win lives in the pink castle up on the hill," she enthused.

And then, I think, I knew everything there was to know. And it occurred to me, and not for the first time, that life really did imitate art, rather than the other way around. If John Winfield and Guy Savarese appeared together in a movie, no one in the audience would ever mistake them. Guy would be the dark, saturnine villain, and Win would be immediately recognizable as the strong, silent hero. Maybe that was the problem with *Hollywood and Vine,* which the studio was trying to revitalize, the reason why the series had been first successful and then, so soon, not. Maybe it was because Guy was unacceptable as the hero-cop.

So if everything I assumed was true, then why were these two idiots sitting here so euphoric, while Guy's presence hovered darkly? How much had Cassie told this hero, and why hadn't he picked her up and carried her away, the way heroes were supposed to? Was he strong enough? Strong enough to wipe out Cassandra Hammond's hold on her daughter, and to withstand the possible onslaught of the malevolent villain. Guy Savarese, I knew, was not the kind to suffer easily having anything he owned taken away from him whether or not he valued it.

Or was I only the victim of my own overactive imagination and was Jon Voight—Win—only what he appeared to be? A very nice handsome neighbor who brought over chicken soup?

I made time to visit Cassie, but Cleo made sure to visit *me* often. Was Cleo's presence simply an expression of friendship? I wondered. Was she taking me under her wing—advising me as to the best gynecologist, the best hairdresser, on the social advantages of being seen at lunch at Ma Maison on a Friday rather than on a Monday—only because I was her good friend and a comparative stranger in town? Or was she devoted to me because her husband worked for my husband, and their future and livelihood depended on our good graces?

Oh, paranoia has set in, I berated myself. Hollywood paranoia. How cynical I had bcome, to think that Cleo was only self-serving. It was probably that Cleo *needed* a friend—one she could confide in and trust, one she could let her hair down with. It had to be difficult to be Cleo, to walk around forever with that play-it-with-enthusiasm façade.

She related a story to me, an innocuous little story about something she had done for Leo that meant very little. And, meaning nothing in particular, I remarked in passing that she was a very good wife.

Suddenly she blurted out, "I left Leo once. It was just a quarrel. He didn't like something I had done. I don't even remember what it was. But he said that since I wasn't a great looker, I had just better shape up. And then he left the house and I brooded over what he had said. Here I thought I was really looking snazzy, and he *had* to say a thing like that. I realized it didn't even matter whether I was a looker or not. It was just a mean thing to say, that Leo was mean. And I brooded and it festered. And I got really worked up. I thought, 'Let him see how well he can get along without me.' I had Maria then and she was dependable, so I just up and left the kids with her. If I had taken the kids with me, I wouldn't have been able to go to a hotel—I would have had to go to my mother's. And that was what I didn't want to do. I thought that if she went on and on about how wonderful it was to be married to Leo, I would strangle her. And you know Mother, she would never let up. So I left the kids with Maria and checked into the Bel Air Hotel. It's quieter there and I didn't want to run into anybody I knew. And I called Maria from the hotel and told her where I was—just in case there was an emergency. But, of course, what I really wanted was for her to tell Leo so that when he came home and found me gone, he would go crazy and come looking for me—that he would *beg* me to come home—beg me on his knees!"

"And did he? *Did* he beg you?"

"No. I never even found out if he would have. I checked into the hotel, called Maria, unpacked my bag, ordered lunch from room service, turned on the TV. I stared at the television, didn't eat the lunch, and I panicked. Suppose Leo came home, found me gone, and *didn't do a damn thing about it?* What the hell would I do then? So I packed my bag and drove home like a mad woman before Leo found out I was gone.

"After that, I've never kidded myself about leaving him. Whenever that feeling comes over me now, I bite my lips and wait until it passes. I mean, suppose I did leave Leo for real? What would I do with myself?"

I had nothing to say—I had no answer. Besides, it was all too easy to tell somebody else what to do with her life.

Then Cleo laughed the way people do after they have revealed a very intimate confidence and are already sorry that they have. "God, you'd think I wasn't happy . . . that I didn't have a perfectly marvelous life."

Suzannah appeared to be having a perfectly marvelous life. Not that I saw her often. She was really tight with her lawyer friend, Lee Philips. When I saw them together it was as if she were really in love. And she *was* different. I guessed that it was Lee who had made the difference. He was not a hunk, as we used to call the really attractive men in our youth, but as Suellen put it, he *was* a smoothie. Very smooth. The first time I laid eyes on him, I was overwhelmed. He was the spitting image of Jack Nicholson! I knew I was falling into that trap again, seeing everybody here as a different actor, but there it was—an indisputable likeness. He wore dark glasses almost constantly and always a three-piece suit. (I eventually discovered that he also wore velour jogging suits when he ran, and breeches when he rode.) Suellen said she distrusted people who were addicted to dark glasses—that they were hiding behind them, and *what* were they hiding? And Cleo said there were only two kinds of men who wore suits in Los Angeles—theatrical agents and lawyers. I suppose she was right. And Lee was a lawyer. But how about a suit *and* dark glasses? What did that mean?

And when Lee Philips wore three-piece suits, Suzannah wore suits too—Adolfos, or beautifully cut blazers with decorous-length skirts and tailored silk blouses. And when Lee Philips jogged in his black or white velours, Suzannah did likewise. They were twins.

Suzannah running? Unbelievable. But there it was. She was different.

"Oh, it's wonderful!" she enthused. "The oxygen goes to your brain and you feel like you're flying! Only my obscene titties get in the way. It's hard to run with titties, did you know that?" She eyed my full breasts with polite disdain. "That's what Lee calls them—obscene. I'm thinking of getting a reversal but Lee doesn't want me to do anything hasty, not to do anything rash. But it's hard to look like a lady with *these*. It's all Heinie's fault. Before I was elegant and now I'm obscene . . . *vulgar.*"

"You are not! And I wouldn't think you'd want to tamper with your breasts again."

"Oh, it's nothing. They put in implants to make them bigger and now all they'll do is take them out. And I'll be able to run much better. I'm telling you, Buffy, if you want to run, you really ought to have your breasts reduced."

"I wasn't thinking about running, just now, Suzannah. I'm concentrating on delivering this bundle I'm carrying and he or she will probably prefer a generous milk container."

"Really, Buffy! *Vul-gar!*" I didn't know whether she was referring to my remark or my breasts.

"After you have the baby though, you'll certainly want to indulge in some form of exercise. Everybody has to do *something.*"

"To tell the truth, I was thinking of having another baby right after this one."

"Are you crazy or something? For God's sake, you're not even Catholic. Not that that means anything these days. *Nobody* has more than one child anymore. And right away? Think of your plumbing!"

As a matter of fact, right at the moment, I was thinking of the plumbing *she* had had removed, and she was calling me crazy. But at least she was no longer using the word "temple" for her body, and for that I was grateful.

"I *am* thinking of my, as you so quaintly put it, plumbing. It's getting older each day and after this child, I'm thinking of not one, but two more."

"Five children? You *are* insane. If that's what Hollywood's done to you, perhaps you should go back to Ohio."

I decided to let that one go, and she drummed clear-polished finger-tips on the coffee table. "I was thinking of inviting you and Todd up to Santa Barbara to Lee's ranch for the weekend. Of course *you'd* have to sit on the sidelines, but maybe Todd could ride. What do you think? Riding is terrific exercise and very *à la mode* these days. As a matter of fact, Lee plays polo. It's become fashionable again. Why don't I ask Lee to kind of break Todd in?"

"Todd's kind of busy these days—too busy to be broken in, I think."

"I suppose. How are things going at the studio?" she asked in an indifferent kind of way.

"Well . . ." So, I thought, now it appeared that Suzannah was more into being an *à la mode* Hollywood wife than a Hollywood superstar. It appeared that once Suzannah had her divorce and her twenty million dollars, she and Lee would ride off into the hills above Sunset on polo ponies.

A month or so later, I gave birth to my son, Matthew. And three weeks after that, Cassie gave birth to a daughter, whom she named Jennifer, and I remembered then that that was the name of the lady who had once lived in the pink castle, Jenny Elmann, John Starr Winfield's mother. And if I had had any doubts at all who was the father of Cassie's baby, I had none at all now. I knew that Win's sabbat-ical from Stanford was over, and I held my breath to see if the man I called hero would take his woman and child and go north. But I should have known better. If he had tried to do this, he had failed, because Cassie told me that Win had accepted a "temporary assignment" at UCLA. So far, the good guy wasn't winning out.

46.

When I became pregnant again only several months after Matthew was born, my most vociferous critic was Suellen.

"How you can think of bringing another child into this world of nuclear destruction, I'll never know."

"You have two children," I pointed out defensively.

"If I had it to do all over again maybe I wouldn't have had *any.*"

"That's a terrible thing to say."

"It's a terrible world out there."

"Really, Suellen, I don't know how Howie puts up with you. You always were a prophet of doom but you used to laugh a little and smile a lot. But you're getting older and you're not getting better. Only more sour."

Suellen laughed at that. "Oh Buff, I'm sorry. I'm sure this baby will be as wonderful as Megan, Mitch, and Matty."

Cassie thought it was lovely that I was pregnant again. She herself was euphoric about her baby, thought about nothing else. She seemed to ignore the fact that there was Guy who came home once in a while. Her feet were still bare, her hair hung down her back in one great braid, and her peasant dress nearly scraped the floor. She carried her baby around with her all day long in a sling that hugged the child to her breast, and when it was time to feed Jennifer, she unbuttoned the dress and proceeded without any further ado.

"What does Guy have to say about all this?" I meant the situation with Win as a constant visitor.

"Oh, I guess he's pleased about the baby. That's practically the only thing he talks to me about—the baby. I go to visit my mother with Jenny and afterwards he asks me what Mother has to say about *his* child . . . *her* heir."

"And what *does* she say?"

"Not much. She's not exactly overwhelmed with emotion. She keeps studying Jenny's face. She's very much into resemblances. She says,

'We'll wait and see.' And then she usually asks me about Guy's career with a sneer."

Nothing much new there then, I sighed.

"And what does she say about Win?" I persisted. "And what does Guy say about Win?"

Cassie looked at me rather coldly. "What *could* Mother say about Win? She doesn't even know he exists. As for Guy, he *barely* knows Win's alive. Guy barely knows *anybody's* alive. He's glad that he has the Blackstone heiress and that's about it. As a matter of fact, Guy's here less than ever. He's taken a little place in Hollywood. He said he wants to be nearer to the studio since he has such early morning calls. I understand that the show's ratings are getting better. Is that right?"

I didn't want to be sidetracked. "That's what Todd says," I mumbled. "But Guy has to think *something* about you and Win."

She just didn't want to talk about it. She said with exasperation at my persistence, "He thinks of Win with contempt. He thinks he's a fool because he works on our landscaping for free."

"Doesn't he ever wonder *why* he works on it for free?"

Cassie laughed bitterly. "What you mean is, doesn't he ever wonder if Win and I are lovers?"

I looked at her and said nothing.

"No, he doesn't. And you know why he doesn't? Because he thinks I'm the original gutless wonder, that's why. He doesn't think I have the backbone to take myself a lover. And you know what else? Even if my mother knew of Win's existence, she, too, wouldn't think I had the backbone. My mother and Guy, they have something in common after all. They *both* think I'm a gutless wonder.

Win . . . baby . . . still, status quo.

Cleo, too, thought I was crazy to be pregnant again but *she* didn't say so. Not in so many words. Dressed in a cowboy hat, breeches, and cowboy boots the color of gun metal, she flitted nervously about my sunroom, something obviously on her mind. Finally she spit it out, "You know what they're saying about the King Studios around town?"

"What?"

"That we're really only TV people, not real Movie Set."

"Now what does that mean, Cleo?"

"It means people think the King Sudios aren't really making movies at all, not movie movies . . . only stuff for TV. The series, the sit-coms, made-for-TV movies. *Recycled* sit-coms and series at that. The only movies, *real* movies, that are being made at King are those being produced by independents who are just renting set facilities. So what if King is going to distribute them? Distribution isn't making movies, is it?"

On one level I could sympathize with Cleo. She had devoted so much of herself to being a genuine Movie Set person that she took this kind of talk personally. I also realized that once again she was acting as emissary for Leo, who, while prospering at the King Studios making the redos, revitalizing the recycles, doing the TV movies, still hungered after the recognition and the art—wanted to be a *movie* movie screenwriter and director. And I suppose that given the climate of Hollywood, I couldn't blame him.

But on another level, how *dared* she come running to me with her whining, her criticism of Todd and what he was doing with the King Studios?

"If a studio is to exist and to grow, it has to make money, Cleo," I said, trying to control my anger. "Todd's got the studio on its feet again after the *Love and Betrayal* fiasco," I said pointedly. "And with all his creativity, Leo was certainly part of that disaster, wasn't he? And I think Todd has been pretty creative in making King Studios financially stable. And *I* don't give a damn if people in this town say I'm TV Set instead of Movie Set. And if it's disturbing to you and Leo, I don't think Todd would hold Leo to his contract. If Leo wants to go someplace else where he would have more prestige I think we would be able to go along with that—"

Cleo's eyes widened at my words. She was shocked, even frightened by my words.

"I don't know why you're talking to me like this, Buffy. I thought we were friends." She looked around her, as if searching for some means of escape, as if now she wanted to get away from me.

"We are friends, Cleo. I hope we remain friends."

She laughed uncertainly. "But you're talking like . . . like one of those people who are into *power*. You were *threatening* me, Buffy, threatening Leo's job."

"No, Cleo, I wasn't. I was just telling you like it is. Honestly. As for my being into power, wasn't it you who told me this was a power town? And if one wants to survive here one plays by the rules?"

"I didn't mean *anything* by what I said. I was just telling you what people were saying about *us* . . . all of us at the King Studios. Why, do you know we can hardly get anybody that's anybody to our Sunday Tennis anymore?"

"I'm sorry to hear that. Maybe I should take over for you? We have a wonderful tennis court here. And we're really not doing anything with it. Maybe we should have the Tennis Sundays here at our house? Maybe *the head* of the King Studios will have better luck in attracting the somebodies?"

Our eyes locked. Cleo was right. I was changing. I *was* getting into power. And I had thought I was merely into pregnancies.

As she left she said in conciliatory fashion, "Everyone always said Todd was a genius. A financial genius. I guess that's what it takes to succeed here these days. A financial genius and not necessarily a creative one."

I repeated some of Cleo's conversation to Todd. I thought he'd get a laugh out of it, but I should have known better. He looked *stricken.*

"Look, Todd, you've only been here a short time. A little over a year. And you've put that damn studio on its feet. It's been making money! You've put a lot of people to work—"

He smiled wistfully. "I put a lot of people to work in Ohio. I didn't come here just to be a good businessman. I could have stayed in Ohio and done that. If you don't take chances on doing something truly good, something really big, then what's the point of being in the business?"

"You've done wonderfully!"

He shook his head. *"Saturday Night's Revenge?"* He referred to a movie he had just sold to a network that would air on some Saturday night in TV's near future. "Or our first feature—*Satan's Child?"*

"You're doing it with taste."

He smiled, shook his head. "A real class project, that one is. Gore and guts and teenage shrieks."

"You've done wonderfully!" I said again.

"No, Buffy. What does wonderful mean? Full of wonder, full of awe! I haven't done anything *awesome,* have I?"

Oh, I ached for him! I threw my arms around him and pressed him close. *Oh, Todd, I'm full of awe for you! I find it awesome that I have you . . . I'm as full of awe by the fact of you as I have ever been. Oh Todd, my love for you is an awesome thing!*

47.

After months of postponements and weeks of testimony and a lot of acrimony, Suzannah's divorce trial was drawing to a close. On the day that Lee Philips was summing up, she asked me to accompany her to court.

"We're going to have a big party afterwards at Jimmy's. A celebration, you may be sure. So see if you can find something to wear that will minimize your shame."

"My shame?"

"Yes. When you walk around pointing that big pregnant belly of yours, why, everybody and his third cousin *knows* you've done it! You're announcing to the world: *I've been screwed!*" she teased.

I wanted to ask her what did the world think when she walked around pointing her big, oversized boobs at them, but I didn't. She had become more and more self-conscious about her outsized appendages since she was going with Lee Philips, and decried them everytime I saw her. She was planning on a revision as soon as the trial was over, after she collected her millions and married her suave attorney. And I wasn't going to spoil the good mood she was in with my teasing.

When she came to pick me up, I was more than surprised at her outfit. I hadn't seen her before on the days she had gone to court but I assumed that she had been wearing the kind of clothes she had adopted since going with Philips: Chanel-type suits, demurely bowed blouses, low-heeled pumps. Now she stood before me in a low-cut, spaghetti-strapped, short short dress, her huge breasts straining against the knit fabric. Her extremely high-heeled white boots matched, and her hair was arranged and sprayed into a huge bouffant structure that hadn't been seen in twenty years. Suzannah didn't look like a high-class model, or a glamorous actress. She didn't even look like a high-class call girl—she looked like your everyday street whore!

I searched for words. "Did Lee tell you to dress like this?" And when Suzannah nodded, I couldn't imagine what he was thinking of.

"He picked this dress out himself. I've been wearing outfits a *little* like this to court every day but this one's the *pièce de résistance,* you might say. I guess he wants the judge to see all the glories that Heinie possessed and threw away." At first she was smiling at me as she talked, enjoying the stunned effect she had had on me. Then her smile turned uncertain. "I do feel kind of foolish. I wish this whole thing was over so I can get back my normal titties."

Lee Philips had an overly large easel set up in the courtroom and an assistant placed a huge blow-up of Suzannah on display—a life-size colored blow-up of Suzannah selling her perfume in an evening gown of stunning elegance. Then he removed it and placed another one, equally large, of Suzannah in a long fur coat that spelled class. They followed, one blow-up after the other, displaying a beautifully refined, tasteful, eloquently glamorous, chicly well-bred, sophisticated, graciously alluring Suzannah. They were spellbinding. I looked at Suzannah. Her mouth hung open, her amber eyes glowed with a longing.

Then Lee Philips called out, "Suzannah, please! Will you step up here?"

Uncertainly Suzannah got to her feet and looked at me and I knew then what Lee Philips was doing. "No, Suzannah! Don't!" I rose too and took her arm, "Don't, Suzannah! Don't go up there!"

Philips said nicely, "Suzannah," calling her, and she hesitated and then went, like a sleepwalker, and walked toward the stand. But Philips put a detaining hand on her arm, and kept her standing there.

The testimony of the previous days had been lurid and the newspaper accounts had packed the courtroom, but it was as still that minute as a graveyard at night. I was only grateful that Heinie was absent.

"Your Honor," Philips began quietly. "You've seen here what Suzannah *was,* before Heinz Muller married her. Now I present to you what Heinz Muller made of her." His voice rose. "A ten dollar hooker!"

Somebody tittered in the quiet, and then the courtroom went wild! I ran up to Suzannah, wanting only to pull her away. Her mouth was open, her head thrown back, and her eyes rolled around in her head.

And then a terrible screech came up from her body, a lamentation, a shrill animal sound:

"He *fuuuuccckkked* me!"

I felt like it was the two of us against the world as I tried to hustle her out of the courtroom, as I hit out against anybody who got in our way. Suzannah was an unseeing rag doll, and I was a weeping pregnant security guard armed with only my pocketbook as I slammed away at the press who crowded in on us. And there was nobody I could even yell at to get the car. It was as if the world were attacking us and there were only the two of us alone. I tugged at Suzannah, and all the while struck out at the cameras. No matter what else happened *nobody* was going to take Suzannah's picture in that dress!

Finally I managed to get Suzannah's driver with her car to pull up and we ducked in and I told him to take us to my house. Leah came to the door and I told her, "Something terrible has happened!" and Leah took Suzannah from me and helped her upstairs. I called Todd at the studio but it seemed the news had already spread and Todd was on his way home.

We took no phone calls for the next few days, and we even hired a security guard to make sure no one approached our house, while Suzannah spoke to no one inside our house either. I wondered if she would ever talk again. Lee Philips called and Todd spoke to him. I heard him say, "If I ever see you, turn around and walk the other way, because I might kill you!"

And he shook his head and told me, "With all of that, he didn't get her the twenty million anyway."

"How much?" I asked.

"I'd say, all things considered, a very nominal amount."

It was as if Suzannah would never be the same again. Todd told her repeatedly, "I've got a great idea for a picture for you, Suzannah," but there was no interest, no response. He described a movie, went on at length with a plotline, even recited lines from the script, but to no avail.

"I had no idea you were planning a movie of this magnitude. *When* was the script written?"

Todd gestured helplessly. "The minute I got a response I was going to put Leo on it."

We decided Suzannah needed a doctor's help and we spoke to her about a psychiatrist, suggested that she think about it. But it was her decision to go out of town, to a small sanitarium in Palm Springs. And we took her there and I promised I would come see her regularly. She kissed me, and then Todd, "You've been my friends—my only true friends. Except—" She made a gesture with her mouth, lifted her shoulders. "Well, it was a good day for me when I walked into your room. Friends to the end?"

I nodded. "Friends to the end."

48.

My son Michael was born that summer, and I congratulated myself on keeping to the schedule I had more or less formulated for myself—I was in California a little more than just two years and I had added two little Kings to the family. One more to go.

Cassie came to visit, presenting me with one of those slings that snuggled the baby against the mother's heart, the same kind she had carried Jennie in.

"So how goes it?" I asked her.

"Wonderfully. Jenny's wonderful."

"And Win? What about Win?"

"He's wonderful."

So she's still euphoric, I thought. And still evading doing anything about her situation.

"I'm glad he's wonderful," I said a trifle sarcastically. *"And* patient. Isn't his year up at UCLA?"

"He's signed on for another year. Win says the study of history teaches one patience."

"How nice for both of you. And Guy? Is he wonderful?" I felt mean to do this to Cassie, to try to burst her bubble of false happiness, but I couldn't help myself. I wanted her to *act,* to do something for her situation that meant some lasting happiness.

"Oh, I hardly ever see Guy. I told you, he has an apartment in Hollywood. It's almost like we're married in name only."

I wanted to shake her. She was willing to go along this way forever, just so she wouldn't have to confront the situation with her mother. And I was mad at Win too. He was an idiot to go along with this situation. That was the problem with students of ancient history. They didn't understand the modern world . . . how one thing affects another and how the world can blow up in your face . . . suddenly . . .

in a minute . . . the way it had with Suzannah. And Suzannah was tough, not as well-born as Cassie and Win. She was a lily of the field, and they were hothouse flowers. If she had folded, how would they survive?

I was right about Suzannah. She was tough and a survivor. Three months later she was back, and almost the old Suzannah, brash and bold and full of enthusiasm, *almost.* Not exactly the same in spirit. And not the same in body either. She had had the revision of her breasts, and she had had a tuck taken in her behind too, she told me. "Gotta keep the old ass high in the air, you know. Who ever heard of a film star with a flabby ass?"

She asked if she could stay with us awhile, while she got herself straightened out, while she got started on her career again. "You will have a film for me soon, won't you, Todd?"

I assured her that she could stay with us and Todd assured her he'd come up with something for her. Neither of us could do any less for her.

Suellen thought I was crazy to let Suzannah stay with us. "To allow her to move in on you like that, take over your lives? Insanity! She's taking advantage."

"Come on, Suellen! You've espoused causes all your life and most of them were thankless and hopeless, but that didn't stop you from doing what you thought you should. Todd and I won't turn our backs on Suzannah when she's in trouble—"

"Suzannah's not in trouble. You two are the ones in trouble," she said ominously.

I pooh-poohed her. But I *was* a little worried. I wasn't completely sure that Suzannah didn't want to move in with us as a subtle form of blackmail—to ensure Todd's giving her a movie to do quickly.

I hired a full-time, live-in maid, Rosita, a recent immigrant from Mexico who spoke little English. I did this *for* Leah, but against Leah's wishes. With Suzannah in the house, there was a lot of extra work, an impossible amount to contend with without extra help. To minimize Leah's sulks, I put Rosita into the chauffeur's quarter above the garage, and not into the small maid's room next to hers. We didn't have a chauffeur anyway.

There were other changes about the house. Suzannah immediately forged an alliance with Megan who was very much impressed with Suzannah's glamour. Suzannah told her amusing stories and treated her to bits of costume jewelry, colorful scarves, a gold kid purse. And she said things to Megan like, "Wouldn't it be wonderful if your Daddy gave me a great big part in a great big movie?" And of course Megan then turned to Todd reproachfully, "Why don't you, Daddy? Suzannah's so beautiful."

This made Todd very nervous. For one thing he was still working himself up to expending the studio's resources to make a really big, really great movie. It was as if he were fighting with himself to do it—fighting the natural caution he felt, still going along with the TV stuff that brought in the money. And he *had* promised Suzannah he would star her, and her presence in the house was a constant spur to him to get moving on the project. And yet if he did it—a really big movie—and gave Suzannah the starring role, could she carry it? And if she carried it, could he trust her not to be a prima donna? A prima donna could be a wonderful actress and still drive up production costs. While he hammered this problem out with himself, he started not being at home as much as before. Suzannah's presence was a subtle form of nagging.

And Suzannah, who had studied Spanish at Ohio State, forged an alliance with Rosita, who poured out her heart to her new confidante—about her persecution at the hands of the surly Leah, about the frightening noises to which she was subjected in her lonely quarters above the garage, separated from the rest of the household. It was Suzannah who comforted her with soft words, gifts—a satin evening dress, a pink marabou wrap, a half-filled bottle of Arpege—until it seemed that Rosita was working for Suzannah exclusively, fetching and carrying for her endlessly, drawing her hot baths, brushing her long red hair, pressing her clothes. Rosita forgot that the rest of the household existed—Todd and I, the three children, the baby, Leah who could have used a hand in spite of herself, and the baby's nurse who *expected* some help.

I decided it was time for me to take a hand in the matter. I told Todd: "You do have those pictures you've been debating doing sitting on the drawing board. Do one of them with Suzannah!"

"But I can't make a decision of this magnitude on the basis of household considerations. Can I? I just can't take a chance on Suzannah in one of those—I'm afraid of her shenanigans. Besides, Leo says she's incapable of a subtle performance. Leo says all she can do is blatant melodrama."

"Leo!" I sneered.

"I don't care what Leo is or does on a personal level, when it comes to moviemaking, I respect his judgment. The thing is Leo does have an idea for a TV movie that might just fill the bill. About a young actress who is stalked and terrified by a psychopath—"

"Hurrah for Leo. That's what I really call an original concept—"

Todd smiled a little at my sarcasm. "It's a natural for a low-budget. We could shoot it almost entirely on the lot. And it's something Suzannah could handle. And since I've decided to cancel *Hollywood and Vine* once and for all, and we still have a contractual commitment to Guy Savarese—He will make a terrific psychopath, you have to admit. That dark brooding quality. And we can shoot this fast. Right now, Guy has a top recognition quotient with TV audiences. And fast is better for Suzannah, too. We would be at least two years away right now from a feature appearing in the movie houses, and Suzannah *needs* something right away. Don't you see?" he appealed to me. "I can sell this idea tomorrow to one of the networks and it's easy money . . . for everybody."

"And you'd have Leo direct? After—"

"Why not? In this town, everybody works with the same people they've been feuding with; actors work for a producer even as they're suing him for the five percent of the net he screwed them out of on their last picture. Yes, the whole thing works—Leo, Suzannah, and Guy. And I can fulfill my promise to Suzannah. That's important, isn't it?"

Yes, I did think it was important for Todd to keep his promise to Suzannah. And I was glad, for Cassie's sake, that Guy would be in a movie, albeit TV, since his series was being canceled. I hoped, for her sake too, that he would be a big success in it so that she could stop using this success business as an excuse not to confront her mother. I was convinced that she was a masochist who really didn't want her life resolved. As for Win, I really didn't know what to make of him either. He was a big disappointment to me. I had so wanted him to take charge of this situation!

I had expected Suzannah to make large squawks about doing a TV film instead of a big movie. But she was delighted. And then I realized she no longer had the confidence she once had. A TV film was less demanding, and not such a frightening spectacle. And she said that she would use the time it took to prepare the script for shooting to find her own place to live.

I suggested she buy a condo, both as an investment and as a good place for a single woman to live. And she did so with Leila Pulitzer's assistance. As a matter of fact, she bought in the same building where

Leila herself lived—on the fashionable Wilshire corridor. And she prepared to leave us.

"It's funny—me moving into a bachelor girl's apartment. Lee . . ." It was the first time since the courtroom debacle that she had mentioned his name. "Lee told me that we would buy that sheik's house on Sunset . . . the one I always loved. You know, Buffy, I think I really loved him. And I thought he loved me. What a fool I was." She looked sick, talking about it.

"Don't look back, Suzannah." I squeezed her hand. "Let's just keep going forward, keeping our eye on the big dream," I said softly.

Then she giggled.

"What is it? What's funny?"

"You know what I'll remember best about Lee Philips?"

"What?"

"He had the *biggest* cock. You wouldn't believe it."

And I started to laugh too. We looked at each other and we couldn't stop laughing.

It was an unbelievable world. Suzannah sweetly asked Cleo to help her decorate her new apartment and Cleo pleasantly complied. Cleo knew where to buy what, and how to get fast delivery. In this case it was a lot of big white furniture with a generous helping of oversized silver kid pillows, which Suzannah adored. "Very *à la mode*," she declared. "Very *au courant!*"

And when she left, she took Rosita with her, to which neither Leah nor I really objected. Still, she might have asked first.

49.

The Stalking went on the air in the spring and was an incredible hit. Everybody, it seemed, loved it: the millions of people who sat in front of the TV sets, the critics who usually gave the kiss of death to this type of fare, and the ratings. It was at the top of the list. The reviewers raved over Guy, equating his sinister performance with those of classic screen fame—a kind of comely Peter Lorre. And while they were more reserved about Suzannah's characterization of the terrorized starlet, they praised her great beauty, a beauty in the tradition of the stars of the thirties and forties, a beauty they found sadly lacking among the current queens of the cinema. As for Leonard Mason's script and direction, they awarded him kudos for subtlety and class, for withstanding the temptation to go for the cheap and obvious, which lesser craftsmen might have done.

Reading that, Todd said, "But that's exactly what *I* did. I grabbed for the cheap and obvious buck when I could have taken that film into the theaters. I could have really gone for it."

"Don't be ridiculous," I rose to his defense immediately. "You produced a quality film. What's wrong with that? That it appeared on TV? Why, you'll probably win an Emmy!"

"But don't you see? If I'm a moviemaker, why didn't I go for the real movie? Because TV was easier . . . an easy sale. But I should have taken the chance. I should have been more creative. I should have seen that Guy can make it on the big screen. I should have seen that Suzannah's looks are unique enough these days to make a difference, could even make up for a less than sterling performance. They used to say that pretty girls were a dime-a-dozen in Hollywood. But today, well-trained good actresses are in abundance—*plain-looking* good actresses. But how many true beauties are there? Women with charisma, with star quality?"

I was nettled, because in discussing Suzannah's obvious beauty, for the first time in our lives, Todd had not prefaced his observation with "second only to yours." So I said perversely, "If that's true, if Suzannah has true star quality, how come no one besides Heinie, who was hooked on her, ever put her in a real movie? She's been around for quite a while now. She *is* into her thirties."

"I'm not sure that means anything," Todd answered thoughtfully. "Marilyn Monroe had been around for years and it wasn't until she was almost thirty that anyone realized her potential."

What kind of an example is Marilyn? Almost thirty before she realized her potential, and dead well before she was forty? And I hugged myself against a sudden chill in the middle of a sunny morning.

Todd went on, talking aloud to himself, as much as to me. "As for Leo's script, I could take Leo any place without being ashamed. And he's an even better director than he is a writer. Don't you see, Buffy Ann? I had everything going for me—the actress, the actor, the screenwriter, and the director. I should have gone for it and I didn't. I had the opportunity and I blew it!"

He was so distraught I yearned only to console him, to kiss it and make it better. "Okay, so you blew it and you'll end up with an Emmy. The next time you won't, and you'll end up with an Oscar. Okay?"

He grinned at me ruefully, with the yellow light in the room making his hazel eyes gleam. "Okay. Next time we'll go for the big one. Okay?"

"Okay," I said softly as he hugged me and whispered in my ear, "I have the most beautiful wife in the world, the most beautiful woman anywhere. So I want to be the best. Is that so terrible?"

Oh Todd, you are the best!

"No, that's not terrible. I told you—it's fine."

And later, whenever I looked back at this moment, I supposed that was the moment that I gave my consent to everything that was to follow.

Todd saw that the reviews had gone to Guy's head. He was strutting, preening, being arrogant and demanding, and Todd realized that despite their contract, unless Guy got a bone quickly, he would be sniffing out bigger and better deals elsewhere. So Todd gave him scripts to read, implying that Guy was a star of the top magnitude and, therefore, had a star's privilege of choice of script and of final approval. At the same time, Todd assured him that they would all be intent on getting together a property of a nature that would establish Guy in the top ranks of stardom.

Actually, I was pleased with Guy's arrogance, pleased that he was being treated as a star of the top magnitude. Since Cassie wasn't about to make a move, wouldn't it be nice, I thought, if Guy walked out on her? It *could* happen. He could think he was so big and so important he didn't *need* the Blackstone money, the Blackstone mansion, or the Blackstone heiress anymore.

Todd set Leo in motion, charged him with coming up with a screenplay of consequence—an original or an adaptation—to co-star Guy and Suzannah.

"And I'll direct too?"

"Yes."

"You can count on me, Todd." And Leo started running with his ball.

The only one with whom Todd was vague was Suzannah. He didn't want to expose himself to her impatience—who knew how long it could be before there was a script ready? I wondered whether it was a mistake —his being so unspecific with Suzannah. He just told her, "I'm working on something big. A big feature. But you know how much time this kind of thing takes. You've been there before. I've been thinking about what you should do in the meantime. We don't want people to forget your name . . . your presence. Remember how Heinie had a campaign laid out for you—a Vegas act. Why don't we revitalize that act? Get you a manager and book you into Vegas? A smash in Vegas, after your TV smash, would really establish you as a top talent."

She was wily. "Are you sure you're not just trying to get rid of me?" She turned to me, "He's not just trying to get rid of me, is he?"

"Just for a little while. We're sure you're going to kill them in Vegas."

50.

While Jenny, in a ruffled pinafore, opened up the bottom cabinet doors and removed pots and pans, Cassie put away the groceries she had bought on the way home from visiting her mother, the ritual that had become only monthly these days, or even less often. She would change Jenny's clothes as soon as she was through with the groceries. She herself was still wearing her visiting clothes—blazer, sweater, skirt, medium-heeled sandals, nylons to be sure. Cassandra deplored bare legs.

She turned to see Win in the doorway. Her face lit up. "Win! I was just about to change my clothes and go up to your house."

But he wasn't smiling and he looked at her with eyes so slitted, she couldn't read them at all. A twinge of anxiety coursed through her. "Is something wrong?"

"That depends. Tell me, did you tell your mother you were leaving Guy? After all, he has just had a big success, hasn't he? And that's what you were waiting for—this big success, wasn't it?"

"No, Win, I didn't. You don't understand. Mother would never call a TV movie a *successful* career." She faltered. Win looked so strange, angry. She had to convince him to wait just a little while more. "But that doesn't matter. What does is that Todd's promised Guy to star him in something so big, it's bound to be the picture of the year. And Todd always keeps his promises. *That's* what we've been waiting for and it's really going to happen."

"Wrong," he said. "That's what you've been waiting for, or what you've told yourself you were waiting for. Me? I've been waiting for you to grow up and be a strong, complete woman, not a cowering, frightened kid. I've been waiting for you to stand up and tell them both to go to hell—Guy, but especially your mother. I've been waiting for you to tell her to fuck off!"

Jenny tugged at his leg and he picked her up, snuggled her close, kissed her cheek.

Cassie stared at him, frightened and cold. Win had never spoken like this to her before. "Oh, Win, you've been so wonderful . . . so patient. But it's almost over, the waiting. The movie . . . it'll be just a tiny bit longer now. We have time—"

Jenny touched Win's cheek. "Winnie," she said and laughed.

"No, Cassie," he said. "No more time. You're not listening. You've got to do it *now, before* Guy is a success in this pipe dream you're talking about. Otherwise it's not going to mean anything. It's now you have to stand up to her in order for you to be really free of her. It's never been a matter of you and Guy. It's always been just you and her!"

"Winnie!" Jenny said again.

He looked at the little girl and a muscle twitched in his face. Then he looked back at Cassie. "Just think. If Jenny's mother grew up and became a real woman, Jenny could call me Daddy. It would be really nice for her if she had a real Daddy."

Then he put his daughter down and walked out of the house.

Cassie came over to visit, but I could tell this wasn't just an ordinary afternoon visit. She was overwrought and when I offered her coffee or tea, she asked for a drink.

"Sure thing," I said, and sent Jenny off to the kitchen to have cookies and milk with Leah and Matty, taking Cassie to the barroom.

She poured out the conversation she had had with Win and I thought: Well, finally! My slow-moving, laconic hero has finally asserted himself.

"But he's wrong, Buffy. Tell me, he's wrong, isn't he?"

"Of course I can't tell you he's wrong. He said only what I've been saying to you for years. I think he's completely on the mark. All these years you've waited—you have been a cripple. You *wasted* those years, while you could have been living and loving. And if you do wait until this big movie comes off for the hollow triumph of impressing your mother—Well, you'll just crawl away, still crippled. Win is right. It won't mean a thing then. You have to be counted now while it does mean something. What if something happens? *What if Guy walks out on you first, divorces you?* If he's going to be so successful, he might just do that. He might not think he needs you anymore. Where would that leave you? No satisfaction, worse off actually than now. Then you'll be standing before your sneering mother with terrible egg on your face. You weren't even worthwhile enough to keep a worthless husband. And what if Win's patience wears so thin it tears? It's been so long, Cassie. Don't lose him," I begged her. "If you don't have the strength to face up to Cassandra for yourself, be strong enough for Win, for Jenny!"

But she only cried. She was hopeless. Too many years of ingrained fear.

I tried to think of something else to say. Anything that would help move her off her position. "There is something else, Cassie. This movie may be a long way off. Between then and now there's something else that can blow up in your face. Something that you would never be able to explain away to your mother. There are rumors going around, Cassie, about Guy cruising the Strip, picking up young girls. Todd's spoken to him about the stories, and Guy denied them, said they weren't true. But he's arrogant—more so than ever before. Who knows what the truth is? Get rid of him before there is a hint of a public scandal. If you don't, well, there's not only your mother to think about, is there? There's Jenny. And the world thinks he, Guy, is her father! What then?"

"I would kill him!"

I knew it was a form of hysteria talking, and I didn't take it seriously, even though it was a shock hearing the words coming from impotent, sweet Cassie's mouth. And it wasn't until later that I remembered the story about Jenny Elmann blasting her husband . . . and that there was a rifle sitting in the closet of Cassie's bedroom . . . waiting.

And then it occurred to me that Cassie hadn't said one word speculating about the truth of those rumors, had not even bothered to say one way or the other, as if the truth of the charges were not even a matter of contention, as if she knew what the truth was.

And there was Todd, making his preparations for the great movie to star Guy Savarese, convinced that the stories were false. "Guy Savarese is too smart to risk everything for a little cheap whoring around."

But was he? How smart could an egomaniac be, an egomaniac who thought he was so hot nothing could touch him?

I found myself wishing that we had never heard of Guy Savarese. And that Todd had never thought of making this picture with him. Guy Savarese was a volatile property . . . he could blow up in all of our faces.

51.

It took several months, but Suzannah finally got her act together. It was more a matter of hard rehearsal than anything. And she worked hard at it—everything that had already been blue-printed by Heinie. And then with Todd's help she acquired a road manager and bookings and went off to Las Vegas. And three weeks later, we flew out for the opening—Todd and I, Cleo and Leo, Howard and Suellen. Suellen, for once, had agreed to go someplace without her children, and of all places—Vegas. She insisted that she was going only for Howard's sake: as head of production he was in bad need of a break in routine.

We were seated at a banquetted front table along with Suzannah's old friend, Poppy, her husband Beau Beaufort, and a friend of theirs, a distinguished-looking middle-aged man with an artificial tan and a fine head of graying black hair. His name was Ben Gardenia.

For some reason, Suellen kept studying Gardenia while I myself was preoccupied with Poppy. I had heard so many stories about her that I had expected a stereotypical tough, gum-chewing, vulgar-mouthed tootsie, covered with Las Vegas glitter. But she was gowned conservatively in a long dinner dress with long tight sleeves and a high neck and only a thin strand of diamonds encircling her neck as adornment. Her midnight-black hair was pulled back tightly in a huge chignon at the nape of her neck, and she seemed to wear no makeup at all except for charcoal-grey eyeshadow and possibly mascara. Her face was perfectly white, as if she had never been out in the sun, and only her eyes seemed to have life—they darted back and forth with a hard intelligence. She was a stunning if offbeat-looking woman.

Her husband had the face of a young but happy boy, with beautifully cut yellow-blond hair, not long but not short either, and a mouthful of exquisitely-capped teeth which he didn't stop revealing for a moment, as if he had been born not to sing but to smile. Only the color of his face was wrong. It wasn't the healthy reddish-brown you'd expect of a boy brought up in the Vegas sun. It was too orange. A sun lamp, I guessed, complimented by makeup. I had heard how he ran to fat, victim of an undisciplined appetite, but he wasn't fat. His face was a bit bloated, but his body, clothed in an impeccable white dinner jacket, was not that corpulent. He was more on the burly side—like a football player who had recently stopped playing.

I asked him where he was currently appearing, said we'd all love to see him perform, and he answered me by suddenly swooping down on the table, playing some riff with his hands while he closed his eyes, moved his head, and sang a snatch of words that I didn't quite catch.

"We just got back from the road a couple of weeks ago," Poppy interjected quickly, smiling only with her pale mouth and not with her sharp eyes. "Beau's having himself a rest, a . . ." she paused, "hiatus." Then she leaned back in her chair as if contemplating the word she had just used while Beau continued using the table as a drum, eyes closed, his head bopping, mouthing words to a melody he heard in his head.

When the waiter took our order, Beau held up a finger and started to say something, but Poppy spoke first: "Nothing for us." And Ben Gardenia smiled.

I felt an incredible tension at the table and I wished that Todd would speak. He was so good at carrying a conversation, making everyone feel comfortable. But he was contemplating Beau, both he and Leo. And then I saw that Poppy was studying Todd just as intently. Howard, good old Howard, conversed with Ben Gardenia. I leaned over Beau trying to engage Poppy in talk, trying at the same time to draw both Cleo and Suellen in too, but unsuccessfully. Then Todd leaned over to join Howard and Ben's conversation, while Leo seemed lost in thought, still watching Beau. And Cleo, usually the most talkative person at any gathering, seemed transfixed, speechless, staring down at the flatware on the tablecloth as if she found it fascinating. And Suellen was observing Beau as if she found *him* fascinating.

The comedian, the lead-in act, was ready to go on. Todd looked around the huge room. "Certainly is a full house," he said, pleased for Suzannah.

Ben laughed. "The first time Beau headlined, I brought about a thousand friends to paper the house. What I didn't know was that Poppy had been standing out on the Strip all afternoon, handing out halved Andy Jacksons—" he looked around the table and explained "—twenty dollar bills. The jokers had to come to the show to get the other half, but only after they had paid their admissions. We damn near had a riot but it was a big evening."

Everyone laughed except Poppy, who managed only a faint smile. Either she wasn't one for laughing or she didn't like to be reminded of the days when she had to hawk torn twenty dollar bills. Actually, it was extremely difficult for me to connect this hard-eyed elegant woman with that hustler of bygone days.

When the comic went off, Suellen and I repaired to the ladies room. Suellen was in a snit. "My God! Did you ever hear such revolting filth?"

"This *is* Vegas, Suellen."

"And that Beau Beaufort!"

"He? He didn't say one dirty word."

"How could he? He's too stoned to talk!"

"Suzannah's always said he wasn't too bright. Maybe that's why. Anyhow, I wouldn't say he was *stoned* exactly. More like . . . a little high."

"A *little* high? He's stoned out of his gourd."

I laughed. "What do you know about such things? Innocent Suellen."

"Oh really! I grew up in the sixties too. And just because I didn't do drugs doesn't mean I'm uninformed. And anybody with children had just better keep herself informed."

"Aren't your kids a little young for you to be worrying?"

"They're never too young, and it's never too soon to be concerned. That man . . . that Ben Gardenia. What is it that he does? Nobody said. I bet he's a drug dealer."

I burst out laughing. "You're so dramatic, Suellen. And you always overreact. I think Ben Gardenia's a business associate of Poppy Beaufort. I think he's in show business."

When we returned to our table, Beau got to his feet. " 'Scuse," he muttered.

Poppy stood up too.

Beau laughed like a naughty child.

"I gotta go to the toilet," he said. "You can't go to the men's room, Poppy."

Poppy looked around, obviously embarrassed, then sat down. Not so dumb, I thought. He had outfoxed his keeper. Beau, triumphant, went off weaving and bopping in and out of the tables, hailing the crowd as he went.

Beau still hadn't returned when there was a tremendous fanfare. Hot, tribal music . . . rockets and fireworks . . . chorus boys in flame-colored tails came spinning out onto the stage. "Suzannah on Fire!" was the name of the show.

In the pitch-black darkness, with the explosions going off on stage, lighting up different parts of the room in succession, I could see Poppy Beaufort's face twist in anger and anxiety. Beau had not returned and in a few seconds, they would no longer open the doors to the room.

And then Suzannah was on stage, somehow caught in a ring of flames, and Suzannah, in a costume of orange, pink, and red, was electric!

There was a commotion in back of the room over by the doors, which in a matter of moments exploded into a barrage of sound. We all turned to see Beau Beaufort struggling with ten members of the management. In a flash Poppy was at his side and she led a triumphant Beau back to our table, her mouth a slit, while he exuded a sublime affability. Now I agreed with Suellen. Before Beau had been a bit high . . . *now* he was stoned out of his gourd.

Poppy pushed him down and the next time I took my eyes off the stage and looked, I could see her hand in his lap. I thought perhaps she was holding his hand, but no—*his* hands were on the table. Apparently she was fondling a different part of his anatomy.

Suzannah came out in one magnificent costume after another, all in shades of a blazing fire. She sang; she danced; at one point she even talked in a deep, hot, breathy voice reciting some kind of strange, voo-doo poetry. All the years of lessons in the various theatrical arts had paid off. The audience was mesmerized. I saw Todd and Leo exchanging significant glances and Ben Gardenia's face covered with sweat, as if he had yielded to the intense heat and excitement emanating from the stage.

Suzannah had sworn that she was going to outdo Ann-Margret, that Vegas darling, and I could not tell if she had or had not, since I hadn't seen Ann-Margret in action. But I knew one thing, as I think everybody else in that room did too, a very exciting star had come to town.

Poppy's mouth was so dry it felt as if it had been seared. She wanted to kill Beau for what he had done tonight when she was hoping to impress Todd King with his screen potential. But when she saw how Ben never took his eyes off the stage—and he certainly wasn't fixing on the chorus boys—Ben, who never sweated and who was never moved by anything or anybody, she got an idea. An idea about control. And when everyone rose after the finale to applaud the star now draped in mere bits of purple-blue-red chiffon, she knew that she was right. Ben Gardenia could barely stand for his erection.

It was a big night for all of us concerned, and still Todd did not tell Suzannah any specifics of the screenplay that was being readied, that it was *almost* completed and that her role was one that the biggest star in Hollywood would kill for. I just knew it was a mistake. In order to keep Guy in line, Todd had reassured him to the point of a contract and a seven-figure sum, and had guaranteed him star co-billing. And at this point, Suzannah was the bigger star, and more inclined to basic insecurity about her future as a movie queen, more inclined to get restless and nervous waiting.

"Do it, Todd," I urged him.

"No. If I tell her a screenplay's near completion, she'll finish her engagement here and run back to Hollywood to help us finish the script. I want her to tour the country with this act until everybody's panting for her in a movie. You know Suzannah. After Vegas, she's going to be bored with the rest of the tour. All I have to do is say one word to her and she'll cancel out Jersey and Reno and Chicago. She'll figure that she can do without the other cities, that she's had all the live adulation she needs."

I had decided to keep my nose out of studio business as much as I could, so I let it go, but with misgivings. No one knew Suzannah as I did. And I knew that underneath all that bravado and flash, she was scared! And people who were scared did unaccountable things.

Another thing had me worried: the way Leo and Todd kept studying Beau and the crowd's reaction to him—even off the stage. Didn't Todd realize that even if the women reached out to grab at him, you couldn't trust a boy-man who was first high, and then stoned, and was only concerned with sneaking away from the woman who had pushed him to stardom?

52.

Cleo had barely spoken a word the whole time we were in Vegas, and after not hearing from her in the few days we had been back, I went to see her.

She wore no makeup, an old gray sweatshirt, a faded pair of Calvin's corduroy jeans. It was the first time I had ever seen Cleo without makeup and so informally dressed. Even her hair was lackluster.

"Leo's leaving me," she blurted.

I couldn't believe it. "When did all this happen?"

"He has a girlfriend," she said in a dead voice, dry-eyed as if beyond tears. "He's been seeing her for a while. Her name's Babette Towne—a divorcée from Houston. These divorcées in their thirties and forties are the worst—not the pretty young things in their twenties. The divorcées on the verge of middle-age are the ones out for blood, the ones who *really* prey on other women's husbands. Babette Towne is rich! Department store money. I've really lost Leo now—"

I wanted to say "no great loss," but it wasn't the time. "But he's still with you. You just went to Vegas with him."

"He's leaving me all the same. Babette's bought a house in Bel Air. An estate. Seven-and-a-half acres. Leo told me all about it. A better court than ours, he said. But she's got two children and she won't let him move into the house with them until he's got the divorce and they marry. So he's staying here until we get the divorce."

I gasped. That was incredible gall, even for Leo.

"I know what you think of Leo," she droned on. "You think he's a crummy husband. But do you know that up until that time with Suzannah, he was never unfaithful. But that kind of triggered something in Leo, like they say something triggers off the cancer potentiality in our bodies. After Suzannah, he went shopping around, sort of looking around and feeling the tomatoes in the supermarket. I knew it but I didn't say anything. I just tried to make everything around the house more attractive and comfortable for him. And to have more parties," she sniveled, "because he liked them so much. And I tried to get the children to be more affectionate with him. So he'd want to be home more. And I thought maybe it was all working. But then he met Babette and it was all over. She was too much for Leo to resist—too much money, too much class—she always wears *all* beige."

"What does that mean? All beige?"

"Oh, she's a socialite. Did I mention that? She's a socialite . . . very ladylike and she wears all beige. Always. Leo told me—beige from the top of her head, her hair's beige too, down to her shoes."

"Sounds pretty boring to me. Do you think this is going to pass? Babette, I mean? Is that why you're letting Leo stay on in the house?"

"No. I don't think it's going to pass. Babette is what Leo always wanted. A real twenty-four carat princess. He's always *needed* me before, you see. I could do things, manage everything. And Leo always had his insecurities. But now Todd's guaranteed him five movies in the next seven years, given him a commitment. And Leo's riding high. He doesn't think he needs anything or anybody except Babette to give him real *tone*. He says I'm too *New Yorkish*."

"And what does that mean?"

"That once I open my mouth everybody knows I'm from New York. And that I'm too aggressive."

"But you're not from New York—you're from New Jersey," I argued foolishly.

"Leo says it's the same thing."

"Is she pretty? Prettier than Suzannah?" The words came out of my mouth by themselves, and under the circumstances, the words were less than tactful. I clapped my hand over my lips.

But Cleo didn't even notice. "Oh, God, no! I just saw her once at a party. She's . . . neat looking . . . and very understated looking. But no one would call her *pretty*. You don't understand Leo. He never *did* fuck Suzannah for any other reason than that he thought it was in his best interest, career-wise. Looks never meant anything to Leo. You know how Suzannah kidded around—called herself a little old hillbilly from Kentucky. Well, that's how Leo always thought of her—as a hillbilly with no class. At least I," Cleo preened herself a little, "was brought up to act like a lady, even if we weren't what you'd call society—"

I was getting really angry. "Did it ever occur to you, Cleo, that you don't have to sit still for everything? That especially *now*, you don't have to go along with what Leo says? If he's divorcing you, throw him the hell out!"

"Oh no. Leo says there's no use in spending the extra money for two households. A divorce can drag out. And Leo says it's better for the children if he stays in the house."

"Better for the children? He's going to move out when that woman allows him into her house, isn't he? What kind of a valid reason is that?" *My* voice was getting louder and shriller by the moment. Leo would say *I* had no class.

"Mother says I should hang on as long as possible. Even after the divorce proceedings start, this thing could still blow over. Mother says I should redouble my efforts to make Leo's home life more pleasant." Cleo looked embarrassed then and whispered, "Mother went to Frederick's in Hollywood and bought me some sexy lingerie."

Now I didn't know whether to be angry or laugh. The image of Leila Pulitzer browsing among the garter belts and G-strings was a bit much.

"Listen, Cleo. I heard what Leo wants. And I heard what your mother wants you to do. But what is it *you* want?"

Cleo started to bawl. "I don't want my life to change. *That's* what I want. What will I do, Buffy?" she whined and sniffled and bawled. "I'll be the odd woman at people's dinner parties. And everybody *hates* the single, divorced woman. They love the single, divorced man but they really hate the odd woman. Oh, you just don't know."

No, I didn't. I didn't know many things. I didn't know why Todd had to go and give Leo a guarantee of five movies so that Leo envisioned himself as the king of Hollywood directors. And I didn't know why Babette Towne with all her understated beige wanted Leo altogether. And I didn't know why Leila wanted her daughter to hang on to a man who had so cruelly rejected her.

53.

At one time Poppy had thought of getting Ben to feed Suzannah to the Old Man, but just for laughs, a little revenge for past slights. But she had given up the idea as not worth bothering with when she had so many real problems to deal with. And that was *before* Ben had seen Suzannah . . . *before* he had become so entranced with her . . . *before* he had started attending Suzannah's performance nightly. *Now* she had a definite plan that had nothing to do with the Old Man but only with Ben and Suzannah, and Suzannah would be in Vegas for some time . . . enough time for her to get something going.

Suzannah came in the door complaining of utter exhaustion, of being really dragged out, and Poppy quickly poured a little powder on the glass coffee table, chopped it up quickly with a razor blade, then cut it into two long, thin white lines.

"I don't know," Suzannah said. "I've never done coke. I've heard it can do things to your nose . . . rot your septum."

"Don't be silly. You have to snort for years before that'd happen. Besides, a plastic surgeon fixes that up in a few minutes. Nothing."

Still, Suzannah hesitated. "You sure it's not habit-forming? I don't like to get into bad habits."

Poppy laughed. "Everyone knows coke isn't addictive. That's why everybody does it. You get the fun without any of the pain. That's why it's so good for performers. You get the high, the extra edge up there on stage, and no aftereffects. It's the best high there is."

"I don't know. Are you going to do it with me?"

"It's my damn luck that I'm allergic. I break into hives. My personal chemistry, you know? But that's my problem. Don't let it stop you."

Suzannah got down on her hands and knees, leaned down to the white lines. "Just put a nostril to it and draw it in," Poppy instructed. "One at a time . . . there you go!"

Suzannah leaned back on her heels. "Wow!" she said.

"I'll give you a teeny bit to take along with you for tonight's show."

54.

It had been almost a year, incredible as it seemed, since the TV movie *The Stalking* had aired. I counted back the months. Yes, it had been the spring of '80 and now it was almost spring again. In the interim Todd had put Guy in a "small" movie which, it appeared, was going to do very well for itself; Suzannah was still performing live; and there had been at least twenty versions of *White Lily,* the "big" movie that was going to star Guy and Suzannah, going back and forth between Todd and Leo. And several script doctors had been called in. Eventually everything had been scrapped. I sensed a certain insecurity in Todd, when never in his life had he been anything but confident, always sure that his instant decisions were the right ones.

But finally he told me, "I think we've got it licked. Kind of a *Star Is Born* concept, mixed in with *Pygmalion . . .*"

"But *Pygmalion* was *My Fair Lady* and there've been three versions already of *A Star Is Born,* haven't there? And didn't that last one with Barbra Streisand bomb? You'd think that after all this time, Leo could have come up with a more original concept?"

Todd was offended. *"I didn't* say we were doing a remake—it's just a *similar* concept, that's all. And I've analyzed why the Streisand picture failed. Analysis of failure *is* my forte, you'll remember—" he said a bit stiffly. "I think it was because the hero was too negative. It was hard to feel for him. And when he died, the audience felt like cheering—to hell with the bum. And then they couldn't mourn with the heroine. She was well rid of him. Heroes should be allowed only very slight flaws. Maybe just one."

Todd had something there. He was right about heroes. In her heart, every girl, every woman, wanted a hero to believe in, and he had to be a sterling hero. If anyone knew that, I did. Hadn't I chosen a hero when I was only eighteen? And I had chosen one without any flaws at all. How many women could say that? Maybe Suellen. She had chosen Howard and he was sweet and good and true. I thought of Cleo. She had picked a hero simply riddled with flaws. How could he not fall apart on her, so full of holes was he? Maybe the problem had been that he had been more Leila's hero than Cleo's, and there was a generation gap there. Maybe different generations needed different heroes.

Suzannah? You couldn't count Suzannah. She wasn't completely real herself. And she had no idea what heroes were all about. Or heroines, for that matter. I knew no one else would agree with me, but somehow I felt that if Suzannah knew what it really meant to be a heroine, she would have tried harder to fit the bill.

As for Cassie, poor, sweet Cassie—she was almost as confused as Suzannah. And like Suzannah, who had let Heinie get away, Cassie had let her hero slip through her fingers. She had allowed him to go back to Stanford University without her, she had let him give up on her. Or maybe he had only given up temporarily? Maybe he would show up again in the hills of Bel Air on a white horse and ride to her rescue?

"My concept now is to have Suzannah as a kind of half-hearted hooker, tiredly plying her trade. And Guy's going to be a Professor Higgins of show business. He spots the heroine's potential and he's going to clean up her act for her, train her—make her into a star. He's the real hero even though the heroine doesn't realize it, nor does our audience. You see, he's not distinguished like Professor Higgins. He's hard and tough and doesn't get the audience's sympathy . . . *not in the beginning.*"

"Who does?"

"The other male lead. The country singer our heroine *thinks* she's in love with. He's sweet and lovable, but weak—the one flaw." Todd paced back and forth while my heart sank. He *was* thinking of Beau Beaufort, which I had feared all along.

"Our heroine grows stronger because of the singer's weakness. She fights to save him, not realizing the flaw is too large. And while she's fighting in vain, the other hero, Guy, is building *her* up, being hard and sometimes unpleasant, but necessarily so. And she's leaning on him, counting on his strength, as she deplores his hardness. The country singer keeps dragging our heroine down, his weakness outweighing his sweetness, and finally that weakness betrays both of them—the singer and the girl. Only then does she realize the great truth . . . not that she didn't really love the singer, but that it was in the wrong way. It was not the way a woman is supposed to love a man, a real man, a real hero. It was a case of mistaken devotion, of mistaken heroes. It was really always Guy she loved because he was the true hero . . . without a flaw except for a minor one of being tough. When she gets all that straightened out, she achieves success and happiness." He was triumphant. "You see—it's not really either *Pygmalion* or *A Star Is Born.* It's a story about heroines and heroes, a fairy tale. You know how you've always loved fairy tales."

He was right. I did love fairy tales with happy endings. But there was a glaring flaw in Todd's scenario. My own hero had chosen Guy Savarese for the true hero, which was a mind-blowing case of miscasting. Not to mention the casting of the country singer.

"And who will play the flawed hero . . . the country singer?" I asked as if I didn't already know. We had of recent months acquired *all* his singles and albums, and had been listening to them, over and over again.

Todd smiled, spread his hands. "Beau Beaufort, who else? As a singer he's one of the best. And as an idol? I've done my homework. When he goes out on tour, they mob him, they tear him apart."

I tried. I said, "But he's . . . he's not *real.* He's a caricature. How is he going to make a picture? You saw him at Suzannah's opening in Vegas. He was drugged out. And he's stupid. How can you put him into a project costing millions?"

Todd's smile was confident, almost smug. "But that's just it. All he has to do is be himself!"

"How about the reliability factor? Without that you've got nothing! Nothing but trouble."

"That wife of his. Poppy the Dragon Lady. She keeps him in line in Vegas and out on the circuit. And she's mean. I tell you *I* wouldn't want to cross her. Did you see those eyes of hers? And I hear she's hot to get him into movies, hot enough to keep him on a very tight chain. But I'm not even going to broach it to her until I have a shooting script. It shouldn't be long now until I have the concept down pat. There's no sense in talking to her now . . . I don't want to give her enough time to figure out how to break my balls. I'll spring it on her at the last minute and she'll have to go with it quickly if she wants it, and I think she wants it hard enough not to give me any trouble.

"In the meantime I'm putting Guy into another picture that I have high hopes for. Leo's finished the script and I'm counting on it being a sleeper. And it really establishes Guy as a hero. In this one he's a private eye . . . tough . . . hard . . . but definitely a hero. Then with Suzannah's success as a concert star, on top of her performance in

The Stalking, White Lily can't miss. For the life of me, Buffy, I can't see how it can."

His enthusiasm was that of the old days, when he talked of the shopping centers. And I couldn't bring myself to express my doubts. I couldn't douse that fire, that happy optimism. All I said was, "You're going to keep that title then, *White Lily?*"

"Yes. Lily is the heroine's name and the white stands for purity, because in spite of all the dirt she's had to wade through on her way to the top, she remains pure in spirit. There's your fairy tale, Buffy. A modern one. I don't see how it can miss," he said again.

His eyes were full of light, his face alive with the excitement of the fight. It was the way I loved to see him. And a true heroine and a good wife just had to know when to keep her mouth closed. But I couldn't. Not completely.

"Suzannah!" I told Todd. "You must tell her that you're going to start production shortly. You must. She's completely dispirited. When I've spoken to her on the phone she told me she hates the road, that she's dying to be back in Hollywood, that she's lonely and feeling really bad."

"Come on, Buffy. She'll last another couple of months. It's not good form to cancel out on bookings. And besides, if she comes back here, she'll be demanding to see the script . . . to see if Guy has more or better lines than she has. This way, it'll be a nice surprise for her. I'll just let her finish out in Vegas again, and a few engagements in the East, and I'll tell them not to book her anyplace else. And she'll call up and say why isn't she getting any new bookings and then we'll say, 'Surprise! Let's go for it, Suzie!' "

It sounded good. And I hoped it would all sound good to Suzannah and soon.

Swallowing the bile that came up with her throat, Poppy opened the door to her bedroom. She had to check that Suzannah was following the rules—she was not to touch the face or the arms, no part of Beau that might be visible to the world. And she was to use nothing that inflicted any serious mark or wound. The first time she had left the two of them alone, there'd been cigarette burns on Beau's thighs. Another time, she had confiscated a metal-tipped cat-o'-nine-tails from Suzannah's Fendi tote bag. Yes, Suzannah had become addicted . . . just as she had become addicted to the coke . . . just as Poppy had known she would.

Forcing herself to look now, she saw Beau spread-eagled on the bed, wrists and ankles tied down, his moans stifled by the gag stuffing in his mouth. Only his head moved from side to side as Suzannah stood over him, a rubber truncheon in hand, wearing only the black stockings and black boots that turned Beau on. Suzannah's hair was wild, matted with perspiration; her body glistened with sweat that dripped down from her onto Beau. She lifted her arm to strike again, invectives flowing from her mouth. Then as the stream of white milky fluid spurted from Beau in an arc, the barrage of filthy mouthings stopped and Suzannah's body convulsed in a series of shakes and contortions, as she screamed in torturous delight.

Poppy's own body sagged against the door jamb. She wanted to be sick in the bathroom but she had to wait. She had to drag herself across the room to the bed, had to hold back the aching tears she could not allow herself to shed.

"Now clean it up!" she commanded Suzannah, who rubbed her hands lingeringly into the sticky substance that coated Beau's thighs and loins, and then one by one, licked her fingers clean.

Yes, Poppy thought. Suzannah was almost ready. Ben, who had lusted after no woman in his life before, lusted for Suzannah. And she had promised Ben to deliver Suzannah to him—lock, stock and barrel —for a price: her and Beau's freedom. No more Ben and company. No more 50 percent off the top. It would be Suzannah who would have to ante up the 50 percent. Or would it be 100 percent, straight down the line?

55.

I got a call from Cleo at seven in the morning. She was hysterical. "I just threw Leo out of the house!"

I felt like cheering, but it was too early in the morning for such an enthusiastic response. Instead, I promised that as soon as my household got going for the day and the temporary nursemaid for Matty and Mikey arrived, I would be over.

"I was just sitting here waiting, you know. Things were pretty quiet. Sort of status quo. I thought maybe Leo was even thinking things over, maybe even changing his mind about a divorce. So I didn't do anything myself. I was still trying to shore things up, making sure Leo was comfortable whenever he was at home. And then I just found out what that worm was doing while I was just sitting, waiting for things to get better."

"What?"

"He's been seeing lawyers all along. Ten or twelve of them!"

"I don't understand. Why so many?"

"Ah! That's the catch. Why indeed?" her voice started to rise. "He was *interviewing* them! Ostensibly to engage one for himself. What he did was interview every top lawyer in the area!" She stood up, arms folded across her chest, waiting for my reaction. I was waiting for further elucidation.

"So?" I said.

"So?" she screamed. "You still don't get it, do you? Once Leo interviewed these lawyers, he shut them out to me. They're no longer available to represent me. Once a party in a divorce proceeding discusses a case with an attorney, that attorney can no longer represent the other party. And that fucking worm made sure to discuss the case with every top divorce lawyer in town, so all that's left for me are the shleps and the incompetents! And all this time he's been staying in *my* house, eating *my* cooking, accepting *my* loving care, letting me fetch and carry for him, even letting me carry the electric footbath full of hot water over to him while he sat there like a fucking king. Every night I massaged his aching neck while he was *cutting* my throat!"

This had to be the sneakiest thing I had ever heard of, even for Leo, even for Hollywood, I thought. "How did you find out about all the lawyers?"

"Some woman on Bedford called my mother in to sell her house. She was getting a divorce and was being forced to sell so they could split the community property. She told my mother this was what *her* husband had done. Interviewed every lawyer in town, so she was left with a second-rater. Otherwise, they might have found a way for her to hold on to the house. Then—wait till you get this—not knowing that my mother was my mother, she told her she had heard that the director, Leonard Mason, was doing exactly the same thing! The goddamn practice is spreading all over Beverly Hills! *It's a trend!*" Then Cleo smiled a little nastily. "Well, if Mother needed something to get her head screwed on right, this was it! She came hot-footing it over here right after she talked to that woman. She said, 'Cleo, if you don't want to lose this house you'd better find a lawyer quick!' " Cleo shook her head up and down. "I never thought I'd live to see the day—"

"So do you know whom Leo chose in the end, out of all those lawyers?"

"Yes, I found out. And do you know how? When Leo came home last night I was waiting for him with a knife!"

"Cleo!"

"Yes, I was. And I took him by surprise and I held it against his throat. And I said, 'Talk to me, Leo. Tell me who your lawyer is and start naming every lawyer in town that you spoke to—' He talked all right! He turned the color of pea soup, let me tell you, that son of a fucking bitch! And my Mother, bless her little mewling heart. Let me tell you she's singing a song of another color. She's lucky I didn't take a knife to her throat too."

"Cleo!"

Her face was ugly, distorted with venom. "It was the best thing I did in years. To watch Leo squirm. And squirm he did, the worm."

"So, *who* is his lawyer?"

"Lee Philips . . . Suzannah's Lee Philips."

I thought about that a moment. "Well, that's good, Cleo. Look at what Lee Philips did to Suzannah. Maybe he'll do something like that to Leo."

"Yeah, but Leo won't care. As long as he keeps me from getting my money he won't care how Philips shows him up. And Philips *did* win Suzannah's case for her, didn't he? He got her her money. That's all Leo will care about."

I wanted to make her feel better. "Oh, Philips didn't get her nearly what they asked for. A paltry sum, really."

"How much?" Cleo's eyes pinned me to the sofa.

I knew the amount would upset her. "I can't say. I promised Suzannah. But it was minimal."

"But think what I could have gotten with Philips on *my* side. Suzannah didn't have much of a leg to stand on. She *had* committed adultery and they weren't married much more than a year. By rights *she* shouldn't have gotten a dime. I've been married to Leo fifteen years! I have two children, and everything Leo's accumulated has been accumulated while I've been married to him . . . helping him every goddamn step of the way. I should collect not only for the past fifteen years, but for the next fifteen years too. Where would Leo be without me? My God, the things I've done for that man! Prostituting my integrity! Besides, look who Heinie had representing *him*. Million dollar lawyers, a whole firm of them. And everybody knows those Texas lawyers are sharper than anything L.A. can come up with—"

"Cleo! If Leo talked to all the good lawyers in town and that means you can't use them, how about those million dollar Texas lawyers? If they could legally represent Heinie in L.A., then they could represent you too, couldn't they?"

A murderous gleam appeared in each of Cleo's eyes. "Of course they could! But of course! But they must charge a fortune. Heinie could afford them, but can I?"

"Of course you can. Their fee is awarded on top of your settlement. It will be Leo, in the end, who'll have to pay them, one way or another, won't it?" I could not help but smile smugly, with satisfaction.

And Cleo smiled back with equal malicious satisfaction. "Since it was Leo who shut me off from the L.A. attorneys, it won't be any more than he deserves. And that will only be the icing on the cake."

When I looked askance, she led me upstairs to her bedroom.

"I threw Leo out last night. He wanted to pack his things but I said no, that he had to get out immediately or I was going to kill him, that as soon as he had a place, I'd send his things over. And I will, as soon as I gather them all up—"

She flung open her bedroom door. All over the floor were Leo's things—his jeans, dinner jackets, tennis rackets and tennis clothes, books, manuscripts, papers, even bottles of shaving lotions and after-shave colognes—all torn, ripped, cut, broken, shredded and smashed.

When I repeated the whole story to Todd he laughed in all the right places until I got to the part where I advised Cleo to hire Heinie's Dallas lawyers. Then he said, "I don't think you should have mixed in . . . given her advice."

"Why not?" I took umbrage.

"Because in a divorce case outsiders shouldn't mix in. You're taking sides and I don't think we should do that. We should remain neutral."

"What are we supposed to be—nations or friends?" I asked resentfully.

"That's just it. We *are* friends . . . of both the husband *and* the wife. That's why we have to stay out of it."

"You're wrong. In a divorce case you always end up taking sides.

And I know which side is the right side. And you know too. For years you took a position on our friend Leo's character and behavioral problems. And suddenly, you don't know who's right and who's wrong? Suddenly, you can't take a position?"

"I *am* involved with Leo professionally. That has to make a difference, Buffy Ann, and if you can't see that, you're being extremely short-sighted."

"What's the matter, Todd? Is there a vocabulary problem in Hollywood? Does integrity suddenly spell short-sighted?"

I got into bed, way over on the edge of the king-size. It was pretty far over from the middle. I was all choked up. What had happened to the position of heroes on damsels of distress? Cleo might not be a damsel, but she certainly was distressed.

We had had *almost* fights over the years but we had never gone to bed mad. It looked like another first for Southern California.

But Todd got into the bed and moved himself past the middle, way over to my side.

"Scarlett honey, ah sure love to see those emerald green eyes flash when you're mad—a prettier sight ah never did see."

Relieved, I giggled. "How can you tell in the dark?" And I knew he would tell me. Still, I knew the difference between integrity and Scarlett and emerald green eyes.

We finally agreed that we would try and remain as neutral as possible in the case of *Mason* v. *Mason*. Then, only a couple of days later, Todd said that he wanted to go to Reno to see Beau Beaufort live, and that Leo would go with us. He wanted Leo to see Beau live too.

Both Beau and Suzannah had engagements in different hotels there, and Todd tried to soften the blow of Leo's joining us by saying, "Of course we'll visit with Suzannah too."

"If we're supposed to be neutral, how come I'm stuck with Leo so fast?"

"Business, Buffy, business. I'm going to have my secretary make a reservation for us this weekend."

I sighed. "All right. But we don't have to share our room with Leo too, do we?"

Todd managed a weak smile but I don't think he was amused.

56.

"I'm sick and tired of everything, Poppy. And I don't like Reno any better than Vegas or Tahoe. I don't know what I'd do if we weren't following the same schedule on the road. I want to go back to Hollywood." Suzannah started to cry. "Oh, if only I hadn't lost Heinie. Heinie wouldn't have let me wither on the vine."

Poppy recognized the symptoms. It was the morning-after blues, the big coming-down. Suzannah would be moaning for her little tootsky, as she so charmingly put it, in about two minutes. She'd take bets on it.

"Well, what do you hear from your boy Todd? It's he who's keeping you out on tour, you know."

"Oh, every time I speak to him on the phone, it's the usual 'patience, patience, patience, Suzannah.' " She lay back on the chaise, holding her head. "Give me a little tootsky, Poppy darling, pu-lease."

"In a while," Poppy said curtly. "You'd better do some serious thinking about what you're going to do. You're sick of Vegas; you're sick of Reno, Jersey, and Wichita. And your big daddy King there keeps giving you crap for answers. He's been saying 'shortly . . . soon . . . patience' for months now."

"Buffy told me they're coming up to see me here in Reno. Maybe he has something to tell me now."

"He's going to tell you shit. Not like Ben—"

"Ben?" Suzannah asked irritably. "I've been dating him like you asked me to, but outside of a few presents, what the hell has *he* done for me?"

"It's not what he's done for you—it's more like what he *could* do for you. Don't you know Todd King is small potatoes next to Ben? Even your ex big-daddy, Heinie, is small potatoes next to Ben. Ben and his friends, people like him, are really the ones who control the Industry. They're the movers behind the scenes. They're the financiers, for one thing. Don't you get it? They're bigger money-men than the Wall Street Crowd. They control everything!"

Suzannah shook her head as if in a daze. "Really? But Ben's never said anything like that to me—like now. He came here to Reno, but still, he doesn't *say* anything."

"Why should he? The way things are now? Ben's a man who wants total commitment."

Suzannah thought about it for a second. "I'll think about it later. But now, can I please have my little tootsky, Poppy darling?"

"All right," Poppy got up. "But you'd better do your thinking quickly. You get old quick out on the road, Suzannah, and we're going to Jersey next with all that humidity, and then back to Vegas. The desert heat . . . the desert winds. All that sand blowing around. It's hell on the complexion."

They both knelt at the coffee table. Poppy's long tapered fingernail cupped a tiny bit of the white powder, but she held it away from Suzannah.

"I'm going to hype Ben for you, Suzannah. I'm going to go all out for you. But of course you have to do your part. *You're* going to hype Todd King for *me.*"

Suzannah was looking at Poppy's fingernail. "But why do you want me to do that? Todd's been stalling me, and you *already have* Ben as your friend?"

Poppy hesitated, bringing her finger a little closer. "Yeah, but Ben won't do for Beau what he'd do for you. Beau and me, we're friends with Ben, but we don't turn him on. I bet I could convince Ben to move the moon and the stars for you. If I do that for you, maybe you could convince Todd King for me." She brought the fingernail that much closer. She laughed. "If nothing else, maybe you could seduce your old pal Todd into doing something for us."

Suzannah's eyes were on the fingernail as she said, "Oh, I couldn't do that. Todd is unseducible, straight as an arrow. And Buffy Ann's my best friend. She's always been my best friend, even when everyone else deserted me."

Finally, the fingernail was a quarter inch away from her nose. "No, Suzannah," Poppy whispered fiercely, "it's *I* who've always been your best friend." She thrust the nail at Suzannah's nostril. "Go!"

57.

Todd, Leo, and I sat at what seemed to be the very best table in the room along with Poppy Beaufort, Suzannah, and Poppy's friend, Ben Gardenia. Although Ben was only a visitor in Reno too, somehow he had managed to become our host for the evening although that certainly had not been Todd's intention.

Todd and Leo were concentrating on Beau who was dynamite on the stage, I had to admit that. He pranced, jumped, shimmied, and shook with an exciting animal sexuality. Then, when he sang his romantic ballads, there was a silence in the room, and hard as it was for me to believe, several women in the audience were actually moved to tears. And one of them was Poppy Beaufort herself. When she saw me looking at her, she smiled almost sheepishly. "I did that the first time I heard him sing . . . years ago." It was the first time I saw those hard eyes cloud over. "I forget sometimes how sweet he can sound, like a honey bird calling out."

And then when Beau cakewalked off the stage for the final time, she got up to go backstage herself, her face closed. I almost wondered if I had only imagined the tears, the words. Then I was distracted by the sight of Ben's hand gliding smoothly down Suzannah's bare white arm, up and down, stroke after stroke after stroke, along Suzannah's bare white back. I remembered Heinie Muller doing much the same thing not so long ago. But Ben Gardenia was no Heinie and I hoped Suzannah realized that. She was smiling but almost as if in a daze; the smile rather disoriented, it seemed to me.

I shivered with goose bumps. Suzannah turned to me, almost as if she felt my goose bumps, and she smiled at me entreatingly. I yearned to put *my* hand on hers and reassure her. *Todd is planning a wonderful picture for you, a picture in which you'll dance and sing and laugh and cry . . . a picture that's going to be the greatest vehicle for a female star since* Gone With the Wind.

Tentatively I started to reach out my hand but I pulled it back with a shudder of revulsion. *His* hand was already there, the tanned hand with the black hairs sprouting on its back. And the moment passed.

We were back in our suite at the hotel and I was already packing up our things for a quick getaway in the morning. Once I had been anxious to leave L.A. to go back to Ohio; now I was anxious to get back to L.A. from Reno. Everything was relative.

"Did you speak to Poppy Beaufort about the movie?"

"Not really. I just felt her out. She's hot for it, I know that. But I can tell you, I don't savor the prospect of doing business with that she-tiger."

I thought of her tears when Beau was singing, "I wish ya coulda loved me the way I hadda loved ya—"

"Maybe underneath that glossy hard finish there's a pussycat."

"No way. I bet that's one pussy lined with broken glass."

I laughed complacently. "So when will you take her on?"

"Soon. I think she knows we're *mildly* interested. But we'll let her simmer awhile. I won't say anything absolutely definite until I have a contract ready for her signature. Then I'll negotiate quickly, if I can. Frankly, I don't want to give her that much time to perfect her bargaining strategy."

"And did you say anything to Suzannah? She seemed spaced out to me."

"Isn't our Suzannah always spaced out? She's booked into Atlantic City for a few weeks, then it's back to Vegas. And then it'll be all over. She'll be through with it all for good. We'll positively be ready to start production by then."

He had been saying that for so many months. It seemed to me we could have erected two shopping centers quicker than it took to get one movie off the ground.

"Are the Beauforts heading for Atlantic City too?" It seemed strange to me that wherever Suzannah went the Beauforts were sure to follow. "Surely they wouldn't stay in Vegas for the summer months? It's so hot. Even with their home, it still must be uncomfortable."

"I think they're going to Jersey too."

I wondered where Ben Gardenia of the traveling hands would be. Surely, no high rollers were in residence in Vegas during the summer heat, and I was sure Ben was always with the smart money.

I had packed everything except for our robes and toiletries, and the clothes we would wear to leave in the morning. I had packed my diaphragm too, but had left out the sheer black nightgown and net hose and lacy garter belt I had purchased that afternoon in one of the stores in the hotel's arcade. Maybe if I started another one of my very own projects tonight, I would beat *White Lily* into production by a couple of months, and surely I would finish months ahead.

Todd was out on the terrace staring down at the gaudy lights. I went out there to present myself in my showgirl ensemble, confident of an enthusiastic reception. And I found it. I looked up at the Nevada sky, dark tonight and starless, then down at the Reno neon. Still, I thought, tonight could be the start of something good.

58.

Beau was sullen in the elevator going up to their suite. He had wanted Suzannah to come back with them. Poppy bit her lips, explained that Ben and Suzannah had business to discuss.

"I don't give a shit for their business," he said meanly, almost viciously.

She was startled, and realized something. She herself had changed, but for some reason, she had kept on thinking that basically Beau had remained the same—that despite all the success and the adulation and all the drugs and all the kink, he had remained the sweet, foolish, good-natured boy she had known since she was fifteen.

She was the one who was the fool.

She slipped her hand into his waistband, put her lips to his ear. "Remember back in the old days," she whispered, "when we used to drive home in the pickup." She cupped his testicles in her hand, squeezing them gently, and looked into his eyes for a response.

He turned to her, his face surly, and with a sudden flash of intelligence, snapped, "Shit, Poppy! That was a fucking long time ago." And his innocent blue eyes looked old and weary.

Oh God! Was it too late? She had received such good vibes tonight from King! She had liked what she'd seen in his face when he was watching Beau onstage. And she had Suzannah all set up. With that one push from Suzannah, it could all happen. And if they went to Hollywood, gave up the tours and all the crap that went with it, kind of started all over, why maybe it could still be the way it *could* have been, instead of the way it was.

When they were inside the suite, he stripped off his clothes on the way into the bedroom, threw himself down on the bed, waiting for her to come to him, to do for him what Suzannah had learned so well to do.

Determined to do it differently this time, Poppy donned a short pink baby doll nightie. "Remember when we used to play you were the stranger in the house and you were going to rape me?" She smiled sweetly, enticingly.

"I don't remember," he said stubbornly, the angry child.

"Sure you do!"

"No!" Then he smiled cunningly, as a child might. "I might remember real good if you gave me something—"

She hesitated but then went into the bathroom, opened a large case that was a miniature safe, and took out two Quaaludes. After he swallowed them, she waited a few minutes, then feigning fright, she said: "What are you doing in my house? You're not going to rape me, are you? Oh, please don't. Please don't rape me!"

He was supposed to say, "Oh yes, little girl. I sure am going to rape you!" That's how the scenario used to go, a long time back. But now he said, "I sure as hell ain't going to rape you, lady. You're going to rape me," he said, determined. Then his voice turned abject, whiny, "You're going to rape me, aren't you?"

Furious, she climbed on top of him, sat astride, jamming him into her, cracking him across the face as hard as she could, back and forth, back and forth, slapping him until she felt and saw the bright red welts form on the pretty baby face. At the sight of the red welts, she became even angrier, and she smashed into his face with her fist, over and over again until she felt him spurt into her, until she felt as if she herself were about to explode. And she did.

Then, his sweetness temporarily restored, and bleeding from the corner of his split lip, he inquired softly, "Why are you crying, Poppy?"

59.

Cleo and I were having lunch at the La Scala Boutique, one of the places on her list of favorite luncheon spots. I knew she actually had such lists written out and filed. Best Places for Lunch. Best Places for Dinner. Best Places for Late Supper.

No reservations were taken for lunch, and we were waiting for a vacant booth. The booths in the window, rather than the tables out on the floor, were the sought-after seating, and Cleo was getting impatient. Pierrette, the charming hostess, held up a finger to Cleo and smiled, indicating that Cleo must be patient—she played no favorites but if she did, Cleo would certainly be one of those favored.

By the time we slid into our booth, the very one Cleo wanted—she told me Suzanne Pleshette sat there every Saturday lunch—I had a brilliant idea.

"I know what you should do, Cleo! Become a professional party-maker for people who need help giving their parties. You could do it for them at home or make the necessary arrangements at restaurants. You'd do weddings, luncheons, whatever it was a client needed. You could utilize all your talents—decorating, food, flowers, and your general humongous organization abilities. You could really have a career!"

"Oh, Buffy, I'd love to. I really want that for myself, but I can't do it now."

"Why not?"

She perched her Porsche sunglasses on top her head. "Because I can't go into court and testify that I can earn a living. They're getting tougher and tougher on women in the courts. The male judges are leaning over backward to be fair to men." She laughed shortly. "That's what the liberation movement has done for us—getting us a screwing in the courts. Before, if you'd been married for even a few years, you got supported for life or until you were foolish enough to get married again. But now, all you have to do is look like you could go out and wash dishes for a living and you can forget all about support. And if you're *already* in the work force, they'll probably make you support your ex-husband, the son-of-a-bitch. No, I have to look as unprepared to make a living for myself as a five-year-old kid."

"Wait a moment. There *is* community property. You *are* going to get half of everything, aren't you?"

"You bet! Half of everything Leo isn't able to hide, that is."

"And you are going to get child support?"

"You better believe it!"

"So then, why do you need alimony? Wouldn't you rather take half of everything you and Leo own, take the child support, and then be independent? Wouldn't you really rather have a career? Earn your own living and be proud, have self-respect?"

She smiled at me mischievously, her eyes sparkling. "I would like to work, but I can't. And it's my pride and self-respect I'm thinking of. If I don't get alimony out of Leo, if I don't stick it to him every way I can, I might never be able to look a mirror in the eye again."

Then the smile evaporated and she said, tough again, "Community property is for the past years. But how about the future? How about all the money Leo's going to make in the future, including the big bucks he's going to get for *White Lily?*" She stabbed her chest with a forefinger. *"I've* already done the work for Leo's future, paved his way with my sweat and my labor. All that dirty work, all that blood—my blood —spilled." She shook her head. "No, Buffy, I can't let him off the hook with all his skin intact!"

She stuck a large forkful of the gourmet salad into her mouth, chewed furiously on the strands of cheese and salami and bits of lettuce as if they were made of iron. "It's easy for you to talk, Buffy. You've got Todd and there isn't one chance in hell he's going to do to you what Leo's done to me. I mean, Todd just bought the beach house for you in the Colony and he put it in your name—"

I was amazed. "How did you know that?"

She looked a bit shamefaced. "I was curious and I asked Todd. Just for my own private store of information. The point is—you're never going to go through what I'm going through. You're never going to suffer through my humiliation, my rejection, and shame. You're never going to know what it feels like. But if you did, you'd know—you don't feel like rolling up your sleeves and earning your own living. All you want is every goddamn cent you can squeeze out . . . you want to pick the bones clean. All you're after is blood!"

I bent my head to my chopped salad as Cleo called out for another glass of white wine. For years I had wanted to see Cleo stand up to Leo and be counted as a real human being, but I had never wanted to see her turn into a vulture.

60.

Cassie spied on Win through her binoculars as he worked on the box hedges that lined the pink castle's uppermost terraces. She herself stood inside the den, behind her French doors, so that he would not see her watching him. She had known, she told herself, that he would be back . . . even if it was only for weekends. He had not really forsaken her.

It was all nearly over anyway. She saw Guy only about once a month, when he stopped by to pick up something or other, at which time she kept out of sight. He usually left a check for her on the kitchen table, sometimes bigger than other times, and sometimes smaller. It didn't matter to her. When there was less money she and Jenny ate eggs instead of fish, or just the vegetables she raised now in back of her house. If there was enough money left over, she paid the electric and gas bills, and if there wasn't she just sent them over to Guy's apartment without comment. A couple of times she was left without electricity and she lit candles. She had enough clothes for herself—she didn't go anywhere that she needed to be dressed in the latest fashion and she had learned how to sew for Jenny.

She assumed that Guy was still making the payments on the house, since nobody appeared to dispossess her. She supposed that he wasn't going to take a chance on losing their valuable piece of property now that the real estate in their area was doubling in value every year.

Since she no longer took the daily newspaper, she hadn't even known that Guy's latest picture, in which he played a private eye, had opened and was a big success. Buffy, who visited every once in a while and told her the latest news, was furious with her. "Don't you even watch TV? They review movies on some of the channels, you know."

Then she had to tell Buffy that her TV was on the blitz and she had never had it repaired. And then Buffy had offered her money. She had refused. She had thought that Buffy didn't understand that it *wasn't* just her pride, it *wasn't* that she didn't want to ask anything of anybody, not of Win, or her mother, or Guy, or even her dear friend Buffy. But then Buffy said something that showed she *did* understand, did have an idea about what was going on in Cassie's head.

"You can't hide away, Cassie. And you can't hide Jenny away either. Both of you can't go on living like this in some kind of a secret fairy tale. The world *will* come in on you. Guy will impose himself on you, somehow. Or your mother will get sick and you'll have to acknowledge that she might die before you show her that you were right. And Jenny, she has to go to school soon, has to go out into the world. Time is creeping up on us. Things change. People change. Maybe Win will marry somebody else and then where will you be? No happy ending to dream about. What happens to the fairy tale when there is no happy ending?"

She had no answer for Buffy that time so she just smiled at her. And the next time Buffy came she gave her the news that the preproduction work on *White Lily* had actually started, so there *was* a happy ending in sight. And she had been right all along. And now, a matter of months, and it was all over. It would be "See, Mother?" and "Bye-bye Guy," and it would be a happy ending with Win. It wasn't too late. If Win had really given up on her, he wouldn't be up there on the hill at their pink castle clipping the boxwood hedges.

She saw him cut a few pink roses and go into the house. Was he going to put them in water? Maybe he was going to surprise her and bring them down the hill to her?

Jenny came over and pulled at her skirt for attention. "Mommy, play with me."

"One moment, Jenny," she said. "In just a few seconds, Jenny darling."

She wanted to see if Win was going to come out of the house again . . . if he was going to resume his work with the clippers. Or if he was on his way down the hill, pink roses in hand. In a few minutes, disappointed, she put down the binoculars. Apparently, he wasn't coming out of the house again and neither was he going to ring her chimes.

61.

I had talked Suellen into coming to lunch with me, to actually leave the Valley and meet me at the Bistro Garden. We spied two of Nancy Reagan's friends at lunch at a nearby table—Betsy Bloomingdale and Jerry Zipkin—and that immediately soured Suellen's mood. She was still very political in her thinking and that gave me an idea. Lately she had complained how busy the studio was keeping Howard, and that he wasn't spending nearly enough time with her and the children at home. What Suellen needed was something to keep *her* busier than she was.

"Why don't you get into politics, Suellen? I mean *really* get involved. Run for something. Get started on a local level. You did work for that rent-control thing. That should give you something of a base—"

"And what do I do with my children?"

"Well, they're not babies anymore. Becky's nine and Petey is what . . . fourteen? You better start thinking about the empty nest syndrome."

Suellen blushed, smiled faintly. "Actually, I *have* given it some thought. But I wasn't thinking about politics. I was thinking more along the lines of a catering business . . . something I could do from home where I could still keep an eye on the kids and run my house. I mentioned it to Howard."

"And?" I prompted. "What did he say?"

"He thought it was a wonderful idea. He thinks working would make me a more fulfilled person. He always says that anybody with my energy should have more outlets."

"Howard's right."

"*You've* got a lot of energy, Buffy, and you haven't gotten very involved with the studio. Maybe you'd like to think about coming into a catering venture with me? I'd do the cooking and you'd handle the business end."

"Oh Suellen, I'd really love to do it if I weren't . . . pregnant."

I watched Suellen's face cloud over with something akin to anger. "What is wrong with you? What are you thinking of? Anybody with four children who even thinks about a fifth child at your age should have her head examined."

"What about my age? I'm not exactly ancient. I'll only be thirty-six when the baby is born. Women are having babies even into their forties these days. There are all kinds of tests now, safeguards—"

"But why? What are you trying to prove?"

"I'm not trying to prove anything! We have so much to give a child— Todd and I—our love, brothers and a sister, our good, happy home and certainly all the material advantages. It's the people who can afford it who should have the big families."

Suellen turned her attention to the menu, not looking at me as she spoke. "I don't know, Buffy. Sometimes I think you're scared, for all your brave talk. That you have each child as a lifeline—to make sure Todd is securely tied to you for eternity."

She turned her eyes from the menu back to me and said earnestly, "You must know by now that's not how it's done . . . I think I'll have the pâté. I'd like to see how they do it here." And then she smiled, and said sweetly, "Since you *are* pregnant, and you're not going to listen to your big sister's advice about a termination, let's order a bottle of champagne and drink to the new little King on the way."

I ordered the champagne but I *knew* Suellen was wrong. I wasn't trying to secure Todd more firmly to me. I didn't have to. We were as one—as much now, if not more, as we ever had been in the beginning. I wanted this child because we had promised each other this child! This one was for the one we had lost to the abortionist's knife in the early days, when we had to sacrifice the present for the future.

Suellen tasted the pâté with a scientist's palate. "Not bad . . . I think I detect brandy in there. But what kind?"

"Perhaps you could ask—"

"I think I'd rather experiment on my own. It's really very exciting. You'd be surprised."

"No . . . I think I understand the appeal—"

"Talk about understanding, Buffy, I'd like to understand what's going on with this picture? *White Lily?* Why is it taking forever?"

"That's the movie business, Suellen. But I think all the preproduction stuff takes longer than anything else. Once they start shooting everything will probably go more quickly and smoothly. Didn't Howard explain any of this to you?"

Suellen deliberately buttered a piece of the crusty bread and then bit into it and crunched. "No. I don't think Howard knows what's going on. He's trying to take care of *everything else* for Todd while Todd's completely engulfed in the movie."

I looked at Suellen sharply, ever sensitive to any implied criticism of Todd. "Of course Todd's immersed in this project. This is the biggest thing he's attempted since taking over the studio. And a lot is going to be riding on its success. Millions and millions before it's over."

We looked at one another, both thinking the same thing. But I wasn't worried. I remembered something Todd once said to me, something brilliant about not putting all your eggs into one basket. I was sure Todd was covering himself in some way, in some manner.

Suellen sipped at her champagne and stabbed at her salad, picking and choosing with her fork instead of eating whatever came up. Her deliberation of each morsel was slightly irritating. "Why can't you just *eat* like a normal person?" I blurted out.

Suellen lifted her eyebrows at me. "I hope you're not going to have a nervous pregnancy, Buffy. You never did before. It's bad for the baby."

I wanted to scream.

"And what's going on with Suzannah and Beau Beaufort? Howard said they're first drawing up their contracts. Isn't it awfully late for that?"

"Todd has his reasons. Besides they're both going to be back in Vegas in about ten days. Todd's going there then to get both of them to sign."

"And then?"

"And then it's go, for God's sake. What are you going to have for dessert? I think you should have both the strawberry tart and the mousse. That way you'll eat for both of us since I have to watch my weight. The doctor doesn't want me to gain more than fifteen pounds."

"I don't approve," Suellen said firmly. "That keeps the babies small. I think big babies are healthy babies."

"I'll be sure to tell the doctor that. That you said so." But I was thinking about what Suellen had said about it being awfully late for Suzannah's and Beau's contracts. Actually I couldn't have agreed more. And it bothered me. I had begged Todd to get them signed long before this, but he had kept putting it off, just not wanting to deal with it.

62.

Poppy knew the fucking signs only too well. After all these years when she should have been in the clear, finally, safe and clean, she had the syph again! Which meant that despite her keeping her eyes open twenty-four hours a day, Beau had managed to get away from her . . . had done God-knew-what without the benefit of the precautions she had tried to instill in his thick head.

She picked up a vase of flowers and smashed it against a wall, watched as flowers, pieces of porcelain, and water exploded. Well, it really was the end now. She was packing up—Beau, the guitar, and herself—and packing the road in for good. And without fulfilling the rest of the commitment too. She didn't give a shit about the remaining nine days. Fuck them all where they breathed! Let them sue her! She had Ben just where she wanted him, and she had Suzannah ready for delivery, and she was going to be free to go any goddamned place she pleased. She was going to make up for all the fucking years Ben had forced her to stay in Vegas. With, or without a movie deal, she and Beau were going to Hollywood. And she and Beau were going to be respectable. Beau was going to have a place in the community if it killed both of them. And his personal act was going to be squeaky clean.

And as for Todd King, he would come running soon enough when he heard that Suzannah wasn't completing her tour either, that she had fired the agent and manager he had engaged for her, that she was back in Vegas days ahead of schedule. Once she got him in Vegas, she would see what she could do about him. At one time her game plan was for Suzannah to seduce Todd, and holding that seduction over his head, she, Poppy, would wangle a contract out of him. But everytime she brought it up, Saint Suzannah protested—citing her great love for Todd and that fucking stuck-up wife of his who thought she was such a great lady her shit didn't stink! She probably could still have gotten Suzannah to agree to do what she told her. But who could tell whether she would have delivered? Coke heads were notoriously unreliable. So the game plan had been changed. She was buying her freedom from Ben with

Suzannah. As for Todd King, she would handle him herself. She *knew* she could depend on herself. After all these years, *only* on herself.

Poppy went to the phone. Suzannah was staying at the hotel two blocks away where she was appearing. All she told Suzannah was that she and Beau were leaving Jersey on the following day. She hung up and looked at her wristwatch. In about ten minutes, Suzannah would be pulling up in her limousine. Only a fool would leave the security of the luxurious hotel to *walk* the bombed-out Atlantic City Streets.

Suzannah was panicking at the news that she and Beau were going back to Vegas.

"But Beau's supposed to appear for another week—"

"I'm canceling."

"They'll sue you."

"Let them. Beau's a star and stars do what they want."

"But Vegas. It's over a hundred degrees there now."

"Oh, for a week or so we'll do just fine. We won't be anyplace that isn't air-conditioned."

"A week?" Suzannah was confused, as she so often was these days.

"Yes, a week. I'm leaving here, and then I'm leaving Vegas. For good. In about ten days from now Beau and I will be holed up at the Beverly Hills Hotel while I'm shopping for a house. You know what house I like? That one on Sunset with the statues . . . that A-rab mansion. It's boarded up but I think I'll buy it. And renovate it. Put in a sound studio, of course. I love it! Right on the Boulevard."

Suzannah was stricken. "Oh . . . that was my house!" she moaned. "Heinie was going to buy it for me. Those Arabs had painted it a sick green. We were going to make it white again. But Heinie said . . ." she tried to remember. "Heinie said it wasn't for sale."

"Forget Heinie. He divorced you, didn't he? And you know what Ben always says?"

"Ben? What?"

"He says *everything's* for sale . . . if the price is right."

"I think . . ." Suzannah's voice faltered, ". . . I think that's exactly what Heinie used to say . . ."

"Forget Heinie, we're talking about Ben. He's richer than Heinie and a thousand times more powerful. He can buy any goddamn thing he wants. And you're lucky. I think I can talk Ben into marrying you."

"Marry?" She wasn't at all sure she wanted to marry Ben. Not sure at all. She didn't like his eyes. Heinie's eyes had been so soft when they looked at her. Ben's never were.

"Yes. I think he'll marry you if you move fast enough. And then you'll be able to tell everybody to go to hell, including Todd King."

Suzannah's eyes opened wide. "But Todd's my friend. He and Buffy have always looked out for me."

"Yeah? What's Todd done for you except string you along? Where's the movie he promised you? The only time you've been in Los Angeles was for that one week engagement at the Amphitheater months ago. *I'm* your friend, Suzannah. Haven't I been taking care of you?"

"Yes . . ."

"And now I'm going to really take care of you. I'm going to talk Ben into marrying you and then Ben will take you to Hollywood and really make you a star. Not just talk about it, like your friend Todd. And probably if you want that A-rab mansion, Ben will get it for you."

"But you said you wanted it—"

"Oh, yeah, but Ben has so much more money than me. Billions. He could easily outbid me."

"But what about the rest of the engagement here? My agent . . . my manager . . . They'll be furious with me."

"Fire them! Look, Suzannah, I'm leaving tomorrow. Do you want to go back with me or do you want to stay here alone? *All alone?*"

63.

Todd called me from the office.

"I'm leaving for Vegas immediately. Will you pack a bag for me and send it over?"

"Why the urgency all of a sudden?"

"I just got a call from Reilly. It seems Suzannah walked out on the Palace in Jersey. She's fired Reilly and she's fired Max Hanft too. Reilly says she's off the wall. So I'm flying out there with her contract. I hope it will calm her down. And I'm taking the contract for Beaufort along with me too. I can't put that off any longer either. I'm not looking forward to wrangling with Poppy the killer lady but I'm really worried about Suzannah. I guess I didn't play it right after all. You were right. I should have given her the goddamn contract months ago."

"And what about Poppy? You're going there with a contract without saying a word to her? What makes you so sure she'll want Beau to make this movie?"

"She's dying for it, I can feel it. And the contract calls for enough money that even she won't argue. I'm paying Beau more money by far than Suzannah or Guy are going to get—*he's* the superstar. But at the same time, I can always get another country singer. It's Suzannah I'm worried about. I think her nerves are shot. Maybe you want to come with me?"

"I would but I promised for weeks now to take the kids to Disneyland. And the date's set for tomorrow. And I'm taking Jenny too. I finally talked Cassie into letting her out of the house. And Petey and Becky are going too. Megan and Petey are going to be my helpers. But you'll do fine without me. And listen, Todd, don't try to talk Suzannah into going back to Atlantic City. Just bring her back with you. We'll put her up for a few weeks until she's as starry-eyed as ever—"

Famous last words.

Todd called from Vegas a few hours later, and as I picked up the phone I had one of those premonitions.

"Suzannah's married!" Todd blurted out. "She married Ben Gardenia."

"Oh no!"

"I'm afraid so."

"And the contract? What happened with her contract?"

"It's signed. Gardenia looked at it for a second and told Suzannah to sign."

"A second only? How strange! I would have thought a man like that would have argued over every clause."

Todd laughed hollowly. "You'd think so, wouldn't you? I think he's made it very clear that contracts don't mean much to him. And that means trouble. I can't tell you how sick I am about this . . . about Suzannah marrying him. If only I had listened to you—If I had given Suzannah her contract a while ago I have a feeling she never would have married Ben."

"Well, don't blame yourself. Suzannah's a big girl. She should know whom she wants to marry. Have you seen Poppy Beaufort yet? Has she signed Beau's contract?"

"I'm going over to see her now. She's expecting me. Suzannah is going with me. It seems Ben has another appointment. He's going to Jersey. So it will be just little me with the two of them. Wish me luck! I've got a splitting headache already. By the time I'm through with Poppy Beaufort, I'll probably be ready for brain surgery."

"Poor baby. I'm sure Suzannah will help you with her."

"Suzannah? I don't think Suzannah can help anybody. She acts like she's already had brain surgery—a lobotomy. Frankly, Buffy, I'd give anything right now to drop this whole thing. *White Lily*, Suzannah, Guy that fucking egomaniac, and Poppy and Beau Beaufort! I must have lost all my nuts and bolts to ever have started this project—"

"Drop it then!" I said urgently. "Drop it this minute!"

"I can't, I can't. We've already got too much invested. And Guy's contract is play or pay."

"So pay. You always told me you have to know when to take a loss—"

"Too much, Buffy . . . too much. It's too late now."

"Call me later. Call me after you've seen Poppy. And give my love to Suzannah. And I guess you have to give her my congratulations too."

"I won't call you tonight. It'll be late. And you have a big day tomorrow at Disneyland. I want you to get your rest. You have to sleep for two now. Forget about everything, will you? What the hell? It's only money . . . *I think,*" he laughed. "Everything will be all right, I'm sure. I'm just a little unnerved at the thought of having Ben Gardenia on the set, in spirit, if not in the flesh. And facing Mrs. Beaufort right now. But it will all be okay. Goodnight, Buffy. Sleep well. I love you, Buffy Ann."

He hung up.

I love you, Todd.

64.

Poppy watched Todd and Suzannah as they sat in her living room. She wanted to laugh but was careful not to. They were both so quiet. She guessed that Todd was still pretty shaken up by Suzannah's marriage to

Ben. Was it concern for Suzannah? Or was it just that he knew that he'd now have to deal through Ben? She shrugged. It didn't mean shit to her now.

She knew what Suzannah wanted. She was just waiting to get her, Poppy, alone for a couple of minutes to ask her, to beg her for something, anything, a few pills—uppers, downers, anything at all. Suzannah wasn't particular anymore. But she had never had the guts the whole time to get her stuff anyplace else. She had relied on her good friend Poppy. And of course, she had made it easy for her. Well, that was all over now too. Now she could ask Ben for whatever she wanted. And she'd see how far she'd get with him. Fat fucking chance! Ben had no use for druggies, in any form.

Todd handed her the contracts. And she looked them over quickly and signed all the copies with a flourish. Then he gave her one for herself and put the others away in his briefcase. *Over!* And goddamn fucking *easy!* She couldn't believe how easy! She hadn't had to do a fucking thing herself.

"I guess this calls for a drink," she said. "I usually only drink wine myself but you name it. I got *everything!*"

Suzannah perked up for a minute but looked around, at Todd, and asked for Scotch dispiritedly, and slumped down in her chair again.

Todd shook his head. "The desert always gives me a sinus headache."

"Is that a fact?" Poppy said. "Me too. And I've lived here for years. But I got a sure-fire cure. You take a shot of vodka—it opens up the veins, and then you take this wonderful sinus pill my doctor prescribed. I don't ever take anything that's not prescribed by my doctor. Well, in a couple of minutes you're only dreaming you had a headache. You want to give it a try?"

Todd smiled tiredly. "Sure. Why not?"

He couldn't feel any worse than he already did. At least the worst was over. Strange as it seemed, she had signed the contracts without a murmur. She hadn't even argued over the money.

He had thought she would want to have her lawyers look it all over. Why hadn't she? But his head hurt too much for him to think about it. He was just grateful it was over.

"I'll give your remedy a try."

"Good." She picked up her contract and got to her feet. "I'll go get the pill." She'd lock her contract up in the safe. It was her most precious possession . . . beside Beau.

She passed through the bedroom to go to her dressing room where the safe was. She smiled at Beau, sprawled on the bed, knocked out on the sleepers she had given him before Todd and Suzannah arrived. He looked sweet lying there, all the dirt of the day gone. He looked like a young boy. An innocent young boy. "It's all over now, Beau. We're going to the land of milk and honey."

She opened the safe. She couldn't believe it had all happened without her doing one fucking thing, except for marrying Suzannah off to Ben. The timing had been perfect. She had married Suzannah off to Ben and had received her papers of independence. There was no way she was going to wait before signing Todd's contract. Anything could happen overnight. It was all a volatile (she had just learned that word and liked it) business. All these volatile people . . . Ben, Suzannah, and not least of all, Beau. And the word was that King was straight anyway.

No, she hadn't had to do anything else. She hadn't needed Suzannah to give Todd a push; she hadn't needed to try and seduce Todd herself once he rushed to Vegas to Suzannah. Not that she was at all sure that would have worked anyway. But it had all fallen into her lap.

The 'lude she was going to give Todd—a dead ringer for a sinus pill was just for the hell of it. For fun. As she put the contract on the shelf, she spotted the gold Suzannah perfume flask she had snitched from Suzannah years and years ago. She thought, *why not?* For the hell of it. Tomorrow she would go to the doctor to get her first treatment for the syph she had so recently contracted. Why not go out in a blaze of glory? Fix Todd King's snooty wife and play one last joke on Suzannah. Was one 'lude and one shot of vodka enough? Two 'ludes, she thought. So good for the libido and how about a couple of drops of the colorless liquid she had stored away and had never used? *Sheet!* Beau had certainly never needed that kind of dreamwalking. A passé drug, these days. But excellent for Todd's vodka. And as for Suzannah, it probably wouldn't take much for her to fly, and then pass out. And Suzannah wouldn't need anything for the libido. Nope. All old Suzie had to do was fly high, pass out, and remember nothing tomorrow. Old Suzie wasn't going to do any fucking tonight. Only she herself and Mr. King were going to do that. And tomorrow morning when Suzannah and Todd woke up together, neither one would be sure about what happened, and what didn't, about who did what to whom.

Just for good luck, what else should she throw into the pot? *Sheet!* She couldn't make up her mind. Her fingers played over the goodies. *Eenie, meenie, meinee, mo . . . catch a sucker by the toe!*

Leah unpacked Todd's bag as I got a few things ready to send to the cleaner's. She removed Todd's beige cashmere sport coat and viewed it critically, rubbing at a brownish stain on the collar.

"Give it to me, Leah, and I'll put it with the things for the cleaner."

She muttered something and threw it over. Automatically I went through the pockets. *Suzannah's gold perfume flask.* She must have given it to Todd to hold for her at some point. Maybe they had gone out for a drink after he had finished up with Poppy? I put it away in a drawer. I'd return it to her when she and her new husband came to town. They would be arriving within the week.

65.

She had her contract, she had her new husband, she was moving into the sheik's house on Sunset Boulevard, shooting was starting on *White Lily*, and Suzannah wished only that she could smoke an opium pipe and forget her nightmare. She thought longingly of the days in New York with Paulie, he who had massaged her feet after each long day and kissed each toe. She thought longingly of the days with Heinie who always laughed and wanted desperately everything she wanted. If she said she was thirsty, *Heinie* salivated and would have moved mountains to get her a glass of something cold, something clinking with ice cubes.

And Ben . . . Ben didn't give a damn what she wanted; he only knew what *he* wanted, a beautiful ice maiden, a mannequin perfect of face and body that he possessed. How could he look at her with eyes so cold and want to possess her so hotly? How could he make her promenade the room naked, back and forth, back and forth while he viewed what he owned, and then so unceremoniously take her, not caring, completely disinterested in her response to him? He would order her to lie down in the bed, run his hands over her body as he would a cold, perfect gem, and then look into her eyes and tell her to turn over. And as he worked himself into her, doing only what he wanted, she would press her face into the pillow and dampen it with her tears. *Oh, Heinie, Heinie!*

What fun they had had. Heinie had wanted only what she wanted, and she used to insist on riding him. She would sit astride him, yelling, "Giddy up! Giddy up, horsie!" and Heinie would love it as much as she did, because *she* liked it that way! And they would both laugh so much. And afterwards he would bathe her and kiss her. Why had he deserted her and left her to the mercies of Ben . . . Ben who slept with a *revolver* under his pillow! And every time she buried her face in that pillow and wet it with her anguish, she imagined she could feel *it,* cold and hard. And she felt it, *not* under her face, but between her thighs—its icy stub digging into her . . . into her warm, moist innermost recesses.

If only she could have *something,* she thought, she would be able to bear it. But it didn't help to beg Ben—"Give me, get me a little tootsky, Ben . . ." as she had begged Poppy, that bitch. He wouldn't even let her have a drink. No, he wanted her to be perfect and pure, but only for himself. And she thought she was going to go crazy. What good did it do her to be a movie star, to be part of the movie set, and live in that big house on Sunset if she was going to go crazy . . . and get screwed every night by a snub-nosed, gleaming, silvery hard, cold gun?

As soon as she could she would have to tell Todd and Buffy, tell them all about Ben and the gun, about the nightmare and they would help her. Buffy and Todd, they wouldn't let him go on doing this to her, would they?

66.

We moved into our new beach house for the summer even though it was something of a trek for Todd to go to Hollywood every day. Now that *White Lily* was finally in production, he was buried in work. And he was working even on Saturdays and Sundays when everyone else at Malibu was going out to brunch. But it was good to be there, peaceful and almost other worldly. Leah was with us, and a young college boy to help with the boys, watch them on the beach and swim with them. Megan had promised to help out there but it was hard to keep a thirteen-year-old at home with her brothers when there was a whole new beach world out there, with tennis lessons, horseback riding, and other giggly teenagers in bikinis to hang out with and watch the bronzed surfers go by. She had become quite a flirt and I was only grateful that she didn't seem to be attracted to our own serious college boy. That might have been a problem.

They were lovely days, with Suellen coming to stay, and even Cassie who visited with Jennie in her car that was almost a relic. And Cleo came too, giving me the latest on her divorce, a blow-by-blow description. And it was Cleo who told me there was trouble on the set. No sooner had they started shooting, she told me, than Ben had placed Suzannah in a sanitarium.

I couldn't believe it! Todd hadn't said a word! And neither had Suellen!

"How could you not tell me?" I demanded of Todd.

"Because I didn't want you upset. Like you are. Look at you. You're shaking. You have to think of the baby."

"Of course I'm shaking. What's wrong with Suzannah? I want the whole truth."

"Ben said she had a drug problem. And he said he tried to deal with it himself but he couldn't. It seems Poppy Beaufort had been supplying her with whatever she wanted."

"Poppy? Oh, my God! Do you think that Ben's telling the truth?"

"I don't know. Poppy says it's a lie. She said Ben must have been giving her stuff. To make her dependent on him so that she would marry him. Poppy says she had no idea that Suzannah was an addict. But I should have known. We saw that she was acting funny. We should have guessed. But I was so goddamn preoccupied with the movie that I was blind!"

"We were both blind! Don't blame yourself. I want to go see her. Where is she?"

"In Palm Springs. But Ben says we can't see her. I guess she's having some kind of nervous breakdown too."

"Do you believe him?"

"We have to."

"But what about the movie? Have you shut down production?"

"No. Not yet. We just started. I'm trying to shoot around her."

"How long will it be?"

Todd shrugged. "Ben says maybe a couple of months."

Now it was *Ben says*.

"Can you afford to wait for her? Maybe it will be longer."

"I have to, Buffy. We have to. I feel responsible. I was insensitive to her needs."

I gripped his hand. *"We* were insensitive to her needs. You're doing the right thing!" I was so proud of him I wanted to cry. He was putting Suzannah before the picture, before the money, before the studio. I was so proud and I loved him so much I could have died of love.

And I prayed for Suzannah that night, as hard as I did for the children and Todd and for the baby inside me.

67.

I went in to town to go to the obstetrician, and then his office called and asked that I come in again, that they needed to take some test or other. Todd insisted I drive in with him, and then busy myself until he called it a day and we would drive back together. A lady in my condition, he said, shouldn't have to brave the terrors of the rush hour on the Pacific Coast Highway alone.

They took some blood and asked that I come back in a couple of hours. I wandered across the street to Neiman Marcus, bought a few things for the children, but the store reminded me of Heinie and I grew depressed.

Dr. Harvey appeared troubled, seemed to find it difficult to tell me exactly what it was that was bothering him. Seeing how troubled he was, I grew apprehensive and I tried to calm myself by calming him. "Oh, come on, Doctor, it can't be that bad."

"A complication, Buffy."

"Okay. Tell me."

"It seems you've contracted syphilis."

I laughed. "Hey, is that what's bothering you? Then it's all right, because your lab made a mistake."

"No, Buffy."

I wasn't amused anymore. "Yes, Doctor. Your lab made some kind of mistake, and I think it's awful. Scaring the hell out of you!"

"Buffy, there's no error. We took the test last time you were in, and we received a positive report. That's why we called you in today. We took samples again and we sent them down to the laboratory in the building. They made several testings."

Still, nothing registered. There just a lot of mumbo-jumbo going on in my head.

"Look, Doctor, there's a missing quotient here. I understand they've outlawed the theory about toilet seats so I don't see how—I don't go to bed with an assorted variety of—"

He picked up several sheets from his desk. "Look, Buffy. Here's the results of the first test we did. And here's the results of the test we did today. If you'll look, Buffy, you'll see—"

I wouldn't look. I stood up. "I don't feel well, Doctor. I think I want to go home."

"You'll have to face it, Buffy. You'll have to accept it, so we can do something."

I sat down again. I remembered the gold perfume flask in Todd's jacket pocket. "Excuse me, Doctor, but could I vomit?"

One of the nurses escorted me to the ladies room, and stayed with me. But when I came back, Doctor Harvey was still alone, waiting for me. He wouldn't go away. I sat there a couple of minutes while he gravely watched me. I found it difficult to breathe. Finally I realized I could not but accept the word of a perfectly good obstetrician who knew more about these things than I did. Hadn't Cleo assured me that he was the top obstetrician in all of L.A.? Obstetrician to the stars, Cleo had said. And what did *I* have to dispute his word? Seventeen years of total absolute love and total trust? What did that mean in the ninth decade of the twentieth century in Los Angeles, California?

I tried to picture Todd's face exactly the way it had looked when he returned from that visit to Las Vegas. What had been hidden there that I had failed to spot? He had been pale, had said he hadn't felt well. I had urged him to see a doctor. He had said he would when he had more time. What else? I tried to conjure up his face again. But I couldn't. It was as if he had died and I could no longer bring his face into focus. But I was wrong. He wasn't dead. It was I who was dead, and the child that I carried—marked for death. Todd King had killed us both.

"I'm a dead one," I muttered.

"What's that?" Dr. Harvey said.

"My Aunt Emily had a phrase . . . 'I'm a dead one.' "

Dr. Harvey was losing patience, I thought, "No, you're not dead, Buffy. You're hysterical. These things happen."

To other people, not me, the lucky one, Doctor. It's never happened to me before, honest, Doctor.

"We'll have to make a decision, Buffy. There's several—"

"Hold it, Steve. You don't mind if I call you Steve, do you, Doctor? That's your name—Steven." *And you're not about to be my doctor for long, are you?*

"Just cut it out, Steve. No vacuums, please. No saline solutions. Just cut it out!"

"It may not be—"

"It *is!* It's absolutely necessary to do it my way. I want to go to the hospital right away. And make it Cedars, Steve! It's definitely *au courant.* See if you can get me a suite. Make sure I have the best room in the house. I always get the best. My husband taught me that."

He smiled sadly. "We'll have to call and see—It's not a hotel."

"And see if you can get me an open-end deal. I'm not sure how long I'll stay."

My children were safe in Malibu. They had Leah, and Robert who excelled in swimming. He was Olympics material, they said. And Megan *was* thirteen. She should be a help to Leah. I might just decide to stay on at Cedars for the summer.

A white-faced Todd collapsed on my bed. I *assumed* he was white-faced. I would not look at him. He was a stranger . . . an alien presence not of my world. "Did you sign up for your treatment?" I was thinking of never looking at him again. "I wouldn't want you to go home and filthy up the toilet seats that my children use. My goodness. Syphilis, of all things! Why not, at the least, herpes? At least that's all the rage, so much more *au courant!*"

"Buffy, I blacked out! I have no recall!—"

I snickered, still facing the wall. "Surely you can come up with a more original scenario? You used to be so creative. Perhaps if you and Leo put your heads together—"

It didn't matter what he said. As they say, he had lost his credibility. I covered my head with my pillow. Then I removed it and looked at him. I thought I would so that I would be able to remember his face at this moment later. But it was too much. "Rule, Todd King! You may never speak to me about this again! Ever! If you're allowed to speak to me at all." And I turned to the wall again.

There were going to be other rules. I had the rest of the summer to figure them out. And I didn't have to talk to him or look at him if I chose not to. I was dead and the dead had certain privileges. They were entitled to peace, for one thing. And the right not to hear any more fairy tales from strangers.

I rang for the nurse. When she appeared, I asked her to have the weeping man in my room removed . . . bodily, if necessary.

"I'll cancel the picture," he cried. "I've already closed down production today," he said.

I turned to him again. *I* could look at *him* if I chose. I was making the rules, and I could change them if I willed. "Oh no you're not! You're going to have to live or, if necessary, die by that picture! Rule number two! *White Lily* lives!"

You're not going to get off that easy—just wiping the picture away!

"You can't do this, Buffy! You can't destroy everything we've had over something that happened when I wasn't even—"

"Out!"

"You can't break up our marriage! I love you!"

I turned back to the wall and finally he allowed the nurse to lead him away.

Love me, he said. If he had studied poetry instead of Accounting, he would have known the line—*You always kill the thing you love.* Or something like that.

As for me breaking up our marriage, he was wrong about that. And it had nothing to do with his lame story about blacking out! The incredible nerve of that story! First he kills me and then he insults my intelligence! But I had no intention of breaking up anything, unless it was the knife that I was going to break off in him, by twisting it and twisting it and twisting it . . . for the rest of his life.

Cleo had stayed with Leo because she wanted to hold on to her marriage for marriage's sake. Cassie had stayed with her husband in order not to admit to her mother that she had made a mistake. Was revenge any less valid?

Yes, this marriage would go on. As far as anyone knew. As far as anyone knew Buffy Ann King still lived. Oh yes. There would be someone who resembled Buffy Ann King, driving Sunset Boulevard, walking the streets of Rodeo Drive. No one would know that it was really Buffy Ann of the *Walking Dead,* of the movie of the same name.

When I was through being smart-assed with myself, and vengeful and hysterical, I thought, *Oh my God, what am I going to do with the rest of my life? How can I live without him?* All the sweetness had gone out of my life, and no matter what happened, no matter what, ever or never, it was never going to be the same . . . it was never going to be worth anything ever again. If I had loved less, I would have hated less. If I had loved less, I would be able to go on.

PART FOUR

Winter
1981–1984

68

I went back to Malibu to finish out the summer while Todd stayed in town and came out only on weekends to spend time with the children. (He advised me that he had been treated for syphilis, still protesting his knowledge of the details—where, how, etc. I would not listen to these protests.) Out of all the members of our household, only Leah and Megan took note of any change in me. And they both assumed that it was due to the despondency I felt over the loss of the baby and reacted accordingly. Leah didn't grunt at me nearly as much and made me nourishing things to eat and Megan stuck closer to home, helping Leah and trying to cheer me up. She told me that it was all just as well—that her friend Saltie (the family name was Pepper) said that I was too old to have a baby, anyway—that it would have been an embarrassment to the rest of the family. I knew she meant only to make me feel better.

I busied myself walking the beach and compiling a long list of Rules for Todd and me to live by. There was to be no personal conversation of any kind. He was allowed to talk to me only about the children, the house, Leah, and about business in as much as it affected me. He was not allowed to speak of Suzannah unless it was in terms of *White Lily,* the production of which was *not* to be halted. I had died, in a manner of speaking, in the making of that movie, and he, too, now was to live or die by it. I knew that this was a challenge that he couldn't back away from.

And he was very definitely not allowed to bullshit me. I would not tolerate one more word about passing out, blackouts, about his waking up with a headache and a passed-out Suzannah in the same room. (Surely this was one passed-out body too many for any sane person to accept.) And I would not listen to how he had wakened with vague feelings of apprehension, about not being sure what was the truth or what was fantasy. Fantasies were for his films. And I added "liar" and "fraud" to the list of things I called him daily in my mind. A charlatan: he whom I had worshiped and adored for millions of real and intangible reasons; he whom I had admired and respected for his honesty and strength under fire.

He was not to interfere in, or speak of, my personal life, and if he inferred that this meant that *I* would be messing around, that was all to the good. The more *he* had to live with, the better. But actually, that was the furthest thing from my mind. A corpse didn't mess around. *He* was free to do whatever he wanted in that department, so long as it did not become public knowledge and embarrass me or my children. All he had to be was discreet.

I ordered two sets of queen-sized beds to replace the king-sized ones in our Malibu and Beverly Hills homes. It would not do to have separate rooms, not with so many inquisitive kiddies who had grown up with the fact that Mommy and Daddy shared the bedroom. Not to mention Leah. *That* was one of the major Rules: the children and the outside world, including my sister Suellen, were not to suspect that there was anything wrong with our marriage. To the outside world, we were to remain as one.

I knew what he would say when I said he was free to do whatever turned him on. He would swear that he had no intention of doing anything with anybody. It didn't even matter whether or not I believed him, for I knew that it wouldn't be the sex that he would miss the most. He had been an orphan-child, after all, and it would be the lack of warmth of our marriage, I knew, that would freeze his cheater's heart until it cracked. And *that* was exactly my intention.

There would be other Rules as we went along. I hoped to be as creative as Todd, or Leo, for that matter, had ever been, and I would include new Rules as they occurred to me.

As for Suzannah, I would speak to her and allow her to speak to me when the occasion demanded it. I had no intention of letting her know that *I* knew. That would have been another petty humiliation on top of a great humiliation—possibly the humiliation of the century. But in no way, of course, would I act in a friendly manner toward her; correct and polite would be my tone. That would cover most situations. I certainly had no intention of ever being alone with her again since I might then be tempted to rake her face with my nails, pull her red hair out by its roots, kick and stomp her with my most lethal stiletto-heeled shoes. (I had a dream one night where I took a knife, thrust it into the creamy skin of her throat, and split her clearly down the long length of her elegant torso until I reached the filthy core of her existence where I went on a rampage and tried to cut it all out—mound, clitoris, lips—completely, just as my baby had been excised.)

But that was my subconscious. Awake, I tried to check these kinds of thoughts. I *would not* be one of those women who blamed the other woman. Suzannah had only vowed to be my friend; it was my husband, my soul mate, who had sworn to be my everything, who had taken my life after I had delivered it up to him, and had sworn to treasure it forever. She was only a thief; he was a murderer. And furthermore, she had never been what anyone would call a great person, while he had been a hero . . . king of the universe.

We went back to Beverly Hills after Labor Day, and we all picked up the threads of our lives and went on. Megan and Mitchell went back to school and friends; Matty was enrolled in a nursery school and I stayed with Mikey at home. Leah and I resumed our usual relationship—I spoke to her and she grunted and we argued back and forth about my hiring extra help, which I wanted to do, and which she still would not allow.

Todd went to the studio day after day, and each day came back to a family dinner, gay with childish chatter, looking more chastened and more tiredly resigned than the day before. After dinner, after the children went to bed, there was mostly silence as I made sure to retire to a different part of the house. If there was something he had to say about the set, some little crisis to relate, I was glad to listen, making no comment, offering no advice. Instead, I started a log for *White Lily*, intended as a diary of disaster. On the very first page was listed Suzannah's defection to the sanitarium in Palm Springs. More, I was sure, would follow and I waited.

We still went out a lot, upon which occasions we would put on our best smiles for the people, and if Todd's smile became a worn, thin thing, that was *his* problem. As for myself, I laughed a lot, and flaunted my ever-growing wardrobe of a more opulent and extreme fashion than I had ever worn before. I was acquiring what could be called a Hollywood-style collection, which meant more Rodeo Roadish than high couture.

I was also busily buying up a large part of the inventories of the jewelry stores in Beverly Hills. I didn't wear any of the pieces very much. I showed them to Suellen who gazed at me askance, and only said, "A wise man once told me that when there was a possible financial problem pending, and possibly bigger financial problems on the far horizon, the wise person buttoned up his purse and waited for another day to do his shopping."

I didn't ask her what financial problem she was envisioning. I did ask her who the wise man was, and she answered, "Todd King." So I made sure to show him my loot too. His only remark each time was that the piece was beautiful—the ruby ring, the diamond and emerald necklace, the gold and diamond bracelet—whatever. And then I put away most of the pieces in the bank vault, waiting for another day.

And then I realized that Todd too was just waiting for another day. He was waiting for my pain to recede and fade. He was counting on my needing him, wanting him, not being able to resist him—as I never had been able to resist him before. He was waiting for some kind of reconciliation, until gradually, we would become *almost* what we had been before.

But my new role in life was to disenchant him of this theory. He should have really known better. We had been living an idyll and Todd should have known that once the spell was broken, an idyll could never be again.

69.

I saw less of Suellen these days. She had gone ahead and started a catering business on a small scale working out of her home. She took orders for cakes, pastries, and special desserts for hostesses who wanted a special touch not available in commercial outlets, and she was enjoying herself hugely. Pink-cheeked and whistling, she bustled about her kitchen. I was pleased for her and pleased that she no longer had either the time or the inclination to lecture me on the dangers of living in Hollywood and environs. Victim now of the Hollywood syndrome, I no longer had the heart to defend the Southern California life in the fast lane.

Cleo came over every once in a while to keep me informed on what was happening with her. She had settled Phase One of the Dissolution of the Marriage—the financial part. So far, she had gotten exactly half of what she and Leo had accumulated; she had received fairly respectable child support and alimony for herself for a period of five years. And it seemed that with the money part settled, much of her resentment had dissipated.

I waited to see what Phase Two would constitute and I found out. "Sex!" Cleo cried. "Getting laid is very relevant to people in our age group. Even if you're getting it on a regular basis as a married lady, you will agree with me—sex has a top priority, right?"

Wrong, Cleo. Sex is not a top priority. Revenge is!

I wondered how Cleo had gotten over her revenge stage so quickly, but the answer to that was simple: the more you loved, the more you lost when you lost it. And the more you lost, the more vengeful you became. And Cleo's loss could only be described as minor when compared to mine.

"So what *are* you doing about your sex life?" I asked.

"Oh, I'm finding it out there."

"Where?"

Cleo giggled. "For years and years I've heard about singles' bars, swingers' clubs, places like that. Well, now I'm experiencing the phenomena."

"You mean you're going to those Roman bath things too? You're picking up men and sleeping with them? *You?*" I asked incredulously.

"But it's perfectly respectable these days. And nobody's inviting me to many dinner parties where I can meet any eligible men, I can tell you. Oh yeah, I still get invited to these big cocktail things but if you get right down to it, these big cocktail dos are no different from going scavenging in singles' bars. At these parties, *everybody's* scavenging, working the crowd, hustling, looking for a connection—sexual, professional—or merely social climbing. What's the diff? At the bars and swing houses, it's just plain sex. Or sex not so plain."

I laughed now that I had gotten past my initial shock. After all, I was a much more sophisticated woman now than I had been a few months ago. "It's just hard for me to picture you, the perfect wife, doing this . . . *scavenging.*"

"Well, all I can say is if it's relevant sex you're looking for, the bars and the swing houses are just the place to go for it. You get the cream of the crop!"

I must have appeared doubtful because Cleo quickly said, "It's true. If it's only sex you want, then it's performance that counts, okay? At a dinner party you're sitting next to a guy who's somebody *else's* leftover mashed potatoes, and if you go home with him, that's exactly what you're going to get. But if one of those guys are out there in a singles' place, they'd better know that they can perform. They're putting it on the line. If you pick them and you go back to their place and you find out you've wasted your time, it's *their* face that's red, it's your turn to laugh, and the next time you're both in the same place, it's you who gets to nudge the woman next to you and say, 'Get him! He can't even get it up!' And *you* get to snicker and sneer. Don't you get it? It's what men have been doing to women for centuries. So if the guy's out there, chances are you're getting a live one. And besides you get pretty bikini underwear, a freshly shaved face, and a freshly washed body, redolent of L'Homme Terrific. He's all pumped up and plumped up, looking like an ad for I'm Hot, I'm Sexy, I'm Raring to Go. Try me! And what do women going to bed with their husbands get? Yesterday's shave and yesterday's shower and limp dicks! And besides, husbands always think they're doing you a favor. Leo always acted like he was bestowing a magnificent gift upon me. And didn't care whether he pleased me or not. Out there you get more equality. He's anxious to please. He's not a great lover unless he makes you poop!"

I had seen many phases of Cleo Pulitzer Mason by now and I didn't like this one best. Not by far. I hoped that soon there would be another one for me to choose from.

"What about your mother?" I asked. "What does she have to say about all this? Or haven't you told her?"

Cleo's eyes rolled in merry anticipation of what she was about to say. "Oh, I didn't tell you about Mother, did I? She's not paying too much attention to my life lately. She has a boyfriend! A live one! One of my Dallas lawyers. He's about sixty-five but really cute. And rich. And he's taken quite a shine to Mother. He says he's tired of chippies . . . that's his word . . . and he respects a woman who's both handsomely mature and self-supporting. Besides, Mother *was* a lawyer back in the olden days, as my kids say, so they have something in common. Well, anyhow, the Duke—that's what he's called—has his own plane and a ranch just outside of Dallas—just like in the series—and he's been flying Mother back and forth. And the wonder of it is Mother's really crazy about him. She says she wants to take him off that unhealthy cowboy food and feed him some California health salads. I think Mother's practicing to become the housemother superior of this Rancho Grande in Dallas and is redecorating it in her head. It'll be just like the old days in Tenafly—the big house, the gracious living—everything attuned to success, only this time—Texas style. And you know what she said to me? 'See, Cleo? See what happens when a woman keeps herself up, doesn't let herself get bogged down and depressed, and keeps herself ready.' " Cleo reached down into her chest and came up with a throaty bass, "Hot and ready."

We both went off into peals of laughter and I thought, "Oh my God! Life *is* a movie! No, not a movie. A soap opera!"

I saw Cassie only infrequently, and I no longer questioned her about what was happening with her scenario. I had commiserated with her for such a long time and advised her, to no avail. And now I had my own scenario and my own obsession. She didn't mention Win at all so I surmised that she wasn't seeing him, and she didn't mention Guy so I assumed she wasn't seeing much of him either. And I knew *he* was being kept pretty busy on the set since they were trying to finish every scene that didn't include Suzannah who was still in Palm Springs at the Percy Institute.

70.

Suzannah sat listlessly in her nicely appointed room at the sanitarium waiting for Ben to take her home. She no longer craved coke, alcohol, or even a cigaret. She craved nothing, not even starhood or fame. She had only one screaming desire—to stay away from Ben and his gun. And the only emotion she felt was terror.

Ben had not been to see her since the day he had brought her to Percy to be made physically perfect once again, or at least by his perceptions. And she had wished only that she could have the strength to violate her own physical perfection so that he would never, ever, come back to claim her. And she had thought only about that.

So one night when Nurse Burry had brought her her sedative and given her a glass of water to swallow it with—Percy Institute did not use those little paper cups—she had broken the glass on the metal nightstand and raised it to her cheek, ready to slice it from the cheekbone to the chin, but she hesitated a moment before she did it . . . and the moment was lost. Nurse Burry had seized her wrist and squeezed it until she dropped the broken glass and sobbed something about a gun.

As a psychiatrist, Dr. Henry Percy knew that Suzannah was far from well, or whole, for that matter. But as owner of the very exclusive, very expensive Percy Institute, he had a problem reconciling that role with his position as Chief of Staff. If the person who paid the patient's bills relied on his, Hank Percy's, expert opinion, there was no problem. But if the payer of the bills was a man like Ben Gardenia who knew exactly what *he*, Ben, wanted, it was an awkward situation.

Hank Percy gave Ben Gardenia his evaluation of the patient's progress and prognosis. She was no longer subject to any physical addiction, indeed, no longer psychologically addicted to any foreign substance. But as for her general mental condition—

Ben cut him short. "You running a charity here, Doc?" which told Percy exactly what was what. He certainly could not detain Suzannah. Her fate was clearly out of his hands.

When a nurse came to help Suzannah dress in the clothes supplied by her husband—a peach lace-trimmed silk satin chemise, a French silk suit with exquisite tailoring, pumps of fine Italian leather—she found the patient sitting like a large, beautiful doll, staring out of big eyes, widened with—? The nurse couldn't find the proper word. Was it terror?

Ben had called in the decorators while she had been in the sanitarium. It was an alien place that they had fashioned. She and Heinie had talked of the home they would have: a real movie star's abode—white satin and white velvet, white plush carpeting, and big upholstered sofas and chaise lounges—a *real* movie star's home with lots of flowers and a great big whirlpool to splash around in.

Ben and his decorators had created a Medici museum. Ionic columns and pillars, black marble walls, marble urns, pedestals, and statues. Louis XIV fauteuils, cut velvet thrones, Flemish tapestries and hard chairs of burnished bronze, huge Grecian urns. Paintings and sculptures, a Roman sarcophagus in yellow marble. A panel-backed fourteenth-century Italian sacristy cupboard. All strange and alien. The master bedroom held religious art as its adornment. Religious art and a Spanish Renaissance bed completely shrouded in tapestry. It looked to her like a richly carved coffin.

It didn't matter. She lay down on the bed, a bed suited more for Cleopatra, or maybe Marie Antoinette, than for a modern-day movie star. But was she a star? Maybe she *was* Cleopatra, or even Marie Antoinette? Both had died premature deaths. Perhaps she too was already dead? Not dead enough, though. Ben, this moment, was in the dressing room, preparing to enjoy his possession, his trophy, as was his right. He owned her. Somehow, he had bought her. And she had not even known that she was for sale . . . nor had she known the price.

And all the people who could have saved her were gone—Paulie, Heinie . . . even Buffy and Todd. They had not come to visit her even once when she was in the sanitarium. They were mad at her. Mad at her for marrying Ben, and would not save her. And she couldn't blame them. They had been friends, the three of them, and she had introduced a new note into the circle of their friendship—an iridescent note of cold, blue steel. No, they would not help her.

She felt under the pillow to her right. Yes, it was there. Still there. Ben's gun. And Ben was approaching her. Would tonight be the night that cold blue iridescence would enter her, explode within her and blow her away?

71.

I was going to the set for Suzannah's first day back. It was not that I was eager to join in the general jubilation that she was again working. It was only that I had not seen her at all since I had gone to the doctor that fateful day. And it seemed important to me that I establish the relationship we would share in the future—that of polite acquaintances.

When she walked on the set, she seemed more lovely than ever. She was not the fresh dazzling eighteen-year-old beauty she had been when first we met, nor the flashy vibrant beauty that had been the Vegas performer. She was now a mature, true beauty in the classic sense. She was exceedingly slender but that only added to the air of vulnerability about her. She was excessively pale and thereby gained more delicacy. Her face *was* drawn but even that only served to accentuate the hollows and the exquisite cheekbones. And if her strange, amber eyes were clouded over with darkness and appeared deeper set, well, that was less in the tradition of the covergirl charmer and more in the tradition of legendary beauties. But lovely as she appeared, something vital *was* missing. I could not immediately put my finger on what it was.

The workers on the set—the cameramen and prop men, the gaffers and the script girls, the gofers and the wardrobe women—all gave her an ovation, clapping as if a vanquished heroine had returned triumphant. But in my bones I felt that this was a lie.

Like a triumphant queen, she turned to her multitude, from one to the other, a smile for each, a nod for this one and that one, a handshake. And then I realized what was wrong, what was missing. It was her radiance, that Suzannah radiance that had always set her apart from the crowd, even in her worst moments. She was now a magnificent, superb, exquisite, empty-eyed mannequin.

I was about to approach her to make my obligatory salutation and be done with it when her husband put a possessive arm about her and for a moment, her eyes registered *something.* And it was fear! I was sure of it. I turned away, sickened, until she called out to me. I turned back again, went over to her and forced myself to put my cheek briefly to hers, kissing the air.

"Glad to see you back in action," I said, as quickly and impersonally as I could manage.

She tried to detain me. "Oh Buffy, I never got a chance to say how sorry I was about your losing the baby. I—" she threw a look at Ben Gardenia, whose insistent hand was already leading her away. She smiled at me in a sick way, and her eyes . . . I couldn't quite believe it . . . actually *beseeched* mine. And then Ben led her away.

I was stunned. How dare she? How *could* she? Was there no end to her gall? *Beseeching me,* whom she had so terribly wronged? And I looked up to see Todd staring at me with an intensity that burned the air between us. What the hell did *he* want? Did he too have the gall to want me to be kind to his vulnerable, empty-eyed starfucker? The very instrument that he had used to destroy me?

Oh, for a second, I had to admit, I *had* wavered. When I had seen that look of fear in her eyes and when that hand of Ben's had come down on her arm, like a manacle of iron, and those eyes had looked into mine so entreatingly. I knew that I would have to steel myself not to fall into her trap again, not to reach out to her with words of warmth and reassurance. But when I saw Todd watching, I straightened up, in a manner of speaking, and I was strong again.

I left the movie set, leaving the film makers to their work. I got into my car, drove through the gate, turning right on Sunset, driving west, back to Beverly Hills, leaving Hollywood behind me. The human psyche was a strange thing, I reflected. For Suzannah, to whom I owed much less, I had less than a strong urge for revenge. Much as I fought it, I *had* felt a stirring of compassion. But for Todd, the more he suffered, the more suffering I desired for him. At the sight and smell of his blood, I only wanted more.

72.

Poppy saw Suzannah come back from the sanitarium clean as a newborn baby. No dope, no pills, no cigarets, not a glass of wine, not even a cup of coffee. Ben had her on decaffeinated herbal tea. *Jesus!* He was on the set, of course, day in and day out. And Poppy understood that. If you owned something valuable, you kept close watch over every little thing that happened to it. But Ben, at least, was getting to enjoy the fruits of his labor.

And she? It was worse than it had ever been—on the road or in Vegas. At least back there, there had been a respite. Beau had done his show for a couple of hours, and in between shows there had been some kind of a hiatus, a chance to keep pulling him back together. But the set was something else again. They were there from ten to fourteen hours a day. Even when Beau wasn't actually filming, they were on call and people came running in and out of their bungalow. It was getting harder and harder to keep Beau going and he was becoming more and more demanding, wanting more of everything, all of the things she had used to keep him in line all those years, more of it all. Even the goddamn burgers and fries. In between his time on the set, he sat there gorging himself. Now she had to add enemas to their nightly routine to rid him of all the shit he consumed. The bottom line was that he was getting completely out of control. Their big chance and he was going to blow it if she didn't do something.

They had it all now, everything within their grasp. The big house on Sunset only a few blocks from Suzannah and Ben, the house Leila

Pulitzer swore had been Rod Stewart's. The pool, the tennis court, the spa, and the sauna . . . even a bidet. And the house was just sitting there, waiting to be decorated the moment she had some time to call in a decorator. Oh, they were ready for the good life, but somehow it was still out of reach.

And what about Beau himself? Presley was gone. Joplin was gone. Jimi Hendrix, dead on his own vomit. Jim Morrison was dead too.

Rolling Stone had had his picture on the cover—*He's hot, he's sexy, he's dead* . . . Jesus! How many of the bastards were just wasted—their careers down the toilet? Unbridled, they had lost it all. Well, she wasn't going to let it happen to them, to Beau. Sweet Beau. She had to save Beau. Above all, she had to save Beau.

She told Todd King that she was taking Beau to that place where Suzannah had been—it was vital! And he looked into her face and saw that she wasn't just whistling Dixie, that she was talking to him straight. She had to hand it to him. He didn't take it too big. He just turned a little pale, and his mouth became more of a straight line. She thought then that he had changed some from that night when she had slipped it to him—but hadn't they all?

73.

When Todd came home from the studio that night, he asked to speak to me before dinner.

"Can't it wait until after dinner? After the children have gone to bed?" My own tone was businesslike.

"No. Now, please."

Very well. I would grant him the audience before dinner. Actually I was eager for this conversation—news of the production was one area of conversation I was willing to entertain, and one area that Todd was never eager to get into.

Still, it wasn't easy for me to have *any* discussion with Todd. It was difficult for me to look into his face, to see the pain in my heart mirrored in his eyes. Yes, I was still torn despite my resolution. Part of me wanted to see that pain and part of me couldn't bear it.

"Buffy!" he cried, all the anguish in him coming through in that one word. "Let me drop it! Let me cut the whole mess loose! Let me! I beg you—"

I knew he referred to the picture.

"What is it now?" Cold.

"Poppy Beaufort wants to take Beau to the Percy Institute. It seems that, like Suzannah, he has a drug dependency and she wants to do something about it before he proceeds with the movie."

I sneered. "But you knew that he was on drugs. Constantly. Everybody in the world knows. How could you not?"

He turned the color of bricks. "Of course I knew. But I thought it was just the usual Hollywood-Vegas thing. I thought once he was on the movie, she'd get it under control."

"And she hasn't. The Dragon Lady hasn't been able to perform this miracle for you so you want to drop the whole thing."

"It's no good, Buffy. And it's not going to get any better. No matter how you feel about me—about us—why do you insist on making me go on with it, destroying everything we've built?"

Because it was you who has made this bed. And now you must lie in it . . . even if it kills you . . . as it has already killed me. Production on White Lily *will go on!*

My voice was toneless: "You worked around Suzannah while she was away on her little vacation. Do the same thing with Beau. Now that you have Star Suzannah back, you can do all the torrid love scenes with Guy while Beau gets back on his untrustworthy feet of clay."

I was enjoying myself. I tried to think of more clever things to say.

"You won't give up then, will you?" he asked.

"No, I won't. Will you?"

And I waited while he struggled with it. It was very complicated. If he said he would give up on the movie, then he was giving up on me. If he gave up I wouldn't have any choice. I would have to walk away from him *completely*. The marriage would be over in its physical form too. We both knew it. It was the primary Rule I had established.

He shook his head. "You're a wonder!" he said with bitterness. "First you let almost twenty years of love and trust go down the drain because you lack faith. Did it ever occur to you that there's an outside chance you might be wrong and that I'm telling you the truth? That I really did black out from a sinus pill and a drink, and whatever I did with Suzannah still remains a mystery to me? That whatever I did do was never performed on a conscious level? Did it ever occur to you that it isn't I who has failed you, but rather the other way around? And now, on top of that, you're letting our future go down the drain because you insist I go on with the picture. Well, I will go on, and whatever happens, I guess we'll both have to share the responsibility, won't we?" He walked out of the room into the small dining room where the children were waiting for us to have dinner. And I was shaken by his words. *Was* it possible that I was wrong?

And then I remembered what Todd did best . . . he, the master of the spoken word. He had always made the impossible *sound* possible. He could always make any absolute *seem* wrong, and he himself larger than the universe. There comes a time when any fool, even a fool in love, had to use her own reason to decide what was truth and what was fantasy.

Later that evening I took out my log book and wrote: "Beau Beaufort leaves the production to go to Palm Springs for a drug cure. Production will continue as long as possible with Guy and Suzannah. Possibilities: Will Guy pull some stunt now? Will Suzannah be able to perform now that she is drug-free, clean as a new white sheet, as full of life as a department store dummy? Will Todd be able, after all, to pull it all together? To put all the pieces together?"

74.

Poppy felt a strange sense of freedom while Beau was at the Percy Institute with the doctors and nurses to help him and guard him. It was the first time in nearly twenty years that she had some time on her hands, and she knew exactly what to do with it. She would hire decorators to go to work on their twenty-three rooms. And no way was she going to use Ben's people either. For God's sake, their place looked like an upholstered morgue. She wanted everything cleanly modern: clean lines, clean colors, everything tiled and scrubbable. One thing she had learned was to keep everything surgically hygienic. Their kitchen would be as sterile as a laboratory. If anybody wanted to eat burgers and fries in *her* kitchen they could eat them off the floor.

And she wanted to join a country club so that when Beau finished this picture, he could get started on his golf right away. Or maybe tennis, if that was what he should be playing. And she had to get in with the right people. Get on those party lists she was forever hearing about. The A list—the Sinatras, the Pecks, the Stewarts, and maybe even the Cary Grants. And Dinah Shore and that Sara Gold Ross. Maybe Beau would turn out to be real good at golf, maybe he could even get to play in one of those celebrity classics. And she could start going to lunch at all those places where celebrities' wives lunched.

Only where would she start? She hadn't the vaguest idea. She knew only two people in town, really. Suzannah and Buffy King. And Suzannah barely spoke to her when they met. She guessed that Suzannah was getting her comeuppance from Ben and blamed her for getting her hooked on coke. She did feel a little sorry about that, but hadn't Suzannah had it coming? She had been so goddamned smug and superior. But maybe *nobody* deserved Ben. If she could, she'd try to think of something to help Suzannah. When she had time to think about it. But Ben? Who knew how to get away from him? She herself had, but she had lucked out.

No, Suzannah wouldn't help her get started in this town, even if she could. As far as she could see, Suzannah couldn't help a newborn babe. And that Buffy King wouldn't help her either. Buffy didn't like her. She could tell. And it wasn't that little incident in Vegas either when she had probably given Todd King a dose. He couldn't have told his wife about it even if he was of a mind to do so. He had been flying so high he didn't know what hit him. And even if he remembered anything about that night, she had arranged it so that later he would think it had been Suzannah, and not her. At that time she had thought it was pretty funny. She was sorry about it now. He was a pretty straight guy and Buffy King wasn't so bad either—a little cold but some people were like that. Well, it was all water under the bridge now, and no lasting harm done. Still, Buffy King wouldn't be her friend. They weren't the same type. Not like her and Suzannah. Jesus! She had *really* screwed Suzannah.

Hold on, Poppy. You do know someone who can help you. That Cleo Mason. The way she heard it, Cleo Mason knew everybody and everything in town and was a regular pro at social climbing.

75.

Cleo and I were at lunch, a new place on Little Santa Monica that Cleo wanted to try out. She tasted the slivered almonds with black olives and bacon quiche very, very deliberately.

"Not nearly as good as Suellen's quiche," she said thoughtfully.

"Hardly anybody's is."

"True, true," she agreed. "That's exactly what I think."

I showed Cleo the new pin I had bought that morning at Tiffany's. It was composed of jade and diamonds set in a surrealistic flower design.

"Interesting. But soon you're going to have enough jewelry to open your own shop."

I laughed depreciatingly. "Hardly."

"Leo always says that when the money's not coming in, that's the time to stop spending."

I looked up from my seafood medley. Was she referring to the studio? To the studio's trouble with *White Lily?* And where did she get off still quoting Leo? I took a swallow of wine. "Leo? Have you been talking to Leo lately?"

"Well, yes. He comes over to see the children."

"And you two are getting along?"

"Well, it's better for the children if we get along, isn't it? And now that the settlement's all done with, there's no reason why we have to go on squabbling, is there?"

"No. Of course not. You should get along for the children's sake. It's great that you are."

I stuck my fork into her quiche to taste it. Yes, Suellen's was decidedly better.

"But the last time I spoke to you, you weren't feeling that generous toward him. Has all that good sex you've been getting of late mellowed you out?"

Cleo smiled sheepishly. "I'm through with all that. No more bed-hopping."

"So quickly? What happened? Did you catch a little herpes?" I was only teasing but even to my ears that sounded a little too snappy. "Only joking," I hastily added.

"Buffy! That's no joke."

"What *did* happen?"

"Nothing really significant. I came home one morning after a long, hard night, and my kids were getting themselves ready to go to school, and everything was a mess. Esmeralda had quit the day before and Josh had burnt himself cooking an egg and Tabby was just sitting on the edge of her bed crying."

"Why was she crying?"

"I don't know. She wouldn't tell me. I was pretty depressed. The guy I had gone home with had a headful of pretty black curls and when we went back to his place, his rug fell off, and I caught him wriggling out of a girdle. A girdle, for God's sake!"

I tried not to laugh.

"And then I come home and see these two kids, nice kids too, whose father had walked out on them and was taking his girlfriends' kids to the zoo instead of spending more of his time with them, and here's their mother who's busy getting her bones jumped while her head's on so crooked she thinks it's fun to go scoring with jerks who wear girdles. And I think to myself, 'Hey, Cleo, maybe it's time you got your head straightened out instead of your cunt.' "

I squirmed at Cleo's language but I was excited. I felt like cheering.

"So what did I do? I hied myself over to the hottest new psychiatrist in town—Gavin Roth."

"That names doesn't sound *real.*"

"Oh it is. Gavin Roth could have only a real name. And what's more, he's the spitting image of Robert Redford!"

Oh my God! Now Cleo's playing the game.

"A psychiatrist who looks like Redford? Sounds too good to be true. But how good can he be, as a doctor? It sounds like his face would come between you and your therapy."

"I was afraid of that myself the first time I saw him. As a matter of fact, I *flashed* him!"

"Oh my God! You *didn't!*"

"Yes, I really did," Cleo smiled, a little proud of herself. "I did. But he completely ignored it. And the man was so good that I got over his face after the first thirty minutes. And I've been seeing him three times a week—"

"Wow! Isn't that a little excessive? I mean, you're still a fairly normal person no matter—"

"Exactly. That's why I can proceed so quickly. The sicker you are, the more time has to elapse, I think. But frankly, handsome as the good doctor is, I don't want to be one of these people who's in therapy for the rest of her life. He balked at first at giving me three hours a week. But I insisted. You know me. I can be very persuasive—"

"Especially when you're flashing—"

She laughed so hard that she choked on her wine. "I was referring to my verbal abilities. As for the flashing, it was only the one time, I swear. And he completely ignored it in the most clinical way. I guess it happens to him all the time. Anyhow, it was after the second session that I realized that I was screwing around not because I was so hot for sex but because I wanted to get even with my mother and Leo. And I saw that I could beat my mother over the head with ten guys that I laid, and she still wouldn't accept the fact that her little Cleo was messing around with dirty sex. And besides, she's so busy with her Dallas cowboy, she's finally let go of *me*. I mean, really. So what the hell do I want to mess around with her head for anyway? Whatever she did, she meant well, and that's the nitty gritty, isn't it?"

She sat back and reflected on that a moment. And so did I. What secret did Cleo possess that she could settle her mother problem so quickly, so easily, and without even a little bit of resentment left over? And Cassie—Cassie couldn't get over her mother problem even a tiny bit. Not even *that* much.

"As for Leo, well, it was ridiculous to go around promiscuously screwing because of Leo. I *had* to face it. Leo doesn't really give a good shit how many times I get reamed. That was what I had to get through my head. All Leo cares about is the money he gives me every month. And every time he writes a check, I'm kicking him where it hurts the most. I'm drawing blood each and every month. So in order to hurt Leo I don't have to go around screwing, demeaning myself, making a fucking whore out of myself. Boy! Was that a relief! Now I can pick and choose. I don't have to be compulsive anymore."

It was incredible. So much truth in two sessions with the head doctor. "Maybe you knew it all along? All by yourself without a psychiatrist?"

"I'm sure I did. But Dr. Roth brought the knowledge out. Made me realize exactly what I did know. And after the third session, I realized I didn't hate Leo at all!"

Now I was beginning to lose all respect for Cleo's doctor. *That* was a step backward, as far as I was concerned. It had taken Cleo almost twenty years to know that she *should* hate Leo.

"Dr. Roth made me see that Leo wasn't really the monster I was making him. Leo isn't a monster—he's just a jerk. He's a brilliant moviemaker but as a man, he's just a stupid, insensitive, egotistical, jerky asshole. And you don't *hate* an asshole, you just stay away from him."

"So now you don't hate Leo anymore. You're just going to take his checks every month and stay away from him?"

"For the most part. But Gavin . . . Dr. Roth . . . made me see that I should try not to be friends but to be *friendly.* For the children's sake. He's their father and the situation is already traumatic enough for them. So now when Leo does come over to pick up the kids or something, I have pleasant little conversations with him. As pleasant as I can bring myself to be."

"And what do you talk about?"

Cleo thought a moment and started to laugh. "He really *is* an asshole. Our house, as you know, is community property. And the court said I don't have to sell the house and split up the money until the children are out of the house, in college, or out on their own. But now with real estate prices so damn high, Leo's positively going crazy to sell the house and reap the profits. So the last time I spoke with him, he tried to persuade me that I really *want* to live someplace else. He said so slimily that I wanted to puke, 'Where is it written that Cleo Mason has to live in the pink house on Lexington Road? Is it ordained in heaven? Wouldn't Cleo Pulitzer Mason really be happier in a swingles condo in Marina del Ray?' "

"The asshole," I muttered. "And you didn't get mad?"

"No, I didn't. It *is* funny. That's the point. It's fun to watch Leo bowing and scraping trying to persuade me, oh so ingratiatingly. *Swingles,* indeed. I just told him that, much as I personally would adore it, I couldn't dream of being so selfish as to take Tabby and Josh out of school in Beverly Hills and drag them off to life in a swingles complex."

"And what else did Leo have to say? Anything about the movie?" I managed to slip that in, innocently enough.

"Yes. As a matter of fact, he said that the scenes with Suzannah and Guy are stupendous. He said he can't believe how good she is. He said that off the set, she's spaced out but that's what makes her so good on camera. She's able to absorb everything he tells her. It all sinks in, it's like she was starting clean, from zero, and is able to go to ten."

I remembered that look of fear on Suzannah's face when Ben put his arm around her and I had my own idea why she was suddenly so good on camera. It was that she found real life so unbearable, she was eager to escape that reality, and was thoroughly able to disappear into the role of the White Lily, escape into its fantasy.

But I didn't want to think about it.

"So Leo thinks the movie's going well?"

She looked at me sharply now. "I didn't say that Leo said *that* exactly. All he said was that Suzannah was superb, that she's turned into a real actress."

She looked like she was struggling with something she wanted to say . . . tactfully. "It *is* awfully hard to make a movie the way they're having to do it—first Suzannah gone for months, and now Beau. There's only so much working around you can do. And it's expensive, to say the least. But what does Todd say?"

I smiled, shrugged. "You know Todd. He doesn't like to talk about problems with the studio at home. He tries to protect me."

"I guess . . ." she said uncertainly. "Well, I didn't tell you *all* my news—"

"Tell me." I was eager now to be on another topic.

"Poppy Beaufort called me up. She wants *me* to help her get started in town on the right foot. She wanted me to recommend an interior designer, all the right clubs and organizations for her to join, only the best places. She said she wanted to join Hillcrest Country Club. Rather, she wanted Beau to join. She wants him to play golf there. She said she'd read all about it. And when I told her that Hillcrest was Jewish, she said, 'Well, Danny Thomas belongs. If Danny Thomas belongs and he's some kind of an Arab, why couldn't Beau? Beau's only a Baptist.' "

We both laughed and Cleo continued, "Then she said in the next breath that she also wanted Beau to join the California Club. I didn't want to get into that the California Club wasn't exactly a country club —that it was a club for nonshow business types, an old-line stuffy sort of place that would drop dead at the mere mention of Beau's name—so I just said that I didn't think Beau would feel at home there—that they didn't have a golf course and hardly any Jews at all."

"Oh, Cleo, you're too much! *Are* you going to help her?"

"I am! I'm making a big luncheon party for her at *my* house, since we're just starting to decorate hers. And I'm inviting everybody that's anybody in town. You're coming too."

"I am not!" I said quickly.

"Why not?"

"Frankly, I'm not all that crazy about Poppy, that's how come."
Even though it had been Suzannah who had committed the perfidy
. . . Suzannah and Todd . . . I would always somehow associate
Poppy Beaufort with the whole thing. She *was* Suzannah's friend and
they had all been there together.

"Well, I must say, that's not like you. First of all, she specifically
asked that you be invited. She said she'd like to get to know you better,
that she looks up to you. She thinks you're a great lady. And furthermore, how does it look? Her husband is the star in the movie your
husband is making."

I was starting to waver.

"Me a great lady? I'm only a small-town girl from Ohio." *A rejected
wife from Ohio.*

"Come on, Buffy. You know what she means. And Cassie's coming."

"Really? How did you talk her into it?"

"It wasn't so difficult. If you ask me, I think she's tiring of her self-
imposed role as princess of the ivory tower. I think she's lonely. I think
she wants to get back into the action."

So, even for Cassie, the fantasy, the hope is wearing thin. Me and
Cassie, we were both hopeless cases. It was all too much. The fantasy
and the reality. Where one ended and the other began. All I knew was
that I wanted the sweet love of my youth back and no matter how much
I yearned, and no matter how long I waited, it was never going to
happen. Not for me, not ever again. And I didn't think it was going to
happen for Cassie. Not anymore.

I heard Cleo say something about Suellen.

"What about Suellen?"

"Suellen's doing all the food. The catering. At first, she wanted to do
only the desserts but I talked her into doing the whole thing and even
hiring assistants. Didn't she tell you?"

Maybe she had. I didn't listen much to what people were saying these
days. My desolation was an island.

"You're *paying* her?"

"Of course. She *is* a professional now. Besides, *I'm* getting paid so
why shouldn't Suellen? In fact, I'm trying to talk Suellen into becoming
my official partner."

I *really* wasn't hearing people these days. *"You're* in business then?"

"Yes. And Poppy's luncheon is my very first project."

"But you said you wouldn't do anything to make money, not until your five years of support from Leo were up."

"But that was before Gavin Roth. Now I realize that it's silly to let that five years of alimony keep me from doing something with my life. It was self-destructive, that kind of thinking. Just for the sake of revenge. Don't you get it? The alimony and Leo are not worth five years of my life." Then she grinned. "Besides, Leo would have to go to court and prove that my business was actually making money. And one thing I learned from my years in Hollywood is that there's an awful lot of money a little creative bookkeeping can hide. My God, Buff! You should know that!"

But all I knew was that I didn't know much anymore. I didn't even know how fairy tales were supposed to turn out, anymore.

76.

Cleo's house looked lovely. It was full of flowers and huge plants, a veritable jungle. "The plants are rented," Cleo whispered. "If you want to know the name of the place where I get them, I'll tell you for free."

I smiled. "For free yet? I'm truly blessed."

"Don't get snide with me, Buffy King. Just circulate. And be nice to Poppy. Don't forget, she's really the hostess today. I don't mind telling you I'm charging her a small fortune. I *am* supplying everything. *My* house and *my* guest list. I decided that anytime I supply the guest list for the parties I throw for people, I'm going to charge through the teeth. It's like when you go to a doctor, you're not only paying for the visit, you're paying for his ten years at med school. And it took me over ten years to get these guest lists together. Am I right?"

"Without a doubt."

"Don't be snide. Go say hello to Poppy."

Poppy Beaufort looked radiant, her usually deadpan face was animated and her eyes had a new sparkle to them. I had seldom seen her in anything but black or white and today she had combined the two to the best advantage. She looked both happy and elegant. Like a chic Parisian. I remembered those Parisian women in the cafés . . . studies in black and white, like paintings . . . from my honeymoon. Then, I didn't want to think any more about my honeymoon.

Dutifully I went over to Poppy, willing myself to be more than polite, more than simply gracious. I would be *warm*. She was surrounded by her guests and seemed so delighted, as if her acceptance by this crowd was a surprise. She should have known that it really wasn't all that difficult—all you had to do was to be rich or famous, connected in the Industry, or be married to a rich or famous man. To be dressed beautifully, or to be beautiful, was only the icing on the cake. And Poppy qualified on all levels.

"Poppy!" I exclaimed and forced myself to put my cheek to each of hers, in succession. "How good to see you! What a great party! And how's Beau?"

And I felt a chill run up and down my spine. What do you do about a person to whom you have a natural aversion? And I felt guilty, trying to be warm and gracious, and knowing that I wasn't quite making it. But it was all right because she must have felt the same way about me. As soon as I pressed my cheek to hers, I felt her body stiffen, saw her smile follow suit, saw her eyes grow hard . . . wary. She had an aversion to me too. Whatever it took between two people to establish a friendship simply wasn't there.

I went to the kitchen to look for Suellen. But she didn't have any time for me. She was wearing a wash-and-wear blouse and skirt with a big white apron over all, her cheeks were pink, and she was in her element, dashing from the oven to the counter to check a large tray of lobster fingers. On her way back to the oven, she paused to peck me on the cheek and to taste a huge pink and white salad. She admonished a helper to dust a bit more paprika over its surface.

"What is that thing?" I asked. "I never saw a pink and white salad before—"

"Go be a guest," Suellen answered me. "Eat and enjoy yourself."

I picked up a chunk of something pink with my fingers and Suellen, my very own sister whom I had brought from Ohio to this position of authority, slapped my hand.

"Go in the other room."

"Very well, I'm going. You don't have to get violent. Will you be coming in later to say hello?"

"I don't think so," she said. "I'm not a guest, I'm a working woman."

Properly put in my place, and feeling much better, I went back to join the party.

Acting out my role as the head of the studio's wife, I worked the room, saying hello to this one, promising to call that one for lunch. And then I saw Cassie. She seemed extremely nervous and was holding a large glass of Scotch.

"Who's minding Jenny?"

"I've enrolled her in nursery school. The same one where Matty goes."

The first thing I thought of was, who was paying for that? It was not inexpensive. Had she broken down and asked her mother for money, or had she broken the agreement she maintained with Guy, passively accepting whatever monies he chose to give her? Asking either for help would have constituted a small act of surrender for her, a concession.

Maybe she read the question in my eyes. "Win sent me a check," she said, "a large one. His note said that he thought it would be best for Jenny, if *she* at least, joined the real world. He said there was no reason she should be a victim of *my* alienation, of my inability to grow up and deal with problems."

I nodded my head in agreement. "Did he say anything else?"

"No." She seemed disoriented, I thought. Extremely agitated today. "He didn't say anything about *us*. I wanted to ask you—what's happening with *White Lily?* How is it going? I read that Beau's been hospitalized for a viral infection. Is that true? Is he really sick? Is he coming back to the picture?" Her hand shook. "Please, Buffy. Tell me. Will that damned picture ever be finished? I've finally decided—the end of the picture is *it* for me. That's my time limit. Win or lose, at the end of the picture I'm going to act. Yes. Win or lose."

I had to reassure her. "Beau's sick," I said, "but he'll be back on the set soon, they say. And the picture's going along fine. It shouldn't be too long." Movie talk.

She turned away only half-convinced.

And then I went after her. I owed her more than reassurance. She was my friend. *I owed her the truth.*

I grabbed her arm. "I don't know about the movie, Cassie. I don't think it's going to turn out fine. It might well turn out to be a complete disaster. Don't wait. Write to Win. Act now. Forget the movie. Do something now."

She smiled at me sickly. "I might as well wait. It's probably too late anyway. I think Win hates me. It's probably too late." And she was silent, thinking of the last time she had been up to the pink castle.

She had been watching the house. Every night the electronic timer put on the lights, and once a week a landscaping crew came in a large truck. But there had not been a sign of Win, not for many weekends now. One night she had decided to go up to the house to try and figure out by what was left in the house if Win ever intended to return. She had a beeper for the electric gates, a key for the front door, and one for the servants' entrance in the back.

She panicked when she found the front gate padlocked. The break in the wall by which she had once entered the grounds had long since been repaired. She couldn't get in unless she somehow vaulted the towering gates and then jumped. Then she thought of the landscapers: they would have a key for the padlock. They would have to.

She waited for them to come—Wednesday was their day—waited for them to enter and disperse themselves over the grounds. She slipped through then and ran up the driveway, careful to be unobserved. She ran up to the front door, stuck her key into the lock . . . and nothing happened. The lock had been changed! She was locked out . . . Win had locked her out.

Frantically she ran around to the back of the house, where once she had entered by way of the servants' quarters. If necessary, if that lock had been changed too, she would do again what she had done before— break one of the panes and stick her hand through . . . open the lock from the inside.

But then she saw that it couldn't be done—everything had been boarded up! Boarded up and iron rails added on top of that! Then she had known that Win had really locked her out.

"Don't say it's probably too late! You've waited for years!" I wanted to shake her. "Try to make up with Win now!"

"No. I set the end of the movie as my time limit."

She was definitely disturbed but still as stubborn as ever, I thought. I shook my head at her . . . hopelessly.

"If it's not already too late, a few more months won't matter. And if it *is* too late, nothing matters." She drained her glass of Scotch as she spoke.

Maybe she was right. Maybe it didn't matter. Win or lose, it was too late for me and Todd. And if the movie won or lost, maybe it *was* too late for Cassie too.

77.

It had been two months since she had last seen Beau. They had told her it would take at least that time but today she was going to see him and possibly take him home with her. She had spoken with the doctor—that Percy—several times, and he had given her the usual doctor shit, all kinds of crap, using terms she didn't understand, like they always did. But certain things were easy to understand. Beau had been on a diet, he had lost eighteen pounds, he was exercising every day, he was dried out and he was only on necessary prescription drugs. And one more thing she knew very well. If she didn't take Beau home with her today, it had better be next week. Todd King and *White Lily* weren't going to wait forever. If she didn't produce Beau in a few days, they would reshoot Beau's scenes with someone else. It couldn't cost them any more than to continue working around him.

Naturally all the lovely plans she had worked on for their life in Hollywood weren't complete. You didn't finish redoing a house like theirs in a couple of months. That kind of decorating took time. There was the sound studio, it hadn't even been started yet. And the gymnasium for Beau to work out in, that too was still only in the planning stages. But the pool house had been renovated already and Beau, when he wasn't working, would be able to lie out in the sun most comfortably and take a daily swim. And their bedroom was done—complete to the rose satin upholstered bed and matching chaise and the draperies covering three walls completely, with the fourth wall mirrored. Beau would love the bedroom.

And the applications for the country clubs were in. Cleo was sure that they would be accepted in at least two. Before anybody knew it, Beau would be teeing off with the best of them. And she had a drawerful of invitations to everything worthwhile going to. She had even hired herself a social secretary to keep track of things. And now that Beau was going to be so much better, she might not even have to spend so much time on the set herself watching over things. She could put her attention to all the other aspects of their life.

So she zipped on down to Palm Springs. Wouldn't Beau just die when he saw her driving herself in the new little yellow sporty Mercedes? She had learned that limos were okay when you went to formal affairs, when you didn't want to be busy parking your own car, when it looked good just to pull up with a guy in a chauffeur's cap. But informally, for your personal life kind of things, it was much more stylish in Southern California to drive yourself, to run around in a little sports job. And now that she wouldn't need the goons with her all the time . . . now that Beau wasn't going to need so much care and all—

Jesus! Maybe she'd just take Beau home with her today and tonight . . . tonight they would make love on the rose satin bed and it would be just like they were starting out fresh like a pair of newlyweds.

Dr. Percy insisted on seeing her before she saw Beau. It was hard to wait, but she supposed she might as well get the doctor over with first. She knew the line of crap he was going to feed her. At the prices they were getting, they probably never wanted to turn a patient loose. She'd bet that if Ben hadn't insisted on taking Suzannah home when he did, Suzannah would still be here too.

Hank Percy was as pompous and as stiff-necked as the day she had brought Beau in. She didn't like him. All the doctors she had ever gone to were a hell of a lot friendlier. And cheaper. She watched him as he kept adjusting the glasses on his nose. He was nervous about something all right.

"Mrs. Beaufort. When we agreed to accept your husband as a patient, I think we were not fully aware . . . cognizant, that is . . . of the extent of his condition."

Cognizant? What did that mean?

"Frankly, if we had . . . Frankly, Mrs. Beaufort, we are not equipped—We do not usually accept patients with as serious . . . um . . . problems is as good a word as any—"

"What are you giving me? Of course he had problems. That's why he was here. What kind of a place do you think you got here? A fat farm?"

"We *are* a sanitarium, Mrs. Beaufort. We accept patients with certain problems . . . and not patients with *other* problems. We are *discretionary.*"

Discretionary? She didn't know what that meant. "Cut the bullshit and spit it out!"

He winced and said, "We here at the Percy Institute think that it would be better for all concerned if your husband was treated at another institution . . . one better equipped to deal with his needs."

She couldn't believe what she was hearing. *They* wanted her to remove Beau! "What needs are you talking about? I thought you people *cured* him. That's what you said on the phone."

"Cured? I beg your pardon. Cured is not a word we *ever* use. And certainly we would not apply it to Mr. Beaufort, if we did. The facts of the situation are such that we cannot deal with Mr. Beaufort. You see, we are not a high-security institution. We are not a prison, Mrs. Beaufort. We do not have walls, locked gates, or security guards for our patients. We do not lock our patients in. In general, they are free to come and go as they please. You see, our patients are people who *choose* to be here. We do not *detain.*"

Still, she didn't fully understand what he was talking about.

"What are you getting at?" Her voice was shrill. "You'd better spit it out and quick!"

"The facts are, Mrs. Beaufort, that your husband has on several occasions accosted other patients . . . sexually." He paused while her mouth fell open. Yes, he *thought* that would slow her down. "And it was the first time we have ever had anything like that happen here."

But he saw her eyes harden. "There's a first time for everything, Doc, and that was your problem, wasn't it? Beau wasn't exactly here to attend a birthday party."

His lips twitched. "And then Mr. Beaufort sneaked out of the Institute into town on several occasions in search of various drugs and alcohol—"

She felt something crumble inside her.

"Several times it was necessary for our attendants to collect Mr. Beaufort in—" he searched for a suitable word—"in undesirable places."

Oh God! Oh God!

"Yeah? So? If he was Rebecca of Sunnybrook Farm he wouldn't have been here in the first place. Sounds to me like *you* fucked up. And besides, you lied to me. You told me on the phone that Beau was doing fine, he had lost weight, was exercising every day, and was only on prescription drugs. What was all that shit?"

Her tone was definitely menacing. He decided that she was very much in need of treatment herself. But not at Percy Institute! Not by a long shot. "Whatever I told you was true, as you will see, Mr. Beaufort was exercising great cunning in his deceptions, as people in his condition often do. Therefore we found it necessary to, in order to try and treat him, to put him under constraints—"

"You mean?—"

"Yes," he smiled tightly, now enjoying himself. "A straightjacket is the term in common usage."

Oh my God! Beau!

"And?" Her voice was ragged, harsh.

"And each time we did this," Percy paused for effect, "he . . . ejaculated!"

Poppy stared at him. "You mean he *came?*"

"Precisely. And of course, you understand, we couldn't have that sort of thing. Not *here.* And needless to say, physical constraint which is something we have never used in my institute, was not to be tolerated for any extended period. Frankly, Mrs. Beaufort, it was the consideration of my staff to have Mr. Beaufort transferred elsewhere immediately. But against theirs and my own better judgment, I decided to keep Mr. Beaufort here a bit longer because I wanted to be able to hand him back to you in a more . . . reasonable condition. Call it, if you will, a healthier condition. I assure you, you will find him much more manageable . . . and thinner, his body tone quite good, quite fit, as I told you on the phone—"

"Hold on. You said you stopped using the fucking straightjacket but you couldn't control him without it—" her tone was quiet again, deadly quiet.

"Yes. I referred to certain prescription drugs. We *sedated* Mr. Beaufort, which is sometimes necessary. A very usual procedure in cases of—So you see for the last three weeks we have maintained enough control to carry through a large part of our program. However, as Mr. Beaufort's problems are not those we deal with here, I have prepared a list of institutions that I can recommend . . . those that can better deal with both his mental and physical problems."

"Physical?" she asked, as if in a trance.

"Yes. Our tests show evidence of damage to the heart, the kidneys . . ."

Oh no! She wasn't going to let him get away with this.

"You fucking liar! I've taken Beau to hundreds of doctors for years. Nobody ever said anything about his heart or his kidneys."

Dr. Percy smiled thinly. "Perhaps the type of practitioner you consulted was not prepared to tell you anything you obviously don't wish to hear—"

"Let me see my husband! I'm going to sue your fucking nuts off!" But there was no heat in her words now, only defeat.

Percy consulted his wristwatch, and then a schedule on his desk. "Mr. Beaufort is receiving his sunbath. Twenty minutes a day, twice a day," he said. "Shall we go to the sunning terrace?"

Beau was lying on a chaise while an attendant sat in a nearby chair. The skimpily cut trunks showed off his beautifully tanned, fairly trim body. His blue eyes, wide and innocent as a child's, were open and staring unseeingly at the huge towering mountainside that bordered the Percy Institute to the east.

Beau was tranquilized out of his skull!

He sat beside her going home. She drove with one hand on the wheel, and one hand on his unmoving thigh, the tears running down her face, her mind going around and around furiously. It was Friday. By Monday she would have to have him on the set, untranquilized, if they were to get a performance out of him. There was only one thing for her to do.

"It's all right, Beau," she squeezed the thigh, her voice coming out in gulps. "Poppy will get you home and take care of you. Just wait until you see our pretty rose bedroom. You're going to love it!"

She didn't do it in three days. It took six, but she had him back at the studio, laughing and singing snatches of melodies as he walked around, saying hello, shaking hands, genial and good natured, looking everywhere but at the person he was hailing. After a couple of hours, Poppy led him off the set back to the dressing room where he threw himself down on the couch. He was shaking by now, uncontrollably, and as she prepared to inject him, he smiled into her eyes. "My honey, Poppy! Shoot me honey, eight to the bar!"

I didn't go to the set this time to welcome back Beau. But when Todd came home that night, grim as the proverbial reaper, I asked about him.

"He looks very fit. Tanned and twenty pounds thinner. In fact, he looks too good for the part. He's supposed to look unhealthy, pallid deterioration."

"And how is he performing?" I asked tonelessly.

"He gave a high performance. Very high."

"Well, in that case don't worry about his appearance. Probably in a couple of weeks he'll be pale and he'll have deteriorated quite a bit."

Todd puffed on a cigaret. He had only recently begun smoking. And I left him standing there with his smoke while I went to get my log. Besides noting Beau's return, I had a footnote. Todd had ceased asking me to let him close down production. It would be a struggle to the finish.

78.

When she came home from the studio at night, Suzannah did everything she could think of to forestall the moment when she entered the mausoleum of her bedroom. The smell of her death was in that room, along with the medieval pictures of the crucifixion and the gun lying ready under the white, tatted lace pillows.

If only she could stay on the set all day, all night. She could have managed that. She didn't sleep anymore. She was sure of it. She couldn't sleep in that room. Not with Ben's body next to her, his gun so near, so ready to extinguish her core, with the pictures of saints staring down at her with eyes almost as anguished as her own.

Sometimes she was still so foolish as to try and wheedle a sleeping pill from Ben. She told him it wasn't *she* that craved the pill, but her body just needing the healing respite of sleep. She didn't tell him that it was her mind that needed a temporary surcease from life, from her thoughts. But Ben was hard as steel, hard as the blue instrument of death that tore apart her thighs every night, her cheeks, her lips. Yes, Ben was hard as his voice was soft. That deadly, soft voice.

Instead of a pill, he gave her hot milk with honey in it, and yeast, and beaten eggs, because she couldn't eat, couldn't keep the food down even if she managed to force it between her lips and down her throat. She managed to keep the hot milk down because Ben threatened that she would be fed intravenously if she didn't. He would not allow his statue of perfection to become less than perfect by passing that slim line that separated splendid slenderness from emaciation. At first, she thought that the intravenous injections would mean a hospital, would mean nights in a bare hospital cell instead of her tapestried bedroom and she eagerly, oh yes eagerly, threw up whatever was given her. But then she learned that Ben meant to add the intravenous equipment to her torture bedchamber. The intravenous feedings would be administered by her head torturer after the premier violation.

So through the sleepless nights she thought only of how to foil the instrument that violated her body night after night after night. And one night, just before they were retiring, she shrewdly thought of the answer. The maid had brought her hot milk in the beautifully thin delicate goblet on a silver salver, and Ben went to his dressing room. Oh yes, she would fool that cunning gun.

She emptied the goblet, rapturously spilling its contents on the many-colored patterned carpet, and struck it against the marble nightstand, leaving the goblet an exquisitely pointed jagged edge, and closing her eyes, smiling, she slashed at her sexual orifice—she would fool that gun, she would gut out her hole. And as the blood seeped out of her, covering pale, cool-as-marble-thighs, dripping onto the stark white linen sheets, she laughed.

I wrote in my book: "Ben has taken Suzannah to a hospital in Santa Barbara, not sure, he says, how long she will have to be there, probably only a few days. She fainted, he said, in the bathroom while holding a glass of water in her hand, making some small plastic surgery necessary. The studio's publicity release will state that Suzannah has a throat infection, in order to forestall speculation about 'an accident.' The location of the hospital will be kept a secret."

I laid down my pen for a second. In answer to my query as to whether production would be temporarily suspended, Todd said no. This time they were going to be really creative—"an accident" would be written into the script. I picked up my pen and wrote: "Script will be revised accordingly."

And I wondered how many more of *White Lily*'s problems would have to be worked out in this creative manner. And I thought about Suzannah's accident. How much fact? How much fiction? And I was furious with myself for not being able to repress tears, not for the Suzannah of today, but for the red-headed, spirited, long-legged creature who had worshiped her body, her temple, so many centuries ago.

79.

As they say, time marched on. Matty entered kindergarten along with Cassie's Jenny, and Mikey took Matty's place in nursery school. Mitch was a Little Leaguer and a Scout, and Megan, in high school, had both ballet lessons and boyfriends. Cassie went back to her job at the museum, and Suellen and Cleo's business prospered, keeping them both busy and happy. Only *White Lily* and I went inexorably on, seemingly in circles, going where?

Each couple of weeks or so, I bought myself a new jeweled trophy and every two or three weeks, it seemed, *White Lily* was, in some way, rewritten to cover some small calamity.

And then Todd decided that the set was to be closed to all persons not directly involved in the production with the exception of Poppy Beaufort, whose presence was very necessary. It was Ben's presence on the set that triggered the new rule. Todd and Leo had decided that ever since Suzannah had come back from Santa Barbara her performance had been inhibited by Ben standing somewhere behind the cameras, watching.

It turned out to be a real Western movie showdown. When Ben was forbidden the set, he pulled Suzannah off the movie, waiting for Todd to give in. And I held my breath, waiting to see what Todd would do. The old Todd, intimidated by nothing—he had had many stand-offs with *whole* unions—would never have backed down when he thought he was right. But this, of course, was no longer the old Todd. And all Hollywood must have been watching this new turn of events at the King Studio. *White Lily,* so long in the making, was turning into a Hollywood joke, maliciously relished by everyone in the Industry.

Again they shot around Suzannah. But then the bankers in New York who had been contributing much of the movie's financing called a halt to their participation. And it looked like Ben's fine network of influence in high places had been put to use. There was no way the picture could continue without a new influx of money. No studio, not even the biggest, could or would finance a picture of this magnitude without outside backing.

I watched Todd pace the library every night seeking a solution to this new problem. I imagined that he had already used any personal resources that he could touch without my permission or signature. And I thought of the rather large fortune in jewels that reposed in a bank vault to which only I held the key—the jewels for which I had been depleting our own personal resources, while Todd had never uttered a word in reproach or told me to desist. And my natural, human instinct told me I wanted the good guy to win out, but I kept telling myself that in this case there was no good guy, *only* black-hearted villains. And I held back even when Suellen came to me—behind Todd's and Howard's back, I assumed—and asked me what I was waiting for. She had read, she told me, that Marion Davies had once sold the jewelry William Hearst had gifted her with, in order to help him when he was in financial trouble. "And that was a *multi-multi*-millionaire! and that was only William Hearst! Not our Todd!" Why wasn't I forthcoming with my valuable collection of jewelry which she had never understood why I had bought in the first place. "You never even cared for jewelry. Not even when Todd used to give you something for a present—"

I shrugged and she looked at me suspiciously.

"Why did you . . . why *do* you keep on buying it?"

"I guess because I changed and started to like jewelry. People do change."

"I don't believe you."

"What, then, do you believe?"

"Oh I believe you've changed. I haven't been so preoccupied with my business and everything that I haven't seen what was happening to you. And I think I know exactly what it is!"

My heart started to beat rapidly.

"I think you've become jealous of Todd. Of his success. I think you've started to resent his being the big cheese in the family. And you're reacting badly, just like a lot of other women who think they're coming face to face with their feminists' rights by acting like bitches. I think you're trying to spend his money like water. Just to show him how little you think of that money . . . that badge of his success. You, Buffy, of all people!"

I laughed in her face. "You're talking nonsense, Suellen."

"If I am, then why won't you give him the jewelry to save him?"

"Save *him?* Aren't you just worried about yourself? You and Howard do have a stake in all this too."

Suellen's face flamed and her hand twitched. I knew she wanted to slap my face and I didn't blame her. *Oh, my God! What was becoming of me?* But still, I was angry at her too. For coming here to speak for Todd, when it was her sister who had been dying by inches for months. So I didn't apologize.

But she said, "I'm going to overlook that remark, Buffy, because I love you, and I don't think you're yourself. I think some devil's gotten into you—"

No, she was wrong. The devil was Todd and he wasn't getting into me at all these days. But I didn't say that to Suellen because then she surely would have slapped my face, and then she might have started to understand what was really going on in my marriage. So all I did was laugh and say, "Maybe you want to take me to an exorcist?"

"Don't give me your wise-ass answers either, Buffy. That's something new too. *Give* Todd the jewelry, Buffy!"

"You really think I should do that, Suellen? You, who always believed in security first? Who lectured me on the folly of always going along with Todd no matter what fool thing he wanted to do? Who hated the idea of the movie business from the first moment Todd spoke of it? Now, you want me to take everything I've salvaged, every goddamn thing that hasn't already been thrown into King's Great Folly, and throw it in the pot, good money after bad? This film is a disaster, Suellen! Don't you know that? There probably won't even be a studio left after this film is through and done. And nothing . . . nothing . . . no amount of good money after bad is going to save it!"

"Shame on you, Buffy. I'm not talking about saving *White Lily.* Nor even the studio. I'm talking about you saving Todd and your marriage. If you *don't* offer him your jewelry, if you don't make this gesture of support, your marriage won't be worth anything."

Poor Suellen. She was so misguided. She didn't know that my marriage was such a poor, sick thing, no amount of money could enrich it.

"Do it, Buffy!" she begged now. "Throw everything you have into it to save him. Even the house. What you and Todd had . . ." Suellen started to sob with the intensity of her emotions, "was so beautiful . . . more beautiful than a million of your lousy emeralds . . . more brilliant than a million stupid diamonds."

I started to cry too, for my lost beautiful, brilliant love, and for my sister who cried for me without really knowing why she had to.

But I reined in my tears. "You're being melodramatic, Suellen. It's only a movie. The studio? It's only a lot with some buildings and sets and equipment." But I knew my words to be false.

"No. It's more than that. It's the fight of Todd's life. And if you don't try to help him win it, even if it's already lost, then *you've* lost everything."

Already lost, already lost.

"But there *is* another way out of this mess," my tone was crisp. "All Todd has to do is give in to Ben . . . to let him back on the set. And then Ben will allow those banks to again pour their good money into the picture. Simple, isn't it?"

Suellen dried her tears. "Don't bullshit me, Buffy King. It sounds simple but you know Todd can't do that. That he never will. If he'd give in to a bully like Ben, then he wouldn't be the man you married, would he?"

Ah! Now Suellen had finally reached the heart of the matter. That was exactly what I was waiting to find out—*if* Todd would cave in. I already knew that he was no longer the Todd I had married. But I said nothing more. And Suellen waited for me to speak, to answer her. When I didn't, she said unbelievingly, "And you're still not going to do it? You're *still,* after all I've said, not going to offer him the jewelry and the house, if need be?"

I made up my mind quickly. "Yes, I will. But only if he *asks* me—"

Suellen's mouth twisted with bitterness.

"You haven't heard a word I said. It can only save your marriage *if* you offer, if you don't wait to be asked."

The days passed . . . five of them. Todd didn't ask for the jewelry and true to my word, I didn't offer it although I could think of nothing else. And then it was all over. Quickly. Todd came home, whistling to himself, and I assumed something had happened . . . something resembling a miracle. I hadn't heard him whistle in months.

I said nothing, watching him, as watchful as a cat. And I saw him struggle with it until he blurted it out: Suzannah was back on the set. Ben had brought her there and left. That was all he said and he proceeded to whistle again. Somehow he had won out, but how? He wasn't going to offer to tell me about that. He was going to wait until I asked.

Obviously the money to go on with the production had come from somewhere, and not from the banks that Ben in some way controlled. Otherwise, Ben *would have* been there—on the set with Suzannah. It *was* permissible for me to ask where the money had come from—it came under the heading of business, and we *were* allowed to discuss that. But I couldn't do it.

I sat through the dinner with him and the children. He was no longer whistling but he was teasing Megan about a new boyfriend, talking baseball with Mitch, teaching silly riddles to Mikey and Matty. He was the triumphant hero again and as much as I fought it, I was dizzy with the flush of sexual desire, so extreme that I couldn't sit in place. Oh, there's no fool bitch like an old fool bitch, I told myself. To grow so excited over the news that somehow he had slain the wicked dragon. And yet there it was and what was I to do with it? All I could do was bear it and wait for it to go away. And I was sick with the need to hear more details. Even with the money coming from somewhere, Ben could *still* have kept Suzannah off the set. But he had caved in quickly, forfeiting his right to supervise his most precious possession. Why?

As the children dispersed to their after-dinner activities I thought of riding over to the Valley to see Suellen and innocently paying a social call on a free evening. Howard would know what happened and even if he weren't home, he would have told Suellen, and I could just sniff out the whole story like a bloodhound. Perhaps the ride might even cool me off, cool me down. All I knew was that I couldn't stay in the house with Todd, not feeling the way I did.

But as these things so often happen, the chimes sounded and it was Suellen and Howard, excited as two kids, just popping in to share in the exultation and the glory of Todd's coup.

"Isn't it wonderful?" Suellen cried watching for my reaction. "Isn't it a wonderful victory?" Sly boots, Suellen, as much a bloodhound as I had intended to be.

"Wonderful," I said, but my eyes met Todd's enigmatic ones over Suellen's head.

As sly as Suellen, or even as sly as Scarlett O'Hara had ever been, I turned to sweet, unsuspecting Howard and batted my lashes. "And you, Howard! Don't you play modest with me! Don't downplay your role in this thing—"

"Me?" Howard cried out in disavowal. "I didn't do a thing! It was Todd all by himself, buying up every old picture he could find, buying out whole film libraries from the other studios, for months now, and setting up another company to do it so nobody knew it was the King Studio. As a matter of fact, I have to say it, *I* was the one who scoffed, telling him he was crazy, buying up all those old turkeys. But as it turned out, he sure had one big ace up his sleeve when he needed it. One minute in the game to go and Todd scores the touchdown. Can you imagine? And he didn't even have to sell the damn things. He gets all the money he needs just by leasing out the old turkeys to all those turkeys at the networks and cables. Whew!"

Howard was really beside himself with admiration. My eyes went beyond him to Todd, who, I could see, was fighting down his own exultation, his pride and his joy. So he's done it again, I thought, the boy genius of Akron . . . this time in Tinseltown, no matter that the boy's auburn curls were slowly turning to gray. His eyes, for a minute, pleaded for my approbation too. And I had to turn away, for the desire rising in me again, from my loins, spreading upward and out, until I was consumed with it. I would fight it! I would fight it on the land, and on the sea, wherever we both were. There would be no giving in to carnal fleshliness. And there would be no approbation either. For what? For proving that he was a master businessman, that he hadn't forgotten to cover himself, to hedge his bets? He had proven all that years ago. No, he didn't get any good marks from me for that.

Now I had learned where the money had come from. But I still didn't know why Ben had bowed to Todd's demands. Had Suzannah somehow broken out from the web of fear that Ben had woven around her and asserted herself? Not likely.

"Even so," I addressed Howard, "it's still a wonder Ben gave in without more of a fight."

"I guess he knows that when Todd King gives an ultimatum, he means it. Like when Kennedy stuck it to Khrushchev."

I laughed. "What did Ben think? That Todd was going to drop a nuclear bomb on him?"

Out of the corner of my eye I saw Suellen looking at me, her face full of something akin to pity, as if I were doing something shabby and she was ashamed for me, and sorry. Sorry I was stooping to petty tricks? Or sorry that I had been found wanting, that I had allowed Todd to save the day without me?

But Howard just laughed this time, and elucidated no further. Then, Todd, probably tired of playing games and *wanting* me to know, said quietly, "I told Ben production was continuing, and if Suzannah was not at the studio on the dot of six this morning, the role of Lily was being terminated. We were going to rewrite the script to include a premature demise for our heroine. And Ben wants to be married not to a bit player but to Suzannah the star. A star is what turns the man on."

He had vanquished his foe all right. To save the picture? Or to show me that he was still strong, still brave, still valiant?

But as I was writing down the event in the *White Lily* log, after Suellen and Howard had gone home, and after Todd had climbed the stairs to bed, a third possibility occurred to me. And it chilled my blood. Had Todd only been playing the role of the shining knight on the white charger to save his princess, his lover? Had *she* asked Todd to keep Ben away from the set? Had Todd done it only for Suzannah?

80.

Leila Pulitzer had pulled off her own coup. She was marrying her Texas lawyer millionaire. And Cleo was almost as excited as Leila herself. The wedding, she told me, was going to be in Dallas at the Duke's ranch on the outskirts of town. And the Duke was flying down all the guests from L.A. in his own jet and putting everybody up in the poshest hotels in Dallas for a whole weekend. And everybody was invited . . . "our whole crowd." Even Suzannah and Ben.

I wanted to say that Suzannah and Ben were hardly my crowd, but I didn't. As far as Cleo knew, Suzannah and I were still friends. But I did ask about Beau and Poppy. Were they on the guest list?

"Of course. Would my mother pass up the chance to have a star like Beau Beaufort at her wedding party? She's counting on getting him to sing too. And besides, ever since I helped Poppy out with her plans to get started socially, we've become . . . friendly."

I didn't comment on that. I asked, "Are you making the arrangements for the wedding? And is Suellen going to do the catering?"

"No sir! The wedding is strictly Texas and you know they do their own thing down there. I'm going to be the maid of honor, and just let anybody say I'm not a maiden. My new stepdaddy will step on him like he was a bug. They're big and strong in Texas. And Tabby's going to be a bridesmaid. Mother wanted her to be a flower girl but I straightened her out. She didn't know Tabby had outgrown that stage. And Suellen is just going to be a guest. I hope, in a designer gown. You know, since we've become partners Suellen and I have grown really close, but I still don't have the nerve to tell her she really should give up her cottony, starched, little white gloves look. But *you* could and should. Get her into a Halston or something."

I didn't tell Cleo that I was rather avoiding my sister these days. I couldn't stand her inquisitive, accusing eyes. I had the feeling Suellen wasn't going to quit probing until she found out what had gone wrong with my marriage, and then planned on trying to straighten things out. As if that could ever happen.

Suddenly, Cleo giggled. "I've even talked Mother into inviting Leo. Has love ever turned to hate! Ever since he tried to screw me on the settlement—"

"Why on earth would you want Leo there?"

"I thought it was the nice thing to do, *civilized,* you know. All one big happy family. He is the kids' father, and both Tabby and Josh are part of the wedding party. Buffy, I really wish Leo well."

"You do?" I asked wistfully. Cleo was a really generous person, I decided. The kind of person I once thought I was, or wanted to be.

She laughed. "Sure, I wish him well. As long as he keeps on making money, he won't have any problem writing us our monthly check. Provided his hand doesn't shake too much from the effort." She did an imitation of Leo signing a check, his hand quivering with the strain.

I smiled but I was unconvinced. She wished Leo well because she was now beyond pettiness.

She giggled again. Had she always laughed so much, I wondered? Or was I only noticing it more these days because *I* didn't feel funny.

"You want to hear the latest in the Leo Mason great funny sayings collection?"

I nodded.

"Leo's still after me to sell the house to get his half of the bucks, right? Now he keeps asking me what's wrong with our kids? Isn't it time they were off to college? And the poor things aren't even in high school yet."

Cleo obviously expected me to laugh, but I couldn't. I wasn't into laughing so much and Leo's nonsense made me mad. "And this is the jackass you insist on inviting to your mother's wedding?"

"Yes. I'm even allowing him to bring his girlfriend."

Crazy. "You're off the wall," I told her.

"She *is* going to be the children's stepmom.

Oh dear. The old poets were right. What tangled lives we lead.

"And Cassie?" I asked. "I suppose she's coming with Guy whom she never eyer sees anymore?" My tone was more ironic than sarcastic.

"Oh no. Cassie probably won't come at all. You really *are* out of it. I'm the one who's working and you're the one who doesn't get around and hear anything. Cassie's mother has had a stroke."

Oh no! I had feared something like this would happen. That when and if Cassie's day to declare her emancipation ever came, it would no longer mean anything. What could it possibly mean to declare you're free of the domination of a sick or crippled person?

"She's home from the hospital but she's almost completely paralyzed. They've got nurses around the clock, but still Cassie goes there every day to sit with her."

Of course. Being Cassie, what else would she do?

81.

Cassie stared at her mother propped up in the big bed. Cassandra looked so little and frail, half-paralyzed as she was, and broken. She'd been coming here every day for two weeks, ever since Cassandra had come back from the hospital, and already all the fear she had had for her mother for so many years was fading into nothing. This woman, this broken ineffectual person who babbled nonsense could not possibly be the specter who had dominated her life, had caused her to live a life of rejection and the bitterest kind of failure. She couldn't even hate her; it was as if there was nothing here worth hating. It was some kind of a cruel joke, that it should all come to this. This broken, dotty old woman was not anyone you could take seriously. With her stroke, her mother had completely invalidated her daughter's old life. With her stroke, her mother had had the last word, had won out for the last time.

Her mother rambled on. "Did I ever tell you that my daddy used to take me to San Simeon? That Marion Davies used to be there all the time. What Mr. Hearst ever saw in her I'll never know. She was a movie person, you know. It was there that I met Howard, you know. I don't remember his last name. But he was very much taken with me. Daddy wanted me to marry him . . . what's his name . . . but he was such a stubborn man. And quite strange. Nutty as a fruitcake, I always thought," she cackled.

With Win gone and her mother no longer a real person, it hardly mattered if she divorced Guy or not. Nothing mattered anymore except for Jenny. And Cassie had gotten just what she deserved. As the Cassandra of old had said, she was a little, worthless fool and little worthless fools deserved everything they got. Yes, richly deserved, to sit here and listen and be Cassandra Blackstone's daughter and Guy Savarese's wife. Forever. As for Win, had he ever existed at all? Had she and Win ever existed together as one? Yes, they had. Of that she had proof. There was Jenny, after all.

Poor Jenny. She, Cassie, had made this bed, but Jenny had to lie in it, alongside of her.

82.

It had taken Leila Pulitzer eighteen years to find a new husband, I reflected. Her first marriage had broken up in that first year of our college life and now it was late in '83. But as if to make up for lost time, her current wedding was certainly a razzle-dazzle affair. It was a true Texas-style wedding. A judge, that legal symbol of the Old West, performed the ceremony. And the setting, Duke's ranch, couldn't have been more authentic if it had been TV's *Dallas* itself. Only now the men wore white tie and the women's costumers read like a designers' who's who—Blass; de la Renta; Valentino; the latest California rage, Peter Mitchell; and even Bruce Oldfield, who not only dressed Princess Diana but Bianca Jagger as well. And while the huge spits boasted succulent carcasses of beef and lamb, tended not by cowboys but tuxedo-dressed chefs, no one was expected to stand eating with barbecue juices dripping down onto his elegant chin. Rather we sat at tables draped in silver and gold lamé cloths, the official colors of Duke's ranch, and the chili was served in silver bowls as all around us the night was lit by florist-supplied flora sprinkled with thousands of tiny lights. And everywhere —arrangements of the yellow roses of Texas.

The wedding on Sunday evening was only the culmination of a week-end long roster of celebrations, and some people arrived in time only for the wedding part of the festivities. Like Suzannah and Ben. Suzannah was wearing a creation in white, looking like an ice princess, or maybe, only a bride. But that was all right since the real bride wore gold lamé that matched one half of the tablecloths, which was only fitting—she was neither young nor a maiden.

It had occurred to me that perhaps Heinie would show up since he was both friend and client of the bridegroom, and what a climax that would have been to the wedding—Suzannah and Heinie together at another Texas-style wedding, but this time with Ben hovering close by, a dark, sinister presence.

Perhaps that is what Suzannah was thinking, I thought, as I watched her eyes dart about nervously, seeking, searching. Or maybe she was just taking note of the wedding decor, this Western-style wedding reminding her of her own on the Twentieth Century lot. But whatever she was thinking of, there would be no Heinie riding to the rescue. Leila had told me that Heinie was in Monte Carlo, probably breaking another bank. (Having given up movie studios, he had turned his attention to the banking industry.)

When Suzannah's eyes met mine, the searching look ceased, the light went out and a film, almost a curtain, came down over the amber irises. She clearly expected no answers from me. And we smiled at each other, two acquaintances being polite. And a feeling of bitter regret came over me, as I realized that I actually *wished* Heinie had been there. But it was nothing personal—personally I felt, why *should* Suzannah be saved? Why shouldn't she suffer in hell as I have? It was *objectively* that I wished Heinie would have shown up . . . for the sake of the script. It would have been one hell of an ending, I told myself.

I turned away, confused and miserable as I most often was these days, and almost ran into Poppy Beaufort, who was standing close by. She and Beau had flown in with Ben and Suzannah. She looked almost as deathly as I felt. She was dressed in her usual black and white, and her face too was a study in these two colors—her dark eyes like two huge black olives staring out of a white, tightly stretched canvas. My mouth got ready to go into its act my lips to stretch over my gritted teeth in a big smile. But Poppy spoke first, in a low, hoarse undertone. "We're not friends, and I don't think we ever will be. I don't have any friends. But your husband's acted like one; at least he's been square. So there's something I want to tell you. You watch out for that Ben! He's not a man to let anybody get the best of him."

I saw her walk back to Beau who was standing nearby, grinning like a little boy at a nice party where they were having ice cream and chocolate cake. Then I stared at Ben's back as he led Suzannah around like a puppy on a leash. No, not a puppy. A great big show dog with long red hair.

I felt like I had been kicked in the gut! *She was right! Poppy was right!* Of course Ben wouldn't take it lying down. Of course he wasn't the kind of man to let anybody get the best of him!

I searched the sea of white-jacketed men and finally lighted on Todd's figure as he stood talking to a circle of tall Texans, sipping a drink, his face sober and thoughtful. Did *he* know to watch out for Ben? Did he know that Ben wasn't the kind of man who would let someone best him? Or did he think it was just a matter of who would get to him first? Ben? Or me . . . his own wife?

But then I calmed myself down with the thought that it wasn't physical violence that Poppy was talking about. No, of course not. A man like Ben didn't have people knocked off. Surely Poppy was referring to simple sabotage . . . one businessman trying to destroy another's business empire. And then, as I would in the future, I brushed off my anxiety with the thought: Todd had risked Ben's wrath all for the sake of Suzannah. He would have to watch out for Ben all by himself.

Leo was subdued for once, squiring his financée about, she dressed in her all-beige. And I was glad that she wore that beige—she looked almost colorless next to the radiant Cleo, resplendent in silver lamé, with hair to match. (Together, she and her mother, in gold, matched the color scheme.) I watched Cleo as she boogied with the six-foot-four Dale Waxler, bridegroom Duke's rugged, oilman son, who had served as best man. Cleo had told me that he was recently divorced, as who indeed was not. Cleo's eyes were shining as she gazed way upward into Dale's eyes, her eyes almost as shiny as her silver dress. Could they too be a match?

Howard and Suellen boogied too until Suellen threw up her hands and yelled "I'm bushed! I'm not used to this anymore!" and came running off the dance floor, her eyes shining almost as brightly as Cleo's. Cleo must have talked Suellen into a departure from her usual style of dress after all, because Suellen was wearing a spectacularly weird evening gown from the house of some newly fashionable Japanese designer who specialized in geometric cut and primary colors. It was hard to believe that this was my sister from Ohio, living and cooking for pay in Southern California, attending an elegant hoe-down wedding in Texas looking like a Tokyo hipster. Incredible! All of it!

It appeared that Suellen had gone over to the other side. From the contingent from L.A., there were three joyous female faces—Leila's, Cleo's and Suellen's. And on the flip side there was Poppy's, Suzannah's, and *mine*. No, maybe it wasn't Suellen who had gone over to the other side after all but her sister.

And you, Cassie, wherever you are tonight, move over! You've got a lot of company.

Then there was the surprise. Beau Beaufort was up on the bandstand making an announcement to the crowd in a very hot, sexy voice, his onstage style. He was going to sing a song from his soon-to-be-released movie, *White Lily*.

There was a noisy response from the crowd. Beau Beaufort was *big* in Texas. And I smiled. *Soon-to-be-released, indeed!*

Poppy, standing right in front of the stage, called up a cue. And then Beau leaned into the microphone again and confided to his audience that the brand-new recording, "Love Grown Cool," would be available in the stores all across the country *the following week* under his new label—King Records!

I spun around, amazed, to look for Todd. But he was directly behind me, smiling at me in his new enigmatic style. He had managed to pull another rabbit out of his ever abundant hat. *Magic man.*

You watch out, Ben Gardenia, I thought. That Todd King—he's a hard man to beat.

As Beau sang, I saw Poppy hang her head, her shoulders drooping, not looking at Beau as his voice carried through the night, plaintive and haunting, sweetly melancholic. Maybe she had looked too many times. Maybe it was better for her to just listen to his voice:

The geese depart, I can't go with them—
I have no wings and many ties.
Each has its place within the vee
That points away across the skies.

Each has its mate and nesting place
In other lands to which it flies,

But still the night in which I wait
Rings desolate with lonely cries.

When love is new it bears strong wings
And makes a home of empty skies,
But love grown cool turns faith to rue
And mocks the heart with lonely lies.

Love grown cool turns faith to rue and mocks the heart with lonely lies.
Yes. Perhaps, I, too, had looked too many times.

83.

I left Dr. Harvey's office that June day after my biannual gynecological examination. We were moving out to Malibu for the summer in about a week and I wanted this checkup behind me. It was nearly two years already since I had had my baby removed from my being—a second anniversary for me and almost a second for *White Lily,* which had been in somewhat intermittent production and *still* the talk of the Industry. The speculation was: would the King Studio survive the production?

It seemed the three leading players were hardly ever ready to work on any given day. The latest problem was that Guy Savarese had developed some kind of skin poisoning from dyeing his hair. No one had suspected before that he was dyeing his hair. The irony of it was that he wasn't even graying. Why would anyone with a thick thatch of nearly white-blond hair be dyeing it black for years? It was a puzzle. Now, he was going to have to wear a black wig to finish the picture as he was forbidden to continue the dyeing until the infection cleared up.

Still, despite this new complication, the official studio word was that the picture was now only a couple of months away from completion. And although its costs were certainly as high as any in the history of motion pictures, the studio had probably averted total disaster. Todd had managed, most likely, to cover the financial necessities with the recording company and the library of old films. And besides, all the publicity, adverse or not, was certain to draw people to the theaters regardless of how bad the reviews might turn out. And so far, Ben Gardenia—the big question mark in my head—hadn't made any more moves.

As I walked to the elevator I thought of the peculiar conversation I had had with a woman in Dr. Harvey's waiting room. A pretty girl with a huge head of frizzed hair had assaulted me, a complete stranger, with the announcement that she had contracted herpes.

"I thought I had found one guy in a thousand. One normal guy in a sea of gays. I mean, I know lots of men. And every time I turn around, another one has slipped over the edge and turned queer. Have you noticed?"

I sighed. I hadn't really noticed. I wasn't into guy-watching like some women I knew who inspected behinds and crotches—measuring, appraising, speculating. But I nodded, waiting to give the young woman some satisfaction to help appease her rage. "There do seem to be more gays around than before. I guess it's because both Hollywood and being gay are kind of last stops on the run. If you haven't stopped off someplace else before you get there—"

She moved her head up and down vehemently. "And then I meet this man, this . . . this animal . . . who passes himself off as a great person. He's great-looking, with a great job selling time, making great money, drives a Mercedes and is *nice* to me. And what does he do? He gives me herpes without a declaration. Don't you think he should have told me? Given me the choice? The right to make up my own mind?"

"You should have had the choice," I said.

"The creep!" she said, unappeased.

The right to choose should definitely be part of a woman's bill of rights, I thought as the elevator door opened and discharged a blond man. As I brushed past him to step into the elevator, I did one of those double takes. And the man's bright blue eyes were doing a double take on me. *Robert Redford spotting Vivien Leigh.* As our eyes met, he smiled a bit sheepishly . . . charmingly. That was Redford's smile, all right.

Why, it must be Cleo's Dr. Roth! She was right. He could be Redford's double, or at least his stand-in.

As the elevator alternately zoomed and stopped for new passengers, all kinds of thoughts were swirling around in my head and messages were shooting out from all parts of my body and my psyche, my id. Id? If I remembered correctly from Psychology 401, the definition of id was: the division of the psyche associated with instinctual impulses and demands for the satisfaction of primitive needs. Yes, my primitive needs were crying out for satisfaction and my broken heart told me there was no surer way to break a heart than through the act of infidelity, and my head justified it all. It told me that the Old Testament said that justice was an eye for an eye. And besides, it would be an exciting and interesting project. Unhappiness was such a boring, dreary thing.

The fact was that adultery had been in the back of my mind for several months.

I went home and called Dr. Roth's office for an appointment. I planned on seducing Dr. Roth and I was prepared to do whatever was necessary. I never even stopped to wonder what kind of man Gavin Roth was and what it would take to bring him to the stage where he would be willing to fornicate with a patient.

I drove in from Malibu all summer, once a week, to see Dr. Roth. And sometimes I grew discouraged. I almost believed that my big seduction scene was never going to happen. Dr. Roth seemed impervious to seduction. But I persevered. New to this game, I did all the things I thought Scarlett O'Hara would do. I was alternately sweet, charming, cute, sexy, provocative, innocent, bold, cold, warm, and I hoped, irresistible. Sometimes I thought he was weakening, that he was taken with me. But still, the visits were immaculately professional. He waited for me to speak, which I assumed was routine with psychiatrists. But I had no intention, of course, of speaking about anything really relevant. I rarely did that with anybody these days. A certain flippancy, the wisecrack, even the provocative joke had become almost second nature to me, a way of life, really. I had become accustomed to *not* revealing my true feelings.

So now it was September already and my last visit had been as uneventful as my first, although I *knew* he found me attractive. Women sensed these things. There was a nervous tension between us and although I did not do anything as overt as Cleo had—flashing poor Dr. Roth—I did do certain things that were not overt. I smiled in a certain way, did things with my eyes, wet my lips repeatedly with my tongue, sucked a finger, suggestively crossed and recrossed my legs, all the things I knew to be body language, and if anyone should have understood body language, it was a psychiatrist.

I took the parking ticket from the attendant. The ticket would be validated by the doctor's receptionist, Rosemary—another of those dead ringers for Marilyn Monroe. Hollywood was crawling with bogus

Marilyns. I rode the elevator up to the fourteenth floor. Today, I decided, I was going to make a move on him. I just had to get this over with. I just had to.

I prattled on for ten minutes, detailing the argument I had had the day before with Leah. *I* knew these squabbles had no psychological consequence—merely familial exercises Leah and I both enjoyed. But it was something to fill in the hour, the $100 fifty-minute hour. Not so terrible, I thought, when broken down into minutes, two dollars per minute. Beverly Hills lawyers asked at least three.

I was in the middle of a sentence—right at that part of the argument when Leah turned her back on me resuming her task of chopping onions *manually,* a spiteful act considering I had bought the Cuisinart just to make her life easier.

"She had the nerve to reaffirm her refusal to use the Cuisinart by shaking her backside negatively in my—"

He interrupted me brusquely. "Mrs. King, why are you wasting my time and yours recreating this ridiculous *gestalt* with your maid? If you don't stop playing your silly games and tell me what's really bugging you, I don't think we—"

Why was he so angry? Was it the sexual tension he was feeling? Or was it the Santa Anas that were blowing hot today making him irritable? Whatever it was, I was tired of this game too. I was ready to throw caution to the winds and hoped he was too.

"Very well, Doctor," I said in a small voice. "I will tell you what's bugging me. I would very much like for you to fuck me."

His face contorted. He seemed furious, although my words couldn't be that much of a shock to him. We both lived in a sophisticated society. Stiffly, he said, "I'm afraid that I'm prohibited from sexual intercourse with my patients, tempting as the individual patient may be."

But I had already made my move and I was determined to go ahead with it no matter how much he resisted, nor even how embarrassed I might be myself. Besides, there were tell-tale signs that the doctor was not unimpressed with my advances.

I smiled sweetly at him and began to unbutton my white silk jacket. "Please, Dr. Roth. You must realize that it is not *your* ethics that are at stake here. *You* are not taking advantage of me nor are you seducing me. Let us say for the record that I am seducing you." I removed the jacket and was unbuttoning my blouse. "And let us say that we are doing this on a friendly basis, not as doctor and patient. And furthermore," I was down now to my lace brassiere and unhooking that, "you really don't have to worry about your ethics. This *is* Hollywood!"

When I was bare-breasted before him he ran to the door and locked it, but it was as if he didn't know what else to do, or as if it were a reflex action. Then he turned back to me, his face burning, prepared to do battle with me, prepared to fight for the honor of his profession. But I put my arms around his neck, pressed my lips to his, pressed my body against his body insinuatingly. He tried to push me away but I clung, determined. He wrestled and slowly, his resistance wavered. Luckily, there was the brown ultrasuede couch close by, because after a few minutes more of our bodies wrangling, he succumbed, as I had known he would. *I* was writing this scenario. Still, I had a feeling that the doctor too must have been fantasizing for weeks. Otherwise, I think, I never would have managed to seduce him, no matter how persistent I had been.

Driving home, I reviewed it all in my mind. It had been hurried and he had been nervous, what with his receptionist just on the other side of the door. And if truth be told, I had been nervous too. Still, it had been exciting . . . and not unsweet.

It would make such an amusing story, I thought, if only I could relate it to *somebody*. The seduction of Dr. Gavin Roth. It was too bad I couldn't tell Todd. He had always enjoyed a funny story. Or Suzannah. Oh my, how Suzannah would have laughed.

I had figured, one glimpse of the old titties and the doctor would both wilt and harden at the same time. And who could blame him? There I was . . . a cute, vivacious young Vivian, fluttering thick lashes, waving my pink-tipped white lovelies before his baby blues. Of course, I had just recently added an extra one-half pound of soft, pale flesh to a faultless figure, but then, one extra half-pound of luminescent flesh is not unattractive, cunningly arranged against brown ultrasuede cushions. That's where the seduction took place, you see, on this handsome ultrasuede couch.

If no laugh were forthcoming, I could have made it even funnier. I could have said, "He fondled my white breast. He bent his head and wrapped his lips around my thoroughly erected rosy-brown nipple. 'That will cost you only three dollars at my current rate of two dollars a minute,' he murmured."

I laughed softly to myself, thinking, oh, what a funny line that was! Then I hit the brake sharply for a red light and burst out crying. I was past thirty-five and I had just experienced a *first*. I had been unfaithful to Todd King for the first time and no matter *what else*, it was an enormously traumatic experience, and it had nothing to do with Gavin Roth at all. *He* had done all the right things, as I sensed he might beforehand. He was tender, with a tenderness I had suspected was there —he had kissed my mouth and then my neck, my ears, my breasts. And he was such a pretty boy with that lovely yellow hair and that little nose, that little nose that disproved the theory of the women's locker rooms regarding the relationship between noses and penises.

Oh, yes, a traumatic experience, and I thought I probably would never get over it.

I turned into my driveway. No, I was not sorry I had done it. I was really glad. But this was not to say I didn't feel a deep sorrow at the same time. One more chunk of space in the widening chasm between the boy and the girl who had fallen in love one fall day nineteen years before.

I walked around to the rear of the house to check on the state of the pool before going inside. It was Monday—Manuel the pool man's day, and I had to make sure he had come and attended to the yellowish smoggy film I had detected on the tiles rimming the edge. Yes, everything was tidy. The water was tranquil, unmarred by a dead insect or a stray fallen leaf. Unlike my life. My life had a lot of stray leaves floating around.

Leah was in the kitchen, standing at the restaurant-sized stove, stirring.

"What's cooking?" I asked and received a dirty look in reply. "Oh, that's nice, Leah. Really nice."

I was tired, I realized, and like Leah, slightly cranky, the afternoon's incident weighing heavily on my conscience, no matter how unaffected I tried to feel.

"Telephone messages." Leah muttered, gestured with her head toward the pad lying on the polished granite countertop next to the matching steel-colored telephone.

I glanced at the pad briefly, tore off the top page, asked, "What are Mikey and Matty up to?"

"Playroom. Their friend Tootie's here."

"That's nice. I'm going upstairs to lie down awhile. Answer the phone, will you?"

"That garbage thing's stuck again." She peered at me suspiciously. "What's the matter with *you?*"

"Nothing's the matter with me," I answered indignantly. "I'm a little tired, that's all. I'll call the man about the garbage disposal later."

"Sick of that machine." I heard her say after my retreating back.

I turned back the white satin coverlet on one of the two queen-sized beds where almost two years ago, one king-sized bed stood, kicked off my shoes, crawled beneath the covers, pulled them over my head. I didn't blame Leah for being sick of the garbage disposal; some days a person was sick of everything.

I pulled the covers down again, stared at the white ceiling, foolishly said aloud to myself, "So, Buffy Ann, what's the matter? Why aren't you happy? You've just been bedded by a very nice, very pretty man, and it *is* the first time in a very long time."

I wondered if Gavin Roth had guessed that, although I had been the aggressor, at the very last second I had almost lost my nerve and that I was definitely riding up and down on an emotional see-saw. I had been subject to a flurry of carnal desire, as well as a desire for revenge. But I had also been overwhelmed with shame and embarrassment at my own boldness. Mixed in was a lot of *I'll show you, Todd King!* And finally, it was all mixed up with a strong sense of regret. I thought of the young girl who had once firmly believed that you did it with only one man in a lifetime.

I conjured up the vision of Gavin and me once again.

He kissed my mouth, my ear, my neck, my breast. I threw my head back, my body arched against his. He pressed me down . . . down . . . down on the brown couch, as I dug fingers into his comely yellow hair.

But try as I could, I couldn't suppress another picture from crowding that one out. I was leaning, stretching out to bury my face in a mass of dark red curls.

Oh, God, he had been so sweet! So sweet! And so funny! So funny! Oh God, you know I loved him so!

The phone beside the bed rang, pierced my pain, I wouldn't answer it. I had told Leah to answer it, hadn't I?

I heard Leah yelling up the stairs. No matter how many times I told her to use the intercom, she wouldn't do it.

Oh Leah, go away! I'm in pain.

She was outside the bedroom door. "Pick up the phone," she snarled.

Instead, I got out of bed and spoke through the door. "I don't want to talk to anybody! Say I'm not home. Take a message."

"It's Megan. She say you better talk to her," Leah rasped ominously. I ran to the phone. "Megan! What's wrong?"

"I'll tell you what's wrong, Moth-ur! What's wrong is that this afternoon is Performance Day at dancing class and you're supposed to be here, that's what's wrong, Moth-ur, if you *really* want to know."

"Well, I'm *going* to be there," I said defensively. "I'll be there in ten minutes! I was almost out the door. So hold on to your leotard, will you?"

"You can't possibly drive here in ten minutes. I assumed you had completely forgotten about Performance Day."

"Well, I hadn't. Now just go back and join the others and I'll be there in fifteen minutes, okay?"

I had remembered, *that* morning, but the unusual event of the day had simply swept everything from my mind. I stepped into my shoes, grabbed my bag and my keys.

"Back in a couple of hours, Leah," I cried into the kitchen on my way out. "Don't let the boys kill each other. And when Mitch comes home, tell him I said he has to practice on the piano."

Back into the car and down the driveway. Right on Sunset. Left on Barrington to the Brentwood Studio of the Dance. Thank God there was a carpool for dance class or I would have to do this twice-a-day, twice-a-week. As it was I spent more time in the car than in bed. When we had first arrived in Los Angeles, I had complained of the eternal driving and Todd had suggested a chauffeur. But I wouldn't hear of it. I had said, "Before you know it, we'll have people screwing in bed for us."

And he had grinned. "You think people here don't?"

Take parking ticket. Slide into a space. Through the little garden and up the stairs to the Salon run by Tanya Stanislawa. Actually a Brooklyn girl who claimed to have danced, twenty years ago, with Martha Graham. *Really! Hadn't everybody?*

Megan came running up.

"I hope you're satisfied. You almost missed me!" she whispered loudly.

She's so pretty, I thought, for the thousandth time. And for the hundred thousandth time, I thought how much she resembled her father.

"But I *didn't* miss you, Megan. That's the important thing. When do you go on?"

"In about five minutes. I'm surprised you got here at all."

"Megan! I'm *here!*"

"Okay," she said grudgingly. "I have to go backstage now or I'll get killed. I just wanted to make sure you were here."

I nodded. "Yes."

"Daddy's supposed to be here any minute now, but I can't wait any longer. I have to go backstage."

"How do you know he's coming?"

"He said he would . . . this morning. While you were still in bed," Megan said accusingly. "And I called him when I called you. His secretary said he had already left."

I nodded.

"You see? *He* didn't forget."

He's forgotten a lot of things, baby daughter.

Somebody hissed for Megan.

"You'd better take a seat, Mother. And save a seat next to you for Daddy."

I've always done that, Megan. Until very, very recently.

84.

When I returned for my session the following week, Gavin made a valiant effort to restore things to a professional level. I felt sorry for him. I knew how hard it was to let go of one's ideals.

But doesn't he know that this isn't Giant Steps? That once you take a leap forward, you can't run back?

I reassured him again. *"You* have not violated any rules. *You* did not make the first overtures to a trusting patient. It was I, the patient, who flatly proposed we take our psycho-sexual ride on your nice brown cushions. It's me. *Blame me."*

But he winced. I saw him wince and I said, "If you insist, if you'd *really* rather, I'll talk. I do have subjects to talk about. Let's see. We've already discussed Leah and the children. Perhaps we could discuss

Bess? Bess comes on Tuesdays, Wednesdays, and Fridays to do the heavy cleaning. But she changes her schedule at will."

"Is she as interesting as Leah?"

"Not nearly. Leah doesn't like Bess, of course. And there's Herman, the windowman. He shows up every month or so. And there's Marlena the laundress—twice a week. Rumor has it that she's changed her name from Elvira."

"Are there any others in your life?" he asked, seemingly fascinated.

"Oh, there's a little man—he calls himself Apex who comes to do the crystal chandeliers. There are three of them, chandeliers, that is. One is in the French living room, recently changed from the fifteenth Louis to Louis Seize. More chic . . . or chicer, if you prefer. And there's one in the English dining room . . . Georgian. The largest one, of course, is in the entrance hall. Italian Renaissance."

"What nationality is the kitchen?" he asked, playing along nervously.

"United States . . . steel . . . stainless, you understand?"

"Is that it?"

"There's Manuel, the pool man. Twice a week. And Hirimoto and his crew. Three times a week. Grounds and watering. The watering is very important. And there's Juan. Juan comes once a week to wash the cars. Do you want to discuss Juan, Doctor, or wouldn't you really rather make love?"

Making love is what it's called.

I *did* remember a certain boy saying: "Making love is not necessarily an act of love."

I started to untie my wrap-around dress, as *I* locked the door.

"We could talk about your husband," Gavin said, somewhat desperately.

I smiled at him kindly. I shook my head. "No, you're wrong. We cannot talk about my husband. Not now." And then I said softly, "There's really no going back, you know."

After three more weekly sessions, to my immense relief, Gavin gave up trying to treat me. He stopped trying to talk to me about my husband and my marriage. We even started to become friends, as well as lovers, although I decided that it was in our best interests to remain *impersonal* friends, impersonal lovers, which was a shame in one way because I truly liked him. If we hadn't been lovers, we might have been good friends. But in the meantime, I was sure that my nerves were benefiting more from his jabbing than from his jabbering. *That* was pretty vulgar, but funny, and it was a shame I couldn't repeat it to anybody.

But the matter of the fee disturbed Gavin considerably. He said he refused to accept payment under what was clearly false pretenses. Fraud, almost. But I insisted that Todd be billed. How would it look to the receptionist, the accountant, to Dr. Silverstein, if there was no billing, no receipts, in view of my weekly visit? As for my husband, he *knew* I was seeing a psychiatrist. He *expected* a bill.

"That is my point. Part of my point," Gavin amended. "We don't *have* to meet here . . . in this office. I *do* live someplace. I would much rather take this . . ." he fumbled for a word and didn't find one—"out of my office into my home. I'd feel much more comfortable about it. The way it is now, I'm violating *my* couch and taking your husband's money for doing it. Do you know what that makes me?"

I giggled. "I think we'd better not think about that."

He *was* sweet, and refreshingly different from the usual L.A. man. How had he remained so innocent?

"Believe me, Gav, *this* is the only way. The safest way."

Was safe what I really wanted?

"I'm *supposed* to be here, we're *supposed* to be locked up in here enjoying privacy and discretion. So just take the money." I giggled again and shook my hand expressively. "You're really *earning* that money!"

Yes, I was satisfied with the arrangement as it was. But it did seem to me that Gavin was certainly *not* the brightest of shrinks. Otherwise he would have figured out by now that screwing away on Todd's money was the only kind of therapy from which I could possibly benefit.

But he could not let the matter drop.

"If you don't wish to come to my apartment then you could come here after hours."

I assumed he meant after Rosemary the receptionist left. She did leave after five, I assumed. She must have another life outside this office. She probably spent her private life searching out a man, or the big break, just like all the rest of the thousands of single women out there. Unlike the wives who merely waited, hoping they could hold on to their husbands.

Then I wondered if Gavin was getting it on with Rosemary? Why not? They were both single. He was handsome and she was pretty. But it was of no concern to me, I told myself. I wasn't jealous. To be jealous, one must feel love, or something like love. One must feel possessive, the desire to possess. But I felt none of this. *I was not in love.* I could not be in love. I could not spare the emotional energy a *real* love affair entailed. My emotional energies were otherwise engaged.

I told Gavin I couldn't possibly come after hours. But he was insistent. He consulted his calendar. "Tuesdays after five are good. And then afterwards, we can have dinner."

I knew what he was trying to do: he was trying to elevate our affair into something more than a quick roll on his precious couch. But dinners were out of the question. Little, intimate dinners in dark restaurants? That would mean planning and intrigue. Intrigue meant more involvement. There simply wasn't room in my life for that. No room, either in my head or my heart.

"Tuesdays are out of the question. Tuesdays I have a piano lesson at five." But then I thought, I *could* try it just once in the office after hours. But no dinner.

"All right," I said. "If it's so important to you, I guess I can trade my five o'clock piano lesson with Leah's two o'clock just this once."

"Leah takes piano lessons?"

"Yes. It seems she wanted to play the piano all her life. So when Miss Gaffney comes to give the lessons on Tuesdays—Matty is at three, Mitchell is at four, I'm at five, and Megan is at six, I have her do Leah at two."

"That's really nice," he smiled, obviously touched.

At least now he won't think I'm such a bitch, I thought.

"I really don't know how nice it is. Now that Leah has her piano lessons, she complains that I forced her into it. What do I care that it makes her arthritic fingers ache?"

He laughed delightedly, consulting his practitioner's watch. "That's wonderful. So I'll see you tomorrow. After five."

He led me to the door a bit hurriedly. I was already into the next patient's fifty-minute hour. We had used up that extra ten minutes from mine, and then some. And one patient was not supposed to see the next one. I strode out, averting my eyes from the patient who was waiting, pacing back and forth, fuming. But still I couldn't resist throwing that Rosemary a triumphant grin: I had squeezed a few extra minutes out of her doctor. In answer, she tossed her head in exasperation, setting her long, streaked, layered hair into motion. I didn't tell her, as I could have, "Cleo Mason says layered hair is out this season. The geometric cut is in."

It wasn't until I was in my car that I realized that if this was Monday, and I was returning to the doctor's office tomorrow, that was two days in a row. And that was accelerating things. And that was exactly what I had to avoid. Involvement and acceleration.

I arrived at the office at exactly a quarter past five. Strangely enough, I felt shy. It would be the first time we would really be alone: the reception room empty, the *outer* door locked.

He had his jacket off, his shirtsleeves rolled, his tie loosened. I had never seen him so. All the other times before, he had been either completely dressed or completely undressed. Either way, a professional costume—the jacket and tie for the practitioner at work; the roseate nudity, the red turgid phallus for the lover at play. Now at quarter past five, he was just a man, relaxed, enjoying an after-work drink.

"Join me?" he asked. "I'm having Scotch, no ice."

I nodded and he handed me a squat glass half-filled with the golden liquid. There *was* a difference in the air and he felt it too. I could tell. There was an intimacy now that had never been present in the afternoons. In spite of the big desk and the shelves lined with professional tomes, I could almost smell the delicate scent of flowers, could almost hear the strains of soft violins in the background. Too much intimacy. Too much warmth. It had been a mistake, after all, to come here after hours. I felt as if I were suffocating from the flowers, the music, the closeness of him. I decided to leave. Quickly. I set down my drink and moved to the door.

He appeared surprised and then hurt. "You've just come."

"I know. But I can't stay. I think I left something on the stove—"

"But you don't cook," he said accusingly. "Leah does."

"Leah's playing the piano. I'm sorry. Really. Another time . . . another hour."

And I was out in the reception area, my heart beating rapidly. A close call. I moved down the hall, toward the elevator. But then I slowed down, walking more slowly, half-expecting, half-hoping that he would come running after me, to put his arms around me, to kiss my hair, my mouth, the tip of my nose, to murmur softly in my ear, to turn me around . . . back to the empty office. But he didn't and I pressed the down button.

I drove around, confused. I was a fool. A fool who didn't know her own mind. By this time in my life I should know what it was I wanted. What *did* I want?

He pushed me down on the cushions, knelt on the floor beside me. I felt the flick of his tongue entering me. It felt thrilling . . . wonderful . . . good.

If it feels good, do it!
But I hadn't.

I was not yet ready to go home. I decided I would drive over and see Cassie. She would be at home now, giving Jenny her dinner. It was always easy for me to be with Cassie. She asked me no questions, passed no judgment. There was a tranquility to our shared misery.

I found Cassie and Jenny doing a jigsaw puzzle together, having already finished their dinner. She put Jenny to bed with some picture books and we settled down in the den without putting on the lights. Somehow, the near dark suited our mutual mood.

She made herself a drink after I refused one. I suspected that she was drinking too much, but I certainly was no longer in a position to give advice. I thought perhaps she would ask me how *White Lily* was coming along. It was funny; it had taken so long for the production to get started on the picture that everyone had been constantly asking when it was going to begin. Now, everyone only wanted to know when it would all end. But Cassie didn't ask. It was as if she had completely lost interest in the whole thing. With her mother ill, and, as Cassie put it—a little silly in the head—the movie and Guy had lost all relevance for her. She *did* ask me what I was doing these days and I told her that I was seeing a psychiatrist.

"You!" she scoffed gently. "But you're probably the only well-adjusted person I know."

"Oh, not so well-adjusted," I smiled.

"You are! I remember years ago you said I should see a head doctor. Maybe I should have. Perhaps I wouldn't have messed up my life so thoroughly. A little, but not so completely."

"It's not too late," I said but without any real conviction. There was no use in my getting excited even if I had the energy to do so. She had never heeded me before and I couldn't expect to convince her of anything at this late stage.

"It's too late," she said flatly.

The hopelessness in her voice got to me as usual, and in spite of myself, I began to warm up. "You just can't give up, Cassie. You're too young to give up. Why don't you call Win? Grant him the right of refusal."

"His silence is refusal enough. He told me it was important that I tell my mother before—well, you know it all. But he made it very clear that was the only way he would have any use for me. And *now,* I can't tell Mother off. She's sick and she wouldn't even know what I was talking about anymore. And I can't even call off my marriage as a gesture for Win. There's nothing to call off anymore. It's dead. It just died by itself. So there's nothing I can do for Win to show him that his love meant something to me. *That our love didn't come in second.* No man wants to think that he comes second . . . even if it's only to a crazy obsession. Now he would think that I'm only choosing him by default. He doesn't want me now. Why *would* he want me now?"

"Because he loves you," I said reasonably. "And no matter what, he must know you love him. And there *is* Jenny."

With my own words, hope surged in my breast. Maybe I *could* convince her now, even if I had never convinced her before. "Cassie," I said urgently. "He couldn't turn down Jenny."

"But I can't *use* Jenny."

"Who says you can't?" I demanded. "You listen to me, Cassie. In this life you've got to use everything you have. And besides, you would be doing it *for* Jenny. Give that kid a break. Give her back a real father!"

That was the clincher. She would do it for Jenny. I could see it in her eyes.

"And don't call. Just go! Go this weekend. And you can have the whole weekend together!"

"But my mother—Jenny—"

"Leave your mother to her nurses and her friends. And leave Jenny with us."

She looked at me and it was the first glimmer of hope I had seen in her face for years—ever since Win had gone away. "Yes?" she asked me for reinforcement.

"Yes!" *Oh yes, Cassie, yes!*

"I'll do it! Oh Buffy, thank you." She threw her arms around me.

"You haven't anything to thank me for."

"Yes I do. I have to thank you for being my friend and not giving up on me."

"Oh hell." I could feel the hot tears in my eyes. "I have to be good for something—"

At least the day hasn't been completely wasted.

85.

For the rest of the week I could think of nothing else but how I had run from Gavin's office on Tuesday. Was it all over? Did I want it to be all over? So quickly? I should have known better, right from the beginning. I should have seen that Gavin was a serious person, that an affair such as the one I envisioned would not be one he could tolerate for long. That it would soon have to be nothing at all or something more meaningful. And he was the doctor—why hadn't *he* realized that I was not in the market for relevant or meaningful. But I couldn't make up my mind whether or not I would keep my regular Monday afternoon appointment with him.

Friday morning, Suellen called. She said that she was going to be home all day and why didn't I drop by for a visit? It had been quite a while since we had talked. I went that afternoon hoping she would not be in one of her more probing moods.

Over the hill and through the Valley, to Suellen's house we go
It's a beautiful day and the horse knows the way . . .

No, this was L.A. and there were few horses—only cars. Lots and lots of cars . . . cutting in from lane to lane and blaring rock music. Girls brushing their hair at stoplights. Most of the cars were extremely sporty and carried messages on bumper stickers. Relevant messages. And who, but who, knew the way?

I drove into the cul de sac of glass and redwood homes. I remembered that Suellen had chosen the cul de sac because the children would be out of the way of traffic, would be that much safer. I ran up the steps laid out in layered terrace fashion, and Suellen came to the door wearing two braids and her white chef's apron. Good cooking smells wafted from the rear of the house.

"I thought you were doing all your cooking in that place you and Cleo renovated."

"This is my day off. I'm cooking for the family. I thought it was time I gave them a treat."

I followed Suellen into her Modern Science kitchen, all bleached oak, with an extended greenhouse filled with geraniums, flowering orchids, and varied herbs.

"What's happening?" Suellen asked casually. Too casually. Ever since the day she had demanded that I hand over my jewelry to save my marriage, she had been suspicious of me.

"Nothing much."

"Are you still going to that analyst?"

"Yes. It's something to do," I said flippantly. "With you and Cleo working all the time and Cassie busy with her mother . . . Suzannah, working too, of course," I mumbled quickly, not to give Suellen a chance to be suspicious at my *not* mentioning Suzannah's name, "I don't have anybody to play with. And if a woman doesn't keep busy, she's too much of a burden to her children and her husband. She nags them too much. Don't you agree?"

She ignored my last remark. "You have other friends—"

I made a face. "No friends like the old friends."

"The trouble with you, Buff, is that you were used to working. And it's good for you."

"You never used to think so. Back in Ohio you used to tell me that I should stay at home with my children."

She opened the oven door, peeked in, and slammed it shut. "That was then and this is now. That was Ohio."

"Now what does that mean?"

"It means that there weren't so many things to . . . distract you—"

"I don't know what that means either."

"Besides, your children are older now. Why don't you go to work at the studio, Buffy? They could use you. They need you. Howard says Todd really needs somebody to run the record company."

I made a face. "Oh that. One of Todd's rejuvenation products. Taking over that old Gold Records Company."

"Howard says Todd's really brought the company back to what it was."

"Yes. Well, I guess having Beau record for them was really fortunate. And if it's doing that well, they don't need me, do they?"

"What *is* it with you? Don't you care that Todd is knocking himself out . . . and Howard too? They're spreading themselves too thin."

"Well then, let Todd delegate more authority to other executives.

And if you don't get off my case, I'm going home. I came here for a little pleasant conversation, not to have you sitting on my back."

"What does Todd say about your going to a psychiatrist?"

"I don't know. I haven't discussed it with him."

"Buffy, are you happy?"

"Oh shitty day, what kind of a question is *that?* Of course I'm happy. I live a life that's the dream of every young woman in America. I live in Beverly Hills, don't I?"

"Does living in Beverly Hills make you happy?"

"Of course. It means that if I'm careful and don't stray too far from home, and stick to Sunset Boulevard, I might never have to go on a freeway. In Southern California, *that's* happiness. And I told you, Suellen, I didn't come here to get hauled over the coals."

"Why did you come?"

"You invited me. And as I said, for some friendly conversation. And to check up on you. To see that *you're* not getting into any trouble." I grinned at her.

"Are *you*, Buff?"

"What?"

"Getting into any trouble?"

I got up and went over to the stove. I picked up a lid, dipped my finger into a pot, and stuck the finger in my mouth. "Dee-lish!"

"Is that an answer?"

"What's going on here, Suellen, with all this family cooking?"

"Well, I'm usually cooking for other people these days, and bringing home what's left for the children and Howard. But when I get a chance, I want to cook Howard a really delicious, heavy, fattening home-cooked meal that he will remember for a month." *Finally,* she broke down and laughed. "I want to spoil Howard for some chick who will make love to him in the hottest, most lascivious, liberated fashion but feed him yogurt."

I laughed, delighted that Suellen hadn't completely forgotten to have a sense of humor. "Remember when we were kids, what we used to say? *Treat 'em nice, but feed 'em doody.* Remember?"

She smiled, remembering. "Yes."

"It *does* smell good in here. It smells like I've died and gone to heaven and Mama's doing the cooking."

"This isn't Mama's cooking. This is *Jewish* cooking that's going on here."

"But when did you start to cook Jewish?"

"I've been reading Jewish cookbooks lately . . . for recreation. I want Howard to have the dishes he grew up with so that he'll *know* this glass and redwood house is really home. And home *is* where the heart is, Buffy."

"Oh my goodness. Will you stop making points? Try for a little more subtlety, will you? So show me what's going on here. Whatever I dipped my finger into was heavenly."

"That was stuffed cabbage."

I looked into the pot again. Plump cabbage rolls swam in a tomato sauce flecked with little golden globules of fat. I stuck my hand in again and this time broke off a bit of one of the rolls, burning myself a little. I put the piece in my mouth. "Hot! But yummy!"

"Sit down. I'll give you a plate and a fork and knife."

I shook my head. "What else did you make?"

"Tzimmes."

"What's *timmes?*"

"Tzimmes—there's a *z* in there, I think. It's sweet potatoes, carrots, and prunes." She opened the pot for me to look, and again I stuck in my hand. "Wait." Suellen said. "I'll give you a plate. Sit down."

"No. As a matter of fact, smarty-pants, we *had* this dish at home. Only Mama called it carrot stew."

"I don't think so. Mama cooked German style."

I shook my head. "I think this cooking is very similar. What do you say to that?"

"Well, I suppose there *is* a similarity," Suellen said judiciously. She opened up one of the double oven doors. I peeked in. "There. That's a noodle pudding," I said triumphantly. "Am I right?"

"Yes. It's a *kugel.* With golden raisins."

"Mama used the dark ones. You know I haven't tasted a piece of noodle pudding since Mama's. Give me the recipe. Maybe I can talk Leah into making it."

"Do you want a piece now?"

"Okay. A tiny piece. And I do mean a sliver. I don't stay skinny by gorging, you know."

"A little piece won't make you fat."

"God! You *do* sound like a Jewish mother. Or what I think a Jewish mother is supposed to sound like."

Suellen cut me a big piece as I knew she would and I groaned but ate it all up. "Mmmm . . . this *is* good," I said, nailing the last crumb with my fork.

"I've got a brisket of beef too."

"I want to see."

"It's in the fridge cooling so I can skim off the fat. Then I'll slice it, put it back in its nice fatless juices, and back into the oven to warm. But let me show you my dessert." She held up a cake with strawberry frosting.

"Is that a Jewish cake?" I asked, keeping a straight face.

"No, this is a love cake." She lowered the cake dish so I could see the top. Written in butter-cream script was *I Love You, Howard.*

"Oh, my!" and I burst into tears.

"What's the matter? Oh, I *knew* something was wrong!"

"Nothing's the matter, you fool," I said, wiping my eyes with her kitchen towel. "I'm just touched, that's all. The cake's beautiful and so is the sentiment. Old Howard is really going to enjoy himself tonight. What a meal to come home to! And that cake! But you know, Suellen, Howard doesn't really need that cake to know you love him."

"Yeah, but you know that old joke—*it can't hurt.*"

"No, I don't know the joke. Tell me."

"An old actor is up on the stage in this Yiddish play when he drops dead. There's a big fuss and finally they carry the body off and the manager comes out and makes the announcement that because of the actor's death, the rest of the play has been canceled. So an old gentleman in the audience gets up and protests. But the manager says, 'Sorry. The man is dead and there's nothing to be done.' So the old guy says, 'Give him an enema.' The manager says, 'He's dead. It can't help.' So the old man says, 'Yes, but it can't *hurt!*'"

I laughed heartily and consulted my watch. "It's almost three. Maybe I'd better go. Cassie's Jenny is supposed to get off the school bus with Matty. They're in the same class, you know, and Jenny's staying with us for the weekend. I want to make sure everything went all right and they did put Jenny off the bus in the right place."

"You just came. Why don't you call Leah and check? Then you can stay with a free mind."

"All right." I dialed my number and after at least ten rings Leah answered. "Is everything all right? Is Jenny there?" Leah grunted. "Oh, good. See you soon." Leah hung up.

"How come you're minding Jenny?"

"Cassie went up to Palo Alto to see Win Winfield."

"The one who was her neighbor?"

"Uh-huh."

Suellen studied me for a moment. "Is Jenny *his* daughter?"

"Yes. But don't say anything to anybody."

"I really don't understand Cassie. She's not living with Guy, hasn't for quite a while. And Win's Jenny's father. And since she went to see him, I assumed she still cares for him. Why isn't she divorced from Guy and married to him? Or at least living with him?"

"Because life isn't as simple or uncomplicated for everyone as it is for you, Suellen. Your path is always clearly revealed to you. You're one of the lucky few. By the way, where are my niece and nephew? Will they be home soon? I'd like to see them while I'm here."

"Oh, kids. They're hardly home anymore. When they're little and you're housebound you think you'd sell your birthright for a few free hours. And then they're grown up and busy more with their friends than with you, and then you actually yearn for their company. Petey's practicing with his band which is all he thinks about, and Becky's at religious instruction."

"Religious instruction? What kind of religious instruction?" Suellen and I had never been much of churchgoers.

"Becky's going to be *bas mitzvah*. Confirmed. She wanted it."

"First all this Jewish cooking, and now Becky's going to be *bas* whatever. Are you all converting?"

I guessed that my tone was flip, too flip, because Suellen became angry. "Nobody said I'm converting. Becky chooses to be Jewish, and that's her decision. And what's so bad about that? What would be so bad if Petey and I converted too? It's good for a family to have religious roots in a heathen town and it doesn't matter what religion it is. Personally, I think religious school is a whole lot better place for a kid to be than Hollywood Boulevard, strung out on dope."

That was Suellen for you. No in-betweens. It was either one or the other. Her path so clearly revealed to her. And mine so obscured. I couldn't even make up my mind whether or not I really wanted to go back to Gavin's office Monday. Was it becoming too dangerous a place to be?

When I arrived home I found there were more heads for dinner than I had counted on. In addition to Jenny, Megan had brought her girlfriend, Fawn, home with her. Fawn, it seemed, had immediately called her mother and asked permission not only to eat dinner at our house, but to spend the night. Fawn's mother had generously assented. And Mitch had come home with his buddy, Hylan. Hylan had also obtained permission to stay for dinner, but unfortunately (depending on whose outlook), not to sleep over.

In honor of Jenny's, Fawn's, and Hylan's presence, Leah had prepared meatballs and spaghetti, not one of my favorite dishes, and had already set the table in the breakfast room, including a place for me.

"I'm going out to dinner, Leah."

"No, you're not."

I waited silently for Leah to continue as I assumed she would, in her own time.

"Mr. King called. Not meeting you for dinner. Canceled." She fished in her pocket for a crumpled slip of paper. "He say you should meet him at screaming. Nine o'clock."

I furrowed my brow. Screaming? Oh, the screening. Of course. We had been supposed to meet the Dunns for dinner, and then go on to a screening at the MGM lot.

"The table in here isn't really big enough for so many people, Leah. Why don't we eat in the dining room?"

"What for?" she asked contemptuously. "So they can drop the spaghetti all over the fancy carpet in there? Is that what you want?"

Oh, you're a wise one, you are, Leah. You can recognize a woman bent on self-destruction when you see one.

I sat down with the kids with a dish of cottage cheese.

"Why don't you eat some spaghetti and meatballs?" Leah asked me angrily. "That ain't real food."

"I'm dieting. Why don't *you* pull up a chair and eat some spaghetti yourself?" I countered.

She was hovering, wiping up, slapping a messy hand here, shoveling out more green beans there. "I et already."

No one had ever actually seen Leah eat a real meal. I had an idea that she stuffed herself with sweets all day long when no one was looking. She was entitled. At her age, and single, she could do any damn thing she pleased.

Mitch and Hylan tried to grab most of the contents of the huge bowl of meatballs for themselves. "Hey there," I said to Mitchell. "No hogging. Leave some of those for somebody else."

"We're growing boys," Mitch crowed, showing off for his friend. "We need red meat more than these girls." He and Hylan laughed uproariously.

"Gross," Megan said.

"I think gross is a gross word," I told her.

"I'm a growing boy too," Matty said, and stood up on his chair to spear another meatball himself.

My God, he's already worrying about his manhood too, I thought, as Leah whacked him on the behind, sat him down in his chair, and passed the bowl around. Mikey grabbed a meatball with his fingers and Leah smacked his hand. Megan muttered, "Gross," again and I said, "Use the meat fork, Mikey," and reflected that instead of worrying about whether to continue with my affair, I should better be at home teaching my children some table manners.

"Leave him alone," Mitch said. "A man's got to eat like a man," and he and Hylan went off into another gale of laughter.

Mitchell certainly was into male chauvinism tonight. I ruffled his dark red hair. "Hey, watch that kind of talk. Everyone here is equal, everyone is courteous, and everyone gets his fair share of the meatballs. Okay?"

Megan and Fawn looked with superior disdain at Mitchell and Hylan. "You know what the boys in the school cafeteria do, Mother? They *throw* food at one another. And *they're* fourteen and fifteen. Can you imagine?"

"Very sophisticated behavior," I laughed.

Jenny chewed her food thoroughly, waited to swallow before she spoke. "Boys' manners are terrible, aren't they, Mrs. King?"

I held back a smile. Chauvinism wasn't limited to boys. "Your manners are very good, Jenny. I hope the boys at this table can learn from you." She smirked with satisfaction.

Leah pushed a few more beans onto Mikey's plate. He pushed them back, off the plate, onto the table, and then onto the floor, and looked at his oldest brother for approbation. I was about to slap his hand myself as Leah muttered, "And *she* wants these wild animals to eat in the dining room." The phone rang. *She,* as Leah referred to me, jumped up to get the phone before Megan could, but I went into the kitchen to do so. It was much too noisy in the breakfast room.

It was Gavin! It was the first time I had heard his voice on the phone and I experienced one of those peculiar sensations—much like a swarm of butterflies fluttering around inside me. Angry at the butterflies, I said, "You shouldn't call me here."

"Why not? A doctor may phone his patient," he chided.

"Are you calling me about my next appointment, Doctor? It's for next Monday—"

"I'm at home," he said. "Are you alone? Can you talk?"

"For the moment, yes," I spoke guardedly. "But I can't really. What is it? What do you want?"

"How unfriendly. I just wanted to see how things were coming along."

"We're having dinner. The children and I, and my children's guests. And Leah."

"I'm going to be home all night. Can you come over when you're through with dinner?"

"No."

"I'll expect you."

How quickly man's conscience falters, I thought. How quickly he sinks into the mire. It was only a few days ago that Gavin was anguishing over carrying on with a married patient, and now he was calling me at home and urging me to leave my family hearth and join him in assignation.

"No. I can't. I have a screening to attend tonight. At nine. I'm meeting my husband there."

For a few seconds he didn't speak. The word husband had apparently brought him to conscience. But then he said, "Come for an hour before the screening."

He hung up quickly then. Yes, it seemed Gavin was getting over certain ethical reservations in a hurry. And I was pleased. A man with ideals was too good, too perfect, and vulnerable. And a man with ideals and vulnerability made me too vulnerable. And that led to commitment, and I already had a commitment. And it had nothing at all to do with Dr. Gavin Roth.

Then I started to think about his apartment. I had told him I wouldn't come, but I didn't think he believed me. And while I hadn't asked for the address, I already knew it. I had it written down . . . for reasons of possible emergency.

Of course, if I did go there, there *were* things I could discuss with him. He *was* a psychiatrist and it would be interesting to get his thinking on certain matters, since I no longer had a husband to discuss things with, matters such as the boys' growing machismo. Should that be squelched or encouraged? Or why was it that Suellen saw life's crossroads so clearly defined, and my vision was so muddled?

Distracted, I hadn't been concentrating on the table conversation. Leah went to get the sundaes she had prepared out of the freezer, and I suddenly heard Mitch tell his audience, ". . . so I slugged him," and everyone laughed, *even* Megan and Fawn.

"That's nice, Mitchell," I said, though I hadn't heard the beginning of his story. "I can't think of a nicer way to settle an argument."

Leah brought in the tray of sundaes and I helped her distribute them. Then I looked up and saw Todd standing in the doorway. The hall behind him was dark and for the moment, in the half-light he was standing in, he looked like the Todd of old and my heart slipped out of place. It seemed like I was having a lot of difficulty with my insides lately. Everything was constantly jumping and fluttering and slipping out of place.

I tried to refocus my eyes so that I would see him only as he was now. He didn't look that much different really. The auburn curls were partially gray, and more carefully arranged these days. And he wore a jacket or a suit with his now perpetual tan. Ah, the grin. It was forced these days, whereas once it had been as natural as the sun coming out in the morning.

What was he doing here? He was supposed to be busy elsewhere. And at the screening at nine.

"Surprise!" I called out for the benefit of the children. "Look who has come home to dinner." And only Leah, who threw me a dark, dirty look, must have noticed the lemon-acid tinge in my dulcet tones. "Too bad that you've just missed it. All the meatballs are gone."

"Yeah, Dad," Mitch said. "If you don't grab quick around here you're out of luck."

Todd put a hand on Mitchell's shoulder and said, "I bet that if I go upstairs to change, by the time I come down, Leah will have found something for me to eat. What do you say, kids?"

"Yeah, Dad."

"I bet she will."

"I'm sure she will, Daddy!"

"And what do you think, Jenny?" he asked Cassie's little girl, tipping up her chin.

"Oh yes, Mr. King, I'm sure she will."

Old charmer, Todd.

Leah disappeared into the kitchen, quick as a bunny for the old charmer.

"I decided to cancel my business meeting that I canceled out the dinner for," he smiled at me appealingly. "And the screening too. If you've seen one screening, you've seen them all." Our private joke, our old private joke.

I looked back at him blankly, as blankly as I could manage.

"I thought we'd all spend the evening at home together for a change. The kids and us."

I still said nothing, and he said to the children, "Okay. Be back in a minute."

By the time he came down again, wearing a white pullover and jeans, Leah had a steak and home fries ready. Well, for Todd she had finally used the microwave!

"Boy oh boy," Mitch said, eyeing the steak. "We only had meatballs and spaghetti. You're a lucky stiff."

"I am, aren't I?" Todd agreed as he doused the steak with catsup. He smiled up at me with determination, but I was careful not to smile back.

"Who's for a game of Frisbee as soon as I'm done eating?"

"Me!"

"Me, too!"

"Me, Daddy!"

"How about you, Megan? And you, Fawn? Don't you want to play?"

Megan and Fawn exchanged looks, and nodded at one another. They'd do him a favor. "Sure, Daddy, we'll play."

"But how can we play outside, Mr. King?" Jenny asked anxiously. "It's dark outside."

"I'm going to make it light outside, Jenny, light enough for us to play." He went into the kitchen where the panels of switches were. And in a second through the French doors, we could see the night light up all around us.

He came back and sat down again. "Well, Jenny, am I magic? Did I make the night light?"

Jenny giggled, delighted. "Yes, Mr. King.

Oh yes. Mr. Magic Man. Playing God. Still, I couldn't help but think of how, once, I, too, thought he was magic.

"How about you, Buffy Ann?" Todd asked, looking down as he cut his steak. "Will you play Frisbee too? Hey kids, don't you all want Mommy to play too?"

They all yelled out the proper affirmative answer but I noticed a distinct letdown in enthusiasm. Obviously, I didn't generate as much enthusiasm as the man of the house.

"That would be nice," I said. "But I have a meeting. The museum's acquisition committee. I was planning on going there before going on to the screening." I said this although Todd and I both knew that up until a couple of hours ago the plan was for me to meet him and the Dunns for dinner before going on to the screening.

Todd did not point this out, but looked at me, his face smooth. "Maybe you could skip it? I thought after the Frisbee I'd read some bedtime stories to Jenny, Mikey, and Matty and then the rest of us would play Monopoly."

He was so clever, mentioning the bedtime stories so that the younger ones wouldn't even raise a fuss about not playing Monopoly. But he was also out of it. The older kids would have much preferred the video games.

"No," I said with finality. "I can't possibly skip my meeting. But maybe Leah will play instead of me? How about it, Leah?"

Leah, predictably, gave me one of her slow, evil looks.

Even as I got into the car I wasn't sure I was going to Gavin's. It had just become important for me to leave the house, to make Todd wonder where it was that I was really going.

I turned east on Sunset, drove aimlessly until I came to Hollywood. Then I turned around, drove west on Sunset, trying to make up my mind. Somehow it was a bigger decision now, whether or not to go to Gavin's apartment, than it had been when I had decided to seduce him in his office. It was a commitment. I knew it, and once I went there, he would know it too, and there would be no going back for either one of us.

Suddenly I was at the corner of Beverly Glenn and I did it—I made a left turn from the right lane, cutting off a silver Jag, and when the young man driving the Jag leaned out his window and called me a cunt, I couldn't have agreed more. I drove over to Wilshire Boulevard furiously. I was going to do it and the sooner the better.

I parked my car in the underground lot, rode the elevator up to the lobby.

"Dr. Roth," I said to the deskman.

"Whom shall I announce, Madam?"

Oh dear. Oh God. This *was* a commitment. Hadn't Gavin realized that I was in no position to be advertising? Why hadn't he just left word I was to be sent right up?

"Mata Hari," I improvised.

The man picked up the house phone. "Mrs. Matty Harry is here,

Sir." He listened. "Dr. Roth says you're to go right up. Take the elevator to the right, please. 1106."

I was annoyed that he wasn't waiting for me at the elevator door. I looked around for 1106. Now I had to hunt his door down, ring the bell, wait for him to answer it like some high-class hooker from the Hollywood Hills.

When he finally opened the door, I was taken aback by the sight of him. Jeans, barefooted, bare-chested, the thick stripe of yellow hair curling down to his waist revealed. I didn't know what I had expected but it wasn't this . . . this informality. It was so . . . intimate.

"Why didn't you manage better?" I asked crankily. "Did I really have to go through that C.I.A. inspection downstairs?"

He smiled at me, that charming Robert Redford smile. "You managed very nicely."

He was such a goddamned pretty boy, prettier than Todd, I thought irritably. And younger by a few years. The thought that Cleo might say, "Oh good. Younger men are *in* this year," made me even more irritable. I looked around the low-lit room. It was well-appointed, even luxurious, but it looked much like his office—the same browns, beiges, stained woods. Still it was different here, warmer . . . so much so, I broke out in perspiration. I could feel it . . . between my thighs.

I went over to a door, peeked into the bedroom. All gray flannel. "A decorator?" I asked crisply, trying to break the mood.

He lifted his arms in a helpless gesture. "A sublet."

Then, "You look very beautiful tonight."

He had never said I was beautiful before. It was disquieting.

I was wearing a man-tailored gray suit, and knee-high burnt crimson boots. Subconscious armor? Perhaps. But here I was, the blood rushing to my head. I shouldn't have come. It was a terrible mistake. Oh, yes, there was too much intensity. The room was too dark, too close. And he stood there looking at me, too close, too warm. Cleo would say: *too hot, too sexy.*

Still, he made no move to touch me and now I wanted him to, my body ached for him to. I wanted him to come over to me, put his arms around me, to put his hands on my breasts. I would breathe easier then. By standing there, looking at me in that awed, hungry way, by not touching me, by not saying anything, the feeling in that room was more eloquent than any words.

Finally he said, as if remembering his manners, "Would you like something to drink?"

I shook my head, unable to speak. And then he came over to me and without touching me with his hands, buried his face in the V of my blouse, and I groaned involuntarily. My knees trembled and buckled and his arms came around and pressed my buttocks to him.

He picked me up, carried me into the bedroom, and undressed me. My eyes were closed and I saw nothing. I only felt his hands undressing me and then his lips moving over my breasts, and I heard him whisper, "You are so beautiful" and then I felt the kiss of his tongue and then those centrifical forces started moving from my core, getting larger and wider until they burst within me, and I moaned and groaned and opened my eyes wide. This, then, was the moment I was first unfaithful to Todd King, and everything that had happened before—in the Doctor's office—was as if nothing to this very moment.

I left him reluctantly, with more reluctance than I would have preferred. I drove home, thinking about the cake Suellen had showed me earlier that day—the *I Love You, Howard* cake. Once I had baked a cake for Todd in that little off-campus, third-floor apartment. The cake had come out misshapen from the old disreputable oven, half-burned on the bottom, concave on top. It must have been some special occasion. I tried to remember what the occasion was, but it was such a long time ago, I no longer could recall.

86.

Saturday passed more or less uneventfully, and bright and early Sunday morning, Howard and Becky came over in the oversized station wagon Suellen sometimes used for her catering, and picked up Todd, Mikey, Matty, Mitchell, Hylan, and Jenny to go to Disneyland. At the very last moment, Megan and Fawn, who had arrived only minutes before, patronizingly allowed themselves to be persuaded to go along. Howard told me Suellen was working and Petey was rehearsing with his band, and tried to talk me into going with them too, but I begged off, saying that I hadn't heard from Cassie and I wanted to be there when she returned from her weekend.

Things must be going smoothly at the studio, I guessed, for Todd and Howard to go off on a Sunday so lightheartedly. Usually Todd spent at least half a Sunday looking at the takes for the week, and the other half in consultation with Leo and the editors.

I drove Leah to church, came home again, wandered around the house, gnawed about whether I would keep my appointment at Gavin's the next day, and waited for Cassie.

Leah arrived home from church in a taxi. As usual, I had told her to call me for a ride home, but this wasn't her way, and I had long since stopped arguing with her.

It must be a good sign, I thought, that I hadn't heard from Cassie. That probably meant that she and Win were having such a wonderful reunion that there was no time for a call.

I was a wreck as the afternoon wore on, torn with ambivalence about the morrow's appointment with the good doctor, wondering what had happened with Cassie and Win, irritated with Leah's suspicious looks directed at my nervous pacing.

Finally, Cassie was there and it was with a great sinking of heart that I saw she was alone. I had been hoping that she would come back triumphant with Win in tow. But I should have known better. She looked terrible. She said she had been driving since dawn.

"Well?" I almost screamed at her, prompting her.

"I never saw Win."

"Oh . . ."

"He wasn't there. He was in Tahoe for the weekend. His housekeeper told me."

"Why didn't you wait for him to come back?"

"Yes. That's what I thought too, at first. I drove from Palo Alto to San Francisco and registered in a hotel. I thought I'd drive back to Palo Alto Sunday night. But last night I realized he must have gone to Tahoe with *somebody*. So I got into the car early this morning and here I am."

I was furious with her. I wanted to shake her.

"He *could* have gone there alone. He could have gone there with another man. A friend. A buddy. To go fishing or something. And he *could* have gone there with a woman. So what? You didn't think he was going to live like a monk, did you?"

"I guess I just got scared. I didn't want to find out the truth in case it was a serious affair. A woman he was serious with—I don't blame

him." She shook her head. "I made my bed . . . a very messy bed
. . . and I don't blame him that he didn't want to lie in it with me."

My frustration was so great I wanted to cry. But I was too exhausted
for tears. And how could one argue with a woman who was too afraid
to face the possibility she would have to give up her dream, her fantasy
of a reconciliation, forever?

She went home. I would drop Jenny off when she came back from
Disneyland. And I made up my mind that no matter what, I would
keep my appointment with Gavin tomorrow. I would not be like Cassie.
I would grab the moment!

Then the gang arrived home and Leah suddenly said she felt sick and
went to bed. I had a feeling about her sudden illness. I was sure it had
something to do with my next day's appointment at the doctor's office. I
think in the dark recesses of Leah's mind she connected my weekly
visits to the doctor with the trouble she *sensed* in our house . . . even
without being in my bedroom at night. I had always suspected that
Leah was a witch.

87.

I held my breath as I furtively tiptoed down the stairs the next morning
at seven o'clock. If Leah was feeling better today, up and about, attending to the children and Todd, I would sneak back upstairs and lie in bed
until Todd had left for the day. I preferred not to watch Todd with the
children, engaged in their early morning play—Todd sweetly teasing
Megan, listening to the boys' stories, helping Mikey with his cereal,
with Leah cheerful as she wouldn't be the rest of the day. It was a lovely
scene, too lovely to bear.

I prayed that Leah would be up, maybe making pancakes this morning, or French toast. If Leah was up and well, then I would be able to
keep my appointment at Gavin's office. And if she wasn't, I would have
to stay home to be there when Mikey arrived home from nursery
school, when Matty came home from kindergarten, to take care of Leah
herself. Even if I could get Bess, who came on Tuesdays to clean, to
come today instead, I couldn't very well ask her to take care of Leah,

who probably would have brained Bess with the lamp if she came near her bed. And now I *needed* to see Gavin. I was consumed with the need to see him.

I listened in the hall, outside the breakfast room. Yes, all was well. Leah was up, insisting Mitchell eat his eggs if he wanted sausage, Todd backing her up, while Megan begged and pouted for a ride to school, and Todd insisting he would be late if he waited for her. Every school-day they had this conversation. Every day, Todd, who liked to get to the office early, warned Megan he would not wait for her—that she should take the school bus . . . and every day almost, he waited for her. It was their private little game and it had become a sweet routine.

I turned around and went back up the stairs, grateful to Leah for deciding to rise from her sick bed. I had a new dress I would wear to Gavin's office—a red silk Chinese dress, thigh-high side slits, the mandarian collar piped in gold, and I thought about how Gavin would think I was beautiful in the dress. I thought about that so that I wouldn't think about the warm breakfast conversation going on in the breakfast room and in my head.

At nine thirty I was in a bubblebath when the phone rang. I picked it up knowing Leah wouldn't, not until it had rung at least twelve times.

It was Rosemary, Gavin's receptionist.

"Buffy," she said. *Buffy!* "I'm calling to say that your afternoon appointment has been canceled."

"What time am I supposed to come?"

"Doctor Roth has not told me to schedule another appointment at this time."

Did I detect a certain gloating satisfaction in her voice?

"Let me talk to the doctor."

"I'm sorry, Buffy, but he is not in now."

"But he has to be in. He has hours."

"Emergency."

"Where is he? I have to speak to him."

"I'm sorry, Buffy," she said cheerfully, "but I'm not able to reach the doctor. When I hear from him, I will be sure to give him your message."

When I didn't hear from Gavin by eleven o'clock, I called the office again. "This is *Mrs. King.* I want to speak to you-know-who."

"I'm sorry, Buffy. Doctor Roth is with a patient now. You know that I may not disturb him when he is with a patient," she chided.

"Did you give him my message?"

"Oh yes. I'm sure he'll get back to you later," she said with enthusiasm.

Clearly, Leah was not the only witch in town.

What was he up to? I wondered. What kind of a game was he playing with me? I had thought he was so innocent, so guileless. But now he was doing *something* . . . was being manipulative. Playing hard to get? Something as ridiculous as that? Or what?

I called back again. "You tell Doctor Roth that I have to talk to him. You tell him I'm having a nervous breakdown and am seriously thinking of doing injury to myself."

She put me on hold, came back after a few moments. "The doctor says he will call you back in twenty minutes. He asks that you try to control yourself and not do injury to yourself until that time. He suggests that you drink a glass of cold water and hold your breath for a count of ten."

He called back in exactly twenty minutes.

"Why was I canceled?" I demanded.

"I'll explain it all to you tonight. At my apartment. And please stop calling my office every five minutes. You're disrupting our schedule."

"I want my appointment! I cannot come to your apartment. Why can't I have my appointment?"

"You can't. It's gone. Your new appointment is at my apartment at eight. I'll expect you and I'll explain it all to you then."

"I can't come."

"In that case I won't be able to explain it all for you, will I?"

"I warn you. I'll ingest twenty-two Valium and a quart of vodka."

"Don't be silly. They don't go together. I'll expect you."

Todd wasn't coming home for dinner. He called. He told me briefly that Guy Savarese had had an altercation the night before and there was a problem on the set. "What kind of an altercation? Where? What happened?" I snapped, frustrated at the lack of information.

"I'll explain it all tonight. When I get home."

Did he think that was enough to keep me waiting at home? Whatever it was, it was as expected. Suzannah had had her turn, and Beau his. It was time for Guy to act up, seeing as how they would be into post-production in a couple of months.

I took out the logbook and wrote in it once more. But my mind wasn't on it. I was thinking about the command performance (that *was* what it was) at Gavin's apartment. *I couldn't go there again.* I had made up my mind about that. I needed the atmosphere of the office back again, that impersonal doctor's couch. Otherwise, I might drown in the darkened intimacy of Gavin's gray flanneled bedroom and really be dead. But I would have to go there once more, just once more, to hear his explanation of why my appointment had been taken away from me. Although I already suspected the reason.

Mitch's friend, Hylan, was a guest for dinner again. He was kind of overdoing it, considering that Mitch himself felt compelled to put on such a show for him.

"I liked your dinner last week, Mrs. King, but I *love* your dinner tonight. I like spaghetti and meatballs, but I *love* steak and mashed potatoes. Specially mashed potatoes!" And he rubbed his stomach in appreciation.

"I'm sure we're all thrilled, Hylan," Megan drawled.

I threw her a warning look, and said, "Well, you'll have to thank Leah, Hylan," I said. "It's her mashed potatoes."

After dinner, I told Leah I was going to a fashion show at the Century Plaza that evening. Then, feeling compelled to give her further explanation, I said, "It's a charity thing, you know. A benefit for—"

But she wasn't listening. She just gave me one of her looks as she turned away, and I wondered if she somehow knew that under my red Chinese dress I wore a red lacy teddy. When she reached for the small of her back and emitted a groan, I thought, *Oh God! She does know.*

She was too much, and I was tired of her antics. "If you're not feeling well, go to bed," I said coldly. "I'll tell Megan to clean up the kitchen and to look in on you and bring you anything you need."

She straightened up immediately.

"You tell that Megan nothing."

Now I wondered why Megan had suddenly become *that* Megan.

His clear blue eyes gazed into mine. "I want to put everything in proper perspective for you. Coming *here,* not to the office, will help you get in touch with your real feelings."

"Oh? And what are my real feelings?"

He touched the tip of my nose with a finger. *"That* is what remains to be found out. I think you have a strong need to cuckold your husband.

But that's your need. As a man I might be weak enough, and foolish enough to help you, but as a doctor, I can't make love to you under the pretense of treating you. And certainly, I cannot go on accepting your husband's money for this duplicity. Our relationship as doctor and patient is at an end, and you may no longer come to my office. Here—" he gestured, "I am only a man. And here you have to answer to me as a man. So you have a little time to figure out why you are here. Is it me? Or is it *just* cuckolding your husband? I warn you. As a man I want to make love to you, but I don't want to be used. Everyone wants to be loved for himself. That's a pretty basic need."

Love? Who is talking about love? Love is the very last thing I want to think about, talk about, feel. I have had enough of love. My heart has no room for love.

He was so earnest, so sincere. He was a doctor, a head doctor, for goodness' sake. Why didn't he know that everything was not simple, was not clear-cut?

"So you *do* want to treat me? You want me to come here, just so you can straighten out my head, just so you can help me get in touch with my feelings?" My voice was cool, mocking. "Then am I to assume you *don't* want to make love to me until that time? Until I'm all straightened out?"

He blushed. An innocent, virginal blush.

"I do want to make love to you . . ." he said hoarsely. "I wish I didn't. I wish I had the strength just to tell you to go to another doctor . . . to refuse to see you at all."

"Why don't you?" I asked, knowing already that it was the wrong question, knowing that I was going to get the wrong answer, an intolerable answer. Instead of asking the question, I should just walk out. Walk out before it was too late.

"Why don't you?" I repeated the question.

"Because I love you, Buffy Ann."

I love you, Buffy Ann.

It was the wrong time and the wrong place, and absolutely the wrong man, but ah . . . could those words ever be the wrong words?

He removed my red dress, and my red lace teddy.

He kissed me there and kissed me here . . . my toes . . . my neck . . . my breasts . . . my thighs. *Oh, yes. Here and . . . yes, there. If you do that for me, and this for me, I will wriggle for you and sigh for you and arch for you and reach out for you, but will I love you? Do I wish to love you? Can I love you?*

I ran my fingers through his yellow hair, then held on tightly to it, as my body responded and crescendoed. I thought of a line from a poem I had read many years before, but I couldn't get it straight. It went something like: "love me for myself alone and not for my yellow hair . . ."

I drove home through the starless night and thought not of yellow hair, but of auburn curls. And I was moved with such longing I had to pull up to the curb.

Oh God, will it never cease?

88.

Todd was waiting at the door for me, his face white, while Leah huddled behind him in her old red bathrobe. Something had happened! Something terrible. . . . *The children!* Something has happened to one of the children while their mother was rutting around like an alley cat.

Todd reached out a hand to me. "It's okay," he said quickly. "It's Petey, but he's going to be all right. He was in an accident. A collision on Sunset."

"But Petey doesn't have a car," I said foolishly, feeling sick.

"His friend Eddy was driving," Todd said.

"How bad is it?"

"He has a concussion, but he's going to be all right."

"Where is he?"

"At UCLA hospital. I was there, but I took Suellen home. She wanted to go home to Becky. Howard's still there."

Then, I first noticed that his arms were around me, comforting me. "Is there something you're not telling me?"

"Petey and Eddy. They were drunk. And there was some evidence of . . . drugs."

"Oh my God! Suellen!"

I jerked out of his arms, turned back toward the door.

"Where are you going? It's so late—"

"I have to go to Suellen."

"I'll go with you."

"No," I said, looking now at Leah who suddenly appeared very old and thin, and very little. She was taking the night's happening very hard. I knew she was fond of Suellen; she *respected* Suellen. "You stay here with the children and Leah."

Suellen answered the door stone-faced. "I thought it would be you."

Suellen who had cried when John Kennedy died and Bobby and Martin Luther King and John Lennon and Natalie Wood, was dry-eyed now with her son lying in the hospital with a concussion. It didn't seem right. I threw my arms around her. *I* was crying.

"He's okay," she consoled me. "The doctors said he was okay."

We went into the kitchen to have coffee. "How is Petey's friend Eddy?" I asked.

"Practically untouched. A bruise."

"Oh, good! And the other car? The people in it?"

"It was just the driver. A girl of sixteen. She has a million fractures. She'll probably be in traction for a year."

"The poor thing. Thank God she's alive."

"She was high on angel dust."

"Oh . . ." Angel dust. Such a pretty name for a deadly drug.

"She was high on angel dust, and *my* son and his friend were not only *drunk* but doped up too. The three of them . . . not one of them over sixteen, driving around with poison in their bloodstreams and poison in their heads. Peter and Ed were coming back from Venice where apparently they bought some Quaaludes to add to their alcoholic content."

"But how do you know?"

"The police pried it out of Eddy."

"Where is Eddy?"

"His parents took him home. He didn't have a scratch on him. They . . . the parents, had just given him the car for his birthday. Well, what can you say when people give *children* cars to drive and turn the other way when they *know* they're doing terrible things!"

"Oh, Suellen, don't dwell on that. Don't think about it now. Just be grateful that they're all alive. That's the important thing now, Suellen."

"Is it?" she asked dully.

"Come on, what kind of a question is that?"

"I thought we were a happy family. A good family. But I was deluded. I thought that if I did all the right things, bad things wouldn't happen to my family. Oh, I was worried about Petey and that band of his. I suspected that some of his friends might be punkers, and I know that a lot of the kids are taking drugs and drinking, but I believed in Petey, in us. I thought I had a home full of love and a lovely son—"

"Don't say *had,* Suellen. You *have* a lovely son. Don't overreact, Suellen. This could have been the first time that he ever—"

"I don't think I'm overreacting. People are always saying that to me, and I'm sick and tired of it! I have a son who's barely sixteen, who gets drunk and ingests dangerous, illegal drugs . . . who has taken God-knows-what-else before, and who will probably go on to take God-knows-what in the future . . . who might, one day, be dead from an overdose of something or other . . . who might be better off dead."

"Suellen! What an awful thing to say! God will punish you!"

"He already has."

"Suellen! Your son's come out of a car accident *alive*—an accident that could just have as easily killed him. Look, maybe this incident will serve as a lesson to him. Scare him good so that he won't do it again."

"Oh Buffy, you *are* a fool! A sixteen-year-old boy doesn't learn anything from an incident like this if he gets away clean. All he learns is that he's beaten the system, beaten the odds. He'll think that he can *always* beat the odds, but *I've* learned something. That there is no such thing as a nice, happy family in Lotus Land. The whole place stinks. Kids take Quaaludes and angel dust, bigger kids snort cocaine, we all take pills and everyone is rotten and cheats on one another. And none of us is safe. And you sit there and offer me platitudes. This is no fairy tale! *You* know that it all stinks. It all stinks and we're all tainted with the stink. And don't think I don't know what's going on between you and Todd. Something has happened to your marriage out here—something has happened to the union that I thought was made in heaven. And what about your children? What makes you so sure your Megan is such a good little girl? How can you be sure when you see what's going on here all around you?"

"Don't, Suellen," I begged. "You're hurting and you're lashing out—" I put my hand on hers.

She snatched her hand away. *"Are* you sure, Buffy? What about Megan? They say half the kids in the L.A. schools smoke grass and drink, not to mention the rest of it. What makes you think your daughter is any different? For all you know, she's screwing her brains out every afternoon when you think she's with her girlfriends or taking dancing lessons."

"No, you're wrong, Suellen. You're just shook up and hurt. You've just received a terrible shock. But everything's going to be all right. You'll see. You'll take care of this problem, Suellen. You and Howard together. You'll straighten Petey out. You're both bright and strong and—"

She shook her head. "It's not enough . . . Oh, Buffy! Why, oh why, did we ever leave Ohio?"

Oh, don't ask me that, Suellen! I've asked myself that a thousand times!

But I couldn't say that to Suellen now, not when she was stone-cold dry-eyed with grief.

I smiled at her, determined to go on with the fairy tale. "We left Ohio for a better life, the good life. You'll see . . . it will all come out all right."

"Oh yeah," she said as if with bile in her mouth. "The good life. Earthquakes and mudslides, burning brush and smog, traffic and absolutely no parking spaces. Drought on one hand and streets slick as ice when it finally does rain. And high prices. And kids gone bad and cheating husbands."

I laughed sadly at her diatribe. "Not your husband, Suellen. At least there's that. You're one of the lucky ones. Look at it this way—you have to be brave to live in California. It's a land for the courageous."

"I don't think I belong here, then. I've lost my courage. I want you to go home now, Buffy. It's so late. I want you home with your family, safe in your bed. I don't want to have to worry about you driving in this lousy night with all those drunken bastards and hopped-up kids on the roads. Go home and call me when you get there. I want to know you're safe, if there is such a thing."

Todd was still up when I got home. I could hear the television in the den from the entry hall. Surely he had heard my car pull in. Was he waiting for me to go in to tell him that I was home safe? I started up the stairs. Todd should certainly know, as Suellen and I did, there was no safety anywhere.

A few days later Peter was ready to leave the hospital. Suellen called me to tell me she was taking him straight to a rehabilitation center in Austin, Texas.

"Why Texas, Suellen? You'll have to take him out of school. Why can't he go to something here? After school."

"No. As I told Howard, he has to be removed from his present environment to get his head screwed on right."

"And what does Howard say?"

"Right now, Howard isn't saying anything. Not to me. We're not talking. Howard said that if I do this, he'll never forgive me."

I gasped. "And you're doing it anyway?"

Her voice was hard. "I have to do what I know is right."

Oh, Suellen, no. Not at the expense of your marriage.

"Change your mind, Suellen!"

Don't let your marriage be one of the shipwrecks on the sands of the Pacific too. Not your marriage, Suellen . . . Please!

"I have to do what's right."

I knew that I wasn't going to change Suellen's mind. There was only one person I knew who could definitely do that—the magic man with the golden tongue. And I couldn't ask any favors of him, not even for Suellen and Howard.

89.

"We're going to Malibu for the weekend," I told Gavin on the phone. "All of us, and Suellen and Howard and their daughter. Suellen and Howard are having a problem . . . about their son. And I want you to come too."

"Oh no!"

"Yes," I insisted. If I couldn't ask the assistance of the master of persuasion, I would have to do with second best.

"I refuse to be put in this position. It's one thing to be having an affair with a married woman. Another to socialize with her husband. What are you trying to do? Flaunt me in your husband's face?"

"Don't be ridiculous. I've already told Todd you're coming. That I asked you to come to talk to Suellen—"

"I don't believe you. You're just trying to tweak his nose . . . with me."

"Don't be ridiculous," I repeated myself. "If you're our houseguest, nobody will suspect anything. No one could possibly think that I would invite someone to our house with whom I was fooling around. You must come. I need your help with Suellen. You can't refuse to help me—I will never forgive you if you won't even try to help."

He was not convinced but in the end, he agreed to come.

And was I being completely honest with him? *Was* Suellen the only reason I wanted him there? Or did I, as Gavin put it, want only to tweak Todd's nose? I wasn't sure.

Our two families went out to the beach on Friday night. Howard and Suellen were barely speaking. Petey, in his absence, stood between them.

Gavin arrived on Saturday morning. Todd took the call from the security gate. "Your doctor is here," he said evenly. "I'm going out to play volleyball with the kids."

"Don't you want to wait a couple of minutes and meet him?" I challenged.

"The kids are already champing at the net. He'll keep till lunch, won't he?" he asked, his hazel eyes meeting mine questioningly. "Or better yet, why don't you bring him out to the beach, after you've settled him in?"

"He *is* here to talk to Suellen," I said primly. "Are Howard and Suellen going to play volleyball too?"

"I don't think so. Howard's out there running, and Suellen's not playing anything."

"As you can see," I said to Gavin, "we're not very fancy out here. It's strictly a beach house."

"It seems pretty spiffy to me," Gavin said a bit sardonically, gazing around at our all-white decor, our dramatically overstuffed sofas, the authentic Spanish-tiled floor. He wandered into the open inner court-yard that featured a round spa, tropical plantings, statuary, and a gur-gling fountain, then came back into the living room and walked over to the wall of glass overlooking the deck that overlooked the sand and the ocean. "It shows how much I know. I would have said this was pretty *luxe.*"

I shrugged. "It *is* the Colony. We don't come out too often during the year. An occasional weekend."

We went out onto the deck. A strong breeze blew in from the ocean, but the sun was warm. For a few seconds he watched the volleyball game—Todd sprinting about energetically, giving the kids pep talk as he moved, encouraging them to play hard. He was wiry but muscular—fit, his body evenly tanned down to the skimpy trunks. In spite of myself, I took satisfaction in the fact that he wasn't fat or sloppy, that I didn't have to feel ashamed of his body in front of Gavin, which, under the circumstances, I knew was plain silly.

Todd was teamed with Mikey and Matty against Megan, Mitch, and Becky, while Suellen sat at some distance from the game at the water's edge, staring out to sea, allowing the tiny foam-capped waves to wash over her feet.

"I don't think it's a very good day for surfing," I said.

Gavin laughed. "I don't surf."

"Why not? You're California, aren't you? A golden, native California boy?"

"I grew up in the desert. We didn't get to the ocean too often."

"Did you feel deprived?"

"I don't remember feeling deprived. Is that Suellen down there? By the water's edge?"

"Yes."

"How *is* her son doing? You never said."

"Better than Suellen, I hope. *And* Howard. It's so damn stupid. Howard and Suellen were Hollywood's last model couple, practically. Now this thing with Petey is tearing them apart. I told you—Suellen is planning to keep Petey in the drug program indefinitely, and Howard wants him home. He says *he* believes Petey, that this one time was the first time. But Suellen, she's acting like a martinet. She usually tries to please Howard, but this time, she's rigid. She won't yield an inch. And Howard, who's *always* mellow, is being as rigid as she. They're barely speaking. Last night was horrible. Todd had us all playing Scrabble but Suellen and Howard were sulking, and then Howard had a second Scotch and Suellen lit into him like he was a confirmed alky."

"Sounds like a barrel of laughs," Gavin said as we went back into the house. "Is that what they mean when they refer to fun and games in Malibu?"

"I don't think that's funny, considering—"

He was contrite. "Look, this disagreement won't last. You'll see. In a couple of days Suellen and Howard will probably be purring at one another."

"That hardly sounds like a professional statement to me," I said harshly, knowing I was probably looking for a fight. "What do you intend to do about Suellen and Howard in a *professional* way? That *is* why I asked you to come. To do something in a professional way."

Now *he* was getting mad. "Why are you so angry? Is it because you're not sure in your own mind why you *made* me come? Maybe it wasn't Suellen and Howard at all. Maybe it was to create another situation here. You. Me. Todd. All of us looking at one another and wondering what the other is thinking. People do that, *create* situations."

"Don't be a fool. Do you think I'd play games with my children around? My children are more important to me than any games!"

"Are they more important than how you feel about Todd?"

"What does that mean?"

"And what about me? Where do I rate? After the children, of course. But before the games? After Todd? After the games?"

"Will you stop this ridiculous inquisition? I told you. I don't want you working on *me.* I want you to work on Suellen. I want you to persuade her that what Petey did is not the end of the world. That the world is not coming to an end because her son took a drink and a Quaalude. And that the last thing in the world she should do is drive this wedge between her and Howard. I want you to tell her to take Petey home."

"You know I can't *tell* her that. All I can do is talk to her. Try and make her see what she's doing and why she's doing it. I just can't up and tell her what to do—"

"Why can't you? Why is it you doctors can only sit on your fat bottoms and let people drone on and on for years without your saying one positive thing to them? How about a little affirmative action?"

"You're upset, Buffy. But I don't think you fully comprehend all the reasons why you are so upset. Part of it, I think, is that you can't bear to see your sister's nice, ordered life come down over your ears. It was something for *you* to hold on to in the face of your own disintegrating marriage."

"How dare you say that?"

"You tell me it isn't so."

"What makes you think my marriage is disintegrating?"

He laughed shortly, hollowly, unbelievingly. "If it isn't why am I in your life?"

"Half of Hollywood is in the middle of affairs that won't necessarily wreck their marriages. It doesn't mean a thing."

"That's a pretty cynical view." He put his hands on either side of my face and held it there between them. "And that's not you. It won't work. You're not one to have an affair that doesn't mean a damn. You may believe it about yourself, but I don't. That's why I'm holding on . . . so far."

Suddenly I wanted to cry and I moved my face away. "Oh what do you know about me really? We scarcely know each other. We may be lovers, but we're still strangers."

"I don't feel like a stranger," he whispered. And he pressed me to him, not in a sexual way but in desperately loving fashion. He hugged me. He just hugged me hard.

Oh, Gavin, don't. Don't be too tender. You don't know what you do when you're too tender. I want you only to make love to my body, and never, never to be too tender.

"You will try, won't you? You'll try to help Suellen?"

"I'll try."

"Change your clothes and we'll go out on the beach. I'll show you your room."

I led him down a corridor to a room separate from the rest of the house. "A special guestroom. Or if you will, the maid's room. But it does have its own dressing room and bath."

"The infamous Leah did not come along?"

"No. She hates the beach."

"Who's doing the housework? Don't tell me it's you?"

His tone was teasing but I was so unglued, I became immediately defensive.

"I'm not your usual Hollywood wife, you know. I know how to work. I've worked hard all my life. Todd and I . . . we both worked very hard for what we have. I—"

He was smiling at me gently, so gently that I felt foolish going on and I laughed. "Frankly speaking, I *was* counting on Suellen to help with the cooking, but I don't think she's about to do anything except sulk. But we'll barbecue or go out to eat. Barbecuing is big at the beach."

He took a pair of tennis shorts out of his bag and went into the dressing room to change, closing the door behind him. I stared at the closed door for a couple of seconds, then opened it, walked in, and closed the door behind me.

"What do you think you're doing?" he asked, incredulous.

That was what, partially anyway, was so wonderful about him: two years in Beverly Hills practicing, and he could still be incredulous.

I came up close, ran my hands over his bare back and into his trousers, lifted my face to his. As my hands grew more urgent he pushed me away . . . hard. "Go wait in the other room."

"Why?" I asked. "We could use the shower stall. It'll be fun."

He was outraged, so outraged he lost his professional aplomb. "Get the hell out of here! You're crazy. I'm not fucking you in the shower stall in your husband's beach house. What's wrong with you? Your children are here—"

I *was* acting crazy. What *did* I want? For Todd to walk in on us?

I turned around, left the dressing room, and walked back to the main part of the house.

Todd came running over to shake hands with Gavin. "Great to meet you, Doctor," he said and excused himself to get back to the game. "Have to settle a fight between the boys," he explained cheerfully.

Howard had come back from his run on the beach and was sitting some distance away, cooling down, but still directly in back of Suellen. He played with the sand, letting it run through his fingers again and again.

"Shall I get you a pail and shovel, Howie?" I asked, bringing Gavin over and introducing him. Then I called out, "Suellen dear, do come over and meet Gavin Roth."

She forced a smile. "Too lazy to get up. You two come over here."

We sat down on either side of Suellen who, as soon as she had said hello to Gavin, got up and ran into the water.

"Look," I said to Gavin, "I'm going back to sit with Howard. You stay put and when Suellen comes out of the water, grab her and start a conversation. Or, better still, go in the water after her."

"I'm wearing shorts, not trunks, and it's not really hot enough to swim today. *You* didn't even put on a suit," he said accusingly. It was true. I was wearing a long embroidered beach dress.

"Gavin! Please!"

He groaned, got to his feet, and walked slowly, uncertainly into the icy surf.

I glanced over toward the volleyball game. Todd was standing perfectly still, watching me as the kids clamored for his attention. I crawled on my hands and knees back to Howard who was deeply engrossed in building a sand castle.

"Can I help?" I asked.

He smiled at me. "Always glad to have some help."

I was reluctant to begin the preparations for lunch. Gavin and Suellen were sitting on the ocean's edge, deep in conversation, and I didn't want to interrupt them with food. So I just sat there as Howard and Todd romped in the water with the kids. It was wonderful the way Megan didn't mind playing with all the younger kids when her father was present. At first she hadn't even wanted to come this weekend once I had refused her permission to bring Fawn along, anticipating enough problems without the complication of the garrulous Fawn. Besides, Megan had to share her room with Becky.

Suellen and Gavin got up and walked away, down the beach. I watched Howard watch them go. God! Everybody was watching everybody else this weekend.

"I'll get the barbecue going," Todd said. "The kids are starving."

I sighed. "All right. I'll get the steaks out and set the table on the deck. Ask Howard if he'd like to make the salad."

"I'll make the salad," Todd offered. "We'll let Howard keep the kids busy."

"*I'll* make the salad," I said, thinking how much we sounded like characters in a book.

"Will Suellen and your doctor friend be back soon, you think?"

"How do I know?" *Your doctor friend!* "He's trying to help."

"I know. That's why you asked him here for the weekend."

Silence followed that remark.

Then Todd asked, "Shall I ask the Weiskinds to come over for lunch?"

"Whatever for?"

"To help relieve some of the tension between Howard and Suellen."

I took the salad greens out of the refrigerator. "Oh, sure! That should do it. Our glitzy neighbors with all their latest 'ins'—their 'in' beach garb, their 'in' recipe for a new beach cocktail: vodka with a twist of seaweed. And then their latest 'in' gossip—'Have you heard? Barry Gorkin is into fucking fish!' Then they'll pass around their latest discovery—'in' Mexican gold, tainted pot. 'You know, darling, they sprayed it with poison and now it's a whole new rush.' And then Suellen would probably dive for Flora's hair and pull the corn rows right out of Flora's silly head."

Todd went out on the deck to the barbecue and I started washing the vegetables for the salad.

Suellen and Gavin came back, had their lunch, then wandered off down the beach again. I put on a swimsuit, a one-piece tank that presented my breasts in the best possible light, and played Frisbee with the kids while Todd and Howard sat on the deck playing gin rummy and drinking Scotch. Then I announced a sand sculpture contest and set up two teams, making sure that Megan helped Mikey. I hoped Howard wouldn't be pie-eyed by the time Suellen came back from her walk.

When Suellen and Gavin did return, she appeared more relaxed, even amiable. I took the first opportunity to speak to Gavin alone. "How did it go?"

"Suellen said she may want to go into therapy."

"Suellen? Therapy? For what problem specifically? Petey?"

"No. Not specifically."

"Then *what* specifically?" I asked with a certain amount of irritation.

"You know I can't discuss that with you."

I looked at him as if I couldn't quite believe what he was saying, as if I couldn't quite believe his gall.

"Don't be angry with me, Buffy. You wanted me to help Suellen and I'm trying. She's really very confused."

"But what about Petey?"

"What about him?"

"*What about him?* He is *the* crux of this whole thing. I specifically wanted you to talk Suellen into taking him out of that damned drug program, not enroll Suellen into therapy. The *drug program* is the prob-. lem, that is what the fight with Howard is all about!" Was he thick? Sweet but thick?

"I *suggested* that she might want to remove her son from the drug program but I couldn't *tell* her that that was the right thing for her to do—"

"Then she's *not* going to bring him home? Is that the bottom line?"

"I don't think she's ready to do that just yet."

"When is she going to be ready? Next year?"

He shook his head at me as if I just didn't understand. But it was he who didn't understand. "I'm sorry, Buffy. I'll talk to her some more, okay?"

We decided on Don the Beachcomber's for dinner. The children loved his barbecued ribs. It turned out not to be the most sanguine of meals. First, Suellen held a rather heated discussion with Becky about her proposed *bas mitzvah* party. Becky wanted it held at the Beverly

Hills Hotel where her friend, Stacey, was going to have her reception. Suellen didn't think that was at all seemly. She told Becky very definitely that the party would either be held at the temple or at home and Becky began with a whine and ended up crying bitterly. Suellen looked to Howard to say something but he ignored her, only downed another Scotch. He was obviously making a point. The point he was silently, if somewhat drunkenly, making was that since Suellen would not allow Petey to leave Texas, he was not prepared to support her in any future endeavors.

Gavin was eating some Oriental dish with chopsticks, and Megan, gazing at him with frank admiration, insisted that he teach her how to use the chopsticks. I could have sworn she already knew how. Gavin, of course, complied, but I realized with a shock that Megan was flirting with him. She was being arch, coy, alternating a sensuous-lipped pout with a low, throaty laugh, accompanied by an open, wet mouth, the tongue delicately darting in and out. Gavin was studiously not noticing, even when she audaciously touched his chin with a tentative finger, forcing me to cast a swift glance at Todd to see how he was reacting to all this—he, who was always so ultraprotective of his teenage daughter. He *was* watching her with set lips, even as he wiped barbecue sauce off Mikey's chin with a tender touch.

I popped Mitch in the arm for wiping sauce on the back of Matty's shirt, while I kept an eye on Megan.

Was this a new problem? And what was to be done about it? I *hated* precociously sexual teenagers, but how did one turn the clock back once the time bomb was already clicking away?

It probably was nothing, I reassured myself. Didn't every young girl practice flirting with an older man? It didn't mean a thing. Then I saw Gavin's face turn pink as he appeared increasingly more uncomfortable. Something apparently was going on that he didn't know how to deal with. Were Megan's pouty mouth and fluttering lashes enough to make a grown man squirm? Or was it Todd's frank, disquieting stare? Then I bent down to retrieve Matty's napkin from the floor and I *saw* Megan's white-jeaned leg rubbing against Gavin's blue one with unsubtle determination.

Was Suellen right? Was it the Hollywood scene forcing Megan to ripen prematurely? Had I been so preoccupied with myself that I hadn't seen what was coming, what was happening? Had Megan already launched her sexual education? Maybe Todd should talk to her? In any case, I would have to take a stronger hand with my daughter. There were so many perverts just waiting around for juicily ripe, adolescent plums to fall into their laps.

Then I saw Gavin's face turn a bright red and I got to my feet, ostensibly to go to the powder room, but in reality to see what was going on under the table. And I saw Megan's hand on Gavin's *thigh!*

Oh, the little bitch!

"Megan!" I ordered. "I want you to come to the ladies' room with me this instant!"

"But I don't *need* to go to the ladies' room, Moth-ur."

"Oh yes you do. You haven't gone to the bathroom in hours."

By the time we got back to the house and put the kids to bed, it was past ten o'clock. Megan insisted that she would not go to bed at the same hour as the little children but I was adamant. I was very angry at her. But after she had gone to her room, I was not so angry. What Megan had done tonight was probably normal, growing-up procedure, and I was making too much of it. Just as Suellen had done with Petey. Overreacting.

As I wondered where the evening would go next, the Weiskinds appeared on our deck behind the expanse of glass, Bernard tapping on the glass door playfully. Todd let them in. Bernard Weiskind wore white shorts and a pink T-shirt emblazoned with the words *Another Shitty Day in Malibu,* while Flora, in sharp contrast, wore a ruffled white shirt, black velvet knickers, white hose, and strappy high-heeled sandals, her corn rows interwoven with gold beads. Cleo would have told her corn rows were out seasons ago.

"We were over at Jon Falker's party. When we didn't see you all there, we decided to pop over and visit with you. You shoulda gone— old J.R. was there."

"J.R.?" Suellen asked sullenly.

"Larry H.," Flora told her, astounded that Suellen needed an explanation. "They've got the house at the end of the road, didn't you know, for heaven's sake? The house with the Texas flag flying. Whenever Larry's in residence, the flag is up."

Oh my God, that was all we needed, I thought. Talk of *Texas.*

"Kids all gone to bed?" Bernie asked coyly. " 'Cause we're holding . . ." He withdrew from his shorts' pocket what appeared to be a pretty enameled compact and snapped it open to reveal a tiny mound of white powder.

Suellen gasped angrily and ran from the room.

"What's the matter with her? She got a bug up her ass?" Bernard wanted to know.

I smiled thinly. "A couple of bugs, I'd say."

Howard coughed. "I think I'll be getting to bed too. Good night, one and all."

"We're all pretty tired, Bernie," Todd said. "Another night, okay?"

The Weiskinds looked at each other, and Bernard snapped his compact shut.

"Yeah, sure. Sorry if we intruded," he said, miffed.

"Let's go see if the Dorseys are in a better mood, Bernie," Flora sniffed as they left the way they had come.

Todd locked the door after them.

"I guess I'll hit the sack too," he said. "It's been kind of an emotional day. Will you be along soon, Buffy Ann?" His tone, as well as his facial expression, was smooth as glass.

"No. Not yet. Gavin and I will talk awhile."

"Good night then. Don't stay up too late. We get a pretty early start on the day at the beach, Gav."

Gav's face flamed.

I reached my hand out to him across the game table. He lifted his, held it upright, the fingers spread. I placed mine to his . . . finger to finger, palm to palm. I rotated my hand slowly against his, felt the dampness of his flesh. His hand pressed harder against mine. My pulse accelerated. He closed his eyes and moved his chair closer so that our legs could entwine . . . pressing . . . pushing . . . rubbing. His eyes were closed, his breath was coming in gulps. I could hear it.

Suddenly he got up, went over to the glass wall, stared out to sea. "I'm a fucking heel," he said, shaking his head in self-disgust. "In your husband's house . . ."

"It's my house too," I offered foolishly.

There was a silence and then he said, "I'm going to put on my trunks. I think I'll take a swim," and went to his room.

When he came back, I said, "I'll walk down to the water with you."

"Maybe you'd better not."

But I did. It was cold but Gavin bravely dove into a wave. I shivered, hugged myself. Instinctively I turned around, looked toward the house. I saw the glow of a cigaret on the deck but I could not make out the form. But of all the people in the house, with the possible exception of Megan who might have sneaked a cigaret, only Todd smoked.

When I awoke the next morning I saw that Todd had already risen. I looked at the little gold clock on my night table. Ten o'clock! Everybody must be up!

There was no one in the house except for Gavin, who was reading the *Times* on the deck. "Where *is* everybody?"

"Your sister went for a walk on the beach with Todd."

"The children?"

"Howard took them all to Venice."

"Why?"

"He said something about buying skateboards."

"Skateboards? Has he gone out of his mind?"

"I suppose he wanted to keep them entertained. There's a fresh pot of coffee. . . ."

"Did Suellen make the coffee?"

"Todd made the first pot. I made the second."

I sniffed.

"There's also toast and bacon and scrambled eggs in the warming oven."

"Very thoughtful of you."

"Todd did that."

"Oh? And what was Suellen doing while all this activity was going on?"

"Sitting out on the sand."

"Did you talk to her again? About Petey?"

"No. I was helping Todd with the breakfast—"

"That's sick! Sick!"

"My mother always told me to help out when I'm a guest in somebody's home."

"Really? And did you make your bed this morning?"

"Of course. And wiped up the bathroom sink."

I went into the kitchen, fixed myself a tray with the food from the oven, poured myself a cup of coffee, and came out on the deck again. I sat down at the table. "Are you sure you're in the right profession?"

"You tell me."

"I'm not at all sure."

"Neither am I." Suddenly, he blurted out: "I'm thinking of giving up on the Beverly Hills practice."

Where did that come from, all of a sudden?

"Don't be silly. You'd be crazy to do that. What would you do?"

"A friend of mine has opened a clinic in San Francisco. He wants me to come in with him."

"What kind of a clinic? A free one?"

"Not exactly. More like mental health for the people who can't afford Beverly Hills prices."

I looked at him as if he said he wanted to go to the moon. "How long has this been going on?"

I wanted to know if he had been thinking of leaving his practice before the Buffy Ann caper, or only since. "When did all this start?"

"A few months ago."

"But why?"

"I don't have any sense of accomplishment in what I'm doing. I'd like to feel I was making a difference. I *was* in Social Service in Sacramento for six years. And then I thought I'd give being the psychiatrist to the stars a whirl. But it doesn't do anything for me, if you know what I mean." He blushed. "I know it sounds corny but I'd . . . I really want to be of help."

It *was* corny. And I was furious with him. Pulling this on me when I wasn't in any state to handle it. But I did know what he meant. And it was just my luck. I had wanted a simple affair—a superficial, moderne, fun affair to flaunt in my husband's face and what had happened was that I had chosen an old-fashioned hero. I was definitely not in the market for heroes.

"What about me? Are you going to run off to San Francisco and leave me with all my problems?"

Cleo could have told him—flower children hadn't been in vogue for nearly twenty years.

"I'm a needy case too, you know."

"You don't need me. All you ever sought was a slight affair." He ruffled his hair. "Getting even with hubby was the name of this game. Unfortunately, I *am* serious and you're afraid of serious. You're using me, and if and when I'm gone, there'll be someone else."

That sounded just awful. I couldn't bear it. "That's not true."

"It is. Accept it. You've just been using me . . ." he said gloomily.

"You keep saying that. Everybody uses everybody else. Don't they?" I appealed to him.

He shrugged, looked at me hopelessly. I wanted to say something flip, something so incredibly flip and amusing, it would save the day, but I couldn't think of anything.

I got up from the table. "You can't go." I stood behind him, slipped my arms around him, hugging him close. "I do need you. I don't have anyone else."

I heard Suellen and Todd coming up the stairs from the sand and I moved away from him. Suellen was smiling for the first time that weekend, but Todd was not. Had he seen me hugging Gavin?

Suellen threw her arms around me. "I'm going to Austin to get Petey. Right away. Where's Howard?"

"He took the children to Venice," Gavin said, searching Suellen's face, then looking to Todd.

"Venice? Why did he do that?" she asked.

"For skateboards. Suellen, what made you change your mind about Petey?" But I already knew it must have been Todd.

Suellen grinned at Todd. "*He* did. As soon as Howard comes back, we're leaving. I'm going to call for a flight. Will you take care of Becky until we get back?"

"Need you ask?" I followed her into the house and to the phone while she made reservations, then followed her to her room where she started packing. "What did Todd say that made such a difference? What did he say that nobody else has said?"

She took my hands. "In a nutshell, he made me cry."

I could believe that. He had made *me* cry.

"But what did he say?"

"He said that every man's dream is to save the world for his loved ones. And Howard has to save his son himself. And Todd pleaded with me—" Her eyes filled with tears. "Todd said, 'Suellen, don't deny Howard this chance. Don't deny Howard the right to save his son himself. This might be his finest hour . . . and Petey's too.' Well, how could I possibly say no to that?"

I covered my face with my hands, and Suellen and I cried together.

"Oh Buffy! That Gavin Roth. He's a lovely man. Really. Very sweet. But he's not Todd King. There's only one of him."

I fled the room.

Suellen and Howard were like two kids getting into their car to go to the airport, excited and happy. And I cried again. I was sure that Howard would save his son, but Todd had saved Suellen and Howard, and I was grateful to him. Even though I had counted on Gavin to do that for me.

At the last moment, Suellen got out of the car and came running over to me. She whispered, "When I come back you and I are going to have a long talk. You've been lucky. First Todd. And then a man like Gavin Roth . . ."

I started to protest.

"Hush up. This *is* your sister talking. You've been lucky, but Buffy, you're pushing your luck."

The good cheer and the sun vanished along with Suellen and Howard. The weather could be changeable in Southern California, no matter what they said. Determinedly, Todd took the kids out on Malibu Road to practice on their newly purchased skateboards while Gavin and I gloomily sat out on the beach. The day had definitely turned chilly and I put on a fur coat over my bathing suit.

"The sun will come out again and burn off this fog," I told Gavin.

"I doubt it," he said pessimistically.

"It happens all the time."

"Is that why you're wearing a mink coat?" he asked with derision.

"It's an old one," I said defensively. "I use it instead of a bathrobe."

"Delightful. That's almost as good a line as 'Let them eat cake.' " He held out his hand, palm upward. "I think it's raining."

"Don't be ridiculous. Are you really going to leave Beverly Hills for San Francisco?"

"I'm *thinking* about it. Very strongly. But it's definitely raining. Don't you feel it?"

"It's just the fog. It never rains this time of year."

Or don't the old rules apply anymore?

Todd came toward us at a run. He looks like a boy running through the sand, I thought.

"There's going to be a big storm. I think we'd better head back to town right away before the roads start to flood."

"I thought you were out front with the kids and the skateboards. Who told you there was going to be a storm? A little birdie?"

"When I felt the first drops of rain I went into the house and listened to the weather report," he said reasonably.

"I told you it was raining," Gavin said.

"But it never rains this time of year," I told him.

Todd grinned at Gavin. "That's the fun of living in Southern California. You can always expect the unexpected."

As the kids scrambled for position in the station wagon, Gavin and Todd shook hands and Gavin got into his Volvo. Then Todd got into the driver's seat of our car, and I went over to say goodbye to Gavin.

"Keep in touch."

He gave me a level look. "He's an awfully nice guy. Unusually so."

I sighed. "So people are forever telling me."

90.

When we arrived home, Megan's friends Fawn and a lanky sixteen-year-old boy named Larry were waiting. How had they so miraculously appeared at the exact moment we did, I wondered, and was immediately enlightened.

"Was I ever thrilled when you called that you were on your way home, Meggie! Just in the nick of time. I thought my mother was going to kill me with her bare hands," Fawn said, brittle thin in a monochromatic color scheme of orchid pink—shirt, harem pants, running shoes and visored cap.

"What did you do to your mother, Fawn?" I asked, convinced beforehand that Fawn undoubtedly deserved killing.

"Well, Laura was picking on me as usual. Ever since my dad left and we were forced to move into that terrible condo, Laura's been in a continuous snit. So when I said something about her taste in men not being of the very, very best, that her latest—Sid—was the epitome of sleaze, she slapped me. She actually slapped me. So I went out on the terrace and screamed. 'Laura Wright has false hair, false tits, false teeth, and a nose job!' "

Larry and Megan laughed but I was stunned, humiliated for the renovated Laura. "Was this before or after the rain started?" I asked, hoping that Fawn's mother had at least been spared the audience of the condos' occupants who might have been sitting out on their terraces.

"Oh, before! It didn't start raining here until about twenty minutes ago."

"That was a terrible thing to do, Fawn!"

She considered, shrugged her thin shoulders.

Todd joined us in the family room. "Leah seems down in the dumps," he told me. "Why don't we take everybody out for an early dinner?"

"Leah won't go out to eat with us," I said. "You know she always gives me an argument when I suggest it—"

"Yes, she will. I've already talked her into it."

"Oh great," Megan said, making eyes at her friends. "It's not bad enough we have to have all these little kids with us—Becky, Mikey, Matty and Mitchell—now we have to have Leah too. Where are we going to go with that mob?"

Instead of reprimanding her, Todd appealed to her: "How about Tony Roma's? You know how you love their babyback ribs. And what about those stacks of french fried onions?"

"She'll *love* Tony Roma's," I said. "I want to talk to you in the other room, Megan."

We went into the library.

Before I could get started on her, she demanded: "Moth-ur, must we take Leah with us? I don't mind for myself or Fawn, even. I love Leah. But what is *Larry* going to think? A family that goes out to eat Sunday dinner with their *maid?*"

"Leah is *not* the maid. She is our housekeeper and our friend. You listen to me, Megan—the Larrys of this world will come and go, believe me. There will be hundreds of Larrys in your life before you're through. But Leah? You'll never be lucky enough to know another Leah. And after the Larrys have come and gone, Leah will still be here. You think about that!"

Megan blushed, ashamed. "Still, Daddy said Tony Roma's. If it weren't for Leah, we could go to Spago's or Pastel's."

"No, you're wrong, Megan. Your father was thinking of your brothers, I'm sure. That they would be much more comfortable at Tony Roma's. As for Leah, he would take *her* to meet the queen."

We were almost out the door when the telephone rang. I jumped and Todd and Leah tensed too. It was as if the three of us expected the phone to ring only with emergencies or bad news. I could think only of Suellen and Howard and Petey.

"I'll get it," Todd said, turning back.

"No, I will," I said, spinning around. "You go ahead and get everyone settled in the car." I steeled myself.

"Guess what?" Cleo's clear, excited voice issued from the receiver.

I breathed a sigh of relief. At least I recognized a voice free of anguish.

"I thought you were in Texas for the weekend!" Cleo had been seeing her mother's new stepson, Dale Waxler, ever since the Pulitzer-Waxler nuptials.

"I am! I'm calling from Dale's ranch. Guess who just got a Texas-sized diamond engagement ring as big as a fist?"

"Oh Cleo!"

"And you know what else?"

"What?"

"I don't give a damn how big the fool diamond is. I'm in love!"

Oh Cleo!

Todd almost sighed with relief as he saw the pleasure reflected in my face as I got into the front seat of the station wagon, next to Leah.

"Good news?"

"It certainly is! Cleo's getting married to Dale Waxler."

His face lit up, and I thought I heard a grunt of satisfaction from Leah.

Then I felt a disquieting pang. This probably meant Cleo would be moving away to Dallas, and this would place another big void in my life. And if Gavin left too. . . . Oh, he was probably just talking . . . not serious. More of his trying to make me get in touch with my real feelings stuff. Why would anyone want to leave a lucrative Beverly Hills practice to go off to a clinic in "it's cold and it's damp" San Francisco?

My thoughts scurried around in my head like so many mice.

Lucky Cleo! To be getting another chance.

We all came back in a pleasant mood from the restaurant. Even Megan and her friends had had a good time, and Leah had actually stopped glowering. Larry took Fawn home in his MG, Todd put the younger boys to bed, and Megan agreed to play PacMan with Becky and Mitchell. Before she went off with them, she had the grace to say, "I'm sorry I was bitchy, Mother. We really had a nice time."

"You weren't bitchy, Sweetie. You were just having growing pains. You're not *all* grown-up yet, but I think you're coming along fine."

She hugged me. Well, maybe I was losing Cleo to Dallas, and possibly certain people to other locales, but at least I had a daughter at home that I was proud to call a friend.

I had just sent Mitch and the two girls to bed and was thinking of going to bed myself. It had been a long day, full of exhausting emotion of one sort or another. I passed the library where Todd was sitting at the desk, going over papers covered with figures. I guessed that he still wasn't out of the woods financially. I almost said goodnight to him but remembered just in time and walked past the room to the staircase, when the phone rang out. I proceeded up the stairs, listening just the same. Todd must have picked up at once because it rang only the one time. But again I thought of Suellen and Howard and turned around, slowly went down the stairs, down the hall to the library.

Todd was slumped in the deskchair, crying.

Oh no!

I was too scared, too sick, to ask what it was that made him cry. So all I asked, in a dead voice was, "Who was on the phone?"

"Dave Ricklaus."

Dave Ricklaus? He was only one of the studio's lawyers. What could he have said to cause a grown man to cry?

"It's Beau!" Todd's voice came out muffled. "It's Beau. He's dead." He buried his face in his hands.

And I, too stupefied to say anything, thought he was only crying for his baby, his film, almost but not quite finished . . . almost certainly a dead issue now.

Finally I found my voice. "How? What happened?"

"The police found him . . . in a motel in Hollywood." He wiped his eyes, breathing heavily. "He was beaten to death!"

Oh my God!

"But who? Why?"

"They found him handcuffed to the bed, with a blindfold over his eyes."

"Oh no."

"Dave said they're looking for a *male prostitute* . . . they think they know who it is." His eyes filled again and he covered them with his hands. "It seems Beau was seen in his company before. I guess this was one time too many. I guess Poppy couldn't watch him all the time. I *really* liked him, you know. I know it's crazy, that he was hardly real . . . he was just a . . . but I *liked* him . . . he was like a big kid, despite everything." He sobbed helplessly.

I was ashamed of myself, ashamed that I had thought that he was only thinking of his picture. And the worst part of it all was not even that Beau was dead, but *how* he had died. It was the how of it that made Todd cry.

He looked at me. "Why, why didn't I try to help? I was so caught up with my own—" He shook his head in despair.

"Poppy!" I said. "We had better go to her. I don't think she has anyone. . . ."

A frightened Mexican maid answered the door. "Missis is in the bedroom," she said. "Nobody else here."

"Will you tell her we're here, please?"

She came back in a couple of minutes. "She no answer. Door locked."

We looked at each other.

"Where's Virgil . . . Smokey?" Todd asked urgently.

"They go away."

"Where's the bedroom?" he demanded, moving fast. I followed.

The maid ran after him to show him the way.

Todd tried the knob, yelling: "Poppy! It's Todd King! Let me in!"

When there was no answer, he heaved himself against the door the way they did in the movies, and he kept doing it over and over again until the door gave and we burst into the room. She was half-lying on the bed, a bottle of pills still clutched in her hand. Todd raced to her, felt for her pulse. "An ambulance, Buffy! Quick! I think she's still alive," and he dragged her from the bed, trying to get the limp body to stand.

They said they were going to keep her in the hospital for two, three days at least, and we went home. I crawled wearily into bed, not looking at Todd who was staring at the ceiling. I turned out the lights. Neither one of us would probably sleep this night.

Then I felt his hand on my shoulder.

"Buffy . . . please. Please, Buffy."

At that moment I wanted to turn around, let him into my bed, into my arms; my whole heart, my body ached to do that; I wanted it, more than I had ever wanted anything in my life, but I *couldn't.* How could I warm him when there was nothing inside me left to warm him with? He had already killed that thing inside me that gave out that kind of comfort, that kind of warmth.

And without even seeing, I *sensed* him going back to his own, empty bed. And I thought of Poppy Beaufort lying in a narrow hospital bed, having failed in her attempt to kill herself. Maybe we had been very wrong to save her. It was going to be very difficult for her to live. I suspected very strongly that like some other people, Poppy Beaufort had killed the thing she loved.

91.

Two days later the hospital released Poppy and we took her home with us. I didn't want to, not really, but I didn't think I had much choice. I couldn't very well let her go back to her house alone. We couldn't ignore the possibility that she might try to take her life again. We had stopped her from killing herself once, and therefore, we had saved her life. There was that old adage that if you saved somebody's life, you were responsible for it. I didn't know for how long that meant, but I supposed it held good for at least two weeks, anyway. We would keep her with us until after the funeral services at least, and those couldn't be held until the coroner's office released Beau's body. In the meantime, production was closed down once again on *White Lily,* and Poppy was very, very *still.*

A walking time bomb? I wondered, or like me, one of the walking dead? That was the way I depicted myself in my more melodramatic moments over the past two years. Now, for the time being, there were two of us in that select group, wandering about my house.

Gavin called. I hadn't seen him since the weekend.

"I'm sorry about Beau Beaufort. I imagine you and Todd and he were close friends."

"Yes."

Well, I suppose one might say that. Todd and Beau, seemingly, *had* been friends.

"When am I going to see you?" he asked.

"I don't know. Poppy Beaufort is staying with us."

"Surely you can leave her for a couple of hours."

"I don't know that I can. She's not—stable." That was as good a word as any. I didn't know if it were right for me to disclose to Gavin that she had tried to take her own life. Surely she had a right to keep that fact private. "And the media people won't leave us alone. They're hanging around the front gate and the phone keeps ringing. Frankly, I'm worried about Leah. She doesn't seem at all well. I think everything is getting to be too much for her. She's old, you know. We don't even know *how* old. She never told us. But I can't leave her here alone with Poppy Beaufort and the children. It's not fair to her. No, I'm too concerned about them both. Poppy and Leah."

"What about me?" he asked hollowly.

"What about you?"

"Aren't you concerned at all about me?"

"Oh you! You're young and strong and so good looking. I don't worry about you."

"I saw a movie last night on the late show. With Irene Dunne. *Back Street*. She had an affair with a married man for about fifty years and every year he threw her a few minutes and she just waited . . . year after year after year."

I knew the movie. I had seen it many years ago at the Cinema on High Street back in Columbus, Ohio. It was a real tearjerker.

"Don't I remind you of her a little? Irene Dunne?"

"A little," I said. "Around the eyes. But your figure's a lot fuller."

We had to hire security guards to make sure none of the newspeople slipped through when the gates were opened to admit the people who were supposed to be here.

Suellen was upset when she came over.

"What are you doing? Living in an armed camp?"

"Those reporters are desperate to get at Poppy. And some of those nutty kids heard that Poppy was here and there's a bunch of them out there too. Didn't you notice them?"

"How could I not? Well, maybe she should be in her own house with those guards. Then you wouldn't be exposing yourself and the children to all this."

"The children love it, believe me," I laughed. "Anyhow, it will only be for a few more days. Once the funeral service is over they'll forget about Poppy . . . and Beau too. They'll be onto something new and Poppy will go home." But I didn't have any idea, really, *what* Poppy would do when all this was over.

"Come in the den and tell me about everything. Tell me about the big reunion in Austin."

"Where's Todd?"

"Still at the studio. Working late. Wondering, I suppose, what to do about the picture."

We went into the den and without asking Suellen if she wanted anything, I fixed myself a drink. And as I suspected she would, she fixed me with a disapproving eye. *Oh dear,* I thought wearily. She was, as I feared, going to turn into one of those nondrinkers who made anybody who took an occasional drink feel like it was time to call A.A. On the other hand, it didn't make sense that just because she had agreed to take Petey out of the drug program, she was going to become an advocate of all the iniquities she had always scorned, either. In time, I supposed, she would go back to being a moderate, well-rounded individual. Didn't they say time cured all problems?

"So now tell me all about everything. What did Petey say when you and Howard got there?"

"What do you think? He cried when Howard told him he was going home. As a matter of record, Howard cried too. And they hugged each other for five minutes before Petey ran to his room to pack. And on the plane going home, he swore to me at least a hundred times that he was going to be a good boy."

"Don't you believe him?"

"Maybe. Howard does. They're home right now having a heart-to-heart. I don't think the important thing now is whether *I* believe Petey or not. I'm not sure I'll be able to ever believe him completely again. The important thing is that he and Howard have their chance together. Todd made me see that."

I nodded and sighed.

"Where's Poppy? I came here tonight to see you, of course, but also to pay my respects to her."

"She's upstairs. She's been keeping pretty much to her room. I'll go up and ask her if she'd like to come down and say hello."

Poppy came down and she and Suellen exchanged a few words, then she asked to be excused, and went upstairs again.

"Well, she's really *controlled,* isn't she?" Suellen said.

"Yes. I think she's just holding on . . . until the funeral. I think she feels she's just got to get through that. And then—I don't know."

"Do you think she'll stay on in L.A.?" Suellen asked.

"I don't have any idea. And I don't think she has either."

"What about you, Buffy?"

I opened my eyes wide. "What about me?"

"Don't give me those innocent green eyes. What are you going to do about your situation?"

"I don't know what you're talking about."

"You're having an affair with Gavin Roth."

"You're off the wall."

"You're talking to me, Buffy. You never could keep a secret from me. I've suspected something's been going on for quite a while. After last weekend, I'm convinced of it. And I don't think I'm the only one who's convinced."

"Whom are you talking about? Howard? Does Howard think I'm having an affair with Gavin too?" My tone was mocking.

"No, not Howard. Howard would never ever think such a thing of you. You know him. He's the world's greatest innocent. And he never thinks anything bad about anybody . . . especially you. Howard doesn't even realize that you and Todd are having problems."

"Of course not, why would he? I never said Todd and I had a problem. It's just you—jumping to conclusions. But if it isn't Howard, who is the other person who suspects I'm having an affair with Gavin? Tell me. Who is it?"

She didn't answer. But of course she didn't have to.

I laughed, got up to fix myself another drink. "You're being silly, Suellen."

"I want to help," she said quietly. "Please let me."

I splashed vodka over the rocks. "There *is* nothing to help with."

"There's trouble here, and you can't tell me there isn't. You and Gavin Roth are having an affair because something happened between you and Todd." She narrowed her eyes. *"Didn't* something happen? Look at me," she commanded. "I have this feeling. Was it Suzannah? I have this distinct feeling that Suzannah made some kind of trouble—"

I had always said Leah was a witch and now I suspected that Suellen was too, possessed of a supernatural clairvoyance. Or was it every woman's primal, female instinct?

The front door slammed and we both jumped.

Todd came into the den smiling broadly. Naturally. He had seen Suellen's car parked in the courtyard. "I could barely get through the gate. I had to show those guys there three kinds of identification before I convinced them I belonged here. Look what I have—" He went back into the hall and dragged in four shopping bags brimming with orange and yellow flowers. Suddenly, the room was filled with the spicy scent of marigolds.

Suellen laughed. "What did you do?" she asked. "Buy out a whole florist shop?"

"Not exactly. A street vendor. Right outside the studio gates. He wanted to call it a night and he offered me all his wares at a reduced price. You know I can't resist a bargain," he grinned. But I resisted a smile. I said coldly, "I thought you didn't like street vendors. You've always said they were bad for the economy. That they don't pay taxes."

"Yeah . . . I know," Todd said, his grin fading. "But I remembered when I was around fourteen. I was selling something or other on the streets and some dude came along and bought me out, gave me a hundred dollar bill! It was the most thrilling thing that had ever happened to me." He shrugged his shoulders. "And when I saw these marigolds, I remembered something else. I remembered that day at the Bois de Boulogne, on our honeymoon, how you rhapsodized about the marigolds." His eyes pleaded with mine to remember.

I picked out an orange flower from one of the bags, held it to my nose. The enchanted French air had been positively filled with their scent that day.

"Flowers just don't smell the way they used to. Have you noticed, Suellen?" I tossed the marigold back into the bag.

Suellen's eyes moved from me to Todd, glistening wetly. Then she looked at the bags again. "There must be hundreds of them."

"Yes," I said. "You must take some home with you. At least half."

Under protest, she took two of the shopping bags with her, and Todd went to the kitchen in search of vases in which to put the remaining flowers. Oh yes, I remembered that day in the Bois de Boulogne . . . we had run and skipped like children, but had kissed like the lovers we had been. Oh yes, I remembered. *How not?*

He came back with one of the vases filled with the blooms. "I think I'll take this one up to Poppy. Maybe it will cheer her up a little."

"That would be nice."

Did he really believe it? That a vase of flowers could actually brighten Poppy's aching despair? Men were such strange creatures. They thought a florist's box could make up for any one of a long string of heinous crimes.

I went to bed.

He entered our darkened room, tiptoed to my bed, whispered hoarsely, "Buffy Ann?" I didn't answer. I was sleeping, wasn't I? He must have brought a vase of the flowers with him into our room too because again I was overwhelmed by the spicy scent.

"When?" I heard him whisper harshly.

Desperately I dug my face deeper into my pillow, my fist under the covers clenching, pressing the dear life out of the lone yellow marigold I had brought to bed.

92.

The authorities were finally ready to release the body, and we moved to complete the arrangements for the funeral services. Todd and I concurred that it was our obligation to get Beau Beaufort buried with as little publicity as possible. We agreed that we wanted the most private affair—a secret funeral service, if we could manage it. The papers had been filled with enough sensational details. Even a picture that some clever journalist had managed to obtain of Beau lying handcuffed and blindfolded in the scroungy little motel room. But so far, the most sensational detail of all had been kept from the media, that Beau's death had *not* been a brutal, robbery-murder, but only a brutal accident—a death resulting from a sadomasochistic paid-for tryst. And we were eager to bury that final secret along with Beau.

We asked Poppy if she had any preference as to where she wanted Beau laid to his final rest. She didn't hesitate for a moment, as if she had been thinking about it ever since she had come to life again in that hospital emergency room. "Forest Lawn," she said. "Where all the other big stars are."

We didn't argue with her; we didn't tell her that it would prove very difficult to keep a burial at Forest Lawn secret. I guessed that she thought she owed Beau that much, at least . . . a place among the stars for all eternity. And secrecy wasn't what she wanted at all. We found this out when we told her it would be wise to have the service at six in the morning, with a very limited attendance of mourners. She told us she didn't want a private service. She wanted Beau *mourned!* And she wanted him properly mourned with all the trimmings, with all the fans who loved him, present. And she didn't mind the newspeople there either. She wanted Beau buried like a star!

It would be mayhem, but it was Poppy's choice. And she asked Todd if he would close down the studio altogether that day so that all the workers on the lot could attend, and Todd agreed. And then she turned to me and asked that I call Suzannah to *make sure* she and Ben would be there. She specially wanted them there. In the absence of relatives, Suzannah and Ben would be like having family present.

It wasn't easy for me to call Suzannah, but I had an obligation and I did it. I delivered Poppy's message, and Suzannah said to tell Poppy that she was thinking of her. She sounded a little strange but I thought nothing of that. We *were,* after all, estranged from one another. But she did ask after everyone—Todd, whom she hadn't seen since the set had been closed down; the children; Suellen and Howard; even Cassie and Cleo and Leo, not even remembering till seconds later that Cleo and Leo were no longer together. Now, *that* was strange, considering. Suzannah must be losing it, I thought. Life with Ben *was* affecting her mind. Or was it only her guilt traumatizing her brain?

It wasn't until after she'd hung up that I realized she hadn't said whether she and Ben would attend the services or not. I thought of calling her back so that I could give Poppy a definite answer, but I changed my mind. It was enough that I had delivered Poppy's message.

93.

After Suzannah had talked to Buffy she collapsed against her pillows. No, she would not be at the funeral. And she wasn't sure where Ben would be, either. All she knew for sure was that Ben wouldn't be at the hospital waiting for her operation to be over, to ask the doctor what, exactly, had been removed. Ben didn't know that she was going to be operated on. She had managed to keep that a secret from him.

The night Beau died she had first discovered the lump in her breast. First terror, and then joy flowed through her. *If* she had cancer of the breast and the breast had to be cut from her, Ben would flee from her like the plague! He would dump her! No more perfection—no more Ben! It was as simple as that. He would flee and free her, praise be to God! She had thought many times of defacing herself; twice she had tried and been thwarted; other times she had lost her courage at the last moment; mostly she had been immobilized by terror. But now it was out of her hands.

She went to the doctor the next day. She told Ben that it was only a routine examination so that he wouldn't go with her, sit in the waiting room to confer with the doctor afterwards.

The doctor tried to reassure her. "Most lumps turn out to be benign, you know."

He would think her insane if she told him the last thing she wanted was the growth to be benign.

He explained it all to her, how they rushed the excised tissue to pathology, getting their answer almost immediately. And *if* there was a morbid growth, a malignancy, there were options: they no longer automatically performed a radical mastectomy, as they once did. Today, some women opted for a simple operation where only the immediate affected tissue was removed, and then they kept a careful watch.

If she could have, if she'd dared, she would have told the doctor to cut off the offending breast even if the tumor was nonmalignant. But he would have sent for the men in the white coats and she had already been *there*.

All she could tell the doctor was that *if* the growth was found to be malignant, she would exercise no options. *Cut it out, cut it off.*

"Wait," he cautioned her. "Don't give me an answer now. Think it over tonight. Go home and talk it over with your husband."

"I don't need his signature on the release form, do I? I myself can sign the form, authorizing you to perform the mastectomy if the biopsy reveals cancer, is that not so, Doctor? It is *my* body, *my* breast, *my* choice."

"It is your choice, Mrs. Gardenia."

He was so perplexed; she was sorry for him. "I have this terrible fear . . . of cancer . . . of dying . . . I'll feel safer this way, Doctor. And I wish to spare my husband the pain of helping me make this decision."

What did the doctor know of a malignant life? Of being torn apart every night by several inches of blue, iridescent steel?

She would enter the hospital under an assumed name, they agreed, to forestall publicity.

She told Ben that she had to go to the hospital for a test, a sophisticated but routine, new procedure that couldn't be performed in the doctor's office. Perhaps Ben would have questioned her more thoroughly as was his way, would have insisted on going to the hospital with her if he had not been so intent on his own business, a new financial scheme, he boasted, that would take Todd's studio away from him —lock, stock, and barrel, every last stick, every last scrap of film.

So, he would not be going with her. He might be flying to New York, as a matter of fact, at the very moment that the doctor, hopefully, would be cutting away at her temple.

She had outsmarted Ben this once. And *if* they removed her breast, and she was free from him, she would outsmart him again, thwart him. She would simply tell Todd, warn him, what Ben was planning to do to him.

94.

Cleo offered to pick up a complete new costume for Poppy to wear to the service—everything—dress, hat, shoes, bag, even hose. But Poppy refused. She said she wanted to wear a black dress that Beau had liked, and she insisted on going back to her house to pick up the things she needed. We went there late at night to elude the hangers-out at the gate. She insisted on being alone in her bedroom to gather up what she needed, *everything* she would need. That's what she kept saying, over and over: "Everything I need."

Cleo came by in the morning to help Poppy dress, to help her with her makeup. Cleo knew exactly how much makeup would be appropriate considering that the cameras would be flashing and that Poppy wanted to do Beau proud. She would be elegant, but discreet, well-groomed, certainly, but not overdone. She said she owed this to Beau and his fans.

Cleo told me that Leo was coming over to ride with us in the limousine. When I appeared surprised, she said, "There's plenty of room, isn't there?"

Yes, there was. Todd and I, Poppy and Cleo . . . and Leo. Certainly there was room. "But why?"

"Leo's girlfriend has dumped him. And he's hurting . . . for Beau, and I guess for his girlfriend too. He would have to go to the funeral alone and it's hard to be alone on occasions like this."

I was filled with admiration for Cleo. She was being most generous. She had always been giving, but now she was being generous beyond the call of duty.

"What happened with the girlfriend?"

"She found somebody new," Cleo drawled. "It's funny. Leo broke up our marriage for her, and it was the most traumatic thing that ever happened to me. And how she has *trivialized* my most traumatic moment. It seems she always adored Leo for his brilliance, but she couldn't resist a young actor she picked up at a party—*twenty-two,* without a brain in his head but full of muscles and a ten-inch cock. I don't know, Buffy. I can't help feeling sorry for Leo. He's so *bewildered."*

So we set off for the services, Todd and Cleo and the bewildered Leo, and a very quiet, very still Poppy, clutching her black purse. I knew that her silence could be a form of hysteria. She was still in shock no matter how dignified she was behaving, and I was afraid for her. As she would stand at the graveside, confronting the grotesqueness of Beau's death, would she break? It would be a madhouse at the cemetery. The police would be there, as well as the private security guards we had hired. Still—the horde of morbid curiosity-seekers, the fans, irrational with grief, and media people from all over the country . . . a madhouse.

"I killed him, you know," Poppy said quietly, suddenly. "Me and— No, not that prostitute who beat him to death. I hope *he's* never found, so nobody finds out that—He wasn't the real killer. The real killer is me."

None of us in the limousine could bear to hear what she was saying.

"No, no." Todd begged her, gripping her hand.

"You were a good wife to him," Cleo said firmly, she who had been the best of wives. "He wouldn't have been *anything* without you!"

"He was crazy about you," Leo said. "He always said, *'My* Poppy . . .' "

"I killed him! Me! And Ben!"

Shocking words, I thought. But Poppy herself was in shock.

"Don't think about it now, Poppy," I said. "Later. Later you'll be able to put everything into perspective." I tried to think what else I could say. "Just hold on to the fact that you loved him and he loved you." I had no idea whether she heard anything any one of us had said. "You tried your best . . . that's what counts."

Ben! I killed him! Me and Ben!

I looked out the window and I didn't see any sun. Where had the goddamn sun gone to?

Poppy had it all figured out. She was going to make Beau's death mean something. She was going to do Beau's memory proud. She was going to stand at Beau's gravesite with her head bowed and as they lowered the coffin into the ground, she was going to *shoot* Ben Gardenia.

She owed that much to Beau. Ben had contributed to Beau's death as much as she herself had. Ben had helped her corrupt Beau; he had insisted on it! Whenever her own hand had faltered.

Through the years in Vegas every time she tried to reverse things . . . to undo all the ugliness, all the harm, Ben had stopped her . . . had forced her hand. If Beau was dead, then Ben had to be dead too. Beau had been sweet, innocent in spite of everything, and Ben was evil. And she would not only avenge Beau, she would settle up all the scores. Suzannah. She had gotten Suzannah hooked on Ben; now she would free her. And she would get rid of the threat of Ben for Todd King and his wife; she had wronged them both and she owed them. They didn't understand about Ben. They didn't know you never got away clean with a man like Ben. She would get them away clean. She would free them. And then with her own books wiped clean, she would turn the gun on herself and fall into the ground next to Beau . . . sweet, innocent Beau. She had loved him more than life itself; life had never been nearly as sweet as Beau. It had turned so sour so soon.

It *was* a mob scene, more so than any movie could have depicted. The photographers. The fans. All the people from the studio down to the last prop man. And Poppy was starting to lose her cool. I could see it happening, sense it happening. It was almost as if she weren't even listening to the clergyman's remarks, how Beau had brought so much happiness to so many people. She kept searching the crowd. Whom was she looking for? And then I remembered how much she wanted Suzannah and Ben to be there. I, myself, didn't see them anywhere.

In front of all the cameras, in front of what seemed like thousands of people, we watched mesmerized as Poppy Beaufort pulled out a revolver from her black snakeskin clutch, still looking around desperately, as they started to lower the coffin into the ground. Then, she dropped the gun and tried to jump into the yawning earth about Beau's box.

"I loved him," she shrieked into the ground as we struggled to restrain her.

Oh, I believed her. *I believed her.*

We sat in the living room with her, tried to get her to take a drink—even Suellen did. But she refused. "Oh, I never drink," she kept saying.

I knew she needed something to give her the strength to live, until she found the strength to forgive herself. I said, "Try to think of it this way. What happened to Beau was an accident of fate, almost as if he had crossed the street and was run over . . . an accident of *living.* And for all the time that Beau was with you, you gave him more than most people ever have. Success and fame and the adulation of millions . . . all the things he never would have had without you. And you gave him love, and *he* knew it. He knew how much love you had in your heart for him . . . so much love."

Her dead black eyes ignited for a moment. *"You* know that, don't you? You believe it. That I loved him. Most people don't know that. That I did it all for love."

I held her close. We were strangers and I had never liked her, if truth be told, but I ached for her. Oh, I ached for her. There were the sinners and the sinned-against. And probably she *had* sinned against Beau. A sin in the name of love. How terrible for her to have sinned against the thing she had loved most.

Everyone went home. And tomorrow, Poppy said, she was going home. Back to her own house. I went to the kitchen to help Leah clean up after the guests. When we were through, and after I finally convinced her to go to bed, I went to check on Poppy.

I found her in the library, sitting side by side with Todd on the leather couch, deep in conversation. Todd looked up at me, his eyes inscrutable, his face closed. He was the one who had explained to me all about the phases a person went through in certain situations. And now I had seen *his* phases. Right after the hospital when I had had the baby within me removed, he kept trying to explain, to proclaim his innocence. Phase One. Then he had given up on that and had moved into Phase Two. Appeasement, charm, being ingratiating, just plain trying to make up with me, hoping to persuade me to forgive and forget . . . forget and forgive . . . alternating with fits of anger that I didn't believe him. (Even his anger had not impressed me—I knew that even liars were angry when you didn't believe their lies.)

And then had come the night of the marigolds, when once more he had come to my bed reaching out, begging for my love and warmth and reassurance, and I had turned him away. The next morning had found him in Phase Three. Closed up, expressionless, no longer reaching out. Now I wondered what would come next. Would there be a fourth phase? Or would we go on like this, immobile, frozen in Phase Three for the rest of our lives?

"Poppy and I have been talking about the picture," he said.

Yes, of course, the picture. There was still that *White Lily* to be dealt with. Surely, with Beau's death that too was doomed to immobility, frozen for all time.

"We've decided, Poppy and I, that the picture should be finished. I want it finished for all the obvious reasons, and Poppy wants it finished as a memorial to Beau."

I looked at Poppy. Her eyes were fastened on mine, pleading. She clearly did not understand the situation here, that *White Lily* was a fight to the death, a private struggle between Todd and me. As far as she knew, all I was concerned with was the economics of it all, and naturally, too, with the studio's pride, its standing. She was begging me with those black eyes not to object.

"But what will you do about—?"

"We're going to include a tragic death into the picture. Lon, Beau's character, will die in a motel room, victim of an overdose, while he's holed up with a street prostitute. We're going to simulate the death scene without showing a face."

I was shocked. I didn't know how Poppy could find this palatable, but then, we weren't the same kind of woman. And Todd was satisfying both their needs, hers and his, and I could not fault him for that certainly.

"And I've persuaded Poppy to come on the picture as an associate producer," he said. "She's been on the set almost every day from the movie's inception. She knows this film inside out. And she's been in the entertainment field for twenty years. *White Lily,* I'm sure, is going to benefit from her assistance."

Poppy did need something to live for and Todd was giving it to her. And he was also giving her something else, maybe something even more important . . . something to help her get through the days.

I squeezed her hand. "I think you'll make a wonderful associate producer."

"Thank you," she said gravely. "You and Todd have been the best friends I've ever had."

He had done it again . . . the magic man. He had saved the shattered *White Lily* once again from the rubble, in a manner of speaking, and at the same time, had managed to give a fellow human being— Poppy Beaufort—something to hang on to.

Later, as I lay in my bed, awake, I heard Poppy's words again in my head. "You and Todd have been the best friends I've ever had." Still, she had said about Ben and Suzannah, that having them at the funeral would be like having family there. And then she had made the shocking statement that she *and Ben* had killed Beau. And when she had pulled that gun out of her bag, had it been only herself that she had intended to shoot? Or was it Ben? Ben, whose face she couldn't find in the crowd?

Ben and Suzannah. They hadn't been there. Why hadn't Suzannah, at least, been there?

Suzannah woke from the anesthesia in her hospital room very late at night. It took her a minute or so to remember what it was she was doing there. And when she did, she felt immediately for her breast. *God, please, don't let it be there.*

Her mouth was very dry. The huge amount of bandage and wrapping reassured her. Too much dressing for a simple biopsy. She was going to be free, free at last.

95.

The next morning I took Poppy back to her own house. I couldn't let her go back there alone. Her maid was there, and a gardener was working outside. There was no sign of Smokey and Virgil, who had not shown up at the funeral. "I guess they're afraid to face me. They didn't do such a good job of keeping an eye on Beau. They'll show up one of these days to collect their pay. I won't be needing them anymore, will I? I'm going to get rid of the limo too. Just for myself, I don't need any limo. Look, you can go on home, Buffy. I'm going to be all right. You've been busy with me for days. You must have things to do. I promise you I'm not going to cut my throat. Honest, you can go. I'm starting at the studio in a couple of days. I can use a little time to be by myself and think about things. I have a lot to think about. I'd like for us to have a long talk one of these days."

"You mean about Ben? But you've already warned us about Ben. Todd's well aware of Ben's animosity. He's not too concerned—"

"No. I have a feeling Todd won't have to worry about Ben for long. But I still want to talk to you, when I get my legs under me."

"Okay," I smiled. "I'll look forward to it. Any time. And, Poppy. Good luck on the movie! I'm really glad you'll be working on it."

I drove home thinking about what she had said, that she wanted to talk to me. And her other remark, *I have a feeling Todd won't have to worry about Ben for long.* Was that a threat against Ben? Who could figure Poppy out? She still was a strange woman to me, alien in many ways.

I would call Gavin when I got home. I hadn't spoken to him in days and the last time I had, he had sounded so, I wasn't sure, but almost as if he were giving up on *us.* And I needed him now more than ever.

But when I got home Leah handed me a message that Gavin had called. Then she announced she was going to bed. I followed her to her room off the kitchen. "What's the matter with you, Leah?" God knew, she looked terrible.

"I hurt," she said.

"I'll call the doctor."

"No doctor!" She fixed me with that look that defied me to defy her, and she knew very well that I wouldn't dare . . . not under threat of the worst torture known to man.

"All right," I sighed. "Get into bed and I'll bring you a cup of tea."

Gavin called again late that afternoon. I took the call in the kitchen. "I've missed you," he said.

"I've missed you too," I whispered back.

"I see by the papers that the funeral is over. Will you come by to-night?"

"I don't think I'll be able to. I think I'll have to stay home with Leah."

"Again? What is it this time?"

He seemed to be losing control. He wasn't even worrying about Todd anymore.

"She's sick. I've been bringing her hot tea and toast and aspirins all day."

"What's wrong with her?"

"I don't know. She just says she hurts."

"I'll come over and take a look at her. I *am* a doctor . . . I think. I'm not even sure of that anymore."

"Oh, God no! You can't come over here and look at her. I suggested calling a doctor this morning and I thought she'd kill me. She doesn't like doctors." *Especially you, even though she hasn't seen you.*

"How about coming over for an hour? Just an hour," he urged.

"No. I really don't think that would be right."

He didn't answer and I said, "Well, would it?"

Still, there was no answer. Then I heard a loud moan from Leah's room. "I'll have to go. I hear Leah moaning. I'll call you tomorrow. I'll come over tomorrow night. Okay?"

"She'll probably still be sick tomorrow."

"How do you know? Is that a medical opinion?"

"I feel it in my bones."

I brought Leah a bowl of broth. "Would you like some crackers or toast?"

She shook her head then raised it slightly from the pillow to sip from the spoon I held to her dry, colorless lips.

"Is it all right? Not too hot?"

She sank back against the pillows, shook her head, and almost smiled. "It's fine," she said. It was the first time, probably, that she had ever used that word to me since first we met.

When Todd came home very late, I was still up. He didn't do more than nod wearily to me.

"Well," I asked, "is Leo busily rewriting the script?"

"Yes."

"So everything is going smoothly, I presume? Production resumed?"

"We can't locate Suzannah."

"What do you mean?"

"Exactly that. We can't reach her. Or Ben. None of her household staff knows where she is. Or if they do, they're not saying."

"Maybe Ben has done away with her? You know, killed her and buried the body on the property? Next to the hot tub."

He didn't think that was very funny apparently, since he didn't even answer me and started up the stairs. Suddenly he turned and said angrily, "I know I'm forbidden to talk about it, but I have one thing to say and I'm going to say it: I know what you *think* happened between me and Suzannah, and from the looks of it, I can't deny that it did. But even if it did, I don't think *she's* any more knowledgeable of the details than I am. She doesn't even know it happened! Whatever it was that hit us, spoiled food or whiskey or those goddamn sinus pills—or whatever —it hit us *both*. We were both victims. . . ." And he proceeded up the stairs to bed.

Things *were* changing, I thought bitterly. Now it was spoiled food or poisoned liquor . . . or whatever. And now it was he, he and Suzannah, who were the victims. And more than two years later he was still trying to protect *her* . . . his lover.

The next day, Leah rose from her sick bed as I had thought she might. I knew she couldn't hold out for too long, and I held my breath all day hoping that no new emergency would arise, but expecting it, as if emergencies had become routine. And I thought about how it would be with Gavin that night. I *was* going to see him that night regardless of whether Todd came home early or late.

He wasn't home yet when I left, after kissing the children good night, checking that Megan and Mitchell were hard at work on their homework, knowing that the minute I was out of the house Megan would be busy on the phone. I wasn't that old that I didn't remember the exquisite pleasure of staying on the phone with girlfriends for hours on end, giggling and talking about men. I said goodnight to Leah who turned her back on me. *Status quo* there.

Wordlessly we kissed and wordlessly we went to bed. Was it my imagination that I felt a certain bittersweet quality to our lovemaking?

Afterwards, he put his hand on my cheek. "Poor Buffy. Very soon you'll have to make a big decision."

Oh no! I couldn't bear any decisions. Not now. Or ultimatums, either. Didn't he know I was in a weakened condition? But I took the bait. "Yes? What decision?"

"I *have* decided that I *am* going to leave my practice here. I *am* going to San Francisco."

"You *can't!*"

"I can and I must."

"No. You're just doing this to spite me."

He looked at me with surprise. "Do you really believe I would live my life out of spite? And why would I want to spite you? Hurt you? I love you, Buffy. Are you so out of touch that you don't recognize love when you see it?"

Recognize love when you see it? Maybe I *was* too far gone from that thing called love to know what true love entailed anymore? Maybe I *had* lived with spite too long.

"You can come with me, you know," he said quietly.

I looked at him as if he were mad. "Don't be ridiculous. How could I possibly go with you?"

"People are doing it every day. If their marriages are really over, they call them over; they leave them and pick up and go on to something else, something better."

It was the most frightening thing I had ever heard of. "Oh yes? And what do I do about my children?"

"Don't hide behind your children. This is between you and me . . . and Todd."

"Don't be ridiculous. My children *are* involved. Do I look like the kind of woman who would abandon her children?"

"No, of course not. You take them along with you," he said reasonably.

I laughed briefly and without amusement. "Sure. Just like that."

He swung his legs out of bed and went into the living room. "You want a drink?" he called out.

"No, thank you. Liquor doesn't help anything," I yelled back.

He laughed, returning with his drink. "You sound like your sister."

My sister! I could just imagine what my sister would say if I picked myself up and my children and went to San Francisco with Gavin Roth. Just the thought of it was terrifying.

He didn't get back into bed. He stood there drinking his drink.

"Come back to bed and let's talk about this," I said in more conciliatory fashion.

"No. I think we can talk better this way. You there and me here. But you don't have to give me a decision this minute, Buffy. I'll still be here for a couple of months, winding things down. You have a little time."

"You *know* it's impossible—"

"I don't know that at all. It's not impossible if you love me."

If you love me.

He had told me he loved me. He had just a few minutes ago said the words again. But I had never said, "I love you," to him. Not that I hadn't been tempted. They were words one wanted to say, *yearned* to say. I love you. And if you were a certain kind of person, you said them easily. Sometimes, not even meaning them a little. And if a person was a woman like me, the me I was now, she was afraid of them. They were frightening, they were a commitment.

But now I needed to say them, to reassure him, to reassure myself, to tie him to me.

"I do love you." There. It wasn't that hard.

"Ah! You love me, but how much?"

So, the *I love you* was not enough. Nothing was ever enough for some people. They always wanted more . . . needed more.

"Do you love me enough to leave your husband, take your children away, and marry me?"

Marry. He wanted to marry me. My second proposal in a lifetime. My second love.

"The question is," he went on evenly, draining his glass, "how dead is your marriage? Whom do you love more? Me or Todd?"

Love Todd? He *was* thick for a psychiatrist. Didn't he know I hated Todd?

"I hate Todd," I said. "I hate him a lot."

He came over to the bed now, sat down on its edge, touched my face again with sweet, tender fingers.

"Poor Buffy. She is so deluded. I don't believe you hate Todd at all."

I was really frightened now. "Why don't you believe that?"

"I don't know what happened between you and Todd. Once I wanted to know, but I don't anymore. But you're still in love with him. You see, I don't think you're the kind of a woman who would choose hate over love. It's such a poor substitute."

I couldn't breathe.

"You're wrong you know. Hate is a very satisfying emotion. It . . . it's fun. It's as much something to live for as love."

"Is it? I don't believe it and I don't think you do either."

"Then why would I do it?" I asked in a scared little voice.

"Moment of truth, Buffy. Why, indeed? You have a few weeks."

Todd was in the entry hall as I opened the door, obviously waiting for me. He looked ghastly.

"Where were you?" he asked.

I didn't answer. I just wanted to get to the stairway and go up to my bed, but he blocked my way. I tried to push past him, but he wouldn't let me.

"What do you want?" I demanded angrily.

"I want you to answer me."

"I'm not going to. I don't have to answer you. Is there anything else?"

"Yes," he said. His voice faltered. "Suzannah called me today."

Whatever it was Suzannah had said to him, it was causing him pain.

"Then she's been located after all? Good! Now can I go up the stairs? *May* I go up the stairs?" I really didn't want to stand there looking at him. He looked too awful and I was upset by all the things Gavin had said. "I'm really very tired. These have been trying days." Days that try men's souls? Women's souls.

"They're not over. Suzannah called me from the hospital. Santa Monica. She's had a mastectomy."

I stared at him, unbelieving. I sat down on the stairs. My legs wouldn't support me.

Oh no! No! This was too much. Was this drama ever going to be over? Would this nightmare ever end?

"Both?" I asked.

"No. Not so far."

All I could think of was that Suzannah was paying for the crime she had perpetrated against me. And I knew I shouldn't be thinking this way, that it just didn't work that way. Did the punishment *ever* fit the crime?

Oh Suzannah, Suzannah!

And then I didn't think of the woman who had betrayed me, who had taken so much—almost everything—from me. I thought of the red-headed girl, so beautiful, so glamorous, who had laughed and thought that the world was hers for the taking, who had worshiped one thing more than anything else—her body, her temple.

And I broke down and sobbed. I didn't want to cry in front of *him,* but I had no choice. I couldn't stop the torrent of tears. He sat down beside me but didn't touch me. "She wants to see us . . . she wants us to come see her tomorrow."

"No! I won't. I can't. I'm not going. I don't have to. What do you want of me?" I wanted to scream, but I couldn't. I would wake the children and Leah if I screamed. I whispered fiercely instead. "Haven't you two done enough to me?"

He took my shoulders in his hands. "She's not even aware of what you think she's done. I swear it! For God's sake, she doesn't *know!* And she may be dying."

Don't say that!

I shook off his hands. "People don't die that easily. Even when they want to. *I know!* You linger for years and you suffer. Don't worry. Your Suzannah won't die. Not her. She always lives for another day. She always wins out in the end!"

But had she?

In the end I must have been screaming because Leah appeared in the hallway to see what was going on, what was happening. Her dark face was pale, her old red bathrobe appearing older than ever. And the sight of her infuriated me too.

"Oh, go back to bed, Leah!" I snapped.

She was too much for me to bear too.

I went to the hospital with Todd, after all. I refused to believe that Suzannah didn't know she had betrayed me with my husband; still I didn't want her to know *that I knew.* That is what I told myself.

Going to that hospital was one of the more difficult things I had had to do in my lifetime, torn as I was with so many clashing emotions: resentment and yes, pity and regret, too.

She didn't look good, but she *was* smiling.

Todd rushed to the bedside and hugged her clumsily, what with all the heavy padding under her bedjacket, as I stood there watching. And then he looked nervously at me, as if the act of hugging Suzannah would offend me. "Where's Ben?" he asked. "Isn't he here?"

"Ben's in New York. That's one of the things I wanted to tell you. He's working on some kind of scheme to take the studio away from you."

"Don't worry about it, Suzannah. I'm not," Todd said easily.

Big, strong, silent hero talk.

"Buffy?" She held out a hand to me and I had no choice but to go over and take it, grip it, squeeze it.

"Does Ben know about this?" I finally spoke. Surely, this would take precedence over his schemes in New York.

"No. He doesn't know. But he will. I'm hoping he'll read about it in the funny papers."

What did that mean? I wondered.

"That's the other thing I wanted to talk to you about."

"Are you supposed to do much talking?" I asked. "Aren't you supposed to rest?"

"I will. I'll rest after I settle certain things."

I grew anxious, more anxious, when she said this. Did she think she was dying? *Was* she dying? And was she going to talk about their deception—hers and Todd's? Was she going to ask my forgiveness? Was this what this damned command appearance was all about? Well, I didn't want to hear it! I wouldn't listen to any deathbed confessions. And I wasn't about to give any dispensations.

And I didn't want Suzannah to die!

Oh, please Suzannah, don't say another word! Hush, Suzannah! Shut your damned mouth, Suzannah!

I thought desperately about fleeing the room, but instead I said, "I think you should rest now. You can always talk later."

Why didn't Todd hush her, urge her to rest?

"No, I want to. I *must* talk now. There's something I want to do, and I want to ask your permission to do it. When Ben hears about this, he won't want me anymore."

I started to protest but Todd put a hand on my arm, staying me.

"No. You don't understand. I don't want him to want me."

I think we did understand, both Todd and I.

"And that's all I thought about at first. That I *wanted* to lose my breast so that I could be free of Ben. And then all day yesterday, I thought about it, my loss, and I cried about my disfigurement. But only for a little while. And then I realized that it was my life I should be crying for, my life is what counts. And that's still in danger. I mean, sometimes the amputation doesn't stop the . . ." She choked up but she was still smiling. *Smiling!*

"So! I'm going to fight it! I'm going to do all the things I'm supposed to do, take those awful treatments. Damn it, I'm going to fight it, and I'm going to win! I mean business!"

Todd sat down on the bed, even though you weren't supposed to, and put his arms awkwardly around her. And I still stood there just determined not to cry, not to be afraid, to try and not let it all get to me.

She was growing tired, too tired to talk, I thought.

"We'd better go now and let you rest. You have to rest, Suzannah, hear?"

"No, not yet. I'm not through." She closed her eyes for a moment, then went on: "But I want my life to mean something this time. If I get another chance at it. Really! My life's been such a poor thing, nothing accomplished, nothing good. I feel so bad about Beau. I always liked him in spite of everything. I won't even go into—" She shook her head. "If you're going on with the picture, Todd, I want to go back and finish too."

He started to say something but she shook her head and he let her speak. "I'll be discharged in about three weeks and I want to go back to work if there's still a picture . . . and if you'll have me . . ."

"Of course I want you! And there *is* going to be a picture—a finished picture. One way or another."

"Okay. But there's something I want to do first. I'm here under an assumed name, as you know. And the hospital is trying to protect my identity too. And I know that it's hard to project the glamorous image of a movie star once people know about, you know, think of you in that way. And most of me doesn't want the world to know. But I think I have to tell. I want my life to mean something. I want to tell the world that Suzannah the movie star has had a mastectomy and is still a star. That to have a mastectomy doesn't mean you're through as a woman, that you can still be strong and beautiful and loving, and you can still have a wonderful life, if you fight for it. You can still be whatever you have the courage to be.

"But you two have a big stake in this movie, and you've had nothing but trouble with it. And I can't do this if you tell me I'll be hurting your picture by deglamorizing the star's image. You're the two best people I know and I haven't always deserved your friendship and your love but I hope you think it will be all right if I do this and try in my small way to be the kind of person you both are."

She closed her eyes, exhausted, and I ran from the room. I could bear no more. But I had no doubt about what Todd would tell her. What would any hero tell a heroine new to the business?

And I realized that I myself had entered another phase. Subtly, they were pushing me over the line to where I had no choice but to start rooting for *White Lily*. These strangers—Poppy, Suzannah, and Todd— were doing it to me against my will. And even Ben was pushing me. How could I root for a man like Ben to win out over the father of my children?

Todd took me home before going on to the studio. As I got out of his car, I said, "Poppy warned you about Ben. And now Suzannah has told you he definitely has a plan to take over the studio."

He looked at me coolly. "I know all about his scheme. Did you really think I wouldn't keep an eye on him? Whatever banks we owe money to —even the ones he hadn't already controlled with influence or whatever —he's been taking over, one by one. And once the picture is finished, before we have a chance to recoup a dime, he plans on calling in all the loans—in one fell swoop. They're all payable on demand."

I gasped. There was no way Todd could come up with that kind of money, not with the house, not with the film library or the recording company, not with every last diamond I owned. Surely Ben Gardenia was going to end up with the King Studio. It really was all over, as far as the studio was concerned.

"Then why are you bothering finishing the picture?" *For Suzannah? Or because old-time heroes didn't quit?*

He grinned at me. It wasn't the old Todd King grin. It was a grin without mirth. "I still have an ace up my sleeve—"

"Yes?" I was incredulous. *Not again?*

"Heinie. Heinie Muller. He's got more money and more banks than even Ben will ever see. He's standing by me. You see, *he's* my friend and *he* believes in me."

He drove away with a triumphant blast of monoxide.

And then it hit me! Damn you! Damn you, Todd King! Don't you know what a man like Ben Gardenia does when he's thwarted? What he does when he can't win out legitimately? Haven't you watched enough old movies? For God's sake, Todd. He has people knocked off! He puts them into bags with cement blocks and drops them into the blue Pacific. Or

*maybe they end up in motel rooms, with their throats cut. Or they get into
their cars, they turn on the ignition, and they're blown to smithereens!*

Or would the magic man come up with another last minute miracle?
Did I believe that? Could I believe that? Maybe I had to believe that. I
had no other choice.

96.

The studio arranged a press conference right at the hospital. Suzannah,
wearing an ultra-glamorous negligee, made up by one of the studio
cosmeticians, her hair a blazing red confection done in the manner of
when she was the Durell woman, eloquently made her statement, and
the television stations and the newspapers played it to the hilt. *People*
did a cover story. It was not a major news story, but it was one hell of
an inspirational feature. The sort of thing *everyone* gobbled up. And the
amazing thing was she was completely sincere and people could tell.
She emerged as some kind of woman!

And she insisted she was coming back to work the very day—no, the
very next day—after she was released from the hospital.

And when that day arrived, I called to offer my services to take her
home from the hospital since she had not heard from Ben the whole
time. It was the right thing to do, I decided. And it would take my mind
off my two anxieties that consumed my every waking hour. Gavin, and
his imminent departure, and his demands. And Ben and his imminent
threat. But Suzannah declined my offer. The studio was sending a car,
she told me.

She felt wonderful. It was one of those beautiful, rare days when the
air sparkled and there wasn't a trace of smog. One of those days when,
if you stood in the right spot, you could see the city views, the hills
outlined against the sky, you could see clear to the Pacific. And tomorrow she was going to work. *Today* she was going home, a home
without Ben in it. She had not seen him, had not heard from him, she
never expected to see or hear from him again. And Todd had told her
not to worry about Ben's plot to grab the studio. Heinie—sweet, dear

Heinie—was going to back him financially. At least she had once picked a real winner, even if she hadn't known enough to walk away from the tables still holding the chips.

The minute she got in the house—the house without Ben and his gun in it—she was going to call the decorators. She was going to remove everything in that house. She would redo it from ceiling to floor, from door to door, until there wasn't a semblance left of the place where Ben and the old Suzannah had lived.

"See you tomorrow, Harry," she said to the driver who would pick her up the next day to take her to work, and she stepped through the door.

The entrance hall was crowded with her luggage—there must have been forty pieces. She glanced quickly at the maid who was hovering, nervously.

"Mr. Gardenia, Ma'am, he told us to pack the luggage."

"He's here?"

"Oh yes, Ma'am. He's upstairs . . . in the bedroom."

She told herself she had nothing to fear. At least the packed luggage meant that he wasn't going to try and hold her. All it meant was that he wasn't letting her keep the house. Stupid of her even to think about keeping it. Why would she want it? A new life, her own house. She should never have come back at all. She should have gone to a hotel. To a bungalow at the Beverly Hills Hotel where she had once been happy. Maybe instead of walking up these stairs at all, she should just turn around and walk out, never see Ben again? Why did she have to see him? She hated him, she was afraid of him, terrified of him. Yes, she was, even now that she knew he didn't want her, wouldn't keep her. How could one not be afraid of Ben Gardenia and his gun?

She should have known he would be here. Was that why she had come back? Because, subconsciously, she knew that she had to face him . . . face him down . . . with her newborn courage? Wasn't that what courage was all about? Doing the thing you most feared?

She opened the door. Ben was wearing a black suit, sitting at the eighteenth century desk under a picture of the Madonna. He must have only recently returned from New York. He *never* wore a black suit in Las Vegas or California. He looked up when he heard the door open and close. He smiled at her, that soft, quiet Ben smile. He spoke softly. He never raised his voice. It was not his way. He was quiet . . . and deadly.

"Welcome home," he said. "Or should I say, welcome and goodbye?

If you had called, I would have sent the luggage. Ben Gardenia doesn't keep what he doesn't need and doesn't want. You know that Suzannah."

She walked over to the bed to sit down because her legs were rubbery. She had made a mistake. A bad one. She could force herself to face him, calling on her will, but her body was too weak. She might be well enough and strong enough to face the cameras for a couple of hours, but she wasn't strong enough for this confrontation.

"Why are you here, Suzannah?" he went on. "Surely you didn't think I wanted you? And I hardly think you wanted to stay. Did you?" he laughed with that low but menacing laugh.

He rose from the chair behind the desk, slowly approached her.

He was going to kill her! Was that why she had come back? Because she wanted to die? Because she deserved to die?

"You hate me. I know that." He came closer and closer. "You were terrified—no, horrified—every time I took your precious body, weren't you? So why are you here?"

Closer and closer.

"I would have thought you'd be happy never to set foot in this house again. Did you come back because you wanted to be punished? Is that it?" He laughed. "No, maybe not. Let me see. Ah! You thought I'd be gone? Yes, that must be it! Because, even in your flawed state, you're a greedy little bitch. Isn't that it? Did you really think I would clear out and leave you my house? Don't you know that I don't give anything away that's mine? Why would I leave you with this house, you with that scarred, disgusting body under that silk dress?" He still smiled. "Don't you know Ben Gardenia doesn't pay for a dead horse?"

She wiggled farther up the bed, toward the headboard, to get away from him.

He laughed. "You don't have to be afraid of me. I'm *not* going to touch you. Why would I touch you, you titless wonder?"

Those were the words that started the blood pounding in her head.

"I'm not afraid of you," she spat out. "You're nothing! You're less than nothing! You're a snake! You're shit! You're scum!"

He raised his hand, but then lowered it. "Your boyfriend won't think I'm nothing when I take that fucking studio away from him, will he?"

Now *she* laughed. "You can't! Did you think Todd King would let a bag of shit like you take away his studio? He's too smart for you. He's got you all figured out! He's got *you* staked out! He's got you covered, scumbag!"

His smile faded, his eyes narrowed. He *was* going to kill her! But no, he was smiling again. "Has your boy really got me covered? Well then, he really better watch out. Nobody gets the best of me. If I don't get the studio, *this is what he gets.*" He stuck his thumb nail between his teeth and pulled it out viciously.

"The little motherfucker, he *dies!*"

Then the blood that was pounding in her head turned to ice, and she stuck her hand under the pillow, there . . . She pulled out the shiny blue instrument of horror, and pulled the trigger. There was barely time for Ben to stare at her with shocked eyes—just like they did in the movies—before he fell to the carpet, his blood staining the precious Oriental only slightly.

She was calm as she picked up the phone and dialed the studio, asked for Todd.

"I've just killed Ben and I'm about to call the police. I don't think I need them, but just in case, do you want to send over a couple of your lawyers before I give the best performance of my life?"

Suzannah didn't start to work at the studio the next day. It wasn't seemly for a bereaved widow who had *accidentally* killed the husband who was trying to wrest the gun away from her, the gun she had picked up while she was smoothing out the pillows on their bed. It seemed that Ben had thought she was about to kill herself because she was depressed over her health problems and her very recent mastectomy.

And the tragedy of it was only more poignant because *that* was the furthest thing from her mind. Indeed, she was looking forward to working again, and was confident that she was going to lick the disease that had assailed her.

As for the gun, that *always* lay beneath her husband's pillow. Ben Gardenia, ironically, had kept that for *her* protection. A devoted husband, he had always worried about the vulnerability of a star of Suzannah's magnitude.

But she did start work five days later, a testament to her strength and fortitude. "Ben would have wanted it that way." The lady had guts.

There was an inquiry, but there never was a question of its outcome.

97.

I looked around and it was nearly Christmas . . . almost time that
Gavin was leaving . . . really leaving. I had told myself that it wasn't
going to happen. And I told myself that there never had been a real
question of my going with him. I could never do that to my children.
And besides—what would Leah say?

Where had the time gone? And how could the end of an affair that
had really only started being an affair in September cause so much pain?
Did it mean that the other, more relevant pain in my life was lessening?
Or was it no longer as relevant? I could not tell. It was as if I was
numbed by all the things that had happened.

I asked Gavin to explain it all to me but he was of no help. He
sounded as confused as I felt.

"I love you," he said again and again.

"Why?" I asked him. "Why do you love me?" I asked him that
knowing all the while that it was too late for those kind of questions. We
were at the end of a love affair and such questions should come at its
beginning. "I'm not really very lovable."

"Hah!"

"Well, maybe I'm a little lovable. But not very. So why do you love
me?"

Why was I torturing him and myself? I didn't want to torture him. I
did love him, didn't I?

"Oh, I love you all right," he said. "Let me count the ways," he
mocked me. "You're cute, you're crazy, and you talk in poetic and
cinematic clichés. You have lovely tits, a very nice ass, and those green
eyes, green as the ocean, green as glass. And underneath your ridicu-
lous-for-Southern-California fur coats and your jewelry, and your supposed hatred for your husband, all those defenses—you're a strong,
warm woman capable of so much love that I cannot bear it. And I envy
Todd for once having been the recipient of all that love, and I feel sorry
for him at the same time, because somehow he has done something to
keep you from expressing it now. But I believe in it, that love, and I

don't think that so much love ever dies. Oh, I think you love me but a little, a secondary kind of love. You love me, but not enough. If you really loved me, you would come away with me."

"But *if you loved me,* you wouldn't leave me. Would you?"

Around and around.

"I love you, that's why I am leaving. I can't live with only a little bit of your love, your leftover love. It's too cold out here with only a little bit of your leftover love."

Around and around. Circles and confusion.

He ran his fingers over my body, followed them with his tongue. He kissed my eyelids, the innermost part of my thighs. A woman could forget herself at times like this, throw everything to the winds and shout, "Oh yes, oh yes, yes. I will go with you to the ends of the earth." And yet I knew I wouldn't, never would, I had already done that once before, and once was enough.

Over and over again.

"You're a strange woman, Buffy."

"Why?" I said as I kissed the pulse in his throat.

"You tell me that you hate, and I offer you love, but you choose hate. That's strange."

Oh yes, strange. I supposed one could call that strange.

Other times, he would grow angry, now that it was all ending. He would get angry and turn nasty.

"Coward! Lousy coward. You're afraid to take a chance. You're afraid that I'll let you down the way Todd did. So you hide behind all your crappy reasons. Buffy, you're full of crap!"

But I knew that it was only the hurt in him talking, the pain he was feeling. So I didn't mind when his words turned nasty. I forgave him and bid him adieu in my head. It was almost Christmas and he was going away. It was almost Christmas and I thought it was all nearly over. Everything. Gavin and the picture and everything. But I was wrong. It wasn't. Not yet.

98.

Cleo called. She said that she wanted to come over; she had a favor to ask of me. I told her to come ahead. I was still not that numb or that confused that I couldn't do a favor for a friend, for a very good friend.

She came breezing into the house, chic as usual, in a dress with huge shoulders and big puffy sleeves. She took one look at me and said, "Don't you feel well? What's the matter?"

"Nothing. I guess it's all this business with Suzannah."

"Yes, Suzannah. But I think she's going to come through it okay. I must admit I was *never* crazy about Suzannah, not in college and not later . . . especially after she had that little affair with Leo, even though I pretended it didn't hurt at the time. But I have to admire her now. Leo says she's going to be the making of the picture yet. And it *was* kind of brilliant for them to write this cancer bit into it. To have the character of Lily go through the experience and emerge stronger for it, and to take advantage of all the publicity."

I didn't know they had written Suzannah's illness into the picture. Todd hadn't told me that. I supposed it was necessary to account in some way for her loss of weight from one scene to the other, and it *did* make the Lily character that much stronger. This picture was going to turn out longer than *War and Peace*. Perhaps it could be a running scenario—life as it was lived, as it evolved—and one would be able to see a chapter a week in the theaters, like they did in the old days. Only this serial would never end. An ongoing *Perils of Lily*. Or better still, they could run it on TV and then they could see which ran longer: *Dallas* or our epic ode to life.

"When did you talk to Leo?"

"I had lunch with him. Just before I came."

"Lunching with Leo? Again? But Cleo, you're engaged. You're not changing your mind?"

She laughed at me. "Of course I'm not changing my mind. Actually

that's why I'm here. But that doesn't mean I can't have lunch with Leo
. . . to discuss things."

"What were you discussing with Leo? Beside Suzannah and the movie."

"Something much more relevant to me at the moment. I want to get married at Christmas. And I want to get married in *your* house. That's the favor I was going to ask of you. If you'd make the wedding in your house. But I'll get back to that in a minute. You see, I was planning on staying on in my business for a while, along with Suellen, and commuting back and forth to Dallas, even after I was married. To tell you the truth, I was kind of reluctant to give it up. I built it and I love it. It's mine. But then I said, 'Cleo, what's more important? You have to give this marriage a real chance.' And commuting back and forth isn't the way. I *can* have another business in Dallas and I probably will, once I get the hang of the city, which are the best restaurants, etc. But I can't have a Dallas marriage in Los Angeles. And I *am committed* to this marriage and Dale. And Dale wants to get married right away. He says he doesn't see any point in people our age waiting. So that would have meant that I would have to uproot the kids in the middle of the school year and take them to Dallas. And I would finally sell the house and Leo could have his money. But Leo doesn't care about selling the house anymore, not since Babette broke up with him. He's really so lost. And lonely. And then I had this idea. Why couldn't Leo stay on in the house with the children? They are his children as much as mine. And he needs them now, and they can finish out the school year. So that's what I was talking over with him at lunch."

"You mean you're actually going to let him have custody?"

"It doesn't necessarily have to be anything legal. It will be an arrangement between friends. A temporary arrangement for now, to keep Leo going; and we'll see. Split custody is the coming thing, you know. Very much in style." She laughed at me. "But seriously, right now, Leo needs the kids to hold on to—"

I was overwhelmed.

"I don't know, Cleo. I don't know how you can be so forgiving. You go *on* being generous and forgiving."

"Why not, Buff? It doesn't take anything from what I am, from what I have today. To deny Leo is to deny part of me, my youth, and what I was then—young, happy, and gay—and romantic. Then I thought everything was going to come up roses. It doesn't even matter what Leo himself *was*. What is important is how *I felt* about him. I *was* in love with what I thought he was. And I thought he was great. He was handsome—he looked like Paul McCartney and he dressed like the Beatles—remember? That Edwardian look? Everyone else then was sloppy, but Leo was so—elegant. And he was the head of that organization—what was it? Students for Peace? I thought he was so idealistic. Every young girl loves an idealist. It was all so sweet and romantic, a fantasy, kind of, *my* fantasy, part of me. What's the point in defacing it now? Calling it names, saying it didn't exist, dirtying it all up? Rather, I'd like to remember it as good, as a positive thing. Those years in college—they had a special sweetness about them that we'll never know again."

Yes . . . a sweetness we would never know again.

I felt full of love for Cleo, and pride. I had picked her years before to be my friend and I had made a good choice. And it wasn't even that she had grown and had become a more wonderful person. It was that all along the way she had made me laugh, had made life a fun place to be. And that was more than I could say for all the others who had been there in the beginning and whom I had loved more. Todd and Suzannah and Cassie and Suellen. Cassie and Suellen had never hurt me and were so very dear, but they had never made me laugh the way Cleo had.

Only I wasn't laughing now. Cleo had talked about the past—about those days that were the beginning—and her own eyes had been shining, remembering. When *I* remembered it, it just hurt too damn much.

"So now, tell me, may I be married in your house Christmas Day? I'll tell you why. If I get married in Dallas, my mother will make it the biggest day to hit Texas since the Alamo, and that is exactly what I don't want. Besides, Mother already did that when she was married. And I can't get married in *my* house because that's where I lived with Leo and it wouldn't be right. And I don't want to get married in a hotel or whatever. I want to be married in a home filled with love, like yours is, Buffy. It will be good luck."

She was wrong, but how could I tell a bride-to-be with stars in her eyes that?

"But at the same time," Cleo went on, "*you* don't have to do a thing. I'll make all the arrangements."

"No, you won't, Cleo Pulitzer!" I said, narrowing my eyes at her. "You may be the bride, but this is my house, and I'm going to fix you! You've bossed me around for the last time. *I'm* going to make all the arrangements for this wedding. And I'm not using the firm of Mason and Rosen either. You're going to be a guest at your own wedding!"

"It'll be a pleasure, Mrs. King."

"What *is* going to happen with your business? Suellen hasn't said a word to me."

"Oh, yes. I thought and Suellen thought that maybe *you'd* like to buy me out. Suellen will keep on doing the food and you'll do what I do. The arrangements and the business end. If you really try I'm sure some-day you'll be as good at it as I am."

"Modesty was never one of your virtues, Cleo."

This *was* something for me to think about. Maybe it would be just the thing to fill a void, several voids.

"And if I don't?"

"Suellen said she would do it all. She said she'd like to have you in with her but if not, she'll delegate but oversee the cooking, and do the business part and the planning herself."

Yes, that would be Suellen. Now. Adapting. Growing. Like Cleo herself. Like Poppy. And finally, even Suzannah. Only Cassie and I stayed where we were, mired in the past; while all around us everyone was moving on, moving away.

99.

The word had been that *White Lily* would be home for Christmas. In the can. In the theaters by spring. Well, it wasn't, not quite. The word now was another week, in the can for the New Year. In the meantime, it was Christmas and Cleo's wedding day. And Gavin was gone to the desert for Christmas with his family and then northward, ho! Going, going, gone.

I was devastated. I knew that the day was coming, but is anyone ever really prepared to say goodbye, done, over? But I had gotten over worse, hadn't I? And I would mourn tomorrow, not today. Today was a happy day. Christmas for the children and a wedding for Cleo.

We had a limited number of guests, Cleo's wish, but we had had lots of fun planning that list. She didn't want half of Texas flying in for the wedding so we had settled on forty people from Dallas: Leila and Leila's husband, Duke, father of the bridegroom, and there was Duke's brother, Deke, and his son Dinkey and his wife.

"Why is he Dinkey?" I asked. "What an awful name."

"It's only a nickname. Wait till you see him—you'll understand."

"Tell me now."

"Well, Duke's six-four, and his brother, Deke, is six-three. Now, Dale, as you know, is six-five. Dinkey, he's only five-eleven!" And she started to giggle.

I smiled politely. "It isn't *that* funny."

But Cleo just kept laughing. "Oh no? Wait till you see his wife. *She's* six-five."

Now that was funny. Oh, I was going to miss Cleo all right.

From the Los Angeles area we had chosen another forty people: Suellen and Howard and their two children, Poppy and Suzannah, Cassie and Jenny but no Guy. "They're not even living together so why do I have to invite *him?* I'm really going to be liberated this time around. I'm not inviting anybody I don't really want. And I *am* inviting Leo, so don't give me any arguments. Then when Dale and I go off on our honeymoon, Leo can go home with Josh and Tabby."

"It's your wedding and I wouldn't think of giving you an argument. Even if I do think it's in bad taste to have your ex-husband at your new wedding."

"Not when you're friends, it's not. And besides, if it's not in the best taste, at least it is sophisticated and chic. Stylish, to say the least."

"How about 'trendy'?" I asked, starting to laugh.

"How about *'au courant,'* or *'à la mode'?*"

"Wait, I have a better one. *Recherché.*"

"Oh, you looked that one up. It doesn't count."

"Yes it does! How about *chichi?*"

She shook her head at me. "Now you're reaching."

Oh yes, I was going to miss Cleo. There was no one to fill her place.

And today, even Leah was rejoicing. Today, Leah, in wine-red taffeta, was a guest. I had told her that since the wedding was being completely catered and Cleo insisted that she be a guest, she needed a new dress and, for once, not black.

"I *like* black," she said.

And although now we spoke less than ever before, I appealed to Todd. "Tell her she *must* have a red dress." I was thinking of how Rhett

Butler had convinced Mammy to wear a red taffeta petticoat, and for some weird, convoluted reason, this became very important to me.

Seriously, Todd took her aside, and when she came back, she granted: "*Dark* red," and dark red it was.

We did have a Texas touch: a Federal judge from Dallas, a friend of Dale's, performed the ceremonies, but the food was definitely L.A. French and Italian dishes, to be sure. With the Japanese sushi thrown in. Plus low-calorie salads, all topped off with the supposedly rejuvenating bean sprout. But definitely no *nouvelle* cuisine. Suellen said—*my* Suellen of all people—she said *nouvelle* was no longer new nor in. *Nouvelle* was *out.*

Suellen . . . moving on.

There was a string quartet and a piano player who set the mood for the afternoon: soft classics and gentle ballads. Cleo and I agreed beforehand that out of consideration for Poppy, we would be sure not to have any tunes that Beau had ever recorded, not even those songs from *White Lily.* But Poppy herself insisted on it, making the request of the piano player personally. She said that she *wanted* Beau and his music remembered. "It hurts," she said, "but it hurts in a good way."

Poppy too . . . moving on.

So when Suzannah sang Beau's song, "Love Grown Cool," the words exuded a special poignancy:

. . . When love is new it bears strong wings
And makes a home of empty skies,
But love grown cool turns faith to rue
And mocks the heart with lonely lies . . .

The funny thing was that I kept expecting Heinie to show up at any moment. I knew that he was a friend of Cleo's new family and I kept expecting that *somebody*—not to mention any names—would have thought to invite him . . . just in the hope of—But no, it didn't happen.

But then when the party was almost over and most of the guests had departed, and after the bride and bridegroom themselves left for the airport, the telephone rang. Now, the telephone had rung all through the afternoon, but this was a fateful call! *I knew it!* How does one somehow separate the fateful rings of the phone from the ordinary ones? Scientists would say that it was only a state of mind, but I would have fought them on that. There *was* an urgency to the ring.

Todd was summoned to the phone, and then he came back, whispered to me to have Cassie stay, and he spoke to Howard and the two of them went into the library, and then Howard came out and called Leo into the library. The call had something to do with Cassie. But what? It couldn't be Jenny. Jenny was here. And it couldn't have to do with her mother, because Leo had been called into the room.

Soon everyone was gone except for Cassie and Suellen and the children, including Leo's Josh and Tabby. The caterers set to work, cleaning up the living room first. Leah had taken off her new red dress and had put on one of her basic blacks, and was now supervising them, having restrained herself all afternoon.

Todd came out of the library, took Cassie aside, put his arm around her, and spoke to her a couple of minutes. She seemed first horrified, and then dazed. Was it Win? But then two of our lawyers arrived, Bill Harris and Hutch Wagner, and the head of publicity, and a fellow from the public relations department. No, it couldn't be Win. Since the lawyers were here and . . . It was Guy! What? Murdered like Beau? Sick? What?

Then Todd dispatched all the kids upstairs and the rest of us went into the library. Howard told us that Guy had been arrested. A girl, fifteen years old, had been found in Hollywood in an alley right off Sunset, badly beaten, half-dead, sexually assaulted, her *insides* ripped apart. She had said enough to make an identification even though her lips had been so swollen she could barely talk. She had said . . . *Guy Savarese.*

I sat with Cassie who didn't move. I took her hand and held on to it tightly and she didn't resist.

The publicity man spoke first. "There's publicity and there's publicity and we've had our share. I'd say, this is overkill."

And the public relations man said, "The girl could be lying. She's *probably* lying."

Hutch Wagner said, "It's quite possible she's lying. The girl lets herself get picked up, she gets more than she bargained for, she wants to get something out of it for her pain. She wants publicity or money. So she names a star. It's happened before. It happens all the time."

"Right," the publicity man said. "Now, she's not only been raped, if it was rape, and beaten. She's been raped and beaten by a star, and she gets an interview in one of the rags and—"

"A big lawsuit," Bill Harris finished. "It figures."

Howard's face was flaming. "Why don't we wait until Dave Ricklaus gets here? He went down to the station. We'll have more facts when he returns."

"What about the picture?" Suellen asked. "How will you finish the picture now?"

Five or six days shooting would have done it, I thought. The picture had been, *almost been,* in the clear.

But Leo said, "We finished with Guy. He did his last day's shoots a few days ago. We've only Suzannah to work with now; we're doing hospital scenes."

So the picture *wasn't* a consideration, I thought. Nobody had to say, "Well, let's help get Guy out of this mess so he can finish the picture."

But then Todd finally spoke. "No, it's not a question of finishing the picture. But there's no way we could release the picture if all this is true. If all this is true and we release a picture with Guy as a hero, spouting moralities, they'd laugh the picture right out of the theaters. It would be a national joke."

"Yeah," Bob Spucci, the publicist, said. "Can't you just see Carson incorporating *that* into his monologue?"

Yes, I could see it. The picture *would* be a joke. So, a decision was going to be made here, with the picture a consideration, after all.

Ray, the public relations man, said, "And think what the reviewers, the critics, could do with it. The funny lines. It would be open season."

Still, Cassie was as quiet as death.

I thought of Cassie's bruised face when I saw her that time, a century ago, before we had actually moved here and become part of this bunch, these movie people. I thought of what Cassie had told me, how she had followed Guy in her car, twice, how he had picked up girls—teenaged girls.

It was true. He was guilty. I knew it and Cassie knew it. And the picture, almost in the clear, was at stake. And there were other considerations: Cassie and her daughter.

"The girl told the police that he was wearing a wig, a big droopy mustache, and large shades, but she said she recognized him anyway. I spoke to Guy. He insists the girl is lying, that he hadn't been anywhere near the Strip all day, that he'd been at his apartment sleeping, that he conked out about noon, after having been up all night the night before, Christmas Eve," Dave Ricklaus told us, when he finally arrived.

"That poor girl," Suellen said. "She's not going to die, is she?"

"No. She's going to live. It's *not* a matter of murder. But rape, rape *and* assault, such a vicious assault, is a serious enough matter . . . if the case is proven."

"If he's guilty. That's a big *if,*" Suellen said severely. "Let *us* not judge." That was Suellen leaning over to be fair.

Dave looked at Cassie, sighed, and looked away. "I spoke to this man Wilkens from the D.A.'s office. The police in the area say they've spotted Guy before. Despite the get-up. They say he frequently cruises the Boulevard, the Strip, picks up girls in that red Ferrari. But they've never had a complaint before. Usually these girls don't, you know, don't complain."

"Hey, man, that doesn't mean he's guilty," Bob Stucci said. "Men do pick up girls, that doesn't mean they beat them up. It doesn't even mean they force themselves on them. If a girl gets into a car, I mean, what does she expect?"

"I say we nip it right now. Tonight. We get to the family. We pay them off. They get the girl to say she made a mistake in the identification. Win or lose, who needs it? Make them an offer they can't refuse." That was Bill Harris.

Hutch Wagner agreed. "Why take a chance? I'd say you got too much riding on this to take a chance."

They were company men, after all. They said what they believed was good for the studio.

Suellen was horrified. "That's not right. You can't do that. You have to give Guy a chance to prove himself. In a court of law. If you pay people off no one will ever know if the girl was lying or not."

Poor Suellen. She *was* innocent. Too innocent. That was her problem.

I looked at Todd. We all looked at Todd. He had hardly said a word. Todd looked at me but his eyes didn't say anything. Was he wondering what I *wanted* him to say? I held my breath while he glanced at Cassie. Still Cassie didn't speak either.

He looked down at his hands, turned them over, looked at the other sides. "I don't think the King Studio wants to buy anybody off. I don't think we're in that kind of business." His voice was toneless. "I don't know if Guy's guilty or not. I certainly wouldn't want to pass judgment on him. But if there's the slightest possibility he *is* guilty . . . well, I don't want to buy that man his freedom. I will not say that our picture is more important than all those young girls unfortunate enough to be out there to be preyed upon. And that's what I would be saying, wouldn't I? That our picture was worth more than their lives, putting a price on their lives." I had thought that was what he would say. I wasn't so out of touch with him, so far gone in how I felt about him, that I didn't know how he would react. And I couldn't have asked for more. I expected no less. But there *was* Cassie.

And finally she spoke. "The world thinks he's Jenny's father. They'll think my daughter has a monster for a father, but she doesn't."

Only Suellen and I knew that Guy wasn't her daughter's father. And Todd. The rest were trying to figure out what she meant.

"Then *you'll* have to stand by him," Suellen said. "You owe that to Jenny. At least until he's *proven* guilty."

"You don't know what you're saying, Suellen!" I cried. "Cassie doesn't have to do anything of the kind. All she has to do is say he's *not* Jenny's father." It would be far too much to have Cassie stand up for that monster.

"Wait a moment," Howard said. "Guy is our . . . associate. We don't buy people off, and we don't lie for him, but until he *is* proven guilty, *if* he is, we do have to stand by him. That is our obligation. That is only right. *We* have to give him the benefit of the doubt, just as the law does. He's not guilty until he is proven guilty. Until he's proven guilty, he's innocent."

"He's guilty," Cassie said and all around us, everyone was stunned.

"You can't be positive of that," Howard said. "You weren't there, Cassie," he said gently. "And if *we* don't stand by him, and you don't, then publicly we're stacking the cards against him. I say we make a statement saying we're behind him. That is our obligation."

"Yes," Todd said. "I think that would be just right."

"I've already arranged for bail," Dave Ricklaus said wearily. "He'll probably be released sometime tomorrow morning. He said to tell you, Cassie, that he'd be coming home. To Bel Air. He wants to present a picture of a devoted family man."

"No!" I protested. She and I knew he was guilty. Standing by him publicly was one thing, but this was too much.

"It's all right," Cassie said. "I owe him. I owe him that."

And she went home, but she left Jenny with us.

In the middle of the night, I suddenly sat up. Why had she left Jenny with us? She was going to kill him! That's why. That was exactly what she was going to do. I knew it! She had the rifle, and she was going to do exactly what Jenny Elmann had done. She was going to stand at her bedroom window and pick him off as he came up the driveway.

"Todd!"

He came awake.

"Yes?" he said expectantly.

"Cassie!" I said and Todd said, "Cassie?" as if he had thought I was going to say something else.

"She's going to kill him. Guy! She is! I just know it. She has the rifle."

"It will be all right, Buffy."

"How can it be?" I pleaded.

"I called Win Winfield. I thought she would need him. He said he'd be here long before morning."

An hour later, I awoke again. Had Todd been right? *Would* everything be okay? Everything and anything had already happened, could go on happening. What if Guy came home and found the two of them together? He was a crazy man, a brutal maniac! Or what if Cassie made a mistake? What if she thought Win was Guy when he came in the middle of the night? And she shot him instead of Guy. Nobody had ever said for sure whether Jenny Elmann shot *her* husband by mistake or by intention.

100.

She sat in the chair by the darkened bedroom window waiting . . . waiting . . . exhausted. Dave Ricklaus had said they wouldn't release Guy until well into the morning, probably nearer to noon. She had a little time, a small reprieve, she could just sit there and let her eyes close for a few minutes. It wouldn't be dawn for at least another hour. The lights of the pink castle were still on. The automatic lights wouldn't go off until dawn.

She never saw the headlights in the dark of the night, but she awakened when she heard the front door open and shut. Oh no! Not so soon! Not yet! She couldn't face him yet. She couldn't! She crept to the door, listened to the foosteps on the stairs. All her courage deserted her, and terror took its place. She wasn't ready. Not ready. And then the voice rang out: "Cassie! Cassie!"

It couldn't be—

The door swung open. As he walked in, she flung herself at him. *Win!*

"I called out . . . I was afraid you'd think it was Guy. I was afraid you were going to blow my head off—"

"I *might* have. You fool! How did you get in?"

He held up his old key, the one she had given him long ago.

"What are you doing here?"

"Todd King called me. He said you might need me."

Oh, I do, I do. Thank you, Todd.

"Frankly, I came here for one thing. I was afraid you were going to kill Guy and I had to stop you. I couldn't let you do that to Jenny. Let her go through life . . . like me . . . not knowing the truth."

Her heart sank.

He had come only for Jenny.

"That's what I *planned* on doing—killing Guy. I was going to stay here and wait for him, and when I saw him approaching, I *was* going to shoot him, kill him! I was afraid he would get off, go free, and would do it again. Beat up some young girl, maybe kill her. Suellen Rosen said that I owed it to him and Jenny—since the world thinks he's her father —to stand by him until he stood trial. She thought that was right, fair, but I knew it wasn't, because I *knew* the truth of what he is, and I knew he deserved to die. And I wanted to wipe him out, wipe him away, so he wouldn't be Jenny's father anymore.

"But then I realized that this would be the coward's way and I had already traveled that road long enough. Shoot him and no confrontation. Shoot him and no trial. The world wouldn't know that Cassie Blackstone Hammond had married a monster. No . . . no more. So I decided I would stand up at last, and stop being a coward. Now I want to stand up *to Guy* and tell him to his face: 'No way am I going to stand beside you and lie, pretend we're one happy family.' And as you said, I'm *not* going to do that to Jenny—kill him and let her go through life wondering whether I meant to kill him, whether I killed him out of hate. No, I want him to stand trial. It isn't enough that I judge him. The world has to judge him, the courts and the people. And as for Jenny, I will tell her later, when she's older, that her father is a man she can be proud of. But in the meantime, I'm going to teach her that a human being is what she makes of herself, not who her mother or father were. And that she doesn't have to live under any burdens, any clouds. All she has to be is herself. Hopefully, a brave, strong person who isn't afraid to live, afraid to reach out.

"I know it's late . . . very late, but I'm going to finally stand up and do the right thing—*for me.*"

She looked into his face and still saw the resentment that she had waited so long. Too long. It was too late for him, then. Too late for *them.* He had said it himself: he had come back only for Jenny.

She smiled at him bravely. "So you see, it's going to be all right. And Jenny will be all right, too. You can go back now, not exactly with a light heart, but reassured."

She watched his eyes narrow the way they did when he was thinking . . . or smiling. She watched him as he struggled with what she had said. She watched as he balanced what she had just said against his grievances against her, the wrong she had done him, letting her obsession and her cowardice come first, before him, and yes, before their daughter. The irony of it all! She had let her fear of her mother—of what her mother would say, of what her mother would think of her—stand between them, and now her mother wasn't even aware of what was going on around her. Well, she couldn't dwell on this now. And she couldn't blame him that he couldn't forgive her. It was too late and she had to let him go.

Or did she? She had sat back for so long, waiting for things to happen. Maybe it was time for her to reach out, to make things happen. Make it happen for the three of them: Jenny, herself, and Win.

She held out her hand to him. "I know what I've done by being afraid. I've wasted over fifteen years of my life, and five years of *ours.* But does it have to go on forever? Can't we put a stop to this waste? Can't we deal, not with the past, but what *is?* The now, the present, and the future. I'm trying to change, trying to grow up. But one thing won't change—the fact that I love you." She smiled at him. "Give me the chance to show you how much. You're the man who told me to let go of the past. Won't you? Won't you let go of the past and come along with me?" She looked into his eyes, tried to laugh. "You won't be sorry, I promise you. I, Jenny and I, will love you so much . . . the more we grow up, the more we'll love you. What do you say?"

She had tried. She had pulled out all stops, even dragging Jenny into it. And she watched him struggle with it for a couple of seconds, before it was his crinkly grin that was narrowing his eyes and not consternation.

"I say that it sounds like a good deal."

"Let's go up to the pink house and wait for morning to come," she begged.

"I think it must already be morning. See." He led her over to the window. "The lights have gone out up there."

He was right. But they would go up to the house to wait for Guy, so that she could tell him she wasn't going to stay with him until his case was decided, that he was going to have to face it alone. That's the way he had lived, with no love in his heart for anyone, and that's the way he would have to go. But when she and Win left the pink house today, she was going to turn on all the lights personally. It was such a long time since anybody had turned the lights on in the pink castle by hand. She would light it up in a blaze of glory . . . a celebration. Her prince had come home.

Guy Savarese was turned loose by eleven thirty.

It had taken the motherfuckers long enough to get him out of that joint. And he was going home, home to that fucking house that he had paid for through the nose all these years. And she had better be there— the fucking daughter of the fucking Cassandra Blackstone Hammond. She had to be good for something! All these years he had paid for that house, had given her money. And what good had she or that mother of hers ever been to him?

If she only knew how he despised her . . . with all her polite, ladylike pretenses . . . that soft voice, the good-little-girl manners, that suffering, holier-than-thou face. Well, she would serve him well now. *And* that mother of hers. Nobody would believe he was capable of—Not if he was living with the sweet, beautiful, perfect, ladylike daughter of that stuck-up, fucking bitch. Shit! He was so close now, so damned close to everything he had always wanted! And after that damned movie came out, he wouldn't need the little bitch again. After he got out of this fucking jam he would cut her loose for sure.

She had never been happier than at this minute, she thought. Here in the castle with Win. But she *was* worried. She *was* afraid for Win, for their future. She didn't want to say anything to Win, she didn't want him to think she was reverting to cowardice, but Guy wasn't a sane person. She was convinced of that. What would he do when he found them together, learned that she was through with him, that she wasn't going to stay with him until the trial? That violence in him . . . Would it erupt? There was no telling what he might do. And what did she owe him? Why should she stay here waiting for him, waiting for just one more confrontation? She wanted to flee.

Guy slammed the door of the cab. Fucking studio. They knew he didn't have his car with him. Why the hell hadn't they sent a car?

He gave the cabdriver the address. "Make time, Buddy!"

"What do you want me to do with this traffic? Eat it? Stick it up? Hey, ain't you Guy Savarese?"

It was wrong to wait now, to risk having everything taken away from them by an unpredictable Guy.

"Let's go, Win. When Guy gets here and doesn't find me, he'll get the message all right. I'm so eager for you to see Jenny, and for Jenny to see you. And my mother!" She giggled. "She won't even realize who you are, you know, but I want you to meet her anyway. She'll probably think you're Howard Hughes. For some reason, that's all she talks about these days. Only sometimes she forgets his name."

She put on all the lights, as she had said she would, even in the boarded-up servants' quarters.

Guy Savarese ran through his house. Where the hell was she? That bitch! That sanctimonious little bitch. With her sanctimonious good manners. Even when he had hit her, she had just stood there, taking it. Well, she deserved it! And if she wasn't there to help him now, he'd kill her! What the hell had he sent her money all this time when he wasn't even living with her? For her health? He had been sending her money while she was screwing around with that fag. That fag in that faggy pink house. What a fool he had been! He had thought nothing was going on there with that creep because the creep was such a fucking lily-livered queen. But apparently that hadn't stopped them. And that kid. Whose kid was she anyway? The fucking lily's? That little bitch! He'd surely kill her.

He ran to the window. He'd just bet that's where she was right now. In the fucking pink house with him. Sure. The lights were on there. In the fucking daytime. She had to be there. He ran to the closet. He was going to get his rifle and flush them out! He'd scare the hell out of them!

He'd stick that rifle right up *his* ass! Up her nose! Up her cunt! And then he'd make them get down and beg him to spare them! Then he'd kick her ass and get her down here where he needed her.

He took the rifle out of the closet. *Wait one minute!* He had a better idea. He remembered those times in La Jolla. Twice. Twice they had torched a house. What a rush! All those pretty flames leaping sky-high. Too bad he didn't have the boys from La Jolla with him now. Oh, he'd flush them out all right! He'd burn them out!

He ran to the garage where he had always kept a spare can of gasoline, ever since that time when they had had those fucking lines at the pumps. He would go in the front, slosh it around, and light it as he went, fast in and fast out—speed was the ticket—from front to rear, in, out, in the front, and out the rear.

He picked up the hatchet he had used for firewood. He'd be through that front door in a minute, in half a minute.

He threw the can and the hatchet over the electric gates, and he himself was over in a matter of seconds. Scaling them was nothing to him, he was in perfect shape. He ran up the driveway. Speed was the ticket! In, out. Fast. Like the old days. He splintered the door in less than a minute. Nothing could stop him! Fuck! He was Superman! He flung aside the hatchet and ran into the entrance hall. He ran, in one room, out another, sprinkling the liquid, dropping the lighted match. The front rooms first, then the dining room, the pantry, the kitchen, into the annex that adjoined the house. He looked back. Yeah! Yeah! He had left a trail of blazing glory behind him. The old place had gone up easy, like a song. He could feel the heat of it on his back. Time to go! He dropped the match to the last of the gasoline before he saw that in front of him the door and all the windows were *boarded up!*

He clawed at the boards with his bare hands, while outside the sky was lit up, almost as brightly as the house, turning the sunny blue to an extraordinarily pretty orange-pink.

101.

Guy Savarese's possible involvement with the girl who had been found beaten and raped was quickly obscured by the news of his death. Guy Savarese had come home, had seen the raging fire, had dashed into his neighbor's house to see if there was anyone to be rescued, had died a hero's death. Irony. Irony and conjecture. Conjecture and fantasy. In the minds of the beholders, fantasy easily became reality.

The case disappeared from the books. The absolute truth would never come out anymore. And even if the absolute truth could possibly be known, what was to be gained? Only the girl in the hospital had to live with her memories. I convinced Todd that since it was no longer a question of a cover-up, of a payoff, the morality of it all was to see to it that at least the girl and her family had their financial requirements taken care of . . . the medical bills. It would certainly be totally wrong —if Guy had been guilty—that she and her family had both the memories and the financial burden to bear. Not hush money, only a tiny bit of justice, something to be salvaged from the ashes.

And now, finally, *White Lily* was a wrap, and the post-production editing would begin. Was it really possible that it was all over? The movie and all that it had precipitated? Over maybe for some of us, but not for me, not ever for me.

The procedure, the usual procedure, was a wrap party, and then after the editing—who knew exactly how long *that* would take?—the first screening. Then, maybe some more editing before a premiere, probably for the benefit of some Hollywood charity, and then release into the theaters. But where and when would *I* ever find release?

It was decided to hold up on the wrap party for three, four weeks anyway, out of respect for Guy Savarese, only a few days dead. And in the meantime, they would forge ahead in the editing room.

And finally, it was Cassie who was moving on and away. To a place, where I was sure, she and her prince and their daughter would live happily ever after. I kissed her goodbye and cried.

She laughed at me. "I'll be back and often. How far is Palo Alto? I *will* come to see Mother, after all, even though I know she'll be well taken care of in her house that she loves so much."

Her eyes fogged over a moment and I wondered if she was thinking of the pink castle that *she* had loved so.

"It was only a house, Cassie, only a house."

She smiled at me brightly. "It was never really *my* house anyway. It was Jenny Elmann's, her house and her past. And now her past is gone, burned up with the house, her past and her secret. Maybe it's just as well." She gave her head a little shake. "But as I said, I will be back to visit when I go to see Mother at Blackstone Manor."

"No resentment?" I marveled.

She and Cleo. No resentments.

"What's the point?" she beseeched me. "It's past history. And if I hold those resentments, it will only make me bitter. And there's no more room for bitterness in my life. No more room!" she said with determination.

"And you know, you *can* come visit me," she said. "Or we can meet in San Francisco; it's very close to Palo Alto, you know. I'll tell you, we'll meet at the Mark Hopkins hotel . . . at their "Top of the Mark." We'll drink a toast, you and I, because *we're* way up there too! At the top of the world! Okay? No, wait a minute. It can't be just you and me. We'll have to include Win and Todd too. Because Win came back to save me, and because it was Todd who knew to send for him! Without Todd, who knows how this story would have turned out?"

I waved goodbye and ran for the bathroom to be sick. Saying goodbye to Cassie, the mention of San Francisco, or that last line—*Without Todd, who knows how this story would have turned out?*—I wasn't sure which of the three made me sick.

And then I realized that I was late and I ran for the calendar. Here it was several days past the New Year and I was supposed to have gotten proof that I wasn't pregnant the day after Christmas—the same day Guy died—four days after I had said my last goodbye to my lover of four months.

I went to bed, to really be sick and to ponder this turn of events—to consider my options and alternatives as so many women . . . millions? . . . before me had done.

The first thing I considered was abortion. Now—only two, three weeks old—the baby within me was nothing more than a speck. *Cut it away,* I told myself. Cut it away with all the other remnants of the past.

Who needs it, this speck conceived out of . . . what? Love? Or just hurt and a desire to reach out and hurt.

But I had already had two abortions in my lifetime and I had never really believed in them. No, that girl from Ohio had believed in children, in life. I had believed only in love. And I *deserved* this child, didn't I? Wasn't that what they told us these days? Be good to yourself, you deserve it? I deserved this child for the ones I had lost. What was it, that slogan they used in the advertising commercials? "It costs a little more, but I'm worth it." I didn't know if I really deserved it, or was worth it, but I wanted it—I *wanted* this baby.

And yes, he, or she, had been conceived in love. *He* had loved me, he had said he loved me, and I believed him. And I had loved him, in a certain way. It hadn't been *the* great love of my life but did that make the love less valid? It *had* existed. It was part of me now, in a corner of my battered heart, and growing within me as a baby.

Maybe it *was* time to let go of the damned past, as Cassie had? It didn't do anybody a damned drop of good. Be through, once and for all, with my first, great love that had turned to ashes. Why was I holding on? Maybe it was really the time to take my children, and the child within me, to the man who swore he would cherish us all, even as Todd had sworn . . . falsely.

If I didn't do that, and I didn't abort, there was only one thing left for me to do: present this baby to the man who knew he couldn't be its father. A final punishment. Reward perfidy with perfidy. Reward perfidy with a baby he would be forced to accept as his own if he wanted to keep our marriage going.

Oh, poor baby. Instrument of revenge. Conceived in love and born into hate? No, not hate. No, Todd wouldn't do that. He wouldn't take out his frustration, his anger, and unhappiness on an innocent babe. No matter what was in his heart he would treat it as his own.

But love? That would be hard. And what right did I have to do that to a child, any child? To deny it the warm love of a father.

Round and round, no solution, no answer, no resolution. So I lay there in my bed, for three, four days with everyone concerned for me. The children coming in to see me, to try and cheer me up; Mikey bringing me his ice cream pop; Megan baking her first cake to surprise me; Matty showing me the picture of his family that he had painted in school (in the picture everyone was smiling); and Mitchell bringing in his friend Hylan to say hello.

Todd asked me gravely each day if there was anything he could do for me, but not looking at me directly. And each day I yearned to cry out: "Yes! Be the magic man and make it go away, that bad thing that happened to us, that destroyed our world the way it was supposed to be." But I knew that this couldn't be, because for me he had lost his magic.

And Leah came bringing me chicken soup and rice pudding, peering at me with questioning eyes, saying nothing, until I was ashamed to have her going up and down the stairs, wasting her strength on the likes of me, and I decided it was time to get out of bed. There were no solutions there.

102.

I wandered around not knowing what else to do with myself. There was something I *could* do, I finally decided. I could go to the doctor and have what I knew to be true, confirmed.

Dr. Harvey gave me his examination, and they took the test—to be absolutely positive, they said. They would call and let me know. But Dr. Harvey was smiling at me so I guessed that he too was already as positive as I. And I guessed that he was glad for me, remembering my last encounter with pregnancy.

I walked down to the hall to the elevator, and on a whim, walked back past Dr. Harvey's door to the door that used to say Dr. Gavin Roth under Dr. Silverstein's name. There it was—the elder doctor's name, and underneath it—Dr. Jeremiah O'Driscoll. An incongruous name if I ever heard one. I recalled that's what I had thought when Cleo first mentioned Gavin's name. Maybe *this* was really Gavin with a new name, just wanting to make me think that he was in San Francisco so I wouldn't bother him anymore, I told myself, playing games with myself as I so often did. And then for no real reason known to me, I opened the door and went in.

There she was, sitting at the desk, Rosemary. Gavin's Rosemary. Only she was dressed very casually for a psychiatrist's office: jeans and a T-shirt with a message on it: "call me anything, but don't call me nuts." Rather tasteless, I thought, considering, and Suellen, I'm sure, would have agreed with me. When Gavin had been here, he always wore a suit, and Rosemary had always worn a skirt. Apparently things had really changed around here.

"Hi, Buffy," she said. "Gavin isn't here anymore."

Why did the words hurt so?

"So I see. Where did he go?"

"To San Francisco," she giggled, although I didn't see how that was funny. "Is there something I can do for you? Did you want an appointment with Jere?"

"Jere?"

"Yeah. Jeremiah. Dr. Jeremiah O'Driscoll. He's taken Dr. Roth—Gav's place." She looked at me sideways, an odd expression on her face. "Would you like an appointment?"

I flushed. "No . . . no. I just saw the name on the door and I wondered what had happened to Dr. Roth."

"Went to Frisco . . . with flowers in his hair . . ."

Now *I* looked at *her* oddly.

"Just an old song," she offered blithely.

The door to the inner office opened and a young man with a head of black curls and a long curly beard, in jeans and a shirt opened almost to the waist, came into the reception room, nodded at me pleasantly, and turned to Rosemary: "When you're ready, I'd like to see you in my office, Rosie." He turned and went back into his office. On his backside was emblazoned Calvin Klein.

She smiled at me. "Well, see you around." And she tripped around the desk on three-inch heels to go into the doctor's inner office. Her behind proclaimed, "Gloria Vanderbilt." Gloria/Rosie was going in to see Cal/Jere. Would Suzannah have said, *"Au courant?"* Maybe. But Cleo, I'm sure, would have said, "Tacké."

I went home and cried some more. But I was glad, in spite of everything, for Gavin. *He* had gone to a far, far better place than he had ever known, to do a far, far better thing than he had ever done before. I was sure of it.

103.

Suellen came to see me a week before the wrap party. She was doing the whole thing herself with a few suggestions from me and she looked pretty tired.

"Look, Buffy, I want you to come into the business with me. I can handle it myself but I'd rather have you with me. It will do us both good."

"I'm sorry, Suellen, but I can't."

"Why not?"

"I just can't!"

"Why not?" she persisted. Suellen always persisted.

I got up to close the doors to the living room. Still standing, I answered her. "Because I'm pregnant. That's why."

She stared at me so long I finally sat down. And then she turned her face away from me as if the sight of me made her sick. She said, "Oh Buffy! Oh Buffy!" She covered her face with her hands and said, "Oh Buffy!" again.

Finally she removed her hands and said, "It's that doctor's, isn't it? Don't bother denying it. It is, isn't it?"

I didn't deny it. I didn't say anything.

"How could you? To a man like Todd? How could you? A saint!"

Oh shit! Good God! I didn't have to listen to this!

I laughed with as much derision as I could muster. "You sound like somebody out of a nineteenth century novel. Nobody calls anybody a *saint!* It must be hundreds of years since anybody said a thing like that."

"I guess I'm not with it. Like my little sister who goes around having affairs when she's married to a saint, to a man who has probably never even squashed a bug, who only tries to be—"

"Will you stop this crap?"

"My God, what has happened to you? Buffy, tell me, what's happened to you?"

"I'll tell you what's happened to me—my husband, your saint, this wonderful man who doesn't hurt bugs, who goes around trying to save the world—he's betrayed me, that's what!"

"I don't believe it!" She was shaking, trembling.

"You better believe it! The saint not only betrayed me; he fucked around on me with my great friend, Suzannah; he fucked a whore; he got syphilis and he murdered my baby."

She gasped, but was still unbelieving. I could see the disbelief in her face.

"Yes! That miscarriage I had over two years ago, that was no miscarriage, that was a therapeutic abortion. A nice word for murder!"

There was a knock on the door, a sharp rap. "Yes?" I screamed.

Leah opened the door, her face like the faces of the Orient, inscrutable.

"You ladies, you hush your voices. There's children upstairs," and she shut the door again.

"That Leah!" I said, furious. *"She* thinks he's some kind of saint too!"

"Yes?" Suellen hissed. "Maybe she's right and maybe *you're* mistaken!" she whispered.

"Oh yeah? He's never denied it, that it happened."

That took her a few seconds to digest.

"Then it was Suzannah's fault," she said flatly, sure. "Not his."

"Why? How do you know that? Why do we always blame the woman? Why is it always the other woman who tempts the woman's husband to stray? Maybe *he* tempted *her.*" I whispered too.

"No. He wouldn't."

I waved a hopeless hand at her.

"It doesn't matter anyway," I said dully. "Don't you see? It doesn't matter about Suzannah. It only matters about him."

"But surely he explained, he must have had an explanation," Suellen said with desperation in her voice.

I laughed bitterly. "Oh sure! He doesn't know what happened. They both drank rotten liquor, they both had eaten poisoned food, they both had some kind of headache pills . . . and they both passed out and woke up in the same room the next morning and, conveniently, both suffered total blackouts! Total nonrecall."

"But you said he didn't deny it? If he said he blacked out, then how does he *know* it happened? How is that explained?"

"He couldn't very well deny it happened, could he? I mean, he did contract syphilis, he did give it to me as a gift, and I had to have the baby removed—cut out. How can anyone deny facts like that?"

"And that's what Suzannah said? She had syphilis? And—"

I looked at Suellen with pity. Bitter pity. "Do you think, do you actually think that I spoke to her about it? Really!"

She thought about that for a few more seconds.

She leaned forward until her face was only inches from mine. "Did it ever occur to you the story—his story—is true? That he really was sick from the pills or the drinks, that he did wake up without knowing what really happened?"

"I might have, maybe, but *both of them?* Two bodies with two heads with no memory?" I scoffed. "Not even a saint would believe that."

Suellen leaned back, closed her eyes. No, even a saint couldn't believe that. Not even an ordinary innocent like Suellen.

Then she said quietly, "You loved him so much, Buffy. He loved you so much. Why didn't you forgive him instead of going out and taking a lover?"

The passion was out of us both now and I answered her very softly, wearily. "I couldn't."

"Why not? To love is to forgive."

"I *couldn't.*"

And I said to her the words I had said to myself so many times when I wanted desperately, with the desperation of the dying, to do just that —forgive him. *"If I had loved less, I could have forgiven more.* I loved him too much to forgive him. Can you understand that?"

She was very quiet now, very sad. "On a certain level, I can. But women, other women, have loved men as deeply and as intensely as you loved. I know you think that it cannot be true. But it is. It must be so. And it happened to them too. Their husbands . . . their men . . . deceived . . . strayed . . . carried on, whatever word you want to use. And those women forgave those men. Most of them did, I'm sure. Maybe they didn't forget—maybe you *never* forget, but they forgave their husbands and went on. Buffy, most women forgive infidelity, even flagrant infidelity, especially today, and they go on. It's better than nothing. It's better than *this.*"

"Is it? Would you forgive Howard? Your standards have always been so, so high, so idealistic. You've always been so demanding when it comes to morality. Unnaturally so for the times. No, Suellen. *You* wouldn't have forgiven this."

"When I was younger, Buffy, when I was first married—I wouldn't have. I used to think about it, what I would do and at first I thought, oh, it would be the absolute end. I would never tolerate it. But I grew older, and I think, wiser. And I learned there are worse things than infidelity and more important things. A forgiving heart, for one."

"I *can't!* I tried. And all I've felt is hate! All I know is I want to hurt him, like he's hurt me. I want to twist the knife in his heart, deeper and deeper."

But was it as true now as it was at first? I didn't know anymore.

"If you did, it would be a better life than the one you're living now. Living with all this hatred. With another man's baby in you. What are you going to do about the baby?" Her voice became urgent. "Get rid of it, Buffy!"

In spite of everything, her words shocked me. They were ugly words.

"No, I can't!"

"You must!"

"I won't!"

"Why won't you?" she implored.

"He *owes* this baby to me! For the one he killed!"

"Stop saying that!"

"I won't. It's the truth!" My voice was rising again, my anger was rising again. "I won't give up this baby!"

"Then what will you do?" she asked reasonably. "If you can't forgive Todd, then you must divorce him. This marriage is a shambles. It's a lie, an ugly, terrible, destructive lie. And if you insist on having this baby, you must go to Gavin Roth. You must marry him—he's the father of the child you can't give up."

The very reasonableness of her voice made me angrier still.

"I have no intention of doing that!" I snapped.

"But why not? This baby, if it's going to be born, has rights too. It has a right to be born into love. You *did* love Gavin? You *do* love him?"

I did. I had already acknowledged that to myself. I loved him. In a certain way, on a certain level. Part of me would always love him. Not the way I had once loved . . . in another time . . . long ago. But love? Yes. I nodded to Suellen. *I loved him.*

"Well, then, it is very simple. If that is the case, you must choose love over hate, Buffy."

The words had a familiar ring. Gavin had said almost the same thing. Suellen went on in her relentless fashion.

"You say you love Gavin. And you have all this unforgiving hatred for Todd. It's wrong to live like this. Loving one man, living with the man you hate. It's more than wrong. It's a malignancy that must be cut away. For all of you. Todd. The unborn baby. Your other children. You. So will you do it, Buffy? Will you choose love over hate?"

And suddenly, the truth dawned on me. No, it wasn't really suddenly. The truth had been growing in me . . . just as surely as the baby growing inside me. I *had* been choosing love all along. But I had fought acknowledging this.

I couldn't go with Gavin because I loved him only in a secondary fashion. And I stayed, had stayed, was staying here with Todd—not because of hatred and revenge, and not because of my children, but only because I couldn't give up my great love, the love that was as strong in me as it had ever been. I *was* obsessed with unforgivingness and hate . . . true. But my love for Todd King was still the greatest force in my life. It was the one obsession that would never die.

Gavin knew it. He had pressed me, but had he really been pressing me to go with him? Or had he, in true psychiatric fashion, been pressing me into discovering the truth for myself? A true gift of love. As much as the baby was.

And Suellen knew it too. She was pressing now as hard as Gavin with her oh-so-reasonable words.

"You cannot present Todd with a child he knows isn't his. Certainly not without forgiving him first. Choose love, Buffy. Choose love."

I walked her to the door.

But she wasn't through yet. Not Suellen.

"Todd must have borne a lot these last couple of years. Not feeling your love. Only your hostility. No matter what he did . . . *maybe what you did was worse.* And how much more do you think he can take? What makes you think he'll accept this last turn of the screw? Maybe he'll walk out on you. Maybe you'll lose him, Buffy. Maybe you'll lose him for good."

I closed the door on her and leaned against it, shivering. I had never felt so cold in my life.

About a half hour later, Suellen called me. Still pressing, although it was no longer necessary.

"I thought about everything you said as I was driving home. Just suppose, Buffy, just suppose that—incredible as it sounds—that everything Todd said *was* the truth. Life *can be* incredible, Buffy."

I had always believed in Suellen, almost as much as I had believed in

Todd. That was why what she said was so terrifying. There had been an expression going around when I was really young. "Keep the faith, baby."

Was it possible that it was I who had not kept the faith?

104.

My conversation with Suellen left me more confused than ever, and with an even heavier heart. Now that I had acknowledged to myself that yes, I loved Todd as much as I had ever loved him, I had lost all desire to go on with my campaign of revenge and torture. And as a result I had to ask myself two questions: was I any nearer to a state of forgivingness? And what was I to do with the baby that I carried? Was it to be sacrificed on the altar of my indecision?

I went to the wrap party expecting to find an atmosphere about as cheerful as the way I felt, which was about as gay as dancing with a corpse might be. But I was wrong. There *was* something in the air. Could it be, could it possibly be the sweet smell of success? I *had* noticed lately, very lately, a kind of optimism on the set when I visited —an enthusiasm—a growing ground swell, if you will. *White Lily,* our ugly duckling so long in the making and earmarked, seemingly, for disaster and disgrace, was beginning to have the look of the child born to beauty and grace. Yes, it was in the air. The sweet scent of optimism. Although no one could really tell, really be sure until that first screening—that first foray into the real world. Yes, it was looking good and all the faces there reflected that state—there was definitely an upbeat note present at the party, as real as any other guest.

Still, I saw only ghosts. Beau, Guy . . . all kinds of phantoms.

My eyes searched the festive throng for familiar faces and found my Suellen, dressed in pink. Bright pink for optimism. Suellen, looking good, half-guest/half-caterer, efficiently directing her people. And there was my Howard talking to the production manager, his hand on the manager's shoulder reassuring him about something or other. And there was Suzannah—not *my* Suzannah—dancing with one of the cameramen, looking good, looking beautiful, looking like a star, her red hair flying, her bright green dress leaping high on her long, wonderful legs. I turned my eyes away quickly. It was still hard for me to look at her. In some way she had the look of the ghost about her too.

And there was Poppy. We had kept her from dying that day, so I supposed that on a certain level, she was *my* Poppy. Poppy was talking to Leo, nodding her head in agreement with something he was saying. As for Leo, I guessed he could properly be called one of Cleo's ghosts.

I had sent invitations to Cassie and to Cleo. I had wanted them to be here today. Happy ghosts. I wanted to touch base with them, needing to be reassured that they, at least, were at peace, finding satisfaction in the new lives they were leading. But neither one of them had been able to make it. Cassie said she was three bare weeks into her pregnancy and her doctor wanted her to stay quiet because of her past pregnancy history and because, quote—she *was* getting on for this sort of thing— unquote.

Godspeed, Cassie, Godspeed.

As for Cleo, she was too busy redecorating her ranch house to come. Of course. What else *would* Cleo be doing? It was really a challenge, she said. What do you do with a Texas ranch house to make it as chic and sophisticated as a New York apartment on the East Side—say, River House?—but also as appealing and sunny and lighthearted as a Spanish villa in the heart of Beverly Hills, and as green and comfortable as a luxurious contemporary in a northern New Jersey suburb, while still keeping its inherent Texas quality?

"How about making it homey, a place to really hang your hat?" I suggested.

"A Stetson."

"A place to hang your umbrella?"

"I never did get to use mine in L.A."

"A place to hang your heart?"

"I've already done that."

Good for you, Cleo, good for you.

And I looked around for more familiar faces. And then Todd was next to me! He kissed me on the mouth, and as the song went, my heart stood still. And a camera flashed. But unlike a movie kiss, it was only a quick brush of the lips. But *like* a movie kiss, it was only something for the public to view.

Quickly, he moved and quickly I sought Suellen's eyes to see if she was watching. She was and she smiled at me and looked quickly down, as if it were too painful for her to look at me.

Then everyone was calling for Suzannah to sing—not the theme song which had just been sung by one of the boys from the band—but "Lady Love," a more upbeat song than "Love Grown Cool."

I went over to one of the white lace-covered tables to get myself a glass of champagne. I needed something to drink if I was going to listen to Suzannah sing Beau's song about love.

Poppy came up behind me. She was dressed very elegantly today but she looked grim . . . so intense. I thought it must be a very hard day for her. "Remember I said I'd like for us to have a talk—?"

I wanted to tell her that it wasn't the time or the place because she did look so grim and so intense, and I already felt that way, but as I knew it *was* a hard day for her I said all right, and we walked over to a corner away from the center of the action.

She looked at me helplessly. "I don't know where to begin—"

I smiled. "They always say begin at the beginning."

"Okay. Remember when Todd came to Las Vegas—he had a contract for me and a contract for Suzannah?"

Remember? I started to feel clammy and nauseated.

"Yes, Poppy, I remember. But I don't think I want to go into it right now. Surely another time." I tried to turn away but she held on to my arm.

"You *know* then, don't you?" she demanded.

That at that time my husband went to bed with Suzannah? Yes, I know. And obviously you know too. But I don't have to discuss it with you. I don't owe you that.

"Know *what*, Poppy?" I said coldly. "I don't know what you're talking about."

"We're only going around in circles. So just let me talk, will you? I have to set you straight."

"I don't want to hear it, Poppy. Can't you—?"

"Look! It wasn't what you think! *It wasn't Suzannah."*

"What did you say?" *Maybe we weren't talking about the same thing after all.*

"It wasn't Suzannah who screwed Todd and gave him the clap. It was me!"

Something was the matter with this woman, I thought, as my head went around and around. Someone should tell her that if she wanted to sound as elegant as she dressed, she should really stop using words like that. Cleo should tell her.

I felt as if I were going to faint. "I have to sit down," I said.

"Here . . . here's a chair . . ." She pulled over two chairs. Stunned, unable to speak, I allowed her to sit me down. Then she sat down beside me. "This isn't easy. I thought maybe you didn't know, and if you didn't know, maybe it was better not to say anything. But then I figured, if you didn't know and I told you the truth, then it wouldn't be bad because you'd know that it wasn't Todd's fault."

Wasn't his fault? I was sitting down, but still, I was about to keel over.

". . . And if you *did know,* you had to know the whole truth. And Todd had to know the truth . . . and Suzannah."

Somehow I found my voice. "I think you're right, Poppy. I think you had better start at the beginning after all."

"Okay." She gripped my hand and I wanted to pull it away but she was holding on too tightly. "I knew Todd was coming to Las Vegas to see Suzannah about the movie. And I wanted a part for Beau in the movie. And I wanted Suzannah to talk him into it—seduce him, if necessary—to get him to give Beau a part. I'm the one who got her to marry Ben, you know."

The horror of that remark didn't get to me. I had no ears at that moment for anything but the rest of what she had to say. "Go on," I said in a very dead voice.

"But she wouldn't do it. I had her on all kinds of stuff and still she wouldn't do it."

"She wouldn't?" I whispered.

"No. So I figured I'd do it myself. With the help of some drugs I was going to get him into the sack, and then I planned on using it, holding it over his head, you know, blackmailing him into giving Beau a part in the movie. I want you to know I was a different person then . . . that I—"

"Get on with your story," I said harshly, cutting her off.

"Well, as it turned out I didn't have to do it. He came with an offer, a contract. That's the hell of it—"

"Go on," I whispered hoarsely. I thought I might retch at that moment but I didn't care. I would vomit all over her.

"But I decided I'd do it anyway. For the fun of it. As a sort of practical joke on Suzannah."

"A practical joke?" I *would* vomit on her, I thought. This piece of garbage. I would vomit on her, I would beat her like her husband had been beaten until she was dead. Dead and rotted. Filth. She was filth!

"Well, more than a practical joke," she went on. "A malicious joke."

With malice aforethought, I would beat her until she dropped and then I would peel the skin from her body with my fingernails. But all I did at that moment was ask, "You *knew* you were infected?"

"Yeah, I knew . . ." she dropped her eyes. "I was going to go to the doctor, but I waited—"

"You mean, you planned it that way?"

I would grind my heel into her belly, into her filthy, rotted thing. . . .

"Yeah, that was part of it. If your husband got it and gave it to you, then you'd be sure to *know*. Don't you get it? I planned on you *knowing* and thinking it was Suzannah. They were sitting ducks. Ben wasn't there and Todd was complaining of a headache and Suzannah was dying for some kind of fix. And I had everything—uppers, downers, relaxants, depressants, speed—and the stuff, the stuff that made you think you were jumping off the moon. And I had Suzannah's perfume flask. I stuck it in Todd's pocket. And I gave them a few drinks. All I had to give Suzannah was something for her to pass out. As for Todd, I gave him the works. And when Suzannah did pass out, I made it with him. He could have been fucking a watermelon for all he knew. And then I lit out . . . and let them wake up together. I knew neither of them would know what hit them. Or what happened. Until Todd went home and passed on the VD to you. With the perfume bottle and Todd waking up with Suzannah, well, the *both of you*—you and him—would think it was her."

She was through speaking, and I was through too. The passion had left me drained, and I just didn't want to look at her. I couldn't bear to look at her.

When I said nothing, she spoke again: "I know what I did was . . ." she shrugged her shoulders, not finding the proper word. "I can never forgive myself."

What did she want of me? Forgiveness? She couldn't forgive herself but she wanted *me* to forgive her. Me? Hardly the queen of forgiveness. Hardly was hardly the word.

"I guess you think I'm lower than whaleshit. . . ."

Indeed! We were both lower than whaleshit, I thought.

We sat silent, and I looked around the room. I couldn't find him. But that was all right too. I could never find him again. I would never be able to look at him again. I deserved to die. As we should have let Poppy die that day.

She shook her head. "It was worse than—No, not worse, but almost as bad as what I did. . . . Making it look like it was Suzannah who did that to you . . . and to him. I hooked Suzannah on Ben and then I did that to her."

I almost laughed. She was more upset about what she had done to Suzannah. In her sick head, that was the greater of her crime. Infidelity, even infecting someone with a terrible disease, those were not as serious offenses as betraying a friend, having *me* believe that it was my friend who had betrayed me. Infidelity? That had been a way of life with her and Beau. Syphilis? Treatable. Not so serious.

She didn't have any idea really of how much she had done. No idea, and I wasn't going to enlighten her. I wasn't going to kill, strip her body of its skin, nothing, and I wasn't going to enlighten her. It really wasn't a question of what she had done so much as it was of what I had done. Me. Myself. All by myself. I had not kept the faith and I had plunged us—Todd and me—into hell.

She looked at me now with those huge, black, tortured eyes. What could I possibly say to her, this woman who had already destroyed the man she had loved? I, who had done no less? Could I judge her? We were two of a kind. And we both had to live with what we had wrought.

"I tried to make up for what I had done to you two and to Suzannah. I tried, you know. I was going to kill Ben. For you two and Suzannah. Only she, Suzannah, beat me to it. We never talked about it, but I have a feeling she killed Ben for you two as much as she did it for herself."

That too was my burden to bear. Not even that I had lost the faith with her too, but that I had turned my back on her when she had needed help. I had known she needed help, and I had turned away from her, my friend Suzannah.

"I got to tell her too. Tell her what I did to her."

I looked over at Suzannah. She was dancing with one of the propmen now. She was at her most vivacious. She was at her most valiant and courageous. She had become a great person, as we used to say in college. *She's a great person. He's a great person. She's a super-great person.* And I had scorned her.

"Leave her be. Leave her be."

"Not tell her?"

"No. It will just make her sad. And she's got enough to bear."

"I'd like to get it off my chest—"

"I know you would. But it's better for Suzannah if you don't. It will just have to be your burden . . . one more burden for you to bear."

She nodded her head.

"But I guess I should tell Todd."

"Yes, I guess you should." He was an honorable man and we, Poppy and I, had made him doubt himself. That shouldn't be. He had to be told.

"Okay. Should I tell him today? I mean now?"

"This afternoon, I think."

"You're a classy lady."

I was too tired—too sick—to laugh. *Hardly classy.* That was not exactly the word I had for myself.

"Most people wouldn't understand. You do understand that I was a different person then?"

It's you who don't understand, Poppy. I have betrayed my love and my friend. I have destroyed my marriage. I am carrying a baby inside me that I don't know what to do with and I cannot believe the pain I am feeling, which doesn't even count. What about the pain I have caused Todd? What about his pain? Do you understand about that?

What was the point? She was only a fellow traveler, another body in pain.

"Yes, I understand," I said.

"Do you forgive me?"

Ah, that was a question. Understand . . . yes. But forgive? It was a word I was not familiar with. And besides, I wasn't sure exactly what it was she wanted forgiveness for. I had a feeling it had less to do with Todd and me than with her own dead husband. All I said was, "I thank you, Poppy. I thank you for straightening me out about . . . about Suzannah."

I got up from the chair and almost fell over. She helped me. "Are you all right?" she asked.

Can it ever be all right again? For either of us? You or me?

"I'll be okay." I said.

"You're not, are you? Okay, that is?"

"Are *you*?" I had to know. I looked deep into her eyes. "If you want me to forgive you, tell me the truth, the whole truth. Are *you* okay?"

"Sometimes I am. And sometimes I'm not. Sometimes it gets so bad I still want to kill myself. But what the hell kind of an answer is that? It's too easy. It doesn't prove a thing. So I'm still working on it. I think I'm going to make it. One way or another."

"Good. I'm glad. And I do forgive you."

"Thank you. I'm going to look for Todd now."

"Good. I'm going home. If anyone should ask for me, be sure and tell them that—that I've gone home. And while you're looking for Todd, keep an eye out for my sister. And give her a message for me. Tell her that the saints are alive and well and some of them are actually living in L.A."

EPILOGUE

I didn't go straight home. I drove around for a while. West on Sunset. Back to Beverly Hills. Left on Rodeo. Right on Wilshire. Right on Whittier and I was back on Sunset. There was a little park at the corner. I had taken Mikey there a few times. I parked my car not checking the posted sign to see if I were parking legally. It was completely immaterial to a practiced lawbreaker. I knew there was a commandment that covered adultery and there should have been one that covered trust.

I crossed the street and sat down on a bench. The sun had set and the late February day was definitely cool. I hugged myself and stared at the silvery spray of the fountain. It wasn't much of a fountain as fountains go. I had known bigger and more magnificent ones in my day. There was a prettier one in my own courtyard. I had even jumped into a couple. That wonderful day in Paris . . . that day in New York at the Plaza. But I wasn't about to jump into any fountains today. For one thing, I was alone and it took two to jump. And it was too cold. And I was too bereft, and at the same time, too burdened. Guilty people didn't jump into fountains. It was too difficult to drown in one. You would really have to work at it.

I should have been rejoicing to find that my hero was, after all, unflawed. And he, unlike me, *would* be forgiving. I didn't doubt it for a moment. His capacity for love, his store of personal strength were so enormous they could encompass almost anything. Without words, without regrets or recriminations. He was a man of infinite resources and fortitude. He could even suffer faithless fools. That was what hurt the most. He deserved better than that, and the faithless fools deserved less than his kindness and his love. And without the proper reproach, without their proper desserts, they, the faithless fools went to their graves unpunished; and without true absolution. They remained burdened with undistilled guilt.

Perhaps that was the answer: guilt was the true punishment.

No, I had no doubt that Todd would forgive me, love me, and cherish me as he always had. But could it ever really be the same again? For him perhaps, but never for me. That was the bittersweet truth. And the bittersweet taste that lingered on the lips far longer than the most honeyed kiss.

It was *I* who had shattered the idyll that had been ours. We *would* pick up the pieces again but it could never be perfectly whole again. We would patch it and glue it, but still there would be hairline cracks. He, with those wonderful eyes, wouldn't look that close, but I would not be able to avert mine. I would see those cracks every day of my life, for it was I who put them there. I, the guilty, would finger those cracks gently, gingerly, for the remainder of our days. That would be my punishment, and I deserved it.

Still, that part was simple. The difficult part was the baby inside me. Gavin's child. What was I to do with it? Was there room in our reconstructed house for Gavin's child?

If—and what an if—if I had forgiven Todd *before* I had found out that there was nothing to forgive, I might have said to him: I forgive you because I love you and I ask that you in return, will love this baby. And it would have been okay; it would have been good. The baby would have been a replacement for the child I had lost, and I was almost positive that Todd would have accepted it as his own and loved it as his own. It might even have been a bond that would have made our reconciliation stronger.

And I knew that even if I did it now . . . tonight . . . asked him to accept and love this child, he would try to do it. He was that kind of a person. *But it could not but hurt him.* The child would be a constant reminder that I had been faithless not once, when I hadn't believed him, but faithless twice. It was too much to ask of him. Every time Todd looked at that child he would feel a tiny chill of pain. He deserved better than that. And so did the child. A baby was born to be loved, not to be the instrument of pain. A baby should be born out of love, and not out of revenge.

A baby should be born out of love—given and received—not out of revenge, and that was the key. I saw, finally, that I had no choice. Not really. I would be forced to practice one last deception, live with one great lie. A lie born out of love. Tonight, Todd and I would make love and Todd's baby would be conceived.

It would be my guilt, my pain only. My secret, and Suellen's. She would have to bear the secret with me, but she would be compensated.

She only wanted the ending to come out right, the way fairy tales were supposed to end. And now it would.

It was almost dark and I walked quickly to my car.

I guessed there might be moments that I would look up and see a question in those brown, flecked-with-orange eyes, but warmth would quickly replace it. *He* was not a man to doubt those he loved.

I thought of stopping to buy a new nightgown—something virginal, lacy, and white. Or a red one, alluring and sexy. But it was getting late and I really didn't need a nightgown and I did need a cake.

I made it into the shop minutes before they closed and talked the girl behind the counter into decorating a big round chocolate-frosted cake for me, writing across it in capital letters: I LOVE YOU, TODD.

"Yellow icing?" she asked. "Yellow goes nice with brown."

"No. Pink. It must be pink. With little red hearts."

"Hearts?" she was doubtful.

"Red hearts and white lilies."

I stowed the cake carefully in the trunk, but my hands were shaking. Nervous as a bride, I thought. I got into the car, gunned the engine, turned on the radio . . . music to soothe the nervous breast. But as life's coincidences went, it was Beau's voice that sweetly filled the twilight night. It was "Lady Love," the song Suzannah had sung at the party.

> . . . It may not be love
> But oh, my lady dove,
> It sure feels like it is,
> It sure hurts like it is.

Oh Suzannah! How I wish you a second chance too! A second chance at life. I thought again of that twilight time in Columbus in the merry month of May when she climbed to the top of that old Pontiac and danced to Elvis's voice, a free spirit dancing for the gods—her own private gods.

It was crazy I knew, but I had done crazier things. I got out of the car and carefully climbed up on the hood, and from there, scrambled to the top of the Eldorado. And I hummed along with Beau's voice as it filled the Beverly Hills parking lot and the few people there stared. I didn't care. I danced not for my gods but for hers, Suzannah's. If I pleased them, maybe they would not be jealous gods, but good and generous ones. And they would send her a second chance at life and someone to love.

The children were already eating when I got home, and they acted pleased to see me, which was nice.

"What do you have in that box, Mother?"

"Something for dessert. But we have to wait until your father gets home to eat it. It's really in his honor. A special cake. To celebrate his new movie and how we all feel about him," I explained, drawing them into it, as I was going to draw in the new baby, into the circle of our love.

I opened the box for them to see and Leah came up behind us. "Store bought?" she sniffed disdainfully.

She had me there and I smiled.

But she took a look and then she looked at me over her glasses perched on the tip of her nose. "Now *that's* a pretty cake," she said and I thought I actually detected a smile.

Magic! But this time it was I, I think, who had wrought the miracle and not the magic man.

We all heard his car screech to a halt in the courtyard. And we all ran to the door to welcome him home. And I started to cry. I *always* cried at happy endings.